THE DROW WILL LEAVE

THE DROW WILL LEAVE

GOTH DROW™ BOOK SIX

MARTHA CARR

MICHAEL ANDERLE

Copyright © 2020 Martha Carr and Michael Anderle
Cover Art by Jake @ J Caleb Design
http://jcalebdesign.com / jcalebdesign@gmail.com
A Michael Anderle Production

LMBPN Publishing
PMB 196, 2540 South Maryland Pkwy
Las Vegas, NV 89109

First US Edition, December, 2020
eBook ISBN: 978-1-64971-366-7
Print ISBN: 978-1-64971-367-4

THE DROW WILL LEAVE TEAM

Thanks to the JIT Readers

Deb Mader
Diane L. Smith
Jackey Hankard-Brodie
Daryl McDaniel
John Ashmore
AllenCollins
Peter Manis
Veronica Stephan-Miller
Daniel Weigert
Larry Omans
Paul Westman
Angel LaVey

If we've missed anyone, please let us know!

Editor
The Skyhunter Editing Team

DEDICATIONS

From Martha

To everyone who still believes in magic
and all the possibilities that holds.
To all the readers who make this
entire ride so much fun.
And to my son, Louie and so many wonderful friends who remind me
all the time of what
really matters and how wonderful
life can be in any given moment.

From Michael

To Family, Friends and
Those Who Love
To Read.
May We All Enjoy Grace
To Live The Life We Are
Called.

CHAPTER ONE

Cheyenne Summerlin stood in the center of Hangivol's drow inner circle, searching the darkness. *Did I seriously think this was gonna work?*

Ember, who was standing beside her, seemed to read the drow's mind. "They'll be here."

"They'd better be." Cheyenne looked at her mom and frowned. "I have a feeling we're running out of time."

Bianca Summerlin stood tall and proud in the center of the wide main avenue despite the rune scars covering her body and the necromancer's flickering ethereal blight collar around her neck. With her chin lifted, the woman listened to Corian's and Maleshi's muttered conversation as their entire group waited for the next step. From next to the nightstalkers, Venga stared at Ambar'ogúl's first human visitor, who was also the Vessel they'd all been waiting for. Byrd and Lumil scowled at the scaleback, bringing even more tension to their already tense wait.

A side door opened and clanged shut again in the outer wall of the Crown's fortress. Persh'al scanned the mostly empty avenue before walking quickly down it to join Cheyenne and the group of magical rebels who'd once followed L'zar Verdys the Weaver. Now they followed his daughter.

"Thought I would come to see you off," the blue troll muttered as he approached Cheyenne and Ember. "Can't say I'm not a little disappointed about missing all the action, but I still think I should stay here. You know, to run the city and rule the world and all that."

Cheyenne's gaze flicked toward him, and she nodded. "Your call. There might not be any action if no drow come with us."

Persh'al thrust his hands into the pockets of his brown trousers and sniffed. The tips of his mohawk's spikes fluttered in the slight breeze rippling across Hangivol's highest level. "You sent 'em a message to be here, right?"

"Yeah."

"From the bazaar," Ember added and exchanged a knowing look with Ambar'ogúl's first troll Crown.

"Oh." Persh'al rubbed his spotted head. "Not a lotta working tech down there. You sure the message was even sent?"

Cheyenne shot him a deadpan stare. "I'm pretty sure I can tell when the tech I'm using works and doesn't. The message went out just fine."

"Sure. Sure." After glancing down the wide avenue again, Persh'al shrugged. "To be fair, the drow do love a grand entrance. I bet that's what they're waiting for."

Ember snorted.

"I'm already here," Cheyenne muttered, frowning at the dark windows and doorways of the drow-owned shops and apartments in the inner circle. "So I don't know what kind of entrance they'd be waiting to make."

Lumil turned toward them and sniggered. "You'd think all the drow in Hangivol would be itching to get outside in the middle of the night. Darkness is kinda your thing, right?"

Cheyenne and Persh'al stared at the goblin woman.

"Hey, I'm just sayin'."

Cheyenne shook her head. *Dark or not, I haven't done anything to win their loyalty. I gave the Crown up to a troll.*

"Hey." Persh'al jerked his chin at her and winked when she met his orange gaze. "Don't sweat it, kid. They'll show up. If these drow are gonna follow anyone into the night, it's you. You're the drow Crown. I'm just a stand-in."

Corian turned away from Maleshi and Bianca to lean toward the troll and mutter, "I wouldn't let anyone else hear you say that."

"Don't worry about it, brother." Persh'al nudged the nightstalker with the back of his hand. "Cheyenne's got this. Hell, I wouldn't know what to do if she wasn't here to step up to the plate and do this whole… What are you tryin' to get them to do again?"

Cheyenne and Ember grinned at each other. "Heal the forest."

"Yeah, that's right." Persh'al cleared his throat. "All the dead Nimlothars that aren't actually dead."

"Are you *sure* your message was sent?" Corian asked.

Cheyenne didn't bother to look at him. "Why is everyone suddenly second-guessing my ability to send a message through the system?"

"I gotta ask, kid."

"No, you don't. I'm sure the message was sent."

Corian tilted his head, silver eyes glowing as he scanned the dark inner-circle streets and alleys branching off from the central avenue. "What about the drow who helped you with all this? Is he on board?"

"As far as I know."

"Then where is he?" Persh'al asked.

Good fucking question. Cheyenne couldn't come up with anything to say that wouldn't make her sound like a clueless idiot. *If R'leer screws me over, all the drow secrets and creepy staring in the world won't stop me from coming after him.*

Almost as if they'd planned it, the second she had the thought, the echoing rattle of bones and beads clacking echoed from the far end of the avenue. Cheyenne picked up the sound before any of the others and turned to see R'leer's feathered and spiked headdress appearing from an alley. He wore some kind of cloak made of oily black feathers that fluttered as he moved. Criss-crossed bones latticed together covered his shoulders to complete the macabre mantle. He walked slowly down the avenue toward her waiting group.

"Hey, look." Byrd sniggered and elbowed Lumil in the side. "It's drow Big Bird."

The goblin woman snorted. "Talk about drow liking their grand entrances."

Persh'al frowned at R'leer's dark, clacking shape. "Your friend's a darkseller."

"I wouldn't call him a friend," Cheyenne muttered. "But yeah. I'd ask if anyone has a problem with that, but at this point, it doesn't matter. He's the only one of us who had any answers that made sense."

Ember nudged her friend and nodded across the avenue at the lightless buildings and the shadows moving between them. "Maybe that was what the rest of them were waiting for."

The circle slowly came alive with movement as the Hangivol drow emerged from their buildings, stepping slowly out of alleys and doorways without a sound. Cheyenne fought back a sigh of relief and tried to look like she'd expected all this to work out from the beginning. *Not like they couldn't see where the message came from. I don't even care if they're following R'leer instead of me as long as we finish this.*

R'leer's rattling bones and beads were the only real sound as the drow gathered around Cheyenne and her group. The darkseller approached her first, his golden eyes wide as he looked her up and down without even a hint of a smile. She stared right back at him and suppressed a humorless laugh. R'leer's face had been darkened even more by black kohl smeared above and below his eyes, accompanied by lines of black and white trailing across his forehead, nose, and high cheekbones like war paint. *He doubled down on the mood makeup for this one. Whatever gets the job done, I guess.*

Stopping in front of her, R'leer looked her over one more time and raised an eyebrow before turning toward Bianca. He pressed a fist to his chest and dipped his head. "R'leer Haldus. You must be Cheyenne's mother."

Bianca's face was expressionless as she looked the darkseller up and down. "You must be the drow who has involved himself with my daughter."

The corner of his mouth twitched as he lifted his head. "I hope so."

Cheyenne glared at him. "Don't get ahead of yourself."

The darkseller leaned closer to Bianca and raised his eyebrows. "I told Cheyenne how much I looked forward to meeting you."

Bianca's head tilted slightly. "She failed to mention it. I hope you're not too disappointed."

"Not at all." R'leer glanced at Cheyenne again, then fell in line with their group and turned to face the hundreds of drow gathered around them.

Cheyenne watched her mom frowning at the darkseller's ridiculous robe of bones and slick, glistening feathers. *Hell of a way to meet the parents. This would be even more of a shitshow if L'zar were here too.*

As the other drow closed in to wait for Ambar'ogúl's Black Flame to make her announcement, Cheyenne caught sight of the drow girl Ki'zi standing solemnly beside two adults. The kid offered her a small smile and a wave when she met Cheyenne's gaze, and the halfling waved back. The drow who must be the girl's parents nodded grimly at the Black Flame. Ki'zi's father gently grabbed the girl's wrist and lowered her arm to her side.

So, they're here because of who they think I am, not how much they like me. Jesus, this is a weird place.

When everyone had come out of their homes and shops, Maleshi stopped scanning the dark side streets and turned to Cheyenne. "Looks like whoever's coming with us is here."

"Yeah." *And they're all staring at me.*

Cheyenne swept her gaze across the waiting crowd. Her activator picked up on the systems flowing through the streets and building walls of the level, which lit her vision in a way that contrasted with the weirdly ritualistic feel of every drow citizen around her conjuring their own orb of golden light in an outstretched hand.

Like candles. No one had died. What was this?

R'leer flicked his wrist and conjured a black light in his hand. The light grew and elongated, and when he thrust his fist toward the ground, it was clenched around a long staff of bone carved like some creature's spine. A small horned skull topped his staff, eyeless sockets staring at the drow who were waiting for this expedition to begin.

"This is your moment," he whispered, his black-painted lips barely moving as he leaned toward Cheyenne without looking away from the gathered drow. "They're ready for you."

"Right." *Ready for me to step up and show them I know what I'm doing here in a world that doesn't belong to me. This is who you are now, Cheyenne. Not the first time you've had to pretend until it's real. Just don't fuck it up.*

"Things have been wrong in Ambar'ogúl for a long time." Her voice carried across the wide avenue. Rolling her shoulders and grimacing at the throbbing in her poisoned wounds, Cheyenne ignored the constant tingles racing across her skin from the hundreds of pairs of golden drow eyes on her. "And especially in Hangivol. You all know what I'm talking about. The Spider went too far, and the only love she showed her kind was to put you all here in the inner circle, where she could keep you close. Keep an eye on you. Make sure nobody stepped out of line. The whole time, she was poisoning this world and everything in it, including the Nimlothar that grows in the Heart."

The main avenue was intensely silent as she stared at more drow than she had known existed in the city. *More than I've seen in my life. Guess I'm getting back to my roots or whatever.*

Behind her, Lumil let out a violent sneeze. Byrd rolled his eyes. Corian and Maleshi both turned to shoot the goblin woman warning looks.

"What? I covered my mouth."

This is already a joke. Cheyenne looked at Ember, and the fae nodded her encouragement.

"We were all told that tree growing in the center of Hangivol was the only one left," Cheyenne continued. "I believed it too. I don't know about the rest of you, but I saw what Ba'rael did to the Nimlothar forest in the mountains outside Ki'uali. I saw the death there, among other things. But the new Cycle turned, and the last Nimlothar showed me what the Spider didn't want any of us to see. Maybe she didn't even know. I promised it I would bring back what she tried to take from all of you."

R'leer's skeletal staff cracked against the ground with an earsplitting echo. "The *mór edhil* are not a dying race!"

Cheyenne rolled her eyes and turned to face him. *This is my moment, huh? Sounds a lot like he wants it to be his.*

The darkseller nodded, the bones and beads clacking on his head-dress and cloak as he lifted his staff to point at the gathered drow with the horned skull. "We will seize what is ours and regain the power our race shared with the Nimlothars before the Spider's Cycle cast us into the darkness we were not meant to inhabit. The Nimlothars are dying, but they are not yet gone. Now, the Black Flame calls on all of us to do what must be done for the source of our magic and for ourselves. I guided her beneath the mountains to speak with the ancient one who saw all this before it came to pass." He shot Cheyenne a sidelong glance and whispered, "Tell them about that."

She said, "I saw Agalyse and spoke to her."

A mutter of surprise rippled through the gathered drow.

Maleshi and Corian frowned at each other, and the general leaned forward to whisper in Cheyenne's ear, "You told us about the mountains, kid, but you left out the part where Agalyse the *Majiya* is still alive."

"Yeah, we can talk about that later." Cheyenne cleared her throat and addressed the crowd of skeptical-looking drow again. "She told me exactly what we have to do. Obviously, you all got my message, but in case anybody is fuzzy on the details, we're going to the Nimlothar forest that isn't dead, and we're bringing them back. Lending our lives to the trees. That was what Agalyse told me to do, so that's where we're going with this, and we need every drow in Hangivol to be part of it. Any objections?"

The Hangivol drow stared at her, stoic and silent. Like anyone's gonna speak up about it right here in front of everyone. We can talk about the deathflame part when we get there.

R'leer scanned the crowd holding up golden orbs toward Cheyenne, looking incredibly pleased with himself. A smug smile flashed across his lips, and he settled the butt of his bone staff on the metal street again. "Then it's time."

When no one moved, Cheyenne looked over her shoulder at the nightstalkers and nodded. "Go ahead, guys. Fingers crossed, right?"

"Uh-huh." Maleshi's silver eyes narrowed at the back of R'leer's head, then she turned with Corian as they both raised their hands. "Just as long as everyone knows you're the one running the show."

If the darkseller heard the comment, he didn't react.

The nightstalkers cast a single huge portal that grew and elongated to a dark window of light ten times the size of what either of them could open on their own.

Ember folded her arms and eyed R'leer with suspicion. "I know he's, like, super into you and this whole healing-the-forest thing, but are you sure you can trust him?"

Cheyenne studied the drow waiting for the portal into the mountains to finish opening. "Nope, but I'm choosing to. He's pretty much the only option for magicals who know how to make this happen, or he thinks he is."

"Yeah, he's real confident."

"If we finish this tonight, Em, I'd say he's earned it."

CHAPTER TWO

Until a few hours ago, Cheyenne hadn't anticipated returning to the dying forest. Even the promise she'd made the last Nimlothar in the Heart hadn't prepared her for being back here, feeling the pain and the loss from so many of the withered black trunks and bare, broken branches. She felt more than heard the strangled, pleading rattle of the trees calling to her, begging her to undo what had been forced upon them by the Spider's blindness and greed.

The blue-tinged O'gúl moon and the stars not visible from Earth shone brightly on the forest growing across the sloping side of the mountain, but it did little to dispel the darkness.

"Jesus," Ember muttered as she stepped through the massive portal behind Cheyenne and R'leer. "This is worse than it was the last time."

"Looks like it, yeah." Cheyenne frowned at the wide expanse of Nimlothar trees stripped of magic, barely clinging to life and hope. *This better work. I don't wanna see what will happen to this place if it doesn't.*

The drow moving swiftly and silently through the huge nightstalker portal felt the same emotions Cheyenne felt in this place: despair, rage, and uselessness. Hushed gasps rose from those porting in. A keening wail rose from a drow man in the back of the crowd. The cry cut off when he dropped to his knees, and the other Hangivol drow stepped away from him, giving him space to grieve for what they'd all known but few had seen with their own eyes.

Corian scratched behind his tawny tufted feline ear. "I thought they were gone."

"Nope." Cheyenne held his silver gaze and shook her head. "Just way less alive than last time."

"You think there's enough left here to bring them back?" Maleshi muttered.

"That's what we're banking on, right?" Cheyenne glanced at R'leer, who faced the twisted, scorched, dying forest stretching out before them. A breeze whipped through the trees, whistling through the bare branches and rustling the bones and beads strung through the darkseller's headdress and in his hair. When he turned to face the crowd of drow staring in horror at what was left of their magic, his golden eyes shimmered.

Yeah, knowing it and seeing it for yourself are two completely different things. If drow could cry, I don't think he'd bother holding it back.

R'leer glanced briefly at her, then cleared his throat and raised his skeletal staff.

"Now you see." His voice rang out over the drow standing like gray and white statues in the heavy, silent darkness. Whispers of remorse and anger washed over the crowd as they hung on the darkseller's every word. "Now you know the legacy the Spider left for us. She was called the Mother during her reign, but not by us. The real *Majiya* still draws breath beneath the mountains, and she has tasked all of us with this grave responsibility. We will lend our lives to the Nimlothars who have lent their power to the *mór edhil* since the beginning, the power Ba'rael Verdys stripped from them to mold Ambar'ogúl in her image. Tonight, we will reshape it in *our* image, and the Vessel has joined us for that purpose."

He gestured toward Bianca with the skull on his staff.

All eyes turned to the first human on this side of the Border. Bianca blinked quickly and wiped the tears from the corners of her eyes. Cheyenne stepped protectively toward her mom, and the woman shook her head a fraction of an inch before whispering, "I have no idea why I'm crying, Cheyenne."

"It's okay." Cheyenne's eyes glistened with tears as well, but she blinked them fiercely back and nodded at her mom. "It's just this place."

"Yes, that's quite apparent."

"Spread out through the forest," R'leer called, spreading his arms to gesture at the trees behind him. "Choose a source for yourself. Call to it. When the Vessel is ready, we will know."

The gathered drow didn't so much shake off their sadness and grief as they took it with them, moving silently through the blackened, empty husks of the Nimlothars Ba'rael had ordered destroyed.

Not empty. Cheyenne watched the Hangivol drow spreading out through the forest. *Not yet.*

Every dark elf moved quietly across the deadened earth, choosing a tree for themself and stopping beside the twisted trunk. Hundreds of golden eyes glowed in the darkness among the ravaged bark, and when Cheyenne briefly closed her eyes, she heard nothing but the wind whistling through the devastation and her own slow breath.

In minutes, every drow who had been sequestered within Hangivol's inner circle for centuries had taken their place beside a dying Nimlothar. Gray hands reached out to softly touch the dying trunks. Sharp indrawn breaths and hushed groans rose from some of them as they felt even more deeply the pain of the trees that had fueled their race since the beginning. Then all eyes turned toward R'leer and Cheyenne again, waiting.

The darkseller met Cheyenne's gaze and dipped his head. "Is the Vessel ready?"

"Hold on a second." She walked toward him, trying to ignore the hundreds of stares directed at her, and leaned close to mutter, "You didn't tell me she was the one who had to be ready."

"She's the Vessel." R'leer's eyes narrowed. "This is her purpose."

"I don't get how Bianca's supposed to do all this healing."

"She's the Vessel."

"The Vessel. Yeah, I know." *Jesus, can't anyone tell me something straight up without repeating it like I'm a toddler?* "This wasn't part of the plan, R'leer. What's she the Vessel for?"

The darkseller cocked his head and studied her face, surprised she hadn't put two and two together yet. "The deathflame."

"Wait, what?" Cheyenne looked quickly over her shoulder at Bianca, who'd returned to staring with wide eyes at the dying forest. "No. You said we had to burn this place down together, not that we'd be burning my mom."

"She will not burn."

"Says the darkseller drow who looks like a freakin' dark-magic priest. You didn't think this was important to tell me before we got everyone out here?"

"If she has withstood those marks on her flesh, Cheyenne, she can withstand this. I promise you."

"Sorry, that doesn't build overwhelming confidence." Cheyenne eyed the drow spread through the forest and lowered her voice. "I trusted you, and you kept this part from me."

"Is something wrong?" Venga asked, his clawed feet whispering across the dry leaves and vegetation on the forest floor as he joined them.

"Not that we need you to fix," Cheyenne hissed. Maleshi and Corian joined them, glancing around to check on Bianca and the other drow watching the scene unfold.

You can be pissed in front of everyone. That's fine. Just don't let them smell your fear, or it's all over.

"Cheyenne?" Maleshi clasped her hands behind her back. "What's going on?"

Cheyenne lowered her voice even more, trying to speak clearly through clenched teeth. "Somebody failed to accurately explain what the hell he was planning out here."

"What *we* planned, Cheyenne." R'leer lifted his chin. "Don't let your emotions stand in your way."

"My emotions? Look, we can't all be dead enough inside to wear our own dad's bones in our hair, okay?"

Corian raised his eyebrows at that new perspective and gave the darkseller an appraising glance.

"There has to be some other way to get this done," Cheyenne whispered harshly. "I'm not putting her through that."

"She is how we'll get this done."

"What are you proposing?" Corian asked.

"The Vessel is just that." R'leer slowly looked away from Cheyenne to meet the nightstalker's gaze. "A conduit for the deathflame."

Maleshi dipped her head. "Ah."

"No, not 'ah.'" Cheyenne glared at the general. "Do you guys seriously not get how fucked up this is?"

Venga trailed a long black-tipped nail down the side of his scaly face. "In all honesty, I have to agree with the darkseller's assessment."

"Nobody asked you, necromancer."

"Cheyenne." Corian raised his eyebrows. "It makes sense."

"That doesn't mean we have to do it," she spat. "You saw what happened in Venga's lab. What if this backfires even worse than *that* screwup, huh?" Cheyenne stopped when she felt her mom's cool, gentle touch on the back of her neck. She stiffened and glared at R'leer as Bianca joined their circle.

"I can't help but notice I'm the subject of this conversation," Bianca muttered, gazing from one magical to the next. "And I would very much appreciate as clear-cut an explanation as possible."

"You are the Vessel," R'leer repeated. "Without you, we cannot purge this darkness."

"I had a suspicion that was the issue. What am I being asked to do?"

"Mom." Cheyenne shook her head. "No one's asking you!"

"Just tell me." Bianca lifted her chin and stared at her daughter, unblinking. "Now."

Gritting her teeth, Cheyenne took a deep breath. "The Vessel is supposed to channel the deathflame for this whole healing thing."

"Hmm. How ominous."

"Yeah, that's one way to put it." Cheyenne snorted. "We're not doing it like this, Mom. Nobody told me you were supposed to be this involved."

"She has to be this involved," Maleshi said. "Come on, kid. You saw what she can do. You know why she's here. Sure, the *andashal* left out one of the most important pieces, but that hardly matters right now. There's no separating Bianca from the rest of it."

"Are you serious?"

The general nodded grimly.

"I agree," Corian added. "We're out of our depth with this, Cheyenne. You and this darkseller are the only magicals here who heard the next steps straight from the source. Did Agalyse mention the Vessel too?"

"Well, yeah."

"It must be this." R'leer eyed Bianca up and down. "What other purpose would she serve?"

"Oh, I don't know, maybe to harness all the orange magic that exploded out of her and almost killed the rest of us?" Cheyenne hissed. "You'd know that if you'd bothered to ask me instead of assuming you know everything."

"I'll be fine."

"What?" Cheyenne spun toward her mom. "Mom, you haven't seen this stuff. The deathflame."

"The Deathflame is the life source fueling our world," Corian interrupted. He looked at Bianca and dipped his head. "It's not exactly a warm tingle, but its purpose hasn't changed. This is how we heal what's too far gone for any other method."

Bianca raised an eyebrow. "Then that's what we'll do."

"Mom."

"I said I'll be fine." The woman trailed her fingers down her daughter's arm in as much reassurance as Bianca Summerlin was known to give. "And if anything happens, at least now we know you can bring it back under control."

Like I did in the lab. Cheyenne clenched her fists and swept an outraged glare around the circle at Maleshi, Corian, and then R'leer. *So, I'm the one who has to make sure the deathflame doesn't hit the fan.* "Fine."

"Fine." R'leer dipped his head, his flickering smile reappearing briefly before he jammed the butt of his staff into the ground. "It is decided."

"Quit looking at me like that."

"We'll keep an objective eye on the whole thing." Maleshi and Corian exchanged knowing smiles, and the general nodded. "If anything goes wrong—"

"If anything goes wrong, we're all fucked." Cheyenne ignored her mom's glance of disapproval. "This doesn't exactly come with a trial run, does it?"

"It doesn't need one." R'leer nodded and turned to face the forest and the drow standing silently with their hands pressed against their Nimlothar tree. He swept his gaze across the destroyed woodland and cocked his head. "The *Majiya* knew."

Cheyenne forced herself not to roll her eyes. "Knew what?"

"Every drow in Hangivol." He looked over his shoulder at her. "How many trees are left without one?"

Scoffing, she scanned the forest with narrowed eyes. *How the fuck should I know how many trees don't have a drow? It's not like we took a head-count.* But as she searched for a dying Nimlothar without a dark elf standing beside it, she couldn't find one. "There aren't any."

"Exactly."

"One drow for every fucked-up tree, huh?" Lumil snorted and shook her head. "You *mór edhil* have always been a metaphor for the wrong things."

Byrd folded his arms with a snigger. "Just watch. They'll start sprouting leaves instead of hair after this."

Maleshi extended a handful of razor-sharp claws toward the goblins without looking away from the forest. "You two need to shut the fuck up and focus on what you're good at."

"You want us to fight the trees, Hi'et?"

The general turned a silver warning glare on Lumil, and both goblins stepped back with raised hands.

R'leer took a deep breath through his nose and tilted his head toward the star-studded sky. "Now we have everything we need."

Cheyenne stepped toward Bianca, keeping her eyes on the darkseller as she whispered, "I won't let anything happen to you."

"I know, Cheyenne. You've proven that more than once."

A lump formed in the drow's throat, and she swallowed it. *Except I couldn't keep her out of this. If she doesn't blame me for that now, she will later.*

R'leer raised his staff and his other hand toward the black sky and cast a spell in a hissing guttural voice. Black light flickered around his body, then expanded and shimmered into another nightstalker portal. His voice took on two different tones, then three, and the ground trembled beneath him. A spray of dead leaves and twigs and underbrush kicked up around him and what little color they had under the night sky faded, replaced by the same black light as was growing around the darkseller.

Cheyenne took a step back and gently pulled Bianca with her. "What's wrong?"

"I have no idea, Mom. It's always better to stand back. Just in case."

A low growl rose from R'leer's throat, and he spun to face the Summerlin women before slamming the butt of his staff into the ground. The swirling leaves and underbrush burst away from him, his entire face now consumed by the black light glowing around him and darkening his golden eyes. Trails of eerie green light twisted and turned across the ground toward him like fracture lines, growing brighter as they pulsed around the darkseller's feet and turned into tendrils of green mist that climbed up his legs. With a hiss, he finished the spell and flicked his wrist, conjuring a vial of dark glass that did nothing to dampen the brightness of the green flames inside it.

R'leer stepped toward Bianca and offered her the vial. "For you."

"I see." Bianca stared at the vial. "This is?"

"The deathflame," Cheyenne muttered.

R'leer extended his hand even farther. "Drink it."

"Are you fucking serious?"

The darkseller's eyes darted toward Cheyenne, and his head twitched like he was trying to avoid a fly buzzing around his ear. "The Vessel is the Vessel. It's time."

Bianca snatched the vial hovering over his outstretched hand and sucked in a sharp breath. Her wide eyes glittered with green light. "No use in waiting around any longer."

"Mom, wait—"

In one swift motion, Bianca raised the vial to her lips and knocked back the deathflame like it was a shot of whiskey.

Shit. She's totally lost it.

CHAPTER THREE

Bianca blinked and let out a delicate burp with her fingers pressed against her lips, then handed the empty vial to R'leer.

The darkseller grinned and flicked his wrist again to make the vial disappear.

Venga's long reptilian neck stretched as he peered at Bianca. "How do you feel?"

"A little warm." The woman let out a soft chuckle and looked at her daughter. "I don't see what all the fuss was about. It's quite pleasant."

Corian choked back a laugh and raised a fist to his mouth as he cleared his throat instead.

Everyone stared at Bianca Summerlin, the human Vessel, waiting for the next step of the process only R'leer seemed to understand.

"So, what now?" Cheyenne asked.

R'leer's golden eyes blazed as he stared hungrily at Bianca, grinning in a way that looked way too much like L'zar holding onto one of his infuriating secrets. "We wait."

Bianca burped again and frowned. "If you're waiting for me to suddenly know how to move forward, you'll be sorely—"

The woman froze mid-sentence, her eyes glazing over with a blankness that made Cheyenne's breath catch in her throat.

"Mom? What's wrong?"

The wind whistled through the silent forest of sickly bare branches like a wail from the other side of the mountains. Bianca's eyes flashed once with orange light, then her body erupted into green flames.

The magicals around her backed away from the deathflame's blazing green light.

"Holy shit," Lumil muttered. "Didn't know that was possible."

Ember looked the woman up and down. "Is she okay?"

"I have no idea." Cheyenne leaned forward. "Mom? Can you hear me?"

"*Móch ethrilis.*" The words came from Bianca's open mouth, barely visible through the thick tongues of the deathflame consuming her body, but it wasn't Bianca's voice.

Great. Now my mom's speaking in tongues with a dozen different voices.

Cheyenne glared at R'leer. "What did she say?"

"It's time." The darkseller's eyes widened.

"Is that a translation?"

More O'gúleesh spilled from Bianca's mouth in dozens of voices in a range of tones.

R'leer nodded, staring at the blazing woman. "The Vessel has been filled. Now it must be emptied."

Maleshi shot Cheyenne a sidelong look. "Translation, I'm pretty sure."

Ember frowned at the general. "You don't know?"

"You have no idea how long it's been since old-world O'gúleesh left everything but the written word." Maleshi shrugged. "I don't even know."

"Cheyenne." R'leer gestured at her. "This is your moment. Empty the Vessel."

"I don't know what the hell that means," she hissed.

"It is your birthright. Do it."

"Do what?"

A breeze kicked up through the dying trees and the bare branches swayed beneath the wind's growing force, groaning and creaking and sounding like injured animals dragging themselves across the ground.

Cheyenne turned her attention to the trees, and the groans rose in volume and urgency. The gathered drow looked at the madly swaying branches that seemed to stretch toward the Black Flame. An inhuman shriek rose from the center of the forest.

They were saying something.

She closed her eyes and tried to listen.

"Empty the Vessel," R'leer whispered harshly. "Now."

"Something's wrong." Cheyenne's eyes flew open, and she spun to face away from the forest. "This isn't right."

Bianca stood motionlessly, encapsulated in flickering deathflame, and nobody moved.

Corian frowned at the trees and cocked his head. "I agree."

"We have everything we need." R'leer gestured at Bianca with the skull. "It's time."

"Wait." Cheyenne lifted a hand to stop him when she heard a faint rumble in the distance. "Something's coming."

"There's nothing out here." R'leer stepped toward her and grabbed her upper arm. "If I hadn't seen for myself what you are meant to do, I would think you intend to sabotage this for all of us."

"Don't touch me." She ripped her arm out of his grip. "I made a promise and I'll keep it, but something's wrong."

"The Vessel is—"

"Quiet," Maleshi spat. "I hear it too."

The general turned to face the slanted mountainside, her tufted ears twitching. Corian's silver eyes blazed, and he turned as well to search the forest of regular trees that thickened the farther north they ran. "What is that?"

The rumbling grew louder. Five miles out, illuminated by the bright O'gúl moon, a massive swath of trees rustled violently and collapsed.

"Sounds like thunder," Ember whispered.

"No." Cheyenne slowly shook her head, unable to look away from the next patch of trees shaking in the distance before turning in on themselves. "Thunder doesn't sound like that."

A wet squelching sound like the ripping of raw flesh rose from the natural forest beyond the Nimlothar trees. Cheyenne had thought the dying forest she'd promised to save looked too dark beneath the bright stars spilled across the sky. *This is so much worse.*

A low growl rose toward them from two miles away as another

wave of living trees fell to the sick, wet sound moving across the mountainside. "It's the blight," Maleshi whispered.

"The Undoing," Venga shouted. "And you can't possibly know."

"We know." Corian pointed at the line of glistening black sludge pouring across the ground toward them between the shriveling trees. "Don't try to tell us what's possible, necromancer. You were locked up in that joke of an Earthside prison, but we've seen this before."

Byrd slapped a hand to his bald head, eyes widening. "It's coming faster now."

Venga's jaw dropped as he connected the sight of the forest being quickly consumed with his creation. "That slippery bitch. The Undoing was not meant for this!"

"Well, that's what it's doing." Cheyenne turned toward her mom and gritted her teeth. "We can't just stand here with her like this. If the blight reaches us—"

A thick branch snapped in the forest behind her, followed by the rustle of movement and a dark shape racing through the trees.

Lumil's fists erupted in red light and the runes spun around them, and she growled. "Looks like someone else wants to join the party."

"Careful," Corian muttered.

The goblin woman smirked at him. "You know who you're talking to, right?"

Another wave of trees fell to the wet slurp of the blight surging toward them.

Maleshi's glinting claws extended from both hands, and she sliced through the air. "Whatever you're supposed to do, kid, now would be the time to get it done."

"If anyone had bothered to *tell* me." Cheyenne glared at R'leer. "You have any other answers hidden up your sleeve?"

A snarl rose from the darkness coming toward them before a troll woman with matted scarlet hair wearing tattered rags lurched from the natural forest and raced toward them. Spit flew from her mouth as she scurried forward, her eyes completely black and the dark, snaking lines of the blight covering every inch of her purple skin.

Maleshi darted toward her in a flash of silver light and stopped with her claws buried in the blighted troll's throat. She slashed upward, and a spray of blood splattered across the ground before the troll dropped.

More dark shapes scurried through the trees, snarling and gnashing their teeth. "Now, Cheyenne!"

"Fuck, yes!" Lumil let out a shrieking battle cry and barreled toward a blighted skaxen who leapt from the living forest. One red rune-swirling fist connected with the skaxen's gut and sent him flying back into the trees.

"We'll hold them off." Corian nodded at Cheyenne. "Do what you came here to do."

A surge of blighted magicals, first displaced from the cities under Ba'rael's rule and now overrun by the spreading sickness the Spider had unleashed, spilled from the living woods along the mountainside. The blight growled and rumbled and didn't slow on its way toward the Nimlothars.

"Shit." Cheyenne looked at Ember with wide eyes. "I don't know what to do."

"You'll figure it out." With a reassuring nod, Ember spun and raced to join Corian, Maleshi, and the goblins as they held the mindless blighted magicals at bay. A column of violet light burst from the fae's hands and blasted into a pair of shrieking trolls missing half their hair.

"Do not move from where you stand!" R'leer pointed his bone staff at the drow standing beside every dying Nimlothar. "This changes nothing. We *will* succeed!"

Cheyenne spun toward Bianca. "Mom, can you hear me?"

Green fire raced across her mom's flesh, but she didn't respond.

"Cheyenne." R'leer's eyes widened. "You are the Black Flame. The Vessel responds to you alone. Unite the drow and the Nimlothars. Empty it now!"

"Okay!"

Byrd and Lumil roared with battle rage as her red fists and his green goblin fire illuminated the darkness between silver nightstalker lightning and Ember's violet fae light. The blight raced closer, growling and slurping across the mountainside.

Come on, Mom. Just you and me. Cheyenne looked Bianca over and gritted her teeth. *Here goes nothing.*

She reached out to snatch Bianca's hand. The instant their fingers touched, the deathflame surged through Cheyenne, rocking her head back and producing green flames behind her eyes. She tried not to scream but wasn't sure she succeeded as the lifeforce of Ambar'ogúl flooded through her.

This is wrong. It's too much.

"Cheyenne!" R'leer roared.

"I can't!"

"Burn."

The cry rose from all around her and within her as the Nimlothar trees groaned and creaked.

"Burn us."

I'm losing my mind. Cheyenne gritted her teeth as the deathflame surged through her body. *Have to redirect it. Get it out.*

Her drow magic pulsed even stronger from the base of her spine, and she called up the black fire. The second the dark flames raced across her flesh and burst from behind her eyes, the deathflame settled into a cold force she could manage, and Bianca moved.

The woman's hand lashed out toward the Nimlothar forest as dozens of voices rose from Bianca's throat to shout something in O'gúleesh nobody could hear. A column of green deathflame wrapped in black drow fire burst from Bianca's palm and hit the closest Nimlothar, and the bark and branches erupted in green and black flames that spread to the trees beside it.

The magical fire spread in seconds from tree to tree, consuming twisted bark and every drow standing firmly on the ground with their hands pressed against their Nimlothar. The blaze of green and black light blinded everyone but grew brighter and hotter as the Nimlothar forest erupted.

Screams filled the air. The drow who'd come to lend their lives to the trees had no choice but to give it now. Some of them fought the tide of energy surging between them and through them. Cheyenne saw a tall, muscular drow try to pull his hand away from the blazing bark in front of him, but he couldn't. Heads rocked back to howl at the sky. White hair streamed in the wind from hundreds of drow heads devoured by twisting flashes of green and black flame.

What the hell did we do?

"Yes." The golden light of R'leer's eyes was drowned by the blaze of the burning forest. "This is it!"

I'm killing them. Cheyenne snarled and tried to release her mom's hand, but Bianca's grip clamped down on her fingers like an enraged animal's jaws.

"Mom!" Cheyenne grunted and fought to keep her black flames racing around her as Bianca unleashed wave after pulsing wave of deathflame into the forest. "Stop. We can't!"

A warbling bellow rose from the forest behind them as a massive creature with matted black fur barreled through the trees toward them. Its blighted horns crashed into the natural trees and splintered wood flew in all directions, but the beast, which was the size of an elephant, stomped forward, tossing its thick head and sending blackened spittle flying across the underbrush.

"Take it down!" R'leer shouted. He clamped a hand on the skull at the top of his staff, and it flashed with white light.

Maleshi ripped her claws free of a blighted orc barely clothed by shreds of rank rags and dropped the magical to the ground. "Sure. Just take down a *vondra.*"

Corian jerked his head away from a raving blighted goblin scrambling to free itself from his grip and gave the magical's head a sharp twist. The goblin's neck snapped, and it dropped to the forest floor.

The shaggy, hooved *vondra* bellowed again and pawed the ground, lowering its horned head toward Cheyenne's friends. Sprays of dead leaves and dirt flew away from the beast's feet as it charged.

Cheyenne heard the fighting, the snarling animals and crashing trees, and the shouts of her friends battling to give her more time, but she couldn't pull away from Bianca's grip. The screams of the burning drow mixed with the shrieking groans of the Nimlothar trees in her head, and all she could see was black and green fire.

The *vondra* charged at Maleshi as the second wave of black-streaked trolls raced from the trees, scrambling across the ground in a mad dash to take down anything and anyone in their way. The general darted back and forth in flashes of silver light, and the blighted trolls fell in sprays of blood.

She was hurled out of enhanced speed by one of the *vondra's* glistening black horns bashing her shoulder. Maleshi skittered across the ground with a snarl, jamming her claws into the dirt to slow her down. Corian blasted the creature with a stream of silver lightning as the *vondra* raced past him with a growling bellow. The ground trembled beneath its pounding hooves. "Look out!"

Cheyenne couldn't see a thing over the blaze of the deathflame and her drow fire. She tried to turn toward the beast she could feel hurtling toward her but could barely move. *This is it. We're almost there, and I'm about to be skewered.*

A harsh cry rose from dozens of guttural, rumbling voices, and bursts of orange light shot toward the *vondra* from the other side of the Nimlothar forest. The beast howled and fell onto its front hooves, then skidded across the ground to stop inches from Cheyenne and Bianca.

Cheyenne tried to focus on the huge gray bodies racing into the fray. *Raug. Where did the raug come from?*

Cazerel shouted something in French and charged the fallen *Vondra*, which was trying to get back to its feet. Steel glistened in the raug chief's hands and sliced the beast's shaggy neck. Hot wetness sprayed across Cheyenne's arm and neck, and she smelled blood mixed with sulfur.

The raug of Hirúl Breach fanned out to join the fight, blasting orange attack spells at the blighted magicals racing across the mountainside ahead of the blight.

Corian sliced up as he ripped his claws out of a wheezing orc's belly, then turned to look at Cazerel. "Your timing is impeccable, *Zokri.*"

"It always is." The raug chief grunted and raced forward to bring his huge, wickedly curved sword down on the shoulder of a large troll dripping blight. The troll fell, and the battle raged on.

R'leer shot a blast of glistening black light at a blighted skaxen leaping toward him. His attacker flew back with a shriek, then Maleshi's claws pierced the magical's back and flung him aside. The darkseller turned to face the burning Nimlothar forest and drow. They'd stopped screaming but stood rigid beside their trees, attached where their hands pressed against the burning bark.

"Why isn't this working?" He stepped toward the closest Nimlothar and eyed it, his face bathed in the flames' light. "We have everything we need. It should be finished!"

"Fell-damn death wave at two o'clock!" Byrd shouted, ducking as a birdlike creature barreled out of the natural forest on two long, thin legs, squawking and warbling. The starjaw's matted feathers, which were smeared with black, dropped from its body with every long stride. The goblin blasted the creature back with two columns of fiery green before turning to kick a slobbering skaxen in the chest.

"Two o'clock?" Maleshi glared at him, then spun and scanned the woodland.

There it was—the blight, rolling across the ground the way they'd seen it consume the mountain village a few weeks ago on their way to Nor'ieth. This time, Cheyenne, her friends, the Nimlothar forest, and all the drow burning with it were directly in the path of the glistening, squelching disease moving with mindless hunger across the land.

The next wave of trees withered and sank toward the earth as the black sludge sucked out their lives.

"Fall back!" Maleshi shouted, slashing a blighted orc's face with her claws before slipping into enhanced speed to throw him back into the woods and the oncoming disease.

Cheyenne heard the general's order and blinked against the glare of the green and black fire around her. *It's coming for us.*

"Cheyenne, we need to get out of here," Corian shouted, retreating with the goblins, Maleshi, and Cazerel's raug warriors.

"She's not finished," R'leer hissed.

"We'll all be finished if we stay!"

Shit. Cheyenne grimaced, her fingers numb within Bianca's vicelike grip as their combined green and black fire fueled the burning Nimlothars and the drow trying to revive the trees.

Her eyes widened, and she looked at her mom's unblinking eyes, still glowing with green flames. The wavering collar of black light flickered around Bianca's neck, pulsing with the magic behind Venga's engineered blight and holding the Vessel's warded power at bay. *Empty the Vessel. It has nothing to do with the trees, does it?*

A raug screamed as the first tendrils of the moving blight reached his boots and crawled in seconds up his legs and the rest of his body.

The blight's wet, sucking squelch drowned out every sound, but Cheyenne ignored it. Pushing against the power of her black fire and the deathflame channeling from Bianca into her, she reached toward the collar around her mom's neck.

"What are you doing?" Venga hissed and raced toward her.

Cheyenne strained with the effort it took to raise her free hand. Her fingers closed on the cold, tingling energy of the necromancer's collar. Bianca was too far gone to notice what her daughter was doing, but the second Cheyenne grasped the collar and jerked it away from her mom's neck, the Vessel reacted.

Bianca's crushing grip on her daughter's fingers was released, and the woman's blazing green visage was overrun by burning bright orange rune scars. She turned toward the oncoming destruction and released its full power.

Blazing orange light burst from her body from head to toe and blasted back one blighted magical attacker after another. Waves of magic pulsed from Bianca, throwing back O'gúl creatures and snarling magicals who were lost to the world's poison. Bodies flew and trees groaned and snapped, crashing into each other and falling into the blight's thick trail of sludge.

Maleshi and Corian staggered forward under the shockwave, then turned to stare as Bianca unleashed the only power strong enough to clear away the blight.

"Cheyenne." R'leer held his staff with both hands in front of his face and staggered toward her like he was fighting hurricane winds. "Don't stop! Keep the fires burning!"

Is he serious? Cheyenne stumbled toward the closest Nimlothar tree, where swirling columns of black and green fire consumed the bark and the drow woman standing rigidly beside it. She pressed her hand to bark that somehow felt both rough and fragile and doubled down on another pulse of drow fire.

The Nimlothar forest burned brighter beneath her touch, every tree and drow connected as life passed back and forth.

Bianca lifted both hands to reinforce the Vessel's destructive force as it blasted everything touched by the blight.

A high-pitched wail like wind and screams and a rising song lifted from the Nimlothar forest. R'leer stared at the burning trees and consumed drow and cackled. "This is it!"

Cheyenne turned to look at her mom as Bianca spun toward her daughter. The runes on the woman's skin pulsed even brighter, and one of her outstretched hands whipped toward her daughter. Cheyenne saw the orange light streaking toward her but couldn't remove her hand from the tree, so she slipped into enhanced speed, hoping to buy a little time.

It didn't work.

The Vessel's magic burst into Cheyenne's chest and seared through her body. Maybe she screamed, but she lost consciousness before her body hit the forest floor.

The deathflame burning through the Nimlothar forest in the mountains beside the Sorren Gán's den surged beneath the earth. The massive shiver ran through Ambar'ogúl, felt in every village of the Outers, every city and tech-dependent town, every den hidden in the caves, and every waystation on the plains.

In Groulco, a goblin tinker engaged in his work felt the rattle and shiver of the earth moving beneath him before the quake rocked his shelves of metal parts and brought them crashing down around him. He hardly noticed, just closed his eyes and tipped his head back, riding the surge.

The tavern owner in Kur Vróst dropped two metal pitchers of grog on the stained and sticky floors of her establishment and sucked in a sharp breath. Her patrons staggered against walls and slumped in their chairs, intoxicated by the renewed magic coursing through the ground and the air around them.

The low thick metal walls around Charibor crackled with green light and sparks as the control box inside the gates' mechanism overheated and burst. Every citizen froze in their daily tasks within the waystation in the barren Outers, jolted by the lifeforce flaring through everything they touched.

Far beneath the mountains north of the Nimlothar forest and the battle no one else could see, Agalyse the *Majiya* drew a rattling, gasping breath. Her ancient, withered drow eyes flew open as dust and clods of dirt fell around her from the cavern ceiling. The dry, dying vines that had held her in place for centuries flared with blazing purple light, infusing her once more with the Nimlothars' restored power. Ambar'ogúl's oldest drow wheezed and pulled away from the cave wall, ripping the vines off her flesh and falling forward on her hands and knees to brace herself against the wave of energy. Her stringy white hair fell around her face and shoulders, and she cackled into the dust-covered stone floor of the cavern.

Slightly over two miles up the mountain from where the Vessel's power released Ba'rael's hold on the Nimlothars and the blight consuming Ambar'ogúl, the Sorren Gán awoke from a dreamless sleep. The creature made of smoke and fire opened its blazing eyes and gazed around its massive cavern. The light from the fiery lake burning at the back of the cave flared brighter, casting flickering shadows over the high walls and creating new images within the Weave.

The Sorren Gán's deep, rumbling laugh echoed like breaking stone within its lair. Dark eyes seared with fiery light as trails of smoke moved behind the creature's hands. "So, a new age dawns. How amusing."

Grinning and chuckling to itself, the beast flicked its clawed hand and a burst of multi-colored light appeared and opened a round portal in front of where it sat. It waited for its intended guest on the other side of the portal to notice its presence, then leaned forward toward the portal and grinned, flames lapping from its open mouth beneath blazing red eyes.

"There you are. You know what has been done, do you not? Come now, don't look so surprised." Another rumbling laugh escaped the creature. "Even you could not see this, could you? We're going to have a lot of fun now, you and me, all thanks to that little drow. She is something, I'll give you that."

The creature sat back and smiled through the portal, tilting its head as the spiked tip of its monstrous tail lashed the cave wall. "So let's talk."

CHAPTER FOUR

Cheyenne groaned and blinked fiercely to dislodge something tickling her cheek and eyelashes, then pushed up off the forest floor. The acrid scent of smoke hit her first, followed by the sweet stink of seared flesh and burnt wood and something like sulfur. When she finally focused her gaze on the Nimlothar trees around her, everything came back in an instant.

"Mom."

She scrambled to her feet, grimacing at the brief soreness in her chest, and froze.

The Nimlothars remained as they'd been for centuries: dead, lifeless, and blackened. Flakes of white and black ash rained down around the drow as she scanned the bodies of nearly two hundred drow sprawled across the ground among the trees. "No."

Cheyenne couldn't breathe. The bodies were everywhere, including blighted magicals tossed about and taken down by her friends and by the Vessel's power Bianca had unleashed. Blight-maddened wildlife had dropped with their hooves and horns and clawed feet half-buried in the earth. She stepped forward and almost tripped over the outstretched hand of a raug lying in the underbrush, unmoving. Then she saw the rest of them—Corian and Maleshi, Byrd and Lumil, Venga, Ember, R'leer, and Bianca.

"No, no, no," Cheyenne staggered over clumps of upturned earth and splintered tree trunks toward her mom. She barely felt the impact when she dropped to her knees at Bianca's side and grabbed the woman's shoulders. "Mom. Mom. Come on. Wake up!"

She couldn't bring herself to shake Bianca as vigorously as she wanted to because somewhere in the back of her mind, she knew it wouldn't work. *This wasn't supposed to happen. We were supposed to make this right.*

Swallowing thickly, Cheyenne stood again and spun, looking for signs of life from anyone or anything. The natural forest, decimated by the blight, was silent, blasted away from where Bianca had stood with nothing left behind but a massive crater on the mountainside and hundreds of bodies.

"Ember?" She took a step toward her best friend, who lay with her legs bent awkwardly beneath her and didn't stir. No one stirred. Nothing moved but the ash fluttering down from the sky like snow.

Don't freak out. Cheyenne closed her eyes and forced herself to take a deep breath. *Just listen.*

But there was nothing. No shallow breath from any of the bodies around her. No wind whistling through what was left of the trees. No rising song or whisper of voices from the Nimlothars.

I did my part. Cheyenne's fists clenched and unclenched at her sides as her nose burned with the onset of tears. *I fucking did my part, and this wasn't the deal.*

Her chest ached as she spun and glared at the Nimlothar trees. Her racing heartbeat pounded in her ears. *This can't be right.*

"I did everything I had to do." She staggered toward the closest Nimlothar and slapped her palm against it, frowning in concentration. "Come on. You talked to me before. What did I miss?"

The trees remained as silent as everything else, and Cheyenne bashed her fist into the rough bark of the tree. "Tell me what I missed!"

Dull pain flared up her arm, and she stepped back to pull down the collar of her shirt and look at her poisoned wound. The black streaks had disappeared; all that remained was a gaping hole she was sure would heal now. She quickly checked her other shoulder and the wound on her hip and found the same result in both. *No. I didn't do this to heal myself while everyone else died.* "What the fuck do I do?"

A shimmer of thin white light appeared within the Nimlothar forest, then elongated and coalesced around a tall figure. The light flashed, and Cheyenne's breath escaped when she found herself staring at one of the Olfarím.

The tall, eerily thin magical in flowing white robes stared back at her. "It is finished."

"No. No, it's not." Cheyenne headed toward the Olfarím. "This wasn't supposed to happen."

"This pattern in the Weave is fully repaired now, Weaver's daughter." The magical dipped his head, those icy-blue eyes piercing through her. "You have completed the threads, as we foresaw."

"As you foresaw? You mean, you knew this would happen?" When the Olfarím said nothing, Cheyenne stormed toward him. "You all sat in your towers in Nor'ieth and saw this playing out, and you show up *now*? Why didn't you step in to stop it? You could have!"

"It is not our place."

Cheyenne roared, black drow fire flaring to life on her body and racing across her skin. She launched a column of flames at the Olfarím, which crashed into an unseen shield around the magical and fizzled away. She doubled down on the flames and kept pushing.

In the back of her mind, she knew it wouldn't work. The Olfarím lived in a different dimension and had more powerful and concentrated magic than existed anywhere else, could open Border portals at will, and could read the Weave to see what would happen when Cheyenne brought every drow in Hangivol out here to heal the Nimlothars.

No, to die. This is all on me.

Screaming, Cheyenne took one more step toward the Olfarím, still funneling the column of black fire against the other magical's unwavering shield. Then all the strength went out of her, and she dropped to her knees again. The black fire flickered out, leaving smoke trailing from her skin, and she drew a ragged breath. "You could have stopped it."

"The Weave unravels in both directions, drow." The Olfarím cocked his head. "Or not at all."

"That doesn't mean anything." Cheyenne's vision blurred with hot tears. "Not now."

The Olfarím raised both hands in front of him, and a low hum filled

Cheyenne's head. She looked at the glowing light around the other magical as silver threads appeared in the air in front of him.

His long pale fingers twitched the illuminated threads, pulling and rearranging. A web of silver lines stretched from the last string of light toward every Nimlothar and the drow lying beside them.

"What are you doing?"

The Olfarím didn't answer.

"Just cut it out with the mysteries, okay? It's not like there's anything left to protect." She swallowed thickly. "Are you even listening to me? They're all dead!"

The new pattern of glowing threads pulsed with white light, then the Olfarím's piercing blue gaze lowered to ensnare Cheyenne's attention once more. "It is the same."

"No, it's not!"

The magical disappeared, and the glowing threads racing across the forest faded into nothing but air.

"Wait!" Cheyenne rose to her feet and stumbled against the closest Nimlothar.

A jolt of warm energy burst from the tree's bark into her hand, followed by faint but very real violet light.

What?

She stepped back and lowered her hand as she gazed into the bare branches looming over her.

The tree swayed, the branches moving on their own without a hint of a breeze. Wood creaked and groaned, and the Nimlothar forest grew. Purple light raced across the deadened bark and flickered up into the tallest branches. The trunks softened, uncurling from their bent and twisted forms. More purple light raced in bright veins across the ground beneath Cheyenne's feet, pulsing into the Nimlothars' roots and fueling their magic as they repaired themselves. Leaves sprouted from every branch, the trees growing and filling out into thicker, deeper-purple versions of the last Nimlothar in the Heart.

Not the last one anymore.

Cheyenne stepped back, glancing from tree to tree as small dark buds like berries appeared on the branches and burst to life. The purple-black blossoms with golden centers unfolded around her and the Nimlothar forest rustled its foliage, shaking its branches with renewed life without wind to make them move.

The purple light filling the trunks of the forest spread over the ground, surging into the fallen drow beside every tree and illuminating the hands they'd placed on the bark to lend their lives.

The first drow stirred, choking on a mouthful of dust as he drew his first breath. Cheyenne spun around when a drow woman behind her heaved herself onto her hands and knees and gasped.

More groans came from the crater in the earth where the battle had raged. Lumil grunted and slammed a fist into the ground. "What the fuck?"

"Shit." Cheyenne darted past the drow woman in front of her, who reached out to brush her fingertips against the halfling's thigh. She paused to look at the drow gazing up at her with wide golden eyes and a flickering smile. "You good?"

The drow woman chuckled and got to her feet.

Cheyenne passed blossoming Nimlothars and rising drow and went to her mom's side first. Bianca bolted upright with a gasp, breathing heavily, but paused when her daughter dropped to the ground beside her. "Mom."

"Cheyenne." Bianca gazed up at lush branches full of purple leaves and purple flowers so dark they were almost black. "I somehow ended up on the ground. Again. Are we ready to start?"

A sharp laugh of relief burst from Cheyenne's mouth, and she grabbed her mom's hand to give it a gentle squeeze. "We already started. Finished, too. It's over."

Bianca cleared her throat, and her eyes widened when she saw the crater of scorched earth stretching out in front of her. "What happened?"

"The balance is returned." R'leer jammed the butt of his bone staff into the ground and used it to climb to his feet. His golden eyes glistened as he stared at the Nimlothars and the drow coming back to life around him. "We are returned."

"Holy shit." Ember ran a hand over her violet-streaked hair, pushing dead leaves and bits of splintered wood off her head. "I don't even know what that was."

Maleshi offered the fae a hand up, and the rest of Cheyenne's friends rose as well. Ember grinned when she saw the blossoming Nimlothar forest behind her. Corian stopped beside Maleshi and set a gentle hand on the general's shoulder.

Venga folded two of his arms and hissed. "This was what she did with it."

"What?" Cheyenne stood and helped Bianca to her feet, making sure her mom could stand on her own before turning her attention to the necromancer. "You mean Ba'rael?"

"Do not say her name!" The scaleback whirled on her and pointed with two clawed hands at the destroyed forest where the blight had almost taken them all down. "I didn't pour hundreds of years into my work for the Spider bitch to unleash it like this!"

"It's done," Corian muttered. "There's nothing left."

"What about them?" Ember nodded at Cazerel and the two dozen raug warriors gathered around three of their fallen. The dead raug didn't look any different from the once-blighted magicals and wildlife who'd attacked their party. All of the blight was gone from their flesh.

"They were too far gone, just like the others." Maleshi frowned at the bodies scattered around the crater. "But the final deathflame brought them peace."

Corian approached Cazerel and his warriors and thumped a fist on his chest. "We're in your debt, *Zokri*."

"No." The raug chief turned away from his fallen tribesmen and thumped his chest in return. "There are no debts when so much is at stake. You gave us a warning, and we offered aid."

They nodded at each other, and Cazerel's orange eyes flicked toward Ember. "Healer."

"*Zokri*." Ember glanced at Cheyenne.

"I must ask." The chief gestured at the three raug on the ground, surrounded by the other warriors. "Is there anything you can do?"

The fae shook her head. "I'm not that kind of healer. I'm sorry."

"I want no apology from you." Cazerel waved her off. "It is the price of battle."

"The price of restoration," R'leer added, walking slowly toward Cheyenne with a crazed grin. "You felt it, didn't you? You must have."

Cheyenne shook her head. "I don't know what you're saying right now, but you need to back up and quit looking at me like that."

The darkseller stopped and stared at her.

I don't think I can handle drow crazy right now.

"What did you see?" he whispered.

She swallowed. "More than I wanted to, but now it's done."

"Yes." R'leer turned to the drow scattered through the blooming Nimlothar forest and raised his staff. "It is finished, *mór edhil*! The Black Flame has restored what was once ours!"

"May the Black Flame reign!" The echoing cry from hundreds of drow mouths made Bianca turn quickly to frown at them.

"No," Cheyenne growled, shaking her head. "I'm not reigning over anything."

R'leer thumped the fist holding the staff to his chest, rattling the beads and bones strung through his headdress, then thrust the end of his staff against the ground again. The Hangivol drow repeated the gesture, each gray-skinned fist flashing with purple Nimlothar light as they struck.

"We see only one O'gúl Crown," shouted a drow with a sharply hooked nose and white hair pulled back in a half-ponytail.

"The Black Flame of Ambar'ogúl."

"We follow the Black Flame."

"Our lives for the *Lainarí*."

Cheyenne swallowed as the drow marked by the Nimlothars shouted their sworn allegiance. She felt Corian approaching behind her and shot him a look over her shoulder. "What is that? *Lainarí*."

"It's like 'Deliverer.'"

"No. No, that's not why I did this."

He shrugged. "Not a direct translation."

"I don't want anyone following me anywhere or giving their lives or calling me *Lainarí*." Cheyenne stepped forward and swept her hand across the forest. *Fuck, it's hard to look them in the eyes.* "Don't give me the credit for this, okay? We needed all of you, and it wouldn't have happened without you here, so just forget this whole Black Flame thing."

Cries of "*Lainarí*," rose again from the drow.

"Hey, cut it out!" Cheyenne shouted back. "Persh'al Tenishi sits the O'gúl throne. The Ironbreak, remember?"

The drow thumped their glowing purple fists on their chests again, and she shook her head.

"I'd just ignore it, kid." Maleshi stopped on the other side of Cheyenne and folded her arms. "Put an idea in a drow's head, and they're the only ones who can change their mind. You know how that goes."

"They won't stop even if I order them to, huh?"

"Probably not." The general placed a hand on Cheyenne's shoulder and gave it a gentle squeeze. "Just think about what we did here today. That's all that matters."

"Yeah." The drow swallowed and frowned at the blossoming branches rustling overhead. *And nobody remembers dying?*

"Look at you, Cheyenne." Lumil stalked toward her and punched the drow in the shoulder. The goblin woman's smile faded instantly when the Cheyenne grimaced. "Oh. Shit. Sorry, kid. Your fucking shoulder."

"Yeah, well." Cheyenne pulled down the collar of her shirt and gazed at a wound that held no traces of the poisoned streaks. "Looks like the blight is gone from everywhere now, so what's a little gaping wound, right?"

"No way!" Byrd shoved Lumil out of the way to get a closer look, then wrinkled his nose. "Still looks nasty, but hey, improvement."

"Man, what the hell are you shoving me around for?" Lumil pushed him back. "You gonna try to heal that shit or something?"

"I just wanted to see."

"Keep your nasty green hands off me, asshole."

"Fuck you."

Cheyenne and Maleshi looked at each other and stepped away to let the goblins duke it out on their own.

Venga rolled his eyes at the bickering goblins.

Corian nodded at Cheyenne with a small smile. "You did it."

"I almost didn't."

Ember frowned. "What are you talking about?"

Cheyenne shook her head. "Not something I wanna go through right now." *But I bet I'll be dreaming about it. Shit.* She turned to Bianca. "You're sure you're okay?"

"I don't have much to compare it to." Bianca raised her eyebrows. "But I *can* say I've felt worse in the last seventy-two hours."

Maleshi leaned toward the woman, "You know, we have a few things in this world that work well for that."

"I'm sure you do."

Cheyenne stared at the general's knowing grin. "If you're thinking about another party…"

"That's exactly what I'm thinking, kid." Maleshi winked at her. "And your mom deserves the best. She did wipe the blight off the face of Ambar'ogúl with magic a human shouldn't be able to wield, after all."

Bianca put her head back and looked at the trees one more time. "I wouldn't object to a good stiff drink."

"Oh, we'll have fun."

"Wait a minute." Cheyenne pointed at the general. "You're not playing drinking games with my mom."

"Cheyenne, I hardly think a drink is going to do more damage than this." Bianca gestured at the crater at the edge of the forest and turned away. "I would like to leave this place as soon as possible."

"As long as there's nothing else that needs to happen here." Cheyenne glanced at R'leer. "Is there?"

"Not at the moment." The darkseller dipped his head but held her gaze, the corners of his mouth flickering. "But the Nimlothars must be guarded."

Ember frowned and leaned away from him. "Against what?"

R'leer looked the fae up and down. "More drow." He gestured at the forest with his bone staff. "Once word of the new power here spreads, many will come to take the seeds for their trials. We have a duty to ensure the Nimlothars remain."

"Whatever you have to do." Cheyenne shrugged. "I promised to heal these things, not set up security."

His eyes narrowed. "I have your permission, then?"

"Well, you don't need it, but sure." *I won't be around for all that anyway. Mom and I can't stay.*

R'leer's smile widened. "My life for the Black Flame."

"Not you too." Cheyenne turned to the nightstalkers and gestured at the empty cratered space in front of them. "Can we go back to Hangivol and figure out the rest from there?"

Corian fought back a laugh and dipped his head. "As you wish."

Maleshi chuckled, and they raised their hands together to cast a massive portal that led to the capital city.

When the portal opened, Corian searched the crowd of magicals gathering to leave the mountains and nodded. Cheyenne turned to see Cazerel and his raug warriors stalking out of the Nimlothar forest for the return journey to Hirúl Breach without a word to anyone. *Best way to leave something like this. I don't blame them.*

The drow filtered out of the forest and headed toward the giant window of dark light that appeared in front of the nightstalkers. As everyone headed through it, Cheyenne stood back to watch her mom walk alongside Maleshi, their heads bent toward each other as they engaged in a low conversation.

Ember nudged her friend in the arm. "I bet we can finally get those dart holes healed now."

"Yeah, Em. That'd be great."

The fae eyed the drow moving past them toward the portal, the ones closest to Cheyenne dipping their heads and thumping fists on their chests as they walked by.

Cheyenne closed her eyes. *They're swearing fealty to the wrong magical. I let them die.*

"Hey, you okay?"

Clearing her throat, Cheyenne ran a hand through her hair. "I have no idea, but a drink sounds like the next best thing right now."

"I'm pretty sure we can dig something up." Ember nodded at the portal and Corian waiting beside it.

The nightstalker stared as R'leer strolled casually through the window into Hangivol and frowned. Then he bowed as he gestured toward their exit.

"The nightstalker's making fun of me," Cheyenne muttered.

Ember fought back a smile. "Better than swearing his undying allegiance, right?"

C H A P T E R   F I V E

By the time everyone re-entered Hangivol's drow inner circle, the sky was pink and orange with the first rays of sunrise. Cheyenne took a deep breath and gazed at the tall metal walls of the buildings rising on both sides of the main avenue. *I can't believe it's over. Still feels like the other shoe's about to drop.*

Maleshi, Bianca, Venga, and the goblins were on their way toward the fortress, Byrd and Lumil shouting at each other about who would drink whom under the table.

"Hey, drow like to party, right?" Lumil turned and spread her arms as she walked backward, grinning at the drow standing motionlessly in the main avenue. "Party in the fortress, bitches. BYOG."

Byrd snorted and tossed a hand in the air. "G for grog. Or whatever else you got up here!"

Maleshi turned to wink at Cheyenne. "We'll save a tankard for you, kid. Don't take too long."

The side door to the fortress burst open and Persh'al stormed out, surrounded by a contingent of eight orc guards who looked just as pissed as their Crown.

"Shit." Cheyenne looked at the drow staring at her. "It's over. You can go home."

Nobody moved as she headed after Maleshi and Bianca and the

39

angry troll ruler marching toward them. Ember jogged to keep up with her friend. "What's going on?"

"Beats me, but I haven't seen him this pissed since—"

They both ducked when they heard a sharp pop and a rain of sparks fell from the top of the building beside them. The drow in the street spoke in low, semi-concerned voices as blue lines of electricity snaked across the metal paving the avenue. Cheyenne stared at the malfunctioning building wall and tried to process the information her activator fed her.

System failure at 42.85.9. Attempting to—

The rest of the notice showed only O'gúl symbols that wouldn't translate, even when she prompted it manually.

Or as manually as an activator got.

"Since when?" Ember frowned at the sparking walls and jumped when a series of building doors opened and banged shut again in quick succession without a magical standing on either side of them.

"Since he couldn't get tech to work for him Earthside. Now it's not working here either."

They hurried toward Persh'al and his guards, joined by Corian as the new O'gúl Crown tried to hold his anger in check. "What the hell did you do?"

"The answer to that question covers an awful lot of ground," Maleshi muttered. "Wanna be a little more specific?"

Persh'al stopped when he saw Cheyenne, and his orange eyes narrowed. "The whole fell-damn city's had some kinda power outage."

Lumil nodded, her mop of yellow hair flopping across her eyes before she shook it back. "Looks pretty well-lit to me."

"It's not the power," Cheyenne said.

"The system! You think I don't know that?" Persh'al's fists clenched at his sides as he scanned the avenue, which was still filled with the drow. "Might as well be the power. Nothing's working."

"Nothing?" Corian swept his gaze across the level. "Things would look a lot different if the whole system was down."

"It's not down, just malfunctioning." The troll spread his arms. "Anyone have an answer for that?"

A muffled shout of anger rose from behind the fortress wall, followed by a zapping electrical charge and the shriek of tearing metal. The side door burst open, sending shards of metal out onto the street, and Elarit stormed toward them. Her violet eyes blazed as she shoved a sparking silver orb into the pocket of her long overcoat. The delicate silver chains strung from ear to ear across her cheeks and nose jingled violently with each step. "I knew it."

Persh'al turned toward her and lifted a hand. "Hold on a sec."

"No." The troll woman slapped his hand away, then pointed at Cheyenne. "We've done everything we could to make things work, and this is how you thank us?"

"What?" Cheyenne leaned away and frowned at the Crown's wife, or whatever her title was on this side of the Border. "I didn't do anything."

"You failed, then?" Elarit folded her arms and glared from Cheyenne to Corian to Maleshi. "You took all the drow out to the middle of nowhere, fucked up your mission, and came right back to tell us not to blame you for it?"

Cheyenne shook her head. "We didn't fail."

"Then explain why the fell-damn system's falling apart at the seams."

"I can't."

Elarit hissed and shook off Persh'al's gentle grip on her arm to stop inches from Cheyenne. "I tried to ignore it, but I always knew what you'd bring with you when you showed up to tell everyone who you are. Of course, L'zar's daughter would be as bad as he is."

"Elarit!"

"You're even worse!" The troll woman shoved Cheyenne with both hands.

"Hey!" Cheyenne ignored the flare of pain in her shoulders. It wasn't as bad as when they were poisoned, but they weren't healed yet. "Don't touch me."

"Or what?" Elarit spat. "You gave away the throne, *nilsch úcat*. You can't challenge to take it back."

"Stop it." Persh'al stepped toward them. "This isn't on her."

"And I don't want the throne," Cheyenne added. "Whatever you think I did, it wasn't on purpose."

"That's the problem. You don't have a plan past how it'll benefit you."

"This isn't the time," Persh'al muttered. "We need to get inside."

Elarit jerked her wrist out of Persh'al's grasp and whirled on him. "Don't protect her. By the fell-damn Crown, Persh'al! She's bringing the whole thing down on our heads!"

A dark streak of light hurdled through the air and struck the avenue at Elarit's feet. She spun again and snarled at the six drow moving swiftly toward the group. Maleshi and Corian stepped aside with wide eyes.

"Whoa, hey." Cheyenne spread her arms to cut the drow off. "You can't do shit like that."

"Neither can she." A drow man with particularly dark gray skin peered around Cheyenne to sneer at Elarit and Persh'al. "She put her hands on you."

"Yeah, and I'm a grown-ass adult. Thanks."

"You are welcome." The dark drow slipped around her, followed by the other five. All of them summoned orbs of magic in their hands, one palm of each flaring purple with Nimlothar magic straight from the source.

"No, I didn't mean go!" She hurried after them, and the drow stopped when Persh'al's guards stepped in front of him and Elarit, banging their massive swords against shields and snarling at the drow. "Stop."

"Cheyenne?" Persh'al glared at the drow in front of his guards. "What is this?"

"It's nothing." She lowered the closest drow's arm, and the woman blinked at her but didn't snuff out the attack magic in her hand. "Don't."

"We swore our—"

"Whatever you swore, I didn't accept, okay? You don't get to come back here and start picking fights with the damn Crown!"

Another drow with rings of gold and silver lining the cartilage of her pointy ears sneered at Persh'al and Elarit. "May the Black Flame reign."

"I told you." Elarit pulled the silver orb from the pocket of her long coat. It flared to life with a low hum, and she glared at her husband. "I told you we couldn't trust her."

"She doesn't want anything from us," Persh'al muttered. "Not like that."

"What you have is what she gave you," snarled the dark-skinned drow man. "It will never truly be yours."

"That's treason, *nilsch úcat*," an orc guard growled. "Hold your tongue."

"Or what?" The drow man raised the hand crackling with drow magic and purple Nimlothar light. "We've already been through the deathflame. You can do nothing."

"Okay, stop. *Stop!*" Cheyenne muscled her way between the threatening drow and the growling orc guards with their weapons at the ready. "This is the last thing we need right now."

"Let us finish it," the drow woman with all the earrings muttered.

"No!"

"At your word, Ironbreak." The guard in front of Persh'al stepped forward and banged his shield with his sword. "I'd love to fight a drow."

"There will be no word. Stand down." Persh'al frowned at the guard when the orc turned in confusion. "I said, stand down. This isn't happening."

Neither the orcs nor the drow moved from their attack stances.

"Seriously?" Cheyenne gestured at the buildings lining the main avenue. "If you're still hopped up on deathflame, fine, but take it somewhere else." She peered around the six drow and found the rest of the inner-circle drow intently watching the brewing tension. "Everybody, go home! Sleep it off or something."

The dark-skinned drow man snuffed out the magic in his palm and stepped back, though his golden eyes still blazed at the orc guards. The other five did the same.

That's as good as it's gonna get right now. And where the hell did R'leer go? She scanned the avenue but didn't see a single feather or hear any bones clacking together. Probably went right back to his darkseller hole. Fine.

Cheyenne raised her eyebrows at Bianca and nodded at the fortress' broken side door. "Come on. Let's get inside."

Her mom raised an eyebrow and followed Cheyenne without a word.

Elarit glared at Persh'al. "You're not gonna say anything?"

"I *was*, before someone decided to pick a fight."

The troll woman shook her head and stormed away, heading for a different side door so she wouldn't have to follow Cheyenne and Bianca.

Byrd snorted and clapped Persh'al roughly on the back. "Trouble in paradise, huh?"

"Shut up." The troll Crown looked at the rest of their party and gestured at the broken door. "We can talk about what happened inside."

"Uh-huh." With her arms folded, Maleshi turned to cast the crowd of drow a confused look. "Probably a good idea."

His orc guards led the way toward the side door, and the rest of their group followed.

A chunk of the broken door clattered to the ground as Cheyenne bashed it aside to clear the way.

Bianca studied the hole in the torn metal. "That's not a very constructive way to channel your frustration."

"Mom." Cheyenne took a deep breath and forced herself to calm down. "This door should've repaired itself already. I'm getting the broken pieces out of the way."

"If you say so. Shall we, then?"

Okay, now *she sounds like herself again.* Cheyenne stepped aside to let the guards through first. None of them met her gaze as they stomped into the armory beyond. She pressed her lips together and gestured inside as Persh'al approached.

He paused slightly. "I didn't know she was gonna do that."

"I didn't know any of this was gonna happen, so it's fine." She shook her head. "Let's go talk somewhere with no guards and no drow hanging around, huh?"

"Good idea." Scowling, the blue troll stepped through the doorway.

"We do all that and still can't keep the shit from hittin' the fan, huh?" Lumil snorted as she passed Cheyenne and Bianca. "Some kinda gratitude."

"Man, are you trying to start a fight too?" Byrd muttered.

"The damn sparksetter almost started a civil war, you moron."

"No, she didn't."

The goblins' bickering echoed through the armory as they followed Persh'al.

"General." Bianca lifted her chin toward Maleshi as the nightstalkers approached the broken door. "I have a few questions for you if you don't mind."

"By all means." Maleshi dipped her head and gestured inside. "Walk with me?"

"Thank you." Bianca didn't look at her daughter as she joined the general, and Corian chuckled as he followed them with his hands clasped behind his back.

Ember stopped beside Cheyenne to wait for Venga to storm into the fortress before they brought up the rear. "That was weird."

"Yeah, like they're suddenly best fucking friends."

"Wait, what?"

Cheyenne glanced over her shoulder at the drow filling the main avenue, yet to disperse, and reflexively waved her hand at the doorway. The sheared metal sparked and trembled, but of course, the door didn't close. "Bianca and Maleshi."

"No, I meant your new bodyguards, but whatever."

"Oh." Cheyenne ran a hand through her hair and scanned the weapons on the armory's shelves and scattered across the metal tables. "Jesus, Em. I seriously hope they're all on some kinda 'We healed the forest' power trip. I don't have it in me to deal with another rebellion."

Ember snorted. "That would be a little counterproductive."

"You heard her, right? She thinks I'm worse than L'zar."

"Yeah, but you're not." The door on the opposite side of the armory slammed shut with a metallic bang and belched blue sparks at them. "What the hell?"

Cheyenne waved at the door, but the command prompt from her activator only managed to open the thing four inches. She grimaced and shoved the door open the rest of the way with her uninjured hip before holding it open for her friend. "I'm trying to help."

When they headed down the hall, the armory door slammed shut again and sent crackling blue lines of electricity racing ahead of them along the walls. Ember shook her head. "Anyone who can't see that is a fucking idiot. Elarit and Persh'al are trying to figure out what they're doing too."

"I know. As long as it doesn't include her trying to kill me in my sleep, it's fine."

Ember fought back a laugh. "You know, before now, I don't think I could've imagined her doing that."

"Oh, but now you can?"

"I mean, maybe."

Cheyenne said, "She can try, but I hope she doesn't. I kinda like her."

"She makes a pretty badass second-in-command, right?"

They laughed softly, then Corian appeared around the corner ahead of them and raised his eyebrows. "Might wanna pick up the pace a little. Maleshi found the Crown's private fellwine cellar."

"To share with Bianca?" Cheyenne picked up the pace, scowling at the nightstalker when he chuckled.

"I think she's earned it."

"She can drink half of DC under the table if she wants to, but that's with scotch. You told her what fellwine is, right?"

Corian shrugged.

"Come on."

CHAPTER SIX

"Whoa." Ember stopped at the open doors into Persh'al's living quarters and cocked her head. "I wasn't expecting this."

"Taking it up a notch from Ba'rael's secret sleeping vault," Cheyenne muttered.

On the far-left side of the massive receiving room, Venga spun away from the banquet laid out on a long table and hissed, "I will not suffer hearing that name, Cheyenne."

"Feel free to leave." She frowned at him as she and Ember followed Corian into the room. "Not gonna censor myself to make you more comfortable."

"You ungrateful—" He stomped toward her, his clawed feet shrieking across the stone floor. "I'm the one who discovered the Vessel's—"

"You're the one who made the Undoing for Ba'rael." Cheyenne glared at him and slowly shook her head. "*We* cleaned up *your* mess today, not the other way around."

"Cheyenne," Maleshi called from the other side of the room, "the fellwine's flowin', kid. Come celebrate with us."

Venga's black eyes twitched as he stared Cheyenne down, then she turned away from him to head toward the huge half-circle of O'gúleesh armchairs, settees, benches, couches, and pillows thrown across the

47

floor at the other end of the room. Bianca and Maleshi were already sitting on one couch. A tray stacked with metal cups occupied on the low table in front of them, and the general raised an open bottle of fellwine with a grin.

Cheyenne met her mom's gaze. "Did she tell you what that is?"

"Yes, Cheyenne. She had me at 'five times stronger than whiskey.'"

"Oh, jeez."

Corian chuckled and dropped into an armchair across from the couch. "Pour the drinks, then."

"Got anything else?" Ember asked.

"Oh." Persh'al hurried toward the far wall at the back of the huge receiving room and passed his hand over the metal, which was spelled to look like stone. The illusion flickered across the wall, metal showing through where it wasn't supposed to as flashes of blue light trailed across the surface instead of the commands he wanted.

"Damnit." The blue troll pounded on the wall with a fist, then leaned closer to try a gentler, more technical approach. "See, this is what I'm talking about. That power surge fried the whole system, and now I can't get…"

His fingers swept up and down the wall, connecting different commands in a long series to get the drawer to open. When it finally did, he grunted and snatched two green glass bottles and a brown one from the drawer but left it open before coming to rejoin everyone else in the sitting area.

Cheyenne was too busy warily watching Maleshi pour Bianca a full cup of fellwine to immediately realize what Persh'al had said. The liquor bottles thumped onto the metal table and made her look up at him. "Did you say, power surge?"

"Yeah." A green bottle of Bloodshine popped open in his hand, and he glanced up at her every few seconds as he filled a cup with the insanely bubbly golden liquid. "About an hour before you all ported back into the city. Would've jolted me awake if I'd been able to sleep."

"Aw, listen to that." Byrd nudged Lumil's shoulder as she lifted a cup of fellwine to her lips. She glared at him until he added, "Little Troll Blue was worried sick about us."

Lumil snorted into her cup and took a long drink.

Persh'al ignored them and handed the Bloodshine to Ember. "Here."

"Thanks." Ember took a small drink and wrinkled her nose like she was about to sneeze.

"The whole city's gone into some kinda half-powered tech malfunction," Persh'al continued. "I checked."

"That would be the deathflame, most likely." Corian crossed one leg over the other and took a long drink from his metal cup.

Cheyenne absently accepted a cup of fellwine from Maleshi but frowned at Persh'al. "What does the deathflame have to do with all the city tech?"

"Beyond both of them being fueled by magic?" Persh'al knocked back a long guzzle of fellwine straight from the bottle, then shrugged. "Beats me."

The bottle thumped back down on the table, and he belched before lowering himself onto a pile of massive pillows.

Bianca stared into her fizzing cup of glowing green fellwine and licked her lips. "Now that I think about it, this looks an awful lot like the last thing I drank."

"The deathflame?" Maleshi chuckled and waved away the comparison. "This is good old-fashioned O'gúl fellwine, woman. Might get you tipsy faster than you expect, but you sure as hell won't burst into flame."

"Ha." Byrd snorted. "Because that happened *last* time."

Bianca lowered the cup into her lap and stared at the sniggering goblins. "Excuse me?"

"What?" Lumil shrugged. "It did."

Slowly closing her eyes, Bianca let out a long, restrained exhale through her nose. "I have no memory of that."

"Wait, for real?"

Byrd snorted. "You were fucking epic, I'll tell you that much. I mean, for a human."

Maleshi leaned away from Bianca and frowned. "What do you remember?"

"Drinking something that looked much like absinthe." Bianca looked at Cheyenne and lifted her chin. "And then I was on the ground. The rest of you seem to know what occurred between those two instances, and I would very much like to hear it. Right now."

The sitting area fell silent, making it impossible to ignore the hungry grunts and slurps coming from Venga at the banquet table on the other side of the receiving room.

"Mom." Cheyenne leaned forward to meet Bianca's gaze. "Maybe now isn't the right time."

"It's precisely the right time." Bianca turned away from her. "I've already spent too long incapacitated or unconscious or cursed. I want to know what happened."

Byrd grinned and pointed sharply at her. A slosh of fellwine spilled over the side of his cup. "You were fucking epic."

"Man, you already said that."

"It's worth saying twice, okay? Hell, I'll say it again. You were—"

"On fire." Lumil grinned at Bianca, her yellow eyes widening. "Green fucking deathflame all over your human ass. Craziest shit I've seen in a long time."

"And you needed the halfling's help to get the job done."

Bianca blinked. "The what?"

"Oh, shit." Byrd sniggered. "I meant Cheyenne. Deathflame, drow fire, burned the whole forest down and every drow with it."

Lumil shrugged. "Then we got attacked by blighted villagers and that fucking rabid *vondra*. The damn blight almost had us, then Cheyenne unleashed the Vessel beast."

Both goblins mimed tugging a collar away from their necks, and Bianca's hand rose reflexively to her neck to find Venga's blight-fueled collar gone.

"You blasted every undead bastard off the map, lady."

Lumil nodded toward Venga, who was still gobbling up the buffet. "And that bastard's blight with it."

The goblins clinked their cups together and drank deeply at the same time.

Bianca pursed her lips and stared at them. "Anything else?"

"Oh." Lumil belched and thumped a fist on her chest, then raised her cup toward Cheyenne. "You attacked your kid. Pretty savage if you ask me, but it got rid of those nasty holes in her."

"No, the holes are still there." Byrd shook his head. "Were you even paying attention?"

"The blight isn't there anymore, shitstain."

"Man, it's not the same thing."

"That's enough, thank you." Bianca turned to Cheyenne and took a deep breath, but the goblins wouldn't stop.

"You wanna go hold her down so I can show you the damn difference?"

"Yeah, good luck trying to hold the Black Flame down for a medical exam."

"Medical? You don't know the difference between fucking poison and a health cure."

"Stop talking!" Bianca shouted, her voice cutting harshly through the receiving room.

The goblins stared at her and blinked. Corian grinned into his cup and slurped loudly.

Bianca cleared her throat and looked at her daughter again. "I attacked you?"

"He means," Cheyenne explained, "you attacked the blight. There happened to be some in me at the time."

"Cheyenne."

"Yeah."

Bianca swallowed thickly, then her eyelids fluttered and she looked away. "It seems not to have hurt you that badly, so I'm glad to see it all worked out."

The woman stared at the low table as she lifted the fellwine to her lips and took a long drink.

"Oh, shit." Lumil burst out laughing. "Fucking epic."

Byrd scowled at her. "That's what *I* said."

Bianca took a deep breath, her eyes widening at the glowing green booze in her cup. "I see what you mean, General."

"Didn't I tell you to call me Maleshi?" The general chuckled.

"Yes, you did." A small smile flickered across Bianca's mouth. "I haven't been paying attention."

Maleshi threw her head back in a roaring laugh. Cheyenne took a huge drink of fellwine when she heard her mom laughing with the nightstalker. *This got way out of hand. Mom's going on a fellwine bender to forget that she doesn't remember attacking me. And I'm the only one who remembers everyone dying.*

The fellwine buzzed through her arms and legs, and she sucked in a deep breath.

"Well, I'd say it's been a long time coming." Corian raised his cup and gazed around their group. "So here's a toast."

"A fucking toast!" Lumil's cup sloshed over onto her hand when she thrust it into the air.

"To Bianca, our human Vessel."

"Bianca!"

"Oh, that's unnecessary," Bianca muttered, but she lifted her cup anyway and chuckled when Maleshi's clinked hers.

Corian met Cheyenne's gaze with his glowing silver eyes and nodded. "And the Black Flame who made it all possible."

"The Black Flame!" the goblins cheered together.

Cheyenne frowned at them, then looked at Persh'al. The blue troll shrugged. She shook her head. "Don't."

"Why the hell not, kid?" Maleshi slammed her now-empty cup on the table and refilled it before topping off Bianca's drink. "You came here for one thing, and it turned into five others. Now it's finished."

"No, it's not." Cheyenne gestured at Persh'al. "If the power surge came from what we did out there, it's our fault the system's down."

"Give yourself a break, kid." Corian leaned forward and propped his forearms on his thighs. "No offense to Persh'al the Ironbreak, but a malfunctioning tech system isn't on the top of the priority list."

"It should be." Persh'al glared at the nightstalker. "Do you have any idea how much information is stored here? It extends to every waystation in the Outers."

"Yeah, I have an idea." Corian snorted. "It's a better idea to take our wins where we can get 'em."

"Easy for you to say." The blue troll snatched the unopened bottle of Bloodshine and uncorked it with a loud pop. "You get to leave whenever the hell you want."

"Hey, no one forced you to take the throne."

"No one forced you to be an asshole either, *vae shra'ni*." Lifting the green bottle toward Corian in a mocking toast, Persh'al stood and headed toward the far end of the room, where the open alcohol drawer still protruded from the wall.

"Aw, come on," Maleshi called after him. "He's only an asshole when he's relieved."

Corian laughed and kept drinking.

Bianca sipped her fellwine and hiccupped softly. "There's a shortage of reasons to celebrate these days. I say we make the most of the ones we have."

"That, Ms. Summerlin, is the best piece of advice I've heard all week." Maleshi clinked her cup against Bianca's again, then the goblins took over the conversation by listing all the recent things they'd had reason to celebrate, and Cheyenne tuned them out.

"Hey." Ember leaned toward her. "Feel like being healed?"

"Might as well before something else goes wrong, right?"

Ember set her cup down on the side table next to one of the empty benches and couldn't help a small smile. "Weird mix in here of 'drink our problems away' and 'we can't party yet,' huh?"

"No kidding." Cheyenne pulled down the collar of her shirt and scanned the far wall of the receiving room, where Persh'al took a slug from the Bloodshine bottle before opening a large metal trunk on the floor. The warmth of Ember's gold healing magic coursed through the drow's shoulder, and Cheyenne took another drink. "Even weirder that Bianca's part of it."

Ember removed her hand from her friend's shoulder, smiled at the slight scar there, then remembered they were having a serious conversation. "Maybe she's not anymore, though. How's that feel?"

"What?"

"Your shoulder, Cheyenne."

"Oh." The drow looked down at the puckered flesh of the new scar. "Hell of a lot better, Em. Thanks."

"Next one."

Cheyenne pulled down the other side of her shirt to expose the second unhealed wound, and Ember's healing magic flooded down her other arm. "What do you mean, maybe she's not part of it anymore?"

Ember waited until her healing spell had finished running its course, then blinked slowly. "Just that she came here to do one thing. Now it's over. Things can go back to normal after this."

"Yeah, right." Cheyenne snorted. "Unless we find a way to wipe her memory of the last week without taking her sanity with it, I don't think that's gonna happen."

"Or maybe she's stronger than you give her credit for. You know, like someone else I know." Ember looked down at her friend's hip and raised her eyebrows. "Last one."

After pulling down the waistband of her pants to expose her hip, Cheyenne watched the fae heal her last wound and frowned. "I have no idea how I'm supposed to act around her once we go home."

The gold light winked out beneath Ember's palm, and she grabbed her metal cup from the side table and took a long, fizzy drink. "It's not like you live with her, and she won't be alone. I mean, sure, Eleanor won't know what the hell to think about all this, but you don't have to babysit your mom. Or whatever."

Right on cue, Bianca let out a sharp laugh at something Maleshi said before drinking deeply from her cup one more time.

"I don't know, Em." Cheyenne shot her friend a sidelong look. "I might have to. At least until we make the crossing again."

"That's up to you, I guess." Ember shrugged. "But for everything she's been through in the last week, she looks happy."

"Yeah. That's the part that worries me."

"Cheyenne." Persh'al took another long pull from the Bloodshine bottle and waved her toward him. "I wanna show you something."

"Yeah, okay." Cheyenne clinked her cup against Ember's and nodded at her mom, who was thoroughly enjoying herself with the two night-stalkers and the squabbling goblins. "Don't let them talk her into anything stupid."

"I'll do my best." With a barely restrained laugh, Ember joined Bianca and the magicals, and Cheyenne headed across the huge room toward Persh'al.

"What's up?"

Persh'al quickly looked up at her, then patted the floor beside him. "Pop a squat, kid. I'm about to show you something no one else in this whole fell-damn world has seen, except for Elarit and me."

"Oh, yeah?" She lowered herself to the floor, smiling when her body didn't protest the act of crossing her legs beneath her. *Pays to have a fae as a best friend, that's for sure.* "So, you're letting me in on a Crown secret, huh?"

"Something like that, yeah." He thumped the side of the open trunk in front of him with his boot. "We made it."

CHAPTER SEVEN

Cheyenne peered over the top of the trunk. "You made this?"

Persh'al snorted and drank from the bottle again before wiping his mouth with the back of a hand. "You look surprised."

"I'm just…well, no. I guess I'm not surprised. I've seen you build stuff Earthside."

"Yep. Way better resources over here." The troll sniffed. "Or at least there were."

They both stared at the complicated device taking up the entire bottom of the trunk, and Cheyenne took a deep breath. "So, I know it's the worst timing, but I didn't—"

"Look, kid," he said and set the Bloodshine bottle on the off-white stone floor beside him. "I know I stormed outside and started yelling at you. For a second there, I thought maybe I did wanna start a fight, but that's gone. I don't blame you for this, all right?"

"Yeah, okay." Cheyenne's gaze flicked toward the partially open door on the right-hand wall, hidden from the sitting area by the recessed niche in the corner. Elarit's scarlet eyes flashed in the room beyond before the troll woman moved away from the door to busy herself with something in the back room. *I guess there's more than one way to get in and out of their quarters. Not surprising.* "Somebody else blames me, though."

Either Persh'al hadn't noticed his wife peeking through the open door at them, or he ignored her. "She'll come around. This whole O'gúl-Crown bit is weird for me, sure, but you gotta understand where she's comin' from too, you know?"

"Except that the trolls are represented at the O'gúl capital now, I'm not sure what's changed for her. She's been here the whole time." Cheyenne downed the rest of her Bloodshine, and Persh'al took her cup from her to refill it. She didn't bother protesting.

"It's not about where we've been for the last few centuries, kid." He handed her the cup and ran blue fingers back and forth across his lips. "I mean, yeah. She still lives in Hangivol, and she spent the last few centuries thinking she'd never see me again. That L'zar would come waltzing back in here with some kid of his he dances around like a puppet on strings to make this whole world one more fucked-up reflection of another drow on the throne with all the wrong intentions."

Cheyenne frowned at him. "So, I screwed up her expectations, and now she's pissed because things aren't as bad as she expected?"

He snorted and picked up a thin gold-wrapped activator from the floor beside him. "I've never seen her happier, Cheyenne. Until over an hour ago when this whole system started scrambling itself, and neither of us can figure out why."

"It's a side effect."

"Yeah, I know. A big one."

"A big side effect from us getting rid of the blight."

Persh'al slowly turned his head to her and nodded. "I know."

"It could've been a lot worse."

"Sure, if you'd failed to heal the Nimlothars and restore the lifeforce to this entire world." He elbowed her in the side. "But come on. We both know failing isn't in your repertoire."

"We could call it failing with style."

Persh'al barked out a laugh. "The self-deprecating humor hits a soft spot in me, kid. I'll give you that. But the way I see it, you haven't failed once since Corian reached out to you and you figured out who you are."

Cheyenne swallowed and stared at the lip of the trunk. "I'm still figuring that out. But trust me. If the deathflame short-circuiting Hangivol's system for a while is the worst thing we have to deal with now, I'd say we got outta this pretty damn lucky."

She said it as he was halfway through another guzzle of Bloodshine, which almost spilled down his face when he quickly lowered the bottle and blinked at her. Persh'al's loud gulp made him grimace. "Something else happened out there, didn't it?"

"Doesn't matter."

"Come on. You know all I'd have to do is ask a nightstalker or one of the terror twins over there, so you might as well tell me yourself."

Cheyenne shook her head. "They don't know. That's why it doesn't matter." *And how the hell am I supposed to sit down and tell everyone that we did fail and they all died? They'd drink every bottle of booze in the city.*

Persh'al squinted at her, then shrugged. "You know where to find me if you change your mind. And since I don't know what could be worse than every piece of tech going haywire, how 'bout you help me figure this out, huh?"

"Sure." She scooted closer to the open trunk and peered over the lip at the long machine at the bottom. "What am I looking at here? Some kinda castle built from scrap metal?"

"Very funny." The troll tilted his head. "Does kinda look like a human castle."

She reached over the side of the trunk toward a panel her activator labeled System Access.

"Whoa, whoa. Hey." Persh'al grabbed her wrist and shook his head. "I didn't say you could touch it."

"Oh, so this is one of those 'help but don't touch' kinda favors."

"You know what? You're gettin' real cocky with your tech skills."

"Okay, fine. I won't touch."

Persh'al chuckled. "Yeah, you will. Just let me show you what's up first. For now, we're calling this thing the motherboard."

Cheyenne shrugged and muttered over the rim of her cup, "For a system that was built way before you became the Crown. I'm not the only one getting cocky."

"It stuck. Maybe I'll think of something better when we get everything back online. But forget the damn name. I wanted something right here in my room that got me access to every part of the system without having to go all the way down to wherever the hell that mainframe vault is."

"Big round room? Feels like the brain of a machine the size of a city?"

"You've been there already." Persh'al shuddered. "Place gives me the creeps."

"Well, L'zar did seem especially happy to be there. Even when he was all wrapped up in the Weave, or whatever."

"Of course he did." With a snigger, Persh'al stuck the gold-wrapped activator behind his ear and hissed as his eyelids fluttered. "Shit. Even the activators are reacting."

The troll thumped the side of his head with the heel of his palm and snorted.

"You okay?"

"That damn pinch makes me feel like a fucking noob all over again." He sniffed and shook his head. "I'm good. So check this out. The control panel you almost touched without permission is the controls, obviously. The rest of this thing is more or less like VR for the whole city system. Sucks you in, you know?"

Cheyenne frowned at him and couldn't hold back a small smile. "Not really. Do you mean, like, literally?"

"Smartass. I want you to go in and see what you can find, yeah? I get blocked every time I try, but I have a feeling the Black Flame can blast her way through almost everything. Including a few technical issues."

"Feel free to stop calling me that."

"What, the Black Flame?"

"Yeah." Cheyenne widened her eyes at him. "Not what I'm trying to be right now."

"That name's going down in history, kid. Like it or not."

"I spent all of twenty minutes as the Crown, okay? I don't need a title."

Persh'al chuckled and shook his head, the tips of his mohawk fluttering. "It's not a title, Cheyenne. It's who you are. That's not going away."

"See that human over there getting wasted on fellwine? She's the one who named me. I'm good with that."

"All right." Smirking, Persh'al pointed at the control panel. "Neither of us is gonna win this one, so go ahead and do your thing."

"So now I can touch it?"

"Yes, you now have the Ironbreak's fell-damn permission to touch the fucking machine, Cheyenne." He snorted. "Just pay attention to the exit command. Should be in the bottom right corner, but it moved the last time I went in. Took me an extra five seconds to pull out."

"Are there virtual monsters in your VR system too?"

"Just do it already."

Smiling despite how funny everything else *wasn't* right now, Cheyenne reached out and placed her hand on the machine's only smooth surface. Sparks flared beneath her palm, and a hot jolt of energy rushed up her arm and into her head.

"Shit. Sorry, kid. That's not supposed to…"

Persh'al's voice faded with everything else: the machine, the trunk, the entire room, all the voices coming from the sitting area as Bianca drank and made merry with nightstalkers and the goblins. Cheyenne sucked in a sharp breath as lines of code flashed and swirled around her. When she looked down at her hand, Persh'al's machine was gone, and she was standing on a surface made of scrolling blue O'gúleesh symbols.

"Huh. Virtual version of the vault he's too scared to walk into." She gazed up at the high walls of code in the shape of the circular room in the fortress' lower levels, but it wasn't anything like standing there in person. Half the coded lines flickered and jerked instead of their usual smooth movement. Most of it translated into English, but huge blocks of the system wouldn't budge from their O'gúleesh symbols.

Not the easiest thing to find out what's wrong if I can't understand it.

She slowly turned in a circle, noting the fragmented command lines interspersed with huge sections of blank blackness. She stopped when she found the entire "back wall" of the virtual room blank in front of her. *It's not even a wall, just nothing.*

The huge black expanse started two inches from where she stood, sucking the light from the room. The scrolling code lines looked like they should have kept moving behind it but disappeared instead. Frowning, Cheyenne reached out to touch the blackness, and a jolt of energy raced up her arm. Yellow and orange O'gúleesh symbols illuminated on the solid-feeling wall in front of her and quickly disappeared again. She pressed the wall with her palm, and her activator's warning alarm simultaneously blared and somehow appeared in her head.

Access denied. Command Alpha-G50ttemblrg_ notfunctionalerrorerrorerror_ withdrawing_ access_ NOT APPLICABLE.

"What the fuck?" As soon as she removed her hand, the activator's alarm and the ridiculous error message disappeared. Cheyenne frowned at the black wall in front of her and nudged it with the toe of her shoe. A ripple of orange and yellow symbols flared up the wall in a scattered array, the symbols toppling back down again over nothing until they disappeared. *Yeah, that's not supposed to happen.*

She moved down the wall, testing it every foot by brushing her fingers against the blackness. The wall's response was the same every time. Stopping in front of the edge of the black wall where it met the other stuttering lines of blue code she could read, Cheyenne scanned the commands racing around her. Her activator illuminated a single command on the circular wall:

Decrypt system failure.

At least there is a built-in option.

She pressed the command and dragged it toward the black wall. Blue sparks raced along the nothingness, and a block a millimeter square revealed a tiny section of moving code. Cheyenne stepped back and gazed at the massive virtual block clogging up Hangivol's living system. *That's gonna take forever.*

It wasn't hard to find another command prompt in the racing blue lines that would tear down another section of the black wall. Her activator illuminated it bright yellow, and she flicked her fingers toward the line she wanted.

She couldn't type in her cloning command, but her fingers moved on their own as if she had a keyboard beneath them. The activator responded instantly to what she wanted, and when she executed the order for a million copies of the decryption line, the alarm blared in her head again.

System malfunction. Command overload. F8runner_ clonecommand_ prompt_ DataZZnonexistent_ errorerrorerror_ kill849it_ switchmalfun_ NOT APPLICABLE.

"You've gotta be kidding me." When she killed the cloning command and pulled the single decryption line onto the black wall, no incomprehensible error message rose in response. Another tiny square of blackness filtered away, and now two pinpricks of blue light from the decrypted code beyond the wall winked at her.

Yeah, keep mocking me. I'll bring a virtual sledgehammer next time. Now, how do I get outta here?

Cheyenne turned slowly around, searching for the exit command. It took her twenty seconds to scan the virtual floor of blue symbols without finding it before she searched higher along the wall. A stuttering code line frozen beneath other racing lines of data flashed a deep orange toward the top of the virtual chamber.

Bottom right corner, my ass.

When she selected her activator's prompts to retrieve the exit command, nothing happened. With a grunt, she stalked toward the round wall and started piecing together different sections of other data streams, building upon what was already there and taking sections she needed from other scrolling lines. The data streams jerked and shuddered beneath her touch, but the walls kept showing blue symbols and half-translated O'gúleesh.

I have to program my way out of here. This is ridiculous.

Swiping the last piece into place, she stepped back and stared at the virtual rope materializing in front of her and racing up to the exit command, now glowing even brighter. The image of Bianca blasting away snarling blighted magicals before turning on her daughter flashed through Cheyenne's mind, and she clenched her eyes tightly shut.

Nope. Not here. Pull it together.

As soon as she opened her eyes, the rope finished materializing, rigged to a metal pulley at the top of the huge round chamber that didn't exist. The other end of it disappeared within the exit command.

"Seriously?" She grabbed the rope with both hands and pulled, defying all natural laws of physics and the way pulleys worked as she yanked hand over hand and the orange code she wanted moved down the wall toward her. "Manual labor to get out of Persh'al's stupid VR. He has no idea what he's doing."

As soon as the exit line was within reach, Cheyenne dropped the rope and slammed her palm on it.

CHAPTER EIGHT

The virtual data room disappeared, and a blast of searing energy raced up her hand and into her arm. With a shout of surprise, she jerked her hand away from the control panel of Persh'al's motherboard, which sprayed blue and yellow sparks.

"Endaru's balls, Cheyenne!" Persh'al stood behind her, his fists clenched at his sides as the walls trembled around them and flashed intermittent bursts of yellow and blue code. "What the fuck were you doing in there?"

"What?"

The orbs of light set in the ceiling fluctuated between near-darkness and way too bright. Corian stood in the center of the room with his arms folded. "You should've pulled her out when I told you to."

"You can't just yank someone out of a system like that!" Persh'al spun to glare at the nightstalker and gestured at the open trunk on the floor. "That's like pulling a fell-damn plug on both of them!"

"Hold on." Cheyenne pushed to her feet and stared at her hand, which was still buzzing with energy. "What the hell are you talking about?"

"You started glowing, kid." Corian nodded at the trunk. "Then a bunch of tech went haywire. You touch anything in there?"

"Yeah. I touched lots of things." She scowled at Persh'al. "That's why you wanted me to go in, right?"

Persh'al vigorously rubbed the side of his shaved head and glanced at the trunk. "Yeah. That was kinda the point."

"So, I do what I'm supposed to do and something goes wrong, and it's my fault?" Cheyenne folded her arms. "Feels like a pattern."

The overhead lights flickered one more time, then let out a low hum and returned to their regular level of illumination. The walls stopped sparking and trembling, and they waited in silence to make sure nothing else malfunctioned.

Finally, Persh'al clapped his hands together, rubbed them vigorously, and stepped toward Cheyenne. "So. You found the block?"

She cocked her head. "Kinda hard to miss in there. It's like you threw a bunch of random programs together and hoped something would stick."

"No. No, it was working perfectly before the surge." The troll wiped his palms on the sides of his trousers and shook his head. "That's what turned everything upside down."

"Well, it's a big block."

"I know it's a big block. Did you get through any of it?"

"Yeah, like this much." Cheyenne squinted at the millimeter of space between her thumb and forefinger. "It's gonna take forever to decrypt. An automatic process-repeat is useless."

"For real?"

Corian looked at them. "Anyone wanna put that into laymen's terms?"

"Fixing this system is gonna be like digging the Chesapeake Bay Bridge with an icepick. Is that a clear enough image?"

The nightstalker wrinkled his nose and turned to head back to the sitting area. "This is why I don't fuck around with magi-tech."

Cheyenne rolled her eyes at his back, then looked at Persh'al and spread her arms. "You had no idea?"

"No. What took you so long to get out?"

"The exit was not in the bottom right corner."

"Huh." The troll's orange eyes flickered across the room, then he thrust a finger in the air and grinned. "So we'll try again."

"Dude."

"No, seriously. Look, maybe you can't replicate the decryption inside, but we can write something externally, and you can take it with you. Lemme get my—"

There was a sharp bang behind them. Cheyenne and Persh'al spun toward the trunk, which was now closed, with Elarit's booted foot on the lid. The troll folded her arms and glared at them. "You two are done with this."

"What?" Persh'al let out a nervous chuckle and headed toward her. "We can fix it."

"I don't care what she found." Elarit's scarlet eyes narrowed at Cheyenne. "The last thing we need is for anyone to go blasting through this system when we have no idea how widespread the damage is."

Cheyenne shrugged. "Seemed pretty contained to me."

"The city's been rewriting itself for centuries." The troll woman's lips twitched into a sneer. "It needs space and time, not you diving in to rip everything apart and try to put it back together later."

"Sure." Cheyenne raised her hands in surrender and stepped away. "Just trying to help."

"Well, stop."

"Come on, *ma gairín*." Persh'al frowned at his wife and cast Cheyenne a distressed grimace over his shoulder. "You know what she can do. If we can get this up and running again sooner rather than later, what's the harm?"

Elarit glared at him and didn't say a word.

Cheyenne looked around for her cup of Bloodshine, realized she'd left it in front of the trunk, and turned toward the sitting area. *I'll get another fucking cup.* "She's right. We should give it time to let the dust settle, or whatever."

"Cheyenne."

"It's fine." The drow headed over to the half-circle of furniture and scanned the table in the center, trying to ignore Persh'al's and Elarit's low, strained voices as they argued about her behind her back. "Is there an extra cup over here?"

"Take the whole damn bottle, kid." Maleshi leaned forward to snatch the other Bloodshine bottle off the table and handed it to her. "You look like you could use two."

"Excellent advice." Bianca nodded and drained the rest of her drink. Another light hiccup escaped her. "Who needs cups?"

Hers flew from her hand and clattered across the floor before rolling under the settee where Ember sat. The fae looked at Bianca with wide eyes and chuckled uncertainly. "Right."

"Having fun, Mom?" Cheyenne didn't mean for it to come out sounding so angry. She frowned at Bianca to cover her surprise. *She hasn't done anything wrong. Rein it in, Cheyenne.*

Bianca snorted. "Normally, Cheyenne, I'd tell you to watch your tone, but I've had one too many cups of moonshine."

"Ha!" Lumil slapped her knee and cackled. "Moonshine."

"This human, man." Byrd's head swung low over his chest as he slowly shook it. "We could make a killing charging assholes to hear the shit that comes out of her mouth."

Ember set her cup on the table with wide eyes and opened her mouth, then thought better of whatever she was going to say and sat back.

Bianca raised an eyebrow at the laughing goblins. "I'll take that as a compliment."

"Go on!" Lumil guffawed and leaned sideways into Byrd. They both toppled over on the couch and cracked up again.

Cheyenne sat beside Ember on the settee, holding the Bloodshine bottle in both hands and staring at her mom. *O'gúl parties seem to have lost that special something. Or maybe it's the company.*

As the goblins' drunken giggling died down, the rest of the magicals gathered around the table stared at anything but each other.

"So." Maleshi cleared her throat. "This is about as good as day-drinking gets on this side, huh?"

Corian snorted and raised his cup toward the general. "Just today."

"We could take it to Vedrosha."

"Fuck yes, Hi'et." Lumil pushed off Byrd and pointed at Maleshi. "To the pits. We need to get down the way we did before the Spider fucked up all our shit."

"Does anyone seriously wanna fight right now? After where we were?" Cheyenne gazed slowly around the circle.

Byrd let out a monstrous belch. "Who doesn't?"

"I've gotten pretty comfortable right here." Corian nestled into the pile of pillows and closed his eyes. "If I passed out right now, I bet I'd sleep like I was fifteen hundred again."

Ember raised her eyebrows. "There's an image."

Cheyenne shook her head. "I don't feel like fighting anyone right now."

Maleshi said, "That might be a first."

"Not really."

"I feel," Bianca began and frowned at the center table, then sat straighter on the couch. "I feel unwell."

"Mom?"

"Hmm." Taking a deep breath, Bianca closed her eyes and waved off her daughter's concern. "I'm sure it's nothing."

"Great. Here's one for the books. General Hi'et got Bianca Summerlin wasted on fellwine." Cheyenne ran a hand through her hair and scanned the sitting area. "Where's the water?"

Lumil snorted. "Who wants water?"

Bianca's fingernails dug into the upholstery of the couch's armrest with a soft scratching sound. "This is quite strange."

Cheyenne and Maleshi exchanged concerned looks, all traces of the general's buzzed amusement gone. The drow knelt in front of the armchair and studied her mom's face. "What's going on?"

"It's not something I—" Bianca swallowed.

She reached toward her daughter, then her eyes rolled back in her head. Bianca's body bucked and jerked on the couch, and she slid forward on the cushion, her feet thumping the floor.

"Shit. Mom!"

Maleshi was on her feet before Cheyenne. "Grab her torso. Get her on the floor."

Cheyenne hooked her arms under Bianca's while the general grabbed the seizing woman's legs. Corian leaned forward to pull the low table away, giving them room to lower Bianca to the floor. Cheyenne sat back on her heels and set her mom's head onto her thigh, trying to hold her still while her mom's body jerked and flailed. "What do we do?"

Maleshi shook her head. "I'm not sure there's anything we *can* do. Not right now, at least."

"Jesus. Mom?" Cheyenne brushed Bianca's hair away from her forehead as the seizure slowly ran its course. Maleshi held the woman's legs gently against the floor, and when they stopped kicking, she said to Cheyenne with a concerned frown, "I thought this was over. She's here. We got rid of the blight. Why is this still happening?"

Bianca's body softened, her limbs now still, but the woman's eyes remained closed, and a soft snore rose from her slack lips.

Drunk and unconscious. Fucking great.

A faint pulse of orange light flared beneath the rune scars burned into Bianca's flesh, but it disappeared a lot more quickly this time.

Corian stroked his chin. "I'm not an expert, but I'd say that's still part of the curse."

"Seriously?"

He raised his eyebrows and studied Bianca's prone form. "We addressed the Vessel part of her, which, if I had to guess, was the largest block to removing the curse."

Maleshi nodded. "There's a good chance it's possible to remove the runes now."

"Then let's do it. Whatever needs to happen. Fine. Just tell me." Cheyenne looked from Maleshi to Corian and back again, but neither of them said a word. "Okay, either there's something you're trying not to tell me right now, or you don't know how to handle this."

Corian cleared his throat. "The latter."

Cheyenne raised her eyebrows at Maleshi. "You too?"

"Kid, I don't know shit about curses. I mean, beyond being able to recognize one. Sometimes." Maleshi sat on the floor and leaned against the couch. "Sorry. That's what banebreakers are for, among other select talents I don't have."

"Fine." Cheyenne stroked her mom's hair. "I'll go talk to someone who might know."

"Who might that be?" Corian asked.

"She's gonna go talk to the darkseller," Ember muttered. "Again."

Cheyenne and both nightstalkers looked at the fae, who was sitting with her legs crossed beneath her on the settee. Maleshi narrowed her eyes. "There's something off about that drow."

"Yeah, I noticed."

Byrd drained the rest of his fellwine and let out a loud, satisfied burp. "Kinda like you, right?"

Cheyenne frowned at him. "What's that supposed to mean?"

"What? Hey, no offense or anything." The goblin man flinched away from Lumil when she scowled at him and spread her arms. "I just mean the off part. You're not exactly the picture-perfect halfling, kid, but when you know what's up, you're fucking good at what you do."

"Wow. You sure took the long way around to give her a shitty compliment," Lumil muttered.

"I'm tellin' it like it is."

"Man, you need to shut up and drink more." The goblin woman snatched a fellwine bottle off the table and sloshed more glowing green booze into both their cups.

Cheyenne shook her head. *I'm nothing like R'leer. We both wanted the same thing for a short time. Now I have to go back down to the bazaar to ask for his help. Again.*

"Can you put her in a bed or something?" she asked Maleshi. "Keep an eye on her?"

"Not a problem." The general scooped Bianca into her arms and met Corian's gaze before nodding at the double doors that led out of Persh'al's private quarters.

"Yep." Corian pushed up off the pillows.

"Want some company?" Ember asked as Cheyenne stood and warily watched Maleshi carry her mom out of the room.

"I'm good, Em. Thanks. This'll be a short visit." The drow looked at her friend. "And I'm pretty sure you don't wanna go down there with me."

The fae let out a relieved laugh. "No. I don't."

"Yeah, okay. I'll be back in a bit."

"Wait, where are you going?" Lumil perked up and blinked heavy, drunken eyelids.

"For a walk." Cheyenne headed across the receiving room and paused at the doors. She turned briefly to look toward Persh'al's motherboard's trunk, but the troll Crown and his wife were gone. *Better that way. Maybe Elarit can cool the hell off while I'm not around.*

CHAPTER NINE

The main avenue of the drow inner circle was mostly empty again when Cheyenne left the fortress and headed across the highest level of the city. *Good. They finally listened to something I said.*

She walked quickly toward the alley that led to the descending passageways to the lower levels. *As long as the disappearing walls are working right now.*

As she passed the rows of doorways and storefronts lining the avenue, the drow stopped what they were doing to watch her. Some of them approached the doors and peered out to follow her with curious stares. A group of drow holding a low conversation inside a fabric shop stopped talking when Cheyenne passed the door.

She stared at them and slowed. *Now what's going on?*

When she faced forward again, she almost walked into the dark-skinned drow with the half-ponytail. "Whoa. Okay, back up."

"I am at your service." He pressed a fist to his chest and bowed his head. His golden gaze might as well have been glued to her face.

"Huh." Cheyenne looked across the avenue at several other drow emerging from their homes and shops to head toward her. "What's your name?"

"Althas."

"Look, Althas. I appreciate the sentiment. I think, but I don't need your service. You and everyone else here did more than enough in the forest this morning, and that's all anyone needs. I'm good." Without waiting for a reply, she skirted around him and kept walking toward the far end of the level.

The dark drow's slow, soft footsteps whispered behind her, and she rolled her eyes. *The lost-puppy thing doesn't work well with drow.*

Three more closed on Althas and joined him in following the Black Flame across the inner circle. Cheyenne tried to ignore them until she reached the alley she wanted between glittering metal buildings and darted quickly into it. Then she spun around and folded her arms.

Althas and the other three drow entered the alley together, stopped when they saw her, and pressed their fists to their chests.

"I said, no thanks." Cheyenne nodded at the avenue. "Go on. I'm sure you have way better things to do than follow me through the city. And I don't need babysitters."

"We swore to follow you." The drow woman with gold and silver rings through her ears dipped her head. "That's our priority."

"Okay, usually when someone says, 'I'll follow you to the end,' they don't mean it literally." Cheyenne shook her head. "We'd all be better off if you waited until the next time I asked for help. Right now, I don't need it."

The short drow man with swirling tattoos stretching up his neck squinted at the end of the alley behind her. "Where are you going?"

"None of your business."

"We'll escort you." The drow woman nodded. "None of us are new to security."

"Yeah, but I don't need security."

"Ban'oru and Haslin fought at Aelmhalk," the woman added without missing a beat. "Althas was one of the *Majiya's* first attendants. Before the Cycle turned for the Spider."

Cheyenne raised her eyebrows. "Okay. Great resumes."

"I oversaw the *marandúr* trials for the last two centuries of the Everbright's rule."

Cheyenne squinted at the drow woman, then passed her gaze over Althas, Ban'oru, and Haslin in turn. *Ex-soldiers and dignitaries who served before Ba'rael?* "So, you've all known the Verdys drow for a while?"

The woman lifted her chin. "We served the Verdys line in our own ways before the Spider strayed. But you haven't."

"You just met me, lady. Trust me, I do plenty of straying all on my own. Nice to meet you." Cheyenne turned and headed toward the back of the alley.

"My name is Glís," the drow woman said.

If I turn around and acknowledge that, they'll never leave me alone.

They didn't leave her alone anyway. All four ridiculously loyal drow followed her down the alley, stopping when she stopped at the end and tried to find the codes scrolling across the metal wall that would open the passage to the lower levels. The system's data streams were as choppy as they'd been in Persh'al's VR room, but she found what she wanted easily enough. With a swipe of her fingers across the wall, Cheyenne studied the code and waited for the tunnel's entrance to appear.

Nothing happened.

Shit. Makes me look like I do need help.

"There's another staircase on the east end."

"I know where it is, Althas. Thanks." Cheyenne didn't look away from the wall. "But this is the one I wanna use."

"Nothing will be the same here after what we accomplished this morning."

Cheyenne looked over her shoulder at the tattooed drow. "Ban'oru, right?"

He nodded.

"What do you mean by that?"

"We restored the lifeforce veins." Ban'oru frowned. "And the forest. And our race. It changed everything."

"So, you're saying the deathflame flooding underground wiped out everything we know about how the city works?"

"And then some."

Cheyenne turned slowly back toward the wall and tried to open it again. "Like what?"

The access code illuminated beneath her fingers and threw a few bright-blue sparks, and the wall shuddered.

"That remains to be discovered." Haslin's voice was the deepest. "Which is why we're coming with you."

"Oh, jeez." Cheyenne tapped her fingers on her thighs as the metal wall folded on itself at a snail's pace to reveal the passage behind it. "If I gave you, like, official orders to stay up here, would that work?"

"We're coming with you," Althas muttered. "That's all that matters."

"Of course it is." The wall finished opening, and Cheyenne stepped into the passage, which was lit by crackling blue sparks and blinking lights scurrying along the walls without any real purpose. "Just stay out of my way, all right? The last drow who tried to escort me through the lower levels pissed me off."

Her new followers said nothing as they stepped into the descending tunnel behind her. The wall clicked and banged back into place without its normal magic-synced functionality.

This is gonna be the weirdest trip through Hangivol to date. Me and four has-beens for the drow Crowns before Ba'rael.

"When was the last time any of you left the inner circle?"

Their silence said more than enough.

That's what I thought.

"It has been difficult to step beyond," Glís muttered. "Not anymore."

"You mean, Ba'rael kept you from leaving, or what?" Again, none of the drow replied, not even Glís. "Okay, don't expect me to be a tour guide. I'll be going in and out, so feel free to turn around whenever you feel like it."

Cheyenne forced herself not to turn around and look at them when the only response she got was more silence and the whisper of their footsteps down the descending corridor. *This was why I gave up the throne. Earthside magicals are way better conversationalists, even the assholes.*

They reached a dead end in the tunnel, and she waved her hand at the wall with the command prompt to open the next passage. The only thing she got was another error message from her activator:

Process nonexistent.

Come on.

Feeling her escorts' gazes on her back, Cheyenne pressed her lips together and scanned the code on the wall for something that worked. Her activator offered another route along the right-hand wall, and she accepted it. Blue sparks rained down around the door that opened into the tunnel. Blinding white light spilled through the slowly retreating metal segments and glittered over the opposite wall.

Detour through Upper Tech, huh? I guess there's more than one way to get from A to B.

Cheyenne stepped onto the brilliantly sparkling ground of Upper Tech's white-tinted metallic courtyard and followed the activator's yellow directional arrow. The passage wall groaned and screeched as the other four drow flanked her, two on each side. With a metallic squeal, the closing segments stuck in place, then erupted in more sparks and a series of high-pitched clicks as whatever mechanism allowed the walls of Hangivol to open and close on command broke.

She tried to shove her hands into the pockets of her black pants, but they were too tight, so she gave up. *I'm not about to fight my own pockets now too.*

Then she realized how weirdly empty Upper Tech was. The fountain in the center of this particular courtyard spilled only a trickle into the basin. Her activator lit up dozens of error codes in dark red on the floors and the walls. As she scanned the doors and alleys between the glittering buildings she passed, Cheyenne narrowed her eyes.

A door flew open on her left, and a frazzled-looking goblin barreled into the courtyard. His matted yellow hair must have once been styled to look like some sort of potted plant, but now half of it was squashed against his head and glistened with metal fragments. An explosion of machine pieces, cogs, wheels, springs, bolts, and sparking panel segments hurtled through the doorway after him and scattered across the metal ground.

"That's it!" the goblin shrieked. "It's never going to work! You can take your promises and all the *veréle* in the world, Ulvich, and shove them in your fell-damn vault. This is an outrage!"

He slipped on random bolts beneath soft foot coverings that weren't either shoes or slippers and stumbled sideways toward Cheyenne and her drow entourage. The goblin stopped immediately, and his eyes got wide when he saw the party.

Ban'oru hissed and loomed over the goblin. "Watch where you step, Upper."

"Well, I never!"

"Okay." Cheyenne nodded at the flustered goblin and leaned toward

Ban'oru to mutter, "He ran out of a store, not into a fight. Loosen up a little."

As if that were her cue to stick her foot in her mouth, the owner of the Upper Tech establishment squeezed through the doorway, which was almost too small for him, and stepped into the light. Ulvich looked like a cross between a raug and a wooly mammoth. Shaggy brown hair covered every inch of his huge body except for his beady red eyes and his wrinkled gray face with huge, wormlike gray lips. Two long, curved horns protruded from the sides of his head and curved over his fore-head. Thin, delicate chains of silver dangled from those horns, which matched the silver threads of the tailored vest bursting at the seams around the magical's large chest. Sparks flew across the ground beneath every step of the shop owner's cloven hooves. "Shall I watch where I step too, *mór edhil?*"

Althas snapped his fingers, which glowed with the purple light of the Nimlothars' magic that had marked them all that morning. Then a blaze of dark crimson energy swirled around his hand. "Only if you enjoy walking."

The wooly magical growled at Cheyenne's escort and took another step out of his shop. Then a sharp pop and the clatter of fallen items came from inside, and Ulvich roared before squeezing back through the doorway to deal with the issue.

Cheyenne kept walking, and the four drow fell in around her again, scanning the blinding streets and only slightly darker alleys as they exited one courtyard of Upper Tech and entered a separate district. *Fine. Tensions are still riding high, and now five drow are walking right out in the open where everyone can see. There goes keeping a low profile and blending in.*

The next courtyard they entered had abandoned all pretense of being reserved for Hangivol's upper-echelon society. The wealthy O'gúleesh who called Upper Tech home raced around the square, snarling and snapping at each other in their fine clothes and ridiculous hairstyles. Floating serving trays and mechanical creatures far more advanced than Ember's borrowed crawler darted around the square, crashing into walls and magicals and each other.

"I don't care about your timepieces," a fae hissed at a hunched, aged troll walking behind her. "Fix it!"

The stooped troll wrung his wrinkled hands, more brown than scarlet in his old age, and lifted a shaking hand to the monocle in his right eye that was flashing every possible color in quick succession. "Fix it? Have you lost your mind? That's a tinker's job!"

The fae woman whirled on him, her pastel-pink skin shimmering with an explosive wave of light. "Then get a tinker. Do you know how much is at stake if we don't get these services back online?"

Two silver orbs spun madly through the air and dropped toward the magicals' heads. They both ducked, and the old troll nearly toppled over, trying to get out of the way. He righted himself and snatched the monocle away from his face before snarling at it. "And I suppose it's that simple to call up a tinker when nothing works!"

A glittering machine that reminded Cheyenne of a metal deer studded with gemstones bounded across the courtyard and crashed into an orc woman wearing a sequined pantsuit. The orc shrieked and smacked the metal deer's bucking head. "Who abandoned the menagerie?"

Two gremlins raced after the deer and tried to wrestle it to the ground, but their white gloves made the machine too slippery.

"For the love of the deathflame, you useless creatures. Shut it down!"

"We can't!" One of the gremlins pulled a sleek metal rectangle from his jacket pocket and swiped frantically across it. The device sparked and hissed at him. "None of the exhibits respond."

A hovering palanquin draped in green and blue silk raced across the courtyard way too fast, the fabric whipping madly behind it as the beaked magical riding inside shrieked and pounded the control panel. "Ollu! Ollu, stop this at once!"

A tall, pale magical with luminescent arms that almost reached the ground lumbered after the hovering palanquin. "It's not me. Try getting out to walk."

"I don't walk. You know that!" Another shriek rose from the palanquin as it struck the back end of the metal deer and sent it flying across the square.

Serving trays and spinning orbs whizzed out of windows and open doors, terrorizing the privileged magicals for as long as possible before clattering uselessly to the ground.

Cheyenne bashed one of the flying serving trays with a fist when it soared toward her carrying an assortment of what looked like prosthetic eyes in multiple colors. The eyes clacked when they hit the ground, and she picked up the pace toward the next descending corridor that would take her out of Upper Tech.

"Ah. Drow!" A scaly magical who looked like a snake with arms, trailing thin, shimmering materials behind its long tail, slithered upright toward Cheyenne and her escort. "Surely one of you must have experience with opening Givers."

"Back off, belly-crawler," Glís growled.

"But the Givers," the snake-thing hissed. The tall feathers bursting from the tiny cap on the magical's head fluttered as it wove and flapped its stunted arms in distress. "They won't open themselves."

Cheyenne turned into the wide alley lit up in her vision by the activator's yellow arrow and shot a look over her shoulder at the chaos in the square. "What are Givers?"

"Feeding mech," Althas muttered.

"That thing can't feed itself?"

Glís rolled her eyes. "Why do it yourself when you can have tech do it for you?"

That was sarcasm, the whole feel of Upper Tech captured in one sentence and a whole lot of attitude.

"These Uppers will learn a valuable lesson," Ban'oru said, brushing his long white hair away from his tattooed neck.

Haslin grunted. "They'll get the lesson. That doesn't mean they'll learn."

Cheyenne had to manually program what would have been another automatic door to open for them at the back of this alley as the shrieks and whimpers and metallic crashes echoed around the courtyard. The wall split apart like elevator doors but stuck halfway and groaned until she pried them apart with both hands. "Hopefully, they can get their shit together."

"Don't pity them." Althas slipped into the corridor behind her, and they descended a flight of steep stairs that was missing every fourth step. "Those O'gúleesh have been bred into dependence."

"I don't pity them." Cheyenne scanned the multi-colored lights crackling along the stairwell walls and hopped over the first missing step. "Just because someone was born with a silver spoon up their ass doesn't mean they can't take it out on their own." *I would know.*

"That seems highly unnatural. Even for Hangivol," Haslin muttered.

Cheyenne shook her head and forced herself not to turn around and stare at the drow in disbelief. "It's a figure of speech I picked up Earthside."

"I assume you have experience with the proverbial metal spoon," Glís added.

"Silver spoon." Cheyenne snorted. "This isn't a meet and greet, okay? I'm trying to get to Halter's Deck so I can have a quick talk with the darkseller and get right back up to the top again."

They descended the rest of the stairs in silence as the walls flickered and sparked around them. Something heavy thumped and clanged behind the wall on their right, and Cheyenne hopped over the last two missing steps onto a round platform meant to take them down an O'gúl elevator tube. The platform sputtered and jerked as she went through one after another of her activator's prompts to get the thing to move. Two seconds after Ban'oru stepped onto the platform with everyone else, they dropped through three lower levels and didn't slow as they neared the bottom.

Fuck. Really?

Cheyenne reached toward the platform's floor and pulled on it with telekinetic force as the walls of the tube rushed past them. She managed to slow their descent enough that the platform didn't crash. Stumbling backward, Cheyenne braced herself against the wall with a hand, and Glís and Althas grabbed her other arm to keep her upright.

"Yeah, I don't like being touched." She shrugged out of their grasps and stalked off the platform. "I don't need to be caught, either."

Althas and Glís looked at each other before stepping off after her, Ban'oru and Haslin following closely. The already dim magical track lighting in the next tunnel flickered on and off like a strobe light, and a growing rumble of voices and activity came from the other side of yet another dead end.

"Seriously, you guys don't need to keep shadowing me." Cheyenne swiped her fingers along the wall, snatching what remained of unbroken code lines to open another nonexistent door. *This was much cooler when all I had to do was wave. So much for technological convenience.*

"You haven't been down to Halter's Deck in forever, right? Go have fun. Mingle with the locals. I promise I'm not as exciting as you think."

The door finally slid open with a bang, spilling dim light into the tunnel as the rumble of voices from Hangivol's lower levels erupted in a roar ahead of them. Two dark streaks hurtled toward the newly opened doorway and Cheyenne's face. A wind whipped up behind her with a sharp crack, then Glís stood in front of her with her fists clenched around two jerking, buzzing mechanical birds. Their beaks looked like knives as they twitched in the drow woman's hands.

Glís squeezed and the metal birds wheezed and clicked, then a rain of broken machine parts pattered to the tunnel floor. The drow dusted off her fingers and looked over her shoulder at Cheyenne. "Exciting or dull, we're coming with you."

She slipped through the doorway, scanning the chaotic mess in the lower-level streets as she waited for Cheyenne and the rest of her escort to do the same.

"I could've handled it," Cheyenne muttered as she passed Glís. "But thanks."

Glís dipped her head. "My life for the—"

"Don't. Just don't say it." And it wasn't her life. It was drow speed and showing off—big difference.

CHAPTER TEN

*J*esus. *If I thought it was bad upstairs, this place makes Upper Tech look like an organized parade.*

Cheyenne skirted a group of orcs jeering and roaring at two magicals with cracked gray shells on their backs who were pummeling each other. Red fire blazed in multiple open doorways, though she couldn't tell if it was meant to destroy the rooms beyond or protect them. A group of rag-covered magicals three feet tall with at least five legs each skittered across the scuffed ground, snatching up discarded tech pieces and pilfering metal implements from at least two arguing passersby's pockets. Cheyenne looked away.

Frayed wires and destroyed machines dangled from vendor carts and shop awnings. Someone hurled a flaming metal can trailing green smoke behind it that ignited with a loud bang. The walls of the ridiculously tall buildings of whatever district they'd stepped into shimmered with half-formed images and neon messages scrolling diagonally toward the ground before winking out. A low warble came from an image projected onto the middle of the street. Cheyenne squinted to make sense of the image before she realized it was a loop of a scarred orc with a third stunted tusk protruding from one side of his mouth who'd recorded himself throwing all his clothes out a window.

Why was that a thing?

Her drow entourage formed a square around her, shoving snarling magicals out of the way as angry citizens darted across the wide street. A skaxen missing a chunk from his ear skidded to a halt before he came within shoving range and hissed at the five drow heading through Halter's Deck. "That's it. Keep walkin'! Not like you give a shit about the sparksetters and tinkers down in the slums, eh?"

Cheyenne looked over her shoulder at him, and the skaxen curled two fingers and extended the other two in the O'gúleesh version of the middle finger before scuttling off across the street.

Red and yellow sparks flew from a troll's fingertips as he hovered over a heap of metal wreckage, trying to bring it back to life. He looked at the passing drow and whipped the dark goggles off his face before spitting in Cheyenne's direction.

She looked him up and down and kept walking, unable to ignore the yellow arrow blinking in the corner of her vision and urging her toward the darkseller bazaar.

They turned the corner around a low building with a round metal roof. The grinding wail of saws cutting through thin sheets of metal came from the open bay door. Inside, yellow and blue flames belched from a long, wide metal tube suspended across the center of the building. Maybe Cheyenne was in the wrong place at the wrong time, or maybe she stared too long at the magicals in leather aprons and gloves working like they were in the Outers instead of Ambar'ogúl's most technologically advanced city. Either way, when one of the orcs looked through the bay door and saw her watching them, he bashed the suspended metal tube with a gloved fist and spun the wide, dark end of it toward the five drow slowing on the side street.

The orc's upper lip twitched in a sneer. The tube gave a series of hollow bangs, and Cheyenne saw the yellow and blue flames shooting down the barrel. She stepped quickly aside and avoided the belch of magical fire redirected at her.

"Hey!" The roar of the flames drowned her voice, so she stopped and waited until the fire disappeared and the tube fell dark again. "Hey, you should watch where you're pointing that thing."

"Nope." The orc grunted and reached for a new saw blade before attaching it half with magic and half with two sharp bangs of his fist against the blade mount. "You should watch where you show your face, Black Flame. Not many O'gúleesh want to see it."

They were dancing in the streets in my name over a week ago.

"Is there a reason for that, or do you just like to hear yourself talk?" When the orc didn't answer, she slapped the side of the metal tube protruding from the bay door, eliciting a hollow gong. "Hey!"

"I would let it be," Glís muttered, glaring at the orc as he tested the new saw blade. "That one calls the final deathflame."

Yellow eyes flashed above the orc's dirt-smeared cheeks. "Yeah. For her."

Cheyenne gritted her teeth and stepped away from the building. "He's talking about me."

"And it's blasphemy." Haslin flicked open his hand and conjured a long, thin, wickedly sharp knife pulsing with silver and violet light. Then he headed for the bay door, his head turning slowly back and forth as he challenged the magicals inside with a silent glare.

"Whoa, wait a minute." Cheyenne moved after him but stopped when Althas lifted his arm to block her path. "What are you doing?"

The dark-skinned drow nodded once. "Haslin will root out the dissenters."

"What dissenters?"

"Traitors to the O'gúl Crown."

"Yeah, which isn't me. How fucking hard is that to understand?" She glared at Althas and shoved his arm away from her before storming after Haslin. "Pack it up, man. This is not why I came down here."

"No. It's why *I'm* here." The conjured dagger flashed in the growling drow's hand. "This *dae'bruj* needs to understand a few things."

"You need to understand that we're not picking fights down here. Or anywhere." Cheyenne grabbed his shoulder and squeezed hard enough to make him turn toward her. "Got it?"

Haslin hissed at the orc sawing through metal, then turned away and headed past the open bay door toward the next corner.

Cheyenne gritted her teeth and shot the orc a final glare. He wiped his nose with the back of his forearm and glared back at her before she turned away to give them both the space they needed. *I can't just say sorry and leave it at that. This is our fault. Not intentionally, but healing the Nimlothars broke the tech. They have every right to be pissed.*

As she turned the corner past the domed workshop with her drow escort, a group of grimy magicals in leather and the closest thing Ambar'ogúl had to denim stepped out of the branching alleys to cut them off. The troll leading the group thumped a sparking club into his opposite palm. Yellow and pink light crackled at the fingertips of the two gremlins and a magical with pastel blue and green fur that looked to be half-human, half-moth. A goblin woman and another orc stood behind them, and all five Halter's Deck citizens sneered at Cheyenne and her self-proclaimed guards.

Guess I should've expected this.

Cheyenne stopped, cocked her head, and raised her hands in as close to a peaceful gesture as she could get. "We're just passing through."

"Oh, sure. The Black Flame and her *mór edhil* want passage through Halter's Deck. Makes sense." The grimacing troll slapped the sparking club into his hand again and shrugged. "None of you would be caught dead down here in any other century, but now you have what you always wanted. Ain't that right?"

"This isn't what I wanted." Cheyenne raised a hand to shoulder height to keep the four scowling drow behind her at bay. *Even if I listed half the things I've done to help this city, it wouldn't make a difference. Just take the heat.* "It wasn't part of the plan, either."

"Favoring your own kind. Taking whatever you want," the goblin woman snarled. "You're just like the Spider."

Cheyenne fought down the blazing heat of the drow magic flaring up her spine and through her limbs. "That's taking it a little too far."

"No, it ain't." The yellow gremlin bashed his fists together, and a halo of yellow light erupted around the two-foot-tall magical. "This is all we have. Setting the spark for the Uppies and their fluffy lives. Selling it down here."

"Now even that's gone," the troll added. "And you're the blood-cursed *nilsch úcat* who took it."

"Watch your tongue." In a burst of air, Glís darted around Cheyenne and stopped between her and the gang of pissed-off magicals. One hand glowed with violet Nimlothar magic, and her other fist erupted in wavering black tendrils like solid smoke. "You are speaking to the Black Flame. Show respect, or I'll take you to the final deathflame myself."

"No, you won't." Cheyenne stepped toward the other drow, but

Althas, Ban'oru, and Haslin stepped past her and quickly fell in line beside Glís, blocking their alleged leader in her path.

The grimy troll sniggered, his scarlet eyes blazing as he scanned the four drow stretching across the side street. "You sure you can fight your way outta this? 'Cause we been watchin' from the slums. Drow ain't had to fight since you was sucked up there into your high towers with all the spark you could ever need."

"When was the last time you fought a drow loyal to their Crown?" Althas growled.

"The Ironbreak sits the throne now, *nilsch úcat*," the orc spat. "You givin' your lives for a reject."

"Jesus, no one's giving their lives for anyone." *They already had.* Cheyenne tried to muscle her way between Ban'oru and Haslin, but they wouldn't budge. "Seriously. Stand down."

"Nah." The troll shook his head and chuckled. "You'd be lyin' on the ground for what you did."

"Look." With a grunt of frustration, Cheyenne peered around Ban'oru and glared at the angry gang. "I can fix it, okay? I know what's wrong with the system. It's gonna take some time."

"The drow are out of time!" the mothlike magical shrieked. A bolt of pink light burst around her fur-tipped wings, which beat heavily and lifted her into the air before she let off a shockwave that blasted all five drow back by half a foot.

The drow charged, moving faster than the angry gang could see. Althas grabbed the moth woman's legs and hurled her against the wall of the building. Glís's tendril-shrouded fist connected with the troll's face, and the black tendrils wrapped around his head and neck before she jerked him to the ground. Haslin threw his conjured knife at the orc, who roared when the blade buried itself in his bicep. The gremlin got a good shot in, crashing a sparking yellow fist into Ban'oru's thigh, which was as high as he could reach, and the goblin woman threw two metal disks at Cheyenne.

Whatever the disks were meant to do, the faulty magic synced with the tech made them as dangerous as chucked bricks. Cheyenne raised a shield in front of herself, and the disks clanged off the dark wall of light before clattering on the ground. The goblin woman's eyes widened, and she charged Cheyenne with a shriek.

Cheyenne burst into enhanced speed long enough to sidestep as the goblin barreled toward her. When she slipped out again, the goblin woman stumbled down the side street under her own momentum and crashed into a discarded pile of scrap metal.

"Stop!" Cheyenne darted toward the fighting magicals and summoned a crackling black energy sphere in each of her hands.

The troll's club swung over Glís's head as the drow ducked and would have crashed into Cheyenne instead if she hadn't leaped aside.

The moth-woman let off another blast with a powerful beat of her wings and sent every magical staggering away from her. Althas snarled and darted toward her in drow speed, backhanding the magical across the face when he reached her. She hit the wall again with a grunt. The orc charged and sank a fist into Althas' lower back, then cracked his forehead against the drow's when Althas whirled toward him with a snarl.

Cheyenne darted toward Ban'oru, who'd pulled the gremlin off the ground by the back of his leather vest and tried to hurl the short yellow magical into the closest wall. "Put the gremlin down."

The gremlin shot a bolt of yellow light at her feet and missed by half an inch. When Ban'oru tried to grab him with the other hand, the gremlin latched on with both arms, both legs, and his sharp teeth chomping down on the drow's forearm. Ban'oru hissed, spun, and slammed the gremlin against the wall, but the short magical held on and didn't release the drow's slate-gray flesh between his jaws.

"I said, *stop!*" Cheyenne's voice took on an otherworldly tone when the Nimlothars' purple light flared behind her eyes. Her body erupted in black flames, and she sent a burst of crackling black lightning flaring across the ground and up the walls of the buildings around them.

The battling magicals paused for two seconds, long enough to stare at Ambar'ogúl's ex-Crown, who was covered in the drow magic that had given her her moniker. Then they went right back to punching and kicking and blasting each other again.

Fuck this. With a roar, Cheyenne darted into drow speed toward Althas and jerked him away from the moth-woman, and he flew across the side street and slowed in suspension. She moved to Haslin next and pried his fingers off the orc's neck. She shoved him away, then grabbed Glís's arm and hurled her away from the troll. The drow woman's tendrils disconnected from the troll's neck with a crack.

Ban'oru slipped into enhanced speed with her and snarled. "What are you doing?"

Cheyenne stormed toward the gremlin suspended in the air, his arms and legs frozen mid-flail on his slowed trajectory toward the frozen goblin woman racing back to the battle. She grabbed the gremlin and set him gently on the ground before spinning to face the tattooed drow. "I said, we're not fighting them."

"These are traitors!"

She cocked her head. "You wanna fight me too?"

Ban'oru scowled at her and slipped out of enhanced speed right after she did.

The magicals she'd disconnected from each other staggered back when time returned to its normal pace, snarling as they toppled over. Althas crashed to the ground and skidded before righting himself with a growl.

Cheyenne glared at Ban'oru and let another burst of black fire flare around her body before snuffing it out.

"The blight's gone," she shouted and turned to glare at the magicals who'd attacked her. "Ba'rael's gone. Persh'al sits the throne, and I *will* fix this. All of you need to get your shit together and think about how much worse it could be right now instead of going for mass bloodshed. Got it?"

The drow and the angry Halter's Deck magicals breathed heavily, all of them scowling at her.

The troll wiped his face, still feeling the sting of Glís's black tendrils, and spat on the ground. "If you don't, the inner circle won't be safe for any drow."

"I will. And I'm calling a fucking truce." Cheyenne nodded at the troll with a grimace, then stormed through the heaving, furious magical gang toward the alley at the far end of the side street. None of them moved to follow her or attack, but they did hiss at the four inner-circle drow who collected themselves to hurry after the Black Flame.

"The deathflame waits for no one," the orc growled, looming over Althas. "Your time will come."

"And yours." The dark-skinned drow didn't look at the orc as he stalked past. Glís, Ban'oru, and Haslin hissed at the other magicals as they stormed down the side street.

Cheyenne turned the corner where her activator prompted her with a flashing yellow arrow. *I can't handle everybody trying to rip each other apart. If that's what this world wants to do when I'm gone, fine, but not until I've done what I can to clean up this whole mess.*

CHAPTER ELEVEN

The drow entourage caught up with her around the corner. Cheyenne could feel their angry stares and the buzzing energy of magic wanting to be released on something. *Everyone wants somebody to blame. Great.*

Althas glared at a pack of skaxen leering at them from a recessed archway. "You cannot let treason slip by unnoticed and unpunished."

"Yes, I can." Cheyenne took another sharp turn at her activator's prompting, then headed down a staircase along a wall unaffected by the brownout. "And it's not treason. I'm not the Crown."

"Perhaps not in name," Glís muttered. "But in everything else? Where it matters? Yes."

"No."

"Who else would have led us to restore the Nimlothars?" Ban'oru snarled at a thin orc who stepped out of another doorway, and the orc went back inside until the group of drow passed. "Who else would have restored the lifeforce vein? Purged the Spider's poison?"

"That makes me the drow who did those things, not the Crown."

"The Crown makes the impossible possible," Althas added.

Cheyenne paused. "What did you say?" *Either that's a drow saying, or L'zar's finding a way to screw with me from across the Border.*

88

The dark-skinned drow spread his arms and held her gaze. "I see no one else willing to shoulder the burden."

She shook her head and kept walking. "Persh'al's shouldering more than enough."

"The Ironbreak is a troll," Haslin spat.

"Yeah, and as far as I know, trolls haven't been screwing things up for this world over the last however many centuries." Cheyenne turned the next corner and studied the crackling lines of disrupted code on the walls. "You're not gonna change my mind, so drop it."

A rumble and squeal of moving metal rose behind them, and all five drow turned to see a section of the alley wall break apart and shift into place, blocking them from returning the way they'd come. Out of the newly formed alley intersecting with theirs stepped an ogre, his yellow eyes blazing. "Found you."

"Not again." Cheyenne shook her head.

Another wall lurched out of the alley in front of her but stuck with a spray of sparks and a groan. A gruff voice cursed behind the half-open doorway, then blasted it the rest of the way open with a bright green light and another squeal of forced metal parts. A hunched troll woman with a glinting knife in each hand barreled into the alley and tossed her scarlet braids over her shoulders. "Try to turn the city against us, huh? Not good enough."

"I've been trying to help this city, okay?" Cheyenne glanced up and down the alley as more magicals filtered in behind the ogre and the knife-wielding troll. "Look, I don't know who's been feeding you guys the idea that I want what the Spider wanted, but it's not true."

"Then turn the city back on." The troll woman gestured at the sparking walls with a blade point. "Unless that would ruin your plans."

"Why me?" Cheyenne spread her arms. "I'm not tearing this place apart. I'm not taking your magic. Hell, I'm not even stealing from you. What else do I have to do for magicals around here to leave me the fuck alone?"

"Get out." The growl came from a dark shadow flickering along the wall down another intersecting passageway. "Now."

"I already said that's what I'm gonna do." Cheyenne squinted at the moving shadow coming toward them. *Great. Now the last route out of here is blocked.*

"I'm not talkin' to you." The shadow's owner pounded a mottled pink-and-gray fist against the wall and emerged into the main alley. "I meant everyone else."

Glís hissed and produced smoky black tendrils around both fists this time. "We were here first."

The magicals converging on Cheyenne and the drow from both sides—at least a dozen now, but she didn't take the time to count—paused when the figure stepped out of the intersecting passage. The newcomer, draped in reeking black rags dragging on the ground, lifted the hood from his face.

Mirl's piglike snout twitched, his blind eyes staring at the wall beside the ogre's head. "But hey. Don't let me interrupt the party. I'm always down for one."

The troll woman wrinkled her nose at the stench coming from the radag. She ran her tongue over her teeth, then jerked her head toward the alley from which she'd emerged. "You smell like *radag* shit, you know that?"

"I'm blind." Mirl cocked his head. "Not ignorant."

The ogre grunted and shoved his way through the magicals who'd come out behind him. "Fell-damn radag. Let him touch you, and you're all on my blacklist."

He disappeared through the newly created alley behind him and the other attacking magicals slowly followed, snarling and snuffing out their magic.

As quickly as they'd cut off Cheyenne and her drow escort, the small angry mob vanished, though the new doorways in the metal walls remained open behind them.

"Well, shit," Cheyenne said, smirking at Mirl. "If I'd known how much everyone loves being around you, I would've brought you with me."

The radag exposed the stained, stunted teeth in his wrinkled mouth and tittered. "I guess you think I should be flattered by that."

"Step aside, radag," Althas growled. "The Black Flame wishes to pass."

"Ooh. Listen to that." Mirl cocked his head toward the dark-skinned drow and sniffed the air. "How'd you get four drow to debase themselves in Halter's Deck, eh?"

Cheyenne headed toward the mouth of the passage where he stood. "Trust me, I tried to tell them it wasn't worth their time."

"Ah." Mirl lifted a mottled finger and wagged it at the four drow, who were grimacing at his overwhelming stench. "You owe her something, don't you?"

"Our lives." Ban'oru cocked his head.

"Save it for a magical who gives a shit." Mirl waved off the threat and turned to follow Cheyenne. "Where you goin', drow?"

"I'm trying to get to the bazaar."

"Huh. I didn't show you this route."

"Yeah, I had to take a few detours." She slapped a hand against the wall, and a wave of blue streaks burst away from the impact point.

"Word travels fast, Cheyenne." Mirl snorted, thumping along behind her in his shuffling gait. "The whole city's on a crusade against *the one who broke Hangivol.*"

"It's not broken, just down for a while. I'll fix it."

"That's the least of your worries."

She stopped and turned to frown at him. "You're threatening me too now?"

Mirl sniggered. "I would never. But your worries are our worries, right?"

"Hardly."

The radag patted the front of his robes, his head tilted far to the side as he searched the folds of his rags. Then he withdrew a bone with half the cooked meat still attached, sniffed it, and popped the whole thing into his mouth with a crunch.

Cheyenne saw the four drow coming up behind him but keeping their distance. *I wouldn't mind getting away from him either.*

"Are you gonna tell me something I can use?"

"Oh, you want that now, do ya? Ha." Flecks of bone spilled from Mirl's mouth as he chewed noisily, his lips smacking. "You and your drow elite turned everything right-side-up again, friend. Been a long time since Ambar'ogúl's seen anything work the way it's supposed to."

"Except for the city system and all the tech."

He swallowed noisily and wiped flecks of spit and meat from his squashed lips. "I'm talkin' about the rest of it. No blight. No torture. No mad drow on the throne. Magic's stronger than ever, thanks to you. Better snag what you can get before the end, know what I'm sayin'?"

"Not really." Cheyenne grimaced when the radag whipped his robes away from his body, sending a wave of stench over her.

He vigorously shook his head and drew a long, blood-stained needle from his robes to use as a toothpick. "Look, all's I'm sayin' is that while everyone's down here freakin' out about their livelihoods, the rest of Ambar'ogúl will figure out pretty quick that there's no consuming plague and no Ba'rael the Spider to stop them from trying to take Hangivol. If they haven't figured it out already. I'm sure some thickskull somewhere's already got an idea or two floatin' through his head. Or hers." Mirl shrugged. "Can't discriminate."

Great. We healed the world and created another power vacuum, all in one morning.

"Thanks for the tip. The O'gúl Crown can handle visitors knocking on the door." Cheyenne turned and headed back down the alley.

"We will stand beside you," Althas added.

She rolled her eyes. "I'm talking about Persh'al."

"Suit yourself." Mirl spun again and hobbled toward the drow entourage. All four of them stopped and pressed themselves against the wall of the alley as the radag shuffled past. "Tell the darkseller I said hello."

"Whatever."

Mirl paused and leaned toward Haslin to sniff the air in front of the drow, then chuckled. "You lot are gonna have some fun down there. A whole new world. Just don't mention my name."

He started walking again, still picking his teeth with the long needle.

The four disgusted drow fell back in line behind Cheyenne.

"No one wants to hear your name, you reeking sack," Ban'oru muttered.

"But you all know it!" Mirl's shout and ensuing cackle echoed down the alley behind them.

Cheyenne swallowed and took a tentative sniff after breathing through her mouth for so long as she thought, *We could station the radag in front of Hangivol. That'd turn everyone right back around again.*

Her activator led her down two more twisting corridors and one last set of stairs. No more Halter's Deck gangs intercepted her to seek vengeance against the drow who'd brought the human Vessel across the Border and healed the blight. She finally found herself in front of the stone wall that enclosed the darkseller bazaar beneath the city on the other side. *There has to be a better way to get back when I'm done here. I can't believe I keep showing up in this place.*

Her activator lit up a short series of commands for the spell that would open the stone wall. Cheyenne's hands moved quickly on their own, and chunks of black rock peeled away from each other without a single spark or hitch in the movement.

"No sparksetter work down here," Haslin muttered, gazing at the walls and ceiling. "What happened here?"

Cheyenne shrugged. "More like what didn't happen. I guess the darksellers knew not to mess with combining magic and tech. Smart move."

She stepped through the open doorway and entered the dusty, grimy avenue of the darkseller bazaar.

"Wait," Althas called behind her as he took one halting step. "This might not be the best place for you."

Cheyenne snorted and turned. "It's not any worse than up there right now."

The four drow gazed with wide golden eyes at the dimly lit bazaar and the rows of shops displaying anything a magical could want—as long as that magical wanted to work with dark powers most of them wouldn't touch.

They look terrified.

She folded her arms. "Are you trying to say this might not be the best place for *you*?"

Haslin took a deep breath and stepped past Althas into the bazaar. "This place."

"Yeah, I know. Creepy and cool at the same time."

"Perhaps we'll wait for you here," Glís muttered. "Until your business is finished."

Ban'oru shot her a strange look, then stepped slowly toward the closest shop to peer through its dust-smeared window. "Your cowardice is overwhelming, Glís."

"It's not cowardice." The drow swallowed thickly. "It's caution."

Looks like I'm not the only drow trying to stay away from the dark stuff.

"This is what we are, right?" Cheyenne asked, glancing at each of the drow in turn. "What drow used to be, at least."

"This should not be beneath the city," Althas muttered.

"I'm pretty sure this built the city." She waved them off. "Do whatever you want, but get it together, okay? Seeing four drow down here looking as lost and freaked out as you do is like blood in the water."

Ban'oru tilted his head and watched a magical with thick black thorns protruding from her face lean her head out of her shop doorway to grin at him. "Whose blood?"

"No sharks in Ambar'ogúl, huh? Figures." Cheyenne turned and headed down the avenue toward R'leer's storefront. *Everyone around here's been holding a grudge against drow for centuries, and these guys aren't half as bad as they're expected to be. L'zar and Ba'rael were, though. Guess it runs in the family.*

CHAPTER TWELVE

Cheyenne stepped away from a massive trembling flesh-colored creature making its way down the side of the avenue toward her. She would have written it off as some kind of living dark magic if it weren't for the thick, slug-like appendages weaving and crossing each other on the creature's skin. A dozen eyes blinked open and closed as the creature squelched across the stone floor, leaving a trail of quickly evaporating white sludge in its wake.

Not gonna see one of those in the upper levels. Where the hell does a thing like that live?

Stepping cautiously over the disappearing slime trail, Cheyenne turned into the doorway of R'leer's shop and pushed aside the curtain of strung bones and beads. The shop was as dark and silent as the last time she'd stepped inside, and the darkseller's orc assistant was present again in the large chair beside the desk on the left wall. The orc woman stared at Cheyenne, her meaty arms folded across her chest.

Turning toward the other side of the shop, Cheyenne scanned the dried, withered, bottled, and dangling items laid out on the counters and shelves. Her gaze fell on what looked like a sea urchin on the center display counter. Its six-inch spikes, which protruded in every direction, pulsed with scarlet light and grew brighter when she stepped toward it.

"I wouldn't." R'leer appeared from the back room and nodded at the urchin-thing. "Unless you want to know what it feels like to have your internal organs drained of all fluid. Then by all means, pick it up."

She leaned away from the counter and turned toward him. "Who would want something like that?"

"It has its uses." The beads threaded throughout the darkseller's long white hair clicked when he lifted his chin and looked her up and down. "I knew you would return eventually, but I honestly did not expect to see you twice in the same day. Certainly not today."

"Trust me, it feels a lot longer." Cheyenne narrowed her eyes as he approached. Her gaze kept returning to that pout of his. *Talk about wearing a mask. The guy puts on drow makeup to heal a forest and takes it off again to run his shop.* "You look way too pleased with yourself right now."

"Why shouldn't I be pleased?" He stopped less than six inches in front of her and tilted his head, his golden eyes flickering across her face. "We accomplished incredible things this morning. Our pattern in the Weave is complete, and you stand in my shop again."

A knot tightened in Cheyenne's stomach. "What did you say?"

"You stand in my shop."

"No, about the Weave." He had been lying on the ground when the Olfarím said it. He was dead like everyone else.

R'leer raised his eyebrows. "Our pattern in the Weave is complete."

"Whose? 'Cause we haven't had much of a pattern beyond you staring at me like that and spouting a bunch of random crap that doesn't make sense."

"Yet here you are." He spread his arms. "You can't seem to stay away."

"This isn't the first place I wanna be right now, trust me." Cheyenne took a step back and pretended to be interested in something else on the display counter so she wouldn't have to look at his infuriating grin. "But I need your help. Again."

R'leer chuckled and placed a dark hand covered in rings on his chest. "My life for the Black Flame."

She looked sharply up at him. "Don't mock me."

His lips twitched. "Mockery and flattery are closely intertwined. Especially when you want neither."

He's right about that, at least. Cut to the chase. "Bianca needs help. With the curse."

"Hmm." Frowning, R'leer steepled his fingers, his narrow-eyed gaze flicking around his shop. "I can only assume it did not break this morning."

"No, it didn't." When he leaned toward her again, she took another step back and folded her arms. "It's still causing a lot of problems."

"Interesting. I expected the Vessel's power to be stronger than an unintended curse." He shrugged. "At the very least, the Nimlothars have been restored, and the necromancer's creation no longer exists."

"Yeah, but I can't let Bianca no longer exist." Cheyenne shook her head. "I don't know how much longer she can hold out."

"Nor do I." A light chuckle seeped through his nose. "I am curious to find out why you came to me about it."

"What do you know about curses?"

Taking a deep breath, R'leer eyed her again. Then he turned away, clasped his hands behind his back, and strolled casually down the side of the display counter. "Not enough to help you."

"What?" She glared at him as he perused his wares, bending to study two dried, horned skulls attached to the same spinal cord. "That's not the answer I was looking for."

"The answers we receive rarely are."

Gritting her teeth, she rounded the corner of the central display counter and stopped beside him at the shelf along the wall. "It sounds like you know something you aren't telling me."

"I know a lot of things, Cheyenne."

"Stop. Just stop it. You said I needed to trust you and I did, so we could do what we had to do with the trees."

R'leer raised his eyebrows but said nothing and didn't look away from his crammed shelves.

He's been using me this whole time.

"Hey." Cheyenne shoved his shoulder to turn him toward her, her fingers slipping on the beads and bones. His oddly decorated tunic felt like wet leather under her touch. "If you wanted to act like I could trust you, you shouldn't have thrown down that card in the first place. I did everything you asked me to do in that forest. I let you feed my mom the deathflame!"

"And it worked."

"But it didn't help *her*. I need to know how to break this curse so I can take her home and quit dragging her back into all this bullshit." They stared at each other, and Cheyenne couldn't take the silence. "This is a drow thing, right? Using me for something only I can do and being a total douchebag about everything else once it's done? I got more than enough of that from L'zar."

"I've been perfectly civil."

"You won't answer my question! If you don't know anything about curses, fine, but you know something. Just point me in the right direction, and I'll be the one who decides whether or not it's enough to help me."

Lifting his chin, R'leer straightened the shoulder of his tunic where she'd shoved him and steepled his long fingers again. "If I dealt in curses, Cheyenne, I would help you. But you need a banebreaker for that, not a darkseller."

"Yeah, I know what banebreakers do." She scowled at the items in his shop. "Not seeing a huge difference between the professions, though."

"They are quite different, I assure you." R'leer pursed his lips. "I cannot cross that line, even though I would like to. For you."

Nice line. Either he's trying to rope me in again, or he means it, and I'm being an asshole.

She raised her arms and let them drop back down against her thighs. "Fine. So where's the banebreaker club in Hangivol?"

R'leer's eyebrows flickered together, and he shook his head. "Not in Hangivol. The closest one I'm aware of is out in Aelmhalk. The transports would only take you half the distance, but I would not trust them to run on their own right now, given the current state of technology in this city."

"You know I have nightstalker friends who can make portals, right?"

"Not to get you into Aelmhalk. And there's no guarantee that particular banebreaker is still in residence. It's been a thousand years since we spoke, and they tend to move about."

Cheyenne fought not to roll her eyes. "Anyone else?"

The beads and bones clicked against each other in his hair when he turned away from her and headed toward the counter beside his orc assistant's chair. "Every other banebreaker I know in Ambar'ogúl has been consumed by their work."

"Don't worry. I can distract anyone from their work if I have to."

"I mean, literally consumed." R'leer stopped at the wall beside the counter and removed a foot-long box Cheyenne thought was made of off-white-painted wood until she noticed that the spikes on the corners of the lid were part of one unbroken piece.

This guy and his bones. What kind of creature did he take that from?

The darkseller set the box on the counter and looked at Gyla. The ogre grunted and pushed herself out of the chair before heading toward the back of the shop to give them privacy. Her yellow eyes passed briefly over Cheyenne, then she was gone.

"Banebreakers work with curses, yes, and forces beyond what most of us can see with our own eyes. Or with our magic."

"So, you're telling me all the banebreakers died because they went too far?" She headed toward the counter and folded her arms. "Kinda hard to believe no one else would step up to take their places."

"Very few are suited to withstand what a banebreaker must endure to be of use to anyone." R'leer passed his hands over the lid of the bone box, and his eyes widened. "But they're not all dead. Some have been overrun by the forces with which they've chosen to commune, and others have been sent away."

"Who takes on that job?" Cheyenne stared at his hands, still hovering over the box. "I'll go ask where all the banebreakers are."

R'leer lowered his hands to the counter and slowly turned his head to look at her. "Then ask."

She blinked. "You?"

"It was not a decision I made lightly. The banebreaker who made a name for herself down here beneath the city was gifted far beyond what the others could manage, and far more reckless."

"So you sent her away."

"I banished the banebreaker, and she will not return. I do not suffer thieves." R'leer undid the clasp of the bone box and gingerly lifted the lid on its hinges. A dark, shimmering light pulsed within the box, casting a flickering web of shadows to cross his face. "Or those who push their limits."

Yeah, that sounded a lot like a threat.

Cheyenne leaned forward to get a closer look at the inside of the box, then thought better of it. "Where'd you banish her to?"

The darkseller looked at her and frowned. "You do not want to go after that one."

"Maybe not, but you're not leaving me with a whole lot of options."

"I banished her to Earth." R'leer looked down at the shimmering bone box. "If she had kept her greedy hands off what did not belong to her, Inolu Rosh would have been here to give you your answers."

Cheyenne's shoulders slumped. "Inolu's in Richmond, Virginia because of you?"

"I do not know where exactly."

"Well, I do, and I spent way more time with her than I wanted to."

R'leer glanced quickly at the stained, dusty front windows of his storefront, then stepped around the counter toward Cheyenne. "You've spoken to her?"

"And then some." She shrugged. "Couldn't have gotten the Vessel across the Border without her." *Or without the Underman laughing in my face as he told me I had no other choice.*

The darkseller cocked his head, then flicked his hand toward the windows of his shop. A dark wall flared behind the shelves and blocked out whatever dim light spilled through from the bazaar's avenue outside. Two heavy doors slammed shut at the back of the main room, closing them off from Gyla and whoever else was hiding back there.

Hopefully not Ur'syth.

Cheyenne stared at the closed doors pulsing with orange light. When the light faded, she saw crude images of unnatural skeletons and piles of bones carved into the wood. "What are you doing?"

"If you've already set foot in the banebreaker's domain, I can't stop you from doing it a second time." R'leer leaned against the counter, gripped the edge with both hands, and stared at her. "I *can* tell you what I know of Inolu Rosh, but it remains between us. Do you understand?"

Not sure he can tell me anything I don't already know about her, but okay. "Fine. I won't go spreading any rumors."

"This information is dangerous, Cheyenne. I need your word."

"Yeah. You have my word. Nobody in Hangivol wants to listen to me anyway."

"But your friends will. You cannot share this, even with them."

"Okay." She folded her arms. "I've been keeping secrets my whole life. I know how it works."

"Not one like this."

CHAPTER THIRTEEN

"Inolu Rosh is a Siliwari, a magical biologically suited for communing with unseen forces."

"How is that different than what Oracles do?"

"Oracles read the Weave, Cheyenne. Some may even grasp the threads, like L'zar, and rearrange them in small fragments, but they do not interact. That's the difference."

"So, banebreakers talk to the Weave?"

The darkseller stepped around the counter. The bones in his hair rustled and clicked against the counter's surface when he bent down behind it. When he straightened, he set a round glass flagon filled with glowing silver liquid on the counter, then stared at Cheyenne and set two metal cups the size of shot glasses beside it. "Given how intertwined you are in all this, your lack of crucial information is astounding."

Cheyenne ignored the jab and stared at the glowing liquid. "I've dealt with more mind-blowing revelations than I can count. Crucial information seems to find me, no matter what." *Eventually.*

The flagon let out a startlingly loud pop and hiss when R'leer uncorked it, and he poured the silver liquid into the tiny cups. The stuff moved like cold syrup in a thick, fluid stream.

"What is that?"

"Nectar."

"Of what?"

"That is merely the name. Made by drow for drow." R'leer stoppered the flagon again and returned it to its place on the other side of the counter. Then he slid one of the shot glasses toward her and stared at the other in his hand. "I find it stills the mind when faced with difficult truths."

Cheyenne approached the counter and peered into the small cup reflecting the nectar's silver glow. "Whatever you're about to tell me, I don't need a drink to deal with it."

R'leer grimaced. "I poured it for myself. It would be rude not to invite you to join me."

"Oh." *Damn.*

The darkseller raised his shot glass toward her, then took a small sip and closed his eyes. "For sipping. Unless you'd like to leave your body again."

Cheyenne lifted the cup and didn't have to sniff it to smell acrid bitterness tinged with overflowing sweetness. She took a small sip and frowned at the sludgy, slimy texture. "Tastes like frosting."

R'leer cocked his head.

"I'm not explaining frosting to you. Just keep talking."

He took another sip first, then placed both hands on the counter and leaned over them. "Inolu stepped into her birthright as Hangivol's banebreaker after I passed the trials. And before you ask, no, it was not before the Spider's reign. I was one of the last to take a Nimlothar seed from a living source beyond the Heart."

Before all the trees we saved were destroyed. Or almost.

"So, you were lucky."

"Hmm." R'leer narrowed his eyes as he stared at the counter. "I was determined, and I went to Inolu for an arrangement. A young drow about to step into his full potential making deals with a newly inducted banebreaker. It was a thrilling combination. And dangerous."

What the hell did this have to do with breaking the curse on her mom?

Cheyenne looked down at her shot glass, then set it down on the counter and waited.

"We both wanted something only the other could offer. I agreed to procure certain items for Inolu in exchange for a curse."

"Who'd you curse?"

R'leer looked at her. "I never used it. I merely wanted it in my possession as a safeguard. The state of flux back then… Hangivol was nothing like it is today. But it wouldn't have mattered if I had used it. I provided Inolu with the means to do what few banebreakers accomplish. Successfully, at least. Most of them meet the final deathflame in the process."

"Yeah, I get it. Always good to have a darkseller on your side, right?"

He blinked quickly at her in surprise. "That's an unpopular sentiment, but I'd have to agree with you."

So he can be flattered.

Cheyenne leaned sideways against the edge of the counter and waited for him to continue.

"What I did for Inolu enabled her to channel these unseen forces. Spirits of the eternal. *Uanáj.*"

"You mean, like demons?"

"I don't know what that is."

"Of course not." Cheyenne ran a hand through her hair. "Evil spirits, I guess. Which I didn't believe existed until I'm pretty sure I saw one in Inolu."

"Ah. Perhaps demons and *uanáj* are the same. Only she would know. Or at this point, she may no longer be aware of herself and the separation between who she is and who they are."

"Oh, she's aware." Shaking her head, Cheyenne let out a small, disbelieving chuckle. "Her business hours revolve around when not to let anyone see her when she's not all there. And she might be a little paranoid about being attacked."

"It makes sense." R'leer took another sip of nectar. "She has been attacked. Many times. Inolu rode the line between sanity and madness for longer than I expected. Then she was overrun. Consumed."

"Possessed."

He dipped his head. "By the *uanáj.* Most likely, yes. She lost control, as so many banebreakers do. Her patrons found themselves facing unpleasant consequences after contracting her services. This bazaar was overrun by swarms of disembodied forces more than once, *uanáj* or demons or whatever you wish to call them, and Inolu lost touch with her responsibilities. It would not surprise me if her lack of control was directly related to why Hangivol has forgotten what used to be its Heart. This city beneath the city. No one wants to face a magical whose power has grown beyond her ability to control it."

Cheyenne watched him knock back another sludgy sip from his shot glass. *Just like Ba'rael. Her power ran away from her too.*

"So you banished her for not being able to control the demons. Or whatever."

R'leer eyebrows twitched into the first sign of regret she'd seen in him. "No. It has never been my duty to decide which magicals deserve to remain here. She flooded the undercity with terrors, but they would have eventually run their course. Either they would have brought her to the final deathflame, or they would fall beneath her command if she found the strength to subdue them. That part was up to her. She struggled with a fractured existence but still had the presence of mind to come to me once more for assistance. I couldn't give her what she needed to keep the *uanáj* from taking over completely, so she stole it from me instead and performed the ritual before I realized what she'd done. When I found out…as I said, Inolu Rosh will not return to Ambar'ogúl. She cannot."

A memory of Inolu's glowing green veins peeking out from the dark hood when the banebreaker finally revealed herself entered Cheyenne's mind. Her green eyes that became the Underman's. The way no other sign of Inolu herself remained when the *uanáj* took control and existed only as glowing eyes and that gaping, grinning mouth suspended in the darkness.

"What did she take from you?"

R'leer's golden eyes blazed when he looked sharply up at her. "Something that was not hers to take, that does not belong in the possession of any banebreaker, let alone a Siliwari. Inolu bound the *uanáj* and whatever other forces she channeled into her physical body. Into her spirit, even, or what remained of it. If she is who you spoke to Earthside, I imagine she's still straddling the line between this realm and the other beyond the Weave. Not entirely there."

"Probably, yeah." Cheyenne pointed at her temple. "She seems mostly normal, or whatever passes for normal, then the next thing out of her mouth sounds like—"

"Like it belongs to someone else." R'leer nodded. "Yes. Most likely because it isn't her. Not entirely. She is highly dangerous on her own, Cheyenne. Combined with whatever forces she channels from within herself now, I cannot fathom what she's capable of." He shook his head.

"She helped me. Mostly. And she made it possible for my mom to make the crossing. So I guess I'll have to go back to her creepy townhouse and ask her to break Ba'rael's curse. Again." *The last time was a consultation. She'll be charging me from here on out, I guarantee it.*

"That is your decision." R'leer set his shot glass down before approaching the open glowing bone box again. He reached inside and pulled out a device that looked like a jeweler's loupe, only it was the size of a golf ball. The shimmering light inside the box pulsed and faded before he shut the lid. "If you choose to treat with the banebreaker, take this with you."

Cheyenne frowned at the device, which let off a faint, shimmering green glow with flecks of purple and black through the glass lens, then she raised an eyebrow at the darkseller. "You seem pretty sure that thing will make it back through the Border with me."

"Well, it isn't Spider-Cycle tech, so no issue there. Even if it were, that's hardly an obstacle for you, is it?"

"You read that in the Weave too, huh?"

"No. I guessed, but now I know. Take it." He extended the device farther toward her and nodded.

"What's it for?" Cheyenne took the device, her fingers tingling from the metal and glass as she slipped it into her back pocket.

"It will get her attention. Don't use it unless you have to, but if you do, don't hold back."

"Okay. Does it come with an instruction guide or anything?"

A low chuckle escaped the darkseller, and he lifted the bone box in both hands to replace it on the shelf.

He thinks I'm joking. Why would I know how to work old-school tech? Shouldn't be that hard.

When R'leer turned toward her again, his eerily intense stare returned to her face, and he stepped slowly toward her. "I'd like to change the subject for a moment. If you don't mind."

"Depends on what it is."

"Nothing onerous, I assure you." He stopped mere inches from her again and looked her over in that creepy, drow-stalker way of his. "I want to thank you."

"Oh." She swallowed and leaned slightly away. "I mean, it wasn't a personal favor or anything. But you're welcome."

"It feels personal." The darkseller dipped his head toward her, all the strung beads and bones clicking as they fell over his shoulders with his hair. "You were willing to listen and to let me show you what was at stake. You brought your mother across the Border to do what had to be done."

Cheyenne said, "You wear your dad's bones, so…"

"You think I killed him."

"Wouldn't be the weirdest thing. I know a nightstalker who drinks out of her mentor's silver-dipped skull."

R'leer's lips twitched into a smile, and he leaned closer. "Now there's an idea."

She stared at him, her arms folded, and lifted her chin. *This is the part where I back up and tell him to get the hell out of my face. Why am I not doing that?*

"You don't seem any different from when I saw you standing in the inner circle under the stars."

"Why would I be?"

He slowly closed his eyes and took a deep breath. "Because of what you did. It wasn't for the trees, Cheyenne. Not even for the drow." Biting his lower lip, his kohl-smeared eyes still closed, R'leer lifted his hand beside his face and twisted his fingers. A spiral of purple light danced like smoke around his hand, and when he opened his eyes, they were centered on hers. "Perhaps you don't feel the balance shifting back into place, but I promise you, the rest of us do. Ambar'ogúl has not been this strong in millennia. For most of living memory if we're being honest with one another."

"But the city's gone haywire." *Why am I still hung up on that right now?*

"The city is as much a construct as the technology running it. You are worrying about new magic when you should be celebrating the revival of the old. Everything will change, thanks to you."

"As long as it's for the better."

"It is." He lowered his hand toward her face and slipped two fingers through a lock of her bone-white hair.

Pull away, Cheyenne. If I stand here like this, he's gonna think I like it. Do I?

"There will always be disappointment with a shift in the status quo." R'leer studied the hair trailing through his fingers and let it drop against her shoulders again. "But those of us who have known what was coming since the beginning, those of us who are prepared to face the new age, will rise stronger than ever."

She couldn't look away from his blazing eyes as he took one more step toward her. The darkseller was so close, she felt his body heat radiating against her chest and shoulders. *Or maybe that's just me. He's playing it up now.*

"So, you'll rise," she muttered. "And do what?"

A feral, dangerous grin spread across R'leer's lips as he searched her eyes. "Whatever we want."

"That doesn't sound very balanced, darkseller."

"Oh, but it's simple." He lifted his chin and looked down at her, his fingers brushing her arm. "I want you to—"

Something crashed in the back of the shop behind the crudely carved wooden doors. R'leer frowned and looked toward the sound.

"Maybe you should take care of that," Cheyenne muttered. *And this would be my perfect exit.*

"It's fine." He narrowed his eyes at her.

Another crash interrupted him, followed by a creaking groan and an explosion of hollow metal banging on the ground. With a hiss, R'leer spun away from her and stormed toward the double doors. They flashed with silver light at a flick of his wrist and swung open into the back. Choking sounds and muffled grunts spilled through the doorway with the repeated thump of heavy thrashing.

Cheyenne quickly followed him, summoning a crackling black sphere in one hand and scanning the dark back room. A puff of white smoke burst around the corner, then Ur'syth's hookah hurtled across the wide hallway and shattered, spilling hot coals, ash, muddy water, and a smear of what looked like chunky peanut butter on the floor.

"What now?" R'leer turned the corner into the dark room in which the old Oracle had been holed up for weeks and froze.

Ur'syth knelt in a pile of spilled metal parts and a shelving unit that had toppled away from the wall. Her withered arms were extended at her sides and thumped the wall as she jerked back and forth. A thin trickle of dark red spilled from the corner of her mouth, and her all-white eyes rolled wildly in their sockets. Her head was thrown back. "It comes!"

Cheyenne folded her arms. "She gives prophecies without being paid now?"

R'leer shot her a scathing glare before stomping on one of the crone's filthy pillows, which had caught fire from a spilled coal burning a hole through it. The coal crunched beneath his boot, and the gray smoke curling toward the ceiling dispersed. "What comes?"

"The new age." Ur'syth's wrinkled, toothless mouth opened and closed without sound as her white eyes darted back and forth, aimed at the ceiling but seeing something else that wasn't there. "In the sister, balance remains. One side falls. The other swells. The new age will rise to break both worlds." She drew a gasping breath and bucked violently. The back of her head cracked into the wall. "Earth! The doorway opens. This should not be!"

R'leer pointed at the front of his shop and looked at Cheyenne. "Out."

"I didn't do this."

"No one said you did." He clapped his hands together, and when he drew them apart, the magical lights suspended below the ceiling flickered. A low rumble rose between the darkseller's palms, growing louder as a hissing mass of black specks and crackling silver light roiled in the air before him.

"He knows!" Ur'syth shrieked. "He sees! He will know before it's too late. Find him!"

"Who's she talking about?" Cheyenne stepped forward, her shoes crunching against shattered glass grinding into the smeared substance the Oracle had been smoking. *Maybe that's what's happening.*

R'leer grimaced as the storm built between his hands. Ur'syth's rag-covered body flashed with multi-colored light, and she let out more strangled chokes. "She is adjusting."

"To what?"

"Everything." He hissed a sharp word in O'gúleesh, and a bolt of black light struck the seizing Oracle's wrist and pinned her to the wall. The flashing lights around her flickered out for two seconds, then reappeared with renewed vigor.

"Find him! Look for the Weave."

Ur'syth screamed when another bolt of black light pinned her other wrist to the wall.

R'leer muttered the rest of his spell in a low growl. The dark magic growing between his hands kicked up a blast of hot air and whipped his bone-laden hair around his head. "Out, Cheyenne. No one else is meant to see this."

Cheyenne stared at Ur'syth, who snarled and jerked against the dark magic holding her to the wall. The thin trickle of red at the corner of her mouth was now a gushing cascade flowing through her lips and splattering all over her robes and the floor. The wrinkled crone cackled through a mouth full of what wasn't thick enough to be blood. Her white gaze dropped to the floor, where a monstrous, clawed shadow covered in spines spread toward her from R'leer's feet.

No way was that his shadow.

The darkseller's golden eyes flickered as he chanted more of his spell. The shadow expanded along the ground, growing and casting itself across Ur'syth and the wall behind her. R'leer didn't move, but the shadow raised a spike-covered arm and opened its claw, preparing to strike the crone Oracle spewing red liquid from her mouth.

Get the fuck out.

Cheyenne spun and stormed down the hall toward the front of the shop.

Ur'syth's bubbling cackle echoed behind her. Then dozens of laughing voices joined her in the same rhythm. "The old laws stand, Darkchild. Stand with us! Repay your debt."

A wet slice cut off the voices. The ground jerked beneath Cheyenne's feet and sent her tumbling through the curtain of strung bones and beads. She batted them away from her face and stumbled into the bazaar's main avenue. "Fuck."

When she straightened and turned to stare at R'leer's storefront, she found only the blacked-out windows. Even in the eerie silence of the bazaar, where the darksellers peddled their wares and services in low voices and scratchy whispers, she couldn't hear a thing inside the bone drow's shop.

Don't get involved. Whatever the hell that was, he can handle it himself.

"You look lost, *hinya.*"

Cheyenne jumped away from a tall, gangly magical with stringy hair like wet seaweed plastered to her face. Two sharp incisors jutted from the seaweed woman's open mouth and a thin film crossed over her lidless eyes before peeling back again.

"I'm not." Cheyenne looked the blue-green magical up and down and turned away. "And I don't need your help."

Tiny scales of black and dark green glinted on the other woman's flesh as she tilted her head. "Come find me if you do. No drow is ever turned away from Sashuyo's open arms!"

Shaking her head, Cheyenne ignored the strange magical's dark laughter and stalked through the bazaar toward the only entrance she knew. *She probably says that to everyone right before she slits their throats and sells their body parts.*

None of the other darksellers and practitioners of dark magic seemed to have a clue about what had happened or still was happening inside R'leer's shop. Only a handful of them watched the scowling drow head past their booths and open doorways, but no one else tried to confront her. *Every magical for themselves down here. No one would step in to help, even if they did know what was happening. Unless it affected business.*

Her drow entourage from the inner circle sat against the stone wall beside the entrance. Glís stood swiftly when she saw Cheyenne storming toward them, and the others followed suit, warily eyeing the underground community who called this place home.

"What happened?" Althas asked.

She let out an angry snort and brushed past him through the stone doorway, which hadn't closed on its own. The four drow waiting for her looked at each other in wide-eyed curiosity, then filtered through the doorway and headed after her without a word.

Cheyenne searched her activator for a better, more hidden route through the city levels back to the fortress. It offered her three different routes and their possible obstacles now that Hangivol's system had a major glitch blocking almost half of its data. She chose the route with the least exposure to the streets and angry crowds of Halter's Deck and made a sharp left turn down a narrow corridor. *I'll blast through the walls if I have to. Better than blasting through another pissed-off mob.*

"We came from this way." Haslin frowned at her and pointed down the much wider corridor leading directly away from the bazaar.

"Don't let me stop you," Cheyenne muttered and didn't bother to wait for them.

Glís sneered at Haslin and hurried after Cheyenne. "We follow you to the end."

"Oh, yeah? You gonna follow me across the Border too?"

The drow woman exhaled heavily through her nose but didn't say a word as she fell in three feet behind Cheyenne. Althas, Haslin, and Ban'oru walked briskly after them, casting looks over their shoulders at the open doorway into the bazaar. No one came after them.

CHAPTER FOURTEEN

The only time Cheyenne slowed down on her way back up through the city levels toward the fortress was to manually program four doorways to open and, in one case, manually pry an unresponsive door apart at the seams. Her activator came through in finding the path least traveled by the lower-level citizens, and she didn't have any more run-ins with magicals who blamed her for the power outage.

Her drow entourage was just as open to conversation as she was, so it was a silent trek back through Hangivol. When they reached the inner circle, the main avenue was livelier than when they'd left it, groups of drow gathered in tight circles for discussion. Some of them had drawn out chairs and tables and arranged them with views of the fortress.

Like they're setting up to watch a concert. What do they think is gonna happen?

Before she reached the shredded side door in the fortress wall, she stopped. "Look, I get that you guys wanted to make yourselves useful or whatever, but now it's seriously time to…" She spun to face her drow escort, but they were gone. "Look before you open your mouth, Cheyenne."

She scanned the avenue, which was slowly filling with more drow joining the remarkably dull party. Glís stood at a table outside a store-front with a tight smile and raised a metal cup to her lips before glancing at Cheyenne. Haslin and Ban'oru were already deeply engaged in a knife-throwing contest with two others, the blades sticking with sharp metallic rings into the side of their target, an empty grog barrel. Althas stood two doors down from the knife-throwers, his hand propped on the door beside him as two drow women spoke to him in low tones. He stared at Cheyenne so intensely that the drow women turned to eye her as well.

Cheyenne ran a hand through her hair and nodded at him. Althas dipped his head, then returned to his previous conversation. *Okay, maybe they do know when to call off unnecessary guard duty. Just gotta work on when not to pick fights with the locals or insist on calling me the Crown.*

She slipped through the shredded side door and made her way through the twisting corridors of the fortress toward Persh'al's quarters. The large double doors were propped open when she reached them.

"Pull!" Byrd shouted.

A silver cup launched across the receiving room and was blasted away by an ensuing burst of green light.

"Damn. You weren't fuckin' around."

"Told ya. Anyone who says you need two eyes for depth perception is full of shit."

"Yeah, but you have two eyes."

"I covered one of them."

Cheyenne cleared her throat.

The goblins jumped and spun toward her.

"Shit, Cheyenne." Byrd chuckled and rubbed his bald head. "Didn't see you come in."

"So your peripheral vision's shit, huh?" Lumil slapped his chest with the back of a hand and turned toward the sitting area. "Good to know."

He hurried after her. "There's nothing wrong with my peripheral vision. I was focused!"

Maleshi snatched a newly opened bottle of Bloodshine off the table before Lumil could grab it. With a snort, the goblin woman settled for more fellwine and filled her cup almost to overflowing. "So, how was your visit with the *andashal?*"

Cheyenne approached the half-circle of furniture and sat on the couch's armrest. "What does that mean, anyway?"

"It's an old-world title." Corian lay sprawled on his back on the pile of cushions, his eyes closed and arms folded behind his head. "Something like a shaman. Sort of. Not sure any drow fully fits the job description these days."

"I wouldn't be so sure." Maleshi crossed one leg over the other and sat back in the armchair. "The darkseller had a pretty *andashal*-ish vibe this morning."

Cheyenne snorted. "He's got a vibe. That's for sure."

"Ah. It went well, then." The general grinned up at her and raised the bottle of Bloodshine.

"Not as well as I hoped." The drow shrugged. "But it could've been worse." *A lot worse.*

"Indeed." Corian chuckled but still didn't move or open his eyes. "It can always be worse."

Cheyenne frowned at him. "He's wasted, isn't he?"

"Hmm. I can't tell." Maleshi squinted at the nightstalker on the pillows, then belched loudly. "Probably because I'm wasted."

A door opened at the back of the receiving room opposite the hidden door leading into the private areas of the Crown's chambers, and Bianca and Ember emerged. The woman used the fae's arm for support as they stepped back into the receiving room as she said, "That's the thing, isn't it? When you're human, no one thinks twice about showing you how to use a magical toilet."

"Mom." Cheyenne stood and gave them both a weak, surprised smile. "I thought you were resting."

"I was. Then I got unbearably bored." Bianca cocked her head and stared across the room at the open double doors as if remembering something she'd rather forget. "Besides, that room had an awful draft, and you know how I feel about drafts."

"Right. You sound like you're feeling better, at least." *She sounds like herself again. Now we wait to see who she pisses off first.*

"Better than before, yes." With Ember's help, Bianca slowly sank onto the couch beside Maleshi, who dipped her head at the woman and took a long, guzzling drink from the Bloodshine bottle. "But not fully recovered. Ember mentioned you'd disappeared to find another solution for that."

Awesome. I get to tell her the fun's not over yet.

"Not quite a solution." Cheyenne had to look away from Bianca's prying gaze. "Just a pointer in the right direction."

"Where are we headed this time?"

The drow swallowed. "Home."

Lumil barked a laugh. "You expect us to believe that darkseller told you to go Earthside for this shit? Man, he must think you're an idiot. He didn't make you pay for that shitty advice, did he?"

"Make me pay?" Cheyenne scoffed. "No. He didn't try to sell me on something I'm gonna do anyway. Apparently, the best banebreaker for the job is the one I saw in Richmond."

"No shit." Byrd slapped his thigh. "How d'ya like them apples?"

"Dude, what the fuck?" Lumil wrinkled her nose in disgust and shook her head. "Nobody says that."

"Somebody has to, or it wouldn't be a saying. Would it?"

Corian finally pushed himself off the cushions and blinked drowsily at Cheyenne. "A banebreaker in Richmond."

"Yeah. Inolu Rosh."

"Never heard of her."

Cheyenne shot Maleshi a questioning look, and the general shrugged. "Hey, if I didn't recognize the name when I was sober, I definitely won't now."

"Before she was Richmond's banebreaker, she was Hangivol's."

The nightstalkers shared a knowing look. Corian smacked his lips. "So?"

Maleshi snorted and took another long drink from the bottle while Bianca stared at her.

"So, it's not that weird to think neither of you knew a banebreaker in Hangivol. Right?"

"Listen, kid." Corian swayed and raised his hand like he meant to drop it on her shoulder. Of course, it landed on air and then his thigh. "I can count on one hand the number of times I set foot in this fell-damn city in the last two hundred years. Before the Cycle turned for you, obviously."

His silver eyes flicked up to meet her gaze and he slowly raised his hand again, turning it around to raise his middle finger at her.

Lumil guffawed. Byrd slapped his thigh again. "Ha! Good one!"

Bianca stared at the smirking nightstalker and pursed her lips. "How charming."

"My pleasure." Corian dropped his hand into his lap and swayed again, his eyelids drooping shut.

"Can we go back to you and Maleshi recounting your war stories for my benefit? I much prefer that version of you."

"Recounting their *what*?" Cheyenne frowned at her mom. "Are you serious?"

"It was very enlightening."

Ember chuckled and covered her mouth. "That got off-topic really fast."

"Yeah." When Cheyenne's stare didn't make Corian open his eyes, she turned it onto the general instead. "I don't care what stories you do and don't tell my mom. But maybe you can tell me why Corian's flipping me the bird when I asked about a banebreaker in Hangivol."

"I wasn't," Corian grunted. "That was one, Cheyenne. One time. That just happened to be with my middle finger."

"Come on."

Maleshi chuckled and raised a hand for Cheyenne to wait. "Neither one of us spent all that much free time here back in the day, kid. I had military campaigns to run, and Corian had L'zar's ass to wipe."

Lumil cracked up again. "And L'zar got into a lotta shit!"

"Yeah!" Byrd almost hyperventilated. "Dragged us through it with him, didn't he? Ha! Good thing only one of us got hanged for his crimes, right?"

The goblin woman's laughter cut off abruptly, and she turned her whole body in the armchair to scowl at him.

Byrd gulped. "And lived."

"Even if we had been here with enough time to consider pursuing a darkseller bazaar," Maleshi continued, "we wouldn't have done it. That was L'zar's business. Not ours."

Cheyenne frowned. "He didn't work down there."

The general chuckled. "First of all, L'zar doesn't work."

Corian snorted and flopped back down on the cushions.

"But he's always had an uncanny ability to make friends in the most unexpected places. Even among darksellers and bottom-feeders."

"Plenty of enemies too," Byrd added.

"That's hardly surprising," Bianca muttered and absently pulled the Bloodshine bottle out of Maleshi's hand to raise it to her lips. She almost spilled the whole thing when the violent bubbles hit her nose and mouth, and she quickly returned the bottle. "I want you to meet my whiskey sommelier. One tasting with him, and you'll never pick up another bottle of this whatever you call it."

"Bloodshine," Lumil muttered.

"Yes, that only proves my point."

"Now I'm intrigued." Maleshi smiled at Cheyenne and winked. "Who could say no to that?"

Cheyenne closed her eyes and blew a long, slow breath. *I picked the worst time for an impossible conversation.*

"Okay, look. The point is that we're making the crossing again to go see Inolu. She'll get rid of this curse, and then we can put the rest of this behind us. That's all I want at this point."

"It sounds like you have it all figured out," Bianca said.

"Not all of it. Just the next step."

"Ah. I trust you." Bianca absently patted Cheyenne's forearm and blinked across the sitting area. "I also suspect it's been far too long since I've eaten something. I'd like to address that if at all possible."

Lumil blew a sharp raspberry through loose lips and waved dismissively. "Just keep drinkin', lady. You'll forget all about hunger."

"If I keep drinking the way you all have been, I'm likely to forget about breathing."

Cheyenne choked back a laugh and turned away from the sitting area. "With the system down like it is, I guess we have to request food the old-fashioned way, right?"

"I don't cook, kid," Corian muttered. "Never have. Never will."

Maleshi rolled her eyes. "That's my cue to stop drinking."

Bianca shook her head. "Don't let his laziness pressure you into doing something he's perfectly capable of on his own. It doesn't do either of you any good."

The general blinked in surprise, then threw her head back and roared with laughter. Bianca looked her up and down with a raised eyebrow.

"You are somethin' else. You know that?" Maleshi wiped a tear from the corner of her eye and shook her head. "I'd slit his throat before I domesticated myself for the *vae shra'ni*. Ha! I was talkin' about him reaching his chronic-liar level of inebriation. This means if I don't stop drinking now, I'll wake up in the morning without a clue as to whose blood is on my hands. But your advice was still excellent."

Grinning at Bianca's startled expression, Maleshi pushed up off the couch and swayed on her feet. "Ironbreak!" she roared, throwing her arms back and puffing her chest out as she turned slowly around the room. "Your council humbly requests an audience with your most prestigiously blue personage!"

Lumil and Byrd fell over each other, laughing.

"We are but unworthy subjects," the general continued, "however loyal. If your imminently mohawked highness would deign to appear before this gathering and tell us how the hell to get some fell-damn food in here?"

The hidden door around the corner burst open, and Persh'al stormed to the center of the receiving room.

"Hey." Maleshi spun drunkenly toward him. "That shit worked."

Persh'al stared at his inebriated friends and spread his arms. "Are you done?"

Maleshi stuck one hand on her hip, raised the other at her side as if carrying a serving tray, and belched. "I'm happy to continue if you want more."

"Fuck, no." Persh'al waved her off. "Just no. Sit down." He turned to the opposite side of the receiving room to glare at the nearly empty banquet table. "You ate all the food."

"It was her." Corian pointed a limp finger at the general.

Maleshi rolled her eyes.

Persh'al cast her a suspicious glance. "He's at the lying stage."

"Obviously. And Venga's the one who went through that entire spread. Hightailed it outta here with his greasy claws two hours ago."

"Fucking necromancers." The troll snorted. "All right. I'll get someone to bring up some grub, but I'm closing the booze drawer, got it?"

Maleshi cocked her head and gave him a one-shouldered shrug. "It's empty anyway, but do what makes you feel good."

"It's empty." He scoffed. "Who needs friends when I have you assholes around, huh?"

Lumil chuckled and jerked her chin at him. Byrd clicked his tongue and shot Persh'al the guns with both hands.

The troll Crown headed toward the back wall and opened a message box that fortunately still worked despite the system outage. "Hasn't even been a week."

"A new record!" Corian shouted, thrusting a fur-backed fist into the air before letting it drop back on the cushions.

Cheyenne looked at her mom and tried to look more amused than concerned about her small smile. "Are you okay with staying here another night and heading back in the morning?"

Bianca turned her hands over and studied first her palms, then the backs of her hands and her fingernails. "I haven't had a full night's sleep in days, Cheyenne. If one more night here can get me that at the very least, I should think that's a rather reasonable request."

"Yeah, I know the feeling."

The woman slowly lifted her head and cast Cheyenne a sideways look. "But I want a room without a draft."

The drow couldn't help but smile, and this time, it was genuine. "We'll make it happen."

CHAPTER FIFTEEN

The Crown's orc guards weren't particularly happy about having to bring up a meal for Persh'al and his guests. They grumbled the whole time about tech malfunctioning and the point of having the city system in the first place if it could be wiped out so easily.

Maleshi stood in the center of the room with her arms folded, somehow managing to pull off an air of sobriety as she directed the orcs where to place which dishes and told them to leave the entire cart of booze where it was. "No use in putting everything away in the wall. It'll get drunk eventually."

The orcs turned to Persh'al with exasperated stares, but they thumped their fists on their chests anyway.

"Thank you." The troll Crown nodded. "I'll let you know if we need anything else tonight."

"One of those things should be servants," the slightly smaller orc muttered. He grunted when his fellow guard smacked him in the back of the head and growled.

"Mind your tongue."

"We're soldiers."

"That's the point."

Persh'al rubbed one side of his shaved head. "I understand. This is only temporary."

Both guards nodded and spun quickly to exit the receiving room. The doors shut behind them with a bang, and Maleshi chuckled. "Crown guards delivering dinner. I have to admit it's amusing."

Persh'al rolled his eyes and cast a spell in the middle of the room. The floor buckled and rippled outward, and a large rectangular table rose through the rearranging metal segments. Sparks flew, the materializing table shuddered, and it stopped halfway out of the floor with stunted legs, tilting slightly to one side.

Maleshi cocked her head. "That takes your redecorating initiative to a whole new level. Care to try for a few chairs?"

The troll blinked at her, then gestured at Corian with a dismissive hand. "Move the useless lump off the cushions and use those. It's something."

"It certainly is something." The general chuckled when Persh'al moved toward the newly restocked banquet table, shaking his head.

Byrd and Lumil jumped at the chance to tug, shove, and roughly peel Corian off the pile of cushions in the sitting area. He was unresponsive until they got him propped in a sitting position. "Damn, he's heavy."

Lumil snorted. "Where does he keep all the weight?"

"Help me get this last one out from under him. Yeah, yeah, just push him forward. He won't feel a thing."

The goblin woman grinned and shoved the nightstalker in the back. Corian lurched toward the ground, then moved with near-lucid speed. One hand smacked on the floor to keep his face from smacking it instead, and the other hand whipped out behind him, glinting claws extended, and stopped less than an inch from Lumil's throat. "Touch me again, and you'll be dining on your own blood tonight."

Lumil smacked her lips and stared at his claws. "I think we have enough pillows without that one."

"Yeah, we're good."

The goblins scrambled to their feet and got to work chucking cushions across the room toward the slanted, half-height dining table.

Byrd looked at Maleshi and grunted as he slung another cushion. "Wanna pitch in?"

She folded her arms and grinned. "You're doing a great job."

Ember helped Bianca off the couch and directed her toward the table. "Want me to make you a plate?"

"That would be lovely, Ember. Thank you." The woman lowered herself gingerly onto two stacked cushions with Ember's support and swiped her brown hair away from her forehead. "Oh, and if there are any of those black berries? You know the ones."

"I'll make sure to pile them on." Ember turned toward the banquet table and met Cheyenne's gaze with a knowing smile.

The drow tried to return it, but she couldn't help the feeling that all this downtime to sit around and eat a real meal together was the calm before another storm. *And it's not only the system malfunction. Mom's done with this place. As soon as we get Inolu to break the curse, that's the last time Bianca Summerlin's involved in any of this. It has to be.*

By the time everyone piled their plates high with O'gúleesh banquet food and sat around the lopsided table on the piled cushions, Corian was acting more like himself. Except that he stabbed each bite with one of his claws and picked it delicately off with his teeth, glaring at everyone around the table.

Ember pressed her lips together to fight back a smile. "You ever worry about stabbing yourself with those things?"

The nightstalker plucked another huge chunk of some type of meat off his claw and ran the razor-sharp tip along his bottom lip as he chewed, then pointed it at Ember. "You ever worry about blasting someone's arm off instead of healing it?"

She snorted and returned her attention to her food. "Fair enough."

Cheyenne watched her mom digging into her meal, which mostly consisted of the small black berries she and Ember loved so much, but she couldn't bring herself to eat much more than a few bites. She grabbed the metal pitcher of water that had fortunately been brought with their meal and refilled Bianca's cup. "You need anything?"

"Many things, as I'm sure you're aware." Bianca nodded her thanks and picked up her metal cup. "But for now, Cheyenne, I am content with what's in front of me. Thank you."

The drow couldn't look her mom in the eye. Bianca didn't seem capable of looking at anyone else, either. *The novelty's worn off. I can't blame her.*

Lumil and Byrd crammed food into their mouths, grunting and slurping like they hadn't eaten in days. Bianca shot them a warning look, but of course, they didn't notice. She turned to Maleshi. "General, I don't believe you finished the story you began earlier."

"Which story was that?" Maleshi popped a chunk of what looked like bread into her mouth.

"A campaign in some city in the cliffs, wasn't it?"

"Ah. Arahk-nahsh." Maleshi nodded. "I don't think that's an appropriate tale to tell over a meal."

Lumil belched as she reached for a huge drumstick of some O'gúleesh bird, then tore into it with her teeth and a sharp jerk of her head. Cooked flesh and melted fat dropped onto the table.

Bianca picked up one berry and looked at the general. "I'm not a squeamish woman, which I'm sure you've picked up on at this point. And I'd much rather listen to an intelligent magical with a flair for storytelling than certain other background noises."

Maleshi chuckled. "Indeed."

The berry disappeared into Bianca's mouth. "Start again at the part where you appeared before Corian could have his pelt stripped from his bones."

Cheyenne choked on her water and lowered her cup. Every magical around the table stared at Corian, whose hand froze an inch from stabbing another bite on his plate. Lumil stopped chewing and gulped down her entire mouthful with a squeezing gurgle.

Corian cocked his head, his eyes narrowing, then burst into uproarious laughter. He pounded his fist against the table, making all the food jump and a few plates slide down the sloping surface. "That is a good story! Tell her, *ma gairín*. It's no secret how many times you've saved my hide."

The goblins chuckled nervously.

Maleshi smiled as Corian stabbed his food with a claw and jammed it into his mouth, his silver eyes flashing as he looked at her. "No. Not a secret. I ported to the top of the chieftain's watchtower."

Cheyenne heard the hidden door open in the recessed corner at the back of the room and turned on her cushion. Persh'al walked slowly through the receiving room toward the banquet table, rubbing his mouth and chin and frowning.

Might not get a better time to talk to him.

She bit into an oblong maroon vegetable that squirted sour juice into her mouth and dropped the other half back onto her plate before standing. No one around the table paid her any attention, and she met Persh'al at the banquet table as he grabbed a plate for himself.

"You finally came out to join us, huh?"

He shrugged, picking absently at the food and dropping it onto the plate. "Even the O'gúl Crown has to eat. Or at least, this one does."

She folded her arms and nodded with a small smile. "True. Hey, when you're done, I can show you the decryption code I put together in your VR if you want. You might be able to chip away at a decent portion of the block in there before I get back."

"Sure. Anything helps." The troll sloshed some kind of gravy onto his plate without paying attention. "Any idea when that'll be?"

"Not yet. I'm trying to take it one step at a time."

"Yeah, I get it."

"You think you can handle things around here on your own for a little while?" Cheyenne tried to smile. "You know, just until I can see a banebreaker about a curse."

He blinked, his small smile as tired-looking as hers felt. "That's why you gave me this gig, isn't it?"

"Yeah. I know you can handle it."

They both turned when a burst of laughter rose from the table at Maleshi's story. "And he said he'd rather suck the wrong end of a steel-worm than hand it over."

Corian pointed at the general. "Which was almost an option."

Cheyenne and Persh'al turned back to the banquet table, and he made his way down the spread of food. "But you're not sure I've reached that point yet, huh?"

She shrugged. "We haven't had the chance to talk about it. You've spent more time in that back room than out here with the rest of us." *Jesus. It sounds like I'm baiting him to say he hates me for handing him the throne.* "Which I get," she added quickly. "And I know it's not personal."

"No, it's not." Persh'al set the plate down and turned to face her head-on. "Has nothin' to do with you, kid. Just hard to think with the whole team spewing useless shit into their drinks. Funny, but useless."

"Yeah, I get that." Cheyenne looked at the table. "So, you've been working on the system the whole time?"

"Working on the system. Piecing together a few ideas. Elarit's not in a social mood right now."

"Got it." *Because she doesn't want to be around me. Drow's outta the bag again.* "That makes sense. You guys took on this huge new job, and you don't wanna let her spend the whole day by herself."

"Cheyenne."

"No, I totally get it. You were separated for centuries. Who would wanna keep doing that when the only other magicals here are a bunch of lunatics who drink all your booze?"

Persh'al laughed and shook his head.

"What?"

"You're nervous about this."

Cheyenne frowned. "I'm not nervous."

"Kid, you're thinking out loud and talking circles around yourself. Normally, it's the other way around."

She dipped her head in acknowledgment. "Okay, fine. I'll shut up and let you get back to your wife."

"*Wadeenesh.* That's the word for it here."

"Right."

Persh'al glanced over his shoulder at the open door into the back room and chuckled. "Elarit doesn't have a problem being on her own. She couldn't care less if I was out here with you guys getting shitfaced and yucking it up with old war stories."

"Oh."

"But I care. I'm trying to get the system back online. It's important." A small, self-conscious smile flickered across his blue lips. "I'm not holing up in there to make her feel better. If I'm perfectly honest, I need her help."

Cheyenne raised her eyebrows and blinked in surprise. "You're working in there?"

"We're working. Listen, kid. However pissed off she was when you brought the drow back this morning, she gets it, and she's the most skilled sparksetter in both damn worlds." He pointed at her. "You've got some kinda crazy gift with working tech, I'll give you that, but Elarit's a master at making it. I couldn't do half of what I do without her."

"Maybe she should make the Earthside crossing with us, then. You know, improve your warehouse systems and everything."

Persh'al's eyes widened, then he caught her smile and gave a relieved chuckle. "You're fucking with me."

"Yeah, a little."

"You've got some nerve, kid." Shaking his head, the troll picked up his randomly piled plate. "Yeah. I can handle things here as the O'gúl Crown while you get rid of that curse and take your mom home. That's what's most important right now, and she deserves it after everything she's been through."

"Thanks."

"She's a real fucking champ. For a human."

Cheyenne snorted. "I'll tell her you said so."

Nodding curtly, Persh'al stared at the table where his friends were eating together and sniffed. "I better get back to it. If I didn't have to eat and sleep and piss, I wouldn't step out of that room until this whole brownout mess is finished. But we'll come to see you off before you leave. I'm guessing that's tomorrow, right?"

"That's the plan, yeah."

"Good." He headed toward the hidden door in the corner.

"Hey, one more thing." Cheyenne went after him, and he turned and eyed her with curiosity. "In your expert opinion, how possible would it be to get a bunch of activators built and ready to go by, say, tomorrow? Before we make the crossing again."

He squinted at her. "How many is a bunch?"

"I don't know. At least a hundred to start. More if it's possible. And a lot more later on if they work the way I want them to Earthside."

"That's assuming you can ferry a bunch of activators across the Border like that top-of-the-line piece behind your ear."

She nodded. "I can."

"You want a backup supply, or what?"

Cheyenne shrugged, unable to hold back a smile. "I'm trying to be smart about when and how often I make the crossing from here on out. I have a feeling crossing back and forth all the time isn't doing me any favors, so this is a trial run."

"Sure. You know there's no telling what the in-between's like now that the blight's gone, right?"

"Yeah, I know. But I need to stick around with Bianca for a while once we see the banebreaker. Make sure she's okay. And I have a meeting with the FRoE on Monday that I can't blow off."

Persh'al scoffed. "Man, those idiots don't have shit on you anymore, kid. Why are you still puttin' yourself through that wringer?"

"The Ironbreak sits the throne." She smirked at him. "Which I prefer, by the way. My other option was to take up the whole Drow royalty on Earth gig. That's where I can be the most useful."

"The FRoE aren't in on what goes down over here. Aren't half of them human, anyway?"

"A lot of them, yeah, and it's run by humans. It wasn't intentional, but I kinda fell into a consultant position with them."

"So, it's a job."

She wrinkled her nose. "Eh, more like an involuntary promotion. I could've told them no, but if things are gonna change for Earthside magicals, and I mean for the better, I couldn't. If they wanna keep thinking of themselves as the Border portal gatekeepers—"

"Then you'll do your royal duty from the inside." Persh'al nodded slowly. "Good thinking, kid. I'm impressed."

"Letting them think they have me in their pocket?"

"Naw, anyone can do that." She laughed, and the troll's smile widened. "Any other magical in your shoes would probably end up using the Earthside royalty thing to wipe out the FRoE or at least turn the refugees and Earthborn against a dumbass organization like that. But you're trying to get everyone to work together. Not humans against magicals and all that bullshit."

"I mean, I am half of both."

"Yeah, and you're something completely different too. You got class, kid."

Cheyenne snorted and looked over her shoulder at Bianca, who listened intently to Maleshi's tale and plucked more black berries off the sprig to pop into her mouth. "I learned from one of the best."

"Ha. It sure as shit wasn't L'zar."

They laughed softly. "No, he'd go in, slit every FRoE operative's throat, and turn the reservations into his Earthside palaces."

"Not that far-fetched." Persh'al nodded. "I'll talk to Elarit about the activators."

She turned back toward him with wide eyes. "Seriously?"

"Seriously. Not that I need her permission or anything, but if you want that many activators by tomorrow, she's the only magical in Hangivol who can make them on time."

"Thanks."

"Yeah, don't thank me 'til you have those babies in your hands. Now, go take a load off. You got some downtime. You should use it."

"Yeah. Okay."

Chuckling, he shook his head and headed for the hidden doorway. "See you tomorrow, kid."

CHAPTER SIXTEEN

Cheyenne managed to eat half of what was on her plate before she couldn't touch another bite. The rest of the magicals around the table filled their cups with grog from a small barrel left with the restocked cart of booze. Byrd and Lumil had taken over the conversation by talking about their home, a small town in what used to be the Outers millennia ago, where they'd been miners in the everstone quarries.

"Tell you what." Lumil picked at her teeth. "Nothing in either world like the grog back home."

"Tastes like butane, but it sure warms your belly when there's not much else to do the job."

"Man, when the fuck have you tasted butane?"

Byrd scowled at her and spread his arms. "You got a better comparison?"

Lumil scoffed and slurped her grog.

Ember leaned forward and rested her forearms on the table. "So, how'd you guys end up fighting with nightstalkers and living in DC?"

"At the warehouse?" Byrd shrugged. "L'zar."

Ember and Cheyenne gave Bianca a wary look. The woman's eyes were closed, her hands folded in her lap.

Didn't think that one through, Em. I probably wouldn't have either.

"Damn drow broke into a mine," Byrd added with a chuckle. "You know, I still don't know if he was trying to get in or just miscalculated."

"I'm sorry to interrupt." Bianca opened her eyes and took a deep breath, then looked at her daughter. "I'd like to lie down."

"Are you feeling okay?"

"Just tired, I think."

Tired of hearing about L'zar.

"Sure." Cheyenne started to push off the cushions, but Ember beat her to it.

"I'll take you."

"Hey, look at you." Byrd raised his cup toward her and grinned. "Fae's back on her feet and jumping around like a damn *carako*."

Ember stared at him and hopped once. Lumil snorted and shook her head.

Cheyenne looked at her friend. "Em, you don't have to."

"Come on." Ember gave her a knowing smile. "You don't even know where the guest rooms are. And I'm pretty sure I can find you one without a draft, Bianca."

"That would be wonderful. Thank you."

Cheyenne helped her mom to her feet, then Bianca placed a hand on Ember's forearm and let the fae support her across the receiving room.

"I appreciate the company tonight. And the stories, General. You've painted quite the picture."

"Happy to entertain." Maleshi nodded at her. "Sleep well."

Corian raised a hand in farewell, then took a long drink of grog.

"I can come with you if you want," Cheyenne added.

"I'm perfectly capable of sleeping in a bed on my own." Bianca raised an eyebrow. "I've been doing it most of my life."

That was a jab at being single if I ever heard one.

"I know, Mom."

"I'll be fine. Sleep will help. I'm fatigued and ready to go home." Bianca reached out with her other hand to pat her daughter's arm. "With you."

Ember tried to hide a smile.

Yep. Still weird to get unprovoked PDA from my mom.

"Yeah, me too." Cheyenne nodded. "Maybe you'll sleep better knowing I found someone in Richmond who can help heal you the rest of the way. We'll head back tomorrow and go see her first thing, okay?"

"Whatever you think is best, Cheyenne. Good night."

"Good night, Mom."

"Don't let the bedbugs bite," Byrd added, wiggling his fingers at Bianca before Lumil slapped his hands away.

"If there are bedbugs in this place, goblin, I'll come for you specifically."

Maleshi barked a laugh.

Byrd scowled. "Why me?"

"I imagine they're likely to have come from one of you. Just an observation."

Lumil cocked her head at the woman and wrinkled her nose as Ember led Bianca toward the doors.

Corian grinned at the goblins. "She's not wrong."

"No one asked you, furface."

The doors swung open on their own, and Ember and Bianca stopped in their tracks when Venga hurried into the receiving room. He blinked at them and cocked his head. "Excellent. You're still here."

"We were just leaving," Ember said. "Bianca's turning in."

"Ah, yes, yes." The necromancer wrung all four hands together and looked Bianca up and down. "Before you go, I was hoping you'd agree to another series of tests. Just a few more blood samples to see what else is possible with your unique makeup as the Vessel."

"No, thank you."

Venga stepped in front of them to block them from the doors. "It won't take long, Bianca."

"I mean this with all due respect, necromancer." Bianca stared into his all-black eyes and lifted her chin. "Go fuck yourself."

She released Ember's arm to walk steadily around the scaleback. Ember forced back a laugh when she met the woman on the other side and offered her arm again to escort Bianca down the hall.

Venga's mouth opened and closed soundlessly as he stared at the empty space where his unwilling test subject had stood.

"Looks like your usefulness ran out, scaleback," Lumil called.

He snarled at her.

"Want a drink instead?" Byrd gestured at the half-empty barrel of grog.

"I'd rather eat my own tail, you insufferable greenskins." Venga whirled and stormed through the open doors, his tail thumping on the ground as his claws threw up sparks with each step.

"That's something I'd like to see," Lumil muttered.

Byrd sniggered. "Fifty *veréle* says he chokes on the first four inches."

"He's not gonna eat his tail, you moron."

"Hey, the guy lives for his experiments. I wouldn't put it past him."

Maleshi raised her eyebrows and gave Cheyenne a thin-lipped smile. "Your mom seems to have come into her own here, don't you think?"

"Just in time for us to leave tomorrow. Yeah." Cheyenne sighed. "Hopefully, she never has to set foot on this world again."

"You've done everything you can do to make that possible," Corian said. "And you've done it well."

"With hardly a complaint, once you accepted your mom was the Vessel." Maleshi shrugged. "I'd call that a win."

"Feels pretty anticlimactic."

Lumil snorted. "Not when you were almost taken by the blight. Man, I wish I'd been there to see that shit."

"Dude." Byrd shook his head. "Not cool."

"Yeah, it is. 'Cause she came the fuck back and healed the world, man."

Cheyenne raised an eyebrow and shot the goblin a deadpan stare. "You know me. Just trying to be cool."

Corian chuckled. "I'm proud of you, Cheyenne. You've come a long way since you showed up at my door with a sandwich."

She playfully rolled her eyes. "Sometimes I wish I hadn't."

"Then where would we be?" Maleshi asked. "We're all proud of you. And grateful. The Earthside O'gúleesh are lucky to have you on the other side."

"Yeah, I'll have to see how all that plays out. It's gotta be a hell of a lot easier than this, though, right?"

The nightstalkers lifted their cups toward her in a silent salute. "For the Black Flame, I'd say anything's possible."

"Thanks." Cheyenne looked around the room, then nodded at the open doors. "I'm gonna take a walk, I think. Clear my head a little."

"Want some company?" Corian asked.

"Not really."

"Good. I don't want to leave this table."

Maleshi snorted and shot him an exasperated glare as he smiled into his cup.

"Then it works out for everyone. I'll probably end up in my apartment after this, so I'll see you guys tomorrow, I guess."

"Wouldn't miss escorting the Black Flame across the Border for all the grog in either world," Corian muttered.

Maleshi nodded. "We'll be there, kid."

"Okay." Raising a hand in farewell, Cheyenne headed into the hallway and turned left without knowing where she was going or where she'd end up.

All this time to do nothing before the next step, and I can't even sit still and take it in. That better change once we get rid of that fucking curse.

She walked aimlessly through the fortress' twisting corridors of light pseudo-stone. The occasional spark and scatter of electric blue light lit the hallways around her, but at least the walls didn't malfunction. A handful of orc guards passed her, thumping fists to chests and dipping their heads when they saw her, but nobody tried to stop her for conversation.

I'm done talking anyway. Not like there's anything to say. Ba'rael's off the throne. The blight's gone. The Nimlothars didn't die. Compared to all that, a little system shutdown's nothing.

Cheyenne didn't pay attention to where she was going or which branching corridors she took one after the other. She followed what felt right, or at least didn't feel wrong, until she passed through a large arch and stepped into the Heart's courtyard.

"Of course, this was where I'd end up," she said, moving slowly across the courtyard and gazing up at the Nimlothar growing from the cracked stone floor.

The tree here had been healed as much as the forest in the mountains, so its sprawling branches were now lush with glowing violet leaves. Purple flowers so dark they were almost black dotted the thick foliage, occasionally flashing golden light at their centers. The tree glistened, rustling when the breeze dipped below the open ceiling of the courtyard and danced across the full branches.

Everything is back to the way it should be, huh? Cheyenne headed toward the tree, noting the occasional streak of purple light racing up bark that no longer looked twisted and decayed but fully restored. Alive.

She stopped in front of the Nimlothar and gazed up into the glimmering branches that formed a wide umbrella above her.

"We did it," she whispered. "Almost didn't, but I guess that doesn't matter in the end. I made you a promise, and I kept it. I hope it's that easy, and you keep things running smoothly for Persh'al."

The tree didn't give her any kind of response, but when Cheyenne pressed her hand against the trunk, her fingers flashed with purple light, and the lush branches above her rustled and murmured their assent.

Look at me, talking to a tree like it talks back. At least the tree told me exactly what it wanted from me and exactly what would happen if I fucked it up.

She grinned at the bark. "I'm not gonna hug you or anything."

Cheyenne lowered herself to the stone floor and found a section that wasn't uncomfortably lumpy above the Nimlothar's root system. She sat with her back against the tree and pulled her knees up to her chest. Closing her eyes, she listened to the sound of the breeze filtering through the open ceiling and rustling the branches. A warm tingle spread through her back, and she smiled.

Yeah, I know.

***

She might have fallen asleep sitting up like that, or maybe it was a deep meditation to clear her mind and quit thinking about anything for a while, but the sound of light footsteps passing across the stone floors brought Cheyenne's awareness back to her. She took a deep breath, lifted her head from where she'd nestled it against the Nimlothar's trunk, and opened her eyes.

And now I'm seeing things.

Elarit stood in front of her, arms clasped behind her back as she stared at the glowing purple blossoms and the healthy, glimmering branches. Thin silver chains draped across her cheeks and over the bridge of her nose.

Cheyenne rested her forearms on her knees. "Hi."

"Hi." Elarit didn't look at her. "I had a feeling I'd find you here."

"Let me guess. You're about to tell me I can't leave before I help you guys decrypt that giant data block in the mainframe."

The troll woman blinked quickly and finally looked down at the drow sitting against the tree. "You can hold your own against the Spider and heal trees and use one of my best activators better than I can, but reading minds is not in your skillset."

Cheyenne snorted. "Fair enough. So why were you looking for me?"

Elarit pursed her lips. "Mind if I sit?"

"It's your courtyard."

With a soft hum, the troll lowered herself fluidly to the stone floor and crossed her legs. A handful of thin scarlet braids fell over her shoulder, but the rest were coiled and pinned at the top of her head. Elarit lifted her chin and held the drow's golden gaze. "I have some questions for you."

"Okay. I might have some answers."

"Why so many?"

Cheyenne raised her eyebrows. "So many what?"

"Activators."

Wow. Persh'al didn't waste any time.

"To put them to good use Earthside." She shrugged. "I'd put in a shipment order, but I'm the only one who can take them across without destroying them."

"I'm sure that's an inconvenience you're willing to bear."

Pressing her lips together to fight back a smile, Cheyenne jerked her chin at the troll. "Something like that."

"Persh'al asked me to make them for you. Said it was for a good cause."

"Did he tell you what that good cause is?"

Elarit looked up at the Nimlothar's branches and barely shook her head. "He told me to ask you about it. Seeing as it's your plan."

He doesn't want her to think he's lying to her and trying to sugarcoat my intentions. I picked the right magical for the job.

Cheyenne nodded. "Have you made the crossing Earthside?"

"No, but I know about the Border reservations."

"Well, hearing about them and seeing them are two different things." Cheyenne hooked her arms around her knees and clasped her hands in front of them. "The FRoE's only as old as I am, but they took over running the reservations from whoever had the job last. Doesn't matter who. Maybe they made some improvements, but not enough. Some of their agents are magicals, at least, but only Earthborn. No refugees. No true O'gúleesh. It might as well be a bunch of humans welcoming the refugees to Earth and telling them all to fend for themselves."

Elarit raised an eyebrow. "That bad, huh?"

"Yeah. Not to mention that when it comes to threats from this side, like the Bull's Head and the war machines smuggled across the border, the agents who are supposed to protect Earthside magicals and humans have no idea how to handle them. They're pretty clueless."

"So you want to hand over my activators to little more than pups running around with fell weapons and calling themselves experts."

Cheyenne snorted, and Elarit let out a soft chuckle. "If I just dropped off a delivery and said, 'Go to town, you're on your own,' then yeah, that'd be a pretty accurate assessment."

"But you have more in mind."

Running a hand through her bone-white hair, Cheyenne nodded. "I do. I chose to give Persh'al the O'gúl throne, and I also chose to step into the same empty role on Earth. Part of my master plan, I guess, is to give activators to agents who can use them and help them understand how magic and tech can work together. Give them some basic training. Maybe teach them what they don't know about life in Ambar'ogúl, which is basically everything. They'll have a better idea of how to handle who and what crosses the Border and why, and they can deal with it in other ways besides locking up refugees or tossing them back through."

"A lofty goal."

"Yeah, tell me about it."

Elarit cocked her head and narrowed her eyes. "What of the Earthside O'gúleesh?"

"That's the other part. As soon as I know the activators work after I bring them across, and as soon as the FRoE agents can use them without blowing themselves up, any magical Earthside who misses O'gúl magi-tech can get an activator for themselves from a reliable source." Cheyenne's smile widened. "This may turn into a long-term business relationship if it works. Not sure yet how I'd pay you for it."

"You wouldn't pay me." Elarit shook her head. "I wouldn't let you."

"Oh. It's 'cause you like me so much, right?"

The corners of the troll woman's mouth twitched into a small smile. "It's because I can't help but feel like I owe you after everything you've done."

Yeesh. Either that's code for "I'll pay you back for breaking the system," or she's opening up a little.

"I hope you're talking about the helpful things."

Elarit took a deep breath and looked around the courtyard. "Persh'al and I wouldn't be here if it weren't for you. Honestly, we wouldn't even be together. As long as you don't screw us over, and as long as what you told me is what you plan to do, then I suppose I can overlook you healing the world and breaking a perfectly good system mainframe that hasn't glitched once in the last five thousand years."

Cheyenne stared at the troll and swallowed. "Sounds fair to me."

"Yes. Fair." It didn't sound like Elarit believed it, but at least she'd attempted to sound agreeable.

They sat there facing each other for a moment longer, with no sounds but the rustling leaves overhead and the occasional rise of voices from the city's lower levels miles from the Heart. Cheyenne took a sharp breath. "You can trust me."

Elarit nodded slowly. "I want to. That's as much as I can truthfully say."

"Because you expect me to find something else that works better for me and leave the rest of you hanging." When the troll woman didn't answer, Cheyenne shook her head. "I'm not L'zar, you know."

"Oh, I know." Elarit pushed to her feet and dusted off her hands. "In some ways, that's even more frightening."

"Why?"

"Because you're better than he ever was at making things happen. Don't let it go to your head." Elarit dipped her head at the drow, then glanced up at the glistening Nimlothar's branches, walked swiftly across the courtyard, and disappeared through one of the large arches.

Cheyenne gave a surprised laugh, then frowned at the stone floor. *Don't let it go to my head. Like being better than someone who's always a disappointment is something to be proud of.*

Despite having been compared to her father again, she felt a little better about her current situation.

Maybe things wouldn't be so hard after this.

CHAPTER SEVENTEEN

The next morning, Cheyenne jolted awake on the platform bed in her Hangivol apartment and snorted. *Jesus. Can't anyone be quiet for a goddamn day?*

The heavy bang that had ripped her out of her sleep echoed outside again, followed by a flicker of blue and green light racing across the apartment walls. The pounding intensified, and the bed trembled beneath her.

"What the fuck?" Cheyenne tossed the covers off, climbed out of bed, and vigorously rubbed her face before snatching up her clothes to get dressed. A bellowing roar outside the building pushed her to move faster.

Jamming her feet into her black Vans, she hurried groggily through the bedroom doorway, which she'd left open instead of trying to struggle with tech that didn't always work, and found Ember doing the same.

"What is it?" Ember groaned and rubbed the sleep out of her eyes.

"Someone's trying to wake up the whole damn city."

"And no one's trying to stop them?"

Several voices cried out in warning, followed by another roar of anger. "Cheyenne!"

"Who's that?"

Cheyenne shook her head, and when the pounding started again, they both rushed toward the front door. She had to manually open it given the lurching code lines in the metal, but the door finally slid into the wall with a jerky hiss. Ember raced behind her friend as the drow barreled down the hallway. Code lines skittered along the walls and floor.

The platform lift at the end was already on their floor, waiting for them. Cheyenne and Ember stepped onto it quickly as the roars and angry shouts continued outside. Ember frowned as the lift sank to the levels below without a hitch. "Back home, people would be coming out of their apartments to see what all the noise is about, or at least start screaming at whoever it is to shut up."

"No windows, right?" Cheyenne shrugged. "Maybe drow don't care as much."

"You don't believe what you just said."

"You're right."

The platform shuddered to a stop on the ground floor, and both girls raced down the hall toward the building's entrance. Even the hall down here was empty, and no doors opened for the inner-circle drow to poke their heads out and investigate the issue. *No way is this a normal part of living up here. This is the quietest level in the whole city.*

The door jammed twice, then Cheyenne finally got decent leverage and wrenched it the rest of the way open. Before she could step outside, a drow hurtled across the front of the building, hissing and sliding backward in a crouch as he landed. The magical who'd tossed him bellowed again.

"Shit."

Nu'ek the Golra whirled left and right in front of the apartment building, bashing the dozens of drow snarling and lunging at her with her thick, red-furred arms. The drow were being thrown aside by the huge magical's unmatched strength and the powerful gusts from her beating wings. Magic was tossed around by both parties but missed the target more often than not.

The Golra stomped toward the front of the apartment building again and stopped short when she saw Cheyenne and Ember. "There you are."

"Back down, *dae'bruj*," Althas snarled, wielding a whip of purple light. It slapped Nu'ek's thigh and singed off a clump of wiry red hair, but that was it. "And show some respect."

"Jesus, enough!" Cheyenne darted forward and pointed sharply at Althas. "Ditch the whip."

"You heard her screaming for you." The dark-skinned drow glared at Nu'ek and cracked the ground with his magical whip in warning. "She thinks she can storm up here and muscle her way into an audience."

"I said, ditch it." Cheyenne spread her arms since he seemed confused. "I'm over this drow-protector bullshit. It's completely unnecessary up here. Especially with her."

"Thank you," Nu'ek grumbled and rubbed the singed hair on her thigh. Her massive black wings beat one more time, making the drow around her stagger under the gust, then folded her arms.

"What is she to you?" another drow asked.

Cheyenne looked at him with wide eyes. "A friend, one who helped us turn the Cycle inside that fortress. But none of you were there to see it, were you?"

The drow fell silent and looked at each other uncertainly. Finally, Althas flicked his wrist, and the purple whip vanished. "Touch her, and there will be no quarter."

"Yeah, shove it up your ass, drow." Nu'ek stomped away from the apartment building to let Ember and Cheyenne out into the avenue. The drow spread out around her but didn't move to attack again.

Cheyenne fought back a laugh and nodded at the Golra. "What's going on?"

"I came to tell you your shipment's ready. Your overzealous guard dogs wanted to tussle."

Ember laughed, then clapped a hand over her mouth.

"What shipment?"

"The activators."

"Wow." Cheyenne raised her eyebrows. "She *is* fast."

With a curt nod, Nu'ek straightened the front of her creaking leather vest and turned toward the fortress. Three drow stood their ground in front of her, and she growled with an exasperated wave of her hand, "Move!"

The drow only stepped aside when Cheyenne and Ember followed the Golra. Cheyenne turned to look at her self-proclaimed bodyguards and spread her arms. "We got it. Thanks."

"Try that again," Nu'ek growled over her shoulder, "and I'll be selling drow jelly by the barrel."

The drow stayed where they were in the center of the avenue, thumping fists on chests at Cheyenne but sneering at the massive Golra's back and the powerful black wings folded against it.

Cheyenne looked at Nu'ek with a raised eyebrow. "Drow jelly?"

"It just came out. I'm trying to be more civilized."

Ember choked back a laugh. "What was the less-civilized version?"

"Turning them into drow jelly." Instead of heading for the broken side door, which was way too small for the Golra, Nu'ek skirted around the round outer wall of the fortress toward the opposite side and nodded for Cheyenne to follow. "They're waiting for you at the closest passage down to the fellfire pits."

"Everyone?"

"Yes, everyone." Nu'ek snorted. "Apparently, you slept in."

"Oh, great." Ember rubbed the side of her face and let out a massive yawn. "Late to our own goodbye party."

"Not the worst thing we've been late to, Em."

"True."

When they reached the far side of the curving alley off the main avenue, they found Persh'al and Elarit, Maleshi and Corian, and the goblins waiting for them. Bianca sat on two stacked medium-sized metal crates. She didn't stand or even look surprised when Nu'ek appeared around the bend with Cheyenne and Ember in tow.

"Look who decided to join us?" Maleshi spread her arms and offered them a semi-mocking bow. "I hope you finally got enough sleep."

"Feels like it, yeah. Mostly." Cheyenne swept her gaze across the waiting party. "Whose bright idea was it to send Nu'ek for the wake-up call?"

The goblins sniggered but shut up when the Golra folded her arms over her creaking leather vest and grunted.

"Mine." Bianca lifted her chin, her hands clasped patiently in her lap. "Yours?"

"I wasn't about to go to your apartment and knock on the door."

Bianca shrugged. "I don't even know how to open most doors in this place."

Cheyenne laughed. "Those drow out there saw everyone here but Nu'ek. They know all of you were with us in the forest yesterday. So why her?" She pointed at the Golra.

Bianca blinked slowly and looked Nu'ek up and down. "She's bigger."

Nu'ek tossed her long red mane over one shoulder. "I like her, Cheyenne."

"Yeah, I bet you do."

The closest side door rattled in place before it crackled with blue light and finally squealed open. Two squat machines like open wagons on stocky legs clambered through the door, bashing into the walls and each other as they skittered clumsily toward Bianca on the crates.

"What the hell is wrong with those things?" Lumil muttered.

Elarit bent her head to rub the bridge of her nose in frustration. Persh'al shot her a look, then cleared his throat. "Took longer than I expected, but at least they're here, right?"

"Only because I let the damn things out like a couple of animals." Venga sheared off the protruding corner of the side door with a quick swipe of his claws, throwing another shower of sparks onto the waiting party. Grunting, he stepped over the wreckage and glared at Corian. "And no one thought to alert me to your departure, is that it?"

"Huh. Let's see." Byrd counted on his fingers. "You ate all the food by yourself, didn't stay for the booze, and locked yourself up in your lab for whatever crazy shit you're cooking up next. Does that sound like a friend we'd want to see us off?"

He looked at Lumil with feigned curiosity. The goblin woman stroked her chin and pretended to consider it. "You know, I think he's run out of anything to offer us."

"Yeah, that's what I thought."

"Oh, you want consolation prizes, is that it?" Venga stuck a claw between his sharp reptilian teeth and grunted. "Fine. The next time you cross over, I'll have a present waiting for you. Maybe even a fell-damn cookie. Happy now?"

"Sure." Byrd folded his arms and nodded vigorously.

"Better yet, now that you offered, you might as well get started."

Venga waved them off. "Find me when you get back."

"Oh, we're staying."

"What?"

The goblins shot him twin looks. "We miss the blue troll. You know, spent centuries with him Earthside. The warehouse isn't the same without him there."

Persh'al mimed wiping a tear from a dry eye. "You guys really get me."

Lumil barked a laugh. "So get crackin', scaleback. Shouldn't take us more than half an hour to get down to the fellfire pits and back. Unless, of course, the word of a necromancer is worthless."

"You!" Venga hissed at them, stepping nimbly aside when the crawling cart machines thumped into the stack of crates.

Bianca rose steadily and backed away, putting plenty of room between herself and the spinning claws on hinged arms that emerged from the machine's bodies to pick up the crates. Gears whirred and clicked under the strain.

"Oh, come on." Elarit folded her arms. "They're not that heavy."

Cheyenne approached the troll and watched the machines struggle to do the one thing they were made to do. "Those are the activators?"

Elarit nodded. "It's not the number you requested, but I did my best."

"Hey, I appreciate you making them at all. I can do a lot with fewer than a hundred activators."

"You'll do even more with two hundred."

"What?" Cheyenne looked away from the sparking machines stumbling under the weight of the crates and couldn't help but laugh. "Two hundred?"

"Only took me about six hours."

"That was ridiculously fast."

Elarit cocked her head and gave Cheyenne a small smile. "I suppose that's relative."

"Thank you."

"Like I said, you get things done." Elarit wagged a finger at the drow. "But if I hear anything about my gear falling into the wrong hands and doing the complete opposite of what you told me—"

"If you ever hear news like that, it's because something happened to me, and I couldn't be there to stop it."

"Well, then. Let's hope I don't hear anything about the Black Flame and her Earthside distribution of *masharun* tech."

"I'm with you on that one." Cheyenne eyed the stumbling, jerking carts on legs and narrowed her eyes. "Assuming we can get those trunks down to the portal."

"Those things are ridiculous." Elarit hurried toward the closest machine lunging sporadically at Bianca and waved at it with a quickly cast spell. The cart shuddered and extended a mechanical pincher to stab the troll woman in the ass. "Hey! That's not even… Persh'al!"

"Great." Persh'al rubbed his head and hurried toward her. "We knew they might not respond to the usual commands."

"Oh, it responded. Look at this. I'm bleeding."

Persh'al gave her a reassuring nod and headed for the closest cart. He scanned the malfunctioning code lines on the bot's control panel and reached toward it. The cart bucked and struck him in the groin with a well-placed kick of its metal leg. The troll wheezed and dropped to his knees.

"Oh, shit." Byrd lifted a fist to his mouth.

Lumil pushed up her sleeves. "Makes me glad I don't keep the good stuff at kicking height."

He eyed her with a frown. "Man, what good stuff?"

"Fuck you." The spinning red runes burst to life on the goblin woman's fists, and she marched toward the carts. "I got this."

"Wow." Cheyenne cocked her head. "She will fight anything."

"Hold on," Persh'al groaned, lifting a hand to stop her.

Lumil sent both fists toward the top of the cart that had scrabbled into her path. A metal bar with a dull, round tip shot from the side of the machine and rammed into her stomach. Lumil stumbled back with a grunt as the cart scuttled after its partner in crime. "Fucking wagon punched me."

Persh'al groaned again, but this time, it was at the sight of Corian's flashing claws extending as he stalked toward the carts. "Just the legs, huh?"

"Not the trunks!" Elarit shouted. "Are you insane?"

As Corian swiped up with his claws at one carrier, the second scurried behind him and bashed its front end into the backs of his knees. The nightstalker roared and stumbled forward, his claws swinging at nothing as his target darted out of the way. Instead, they sliced inches away from Bianca's face.

"Hey!" Cheyenne shouted.

Corian righted himself and spun to face Bianca with wide eyes. "Sorry. I'm sorry."

"I should hope so."

"That was—"

Maleshi chuckled. "Bested by a carrier, *vae shra'ni.*"

He glared at her. "You take them down, then."

"Don't take them down." Persh'al lurched to his feet, grimacing. "Just deactivate them."

One of the carts sailed over his head. The troll ducked and spun around as the machine's body bashed into the wall of the alley and toppled to the ground on its back, legs jerking like a flipped turtle's.

Nu'ek dropped the trunk she'd snatched off the carrier's back and stomped toward the other cart.

"Hey, hey." Persh'al raised both hands. "Come on."

The Golra kicked the front of the second carrier, sending the trunk sliding off the back and onto the ground. The machine scuttled in a circle around her, clicking and whirring before striking with two metal barbs. Nu'ek was faster. Her fist crashed down on the top of the cart and smashed it to the ground with a screech of bending and ripping metal. The cart's legs twitched, and the crater in its back sparked and hissed before it finally fell still. The whirring clicks slowed and finally ground to a halt.

Everyone stared at the smashed cart with wide eyes. Elarit turned to Persh'al and folded her arms. "Still worth saving, *ma gairín?*"

He tilted his head from side to side. "Well, not now."

Nu'ek grunted and picked up a trunk of activators in each hand. "Problem solved."

"I can carry those," Cheyenne said as the Golra stomped past her toward the descending passage across from the wall.

"You will. This carrier stops at the fellfire pits." The huge magical squeezed through the opening in the wall and disappeared.

"What?"

Maleshi shook her head. "I don't understand the reasoning behind half of what she does, but it's two miles you don't have to carry two hundred activators."

"Yeah, I guess."

Corian clapped a hand on Persh'al's shoulder and gave the troll a little shake. "You don't have to walk us out, brother. Might not wanna walk at all for a while."

Persh'al looked at him with twitching eyes. "Thanks."

"See you on the other side. Whenever that happens to be." The nightstalker clasped the troll Crown's forearm, then stepped past him with a chuckle. He paused in front of Elarit and dipped his head toward her. "Be gentle with him."

She smiled. "Blood and honor, Corian."

"Ha."

Elarit smiled at Cheyenne and nodded. "Good luck."

"Yeah, you too." Cheyenne gestured at her mom. "You ready?"

"Quite." Bianca stepped over the scattered fragments of the smashed carrier machine and took Ember's offered arm.

She'll take everyone's help but mine, huh? Whatever.

"Now, wait just a moment!" Venga stomped across the broken metal pieces, extending all four hands toward them. "Bianca! Bianca, *please* let me take a few more samples."

"No. Goodbye."

"Please!"

"She's not a fucking science experiment, man." Cheyenne spun toward him and pointed at the other broken side door in the fortress wall. "Those are in your lab."

"But if I can just—"

"Dude, I'd listen to her." Lumil folded her arms and nodded, her eyes wide. "You don't wanna get on Cheyenne's bad side."

The necromancer looked her up and down and hissed. "If this is your good side, it's useless to me."

He stormed toward the door.

"Yeah, good luck to you too. Hey, it was nice saving the world together. Go, team!"

Venga waved her off with a sharp toss of his hand before disappearing inside.

The goblins snickered and nudged each other. "He hates us."

"Yeah. What a loser."

Cheyenne nodded at Persh'al. "You'll hear from us one way or the other."

He grimaced and readjusted the front of his pants. "I'm counting on it, kid."

"Cheyenne! Wait!"

The drow squinted at a small figure darting around the side of the curving fortress and made out the two fully grown drow walking slowly behind the first. A streak of white and gray rushed toward her, then Ki'zi stood in front of her, trying to catch her breath.

Cheyenne chuckled. "Hey."

The young drow smiled self-consciously, then shrugged. "I figured out how to do it."

Before Cheyenne could ask, Ki'zi held up a dark metal spiral five inches long. The curving sides were smooth, and at each end of the spiral was a Nimlothar leaf crafted in striking detail. Cheyenne looked between the spiral and the drow's wide, eager eyes. "You made this?"

"Yeah. For you."

Cheyenne swallowed and couldn't decide whether to frown or smile. *After everything, it's a damn kid making me a present that makes me fall apart.*

"Thanks, kid."

Ki'zi stared at the coil as Cheyenne took it and lifted a shoulder in another awkward shrug. "See you when you come back."

"Yeah." Cheyenne slid the spiral toward her back pocket, felt R'leer's weird darkseller's loupe there, and stuck her present in the other pocket behind her phone instead. She looked at Ki'zi's parents standing proudly at the end of the curving alley and nodded. They dipped their heads. "You gonna train for your trials now?"

"I think so. I actually can now."

"If you don't pass before the next time I see you, you'll have to show me what you're working on." Cheyenne winked at the girl, who snorted and scuffed a shoe against the smooth alley floor.

"I probably won't."

"Give yourself more credit, huh? You got this. Prove 'em all wrong."

Ki'zi slowly looked up. Her golden eyes widened when Cheyenne pressed a fist to her chest and nodded.

Then she turned and headed toward the descending passage where Maleshi, Ember, and Bianca waited for her. Persh'al hissed a laugh. "Now you're showing off."

"No, I'm leaving."

"Maji! Maji, did you see?" Ki'zi raced back toward her parents. Her mom lifted her chin and the drow girl slowed, straightening her back and re-adopting the slow, confident stride that was expected of her. But she looked over her shoulder and grinned at the last glimpse of the Black Flame disappearing down the corridor.

CHAPTER EIGHTEEN

"Never thought I'd say this to a drow about a drow," Maleshi said, cocking her head as they moved down the sloping corridor. "But that was a pretty cute kid."

"Trust me, it's new for me too." Cheyenne let out a wry chuckle and shook her head. "Not sure what it means when I make better friends with drow kids than adults, but hey."

"You've got one of those super-friendly faces."

Cheyenne and Ember both snorted.

Bianca took a sharp breath, and everyone paused in the passage to look at her.

"Mom?"

"I'm fine, Cheyenne. It's nothing." The woman raised a trembling hand to her eye and sniffed.

Ember leaned toward her, still steadying Bianca with her arm. "You're shaking."

"Did you expect me to run down this ramp?" Lifting her head and blinking, Bianca nodded down it. "We're going home. I don't wish to delay that any longer, so if you don't mind?"

"Sure," Ember said. "If you need to stop or take a break—"

"I will let you know, Ember. Thank you." Bianca cleared her throat and practically dragged the fae along by the arm.

She was crying. Cheyenne tried not to stare at her mom, who was shaking her dark hair out of her eyes. *No way is it because she's gonna miss this place.*

"That child handed you something," Bianca muttered, staring straight ahead.

Cheyenne reached back and felt the metal spiral in her pocket. "Yeah. Just a goodbye gift, I guess. It doesn't do anything."

Maleshi dipped her head. "I wouldn't be so sure."

An image of the four-pointed star crafted from Cheyenne's magic more than once and again from Neros' entered her mind. *Okay, but technically, Ki'zi made the shape* of her family's magic. I think.

"I think she wanted to show off a little." Cheyenne forced herself to smile at Bianca even though her mom didn't look at her.

"That was the first child I've seen in this place." Bianca took a deep breath and looked at the faint blue lights crackling across the passage ceiling. "It hadn't occurred to me that there *were* children here until I saw her in the forest."

Cheyenne's heart sank into her gut. And she almost wasn't here anymore, just like the rest of them.

"Yeah, somebody's gotta have kids to keep the population growing, right? Even when everyone lives to be who-knows-how-old."

"Someone has to raise them, too," Bianca added.

Shit. That's what this is about? Does she think I should've been raised here instead?

"Mom?"

"She reminded me so much of you, Cheyenne. For a moment, I thought I'd gone back in time as well as a different world." Bianca slowly turned her head to shoot her daughter a look. "I'm quite glad that's not the case."

Cheyenne stopped and stared at her mom, who was walking with her chin lifted and her hand rigidly clamped on Ember's arm. *What the hell is that supposed to mean?*

Maleshi leaned down to mutter in her ear, "Don't hurt yourself trying to unravel that one, kid. I'm pretty sure it was a compliment."

"How?"

The general put a gentle hand on Cheyenne's back and guided her forward until they were walking again. "She drank the banebreaker's potion, made the crossing with a bunch of magicals who repeatedly trespassed on her property, and subjected herself to the necromancer's bumbling tests. You think she did all that to save a bunch of strangers she thinks are barbaric and a bad influence on her daughter?"

"She didn't say that."

Maleshi chuckled. "It's an observation. And you're avoiding the question."

"No, I mean, she did all that because we thought it would break Ba'rael's curse."

"Ah. That's a nice thought. I can't say that didn't have anything to do with it, but that's not the reason."

Cheyenne shrugged. "Then I'm out of answers."

"She did it for you, Cheyenne."

Swallowing thickly, Cheyenne stared at the slanting passage's floor. "Did she say that?"

"She didn't have to."

"Right." The drow huffed a wry laugh. "I think you're being overly sentimental here."

"Trust me. I know exactly what a mother's willing to do for her child."

Cheyenne whipped her head up to frown at the general in disbelief. "You?"

With a coy smile, Maleshi cocked her head and shrugged. "If you want to change the subject, pick something else."

Blinking in surprise, Cheyenne rubbed her hands down her pantlegs but didn't quite know what to do with them after that. *She's fucking with me. I would've heard something about Maleshi Hi'et having a kid. Oh, gross. Is it Corian's?*

Maleshi chuckled and clasped her hands behind her back. "You look like you just bit into a lemon."

"My brain did, I think." *Yeah, change the subject.* "I ran into Mirl on my way down to the bazaar yesterday."

"Hmm. Not literally, I hope."

"No, definitely not," Cheyenne said. "He said other O'gúleesh are gonna try to take Hangivol after this. Or at least whatever they can get away with."

"Because now every O'gúleesh on this side knows the blight's gone and the lifeforce veins have been fully restored. It makes sense."

"You think there's any truth to it?"

"Mirl is startlingly astute when it comes to his predictions, for a blind radag." Maleshi shook her head. "I wouldn't worry about it."

"You wouldn't worry about other clans or whatever trying to stage another coup after the one we just pulled off?"

"You chose Persh'al for a reason. The rest of us agreed with that choice for the same reason, kid. He knows what he's doing."

Cheyenne shook her head. "I thought it would be a bigger issue."

"It's all relative, isn't it?" Maleshi snorted. "If it makes you feel better, we'll check in on him from time to time. Offer our specialized services if they're needed."

"Ha. I hope they're not."

"That makes two of us."

The passageway started to level out, and Bianca and Ember disappeared ahead of them beneath the tunnel ceiling. Cheyenne squinted against the morning light spilling toward them. "I'm not sure I wanna keep coming back here as often as I have been. I mean, if no one needs me here."

"You can do whatever you want now. Drow royalty on Earth and everything, right?"

"Yeah, I guess." She looked sideways at the general, and Maleshi winked.

"Perks of high status, kid. Which you're not a stranger to."

"This is a little different."

The general's smile widened as they exited the passage and stepped onto the walkway that ran around Hangivol's outer wall. "So are you."

Cheyenne opened her mouth to ask where Maleshi was going with that, but she didn't get the chance.

"I do hope you're not having second thoughts," Bianca called over her shoulder. "Because I'm not walking back up that tunnel."

"No second thoughts, Mom." Cheyenne couldn't hold back a short laugh. "We're coming."

"Good." Bianca and Ember headed down the walkway toward the larger, wider enclosed ramp down to the fellfire pits.

Nu'ek and Corian emerged at the bottom of the ramp and headed across the industrial field toward the shimmering pool of the Sorren Gán's multicolored fire and Hangivol's newest Border portal. The sounds of the city echoed faintly over the capital's high wall, and Cheyenne frowned at the empty fellfire pits spouting occasional columns of green flame into the air. *I can't look at this place without thinking about carrying Mom through it. But we made it. As soon as Inolu breaks this curse, it's finally over. For real.*

When she and Maleshi caught up with the others at the edge of the fiery pond, Nu'ek stacked the trunks of activators one on top of the other and slugged them against Cheyenne's chest.

"Jeez." Cheyenne grimaced under their weight and readjusted her hold on the trunks. "She said there were two hundred in here. Feels like a thousand."

Nu'ek grunted. "You're the one who has to carry them through."

"Why is that, exactly?" Bianca raised an eyebrow at the stacked-up trunks.

"Cheyenne's the only magical we know who can take advanced tech across the Border," Ember said, "and have it still work on the other side. Maybe the only one ever who can do it."

"I see." Bianca turned to the pool of fire and looked more confused than she would admit. "I don't remember seeing this. Is this the way we came in?"

"It is." Maleshi stuck her hands on her hips and shared a knowing look with Corian. "And it's the way we go out."

"Fine." Nu'ek stretched her neck from side to side, rolled her shoulders with a quick twitch of her wings, and laced her clawed fingers to crack her knuckles. "I'll come with you."

Ember smiled at the huge, horned magical, her nose wrinkling in surprise. "You don't have to."

"You've got the Vessel on your arm, and Cheyenne won't be able to fight with her luggage in her arms."

Cheyenne scoffed. "Says who?"

"You drop the trunks to strangle one of those creatures, and Elar-it's gonna rip your head off the next time you show your face in this city."

Maleshi shrugged. "She has a point."

"I'm wondering why you don't think two nightstalkers can handle it for all five of us." Corian tapped his chest and spread his arms. "Especially these two."

"Call it a courtesy, *vae shra'ni.*" Nu'ek grinned and stepped into the pool of flames. "Better keep up."

She disappeared in a burst of multi-colored light.

Corian narrowed his eyes. "Sounds more like an insult to me."

"Don't insult her back." Maleshi gestured at the portal and grinned. "I'll take the rear."

"Uh-huh." He stepped quickly into the flames and vanished.

"Think you can move fast enough with all that heavy cargo, kid?"

"Very funny. Em, you and Bianca go first. I'm right behind you."

Ember guided Bianca forward, and the woman's eyes widened. "That's fire."

"It's our ticket home." Ember fought back a laugh. "You can close your eyes if you want."

"Don't be absurd." Lifting her chin, Bianca stepped into the portal with her hand on Ember's arm.

"I can't wait 'til she's back to normal," Cheyenne muttered and headed after them.

"I rather enjoy her the way she is." Chuckling, Maleshi turned to scan the city's outer wall, then followed the drow into the in-between.

CHAPTER NINETEEN

The breath was squeezed out of Cheyenne's lungs the second she entered the portal. Corian and Nu'ek had already recovered, and Bianca temporarily supported Ember instead as the fae fought to catch her breath. Maleshi grunted when she stepped through and cleared her throat. "Keep moving."

"I do remember this," Bianca muttered as they walked. "Though it seems there's a bit more of a draft this time around."

"Not a draft, Mom." *She's got a real thing about that, huh?* "This is the way it's supposed to be in here."

"It does look like the blight's been removed from the in-between as well." Maleshi extended the claws on both hands and held them at the ready by her sides. "Which means we know what to expect again."

"Which is what?" Bianca leaned away from a particularly thick streak of black smoke drifting in front of her face.

"Let us take care of that," Nu'ek said, gazing through the swirling black smoke and the gusts of thick mist bursting up from the unseen ground. "You focus on following close behind. Don't wander off."

"One would have to be an idiot to wander off in all this," Bianca muttered. "I can't see a thing."

"You'd be surprised how many don't make it." Corian jerked his head away from a burst of black smoke rising from the ground beside him. His claws extended with a sharp, metallic slice.

"There's something none of you want to tell me." Bianca gently squeezed Ember's forearm and leaned toward her. "She mentioned having to fight. The large one up there."

"Nu'ek?" Ember whispered. "Yeah, usually we do. Have to fight."

"Fight what, Ember?" Bianca focused on Ember, oblivious to the shadows moving around them through the smoke and looming closer. "We didn't fight anything the last time."

"Last time was a fluke," Corian muttered. "Things are different now."

"Like I said. Back to the way they're supposed to be." Cheyenne couldn't see nearly as much as she wanted to with the trunks in her arms blocking her ability to fully turn her head. *I would've strapped these to some rope and dragged the damn things if I didn't have to physically hold them for this. The activators better make it across.*

A rumbling growl filled the not-quite air around them, making the ground and the billowing black smoke tremble beneath the gray, washed-out sky.

Bianca turned her head slowly away from Ember and scanned the nothingness. "I certainly didn't hear that the last time."

"I think it's best to release all expectations," Corian muttered as they walked, his silver eyes flashing through the black smoke, "and focus on staying in line."

"Hmm." The woman frowned at his back and muttered to Ember, "He sounds more like he's leading troops than the general."

A warbling shriek came from their right. Another rose on their left. Stomping footsteps traveled across the unseen ground toward them.

"Be ready," Nu'ek growled and stretched out her thick black wings tipped with spikes to their fullest span, her clawed hands open in anticipation.

A barbed appendage lashed out at her from the thick smoke and roiling shadows. Nu'ek moved with surprising speed for her size, rearing back to dodge the sharp attack. Her hand shot out and clamped down around the glistening black tentacle that looked more like a tail, and she jerked it toward her before snapping it in half with both hands. Black fluid sprayed from the tentacle and disappeared beneath the fog. The in-between monster bellowed in rage and stepped out of the black smoke, standing three times the Golra's height.

"My word," Bianca whispered, staring at the five red eyes blazing in what served as the monster's face.

A massive tentacle without barbs rose into the air on the party's right and slapped at Corian.

"Watch out!" Ember shouted.

The nightstalker slipped into enhanced speed and sidestepped the tentacle before slicing down with his claws. Chunks of glistening black flesh flew through the air. Bianca jolted when a piece bounced off her shoulder and hit the ground, leaving a black smear down her gray zip-up.

The other monster screamed and flung two more tentacles and claws tipped in extra spikes at them.

Nu'ek fought the larger monster mostly with her fists, ripping apart the barbed appendages flailing at her and whirling to catch the next ones. Red light glimmered in her hands as she blasted the massive thing backward. "Keep moving!"

Maleshi spun around and launched crackling silver lightning from her fingertips at the two winged beasts descending toward her. One of them crashed to the ground and flailed, kicking up gusts of black smoke. The other landed on its two clawed feet and screeched. "They're closing in from behind!"

Cheyenne's hands crackled with purple sparks. *I'm not a damn pack mule. I should be fighting with them.*

The general darted away from the hooked claws at the edge of the creature's wings and sliced up with the silver blades at the ends of her fingers. The monster's wing was shredded and flapped uselessly at its side before shifting into one solid, muscular black arm with a clenched fist at the end. She dodged the blow and ripped the arm apart.

As the one-winged monster screamed, Maleshi caught sight of Cheyenne glaring at the beast and the purple sparks flaring from the drow's hand. "Don't you dare drop those trunks!"

"I'm trying not to."

Nu'ek launched into the air with swift, gusting beats of her powerful wings and sent both hooved feet crashing into the largest monster's face. Two of its eyes burst in sprays of black sludge and red light, and it fell back as the Golra's massive form dropped back to the ground. "Move!"

Corian darted and sliced in a flurry of flashing silver light and glinting claws. "Hurry."

"Stay close." Ember pulled Bianca along as gently as she could under the urgency. A thick tentacle swung toward their heads out of the black smoke. Ember ducked and blasted a column of violet light at the beast's appendage, but its momentum kept it moving right for Bianca. The woman gasped and froze.

Cheyenne flicked her hand out toward her mom and raised a glimmering shield of black light. The trunks toppled sideways out of her other arm, and she dropped to the ground on one knee to catch them between her thigh and her chest.

The monster's tentacle bashed against her shield, then dropped under Corian's slicing claws.

"Come on." Ember guided Bianca forward, staying as close to the nightstalker as she could while he darted back and forth on the straight path Nu'ek cut for them. The Golra bashed aside monstrous limbs and black flesh as she stomped across the in-between, roaring at the beasts as she cut them down.

Maleshi grabbed Cheyenne's arm and helped the drow to her feet. "Don't do that again."

"Two hundred activators aren't worth her life." Cheyenne got a better grip on the trunks with both hands and hurried after the others.

"What you're meant to do Earthside just might be. Let us handle it."

Cheyenne scowled at the general as Maleshi spun to fire bolts of silver lightning at the monsters slithering and lurching across the ground after them. *None of this is worth losing my family. Why would she say something like that?*

The general swung up with her claws and ripped through the glistening carapace of a beast darting toward her. The hard shell exploded into thousands of fragments and darted around Maleshi before combining again in mid-air and hurtling toward Cheyenne. "Duck!"

Cheyenne dropped, grunting against the awkward bulk of the trunks as the writhing, flapping new monster swooped above her head. The end of its lashing tail cracked against the back of her head and knocked her forward.

She reached out with one hand again to let off a tiny blast of telekinetic force that kept her from falling forward. A barbed tentacle shot from the thick black smoke and struck her in the thigh. The drow shouted in frustration, and Maleshi sliced the tentacle in two before helping Cheyenne back to her feet.

"Keep moving."

"The doorway," Nu'ek shouted as she grabbed a monster's long, sinewy tentacle and jerked it down on top of the thing's head. One hooved foot kicked out in the opposite direction and sent a skittering black beetle flying away into the smoke. "Almost there."

"Time to run." Ember coaxed Bianca forward and the woman nodded, her eyes wide.

The party moved quickly toward the shimmering rectangle of light in the middle of the in-between's nothingness. The monsters swarming around them blocked the doorway before being bashed aside or broken in half by Nu'ek's powerful limbs.

Maleshi roared and jerked sideways when two thin tentacles like vines wrapped around her calf and pulled. "Go!" She waved Cheyenne forward and shredded the things clamped around her legs. "I'm coming."

The closer they got to the doorway, the thicker the swarm of monsters became. Nu'ek and the nightstalkers fought unfailingly, even as the dim gray light darkened as the monsters closed in. Ember shot the occasional blast of purple light to toss the creatures away, but most of her focus was on guiding Bianca after Corian. The woman seemed to have lost her wits, wide-eyed and nearly catatonic as the fae half-guided, half-dragged her along.

Cheyenne gritted her teeth and held tight to the trunks, kicking away the tentacles writhing at her feet and stepping aside from the spray of severed limbs flying around her.

Ten yards from the doorway, the darkness rose from the ground in a writhing wall of undulating tentacles, snapping jaws, and swiping talons. Nu'ek blasted a column of red magic from both hands, but the light of her attack was absorbed by the thick wall of squirming monsters. The creatures screamed in rage and pain but didn't fall.

"I would not call this a return to normal, *vae shra'ni*," she spat as she doubled down for another attack.

"We move through it, just like we always have." Corian jerked his hands toward the ground and sent a wave of silver lightning through the thick black smoke toward the monster-wall. The beasts screamed and bucked. A hand as big as the Golra shot from the wall to swipe at the nightstalker. He and Nu'ek both attacked it and ripped it to pieces.

"Perhaps we should walk around it," Bianca muttered blankly.

"Straight line only in here," Ember replied. "And I have a feeling that wall's a lot wider than we can see."

"What's stopping you?" Maleshi growled, walking backward toward them and slicing at anything that moved.

"A wall," Corian shouted back.

"There's one closing in at the rear too, so hurry the hell up."

Cheyenne ducked a flying tentacle that shifted into a hissing, twisted snake with two heads as it sailed toward her. It hit the ground with a wet smack, then rose from the thick layer of black smoke to five times its previous size and coiled to strike. She kicked the thing in one of its heads and staggered to regain her balance as the thing went flying into the looming wall of monsters on their left. The wall reabsorbed the snake and rumbled.

"I've never seen anything like this." Maleshi stepped backward toward Cheyenne, staring at the writhing walls of monstrous creatures closing in on them. "You might have to drop the trunks, kid."

"What?"

"I know what I said, but we're all monster food if we can't blast our way out of here."

Nu'ek roared and redoubled her efforts with the column of red light bursting from her hands. It did nothing, and she finally stopped. "We're running out of time."

The thick walls of snarling, writhing creatures erupted around them in bellows and shrieks and screaming wails. A massive wave of multi-colored light, mostly mottled brown, green, and purple like oil-streaked mud, descended in seconds from the washed-out sky, struck the walls of in-between monsters, and cut through them like a knife from top to bottom. The light flashed brighter, and every glistening black creature it touched exploded one right after the other into millions of fluttering black specks.

The final beasts writhing on the ground disintegrated. Only their screams remained, echoing through the nothingness until the in-between fell eerily silent again.

Nu'ek grunted. "What in the abyss was that?"

Bianca craned her neck and stared blankly at the wisps of black smoke trailing overhead. "It came from the sky."

"Whatever it was, I think we should say thanks for the help and keep moving." Cheyenne stormed forward, sharing a surprised grimace with Ember as she passed. "Doorway's still there."

"Yes, it is." Corian stopped by the doorway and motioned their party through. Nu'ek stomped forward with a snort and disappeared. Cheyenne nodded for Ember and Bianca to go ahead of her, and as soon as they vanished through the glimmering rectangle, Corian and Maleshi fell in beside the drow. They passed through the doorway without issue and found themselves in the barn at Colonial Williamsburg in broad daylight.

CHAPTER TWENTY

orian's quickly cast spell cloaked them all from sight two seconds after they passed through. A barely visible wall of light blazed around the party and disappeared before one of the day's first tourist groups rounded the corner of the dirt road.

"Our horses are not mere pets," the guide said, smiling as he gestured at the barn. "Many of them are beasts of burden, as I am certain you witnessed with the carriage we passed on the road. But they are also the swiftest means of travel, and caring for these animals is no simple feat. If you return around midday, you'll find the hands brushing down these useful creatures and perhaps even feeding them."

The back of Cheyenne's neck tingled, and it spread across the tops of her shoulders without fading. She scanned the dirt road and the tour group as the sensation intensified. *There's someone else's magic here. Not a good sign.*

The man dressed in full eighteenth-century garb gestured across the road behind his tourist group. "And yonder lies the pen. We keep the sheep and cows in there during the day. At ten o'clock, you'll see the milkmaid out here with Minerva, our most productive cow. Perhaps you'll have the opportunity to churn your own butter. Let us continue."

The tour group ambled down the road after their guide, snapping pictures with camera phones and talking, all smiles and carefree laughter.

Cheyenne caught a flicker of multi-colored light racing across the air above the road from the roof of the stables toward the pen. It looked like flames, but they disappeared and took the tingling sensation across her neck and shoulders with them.

Bianca blinked. "He failed to mention the other furry creatures in the barn."

Corian smoothed down the front of his shirt. "Because they can't see us."

"Is that so?" The woman's voice grew louder in agitation. "Whose idea was it to put a portal to another world right here?"

"Shh!" Corian raised a finger to his lips and stared at the tour group's last few stragglers. "They can still hear us."

"Who put this in Colonial Williamsburg?" Bianca whispered harshly.

"A creature who does what it wants and doesn't care about what happens next," Cheyenne muttered. "You didn't seem that bothered by it the first time."

"That was at night, Cheyenne. This is broad daylight."

"With nightstalkers." Corian raised an eyebrow at Bianca and dipped his head. "We're safe here."

"It hardly feels like it."

Cheyenne stared at her mom while Maleshi opened a portal within their cloaked bubble at the back of the barn. *Yep, she's back to her old self. Now she's pissed off about everything.*

The dark oval of light bloomed in front of Maleshi's hands and grew. Nu'ek, who had to stoop to avoid poking her head through the roof of the stables, leaned forward to peer through the portal. "Where does this lead?"

Ember's eyes lit up when she looked through the dark window. "That's our apartment."

"Wonderful."

Cheyenne grunted when the Golra snatched both trunks of activators out of her arms. "What are you doing?"

"Helping." Nu'ek flung the first trunk through, and it landed on the apartment floor with a thump. The second followed it. Dusting off her black hands, the Golra looked down at Cheyenne. "There. Your burden is relieved."

"Okay, thanks." Cheyenne tried to smile back at her, then remembered what she'd seen. "Hey, did anybody feel that when we crossed over?"

"Feel what?" Maleshi waved her hand, and the portal disappeared with a pop.

"Something like concentrated magic," Cheyenne said, pointing above the road, "and flames in the air."

The nightstalkers exchanged quick looks.

"Might've just been residual from the crossing." Corian shrugged. "I didn't pick up on any of it."

Maleshi and Ember both shook their heads.

"All right." Cheyenne ran a hand through her hair, finally noticing how cramped her fingers felt after holding onto the trunks for so long. *I know I did not just imagine it. Something was here right before we were.* "So now we go see the banebreaker, right?"

"Not me." Nu'ek's wings twitched as she turned to face the stables' back wall. She nodded at Cheyenne. "I don't feel the need to stick around. This world smells like shit."

Ember chuckled. "We are surrounded by a barn and farm animals."

The Golra frowned at her. "That's not what I mean. See you on the other side."

Nu'ek tossed her head and lumbered toward the wall. It looked like she'd crash right through it before she disappeared with a brief shimmer through the portal.

"It seems she has a fondness for that ghastly place," Bianca said.

Maleshi replied, "She has a fondness for Hangivol, at the very least."

Ember blinked at the wall where Nu'ek had vanished. "You think she'll be okay in there by herself?"

"Golra are solitary creatures by nature." The general shrugged. "And something tells me whatever took the monsters out for us is not temporary."

Cheyenne frowned. "Like, they're gone forever?"

"It's a hunch." With a shrug, Maleshi raised her hands again. "This banebreaker is where, exactly?"

"South Richmond. The garage across the street might be better than her front door." Cheyenne shot her mom a sidelong glance. "Broad daylight and everything."

She pulled her phone out of her back pocket and had to turn it on before she could pull up the address to show Maleshi.

The general looked at the map and cocked her head. "Huh. Interesting choice."

"Can we make this quick, please?" Bianca clasped her hands in front of her and lifted her chin. "I'd like to be home by lunchtime, if at all possible."

Corian fought back a smile. "We'll do the best we can. There's no telling how long a meeting with a banebreaker will last."

"I assume that's based on your personal experience."

He laughed and replied, "No, only on what I've heard."

"So, my daughter is the only one who knows what she's doing, is that it?"

Cheyenne snorted and cleared her throat when her mom looked at her.

Maleshi finished opening the next portal and turned to offer Bianca a small, restrained smile. "That's exactly it, Bianca. Does that worry you?"

"Not at all. I'd be more concerned if it were the other way around. Shall we?" Without waiting for a reply, Bianca stepped through the portal on her own and vanished from the stables.

The general raised her eyebrows at Cheyenne.

"She's just ready to go home."

"Apparently." With a snort, the general stepped through the portal. Corian slipped through without a word, and Ember and Cheyenne went together.

The whir of cars on the street drowned out the pop of the portal closing behind them inside the parking garage. Fortunately, no one was around to see four magicals and a human appear out of nowhere between a silver SUV and the garage's elevators.

Maleshi snapped her fingers, and her body shimmered before her human illusion took over. She studied the row of townhomes across the street as Corian and Ember cast their illusion spells. "Which one is it?"

"The gross yellow one." Cheyenne pulled up Inolu's number on her phone and made the call. "Give me a minute."

"Oh." Corian cocked his head. "Are we running into your personal time?"

She rolled her eyes as the line rang. "The best way *not* to get inside is to show up at the front door without telling her first." When the nightstalkers stared at her, she added quickly, "It was on the really long, really weird voicemail she left me." *And the last thing I wanna do is piss her off before we even have a chance.*

The line clicked, and a long sigh rustled in Cheyenne's ear. "What?"

"It's Cheyenne Summerlin."

"Please tell me you weren't a complete idiot and acted against my advice."

Cheyenne glared at the navy-blue door of the banebreaker's house across the street. "I took your advice, and it worked."

"So why are you calling me?"

"It worked for everything but the curse. We still need your help for the rest of it."

"Just you and the Vessel?"

Cheyenne wrinkled her nose. "Plus a fae and two nightstalkers."

"I don't host parties, drow. Do they expect me to entertain them with some twisted fucking idea of fun?"

"No, they're friends. They wanna help."

"I don't need help."

Closing her eyes and forcing herself not to scream, Cheyenne slowly muttered, "Me. They're here to help me."

"Fine. I assume you'll be here soon with two nightstalkers."

"Yep."

The line clicked and went dead. Cheyenne glared at her phone and jammed it back into her pocket, feeling Ki'zi's metal spiral. Then she pulled the thick metal cuff keeping her in drow form off her wrist. Her bone-white hair darkened instantly to jet-black, and the paleness of her human skin replaced the slate-gray. "We can go now."

"By all means." Maleshi gestured toward the street. "Lead the way."

Cheyenne flipped the silver cuff over and over in her hand. *I wish I had my jacket.*

"Want me to hold onto that for you?" Ember asked as they all walked toward the parking garage exit. "I have bigger pockets."

Glancing at her friend's cargo pants, Cheyenne handed Ember the cuff. "Thanks."

Hopefully, I won't need to put it back on for a while. My job's on Earth now.

They waited for a gap in the mid-morning traffic, then hurried across the street toward the row of townhomes. Cheyenne grimaced at the puke-yellow paint of Inolu's house and waited until everyone else stood on the front stoop with her before knocking.

"What a ghastly color," Bianca muttered.

"I wouldn't say she's all that concerned about how things look on the outside." Cheyenne blew a quick breath and stared up at the black panel on the side wall. *Come on. Let's get this over with.*

The black box's front panel slid open, and the camera lens extended on a hinged arm, spinning and clicking.

"That was fast." Inolu's voice came through in a metallic buzz. "What do you want?"

Bianca cleared her throat and gazed up at the lens. "I was told you could—"

"I wasn't talking to you. Shut up."

The woman blinked. "Cheyenne, are you positive this is our only option?"

"I got this, Mom." The drow spread her arms and stared at the camera. "We need your services, Inolu. I just called you."

"I know that." The camera spun again and swung sideways to focus on Ember, Maleshi, and Corian in turn. "You had your consultation and way more freebies than I ever give out. This one will cost you."

"Fine."

"Five thousand dollars."

"Holy shit, that's a lot," Ember muttered.

"And you get one hour."

"Great." Cheyenne nodded. "If you can break this curse in under thirty minutes, I'll double it."

"Listen to you." A sharp, metallic laugh came through the intercom. "You have to be the worst haggler I've ever met. Step inside and stand on the red circle. You know the drill."

"Yep."

"Tell your servants to wipe off their shoes. The mat's in front of you." A loud click came from the intercom, then the camera lens spun quickly and retracted into the black box.

"Servants." Maleshi folded her arms. "I have a hard time picturing you calling us that, kid."

"I didn't." Cheyenne grabbed the doorknob and turned it. "She's just insulting you." *I would be too if I'd bound demons into my body. Or whatever they are.*

Corian snorted and shook his head. "Banebreakers."

"Oh, don't say it like you know what we're walking into." Bianca shot him a stern look. "You have no idea."

He blinked at her and dipped his head. "If I offended you, I apologize."

"No need." Bianca tossed her hair away from her forehead as Cheyenne pushed the front door open and stepped over the threshold. "I'm tired."

"This'll be over soon, Mom." *It better be.*

CHAPTER TWENTY-ONE

The foyer was dark, like the last time. Cheyenne stepped onto the red circle and waved the others in behind her. "Just spread out, I guess."

"Who doesn't light their entryway?" Bianca scowled at the darkness but sidestepped along the wall as Ember and the nightstalkers came in behind her.

Cheyenne ignored her mom's question and looked back at the door.

Ember reached out to pull it shut behind her, but the door closed on its own with a slam. "Ow."

The fae shook out her hand as an orange rectangle appeared in the air around Cheyenne.

Maleshi's eyes reflected the orange light as she hissed at Inolu's magical security ward. "Is this part of the process?"

"Yeah. Takes something like thirty seconds."

The orange light pulsed around Cheyenne. She folded her arms and waited. *This thing better not take me out again. No more blight in my body.*

After the scan finished, a trail of red arrows illuminated in front of the drow's feet. She stepped forward and turned in the semi-darkness to wave Bianca forward. "Same for you, Mom."

"This is absurd. You're paying this woman five thousand dollars to stand under a light?"

Yeah, she's about to lose it.

"Just stand on the red circle."

Bianca stepped forward. "This is why I don't fly."

Corian stepped back against the wall and glared at the rectangle pulsing orange around the woman. "I don't like this, either."

"We're not getting in otherwise." Cheyenne gazed around the darkness as the banebreaker's security scan hummed and clicked. "She's a little paranoid."

"I don't enjoy trusting my well-being to an insane person, Cheyenne. You failed to mention that part."

"She's the one who gave me the potion so you could make the crossing, okay? She's the best shot we have. Just hold still."

The orange light grew brighter around Bianca, and the buzzing hum intensified. "Is this necessary?"

"Mom."

A loud crack split through the entryway. Sparks flew from the orange rectangle, and the security device let out a blazing shriek.

Not again.

"Cheyenne, what is this?"

A warbling alarm blared in a low tone and quickly rose in pitch. The orange light blazed around Bianca, then the lights came on with a crack, blinding them, and a door flew open.

"No, no, no. Goddamnit." Inolu stormed into the entryway and slapped her hands against a long series of control panels on the wall. The alarm cut off abruptly, but the bright orange rectangle around Bianca still blazed. Another shower of sparks flew from the top of the security system. The banebreaker spun toward it, her glowing green eyes wide. "Fuck. Are you insane? Get out of that."

"Excuse me?"

"Now!"

Bianca was thrown forward by an unseen force and fortunately stumbled into Cheyenne's arms.

"Hey!" Cheyenne steadied her mom and glared at Inolu. "You don't get to throw her around like that."

"If I want to throw a human around in my own house, that's my business. You don't get to come in here and break all my shit." Inolu flicked her hands at the sparking orange rectangle and muttered a spell.

The green veins in her light-gray skin pulsed brighter, and the security system buzzed before falling silent. The orange light winked out. "It seems your entire bloodline's a ticking timebomb. On both sides."

"What is she talking about?" Bianca muttered.

"I'm talking about you, Vessel," Inolu hissed, pointing a glowing finger at the woman. "Your Weave-enshrouded spawn knocked herself out the last time."

"No, that was you."

"And now you nearly destroyed one of my most useful tools." Breathing heavily, the banebreaker glared at Bianca. "What are you staring at?"

Corian cleared his throat. "She's never seen a Siliwari."

"Who the fuck are you?" Inolu whirled on him and summoned a glowing green orb on the tip of her finger.

The nightstalker hissed and released his human illusion. His silver claws extended from one fur-covered hand with a hiss, and he pointed right back at her. "Be very careful about how you use that, banebreaker."

They glared at each other, then Inolu burst out laughing. It was a startlingly pleasant, polite laugh for how pissed off she'd just been. She looked down at the green orb connected to her finger and grinned. "What, this? Ha. Put those little needles away, nightstalker. They're useless here."

"I think I'll keep them," he growled.

The banebreaker's smile vanished, and her eyes blazed with green light. "Then get out."

Maleshi looked at them. "Corian?"

"Don't." His silver eyes narrowed at the banebreaker, but he retracted his claws and straightened. "I'm not the one you're being paid to focus on today."

"Of course not." Inolu's mad grin returned, and she batted her eyelashes. "But I'd play with you for free. Just for a good laugh."

The green orb disappeared from her finger, and she smiled at Ember. "And you are?"

"Ember."

"The Black Flame's *nós aní*, isn't that right?"

Ember frowned. "Yep."

Inolu looked sharply at Maleshi next and chuckled wryly. "Don't take it personally, but I wouldn't have chosen that particular look if I were you."

"What look?" Maleshi growled.

"Come on, General. Anyone who's seen you for five seconds would agree with me. It's too soft." Inolu spun and headed across the entryway toward the door she'd nearly knocked off its hinges. "One might think you were using it to hide in a different world. Hmm. Imagine that."

The banebreaker disappeared through the doorway, leaving the rest of them to stare at each other in confusion.

"What just happened?" Ember muttered.

"Inolu Rosh." Cheyenne gently set her hand on Bianca's shoulder. "You okay?"

The woman blinked at the doorway, grumbling, "I will be when we're finished here."

"Yeah. Come on."

"I don't like her," Maleshi said as she gave Cheyenne a warning look.

"Join the club. But I'm pretty sure that was our invitation." Cheyenne gestured after Inolu, and the others grudgingly followed her out of the entryway.

The room they entered was another in the banebreaker's home Cheyenne hadn't seen. Instead of the dark, dusty study straight from the nineteenth century or the well-lit kitchen covered with potted houseplants, this one was decorated like a nightclub. A large dance floor took up the back third of the room, covered in specks of light reflected from the disco ball hanging from the ceiling. The cement floor was painted black. Neon signs with phrases like Dance the Night Away and YOLO hung from walls painted a sparkly dark purple, and a fully stocked bar with chrome barstools ran along the back wall. Every ten seconds, the track lighting on the ceiling changed the color of its low glow, red to yellow, purple to green, orange to white. The huge mirror in back of the bar reflected the group's confused expressions as they filtered through the doorway, but Cheyenne was focused on the corner straight ahead.

A curving booth covered in maroon pleather hugged one wall, the sitting area was furnished with a massive floor pouf and four captain's chairs upholstered the same way. There was no table.

Her townhouse was not big enough to hold all this.

Inolu sat in the center, her arms spread and propped up on the booth's wall behind her. She smiled at them and crossed one leg over the other. "Join me, why don't you?"

"She's insane," Ember whispered.

"But she was right the last time," Cheyenne replied. "Just gotta keep reminding ourselves of that."

Inolu chuckled. "The five of you look like a bunch of terrified squirrels. I hate squirrels. Come sit."

They moved slowly across the cement floor toward the booth. Cheyenne and Bianca lowered themselves into the chairs on one side of the gigantic stuffed pouf, and Maleshi took one on the other side. Ember pointed at the pouf, and a flash of purple light illuminated around it and dragged it away from the booth toward her. She stepped around it and sat, placing her hands in her lap.

Inolu looked at Corian. "Well?"

"I'll stand."

"Ooh." She lifted her shoulders in a mock shiver. "So serious."

So this is how she doesn't host parties. Like, she's a completely different person.

Inolu's green eyes flicked toward Cheyenne. The green veins running across every inch of her skin made her look at home with the neon signs around her weird nightclub room. She looked at Cheyenne's shoulders and raised an eyebrow. "Ah. I see you've solved your little poison problem."

"Yeah. And a few bigger problems with it."

Inolu snapped her fingers and pointed at the center of the ceiling. The Bee Gees' *Stayin' Alive* played from a sound system's speakers hidden in what sounded like every wall.

Cheyenne sighed. Guess she doesn't wanna double her fee by getting through this quickly.

Maleshi scowled and scanned the room. "Please turn that off."

"No!" Inolu hissed, her eyes flashing brighter. A pulse of dark energy and faint green light burst around her figure and quickly disappeared. "We like it."

"So, you throw parties in here?" Ember asked, unamused.

"Sometimes. Don't worry, fae. You won't be invited."

I need to steer this back on track before somebody loses their shit.

"Inolu."

"Cheyenne." The banebreaker grinned.

"You said I had to take my mom across the Border to break this curse."

Cocking her head, Inolu looked at the drow and her mother. "No."

"Seriously?"

"You're wrong on so many levels. Take it from someone who understands. You need to get your memory checked." Inolu dropped her arm onto the back of the booth again and wiggled against the cushion. "The Underman told you the Vessel's fate and the fate of both worlds were one and the same. Ambar'ogúl is healed, and now the human can finally be healed as well."

"My name is Bianca."

The banebreaker didn't look at her. "Good for you."

"How do you know Ambar'ogúl is healed?" Maleshi asked. "I assume you've been right here over the last few days."

"Not in this room. But I have missed it." Inolu chortled. When no one else said anything, she leaned forward toward Cheyenne. "The Border portals are not the only way between worlds, drow. Don't tell me you haven't figured that out."

"Well, now I know." *Just keep it together until she breaks the curse.* Cheyenne took a deep breath and gestured at Bianca.

"You're very boring. Did you know that?" Inolu's back thumped against the pleather cushion again. "Especially for someone who's supposed to be so important."

"This is a waste of time," Corian growled. "We'll find another way."

The banebreaker snapped her head sharply to the side to glare at him. "No, you won't."

"I won't stand here listening to one useless string of craziness after another, Cheyenne."

"You will until we get what we came here for." She shook her head but didn't take her eyes off the smirking gray-skinned woman with glowing green veins. "I'm not leaving until it's done."

"Hmm." Rolling her eyes, Inolu smacked her lips and pushed herself off the booth. "Stand up."

No one moved.

"You, Beatrice—"

"Bianca."

"Whatever. On your feet."

Bianca pressed her lips together and blinked furiously at Cheyenne.

"It's okay." *I couldn't even convince myself, saying it like that.*

"I don't want this woman touching me."

"That makes two of us." Inolu's hands fluttered toward the woman. "Now do as I say. Your mini-me is paying for my time, not your laziness."

With a frustrated exhalation, Bianca stood slowly and lifted her chin at the banebreaker. "What is this for?"

"So I can see you. I didn't think humans were this fucking stupid."

"Watch it," Cheyenne muttered.

"So uptight. Everyone's so uptight." Inolu pointed at Corian as she stepped toward Bianca. "When was the last time you got laid?"

He folded his arms and glared at her.

"That long, huh? Sucks to be you."

What the hell was going on with this chick?

Inolu leaned away from Bianca, looking her up and down like a tailor fitting a client. She tapped her lip, then walked halfway around the woman and nodded. "Show me your hands."

Bianca slowly lifted both hands and turned them back and forth. One of her eyes twitched.

The sleeve of her zip-up sweatshirt jerked up her arm on its own, and a single rune on her wrist flashed with orange light. Bianca sucked in a hissing breath and grabbed her wrist to cradle it against her chest.

Cheyenne leaped to her feet. "What are you doing?"

"What makes you think it was me?" Inolu chuckled. "She's cursed all right. Like shrapnel after everything goes boom."

"We already knew that," Ember said, leaning forward in preparation to stand if things got messy. "The necromancer said—"

"Ha! Necromancer?" The banebreaker stuck both hands on her hips. "A necromancer would only understand his own magic, which isn't worth much of anything if you think about it. Why was it even part of the equation?"

"He made the blight," Cheyenne replied.

"Oh, *that* necromancer. Venga's an asshole. Turn around." Inolu spun a finger in the air, and after an exasperated glare at Cheyenne, Bianca slowly turned. "So, the scaleback activated the Vessel's power, is that it? No, don't answer. I already know it was a mistake." Her eyes trailed up and down Bianca as the woman spun. "Of course, he didn't know shit about this curse. But I do."

"Great." Cheyenne nodded. *Finally.* "So whatever you have to do to break it, go ahead."

The banebreaker paused, her eyelids fluttering rapidly. Then she took a sharp breath and looked at Cheyenne. "You are clueless where it counts."

"Just do it."

"Believe it or not, I very much enjoy a bit of magical surgery." Inolu shrugged. "But I can't break this curse."

CHAPTER TWENTY-TWO

"Excuse me?" Bianca's eyes bulged.

"I said, I can't. It doesn't get any simpler than that, Bernice."

"You're a banebreaker." Cheyenne clenched her fists. "And I know you're the best."

"Oh, flattery now," Inolu said. "That's new. It won't work."

"Why the fuck not?" Cheyenne's anger flared with the heat of the drow magic racing up her spine, and she didn't bother trying to keep her drow form at bay.

The banebreaker simply looked her up and down and cocked her head. "It's not an issue with my abilities, drow. Bring me anything else, and I will rip it to shreds for you. With pleasure. But the caster of this curse made its intended effects remarkably specific, and none of them were meant for her." She pointed at Bianca, who slowly lowered herself back onto the captain's chair and stared blankly at the ground.

"Then how do we get rid of it?" Maleshi asked in a low growl.

"You don't. As long as the Spider lives in Ambar'ogúl, the curse remains." Scanning the stunned magicals and one highly disheartened human in front of her, Inolu clapped her hands together. "Time for a drink."

She slipped between the end of the booth and Bianca's chair and headed for the opening behind the bar. Her head bobbed to the music as she grabbed a glass and turned to view her vast collection of booze.

"It can't be broken?" Ember shook her head. "That doesn't make sense."

"That's not what she said. *She* can't break it, but there has to be a way."

"Cheyenne." Bianca tried to reach toward her but only managed to place a hand on the chair's armrest. "I want to go home."

"I know. You will as soon as we break this curse."

"You heard what she said. There's nothing more."

"No, there's something." Cheyenne narrowed her eyes at the bar, which flashed different colors intermittently. The clink of bottles and shot glasses carried over the disco music as Inolu mixed herself a remarkably stiff drink. "As long as the Spider lives in Ambar'ogúl." She looked quickly at Maleshi. "Nobody says 'as long as' if there's not another option."

The general pushed to her feet, looking back and forth across the room as she followed that train of thought. "That was a rather cryptic way to put it."

"Don't just stand there," Inolu called, her head weaving from side to side with the music. She held up a highball glass filled with a glowing yellow liquid and plopped a handful of the tiny black O'gúleesh berries into it. "I call this a Mindbomb. It'll blow you away. Come on."

"Yeah, it looks radioactive," Ember muttered.

"It looks like piss." Corian stepped away from the wall and paused beside Maleshi. "Are we digging into this?"

"That's up to Cheyenne."

"Yeah, I'm not letting that hidden message slide by. We're not done." Cheyenne stalked toward the bar.

"Can I help you up?" Ember extended a hand toward Bianca, who waved her away without taking her gaze off the ground.

"I think I'll sit."

"Okay."

Ember and the nightstalkers followed Cheyenne toward the bar. One of the barstools screeched across the ground when Corian kicked it aside to make room for himself.

Inolu said, "Careful. That kind of behavior will get you kicked out."

"So will wringing your neck if you don't start making sense."

The banebreaker clicked her tongue and took a long sip of her glowing yellow drink. With a hum of approval, she studied her cocktail. "You don't want to touch me, nightstalker. For your own sake, not mine."

Cheyenne leaned forward over the bar. "You know how to break the curse, though."

"I know what must be done. I told you I can't do it."

"Maybe not right now," Maleshi added. "But if circumstances changed?"

"Sure. Change changes everything." Inolu took another sip. "Are you sure you don't want to try this?"

Cheyenne slapped the wooden bar. "What has to change?"

"You haven't been listening."

"I know what you said. What, we have to kill Ba'rael to break her curse on my mom?"

Inolu cocked her head and pursed her lips. "That's one way to do it."

"And the other is?"

Staring at Maleshi the whole time, the banebreaker placed another highball glass on the bar and filled it with the rest of her cocktail from the shaker. Then she slid the glass along the bar toward her. "Come on, General. Drink with me."

"No."

"As long as she lives in Ambar'ogúl." Ember's eyes widened. "Hey, what if she came Earthside? Ba'rael?"

Corian grimaced and scowled at the banebreaker, who was making eyes at him as she drank again. "Ba'rael would never make the crossing."

"If she were tied up in a bag and dragged through, she'd make the crossing." Maleshi shrugged. "As far as I know, there aren't any limitations to involuntary portal passage."

Ember wrinkled her nose. "You want to kidnap Ba'rael and bring her Earthside?"

The general grinned. "Oh, I would love to."

"We have no idea where she is," Corian added. "Haven't heard a word about her since Cheyenne turned the Cycle."

"I think she's in Nor'ieth."

They all turned to look at Cheyenne. Maleshi folded her arms. "What makes you say that?"

"That's where Neros was. It makes sense that he'd take her back." *And I saw her frozen there in my dreams more than once.*

"That's a hell of a guess." Corian turned away from Inolu when she slid the untouched second cocktail toward him instead and wiggled her eyebrows. "And we'd need a dozen raugs to cast their portal into another dimension again."

"No, that would take way too long." Cheyenne glanced at her mom. Bianca hadn't moved an inch since they'd left her alone in the sitting area. "We need something else."

"Like a drink, perhaps?" Inolu nodded at the untouched cocktail. "It's been a long time since I've partied with a drow. Anything could happen."

Cheyenne ignored her. *I think I know the last drow she "partied" with, and he banished her because of it.*

She looked at the banebreaker swaying to the music. "You said there are other ways besides the portals to get between worlds."

"Hmm. Someone has selective hearing."

"And there are other ways to track Ba'racl down and bring her Earthside, aren't there?"

Inolu set her half-empty cocktail down and glared at Cheyenne. "You think you're so clever."

Maleshi looked quickly at the banebreaker. "That sounds like a yes."

"You're not the one paying me, are you?" Inolu snapped. "If you're not going to drink, keep your mouth shut."

"How do we do it?" Cheyenne asked. Inolu rolled her eyes and headed farther down the bar to get away from her. Cheyenne brushed past Maleshi and Ember to follow her. "You know what it is. Tell me!"

"I highly doubt you want to go down that road," Inolu hissed. "It is not for you."

"Listen, the list of people I'd do whatever it takes to help is ridiculously small." Cheyenne leaned over the bar and pointed back at Bianca. "She's one of them. I came here to break that curse, and I'm not leaving until that happens."

"Then you'll be here for quite some time. And it'll be expensive."

Cheyenne spoke through gritted teeth and fought down her anger. "Get us to Ba'rael."

The banebreaker chuckled again, but this time, it sounded a lot more nervous. "Did you forget what happened the last time you tried to kill her?"

"I don't have to kill her. I just have to bring her Earthside. We'll break the curse, then the Spider can go back to her dark little hidey-hole, wherever the hell that is. Just make it happen."

Inolu stared at her, then lifted her chin. "I don't want to."

"Well, now you don't have a choice." Cheyenne shoved away from the bar and reached into her back pocket for R'leer's giant jeweler's loupe. She thrust it toward Inolu, who jolted and staggered against the back shelf of the bar.

"Get that the fuck away from me!" Two liquor bottles toppled and shattered on the floor. The glowing veins running across Inolu's skin pulsed as she gripped the edge of the shelf behind her with trembling hands.

Cheyenne cocked her head. "Do it."

The banebreaker's lips trembled as she stared at the darkseller's device. "That shouldn't be here." A low growl escaped her. "You're so fucking stupid. How did you get that?"

"I'm friends with the one who banished you here, Inolu. I know all about what you can do. So whatever it is, make it happen and break the damn curse." Cheyenne wiggled the device. "Right now."

The banebreaker tried to retreat even farther, sending another wave of liquor bottles crashing to the floor. She glanced between R'leer's contraption and Cheyenne's blazing golden eyes, then nervously licked her lips. "Do you even know how to use that thing?"

Cheyenne slammed her fist on the bar, splintering the wood. "Does it look like I'm fucking around?"

I seriously hope not 'cause I have no idea what the hell this thing does.

"You can't. No, no. You can't." Inolu shook her head vigorously and clenched her eyes shut. "It's been invoked, banebreaker, but don't try to make excuses." A terrified whimper rose from her lips as she muttered something unintelligible.

"Cheyenne." Maleshi took one step toward them and stopped. "What did you do?"

"Nothing. Yet." Cheyenne squinted at the banebreaker but didn't lower R'leer's device.

"We talked about this," Inolu muttered as if reassuring someone in front of her. "You agreed. I didn't agree to anything, and that wasn't a conversation." Her hand smacked her face, and she staggered back down the bar beneath the impact, sweeping half the bottles off the shelf as she tried to keep her footing.

Cheyenne backed away with wide eyes. *Holy shit. She's insane.*

"Oh, now you're crossing a line. You've already crossed every line there is. Do it. No. They'll ruin everything. Do it! No!" The banebreaker bucked and jerked like someone had grabbed her shoulders to give her a good shake. "We want to. Don't we? Don't speak for the rest of us. Stop it!"

The banebreaker crumpled to the floor with a shriek.

"Hey." Cheyenne leaned over the bar, but it was too wide to see the floor behind it. "Inolu?"

A blood-smeared hand covered in blazing green veins slapped down on the edge of the bar. Cheyenne jumped back and looked at her friends. Everyone stared at the banebreaker slowly hauling herself back up onto her shaky legs. Inolu's short bob hung in dark strands beside her face as she breathed heavily, her head bent to her chest. Then a low chuckle escaped her.

Ember swallowed. "Maybe we should go with the 'raug portal to Nor'ieth' plan."

"You're not going anywhere." This time, the voice echoing from Inolu's mouth wasn't anything close to hers.

Shit. That's the Underman.

Inolu groaned and whipped her head from side to side. Then her head rocked back, and that growling voice in dozens of tones laughed hysterically. The lights flickered. Taking breath after deep breath, the Underman laughed through the banebreaker's mouth, then stopped abruptly. Inolu's head slowly lowered, her green eyes blazing brighter than ever, and smirked at Cheyenne. "Give the Black Flame what she wants."

The disco music squealed to a halt a second before all the lights went out.

CHAPTER TWENTY-THREE

F uck.

"Cheyenne?" Bianca called weakly from her chair. "What's happening."

"Just stay over there." Cheyenne backed away from the gaping, disembodied green grin floating below the banebreaker's blazing eyes, now the Underman's.

"I don't like the way this looks," Maleshi muttered.

"Yeah, me neither."

A cold blast of air hurtled around the room, and only Inolu's eyes, mouth, and the glowing veins on her skin were visible in the thick darkness. The Underman slammed one hand on the bar, then the other, grinning madly as he forced Inolu's body up and onto the bar.

Jesus, she's crawling over.

Cheyenne stepped back and kept a firm grip on the weird jeweler's loupe that had started this whole thing.

"You didn't say anything about having to fight her," Ember whispered.

"I'd be happy to," Corian growled.

"It's not her." Cheyenne tried to look at her friends but couldn't see a thing. "It's an *uanáj*. I think."

"Where the hell did you learn about *uanáj*, kid?"

"Long story."

Another blast of frigid air made her stumble backward, and the Underman stood fully erect on the bar. The two sets of glowing veins vaguely shaped like hands stretched out on either side of two wide green eyes were the only indication that he'd spread Inolu's arms wide. "So you want to see all the other players and the board, do you?"

Cheyenne tightened her grip around R'leer's device. "If you mean Ba'rael Verdys, then yeah."

"Oh, it's so much more than that. You frighten her, drow. Did you know?" Without waiting for a reply, the Underman whirled and shot both veined hands out toward the back of the room. Brilliant white light grew above the dancefloor, its edges roiling black smoke glowing green. It lit the entire room, Cheyenne, her friends, and Inolu Rosh as the Underman stood atop the bar and grinned.

"What is this?" Cheyenne muttered. *This has to be another portal, right? To where?*

No one said a word.

The faint outline of a figure wavered inside the white light. It darkened and took on a more solid form, growing closer. The figure stiffened and turned slowly around. "Cheyenne."

"Neros?"

The light-skinned drow grinned as Cheyenne walked slowly toward him.

"Hey, maybe that's not such a good idea," Ember cautioned.

Maleshi brushed the fae's arm with a hand. "Just wait."

Neros looked his cousin up and down, his pale eyes gleaming in the bright light with nothing else around him. "It is good to see you. In person, of course."

"Yeah, this isn't anything like the last few times, huh?" Cheyenne stared behind him and saw exactly what she'd seen in her dream: Ba'rael suspended within a wall of shimmering light, arms outstretched and face contorted in a frozen scream of rage. *There she is.*

"We're proud of you, Cheyenne. *I'm* proud of you. You finished your part in the Weave, and the pattern is restored."

"I probably wouldn't have made it half this far without your help."

"Cheyenne, who are you talking to?"

Cheyenne looked over her shoulder to see Bianca standing beside

Corian, one hand on the bar to steady herself as she tried to peer into the newly opened portal. "This is Neros."

Not a good idea to mention the familial connection right now.

"I am curious," Neros said, gazing around the room and smiling at Ember and Maleshi. "How did you manage to—"

He froze when he caught sight of the Underman in Inolu's body slowly lowering themselves to sit on the bar, legs dangling over the edge. They cocked their head and grinned at the Nor'ieth drow.

"No." Neros shook his head. "Cheyenne, you can't. Not like this. Whatever you mean to do, end it. It's all wrong."

"We had to do it this way. And we need to bring Ba'rael through right now."

"Ba'rael?" He waved his hand at his frozen mother behind him. "She's safe here, Cheyenne. Everyone's safe with her here."

"Not everyone. L'zar's not the only one she cursed." Cheyenne gestured at Bianca. "That's my mom."

Neros tilted his head, and a small smile flickered on his lips. "I see. The Vessel carries an extra burden. All right."

"Okay?"

"Yes, Cheyenne. I can help in this way as well." He turned to the frozen Ba'rael and flicked his fingers at her. The block of magic holding her in place moved through the white nothingness of wherever they were beyond the portal. The Spider's open golden eyes blazed, but of course, she didn't move.

Why would she? Her son was the only one more powerful than her, and he had locked her up in a magical wall.

"That is seriously creepy." Ember stepped forward as Ba'rael floated toward the portal opening. "How did you do that?"

Neros shook his head with a small, sad smile. "She did it to herself. I've merely been keeping an eye on her."

The Underman let out a dark, rumbling laugh. "Now we all will."

"Wait." Cheyenne spun toward the bar as the Underman reached out a glowing hand toward Ba'rael. "No!"

A thin dart of green light raced from that outstretched hand and struck the wall of shimmering magic around Ba'rael. The sound of fracturing ice and a scream from very far away filled the room.

"Damnit." Corian hissed and turned to Bianca, gently nudging her away. "Go sit down."

"Why? What's happening?"

"Just go."

Neros stared at the Underman. "Why?"

"You need an answer?"

"I see you, *uanáj*. And I know you see the ripples."

The Underman cackled. "Of course you do. If we let it be that easy, we'd ruin all the fun."

The wall around Ba'rael fractured and splintered even more, groaning and shuddering from within.

"Can you fix that?" Cheyenne asked.

"There's nothing to fix."

The wall shattered and sent sharp fragments of frozen magic exploding around the room. The quiet, faraway scream was unleashed as Ba'rael stumbled forward. It died in a snarl of surprise, and she whirled on Neros. "This isn't yours!"

He stared at her with a small frown. "It isn't yours, either."

Hissing, Ba'rael drew her hand back to smack her son's cheek. White light flashed in front of his face and stopped her from striking him. The Spider screamed again and lunged toward him.

"Hmm." The Underman cocked his head and flicked his fingers at the portal. "Let's try."

Ba'rael and Neros were jerked through the open portal and stumbled across the dancefloor. Inolu's body slumped over on the bar, and Ba'rael saw Cheyenne, Ember, and the nightstalkers staring at her. "You! What is this?"

The blinding white light of the portal into Nor'ieth winked out and cast the room into darkness again. The Underman's rumbling laughter came not from Inolu but from the gust of cold air blasting them.

A flicker of purple light bloomed in Ba'rael's hand, illuminating her snarl and half the room. Then the lights came back on.

"Get her," Maleshi muttered.

With a roar, Ba'rael flung the purple light at Maleshi. The night-stalker ducked and shot a bolt of silver lightning onto the floor that crackled toward the Spider's feet. Ba'rael darted into enhanced speed, followed quickly by Cheyenne and the nightstalkers. They all raced toward her as Maleshi's silver lightning inched across the floor.

"You have no right!" Ba'rael snarled, shooting black light from both hands at Corian.

Cheyenne lifted a shield in front of the nightstalker, sending the Spider's attack ricocheting into the ceiling. The crumbling plaster fell slowly, taking forever to reach the floor. Corian darted around the shield and swung a fist at her. Ba'rael blocked him and sent an orb of black shards into his chest, knocking him back against the wall at the end of the bar.

Maleshi let off another lightning attack that struck the Spider in the shoulder and spun her sideways and out of enhanced speed. Cheyenne and the general slipped out after her, and the chunks of plaster finally hit the ground. Ember jumped in surprise and backed away from the battle.

"I should have had you gutted for your betrayal." Ba'rael lashed out at Maleshi with a shimmering wave of silver. The general darted aside.

"You were too scared to come after me." She darted around the Spider and punched the drow in the lower back with a lightning-enclosed fist. Ba'rael snarled and spun, but the nightstalker had already darted away.

Then Ba'rael's gaze landed on Cheyenne as if she'd just realized it was her niece standing there and not some other drow. "You should be dead!"

"Yeah, you too." Cheyenne's skin erupted in black fire, and she shot a streak of it at her aunt.

Ba'rael screamed and caught the flaming attack with both hands, black and silver light erupting on contact. Cheyenne saw Neros standing against the far wall, watching the whole thing with objective detachment and his hands clasped behind his back.

The ground trembled as Ba'rael fought for control over Cheyenne's black drow fire. A harsh, mad laugh escaped her as she drew her hands apart and let the flames race up her arms.

Corian appeared behind her in a burst of silver light and sent a swift kick into her back. She staggered forward, the black flames snuffed out, and she whirled toward him, only to meet Maleshi's fist in the side of her face instead.

The drow woman dropped to the floor with a snarl, jerking against the general's grasp as Maleshi worked quickly to tie Ba'rael's hands behind her back with writhing ropes of silver magic. Flesh sizzled and smoke trailed from Ba'rael's wrists, filling the room with the stench of singed hair.

The Spider hissed and lurched away from Maleshi. "You're a coward."

"And you have nothing to stand on anymore." Cheyenne stepped toward her aunt, summoning crackling black energy spheres in both hands. "Not such a great warrior without your poisoned darts or the old laws of a challenge in the Heart to stop you, huh?"

Ba'rael spat at her niece's feet. "When the drow hear I've returned—"

"The drow don't want anything to do with you. They've even stopped cursing your name, like you never existed. And you haven't returned anywhere. You're in my world now." Cheyenne gestured at the room dusted in plaster, where a cracked neon sign ripped from one of its mounts hung precariously sideways. The light flickered with a stuttering buzz.

Okay, not the best intro.

Ba'rael struggled against Maleshi's bonds and sneered at the magicals around her. "I will ruin you. All of you."

"You already ruined yourself."

"Do it, then." Ba'rael twisted around where she knelt, the silver bonds burning into her wrists, and glared at Neros. "Send your mother to the final deathflame. You've chosen to serve this *nilsch úcat* to take down the one who birthed you."

Neros slowly tilted his head and blinked at her. "I serve the Weave, Ba'rael. Your part in it is nearly at an end."

The Spider screamed and lurched to her feet to stagger toward him. Maleshi jumped into enhanced speed and ran around Ba'rael, kicking up fallen plaster and dust and shattered glass. Three seconds later, she stopped behind the drow, grabbed a fistful of Ba'rael's white hair, and jerked her head back. Ba'rael snarled as the silver ropes tightly wrapped at least a dozen times around her body burned through her black clothes and into her flesh.

Maleshi brought her mouth down to the drow's ear and muttered, "You have no idea how many times I dreamed about doing this."

Ba'rael's eyes widened.

"Maleshi." Cheyenne shook her head. "That's not why we did this."

The general shoved Ba'rael's head away, making the drow fall to her knees again to keep from falling on her face, and wiped her hand off on her pants. "I meant tying her up, kid. Real tight like that, so it hurts."

Black light erupted around Ba'rael's fingers, and the silver bonds flashed brightly. She screamed and toppled sideways on the floor, her chest heaving as acrid smoke rose from the ropes around her.

"Oh, yeah." Maleshi circled the Spider. "Cuts off your magic, too."

Cheyenne raised an eyebrow. "You mean, like dampening cuffs?"

Corian snorted. "Another human rip-off of magic. Everyone wants to be a nightstalker, and they just can't pull it off."

Maleshi chuckled and stepped away from the Spider, who lay smoking on the floor and glaring up at them.

"Wow." Ember stepped forward with wide eyes, sliding her hand along the edge of the bar to reassure herself that it was there. "I'm surprised Venga didn't try to experiment on you two."

"Oh, he tried." Maleshi shrugged. "And I'm sure we weren't the first."

Inolu groaned where she lay sprawled across the bar. Ember jumped and quickly snatched her hand away before taking a few halting steps back.

"No drinking with the clients," Inolu growled, pushing up to half-sit, half-lean over her arms. "I don't know why that's the one rule you constantly choose to ignore."

"Inolu?" Cheyenne leaned forward to get a better look at the banebreaker's face. *Not like I could tell the difference between her and some other spirit. Or whatever.*

"I have no idea why you'd think it would be anyone else." Inolu sat fully upright and tossed her hair out of her glowing eyes. She swept her gaze around the room at the smashed décor and the hole in the ceiling and the two drow who hadn't previously been in their company. "What the fuck did you do to my house? And why is the Spider tied up on my dancefloor?"

"So you can break the curse," Cheyenne said. "Not alive in Ambar'ogúl."

"Ugh. Fine." Rolling her eyes, the banebreaker pushed off the edge of the bar and dropped to the ground. She swayed and widened her eyes, blinking heavily, then stumbled not toward Ba'rael but for the sitting area across the room. "Always moving the pieces around when it's not your turn."

"What?"

"I'm not talking to you." Inolu shook out her hands at her sides and waved her guests forward. "Let's get this over with. I don't have all day, and you've already wasted more of it than I can stomach."

"Go ahead, kid." Maleshi folded her arms and looked at Ba'rael. "I'm staying right here."

Ba'rael jerked against her magical bonds and snarled a long string of O'gúleesh.

"Yeah, back at ya."

Ember's mouth fell open when Cheyenne passed her, and she fell in line beside her friend to head toward the sitting area. "I think that was the craziest thing we've seen."

"Maybe, yeah." *Not the craziest I've seen, but I'm the only one who sees it half the time.*

"All right, whatever your name is." Inolu stepped through the chairs and turned to face Bianca. "At least someone knows how to accept decent hospitality."

Bianca sat in the captain's chair, her feet planted firmly on the floor with the half-empty second cocktail of glowing yellow nestled in her lap. "It's quite good."

"Hmm. Wait 'til you finish the whole thing."

"I don't think so." Cheyenne reached around the chair and gently pulled the glass out of her mom's hands. Bianca didn't resist.

Maybe because she was glowing again.

The runes burned into the woman's flesh pulsed with orange light. Cheyenne sniffed the drink, wrinkled her nose, and set the glass on the wall of the booth. "Mom?"

"Yes, Cheyenne?" Her voice was dull and monotone.

"You feeling okay?"

"Not really."

"Of course she's not feeling okay." Inolu snorted. "Just leave the critical thinking to me and quit getting in the way." She reached down to grab Bianca's hands and gently pulled. "Come on. Get up."

"Careful," Cheyenne muttered.

The banebreaker shot her a harsh warning glare. "Do I need to send you outside?"

Bianca got to her feet and didn't move. She just stared at the wall above the booth, the runes blinking intermittently with orange light.

"This almost went too far." Inolu clicked her tongue and leaned to one side, then the other as she studied Bianca's nearly catatonic state. "Most of my clients want to see the whole show."

"The what?"

"You know. Subconsciously, of course. The glitz and glam of curse work." Inolu waved a green-veined hand in the air. "A few shiny baubles. A burst of smoke. I have a cauldron, but it's in the other room. And no, I do not dance and chant. Unless you want to double your fee."

Cheyenne stared at the banebreaker in disbelief. "I don't give a shit what it looks like. Fix her."

"Right. Obviously, you don't hold physical appearance in high regard." Inolu gave the drow a flippant wave, then rubbed her palms vigorously together and smacked her lips.

Uanáj or no uanáj, *I'll break more than her house if she doesn't get this done.*

The veins covering Inolu's skin flared brighter the longer she rubbed her hands. She eyed Bianca and stepped closer. Thick globs of dark-green sludge dropped from her rubbing palms and landed with a smack on the floor between them. "You, little Vessel, are in for the time of your life. Or perhaps you've already had it. Either way."

Inolu flung her hands away from each other, splattering green globs against the walls and across the bar and on the pleather chairs and booth. Cheyenne jerked her head away from a sailing droplet and scowled.

When the banebreaker pressed a finger briefly to the center of Bianca's chest, the woman gasped, and her eyelids fluttered.

Cheyenne gritted her teeth. "If you hurt her—"

"Shut up." Inolu poked and prodded different points of Bianca's body, her green gaze intently focused on her work: right arm, left arm, the side of her neck, above her hip on the opposite side. Everywhere she touched, Bianca's body jerked in response. The woman swayed, but she stayed standing. When the banebreaker pointed at the middle of

Bianca's forehead and leaned forward for a final light poke, Bianca drew in a gasping breath and choked.

"What's happening?"

Inolu raised both hands and stepped away, smiling as Bianca fell into a fit of wheezing coughs. "She'll be fine."

"Mom?"

The runes on Bianca's skin glowed intensely, then peeled away, floating through her gray zip-up and joggers like decals instead of part of her flesh. Bianca groaned, trembling where she stood without moving a muscle. Her coughing fit grew harsher as she gasped for breath, oblivious to the rune marks swirling slowly overhead.

Ember wrinkled her nose. "That's not her skin, is it?"

"Oh, that would be delightful, wouldn't it?" Inolu grinned at the swirling runes now graying at the edges as the orange light sputtered out. She reached into the pocket of her cloak and pulled out a large square vial before uncorking it. "Any second now."

The floating runes burst into thousands of fluttering pieces like ash and swarmed toward the mouth of the banebreaker's vial. The second the last speck dropped into the opening, Inolu slammed the cork back in, and Bianca collapsed into the chair.

"Mom?" Cheyenne dropped to her knees beside the chair and reached tentatively toward Bianca's shoulder. "Hey! Mom, can you hear me?"

Bianca didn't move.

CHAPTER TWENTY-FOUR

A low, scratchy chuckle rose from Ba'rael. "Your mother, Cheyenne?" She wriggled against the bonds, ignoring the burns in her flesh, and shrieked with laughter. "I thought you had nothing."

Maleshi dropped into a squat and slapped Ba'rael's cheek. The force of it sent Ba'rael's other cheek cracking against the floor, and she grunted. The general's claws shot from her fingertips as she loomed over the Spider. "Say another word, and the next one'll be with these."

Ba'rael spat bloody mist at the nightstalker's face, and Maleshi smiled. "That's better."

"Why isn't she moving?" Cheyenne asked.

"Give her a minute." Inolu swirled the vial in her hand, the ashy specks spinning round and round before settling into a fluffy pile at the bottom again. "Always good to have one of these on hand."

"Mom." Cheyenne studied her mom's slack face. "Hey, she's not breathing."

"Uh-huh."

"Look at her!" The drow leaped to her feet and stormed toward the banebreaker. "I said to break the curse, not kill my mom!"

"Please. Killing the Vessel would be much harder than a little—"

Bianca gasped and lurched forward in the chair. Ember stepped back with wide eyes. Cheyenne spun and couldn't think of anything to say when her mom blinked rapidly. "I'm sorry. Who are you?"

"There." Inolu pointed at her and raised an eyebrow at Cheyenne. "Good as new."

"I asked you a question." Bianca lifted her hands to grip the armrests.

"Oh, we were never properly introduced. And we won't be." With a curt nod, the banebreaker whisked past the chair and headed across the room toward Ba'rael and Maleshi standing guard over her.

"Okay." Cheyenne studied her mom and blinked. "How do you feel?"

Bianca glanced down at her lap with a frown, then pushed to her feet. "Perfectly fine, Cheyenne. I don't see why I shouldn't be."

Cheyenne didn't think about it before throwing her arms around her mom and hugging her as tightly as she dared.

"What's gotten into you?" Bianca gently patted her daughter's back, then slowly pried Cheyenne away to look her in the eyes. "This isn't the time or place."

"I don't care." Cheyenne laughed in disbelief, blinking back the tears she wouldn't let spill over. "That actually worked."

"I certainly hope so." Bianca released her daughter's arms and smoothed down the front of her zip-up. "I have no desire to repeat an ordeal like that. Or discuss it."

Ember turned slowly around to stare at the banebreaker standing in the center of the room and glaring at Ba'rael. "Your clients want more of a show than that?"

"The things my other clients want would blow your little fae mind." Inolu flicked a speck of dried sludge off her palm, then spun to Cheyenne. "So. Cash or credit card? I accept debit as well if I have to, but no personal checks. They always go missing."

"Yeah." Cheyenne forced herself to turn away from her mom and shrugged. "Whatever you want."

"What I want is for you to get the fucking Spider out of my home." Inolu pointed sharply at Ba'rael, who spat out another glob of bloody spittle in reply.

"I'll pay you for that too."

Bianca clicked her tongue. "Really, Cheyenne."

"It's fine. Totally worth it."

Inolu barked a laugh and patted her cheek. "You want to pay me to dispose of the vermin?"

"Yeah. I'm done with her."

"Who is that?" Bianca asked, stepping slowly around the chair.

"Ba'rael Verdys."

"So that would make her…"

Cheyenne wrinkled her nose. "My aunt, yeah. Only by blood."

"I see we have an additional companion." Bianca gestured at Neros, who stood where they'd left him on the far side of the room, hands clasped behind his back as he gazed at the walls and the décor and the bar with wide-eyed fascination.

"That's her son. We can draw the family tree later, okay?"

"Fifteen thousand," Inolu barked.

"Fine."

"I don't mean total, drow. That's to take her off your hands."

Cheyenne shrugged. "Great."

"So we're settled on twenty-five thousand dollars for the entire package."

"Whatever."

"Wait, wait." Ember shut her eyes and raised a hand. "It would've been that much if you'd done all this in half an hour. That didn't happen."

"No, but the rest of it is to cover the damages to my happy place." Inolu thrust a finger at the hole in the ceiling. The dangling neon sign finally tore free of its last mount and crashed to the floor.

"That's insane."

"It's fine, Em. Seriously."

"It's the principle of the thing. Come on."

"I know."

"Oh." Inolu gestured at the bar. "And I'll throw in the extra drink for free."

With a snort, Cheyenne stepped toward the banebreaker and nodded. "Twenty-five. We good?"

"Absolutely. I'd shake your hand, but—"

"Yeah, I don't need that." *I wouldn't poke her with a stick.*

"Excellent!" Inolu whirled and pointed at Ba'rael. The silver dampening ropes unraveled in an instant, writhing away from the drow woman's body before disintegrating on the floor.

"Hey, hey." Maleshi stepped away from Ba'rael and pointed at the banebreaker.

Ba'rael hissed and leaped toward the general. Metal bars materialized out of thin air and banged into place around the Spider, closing her in before she realized what was happening. She shrieked when her face crashed into the bars of the cage and staggered back with both hands clamped around her nose. Her back hit the other wall, and she fired a bolt of black light that bounced off an invisible barrier and struck her in the thigh. Screaming, the Spider bashed against the metal bars, trying to break free without finding any weaknesses.

"Get over here, banebreaker," she hissed. "No more tricks. I'll rip you to shreds."

"Mmhmm." Inolu flicked another finger at the cage, and Ba'rael's words were abruptly cut off despite her mouth still moving in a soundless snarl. "I always did think you talked too much. And after where you've been held for the last several weeks, it might serve you to know that your magic will be considerably weakened for quite some time. If not permanently."

Ba'rael lashed out at the bars of the cage, screaming without sound.

Cheyenne folded her arms and stared at her silently raving aunt. *I would love to get my hands on that mute button.*

The banebreaker skipped toward the cage and stopped less than a foot away, clasping her hands behind her back. With an unrestrained giggle, she leaned so close to the bars that Ba'rael could have slashed at her face if she were able to get her hands through the barrier. She looked like she wanted to.

Inolu grinned and looked the Spider up and down. "I'm going to make so much money off you, drow. Make yourself comfortable."

"You don't plan on keeping her like this forever, do you?" Maleshi smirked at the cage. "Of course, I can't say I don't appreciate the aesthetic. But that one, at the very least, will want to go home." She jerked her head toward Neros, who seemed to be ignoring everything in his attempts to study the room.

"Ah. The Olfarím drow." Inolu sniggered. "Right. He may go back eventually."

"Can you open that portal again to send them back?" Cheyenne asked.

The banebreaker rolled her eyes and shrugged. "Not unless the Underman decides that's something he wants to do. He calls the shots with that one."

"Let me know when he decides." Cheyenne frowned at her light-skinned cousin, who was completely ignorant of everywhere but Nor'i-eth. "Neros doesn't belong here either."

"Then none of us do. Isn't that the way of it?"

"The Underman." Corian rubbed the side of his face. "You name them?"

"I thought nightstalkers were intelligent." Inolu stared at him insolently. "They name themselves, you idiot."

Ba'rael bashed her fists against the cage again, and Inolu spun sharply to nod at Cheyenne. "You look like a credit-card kind of girl to me."

"Whatever works."

"Stay here. Don't go anywhere." Inolu clapped her hands together and shuffled her feet in an excited dance. "I'll get my card reader."

She grinned at the magicals in her private home nightclub, then giggled again and danced around the side of the bar. She disappeared below the edge and popped back up with a card reader in hand. "Pleasure doing business with you, Miss Summerlin."

"Yep." Cheyenne headed toward the bar. "Just one little thing."

An alarm blazed in the hall, though it wasn't nearly as loud as the one when they'd arrived. A green and red flashing light lit up outside the nightclub room, and Inolu slammed the card-reader down on the bar. "No. That's impossible."

"Everything okay?"

"Not fucking likely, is it?" Racing around the bar, the banebreaker shook her head. "Everybody out."

"That's the best idea you've had since we got here," Corian muttered.

She ignored him and stormed across the room, then stopped and glared at Ba'rael in the cage. "Get out. Now." Her finger jabbed toward Cheyenne. "I'll bill you. Right now, it seems I have a little problem, and I don't want you here while I deal with it."

"You'll bill me."

"I have your damn number, Cheyenne. Get the hell out!"

Corian raised his hands to open a portal out of the banebreaker's home.

"Neros."

"Hmm?"

Cheyenne waved him forward. "We're going."

"Of course." He walked swiftly past the cage built around his mother and didn't look at her as he joined everyone in the center of the room.

Inolu stalked back and forth, glancing at the flashing door letting out that wailing alarm. "Hurry up. Just because you got what you wanted, it doesn't make my time any less precious."

"You can go take care of that if you want." Cheyenne gestured at the door.

"And leave you all in here by yourselves? Don't be absurd."

The portal opened into the foyer of the Summerlin estate. Cheyenne shrugged. "Well, thanks for everything."

"Yeah, we'll be in touch. Move it!" Inolu gestured at the gathered magicals and Bianca and sent them all flying through the portal. She let out an enraged shriek, then the window of dark light closed behind them with a pop as Cheyenne and the others stumbled across the well-polished wooden floors.

Bianca righted herself, her coordination fully restored now that the curse was gone. "That woman knows nothing about hosting guests."

Cheyenne gently nudged Ember away after her friend bumped into her and nearly knocked them both over. "At least she knows a hell of a lot about curses, right?"

Bianca stared at her daughter with wide eyes.

Corian snorted. "And cages."

"Ba'rael Verdys in a cage." Maleshi choked back a laugh. "Feels like karma, doesn't it?"

The nightstalkers looked at each other and stifled laughter.

Bianca watched them with a raised eyebrow.

Great. She's on the edge of kicking them out too.

But the corner of the woman's mouth flickered into the hint of a smile, and she took a deep breath through her nose. "I will say, that Ba'rael character seemed much more agreeable when she couldn't speak."

Corian and Maleshi howled with laughter and could do nothing but point at Cheyenne before doubling over and cracking up again.

Smirking, Bianca shook her head. "I've missed something."

"Wow." Maleshi smoothed her black hair away from her tufted face, silver eyes glistening, and took a deep breath. "That's basically what Cheyenne said right before—" A hissing laugh burst out of her, and she turned away to collect herself.

Cheyenne rolled her eyes. "It's not that funny."

"What?"

Ember nudged her friend in the side and grinned at Bianca. "It's what she told Ba'rael right before we all thought the Spider was gonna… I mean…"

"Somebody better spit it out."

"Right before we all thought she was gonna kill me, Mom. Okay?" Cheyenne spread her arms. "I told her she talked too much."

"Oh." Bianca blinked quickly and cleared her throat. For a moment, she looked to be at a loss for words, then she blurted, "At the very least, you managed to maintain some dignity when you thought you faced the end."

Corian roared with laughter, slapping his gut with both hands as Maleshi dropped into a squat, her shoulders shaking with mirth but no sound coming out.

Cheyenne scoffed at her mom. "How pragmatic of you."

"It's a compliment, Cheyenne." Bianca chuckled. "One I would hope to someday receive myself."

Jesus. That's as much as a "Way to go" as I'm gonna get, isn't it?

The woman smoothed down the front of her zip-up again and turned to look up the staircase. "Now, if you and these laughing clowns will excuse me?"

"Bianca? Cheyenne?" Eleanor raced around the corner of the staircase from the kitchen and staggered to a halt when she saw them at the foot of the stairs. The housekeeper tossed her hands in the air and let out a joyful shriek. "You're back! You're alive!"

"Yes, Eleanor, we're very much alive."

Eleanor shrieked again, sprinted toward them, and nearly knocked Bianca over when she wrapped her in a crushing embrace.

"Oof. Eleanor!"

"Sorry. I'm so sorry. Oh!" The housekeeper released Bianca, raising her hands cautiously as she looked the other woman up and down. "Did I hurt you?"

"Not at all." Bianca rubbed her side. "Except for a bruised rib, perhaps."

"If that's the worst of it, I'll happily take the blame and call it a job well done."

"That better be the worst thing," Cheyenne said, grinning as Eleanor turned toward her with wide eyes and a blooming grin.

"You did it? It's over?"

"Yep."

"Ah!" Eleanor pulled Cheyenne in for the same crushing embrace and might have even squeezed a little tighter. "Oh, I'm so happy I could cry!" She thrust the drow away from her and shook her head. "I won't cry. Too much of that already. And Ember! Look at you. Oh, look at you!"

The fae laughed. "What?"

"You're walking!"

"Oh. Yeah. Not as big of a deal."

"No, no. Don't you even think about downplaying what a miracle that is!"

"I'd call it magic. Oh!" Ember wheezed when the housekeeper pulled her into a hug. She coughed when Eleanor released her and chuckled. "Thanks, Eleanor."

"I haven't done anything other than rattle around in this house worrying about all of you. I can't believe it! I mean, of course, I believe it. I knew you'd succeed." She chucked Cheyenne's chin and barked a laugh, her eyes glimmering. "We should celebrate. Are you hungry? It's nearly lunchtime, and I can whip up something quickly. Twenty minutes. Just give me twenty minutes. Bianca, let me pour you a drink."

Bianca snorted. "It's not even noon."

"Do you think anyone here gives a shit?" Eleanor clapped a hand over her mouth and chuckled. "I'm sorry. I'm just so relieved."

"I'll pass on the drinks, Eleanor. Thank you. I've had more than enough in the last few days to last me until the end of next week."

"Ha. Unlikely."

Cheyenne snorted and ran a hand through her hair. *If I look at Mom right now, I'll get the death glare.*

"Oh, you're serious?" Eleanor bustled toward Bianca, quickly touching her shoulders, then her cheeks, then her hair. "Look at you. Nothing hurt?"

"Eleanor, what are you doing?"

"Making sure you're really here."

"Stop fussing. I can't stand it."

The housekeeper took two quick steps back and swiped at her apron. "Well."

Corian spread his arms. "No hugs for us?"

"Huh." She pointed at him. "I'll forget you said that, and you can stay for lunch. Without any interruptions this time."

He chuckled. "I won't take it personally."

"Good. Because there won't be any interruptions this time, right? It's really over?"

"I can't make any promises, Eleanor." Bianca headed for the staircase. "But I assume things will be a lot quieter around here. Cheyenne succeeded remarkably well in ensuring that."

Cheyenne blinked as her mom headed up the stairs. "Thanks."

"Of course she did." Eleanor patted Cheyenne's cheek and winked. "You always work things out in the end. Where are you going?"

Bianca lifted a hand in a dismissive wave as she climbed. "To change my clothes and lie down on my own bed."

"Oh. Shall I?"

"Yes."

"And you want the—"

"Yes, Eleanor. Thank you. Please ensure our guests have everything they need. They can stay as long as they like."

"Right." Everyone watched as Bianca headed quickly around the top banister. The doors to her bedroom opened smoothly and clicked quietly shut again behind her. Eleanor cleared her throat. "You *will* stay for lunch, won't you?"

"I mean, I could eat. Probably."

Ember leaned forward and nodded. "I'm starving."

"Excellent. Twenty minutes." Eleanor spun toward the kitchen again. "Make yourselves at home."

Corian gazed up the staircase again, then peered around the wide landing. "Where's L'zar?"

Eleanor whirled and frowned at the nightstalker. "I kicked him out the second you left."

"Ah. I suppose that's not surprising." He let out a low chuckle. "Then it may be time to hunt down the Weaver. After lunch, of course."

"Yes. After lunch." The housekeeper eyed him and raised her eyebrows at Cheyenne, then bustled into the kitchen.

Ember put her hands on her hips. "You know, she has the best reactions. Nobody else got anywhere near that excited about everything we've done, and she wasn't even there with us."

"Makes it good to be home, right?"

Neros gazed around the massive foyer of the Summerlin estate. "Are all homes on Earth like this?"

Cheyenne snorted. "Not exactly. This place is one of a kind."

CHAPTER TWENTY-FIVE

After Eleanor's lunch of chicken salad and iced tea, which Neros guzzled like he hadn't had anything to drink in days, Cheyenne and her friends thanked Eleanor for the meal and got ready to leave Bianca's home.

Cheyenne went up to check on her mom and make sure she had everything she needed, and that she was okay, the curse was broken, and there wouldn't be any more emergencies popping up in the drow's life, at least when it came to her mom. The sight of Bianca curled up in her bed, fast asleep in the middle of the day, told Cheyenne everything she needed to know.

She wouldn't be lying there like that if anything still hurt. I'll come back in a few days.

Eleanor had disappeared to finish whatever she'd been doing when they arrived, and Maleshi opened a portal into Cheyenne's apartment when she saw the drow heading back down the stairs.

"She doing okay?" Ember asked.

"Sleeping like a baby. Normally I wouldn't say that about Bianca, but she gets a pass on this one. I'm ready to go home too."

They stepped through the portal with the nightstalkers and Neros trailing close behind. Neros stared in wide-eyed fascination at his cousin's apartment, the black leather couches, the north-facing wall of windows, and the mini-loft with Glen and all Cheyenne's gear above the bathroom. "What's up there?"

"My rig. Computer." When he still looked clueless, Cheyenne snorted. "Earthside tech, man. Really great Earthside tech."

"Can I see?" White light flared on the light-skinned drow's fingertips as he stared at the mini-loft.

"Yeah, maybe when I'm sure you won't blow anything up trying to study it." She clapped a hand on his shoulder and gestured at one of the leather recliners. "But you can take a seat."

Neros didn't argue as she guided him toward the chair. His eyes widened when he sat, and he wiggled against the cushions. "This is like floating and sitting at the same time."

Maleshi chuckled. "They don't have comfy furniture in Nor'ieth?"

"Not like this."

"Lean back." Cheyenne and bent to pull up the recliner's handle.

The chair stretched out, and Neros drew a sharp breath, his mouth open in a lazy smile of surprise. "I like this chair."

"Well, good." *Everything's brand-new to this guy, huh? Like a kid. Or an alien dropped on Earth for the first time.*

Neros laid back in the recliner and closed his eyes, enjoying the moment. Maleshi joined Cheyenne by the trunks of activators and muttered, "Probably a good idea to keep a close eye on him until he heads back to the other side."

"Yeah, I know. Letting a lost drow with no idea about how to interact with humans or magicals wander around Richmond? I don't think so."

Corian paced beside the wall of windows, growing increasingly agitated as he dialed his cell phone and pressed it to his ear over and over. "Damn."

"More drow trouble?" Maleshi asked.

He jammed his phone back into his pocket and shook his head. "No one's picking up at the warehouse. I told L'zar he needed a cell phone."

"Hey, so did I." Cheyenne shrugged.

"I need to find him. He might not be as bad as your cousin, kid, but letting L'zar run around town on his own isn't my number one choice, either."

"Yeah, okay."

Corian's silver gaze settled on hers for a moment. "You wouldn't happen to know where he might be hanging out these days, would you?"

Cheyenne barked a laugh. "I've only seen him in the middle of the road, at the warehouse, and at my mom's, in that order."

"Yeah, I didn't think so." Corian raised his hand and quickly summoned a portal into the warehouse. "Guess I'm going hunting. Keep in touch, kid."

"Definitely."

Maleshi grinned at him as he paused in front of the portal. "Oh, you can count on a call from me."

"Great." He smiled briefly at her, then scowled at the portal into Persh'al's warehouse and disappeared.

Maleshi cleared her throat and nodded at Cheyenne and Ember. "I've got a bed with my name on it and an entire two weeks' worth of laundry to tackle. I guess I'll see you on campus."

"I said I'd be out 'til Wednesday."

"Ah. I guess it goes without saying that if you think you need more time…"

"I don't think I will." Cheyenne shook her head. "Assuming everything else I'm trying to do over here isn't nearly as hard as purging the blight with my mom and burning a bunch of drow trees to save everyone."

Maleshi thrust a finger into the air. "All in one go, I might add."

"Right. That's kind of hard to beat."

The general winked at her, then raised her hands to open her own portal home. "You'll do great, kid. Those FRoE bastards are gonna get a run for their money with you at the helm. Let me know how it works with those activators, huh?"

"Yep. Thanks."

"Nah. You don't need to thank me for anything. May the Black Flame reign."

Cheyenne sighed, her shoulders slumping. "Seriously?"

The portal closed with a soft pop behind Maleshi, cutting off her low chuckle.

Ember lowered herself slowly onto the couch with a smile. "Why are you so against that name, anyway? I thought you said it was badass."

"It *is* badass." Cheyenne dropped into the other recliner. Neros hadn't moved a muscle since she'd pulled back the chair for him. *Let me guess. He's meditating.* "I have a thing about the reigning part."

"I mean, you do have a few extra skillsets no one else does. Crown or no Crown."

"I guess." Cheyenne ran a hand through her hair and sank back into the cushions. "But I don't have to be the O'gúl Crown to get things done. I never did."

"It has nothing to do with being the Crown," Neros muttered. Cheyenne and Ember looked at him in surprise, and he kept talking without opening his eyes. "The name binds you to who you are, Cheyenne. What you've done and what you have yet to do."

"What do they think I'm supposed to reign over when they say it?"

Neros shrugged where he lay in the recliner. "Your destiny."

"Whoa." Ember chuckled. "That puts a whole new spin on it."

Cheyenne frowned at her cousin, but a small smile played on her lips. "Okay. I can get behind that reasoning."

"I'm glad. Stop fighting who you are, and you won't be disappointed by others cheering you on."

She snorted. "I'm not disappointed. You know what? Let's table this conversation. I wanna make sure these activators made it through in one piece."

Cheyenne pushed out of the chair, went to the two trunks in front of the coffee table, and bent down to open the first one. As promised, a hundred pieces of metal were stacked on top of each other in the crates, nestled tightly to prevent them from moving around.

"Wow." Ember leaned forward for a closer look. "That's some serious tech."

"You've gotta be kidding me." Cheyenne picked up an activator and held it toward her friend. "She chose this as the layout?"

"It fits."

"Yeah, but I'm not gonna be using two hundred activators in the shape of a four-pointed star." The piece of delicately made metal tech clinked back down on the others, and Cheyenne shut the trunk before opening the second. "Yep. All two hundred. Jesus. She's either way cooler with me than she let on, or she's mocking me."

"Might be a little of both."

"Yeah, thanks, Em." Cheyenne slumped back to sit on her heels and shook her head. "I'm gonna have two hundred FRoE agents and refugee O'gúleesh running around Earth with my magical emblem behind their ears."

Ember choked back a snort, but when they looked at each other, they both burst out laughing.

"That belongs to our bloodline, does it not?" Neros picked his head up off the back of the recliner, struggling to rise from the nearly horizontal chair.

"I mean, it's not like the Verdys drow trademarked it or anything. It's just a shape."

"A very specific shape magicals are gonna recognize," Ember added.

"Maybe. Neros, you gotta push down on the lever on the side." Cheyenne forced herself not to laugh as her cousin flailed in the reclined chair, slapping at the sides and trying to sit up.

"What lever?"

"Right there on the outside. On the right."

"I can't."

"Well, don't break my chair, man."

Ember pointed at the recliner, which flashed purple and jerked into its upright position.

Neros thumped back against the cushion and blinked, his pale eyes wide. "Does that long chair do the same thing?"

"The couch?" Ember laughed. "Nope. This is just a couch."

"I think I'd prefer that." Neros rose from the recliner and gave the coffee table a wide berth, staring at it like he thought it would lash out at him at any second. Then he slowly turned, glanced at Ember, and cautiously lowered himself onto the opposite side of the couch. "This will do."

Cheyenne shook her head, unable to wipe the smile off her face. "Yeah, but what are we gonna do with you? That's what I'm wondering."

"I do not need much, Cheyenne, and I would like to return to Nor'ieth as soon as possible. This world is strange."

Ember clapped her hands together. "Wait 'til you get outside."

"Okay, hold on." Cheyenne pointed at her. "Let's take it one step at a time, huh? For now, I guess Neros is gonna have to couch-surf 'til we figure out how to get him back across."

"Surf?" Her cousin frowned at her. "What is 'surf?'"

"Ridin' the waves, dude." Ember mimed a wave with her hand. Neros' eyes widened, and he looked quickly around their apartment.

"Where?"

"Jeez, Em. Will you stop torturing the guy?"

Ember bit her lip and nestled back into the couch with a small laugh.

"It means you'll stay with us for a while. You can sleep on the couch."

"Hmm." Neros ran a hand over the armrest. "When do I return?"

"I don't know. I can't take you back across the Border right now. I've got all these activators to set up and a meeting with the FRoE to prepare for, whatever the hell that's supposed to look like."

"We could drop him off in Colonial Williamsburg. Easy access to a portal there."

"Yeah, that would be a good idea, Em. Except for the part where I'm not so sure he'd make it on his own."

"Why not?"

Cheyenne grinned and jerked her chin at her cousin. "Neros."

"Yes, Cheyenne?"

"If you were walking through the middle of nowhere and a bunch of creepy monsters came out of the shadows to attack you, what would you do?"

He blinked at her, completely expressionless. "Nothing."

"Yeah, that's what I thought. You hugged Ba'rael into Nor'ieth, and you'd probably try to hug the in-between monsters too. Only we have no idea if that would work to get you out of there."

Ember chuckled. "Lover not a fighter, huh?"

Neros stared at her. "I have no reason to fight."

"Okay, see?"

"Yep." Ember grinned at the light-skinned drow and nodded. "Point taken."

Cheyenne tapped the top of the crates and eyed her confused-looking cousin. "Think you can handle hanging out with us for a while until we can get you back home?"

"Back where I belong." A small smile lifted the corners of his mouth. "Where you belong with me."

"Yeesh. Let's hold off on the creepy cousin thing for a while, okay?

Better yet, don't bring it up. We'll have fun." *I hope.* Cheyenne pushed herself off the floor and stacked the activator trunks.

"Do you have any icy teeth?"

The women shot him puzzled looks, and Ember let out something that was half-laugh, half-groan. "Say what?"

"We drank it at your other home, Cheyenne. With the human."

"Um."

Ember burst out laughing and vigorously shook her head. "You mean, 'iced tea?'"

Neros blinked at her. "If that is what you call it. I would like more."

"Great. Eleanor got my looney-toon cousin hooked on caffeine."

Ember howled on the couch, sliding down on the cushions and fighting for breath.

"Do you have any?"

"No, Neros. We don't have any tea. Just water."

"Or coffee!"

Cheyenne shot her friend a warning glare, but the laughter was contagious.

Neros looked at them and cracked a small smile. "I like it here."

"Great. At least you're going with the flow." Cheyenne blinked the tears of laughter away and pointed at him as she bent toward the trunks. "Just don't get too used to it."

"I have no intention of staying in your world, Cheyenne."

A sharp knock came on the door, and Neros quickly stood. "Why is someone hitting your door?"

"You guys don't knock in Nor'ieth?"

"Why would we?"

"Okay, you can sit down now. It's fine." Cheyenne shook her head as she walked to the door. *I hope doors and privacy aren't gonna be an issue with him staying here.*

She looked through the peephole in the door, rolled her eyes, and jerked open the front door. "Matthew. What's up?"

"Can I come in?" Their neighbor ran a hand through his hair, his eyes wide with concern. "I think we need to talk."

"I mean, I guess."

"Thanks, Cheyenne." He stormed past her before she'd finished opening the door all the way and laughed.

"That settles it then, huh?" She closed the door behind her, and Matthew stopped short.

"Ember."

"Hey." She raised her eyebrows but didn't offer him a warm smile as she stood. "What's going on?"

"You're standing."

"Oh. Yeah. Recent development. Thanks for noticing."

Matthew blinked at the light-skinned drow with wide, washed-out golden eyes, looked at Cheyenne, and did a quick double-take.

"Yeah, I know. The resemblance is uncanny, right?"

Matthew rubbed his mouth. "Should I come back later? Kinda looks like you guys are busy."

"He'll probably still be here later, so it doesn't matter."

"Oh." Matthew's face scrunched in confusion. "Who is he?"

"Matthew, meet Neros," Cheyenne said dryly, gesturing between them. "My cousin."

"Okay."

"Cheyenne, do you often invite humans into your home?" Neros asked with pure curiosity.

"No. Matthew here is our super-awesome neighbor, huh?" She shrugged. "And maybe the only human who's been here since we moved in."

"Moved what?"

"Since we've lived here," Ember clarified.

"Has that been long?"

Matthew pointed at Neros. "Is he okay?"

"I mean, depends on how you define 'okay.' But yeah. He's just foreign."

Cheyenne and Ember snorted and immediately tried to cover it.

Ember lifted her chin and composed herself, blinking quickly at Matthew. "You said we needed to talk."

"Yeah. Does your cousin know about what's going on?"

"In his own way. He's not gonna tell anyone. Trust me." Cheyenne gestured briefly at the recliners. "Have a seat, then."

Matthew stared at her in surprise.

"Yes, I'm inviting you to sit down in my living room. Get over it." Cheyenne shut the door, then headed for her regular recliner and sat.

Matthew headed cautiously toward the second chair, staring at the magicals. Neros sank back on the couch and reached toward the recliner. "Be careful. That one moves, and it is difficult to get out again."

"Wait, what?"

"Just ignore him. It's fine." Cheyenne sat and nodded. "We're listening."

CHAPTER TWENTY-SIX

"I got a visit from some odd people this morning," Matthew started. He leaned forward in the recliner, propping his forearms on his thighs. Neros stared at him, waiting for the chair to move in some odd way. "I think they were government. Maybe Feds."

"Were they FRoE?" Cheyenne asked.

"I don't know. They didn't identify themselves, but they had that look, you know?"

"That 'government-y' look?" Ember muttered.

"Yeah." He dropped his head forward between hunched shoulders. "It was the way they were asking about everything. They knew about Combined Reality, which isn't that big of a deal. It's not a secret, just not publicized."

"Okay."

"Then they started talking about Les. You know, my uncle."

Cheyenne straightened in her chair. "Yeah, we know who he is."

"Right. They brought up his involvement with the FRoE and the war machines, they called it. Wanted to know how I was planning to move forward now that my uncle's been indicted, but that isn't a public thing either, right?"

Ember shrugged. "Probably not. We don't know."

"You want our help because some government-y people knocked on your door to follow up on your uncle's arrest?"

Matthew shook his head. "No, that was just the small talk. They know about my program too. For the new tech, right? The kind you magical people wanna use."

Cheyenne snorted. "Yeah, we magical people love tech."

"Okay, you know what I mean. I have no idea how they found out about it if they're not with the FRoE. They still could be. I don't know. But they offered to buy the program from me."

"Really." Cheyenne folded her arms and frowned at him.

"Yeah. And all of Combined Reality. Proprietary tech. Research. Personnel. Security. All of it."

Ember draped her arm over the armrest. "How much did they offer?"

Matthew looked sharply at her. "Enough to make me think they know exactly what they want to do with my company. And no, their plan wasn't part of the offer."

"What did you tell them?" Cheyenne asked.

"I said I had to think about it." He shrugged. "I'm not an idiot, Cheyenne. They didn't give me names, or at least not real ones, and the card they handed me doesn't have anything but a phone number. Which I couldn't trace."

"Interesting." Cheyenne nodded slowly. "Good job not cashing in like an idiot. Which you clearly aren't." He rolled his eyes. "It's a good idea to figure out who these people are and why they want your program so badly first. You never know who's trying to get their hands on your stuff, right?"

"Well, yeah. I told you I wasn't gonna make that kind of mistake again."

"Smart move."

"Thanks, Matthew." Ember leaned forward on the couch and nodded. "Seriously."

"Yeah. It seemed like the right thing to do."

"Hey, speaking of your tech system." Cheyenne slapped her thighs and stood. "You still owe us after that last little slip-up with your products in the wrong hands."

Matthew stared at her as she approached the stacked trunks of activators and frowned. "I know. You kind of make that hard to forget."

"Here's how you can pay off some of that debt." She opened the lid of the top trunk, grabbed a four-pointed-star activator, and tossed it to him.

Matthew caught it with a jerky, fumbling motion, then stared at the activator, turning it over in his hands. "What's this?"

"This, Matt, is more O'gúl tech from across the Border."

"What?"

Cheyenne chuckled. "Better tech. Way better. So, how about it? You and your program help me get these activators working for magicals here on Earth, and we'll call your debt paid."

"Are you sure? I mean, after what happened last time?"

"Look, I'm not with the Bull's Head, and I definitely don't want to program anything that's gonna start a war between magicals and humans."

Matthew looked slowly at Ember.

"She's trying to make it better for everyone over here," Ember assured him. "And it'll be a lot easier to do with your help."

"We've got four days to make this happen, neighbor." Cheyenne closed the trunk and latched the lid again, then folded her arms. "Four days for you to work your magic and get your program up and running inside that."

"Magic." A nervous chuckle escaped him. "Right. I don't even know what this thing is."

"That didn't stop you the last time. And I'll be around."

"I don't know."

"I'll pay you."

Matthew straightened in the recliner. "You're serious."

"Come on. You know me. I don't fuck around."

Ember snorted.

"Okay. I'll help you."

"Good choice."

"But I can't take your money, Cheyenne. I screwed up when I did all that with my uncle for business and didn't ask the right questions. I'll do it again with you to make things right, not to make a profit."

Cheyenne looked at Ember in surprise, and the fae pursed her lips, then gave a small shrug.

Yeah. I'd say that's an impressive improvement of character.

"You know, Matthew," she said, turning toward their neighbor and pointing at him, "I wasn't sure about you at first."

He scoffed. "Oh, yeah? I had no idea."

"But now I have the feeling we'll get along fine as neighbors. Hey, maybe even business partners."

With a crooked smile, Matthew shook his head and studied the activator again. "Don't take it too far."

"Never say never."

CHAPTER TWENTY-SEVEN

Okay. Got a hundred ninety-nine activators and a hell of a lot of work to do in four days.

Cheyenne Summerlin sat on the floor in her living room with the two heavy metal trunks she had smuggled across the Border in front of her. Only one of them was open, and the cold, lightweight metal of one of Elarit's newest activators made her smile.

Compared to all the other tight deadlines I've worked with, this should be a piece of cake.

The toilet flushed in the bathroom beneath the mini-loft, followed by water running in the sink. When Ember stepped out and shut the door behind her, she was grinning.

"I can't even tell you how awesome it is to be able to walk in and out of the bathroom. I mean, sure, floating with fae magic is a hell of a lot better than a wheelchair, but this?" She slapped her thighs and laughed. "This is what it's all about."

Cheyenne smiled at her friend. "I seriously hope the bathroom's not the highlight of you getting your legs back, Em."

"Well, not the highlight." Ember strutted across the living room and slumped down into her usual seat on the couch. "But one of them, for sure."

On the opposite side of the couch, Neros leaned forward and stared at the bathroom with his wide, washed-out golden eyes. "What is behind that door?"

Ember and Cheyenne exchanged amused looks. "The bathroom."

"And it's a wonderful place to walk into?"

Cheyenne snorted. "Only if you've been holding it long enough."

"Holding what?" Neros slowly turned to look at her.

For real? My crazy cousin gets stranded on Earth and doesn't even know what a bathroom is?

"Don't tell me you and the Olfarím never had to relieve yourselves in Nor'ieth."

The pale-skinned drow frowned. "Of course. That's a natural process." The point dawned on him, and he stared at the bathroom door again. "Why would anyone build a room for that? Then it's all in the same place."

Ember fought back a laugh. "Indoor plumbing, Neros. Conveniences of the modern world, right? Kind of weird to say, seeing as all the tech in Ambar'ogúl is way more advanced than anything we have going on Earthside."

"Not if Persh'al doesn't figure out how to break down that power-surge block in Hangivol's system." Cheyenne returned her attention to the activator in her hand, which was shaped like a four-pointed star. "If Matthew Thomas the tech mogul can get these things up and running for us like he did with the war machines, this world might be more advanced than the other side. For magicals, at least."

Ember crossed one leg over the other and flung an arm over the armrest. "I can't believe she made you two hundred activators shaped like that."

"I know." The drow shook her head. "Still feels like a joke."

"Or a compliment," Neros added. "That is the physical form of our magic, Cheyenne."

"Yep." She glanced at her cousin, who leaned so far forward on the couch to peer into the open trunk that she expected him to fall on his face at any minute. "I feel like we just had this conversation."

"We did not." Neros cocked his head comically far until his ear almost reached his shoulder, his pale drow eyes leaping from one stack of unused activators to the next beside it. "What is the purpose of so many?"

Cheyenne shrugged. "Party favors."

Ember snorted and covered her mouth.

Neros stared blankly at his cousin.

"Right. No party favors in Nor'ieth." *No parties either, probably. Just a bunch of alien-looking Olfarím and concentrated magic that smells like vinegar.* "They're for the O'gúleesh on this side, Neros. And a handful of Earthside magicals to start. If they can handle it."

"You would give the physical form of your magic to others to use?"

"It's not my magic, it's only a shape." Cheyenne studied the star activator. *Same as the piece of his magic I still have locked up in that Darkglass box. I still have no idea how to use that. Good thing I haven't had to.* "You don't know what an activator is either, do you?"

Neros sat up and looked at his cousin and the fae sitting on the other end of the couch. "I do not."

"And why would you?" Ember asked, grinning at him. "All the magic you could ever possibly want right at your fingertips in Nor'ieth and no tech to sync it with. Sounds like a good life to me."

Cheyenne snorted. "Sounds boring as hell."

"As soon as Cheyenne sets up these activators and hands them out to the right magicals, we'll figure out how to get you back there." Ember nodded at the light-skinned drow. "I bet you miss it."

"Not particularly." Neros slowly gazed around their apartment. "I will return when it is time. But this world, I do not understand."

Cheyenne nodded, not bothering to conceal her smile as she studied the star activator. "I don't think you'd understand the rest of Ambar'ogúl either."

"But there, the Everweave shines brightly. Here it is dark." Neros spoke with contemplative flatness. "It is fascinating."

"Well, at least you're not pissed about being dragged out of your home plane by a *uanáj.*"

"Why would I be?"

Cheyenne looked at him and raised her eyebrows. *He's so disconnected from reality, I don't even know how to answer that.*

"I'm gonna see what I can find in this thing." She lifted the activator, then rose from the floor and closed the lid of the trunk with her shoe. "These are off-limits too, by the way. Got it?"

"I will not touch your boxes of magic, Cheyenne."

"They're not…never mind." With a sigh, she turned around and headed toward the metal-grate stairs up to the mini-loft. "If you have to touch anything else, ask Ember about it first, huh?"

Neros looked at Ember, expressionless.

The fae chuckled. "That was Cheyenne-code for 'Ember, keep an eye on Neros.' Which'll be fun." When Cheyenne's cousin merely kept staring at her, she clapped her hands together and nodded. "So. You hungry?"

"No."

"Right. I am, so come on. Let's go see what's in the fridge."

"What is that?"

"Oh, boy." Ember waved him along with her as she stood and headed around the couch toward the kitchen. "This is what it would be like if babies could talk right out of the womb, isn't it?"

"I am not a baby."

"Here on Earth, Neros, you might as well be. You and I are gonna fix that."

With a snort, Cheyenne reached the top of the stairs and headed for her office chair in front of her computer setup. *As long as he stays curious and doesn't try to do anything on his own, he'll be fine here.*

"This is a fridge." The door opened with a sucking hiss, bottles of salad dressing and condiments rattling on the shelves. "Stores our food and keeps it cold all in one place."

"I do not understand."

"Uh, okay. Which part?"

"Does your food not grow from the earth on this world?"

Ember squinted at him. "I mean, it does. And then it gets bagged up and processed and shipped out to stores and… You know what? Let's start with something easy." A jar popped open. "Pickle?"

His first taste of Earth food. Only Ember would choose pickles.

Cheyenne laughed silently at her desk and tried to focus on the star activator in her hand. The silver-coil activator behind her ear didn't pull up anything, which could have meant either Elarit's activator still needed to be turned on somehow, or Cheyenne's had stopped working on this side.

I'm a fan of what's behind Door Number One.

She powered up her computer and grinned as Glenn's liquid cooling system gurgled and the fans kicked on. Lines of simple human-tech code scrolled across her vision, and she looked back down at the four-pointed star.

So it needs a power-up. Might as well take a look at what we're working with while good ol' Matt figures out how to improve it across the hall.

The silver coil behind her ear offered slight resistance as she pulled it away, the pinch a little more prominent. Blinking away the sensation, Cheyenne set down her activator and brought the new one up to her ear.

The cold metal of the four-pointed star felt like ice, then a much more intense pinch and a flood of magical energy raced up the side of her head and into the space behind her eyes. "Shit."

"Cheyenne?" Neros called. "Are you unwell?"

"No, I'm good." Gritting her teeth, she shut her eyes against the sensation of the activator trying to sync with her magic. *And no system to tap into to help that happen.* She quickly removed the star activator and set it down before leaning back in her chair.

"Hey, where are you going?" Ember asked.

"She's hurt."

"Uh, no, she's not." Ember chuckled and looked up at Cheyenne's not-so-private office. "Trust me, Neros. That's her thinking face. When she's hurt, she bottles it all up inside and won't let anyone see it."

"Cheyenne?"

The drow raised a dismissive hand as she replaced her activator behind her ear. "Listen to the fae. She knows what she's talking about." Cheyenne peered around Glenn's monitor and nodded at her cousin. "I'm fine."

"See? She's fine. And she said, 'Listen to the fae.'" Ember grabbed Neros by the shoulders and guided him back to the kitchen's center island. "So stand here and eat your pickle, huh?"

"Is it magic?"

Ember laughed. "What? No, it's a pickle!"

"It smells like home."

"Oh. Huh. Yeah, I guess it kinda does." The fae slowly lowered her half-eaten pickle to the counter. "But I'm willing to bet you've never tasted anything like this. Come on, man. It's part of the whole Earthside experience."

The crunch of Neros thoughtfully chewing on a dill pickle spear filled the apartment. Cheyenne shook her head and tuned the two of them out as her activator pulled up only two scrolling lines of code on the metal star on her desk.

Command Alpha000. System not detected

Okay. Advanced tech Earthside. Didn't disappear or blow up, and apparently, I am the on-switch. We don't need Hangivol's system, just our own.

She turned the metal star over in her hands, studying the same message scrolling across the surface in at least three variations. Her activator displayed multiple prompts for digging out whatever layers of information were hidden inside, but all of those pulled up the same thing.

Command Alpha000. System not detected

A new one caught her eye in a brief flash of yellow light.

Awaiting system pairing

Yeah, okay. I can't do shit without Matthew's program. He better be as good at this as he says he is. Or better.

Cheyenne's phone buzzed in her pocket, and she pulled it out to see Inolu Rosh's number on the screen. *Great.*

She answered the call and raised the phone to her ear. "Please tell me your new houseguest is still locked up."

"Shut the fuck up, drow, and tell me where it is!"

Cheyenne held the phone away from her ear and frowned at it. "Sure thing, *Siliwari.* Wanna tell me what the hell you're talking about?"

"I don't have time for your useless games, Cheyenne," Inolu snarled. "You may have handed over the Spider willingly, but I'm not a fucking moron. What kind of shit are you trying to pull, huh? You step into my house, break my security scanner, and force the Underman out into the open for your fucking family reunion. I have half a mind to bill you double for that!"

"Okay, first of all, I'm not paying you more than we agreed on to sit here and listen to you cuss me out and accuse me of taking whatever it is."

"My calibrax is gone." The banebreaker's snarl made Cheyenne jerk her head away from the phone again. "Do you understand English? Gone. And the only thing that changed between the time I had it and the time I didn't is that you were in my house playing with portals. Where is it?"

"I have no idea what that is," Cheyenne muttered.

"No idea, huh?"

"Yeah. We both understand English. Sorry you lost your calibrax."

"Ha! Lost!" The other end of the line rustled, and Cheyenne could picture Inolu mashing her mouth against her phone's speaker when her words came out muffled and squashed. "I didn't lose it, drow. It was stolen!"

"Well, it wasn't me. I got everything I needed from you, and then I left. We all did."

"You're useless."

"Thanks." Cheyenne rolled her eyes. "I'm guessing you're not gonna try to turn this around and ask me to help you find this thing then, right?"

"I don't want anything from you. We're finished. Stay away from my home, do you understand? You're no longer welcome."

"Great. Clears up a few hours in my schedule. Anything else?"

"Yeah. Keep an eye out for your bill. I'd add this on top of it too, but the calibrax doesn't have a fucking price!" There was a sharp click, then the line went dead.

"Jesus." Cheyenne lowered her phone and blinked. *Leave it to the banebreaker. Always an exciting conversation.*

"Everything okay?" Ember asked, sliding a full glass of water across the island toward Neros.

"Inolu thinks I stole something from her." Cheyenne slid her phone back into her pocket and leaned toward the iron railing around the mini-loft to meet her friend's gaze. "Ever heard of a calibrax?"

Ember shook her head. "Sounds like a fancy watch. What about you, Nor'ieth boy?"

Neros noisily slurped water from the glass and stared at her.

"Yeah, didn't think so. I wouldn't worry about it too much,

Cheyenne. That banebreaker's not the sanest Siliwari in the wherever-she-came-from."

"Right." The drow glanced down at the star activator on her desk again, its repeating lines of code reminding her that there was no system to connect to to bring the thing online. *Something tells me Inolu's not the type of magical to leave her valuables around where anyone could find them. And that alarm went off right before she kicked us out.*

"Whoa, whoa. Hey." Ember lurched after Neros, who stood beside an open drawer at the counter. "If you're looking for something, man, tell me. And be careful, okay? Not everything in a kitchen's childproof."

"What is this?"

Ember folded her arms. "That's a fork."

The pale-skinned drow cocked his head and twirled the silverware in his fingers. He brought the tip of it to his mouth for a quick taste, wrinkled his nose, stuck the tines into the thick waves of his bone-white hair, and pulled it through like a comb.

"Ha! Okay, Ariel. That's not what it's for." She headed toward him and grabbed the fork. "Let's leave the dishes where they are, or I have a feeling we'll be running the dishwasher more than anyone in their right mind ever should."

"Who is Ariel?"

"What? Shit. Of course, you've never seen *The Little Mermaid*. Okay. Moving on. You wanna try any more food?"

"I want to see the other rooms." Neros turned toward Ember's bedroom.

"Yeah, okay. I guess." She shoved the silverware drawer shut with her hip and followed him. "But don't touch anything. And no, I don't share my hairbrush, either. Not even with your cousin."

Cheyenne snorted. *It's gonna be a long night.*

CHAPTER TWENTY-EIGHT

Neros slurped the last noodle of the Chinese takeout they'd had delivered before the place closed, blinking as teriyaki sauce splattered his cheek. "I do like this."

"Yeah, it's kind of a staple." Ember stuck her chopsticks in the empty takeout box and set it on the coffee table. "At least for me. Here." She handed him a wrapped fortune cookie and a napkin.

Neros sat on the couch beside her, pinching the napkin between his fingers and cupping the fortune cookie in his other palm, and stared at her.

"One's for wiping your face," Cheyenne said with her last bite of kung pao chicken halfway to her mouth. "The other one you get to eat."

"For dessert," Ember added.

"If I'd wanted to desert this meal, I wouldn't have eaten so much."

Both women laughed. Ember tossed Cheyenne a fortune cookie and took one for herself. "Something delicious at the end of the meal, Neros. It's fun. You get to read your fortune inside."

The pale drow's eyes widened. "This is where we read the Weave in your world?"

"What?"

Cheyenne snorted and pulled up the lever on the black leather recliner to lay back, crossing one ankle over the other. "It's not the Weave, cuz. Just a game."

"That seems rather empty." Neros stared at the napkin, licked his lips, then gently pressed the paper to his face without wiping. He held onto it, still pinching it between his fingers like it was a mildewed rag.

"Well, yeah. I guess some of the things we do Earthside feel pretty empty when you think about it like that."

Cheyenne peeled open the wrapper around her cookie. "One might even say most of it is empty."

"Oh, come on. Easy for you to say. You're the prophesied drow halfling with the Vessel as her mom, a trust fund, and some kinda crazy-weird ability to read technology the way Neros here reads the Weave. Just because you'd rather sit with your computer all day trying to program activators, it doesn't mean the rest of us have the luxury of handing over the throne of an entire world to someone else."

"Wow, Em. You really packed a lot in there."

"It just came to me." Ember shrugged, then nodded at the fortune cookie in Neros' other hand. "Go on. Try it."

The fae ripped open the package of her cookie and broke the hard, processed shell of sugar in half. Grinning, she popped one half in her mouth and crunched, then pulled out the thin slip of paper and straightened it out to read it. "'The test of true friendship lies in how much you are willing to endure when times are hard.' Huh."

Cheyenne snorted and cracked her cookie in half. "Didn't need to order Chinese food to get that brilliant bit of wisdom."

"Oh, come on. It's true. You know, I wish they'd keep the fortune in fortune cookies. This is telling me something I already know."

"Well, maybe next time, we'll order a giant side of Oracle cookies for you, huh?" Cheyenne crunched down on her cookie and tried to catch the sharp, hard fragments flying out of her mouth. "You know, crack it open and *bam*. There's your Oracle with your private prophecy waiting to be unleashed."

Ember flicked the side of the empty to-go carton. "They're gonna need a bigger box."

The crunch and rustle of plastic came from Neros. Both women stared at him and burst out laughing as the drow bit down even harder on the crushed cookie and the unopened wrapper around it.

"Dude." Ember cocked her head at him.

"Is this not desert?"

"Okay, stop. Just stop." She grabbed another napkin from the table, chuckling as she used it as a glove to take the whole package from his hand. "Did you not see us open ours?"

"Most peels of the fruit in Nor'ieth can be eaten if we choose."

"Fruit!" Ember ripped open the plastic, lifted Neros' hand toward her, and dumped the crushed cookie pieces into his cupped palm, then shot Cheyenne a sidelong glance. "I never thought I'd have to explain processed sugar and plastic wrappers to anyone. Maybe that should be your job. Family priorities and all."

"You're doing great, Em."

Ember snorted, chucked the wrapper into another empty to-go container, and pointed at Neros' hand. "There. Eat the cookie. Crumbs. And not that little paper in there. Yes, technically paper comes from plants too, but it's not the food kind."

Neros picked up one of the larger pieces and stuck it in his mouth. His eyes widened even before he bit down, and the tiniest smile flickered at the corner of his mouth. "I like this too."

"Yeah. That's what it's for." Ember popped the other half of her cookie into her mouth. "Time to read your fortune."

Neros plucked the strip of paper from the pile of crumbs and frowned as he turned it back and forth. "I do not know these signs."

"The what?"

"See, that right there is why Elarit made me two hundred activators to smuggle across the Border." Cheyenne pointed at the strip of paper between her cousin's fingers. "The O'gúleesh making the crossing Earthside have no idea how to read English."

"For real?" Ember's chewing slowed. "So, the other side has French-speaking raug and Golras are fluent in every Chinese dialect, but no one can read and write."

"They don't have to, Em. I mean, they can read O'gúleesh in all the tech, but why would anyone have to write anything when they can put it down in the system?"

"Still. That's one of the first things anybody learns."

"And not even the last thing on the list of what the FRoE thinks is important to teach the refugees. They let them off the reservations with a pat on the back and wish them luck. R'mahr still doesn't remember the word for car."

"Okay, I get that. No cars in Ambar'ogúl. But there have to be pens and paper, right?"

"When was the last time you pulled out a pen and paper to write anything, Em?"

The fae shot her friend a playful frown. "Can't remember. Probably not since I started using the Notes app on my phone—Oh."

"Yeah."

"Okay." Ember turned toward Neros and wiggled her fingers at his fortune as he crunched another mouthful of crumbs. "Give me that. I'll read it for you."

He offered it to her, then crammed what was left of the cookie bits into his mouth and smiled happily.

"Fortune for Neros Verdys."

"That is not my name."

"Oh. Sorry." Ember glanced at Cheyenne, the corners of her mouth turned down in a sheepish grimace. "I assumed. Hey, look. One more thing you and Cheyenne have in common, right? No Verdys."

Neros stared at her and licked the cookie dust off his palm.

"Do you have a last name?"

The pale drow swallowed. "I only need the one. And none at all in Nor'ieth."

"Right. 'Cause you're all connected and everybody's one and all that. They call you *Aut Na'mor*, huh?" When he didn't reply, Ember chuckled wryly and returned her attention to his fortune. "Moving on. 'Home is where the heart is.' Jesus, the creativity levels are really running low with these things." She dropped the slip into an empty container with the rest of the trash and shrugged. "Sorry, Neros. Nothing fun and exciting for you today."

He stared at the container and slowly tilted his head. "I appreciate it. The message. Truth cookies would be a more fitting name."

Ember barked a laugh and shook her head. "You wanna introduce the truth cookie to Earth, man, I'm behind you one hundred percent."

Cheyenne ate the rest of her broken first half and smiled. "It's better than Weave cookies."

"Okay, you're up." The drow stared at her friend. "Come on. Read your fortune."

"I didn't know we were hosting a sharing circle, Em."

"Oh, my god." The fae playfully rolled her eyes. "It's not like we're sitting around sharing our deepest, darkest secrets. What, you've never had fortune cookies with your friends?"

Cheyenne raised an eyebrow. "The only people I spent any time with until I started at VCU were Bianca, Eleanor, and a stable of private doctors. Try to picture my mom sitting at the dining table with a spread like this and reading a piece of paper she took out of what isn't even really a cookie."

Ember scrunched her face and said, "As weird as this sounds, it's easier to picture Bianca drinking with nightstalkers and goblins."

"Yeah, because that actually happened."

"So that makes this your first time." Ember grinned. "Don't make me come over there, drow. Read your damn fortune."

"Yes, Cheyenne." Neros nodded and leaned forward over his lap. "I want to hear your truth as well."

Cheyenne snorted. "Not my truth. These are randomly tossed into a bag, by the way."

"Just do it!"

"Jesus, Em. Fine." Drawing the thin paper from the other half of her cookie, Cheyenne rolled her eyes and looked down. "Huh."

"What?" Ember chuckled. "I bet it's good."

"Sure. So good, a tiny piece of paper couldn't possibly encompass the power of my truth."

"Okay, now you're being an ass."

"Nope. It's blank."

Ember's eager smile morphed into a scowl. "What? Give me that." She leaned across the coffee table to take the paper, then squinted at it, flipped it over twice, and held it up to the light. "Those bastards. Cheated you out of your fortune. They can't do that."

The blank paper joined the rest of the trash in the empty containers.

"Maybe it's karma." Cheyenne shrugged and stuck the other half of the cookie into her mouth. "I've had so many real prophecies in the last few months, everything else is tapped out."

Ember glared at the remains of their dinner. "Someone needs to do something about that."

"I don't think anyone's gonna give us a refund for our malfunctioning free cookie, Em."

"Very funny. Let me tell you something. If it wasn't for fortune cookies with my cousins, Chicago would've been a hell of a lot crappier where I grew up."

"But you got out, and they didn't."

"Did their truths tell them to stay?" Neros asked.

"What?" Ember frowned at him, and Cheyenne laughed. "No. These things aren't real, anyway."

"I would like to see what is real." Neros stood from the couch and seemed to float as he approached the window wall. "Like those lights."

"That's the north end of Richmond and probably a little bit of DC." Cheyenne leaned back in the recliner again and folded her hands behind her head. "Best view you're gonna get of all that is from right here."

"Take me to them."

"Yeah, it's a little late for that, Neros." Ember stood and headed toward him. "Maybe step away from the windows before you throw yourself through them or something."

"Why would I do that?"

"I don't know. You opened a portal to the Heart on the back of a flying stingray and saved Cheyenne's life by hugging your mom into oblivion. There's no telling with you." She guided him back to the couch.

"It was not oblivion," he muttered.

"Yeah, well, we didn't know that until a demon opened a portal right to you, did we?"

"It was an *uanáj*."

"We figured that part out too," Cheyenne added as she sat up and cranked the recliner back into place. "Perks of dealing with the most powerful banebreaker banished to Earth, right?"

The pale drow didn't resist as Ember gently pushed him back onto the couch. "That banebreaker has no idea what she's doing, Cheyenne."

"Funny. She broke the curse on my mom and sucked all the glowing runes out of her body. On purpose. I'd say that's a pretty good start.

"She has no business summoning her *uanáj* to open doors."

Ember shrugged. "It looked a lot more like a takeover than a summons, honestly."

"Which is precisely my point." Neros turned slowly to look up at the fae, watching her intently as she sank back down onto the couch. "The balance has been restored. The threads were completed, as was foreseen."

A brief, flashing image of the Nimlothar forest passed through Cheyenne's mind, every Hangivol drow, Cazerel and his raug, Maleshi and the goblins, Ember and Bianca, all of them lying dead amidst the ruins of their final battle with the blight as ash from the burned trees rained down around her. She blinked quickly and shook her head.

"A new age has begun for all of us," Neros continued in his creepily intense way, "and the *uanáj* do not care one way or the other how it is handled. It doesn't affect them the same way."

"I mean, yeah, that makes sense," Ember said. "From what I've seen, it doesn't look like matters of life and death apply to them."

"Okay, I think that's enough about life and death and *uanáj*." Cheyenne slapped her thighs and pushed to her feet. "And it's late."

Ember looked at her in surprise. "You okay?"

"We had a hell of a day. Breaking curses and locking the Spider up in a banebreaker's cage. You know, the usual." Cheyenne ran a hand through her hair and sighed. "Sleep might be the best thing for all of us, right? Especially Mr. Curious over here."

Neros cocked his head at her. "I don't require sleep, Cheyenne."

"Well, you're on Earth now, so you should probably try it."

"I don't see why there would be a difference."

Cheyenne shot Ember a "help me out or I might kill him" look.

"The difference," Ember said, eyeing her friend back and hoping Cheyenne got the silent message about patience, "is that you're on a couch in our apartment. I'd bet everything in it that you haven't slept under anything nearly as soft as what I'm about to pull out for you."

"An easy bet to make when I don't sleep."

"So, bodily functions requiring a bathroom are natural, but you get to stay up for days on end without needing to lay down, huh?" Neros said nothing. Ember rolled her shoulders as she headed toward her room. "Don't go anywhere."

The living room fell silent once Ember disappeared into the kitchen. Neros scanned the apartment one more time, then settled his gaze on his cousin. "There is an Oracle here, is there not? Close to us now?"

"I mean, it's about a twenty-minute drive, but yeah." Cheyenne looked him up and down. "Don't even think about it. I've had enough of Oracles."

"An Oracle would have the means to—"

"The answer's no. So drop it," she snapped, and added, "Please. The only thing I'm trying to focus on right now is getting those activators powered up so I can help a bunch of O'gúleesh with their problems. The last thing I need is to stir up more of my problems by taking you to see Gúrdu. Or any Oracle."

"That is the Oracle's name?"

"Yeah. The raug. And I'm sure he's doing fine."

"Okay!" Ember pulled her bedroom door shut behind her and rejoined them with an extra pillow and a massively puffy blanket of gray-blue faux fur. "You may not have to sleep, but pull this over yourself, and I promise you won't be able to stay awake."

Neros frowned when she offered it to him. "What creature is this?"

Ember fought back a laugh. "The kind that doesn't need to be fed, cleaned up after, or let outside. 'Cause it's a blanket."

"You good, Em?"

The fae thumped the pillow against the armrest and fluffed it, then shook out the blanket. "You're trying to sneak off to bed, aren't you?"

"Yes."

"Yeah, sure. You go take a load off. I'll tuck in your five-thousand-year-old cousin like it's his first night camping in the woods. No problem."

Neros reached out slowly to stroke the blue furry blanket beside him. "Not quite two thousand."

Ember stuck her hands on her hips. "That young, huh? Well, don't expect a bedtime story or anything."

He stared blankly at her.

"Right. It's funny if you know anything about Earth kids. Forget it. Don't get up off this couch until one of us steps out of our rooms, okay?"

"Understood."

Ember grinned at Cheyenne. "Look at that. Something he *does* understand."

"We're getting through." Cheyenne pointed at her cousin. "We're serious about the staying on the couch part."

Neros leaned over to get a closer look at the fuzzy blanket. "Good night, Cheyenne."

"Yeah. 'Night."

"Good night, Ember."

Laughing, the fae turned to her bedroom and slapped the light switch on the wall beside the door. The overhead lights clicked off. "See you in the morning, you kook."

CHAPTER TWENTY-NINE

As exhausted as she was, Cheyenne spent at least an hour tossing around in her bed, unable to fall asleep. *Just my luck. I get knocked out over and over when there's no time to waste, and now that the imminent threat of two worlds' destruction is gone, I'm too wired to pass out.*

When she finally managed to doze off, her dreams replayed that final battle at the Nimlothar forest, the trees and drow burning with green and black flames, screaming, lending their lives to the twisted trunks and near-dead husks of what used to give them power. And Bianca turning on her to blast the blight out of her daughter as she had with the land and the creatures and the magicals too far gone to the poison.

Then those images disappeared and she was sitting up in her bed, staring through the darkness at the glow of Neros' golden eyes. "What the fuck?"

"You plague yourself uselessly, Cheyenne." Only his glowing eyes moved within his silhouette. "The Weave unravels in both directions or not at all. If it was not meant to be, it would not be so."

Cheyenne whipped the heavy velvet comforter off her legs and reached for the lamp on her bedside table. "We told you to stay on the couch, man. You can't walk into somebody's bedroom while they're sleeping."

The light switched on, and Cheyenne blinked against the glare. Her room was empty.

You've gotta be kidding me.

Gritting her teeth, she pulled the comforter off the rest of the way and slipped out of bed. Once she'd pulled on a pair of loose black sweatpants and an oversized Tool t-shirt, she threw open her bedroom door and stormed into the living room. "Maybe I should've been more specific."

Beside the brewing coffee pot in the kitchen, Ember gave her friend a cautious smile. "That's one way to say good morning."

Neros sat perfectly straight on the couch, eyes closed, hands resting palms-up on his thighs. "I assumed you were referring to my physical body."

"Yeah, well, now you can assume I mean all of it. I don't know what kind of boundaries you guys have in Nor'ieth—my guess is none—but in this world, privacy is a thing. Private bedroom. Private head. Got it?"

He opened his eyes and blinked at her. "And your dreams?"

"My dreams are in my head, Neros." Cheyenne pointed at her temple. "There's only room for one drow in there, and that's a tight fit."

"Your dreams are everywhere, Cheyenne. Right there for anyone who knows how to pluck from the Weave."

"Screw the Weave. And stay out of my dreams." Cheyenne stalked toward the kitchen, breathing in the scent of fresh coffee and trying to force her bad mood back down. *First, it was L'zar with the stupid drow mind-meld, now it's this crazy watching me relive everything I'd much rather forget.*

"Couldn't sleep, huh?" Ember handed her a full cup of coffee.

"No, I slept eventually. Then the Kumbaya drow over there thought it would be fun to hang around in my head for most of it."

"I do not find it amusing, Cheyenne," Neros called from the couch. "Concerning, yes. You need to release the weight of a blame that is not yours."

Cheyenne blew on the coffee as Ember filled herself a cup. *Easy for him to say. This guy probably can't die, either.*

"Blame for what?" Ember asked.

Neros finally moved from the meditative position that made him look like L'zar and turned to gaze at them over the back of the couch. "Your *Nós Aní* is unaware."

"She wasn't asking you," Cheyenne muttered and stared into her coffee as she took a sip.

"I'm definitely unaware." Ember flicked her finger at the fridge, which opened in a flash of violet light. The flavored creamer sailed out of the door and into her hand. "Feel like enlightening me?"

"Not really."

"You should, Cheyenne." Neros nodded. "It will lighten your burden."

Nope. It'll just make Ember carry the same weight. Maybe more, if she hears she died and was brought back to life by that nutjob's creepy keepers.

Ember stared at her as she stirred her fixed-up coffee. "It's about the forest, isn't it?"

The drow met her friend's gaze and looked away again. "If you wanna know, Em, ask me again when Peeping Tom isn't here to butt in."

"Or I could ask him." The fae waited until Cheyenne looked up at her again. Ember pointed at the dishwasher, which fell open in a burst of violet light, and the coffee spoon sailed into the caddy with a metallic ping. "But I won't. If you promise that was an actual offer and not you just trying to brush whatever it is away and hoping I'll forget about it."

Cheyenne shook her head. "No. We should talk about it. Later. And even if I could forget about it, I know you won't."

"Okay."

Neros slumped back onto the couch and stared across the apartment. "Someone is at the door."

"Oh, yeah? You jumping into random strangers' heads now too?" As she said it, Cheyenne heard footsteps stop outside their apartment. Two seconds later, a brisk knock followed.

"Well, now we know he'd make a good guard drow," Ember muttered, taking her coffee with her to answer the door.

Yeah, and his hearing's even better than mine. Cheyenne stared at the back of her cousin's head and sipped more coffee. *He probably expected that portal to open in Inolu's house. Played along the whole time so he could take a little side trip to Earth and slip into my head that much more easily.*

"Matthew." Ember opened the door a little wider and looked their neighbor up and down. "What's up?"

"Hi, Ember. Cheyenne's still here, right?"

"She lives here too."

"Can I come in?"

Ember stepped aside, pulling the door open all the way.

Matthew walked in and nodded at Neros. "Hey, man."

The drow said nothing.

"Right." Setting down the huge metal briefcase in his hand, Matthew scanned the apartment and jumped when he saw Cheyenne standing on the other side of the kitchen island. "Shit."

"I usually only scare people the first time they look at me."

"Sorry. You're always in that chair or heading out the door when I come over."

Cheyenne slurped her hot black coffee, then nodded at the briefcase. "What's in the case?"

"Programmer. Sort of. For your little metal stars or whatever."

"Activators." Ember stepped past him and took her seat on the couch. "That's what they're called."

"Okay. I think I found something last night, and I figured we should do a trial run, right?" Matthew gazed at Cheyenne with wide eyes and shrugged. "You know. Make sure the tweaks I made are headed in the right direction and not—"

"The complete opposite of what we need?" Cheyenne stepped around the island and nodded at the briefcase. "That thing has your whole system?"

"What? No!" he said. "It's just a syncing dock. Portable."

"Right. Can't carry around a whole room full of buzzing servers. Open it. Let's check it out."

"Yeah. Cool." Matthew put the case on the coffee table and opened it as Cheyenne brought her coffee with her to the recliner. In his eagerness, the guy sat down in the middle of the couch between Ember and Neros and drew the activator Cheyenne had given him from his pocket. "I wanted to make sure you were around before I tested it. This thing is a lot smaller than the last order."

"Well, war machines do tend to be pretty big," Ember muttered.

Matthew looked quickly at her as if he hadn't realized she was right there, then glanced at Neros on the other side of him and shifted on the couch cushion. "They probably weren't as valuable either, I'm guessing."

"You have no idea." Cheyenne studied the inside of the case, which was lined with black polystyrene and looked pretty much like she'd expect from a syncing dock à la Matthew Thomas. "And you think your program's up to the challenge with these things, huh?"

"I mean, yeah. I hope so. It didn't take that much work. A few changes, mostly input redirects, and I had to cut a few lines and replicate an addition on the back end, but this thing was way easier to work on than the other stuff. Maybe because it's smaller. I don't know."

"Well, now you know." Cheyenne raised an eyebrow at him. "Bigger isn't always better, Matthew. Remember that."

"Um, okay."

"You rewrote your whole program to work with this in less than twenty-four hours?" Ember wrinkled her nose as she studied the case.

"Not the whole program. But yeah." He flashed her a proud smile. "Cheyenne said we only had four days. Trust me, it's not the first time I've pulled an all-nighter to get the job done."

"Let's test this thing before we call it that, huh?" Cheyenne jerked her chin up at him. "Demo time."

"Right." Matthew scooted forward on the couch cushion, moving slightly away from Neros, who didn't bother to scoot over toward the armchair to give him more room, and settled the star activator into the recessed square of the syncing doc. "Give me a minute to pull every-thing up."

He grabbed his phone out of his pocket, swiping and tapping the screen.

"I'll be right back." Cheyenne set her coffee cup on the table and stood.

"Whoa, whoa. Hey." Matthew wagged a finger at the table. "Coffee. Expensive tech. You of all people should know that's a bad combination."

"Yep. I also know how not to spill my coffee on my expensive tech. I'm sure you can figure it out." She turned and headed for her bedroom, followed by the sound of Ember choking back a laugh.

Can't be too nice to the guy. Not until we know he's not still jerking us around and can do what he said he could do.

She crossed her bedroom to grab her activator off the bedside table and her phone just in case. Slipping into drow mode, she stuck the silver coil behind her ear and walked casually back into the living room. The metal case on the coffee table lit up in her vision with a burst of scrolling code lines racing back and forth across the surface. Her eyes widened.

Okay. Simple on the outside. Way more beneath the surface. I guess he gets points for presentation, at least.

Matthew looked at her when she bent to retrieve her coffee cup and nearly dropped his phone. "Jesus!"

"Not even close. Wanna try again?" She sat and stared at him.

"Sorry. I'm not used to seeing you like that."

"Ember's sitting next to you without any illusion charms at all. Not even a little one."

"Yeah." Matthew turned slowly to look Ember up and down, taking in her fae-pink skin, luminous violet eyes, which were larger than human eyes, and the streaks of purple through her light-brown hair, and smiled. "Ember doesn't look all that different. At least not to me."

The fae raised an eyebrow at him but couldn't hide a smile in return.

Great. If they're not careful, Neros' new age is gonna be overrun by fae halflings.

Cheyenne cleared her throat. "Are you ready?"

"Oh." Matthew whipped his head back toward his phone. "Yeah, just a sec."

Ember looked at her friend with a mock scowl.

Uh-huh. There's no way she's still the same level of pissed at him either.

"Okay. Here." Matthew held his phone toward Cheyenne. "The startup sequence. You wanna do it?"

"It's your program, Matthew. I'm not trying to take over or anything."

"I know that. Right." He tapped his phone, and the syncing doc in the briefcase lit up with blue and green light.

Cheyenne knew it was right from the dock when she saw it reflected in Ember's wide eyes as the fae leaned forward in curiosity. When Cheyenne looked down, she couldn't have held back her grin if she'd tried. "Holy shit."

CHAPTER THIRTY

"I know, right?" Matthew looked between his phone and the case. "It looks cool from here, but all the data running through this thing right now, that's where the real magic is. I mean, not real magic. I've always wanted to know what that looks like. Like, if we could see inside all these devices around us. Not the actual parts, though. I mean the—"

"Energy of it," Cheyenne muttered. Her gaze flickered across the suitcase and the brilliant bursts of code illuminating it from within. *Might as well call it magic in a box. This almost looks like the walls in Hangivol. How the hell did he come up with this?*

"Yeah, I guess 'energy' isn't that far off."

"Trust me, Matt." Cheyenne tilted her head and studied the syncing dock, which was lighting up with line after line of the program he'd written and stored inside. "It's fucking beautiful."

He turned to Ember with a self-conscious smile. "Wait. What?"

Ember studied the near-rapture on her friend's face and snorted. "Apparently, it's beautiful."

Matthew frowned at Cheyenne, whose slate-gray face was lit by more than the blue and green glow from his device. "You can see it?"

"Oh, yeah."

"How is that even possible?"

She pointed at the star activator nestled in the dock. "That's what those are for."

"To be clear," Ember added, "not everyone with an activator can see what she sees when they use one. That's a special Cheyenne thing. I mean, none of us thought it was possible to move through the city, solid walls and everything, until she did it when her mom... Actually, now's probably not the best time for that story."

Matthew stared at the drow, who was still grinning at his briefcase. "You can move through walls?"

"Just a certain kind." She looked at him and snorted. "I promise you I didn't ask you to rewrite your program so I can give a bunch of Earth-side magicals superpowers when I hand these out."

"That wasn't even..."

"Yeah, it's written all over your face."

Ember bit her lip to hold in a laugh and shrugged when Matthew looked at her for validation.

"Okay, well, it's not *that* impossible," he muttered, hunching his shoulders as he leaned over his lap.

"It is in this world." Cheyenne nodded at the star activator, which was starting to glow a dull red in the dock. "I think it's ready."

"No." Matthew glanced at his phone. "We still have three minutes. Takes five to fully cycle through." Everyone but the human stared at the briefcase, and he cleared his throat. "So if you're the only one who can walk through walls or whatever with one of these things, what are they supposed to do for everyone else?"

Cheyenne ran a hand through her hair and forced herself to look away from the glowing magi-tech in her living room. *On Earth. Away from Hangivol's system. Like somebody cut off a lizard's tail and it regenerated a whole body.*

"Think of them as translators," she said, trying to explain how they worked to their human neighbor.

"For code?"

"Sure. Mostly, that's a bonus on the other side of the Border. They translate other things too. Words. Energy."

"Magic," Ember added, wiggling her eyebrows at him.

"A translator for magic." Matthew shook his head in disbelief. "I don't know how to wrap my head around that."

"Example." Ember gestured at Cheyenne. "This magical, for instance, couldn't cast a simple spell to save her life before we found out she can bring O'gúl tech across the Border without it blowing up or melting or disappearing."

"Hey, I remember giving someone an illusion charm I cast on that ring."

"Yeah, after what? Six hours of trying?"

Cheyenne snorted. "Four."

"The activators sync our magic with technology, mostly O'gúl tech because there isn't anything Earthside that works the same way. Except for maybe this thing. And the activators." Ember drummed her fingers on her thighs. "And in Cheyenne's case, her activator helps her cast spells she'd never be able to learn without blowing holes in our apartment."

"Delicately put, Em. Thanks."

"I got your back."

Matthew chewed the inside of his cheek and checked the cycle countdown on his phone. "Would it work for people without magic?"

Ember folded her arms. "About as well as a pair of hiking boots would work for someone in a wheelchair." Cheyenne and Matthew both looked sharply at her in surprise. "What? I can say that. I've been in a wheelchair. Bullet through the spine, remember?"

Their neighbor's eyes widened. "You never told me what happened."

"Oh. I guess not. Well, it's all behind me now. That's also a story for another time." Pressing her lips together, she gave his shoulder a few hesitant pats.

"Most of these are for the refugees," Cheyenne added. "The magicals coming into the reservations from across the Border. To help them get used to life Earthside, and, you know, be able to read signs and directions and shit."

"It doesn't give them extra powers?"

"Nope. I'm not interested in pumping up anyone's power supply. Not even mine."

Ember snorted. "You should see her when the black flames show up." She caught Cheyenne's warning look and the shake of her head. "Yeah. She doesn't need a power boost."

"And the rest of them?" Matthew asked.

"The rest of what?"

"You said most of these things are for refugees."

"Right." Cheyenne studied him. *As fidgety as he is in conversations about magic, he's paying attention to detail. Ember talks too much around him.* "The rest, if it all works out, will go to Earthborn magicals who know less about casting spells than I do."

"I doubt they even know what spells are," Ember muttered.

"Sounds like you have someone specific in mind," Matthew said.

"Sure do, neighbor." Cheyenne plastered on a fake smile that made Matthew and Ember eye her warily. "The same magicals who had no idea how to stop your magical-hating uncle because he made sure the FRoE only hires magicals who have no idea how to stop the kind of threat he posed to the whole world."

Matthew pressed his lips together and nodded. "Makes sense."

A gentle chime came from his phone, and he tapped the screen a few times.

"Ready to pull this thing outta the cooker?" Ember asked.

"It's ready." Cheyenne reached for the star activator, still glowing slightly in the dock.

"Wait, wait." Matthew reached toward her, shaking his head and studying his phone. "I have to confirm the—"

"Dude. I can see it." She grabbed the star activator and turned it over in her hands as Matthew grimaced in frustration. "It's ready."

"Try it." Ember raised her eyebrows. "Moment of truth, right?"

"Not for me, Em. I already have one. Here." Cheyenne handed it across the table to her friend. "Go for it."

"Oh, boy." The fae stared at the piece of O'gúl metal and let out an uncertain chuckle, then shot Matthew a sidelong glance. "I just got used to using these on the other side."

"Wait, you mean you don't know how to use this thing?"

"I didn't say that, Matthew."

"Maybe I should run some more tests."

"This *is* the test, and I'm gonna be the second magical in existence to use a working activator on this side of the Border." Ember grinned and stuck the four-pointed star behind her ear. "Ow!"

"Whoa, whoa. What's wrong?" Matthew leaned forward, studied her face, and set a gentle hand on her shoulder.

Ember leaned away from him, clenching her eyes shut. "I'm fine. Damn. That pinch."

Cheyenne said, "I know, right?"

"What pinch?" Matthew looked like he was about to have a heart attack. "Does it open or something? I didn't see any kind of—"

"Slow down, buddy." Ember lifted a hand to make him wait. "For a guy who made millions on tech and cybersecurity, you worry way too much."

"I didn't build my company on this," he muttered. "Are you okay?"

The fae blinked quickly, adjusting to the activator's first sync-up in a new world, and gazed around the living room. "Oh, my."

"Ember."

"Relax, would you?" She chuckled and scanned the back of Cheyenne's computer in the mini-loft, then the briefcase on the table, then the phone clutched tightly in Matthew's hand. "It totally works."

"How's it compare to the one you had in Hangivol?" Cheyenne asked.

"Well, so far, I'd say it's about the same." Ember flicked her fingers at the entry table beside the front door. Purple light appeared at her fingertips and on the table, then the TV rose from its recessed stand with a low hum. Before it finished rising all the way, the screen turned on, and the volume turned up almost as far as it would go.

The sound jolted Neros out of his expressionless and reactionless stupor, and he clapped both hands over his ears. "What is that?"

"Ha!" Ember's violet eyes flickered back and forth, reading prompts only she could see. The TV went to mute with another flick of her hand. "Holy shit! That was so easy! Is this what it's like for you on the other side?"

Cheyenne folded her arms and sat back in the recliner. "Maybe if Ambar'ogúl had TVs. I don't know."

"Yeah, this is way better than the last one." Grinning, the fae turned to look at Matthew. "Nice work."

He blew out a heavy sigh of relief, then hung his head.

"Cheer up, man." Cheyenne gestured at her Nós Aní. "You see the look on her face right now? Remember that. That's the look we're gonna see on the faces of a whole bunch of O'gúleesh refugees who thought they were gonna have to blaze a new trail through Earth without any help from anyone."

"Neros." Ember leaned forward to peer past Matthew at the drow. "You wanna try this?"

Neros blinked once. "I would like another pickle."

She burst out laughing.

"I'm pretty sure we can find you something better than a pickle for breakfast." Cheyenne pushed out of the chair and headed for the kitchen. "I'm hungry too. How do you feel about toast?"

Her cousin turned in his seat to follow her with his gaze. "How *should* one feel about toast?"

"I'll leave that up to you. Em?"

"Absolutely."

"Matthew Thomas. You want toast?"

He looked up and blinked. "I guess so?"

"Come on. Celebratory breakfast. We just made magical history, my friend."

Matthew scoffed. "We're friends now?"

"Sure. All it took was a rewritten program for O'gúl tech and you almost pissing yourself when Ember said, 'Ow,' but hey. I'd call that a job well done."

He let out a wry chuckle.

"Thank you," Ember said, turning to face him full-on with a wide grin. "You have no idea how awesome this is."

"It's better than powering machines for someone who wants to take over the world or whatever, right?"

"Yes, Matthew. Much better than that."

"Hey, Matt," Cheyenne called as she pulled a loaf of bread out of the pantry and slammed the cabinet door shut. "While I'm slaving over the toaster, go ahead and get three more of those things up and running for me, huh?"

"Sure." When Ember pointed at the trunks on the floor, he stood and stepped toward them to open the closest one. "Do you think you should test them a little more before you start telling everyone they work the way they're supposed to?"

Cheyenne snorted. "I'm surprised to be more confident about this than you are, and you wrote the damn program."

"Which is why I'm trying to be a lot more responsible about it this time." Matthew stared wide-eyed at the contents of the trunk.

"And you're doing fine." Cheyenne pushed down the lever in the full toaster and winked at the appliance as it started to heat up. "Listen, Ember's a good start, but I wanna test these on someone who hasn't touched an activator in a few years. I know the perfect magicals, who might fall all over themselves when I ask them to be my guinea pigs."

CHAPTER THIRTY-ONE

Cheyenne's Gothed-out Panamera pulled up in the parking lot of her old apartment complex in Jackson Ward. She leaned over the steering wheel to look up at the second floor of her building. "Feels like forever since I've been here."

"Well, yeah." Ember unbuckled her seatbelt, then shrugged. "I mean, you overthrew the O'gúl Crown, gave away the throne, and lugged your human mom across the Border to burn down the most magically powerful forest in two worlds and save both of them in the process, all in a few weeks since the last time you were here. Even one of those things would seem like forever."

The drow snorted and turned off the engine. "We stopped by right after item number two, remember?"

"Oh." Ember gazed at the apartment building, which seemed abandoned and empty in the early-November chill. "That's right. When we thought Ruuv'i was stalking you."

"Bingo."

"That does feel like forever ago." Ember opened the passenger side door to get out, and Cheyenne almost did the same before Neros' grunt of frustration rose from the back seat.

He pounded on the door's armrest, waved a hand in front of the window, and jiggled the handle. "This contraption is a useless demonstration of—"

She pressed the automatic unlock button, and her cousin froze. Ember opened the back door for him and gestured with an exaggerated bow for him to exit the vehicle.

All three doors shut, echoing across the parking lot.

Neros stared at Cheyenne over the roof of the Porsche and narrowed his eyes, now a washed-out light blue beneath the close-cropped black hair of the human illusion charm Ember had cast on him. "I do not enjoy traveling this way, Cheyenne."

"Tough it out, cuz." Shrugging, she locked the car with the remote fob and grinned at the delicate chirp and the purple light that flashed above the headlights. "Unless the Olfarím taught you how to open nightstalker portals, this is how drow in Richmond get around."

"There are other drow in this territory?"

"Territory, huh?" Ember grinned at him as they followed Cheyenne up the outdoor staircase leading to the second floor. "Most of our territories aren't part of the Continental US. Not physically connected, and there aren't many. Over here, we have continents, countries, states, cities, and towns. The rest of it, I guess, is like Bianca's house. Somewhere out in the middle of nowhere."

Neros frowned at the fae without blinking.

"I think you're hurting his brain, Em."

"What? This is practical-application teaching right here." Ember shrugged. "If the Nor'ieth drow's taking an Earthside detour, he might as well learn about Earth."

"I think that only applies to useful information."

The fae stopped at the top of the staircase as Cheyenne headed down the hall toward her old apartment. "You don't think that was useful? Jeez. It's amazing the Computer Sciences Department thought it was a good idea to give you a whole class to teach."

"Not a US geography class."

Neros stopped beside Ember to gaze around the hallway of the second floor, then took off after Cheyenne. "There are other drow here?"

Cheyenne snorted. "There are at least three. Technically four, if you count Ba'rael. But the fact that Inolu put her in a cage might cancel that out." She stopped one door down from her old apartment, eyeing what used to be her front door. It was still covered in O'gúleesh symbols, though most of them had already faded into lighter ghosts of themselves.

The ones painted in blood will be the hardest to scrub off. And I'm still paying for this place.

Ember caught up with them outside her old neighbors' apartment and grinned. "These guys about lost it when you told them the new O'gúl Crown was a troll. This might break them into a million pieces."

"They lost their farm to the Spider, made the crossing over two years ago with only a fraction of our ability to fight, and carved an Earthside life for themselves as magical refugees in hiding without anyone to show them how it works." The drow slipped a hand into the pocket of her black trench coat and fingered the three activators in it. "I'd call this family tough as hell. They'll do great."

"Yeah, I guess being tough and being emotional aren't mutually exclusive," Ember replied when her friend rolled her eyes and knocked briskly.

The door opened almost immediately to reveal Yadje's wide grin. "Cheyenne! You have returned so soon!"

Cheyenne returned the smile. "I mean, it's been a few weeks."

The troll nodded at Ember and shot Neros a curious frown. "Come in. Please. Come, come." She waved them in and stepped aside. "How are you? Any news from home? Cheyenne, we have been thinking and talking and dreaming about what you told us the last time you were here. Are things well in the capital?"

"Maji!" The girl's cry rose from the far end of the hall on the other side of the small, cramped living room. "Have you seen *The Road*?"

"Have I seen what?"

"It's a book. From the library. I had it last night, and now it's—" The kid stopped when she reached the front of the hall and noticed three more magicals than usual standing in her apartment. "Cheyenne!"

"Hey, kid…whoa." Cheyenne took a balancing step back when Bryl threw her skinny arms around the drow's waist for a tight hug. The girl's scarlet braids thumped against her back. "Yeah, it's good to see you too."

I have no idea why magical kids like me so much.

Bryl pulled away and grinned up at her. "Everything's awesome."

Cheyenne laughed. "Glad to hear it."

"Stop hanging on her like that, *hinya*." Yadje shooed her daughter away with both hands, clicking her tongue in disapproval. Bryl let Cheyenne go and playfully rolled her eyes. "And here is your *Nós Aní*. So wonderful to see you again."

Ember nodded. "You too."

The troll tilted her head and eyed Neros. "Now, who is this one?"

"Oh, this is—"

"By the life-giving teat of Agriván, Yadje," R'mahr grumbled from a bedroom down the hall. "I thought you said you were taking everything to the wash, and now I can't find the fell-damn pants I was supposed to —" He stopped when his wife spun to hiss at him. He was standing frozen in the hallway in a pair of tighty-whiteys and nothing else. Then he noticed their guests. "*Hishmál*! Why didn't you tell me?" The troll darted two steps forward, then yelped and leaped back into the bedroom.

Bryl burst out laughing, holding herself around the middle as she stumbled toward the couch on the back wall.

"No one wants to see that," Yadje muttered, glaring down the hall and folding her arms. "Especially not you, *phér móre*. I am so sorry."

Cheyenne fought back a laugh. "You guys weren't expecting guests. Can't blame him for thinking it was safe."

"Someone still needs to dig the mud out of his ears." Yadje's scowl melted into another broad grin when she returned to her guests. "You were saying, Cheyenne?"

"Right. This is Neros. My cousin."

"Oh, you have family with you now!"

"Temporarily."

Yadje chuckled and clapped her hands. "Family and friends of the *phér móre*. I do not know what we did to deserve such an honor, Cheyenne. You give us so many of them."

"You were good neighbors." The drow shrugged. "That's all."

The troll tried to cover her proud smile by shooing Cheyenne away and clicking her tongue. R'mahr stepped out of the bedroom again, closing the door tensely behind him. He lifted his head, rolled his shoulders, and made a much better attempt at an entrance this time.

"Cheyenne!" The troll spread his arms and chuckled. "I cannot believe it is you again. In our home."

"Sorry for dropping by without notice." Cheyenne nodded and fought the urge to pull away when he clapped both hands on her shoulders and gazed intently at her.

"You do not apologize to us. Not now, not ever. I will not allow it." He looked quickly at his wife with a tiny frown. "No blame on you for the washing left undone."

"Stop," Yadje hissed, smacking his arm with the back of a hand. R'mahr chuckled. "You know exactly when and where, you brain-addled troll."

"Very nice to see your friend again as well." R'mahr nodded at Ember. "And another friend?"

"Cousin." Cheyenne stuck her hands deeper in her pockets. *All the introductions, and it's still weird to say.* "Neros."

"A pleasure." R'mahr pressed a fist firmly to his chest. Neros merely raised an eyebrow.

"He's a little out of the loop when it comes to regular interaction," Ember explained, trying not to laugh.

"Ah. I could have said the same of myself after we made the crossing here. It will fade eventually, brother."

Ember and Cheyenne exchanged amused glances, but neither of them bothered to correct the troll.

"So." R'mahr grinned at them happily. "Have you come to bring us more joyous news from the capital?"

"The only news is that everything's running the way it should be. No problems."

"Yes, as it should be." Yadje shook a finger at the drow. "A troll sits on the O'gúl throne now. Of course, there are no problems."

Someone else has complete faith in Persh'al. He'd be thrilled.

"I brought something for each of you." Cheyenne smiled at Bryl, who had curled up on the couch and was staring at the talking grownups. "I think it might be even better than news from the other side."

Yadje and R'mahr gazed at each other in disbelief. "Better than news of a troll Crown?"

"Better than the Spider flushed out of her web? Never, Cheyenne.

You could not possibly have—" R'mahr flinched away from his wife's swatting hand again. "For what?"

"Let her speak, *ma gairin*," she whispered fiercely. "You do enough of that as it is."

"Okay, fine." Cheyenne shrugged, shooting them a smile. "Maybe it's not better, but I'd call it a close second. The next best thing."

"You might even say it's just like home," Ember added.

Bryl leaped to her feet on the couch and jumped up and down on the cushion. "You brought something for us? What is it? What is it?" Her bare purple feet thumped onto the old carpet, and she darted toward the adults. "Cheyenne, I want to see!"

"Maybe we should all sit down for this one."

Yadje shrieked and spun away from the front door to race into the kitchen, gesturing everyone into the living room. "Go, go, go. Yes. Sit down. I'll get chairs."

Cheyenne watched her disappear. "I meant the three of you—"

"I will help you." R'mahr stared at Cheyenne, then raced after his wife.

"I don't need your help, you bumbling *dae'bruj*."

"She wants us to sit down, Yadje. It must be incredible."

"Of course it is. It's Cheyenne. No, don't take the...oh! Stop. Just stop. Bryl! Get your father out of my kitchen this instant. He will break everything!"

"Da." Bryl crept toward the kitchen and waved urgently. "She'll smack you if you don't do what she says."

The scuffling and grunting in the kitchen stopped, then R'mahr stepped sheepishly through the door, rubbing his head. A nervous chuckle escaped him as he looked at Cheyenne. "This pup of mine, eh? So young, yet so wise."

As soon as the troll and his daughter reached the couch in the tiny living room, Yadje reemerged, dragging two kitchen chairs behind her and huffing fiercely. "Here we are. Come, come. Seats for everyone."

She set them up on the other side of the wobbly coffee table, then turned back to the kitchen. When she saw Neros drop wordlessly to the floor beside the door and close his eyes with his legs crossed beneath him, she stopped.

"Well. I suppose two chairs is enough."

"More than enough." Cheyenne eyed her cousin as she and Ember stepped into the living room for the highly-anticipated reveal.

Yadje grinned and lowered herself to the couch between her husband and daughter, smoothing her layered skirts over her lap. "If you say we should sit, Cheyenne, we will all sit. Please."

R'mahr nodded eagerly. Bryl gripped her mother's arm and held on tight.

"Okay." Cheyenne and Ember exchanged glances again as they sat slowly in the rickety kitchen chairs. *Maybe I shouldn't have played this up so much, 'cause if they're disappointed by these smuggled activators, I'll be the drow who crushed all their dreams.*

CHAPTER THIRTY-TWO

"What are you waiting for?" Bryl shouted.

Yadje brusquely jostled her daughter, who still hadn't loosened her grip on the troll's arm. "You hush now."

Cheyenne withdrew the activators from her jacket pocket and had to stand to lean over the coffee table and deliver them. "These are for you."

Yadje was the only one who moved to receive the three small, relatively nondescript pieces of metal. She cupped both palms together and stared at the activators like Cheyenne had dropped a handful of gemstones worth a fortune into them.

I guess it might as well be the same thing. Not sure Ambar'ogúl puts the same kinda value on precious gems.

"What are they?" Yadje whispered. "Wait, wait. Do not say. We are supposed to know already, yes?"

"Well, it might be kinda hard to—"

"Let me look at it first, Cheyenne," R'mahr butted in. "If you don't mind."

"Go ahead." Cheyenne stuck her hands in her pockets again.

Three pairs of eyes gazed into Yadje's hands, and her husband reached in to pluck out a metal four-pointed star. Bryl's usual playfulness was replaced with a reverence that rivaled her parents', and she gingerly took an activator from her mother's hands.

"This is incredible workmanship," R'mahr muttered. "So simple. Very neat lines."

"They are beautiful, Cheyenne." Yadje took a deep, shuddering breath. "Beautiful. And yes, very much a reminder of home."

"What do they do?" Bryl asked and was quickly shushed again by her mother.

R'mahr looked at the drow and the fae sitting in his living room, his eyes narrowing as he studied them. "We already know, don't we?"

"I have no idea," Cheyenne replied. "But they—"

"This is too much, Cheyenne." Yadje shook her head fervently and held the star-shaped piece of metal back out toward the drow. "We cannot accept."

"What?" her husband and daughter shouted at the same time.

"Too much. Give them back."

"*Maji*, you can't!"

"No, you can't."

"*Ma gairín.*" R'mahr set a hand on his wife's thigh and stared at her. "Do you realize what we have been given? By the *phér móre*, no less?"

"I realize more than enough." The troll wouldn't stop shaking her head, and she clenched her eyes tightly shut. "I am a fool to dare hope this is what it seems. And if it's not…" Yadje's scarlet eyes flickered toward her guests. "Cheyenne, if it's not, I beg you not to drag it out. Tell us right now what we are to do with these, and we will do it."

R'mahr patted her thigh. "But you know."

"I cannot ask, R'mahr!"

Bryl and her father looked up again with fearful expectation. The troll cleared his throat. "Cheyenne?"

Jesus. These mean way more to them than I realized.

Forcing herself to smile and hoping the troll family had guessed correctly, Cheyenne slowly raised her hand and tapped twice behind her ear.

"Are you serious?" Bryl squealed.

Yadje opened her eyes and shrieked. She looked down at the star activator cupped in her hand and shrieked again.

"No." R'mahr looked at Ember and Cheyenne. "Yes?"

The drow couldn't hold back a wry chuckle. "Okay, you have to try it."

"Yes! Aha!" The troll gaped at his wife, who kept shrieking. "It is! Yadje, they are!"

"Stop yelling in my face!" Yadje shouted, then picked up the activator between two fingers, moving as if she were in a trance.

Bryl fumbled with the activator and had to swipe aside her scarlet braids twice before she could place the device behind her ear. Laughing maniacally, her father quickly followed suit. Yadje sucked in a breath and looked like she was about to pass out before she put hers on.

All three trolls grew rigid on the couch as the brand-new activators synced with their magic. Eyelids fluttered. R'mahr gritted his teeth, his wife winced, and their daughter's mouth dropped open in surprise and pain. Then they blinked quickly, one right after the other, and gazed around their tiny, cramped living room.

"*Majiya iya*," Yadje muttered.

"It is." R'mahr stood halfway off the couch, knees still bent and arms stretched out in front of him like he was trying to walk through a pitch-black room. "Ah! It is!"

"Holy shit!" Bryl screamed. Her parents turned to stare at her, and the girl jumped off the couch, flapping her arms at them. "They work! They work, they work, they really work!"

The troll's shriek of joy sounded more like a keening wail, interrupted by her husband's wordless screeches. He straightened and pulled her up off the couch, then cupped both her cheeks, then grabbed her shoulders, then cupped her cheeks again as they half-laughed, half-cried.

Bryl screamed again and took off running down the hall in the back, her footsteps pounding across the creaking floors. A door flew open and banged against the wall. "Holy shit!"

Another bang. "Holy shit!"

Two more bangs in quick succession, then a sizzling crack that sounded like magic hitting something it wasn't supposed to. "Ah! *Maji*! Da! I can see it!"

The girl raced back down the hall, her scarlet braids flying behind her, and skidded to a halt on the carpet. She gaped at Cheyenne and spread her arms wide. "Holy shit!"

Choking back a laugh, Ember leaned toward Cheyenne and muttered, "What is she? Six?"

"I'm pretty sure that's only in looks," the drow muttered back. *Kid's smart enough to be in high school and probably old enough to have graduated at least ten times over.*

"*Bída,*" Yadje warned in a low hiss, composing herself enough to shoot her daughter a glance over her shoulder. But a small smile broke across her face as she flicked a hand toward Bryl. A sparkling mist of pale light snaked from her fingertips and billowed across the apartment toward her daughter.

When the light curled around the kid's face, caressing her like a loving hand, Bryl closed her eyes. Tears slipped from beneath her eyelids and ran down her cheeks, but she was silent.

"Cheyenne," R'mahr whispered, turning away from his wife to walk around the coffee table toward the drow. "There are no words."

"It's okay."

The troll man shoved the coffee table toward the couch and fell to his knees in front of her. One fist thumped his chest, and the other pressed firmly against his purple forehead.

Cheyenne stood so quickly, the wooden kitchen chair toppled onto the floor behind her. The trolls didn't even notice. "You don't have to!"

"My life for the *phér móre,*" he whispered. "*Lainari.*"

Not that fucking Deliverer shit again.

"Don't. R'mahr, come on. Stand up."

Yadje and Bryl walked around the other side of the forcefully moved coffee table and approached Cheyenne too. When the troll woman lifted her skirts with one hand and started to lower herself to her knees, Cheyenne couldn't control herself.

"Enough with the kneeling and bowing and pledging lives, okay?" She stepped toward the troll and grabbed her shoulders to guide Yadje back to standing.

The troll blinked at her in surprise. "What is it?"

"You guys don't owe me all that, okay? You don't owe me anything."

"We owe you everything," R'mahr muttered, his head still bowed with a fist pressed against it.

"Nope. You sure don't. Please don't do this again." Cheyenne pulled him to his feet too and stopped when she saw the tears welling in his scarlet eyes. *Oh, jeez.*

"You cannot imagine what this means to us, Cheyenne."

"Yeah, I think I have a pretty good idea." She smiled thinly and nudged his shoulder with her fist. "And you deserve it. All of you."

"That is not a reason for delivering such gifts as these," Yadje whispered. "Why us? Why now?"

"Honestly?"

The trolls nodded vigorously, even Bryl as she gazed around their apartment like she was seeing it all for the first time. In a way, with the activator lighting up in her vision, she was.

Cheyenne shrugged. "You guys were the first magicals I ever met who didn't try to threaten or hurt anyone or shoot my best friend at a skate park."

Ember snorted.

"I had no idea I'd been living next to a troll family for two years, but you didn't think twice about giving me your charms or feeding me. And you told me a hell of a lot more about the other side and how bad things are for the O'gúleesh on this side than anyone else because you're a good family. That's who you are."

"And this is who you are, *phér móre.*" Yadje pressed a fist to her chest and reached out with the other hand to grab Cheyenne's shoulder. "You have brought us more than we could have hoped for."

"And it's so much better than hearing about a troll Crown," Bryl whispered.

Yadje's eyes narrowed, and she fought to hold Cheyenne's gaze instead of turning to scold her daughter. "It is."

R'mahr shook his head. "We are not worthy of such an honor, Cheyenne."

"That's bullshit."

The troll couple blinked at her, and Bryl barked a laugh.

"It's not so much an honor as it is your right, okay?" The drow's smile widened when she saw the realization dawning on the family's faces. *Realization of what? I'm gonna go with they're finally figuring out I'm doing this for them, not for myself.* "Every O'gúleesh who makes the crossing deserves an actual shot at a new life Earthside, and the reservations aren't doing anything to make that happen. Trust me, I do know how bad things were on the other side. If I were you, I would've made the same choice."

Forget that they left a shitty life with the Spider for a shitty life without her.

"I do not understand." R'mahr stared down at his hand, where a soft light the same color as his wife's magic swirled playfully around his fingers, and chuckled. "Why would you do this?"

Cheyenne looked at each of them and shrugged. "Because I can, and because it's pretty much my job now. You couldn't give those activators back even if you wanted to."

"We don't want to." Bryl vigorously shook her head. "Never."

Ember laughed and bent to pick up Cheyenne's chair from the floor. "You won't have to."

"I do have a favor to ask you, though."

"Anything." Yadje nodded.

"Whatever it is," R'mahr added, "we will do it."

"Well, it shouldn't be too hard," Cheyenne said to the girl and winked. Bryl grinned. "I want you guys to test these things as much as you can in the next few days. Safely." She pointed at the youngster, her smile widening.

"This does not sound like a favor to you, Cheyenne." The troll man stepped closer to his wife and wrapped an arm around her shoulders.

"Trust me, it is. I'll be back in a few days to see how you're doing and if they're working the way they're supposed to."

"These are worlds better than what we had back home," Yadje said.

Cheyenne grinned. "I know a sparksetter who's gonna be pretty happy to hear that."

R'mahr raised his hand to brush his fingers across the activator behind his ear. "I want to ask you if I may?"

"Yeah."

"How in the fell-damn abyss did you get these across the Border?"

Yadje clicked her tongue at him and nudged her husband's ribs with an elbow. "Watch your mouth."

"It's an important question, *ma gairín.*" The troll chuckled. "This has never been done before. O'gúl technology Earthside for magicals like us to use as we wish?"

"That is her business and hers to keep. She gives us these, and you ask her for more? To share her secrets?"

He gaped at his wife, his purple skin paling along his cheekbones. "I did not—"

"It's not a secret," Cheyenne interrupted. "Not a trick. I didn't do anything crazy or risk more than I should've to get them here. I had them made and brought them across. Really. Don't read into this any more than that, okay?"

The troll couple stared blankly at her.

Damn. I went way in over my head on this one. Time to go.

"Okay." She nodded. "So, we're gonna go. If anything happens that seems a little off or they give you any issues, I wanna hear all about it the next time I stop by."

"*Maji,*" Bryl whispered, tugging on her mother's sleeve.

"Hush, girl."

"*Maji!*"

"What?"

The girl grinned. "Peridosh."

"What does that have to do with this?"

"*Yes.*" R'mahr turned to his wife, grinning like a lunatic. "The market."

"I know what it is, you stone-headed buffoon."

"Yadje, it is the perfect place!" He grabbed her by the shoulders and managed to get in a few good shakes before she slapped his hands away.

"I swear, how you two ever manage to get anything done with all the crazed ideas in your heads." She shot her husband a sidelong glance. "Perfect place for what?"

"To use these gifts." Laughing, R'mahr gazed at Cheyenne with renewed excitement.

This guy's riding an emotional rollercoaster, that's for sure. "You can use them wherever you want," she told him.

"Yes. We'll see if they do what they were meant to do with so many magicals around and so many things from home."

"It is the perfect place to test them for her," Yadje whispered.

"Yes. You always have such brilliant ideas in that beautiful head of yours." He grabbed her head and kissed the side of it before she pushed him away, chuckling self-consciously.

"Sounds like you guys have it all figured out." Cheyenne nodded at them and turned toward the door. "Can't wait to hear how it goes."

Beside the front door, Neros unfolded his legs and rose to his feet in one quick, fluid motion, startling the woman and making her jump. R'mahr yelped in surprise, and Yadje jumped again before smacking his arm.

"I would like to see it."

"See what?" Ember asked.

"This Peridosh market." Neros blankly scanned the troll family's faces before settling his gaze on his cousin. "You will take me there, Cheyenne. Won't you?"

Cheyenne thought, *Shit.* "That wasn't part of the plan."

"Oh, please, Cheyenne." Bryl bounced up and down, her braids flying around her head. "Please, please, please. This is better than any other time. We have activators now. Come with us."

"Your cousin has never been?" Yadje asked.

"No, but—"

"Then we must go together!" R'mahr clapped his hands and laughed. "It is a fine plan."

Cheyenne looked at Ember. "I wasn't going to go underground today."

The fae shrugged. "I mean, did you have any other plans?"

The drow snorted. *Way to throw me under the bus, Em.*

"Please come," Bryl repeated. "Please, please, please!"

"Yes, Cheyenne," Neros said. When she turned to look at him, his lips slowly peeled back into a wide grin. The expression on his human illusion made him look even more insane. "Please."

"Dammit." She rolled her eyes and grabbed the doorknob. "Fine. Let's go. But it's a quick trip for us, got it?"

"I look forward to it." Neros stopped in the front doorway as the troll family scurried around to get ready to go. He craned his neck to study the doorframe above him.

"Nothing special about this one." Ember nudged him into the hallway. "They're all the same."

"I like doorways."

"Even the kind that don't pop you in and out of different dimensions? Huh. Go figure."

CHAPTER THIRTY-THREE

"Hey, Tony." Cheyenne jerked her chin at the scowling man behind the back counter of the froyo shop in Union Hill. "Been a while."

"Not long enough, drow." The magical looked her up and down, then glanced at the troll family in their human illusions but ignored Ember and Neros. "It's always either this bunch of yups or those three yahoos who show up sober and way too loud and leave plastered and even louder. These the only friends you got?"

She raised an eyebrow at him, then snorted. "Only ones worth dragging past your grumpy ass."

Tony chuckled and straightened the open magazine in his hand with a quick flick. He didn't bother to look away and pretend to read when Ember shot him a confused smile over her shoulder.

"This is awesome," Bryl muttered, bouncing on her toes as they waited for the nod from Tony to enter the Employees Only door in the back of the shop. "This is so awesome. I can see everything."

"Stop bouncing, *hinya*." Yadje stroked her daughter's illusioned blonde pigtails and smiled. "Or I will catch it from you."

"To see the world again. Ha." R'mahr grinned at his wife and daughter. "Can you imagine?"

"Vividly." The woman's smile faded. "That is why we are here."

Ember stuck her hands into her jacket's pockets and gazed around the empty froyo shop. "I wonder how many people come here in the winter."

"More'n you'd think," Tony grumbled. "And I *still* don't make any money." He nodded at the door marked for employees, then returned his attention to his magazine.

"Time to go." Cheyenne opened the door and held it for the troll family, Ember, and Neros to step inside. She followed, shut the door, and joined them in the pitch-black of the supply closet that wasn't a supply closet.

When the lights clicked on, Bryl was grinning as she studied the steel walls. "It's not as cool as Groulco or Kur Vróst, but it's still awesome."

The elevator shuddered, and the only magical inside who didn't look quickly at the double doors was Neros. The drow's human illusion fell away, and he stood in the far corner with his hands clasped behind his back, staring at the trolls.

"Groulco and Kur Vróst?" Yadje frowned at her daughter. "When were you in either of those places?"

The girl looked nervously at her parents. "Da took me."

"You did what?"

"Please, *ma gairín*." R'mahr chuckled through a tight grimace. "We can talk about this later, yes?"

His wife scowled at him. "Oh, we'll talk. Years, we've spent Earthside, and now I hear you took our child to two of the most—"

He cleared his throat, nodding briefly at Cheyenne and Ember, and Yadje pursed her lips without another word.

Cheyenne stuck her hands in her pockets and studied the elevator walls as they slowly descended. *Activators can't fix everything.*

Ember raised her eyebrows. "So, is there anything specific you guys wanna look for while we're down here?"

"Ah." R'mahr bobbed his head, his smile returning now that the subject had been changed. "I merely wish to see the magic again. To sift through wares and choose a gift or two for my *wadeenesh* without having to buy ingredients for a spell that would find me the best ingredients for a spell."

Cheyenne squinted. "It's that complicated, huh?"

"Without an activator, Cheyenne? Yes. Everything is complicated."

"I want to watch the crafters!" Bryl added. "*Maji*, you think it'll look anything like back home?"

"Well, they're not sparksetters over here. That much I do know."

"That's the main difference," Cheyenne added. "There isn't a system over here that runs all the tech the way it does on the other side, but the translators should work. Make things a little easier to understand, at the very least."

"*Hishmál*." R'mahr's eyes widened, and he leaned so far toward her, she expected him to stumble across the elevator and crush her against the wall. "Cheyenne. If you can bring activators across, do you think you could bring other things too?"

"Like what?" Ember asked.

"Building mechanisms. Speeders. Other tech."

"We could make a house like ours back home!" Bryl shouted. Yadje hushed her and drew her daughter toward her, wrapping her arms around the girl's chest.

"Just imagine." R'mahr laughed. "Earthside sparksetters. Devices we wouldn't have to make ourselves."

"Or fail to make because we're farmers," Yadje muttered.

"We *were* farmers." He pointed at his wife. "Now, we are O'gúleesh in a new world, a world that could be changed to help us live the way we were intended to live. Better, yes?"

"Okay, don't get too far ahead of yourself," Cheyenne said with a shrug. "I know it's exciting."

"It is very exciting, Cheyenne."

"But we have to take this one step at a time. I want to make sure those activators work well enough that I can hand them out to the magicals who need them the most without wondering if I'm lying to their faces."

"About what?" Yadje's eyes widened.

"About whether they can do what I'm hoping they can do. Make things easier."

"And once the sparksetters can make the crossing—"

"Whoa, R'mahr." Cheyenne spread her arms and laughed. "I'm not even trying to look that far ahead right now, okay? It's one thing to keep refugees safe and able to take care of themselves on this side.

Trying to set up every single Earthside O'gúleesh in the lap of magi-tech luxury is completely different."

"Yes. Yes, I understand." R'mahr dipped his head, looking a little abashed but still failing to hide his excitement about the whole idea. "It would be wonderful, would it not?"

"In the best-case scenario, yeah." Ember smiled at Bryl. "But there'd still be a lot of kinks to work out if O'gúl tech ever became an everyday occurrence for magicals on this side."

"The focus should remain on the magic," Neros muttered, his face two inches away from the elevator wall as he studied it.

Everyone else looked at him.

"What does that mean?" Cheyenne asked.

Her cousin tilted his head and pressed his finger against the metal wall. "The balance is restored in both worlds. It must still be protected."

The elevator fell silent, then R'mahr snorted out a laugh. "Your cousin is an interesting drow, Cheyenne."

"Yeah, that's one way to put it." She shook her head at Neros, who'd stopped inspecting the wall and now leaned his head against it instead, closing his eyes. *And here I thought I was done with vague riddles about magic and both worlds, blah, blah, blah. The rest should work itself out anyway.* "Oh, and before you guys run off through the market, I wanna make sure we're all on the same page about the activators."

"Oh." Yadje reached behind her ear to touch the star activator as her husband and daughter removed their illusions. "Would you like to use one?"

"What? No. I have my own. And those are for you to keep."

"Really?" Bryl's eyes grew impossibly wide. "You mean, forever?"

"If you want them that long, yeah." The drow couldn't help but chuckle at the kid's amazement. "But for now, let's keep it a secret between all of us in this elevator, okay?"

"I can keep a secret."

"I thought so."

R'mahr frowned. "You do not want us to reveal the gift before its time. I understand."

"Thanks."

"I do want to know. Do you know how long you will be keeping this secret?"

Yadje clicked her tongue at him. "None of your business how long she does or doesn't plan anything."

The troll shook his head. "I do not mean to offend, Cheyenne."

"No, I know." She shot Ember a sidelong glance. *These guys are impossible to figure out sometimes.* "I'm not offended. The best answer I can give you is that if everything goes well with your activators and a few others on Monday, you might not have to keep the secret much longer than that."

"So soon?" Yadje's smile grew. "The old tales all said the *Lainari* would act quickly. I do not think anyone expected mere days."

"Okay, first, I'm not the *Lainari*. Or any *Lainari*." Cheyenne looked impatiently at the elevator doors. "And this is still just a maybe. For now."

"Of course."

"So, we're all keeping a huge secret from the rest of the world." Bryl gazed from one magical to the next, stuffed into the elevator with her. "This is the coolest thing I've done since we came to this world."

The elevator groaned and shuddered as it ground to a slow stop. The double doors slid apart, and the girl darted out onto the wide avenue of the underground marketplace before anyone could stop her.

"Don't you dare pass that first booth, Bryl!" Yadje hissed, holding herself back from jumping after the girl in panic. "You will not like what happens otherwise."

"*Maji!*"

"Don't '*Maji*' me. Mind yourself."

The troll stepped out of the elevator to walk beneath the wide, curving stone ceiling of Peridosh's tunnel, which stretched for miles beneath Union Hill and even more of Richmond. Ember bit back a laugh as she joined them. Cheyenne stepped out of the elevator and turned around to eye her cousin.

Neros seemed entranced by the plain, rough-hewn stone wall on the opposite side of the tunnel.

"Those doors are gonna close all on their own." She waved him forward. "And I have no idea how to stop them or open them up again if you take too long. Come on."

His pale eyes moved slowly toward her face, then the elevator doors did start to close. Neros took two steps across the metal box and slipped sideways through the closing panels, barely making it. He stared over his shoulder at the elevator like the thing had insulted him. "I do not understand these elevations, Cheyenne."

"Elevators."

A small frown flickered across his eyebrows. "But we went down."

"Okay, Mr. Nor'ieth." She put a hand on his back to guide him away from the end of the tunnel toward the crowded, bustling avenue of Peridosh. "Some things have weird names that don't make sense. All you need to remember is that if I tell you to hurry up or stay close or not to touch something, it's 'cause I've spent my whole life on this world, and I know what I'm talking about. Got it?"

"I understand." Neros' gaze fell on the first vendor stall to their left, where a toothless, grinning old goblin displayed a bunch of dented metal plates, worn leather straps, and something that looked a lot like a severed head covered in stringy, matted hair. "Tell me what this is."

The goblin's grin widened into a crazed leer as he looked the pale-skinned drow up and down in disbelief.

"Let's stick to the center aisle for now." Cheyenne grabbed a fistful of her cousin's jacket and yanked him toward her. "Right now, I'm telling you to stay close. There are way too many tables and shops here for you to sniff around at every single one. Anything that looks like a body part is off-limits too, got it?"

"Is that a regular occurrence in your world?" Neros stared at the curved ceiling draped in colorful banners that fluttered violently when the occasional winged magical darted past overhead. "The severing of body parts to sell?"

She snorted. "Not nearly as regular as it is in yours."

"Nor'ieth has no such customs."

"Of course it doesn't. I meant the rest of Ambar'ogúl. Come on. I wanna keep an eye on those ecstatic trolls."

CHAPTER THIRTY-FOUR

Ember stayed close enough to the troll family to keep an eye on them as they moved through the busy underground marketplace. Yadje tried to keep the bouncing, shouting Bryl in line, and R'mahr stared at the storefronts and vendor booths like he was walking through a dream.

I wonder how many magicals grin like lunatics in their dreams?

Cheyenne tried to keep an eye on the trolls too, but her attention was torn between making sure Neros didn't break away and get into trouble and trying to ignore the magicals staring at her through grime-streaked windows and dark doorways built into the rock walls. The magicals of Peridosh grinned as insanely as R'mahr.

It's not my first time down here.

She swerved away from a hunched skaxen dragging a large metal trunk into the alley. The old rat-faced orange magical beat a steady rhythm on the trunk with a mallet that looked a hell of a lot like a femur. A portly troll wearing two long overcoats one on top of the other took up the banging next, striking the metal table in front of the shop labeled Bloodtales with his fist.

"To the Black Flame," the old skaxen screeched. "The Black flame walks Peridosh!"

The magical cackled and kept up her banging.

Cheyenne widened her eyes at the skaxen and forced herself not to roll them. *Not this again. Earth was supposed to be an escape from this shit.*

Twenty seconds later, every vendor and shop owner in the magical marketplace, as well as the Earthside magical citizens browsing the market selection, had stopped what they were doing to take up the banging and the echoed cry of Cheyenne's O'gúleesh title.

Neros turned toward her, his lips twitching into a half-smile. "They crow for you, cousin."

"Yeah, I picked up on that." She shoved her hands into her pockets and kept walking through the crowd. "Why are you smirking at me like that?"

"You deserve this praise, Cheyenne." Neros gestured at the group of yellow-skinned gremlins whacking metal implements on huge iron keyrings in the doorway where they'd gathered. "And far more than this."

"You know, I'm starting to think I'm getting a lot more than I deserve." The crowd of Peridosh shoppers parted in front of her like a wave, grinning and thumping fists to their chests if they didn't have anything metal to bang on. Cheyenne nodded slowly, feeling the grimace on her face and unable to remove it. Then she saw Ember and the trolls up ahead, all of them smiling at her now. *At least they're not going full O'gúl native on me down here too.*

"Blood and honor for the Black Flame," a massive stone ogre roared from a recessed doorway on the right.

"*Lainarí* and wielder of the deathflame!"

"The Spider's bane!"

"Blood and honor!"

Cheyenne finally reached Ember and the trolls, feeling hundreds of magicals' eyes on her and a strong itch burning across the back of her neck that was growing stronger.

Ember chuckled. "You can take the magicals out of Ambar'ogúl…"

"Yeah, I get the point."

"You look like you're about to punch something."

"I wasn't expecting all the fanfare, Em." Cheyenne turned and briefly scanned the opposite side of the avenue and the magicals banging and stomping and shouting their allegiance and approval. *I don't want it either.* "This doesn't make sense."

"A whole bunch of Earthside magicals thanking you for overthrowing the worst dictator they've ever had is confusing to you?" Ember folded her arms and smiled at a young troll couple, each with one arm around their partner and the other pounding the metal door behind them. Neither saw the fae's expression. "Seems pretty cool to me."

"Well, yeah. It's not directed at you." Cheyenne frowned and scanned the wide avenue in both directions. The burning itch along the back of her neck intensified, bringing with it the tingle of strong magic she'd come to recognize.

"It's only been a few weeks. I'd take it in while it lasts and not let it bother you. This'll die down in a few more weeks anyway." Ember shrugged. "Probably."

"It's not the attention that's bothering me the most right now, Em." Cheyenne looked at her friend and caught a glimpse of the troll family behind Ember in front of the next shop down. Caught up in the excitement, R'mahr and Yadje thumped their fists on their chests and grinned at her. Bryl scanned the vials of roots and dried plant stems on the table beside her parents. "I'm more bothered that everyone down here has a clue about what happened."

"What?" Ember stepped toward her, laughing at the growing ruckus around them. "I can't hear you."

Cheyenne leaned closer to say it in Ember's ear. "How do they know about the new Cycle? About Ba'rael being overthrown and the whole Black Flame thing?"

The fae leaned back to look at Cheyenne with a playful frown. "Word gets around. Does it matter?"

"Yeah, kind of." Scanning the avenue again, Cheyenne fought the urge to reach back and slap the growing tingle of magical energy along her upper back and shoulders. *There's no communication between worlds and no way anyone crossed over before we did to tell the entire city about what happened. Word doesn't spread that fast.*

The buzzing itch flared with renewed strength, and she jerked her shoulders back at the sensation. A flicker of light in the corner of her eye caught her attention, and Cheyenne whipped her head up and to the right. Farther down the marketplace, a pale burst of opalescent flames raced across the avenue five feet above the tallest magical's head.

A second later, only the trail behind the flames remained, then that too disappeared.

"You okay?" Ember practically had to shout to be heard over the noise.

Cheyenne shook her head. "Something's wrong."

"Okay, before you jump to conclusions… Hey! Cheyenne, hold on a second." Ember raced after her friend through the crowd as Cheyenne headed toward the shop doorway above which the flames had disappeared. "What's going on?"

"You feel or see anything weird down here? I mean, besides the obvious." Cheyenne tossed her hand toward a drooling gremlin banging his fists on what looked like a miniature dumpster.

"No, but the look on your face says you do."

"Yeah. Same thing I—"

The huge, heavy wooden door of the Empty Barrel burst open and crashed against the wall of the tavern. Three magicals darted down the steps, roaring and slapping their hands against the metal plates they'd brought with them from inside. Right behind them was Ogsa, carrying a metal tankard in each hand and bashing them together.

"May the Black Flame reign," the orc bartender shouted. "For a thousand times as long as the last! Cheyenne!"

"Great." Cheyenne turned toward the orc with a tight smile. "Hey."

"Hey? Ha! That's all I get from you after weeks of nothing?" Ogsa bellowed laughter and clanged the tankards together. "Get inside, *Lainari*. Drinks on me today!"

"I'm not the damn—"

"Bring your fae friend, eh? I have enough Bloodshine for her too."

Cheyenne's shoulders sagged as the crowd around her bellowed and roared in approval.

"Come on," Ember said, taking her by the arm. "Might as well take it when it's offered, right?"

"You really wanna drink right now, Em?"

"I would enjoy a tankard of grog or two," R'mahr cut in from right behind them.

Ember laughed. "See? Hey, Ogsa! How about the trolls?"

"If they're with you two, why the hell not?" Ogsa bashed the tankards together again, then waved them inside as she disappeared into the dark tavern.

Cheyenne stared at the fae. "We didn't come here to throw a party in a tavern, Em."

"We're not. She is. Why not let her, huh?"

Yadje approached, towing Bryl behind her by the hand. "Do not buy us anything here, Cheyenne."

"She isn't." R'mahr laughed and threw an arm around his wife's shoulders. "It's free!"

"Nothing is free," Yadje muttered.

"Ah, but today—"

An explosion four shops down ripped through the air. Glass shattered in a shop window, spraying across the avenue and into the crowd of magicals, all pounding and shouting for the Black Flame. Now, as the ground beneath Peridosh trembled, the magicals shouted in surprise and leapt away from the broken windows. A burst of opalescent flames shot through the destroyed shop, though no one ducked or jumped away.

Because no one else can see it. Why the hell is it always me?

Half a dozen magicals ran out of the shop, shouting and glancing over their shoulders. An orc in gym shorts and a tight white t-shirt got caught in the flap of brightly dyed fabric hanging from the shop doorway and ripped it down with him as he stumbled into the avenue. Someone screamed inside, and Cheyenne rolled her eyes as she headed toward the shop.

"Cheyenne!" Ember took two hesitant steps after her.

The drow turned around and spread her arms. "If I can help, might as well, right?"

"I mean, yeah, but…"

Cheyenne hurried through the crowd, which was now scattering away from the exploded storefront. They made a clear path for her as she picked up the pace. A goblin woman tore away the colorful fabric hanging from the orc's face before stepping aside to allow Cheyenne through.

Broken glass crunched under her feet, then she stepped beneath the hanging wooden sign labeling the shop as Old-World Promises and entered.

Two identical gremlins in oversized bomber jackets and baseball caps stood on an elevated platform behind the checkout counter. Only one of them wore glasses, which he whisked off his face to rub clean with a soft cloth before slipping them back on again.

Cheyenne looked around the store. No trace of floating fire, but the tingle of magical warning still flared across her back. "What happened?"

Both gremlins jumped and blinked their yellow eyes at her.

"Fuck if I know, man." The one without the glasses shrugged. "Just some damn explosion."

"We don't even sell explosives."

"Weird shit, man."

"Totally weird."

Cheyenne walked along the wall where the windows had been blown out and studied the destroyed shelves. "What exploded, exactly?"

Glasses shrugged. "The air?"

"The air."

"Just because we're magicals, it doesn't mean we understand how all magic works." The other gremlin raised both hands in clueless surrender. "Honest."

"Yeah, okay." Cheyenne scanned the wreckage in the shop. "And you have no idea why someone would try to blow up the air in your shop?"

"For fun?"

"Nah, whoever it was wanted some shit." The gremlin without the glasses slapped the back of his hand against his brother's chest, then pointed at the broken shelf along the wall right behind where Cheyenne stood. "Took the snaregut."

"Aw, man." Glasses bobbed his head from side to side and grimaced, slapping his hands down on the desk. "That was our only one."

"Only one in all of Virginia, probably."

Cheyenne frowned. "What does a snaregut do?"

Another explosion wracked the marketplace two doors down. She looked at the gremlins, who stumbled against the desk as they tried to right themselves. *Shit. More attacks in the damn market.*

CHAPTER THIRTY-FIVE

Cheyenne darted out of the shop.

"Wait, wait! Ain't you gonna help us?"

"Yeah, cleanup on aisle one!"

She ignored the gremlins and skidded to a halt in the avenue as more magical shoppers darted away from the next storefront. Everyone stared at the busted-out front door. Summoning a crackling black energy sphere in one hand, Cheyenne headed for the next attacked shop, her shoulders burning now with the influx of powerfully concentrated magic around her. *This asshole just got a serious power boost, whoever it is.*

Before she got within five feet of the newest attack, the same heavy explosion with a burst of opalescent flames came from the shop behind her on the other side of the marketplace. Tables toppled over, spilling their wares across the ground while the ogre selling suspicious-looking vials of "miracle wart remover" roared and tried to collect everything.

"Cheyenne!" Ember ran toward her out of the panicking crowd. "What the hell is happening?"

"Another attack, Em."

"Not the war machines, though."

"Definitely not. This is something else."

The fae's luminous violet eyes widened. "Like what?"

The old goblin's potions shop erupted in a spray of tinkling glass and magical fire only Cheyenne could see. The goblin owner screeched in frustration and launched a stream of dark-green magic at the source of the explosion, but whoever was darting in and out of the shops was already gone and onto the next.

The goblin's attack sailed through the splintered doorway of the shop toward the crowd. Cheyenne threw up a huge shield of shimmering black light to catch the wayward attack, then spun toward the next burst of opalescent flames, shattered glass, and destroyed displays in another store across from the potions shop. A chunk of the stone wall above the doorway cracked and dislodged from the rest of the wall.

She reached out with her drow magic, feeling for that hook of resistance in the stone's makeup. When she pulled on it, spreading her hands apart and running toward the wreckage, the huge slab of stone burst into thousands of pebbles that dropped harmlessly to the ground in the center of the avenue.

There's a pattern here. She scanned the destroyed shops as another exploded farther down toward Peridosh's elevator entrance. Someone in that shop threw another attack at the unseen perpetrator, and the purple flames sailed across the shouting, scattering crowd of magicals and struck a stack of wooden barrels on the other side of the marketplace.

Cheyenne slipped into drow speed and took off toward the next shop she expected to be hit at any second. *Gotcha now, asshole.*

A circle of shimmering opalescent flames burst into existence at the shop in front of her, erupting with the thick, unbearably strong vinegar scent of concentrated magic. She raised her hand with the black energy sphere crackling in her palm and aimed at the fire.

Even though she was in enhanced speed, the magical behind what looked like a manufactured portal moved too fast for her to see. A blur of colors streaked from the portal into the shop, and before Cheyenne could launch her attack to stop whoever it was, a bolt of white light surrounded by the same shimmering flames struck her in the chest and sent her flying back across the avenue. She fell out of drow speed and crashed into a table of cages filled with some kind of O'gúleesh chicken.

The birds squawked and flailed, shooting brown and silver sparks in every direction as they fell around her.

Two more shops erupted in quick succession, then one more streak of the flames only Cheyenne could see raced across the air above the marketplace and disappeared.

What the fuck was that?

A puff of agitated bird feathers fluttered down in front of Cheyenne's face as she sat there against the fallen table. She blew them forcefully away and climbed to her feet.

"My birds! My fuckin' birds, man!" A squat, almost square magical with four-pointed tusks emerging from his toadlike head hobbled toward her, arms spread as he surveyed the damage. "You coulda squashed 'em, you know that?"

"Sorry." Cheyenne righted the table, and the toad-guy blinked his huge watery eyes at her.

"Aw, shit. Don't worry about it." Thumping a fist to his chest, he dipped his head. "Wasn't your fault, right? You got tossed around like the rest of us."

Frowning, she picked up one of the birdcages and set it back on the table. "You saw someone else get tossed around too?"

The bird shrieked at her, spouting silver sparks until she removed her hand from the cage.

The toad-guy scratched his square, wart-covered head. "Ah, not really. Figure of speech, right?"

"Sure." Grimacing at the ache in her back where she'd struck the table, Cheyenne rolled her shoulders back and surveyed the rest of the damage. No more invisible flames, no more explosions, but the shop-keepers who'd fallen victim to the strange attack were shouting from their doorways and behind shattered storefront windows.

"I don't hike prices. What the fuck's the point of stealing?"

"Asshole took my idlewór collection. Someone needs to learn some fell-damn manners."

"Endaru's balls, man! I didn't make the crossing to deal with the same fucking shit as I did in Kur Vróst."

The magicals who'd come to spend a peaceful morning in Peridosh shopping for O'gúleesh wares on Earth picked themselves up off the ground or helped their neighbors do the same. Most of them stared in surprise at the damage. A random few scattered through the crowd before it could pick up again with its usual bustle, heading for either the elevator doors at one end or whatever entrances they'd used farther down the underground tunnel.

"Cheyenne!" R'mahr enthusiastically waved both hands above his head before his wife yanked one of his arms down. They ran through the crowd toward her, Bryl bobbing and weaving through passing magicals to keep up with her parents. "*Hishmál*, Cheyenne. What a surprise, eh?"

"Something like that." She tried to smile at the trolls as they reached her. "You guys see anything weird? Besides exploding shops, I mean."

"Not a thing." R'mahr touched the activator behind his ear, his eyes growing wide. "Not even with these. Exciting, though, was it not? So much action!"

Yadje hissed at him and slapped his arm. "Destruction and stolen goods are not exciting, you big-mouthed *dae'bruj*. Someone attacked the market!"

"But no one was hurt." The troll man shot his wife a sideways look, then reached out to pat the top of Bryl's head. "And we are safe."

"Are we really? After all that?"

"I'm pretty sure that's a safe bet," Cheyenne added. "Doesn't look like anybody got hurt."

Ember jogged across the avenue toward them from the last pilfered shop, blowing strands of purple-streaked hair out of her face. "What the hell was that?"

"Somebody who obviously isn't into making legal transactions like the rest of us."

"Yeah, no kidding." The fae straightened the front of her jacket and studied the wreckage scattered across Peridosh. "You get a look at the guy?"

Cheyenne shook her head. "Not before I was blasted into the chicken booth over there."

"Me neither." Ember shrugged. "Doesn't look like anybody got hurt, though. As far as I can tell."

"That might be the only plus. Where's Neros?"

They turned in slow circles, searching for the pale-skinned drow.

They found him standing in the center of the wide avenue as magicals fell back into their normal shopping routine around him. He stood stock-still, his neck craned back as he stared at the curving stone ceiling of the marketplace. The magicals passing on either side of him cast him wary glances but didn't comment on his appearance or his odd interest in the ceiling.

Same on both sides, at least. Nobody questions a drow.

Cheyenne rolled her eyes and made her way toward her cousin, easily passing through the crowd of O'gúleesh refugees and Earthborn magicals, who cleared a path in front of her. Most bowed their heads or thumped fists to their chests, and she ignored the muttered addresses of "Black Flame" and "*Lainari.*"

"Neros." She grabbed her cousin's arm and looked at the ceiling. "Find something interesting in the rock?"

"All of this interests me, Cheyenne." He lowered his head to look at her. "You?"

"I'm not so much interested as pissed off about being thrown across a busy market. Come on. Time to go." She pulled him behind her until he picked up the pace on his own.

"Where are we going?"

"I don't know. Somewhere I can think without someone bowing and swearing their allegiance."

They reached Ember and the trolls again. R'mahr eyed the closest booth covered in brightly decorated tapestries and grinned. "I would very much like to continue our shopping."

"After all this?" Yadje hissed.

"Yes, *ma gairin.* No damage done."

"No damage?" She clicked her tongue. "Cheyenne is leaving."

"Not because I think it's unsafe here." The drow nodded. "Trust me. I'd tell you if it was. Whoever hit this place got what they needed and split."

"See?" R'mahr wrapped his arm around his wife's shoulders and gave her a little shake. "We are safe, so we will stay."

Yadje rolled her eyes.

I'm the wrong drow to ask for backup on that one. "You guys stay and do your thing. Or whatever you want. I have a few more things to get done today."

"We can keep the activators, yes?" R'mahr hunched his shoulders and looked around to be sure no one was listening.

"That hasn't changed." Cheyenne nodded at him, trying to pull up a reassuring smile. "And I'll stop by again in a few days to check in."

Bryl grinned up at her. "I can't wait."

"Remember." Cheyenne pressed a finger against her lips. "Our secret, right?"

The girl pressed her finger to her lips as her parents nodded.

"Good. See you guys later."

"Be well, Cheyenne!" R'mahr called after her.

Ember turned and waved at them before following her friend and Neros, who was being tugged along by his cousin's grip on his flowing white tunic. When they reached the end of the marketplace and stopped in front of the closed elevator doors, the fae folded her arms. "Okay. Now would be the time to spill whatever you didn't want the troll family to hear."

Cheyenne said, "I have no idea who that magical was."

Ember snorted. "Not exactly a secret, though."

With a quick look around to make sure nobody else had plans to join them on the ride back up, Cheyenne stuck her hands in her pockets, then leaned toward her friend. "They were faster than me in drow speed, Em."

"Really?"

"Yeah. Got a shot in before I could get a good look. And I think—"

"What?" Ember frowned. "Seriously. Spill it."

"I think they were opening their own portals. At least, that's what it looked like."

"You think a nightstalker attacked Peridosh to blow up a bunch of shops?"

The elevator doors shuddered open with a metallic growl, and they waited for the two orcs inside to clear out and walk down the avenue. Then Cheyenne stepped into the elevator. Ember joined her and grabbed Neros' hand to jerk him inside with them before the doors closed.

"Not nightstalkers, Em." Cheyenne leaned back against the wall and briefly closed her eyes. *Finally. Quiet.*

"Then what?"

"That's the million-dollar question, isn't it?" With a shrug, the drow kicked up one foot to brace it against the elevator wall. "Some magical who can open half a dozen portals one right after the other that look nothing like nightstalker portals to blow up a bunch of shops."

"Snaregut. Idlewór," Neros muttered.

"What?"

Her cousin listed a string of words she'd never heard before, his voice low and monotonous like he was talking in his sleep. Cheyenne and Ember exchanged confused looks, and when Neros finished, he settled his pale golden gaze on his cousin.

"Feel better?" Cheyenne asked.

Ember cocked her head. "What was all that?"

"What was stolen." Neros clasped his hands behind his back. "Items gathered for a spell."

"Great," Cheyenne replied. "What kind of spell?"

"A big one."

"Very helpful, Neros." Ember shot him a tight, pseudo-encouraging smile. "Care to elaborate any further on this 'big one?'"

Neros swept his gaze across the walls and ceiling of the elevator and took a long, slow inhale. "Where is this Oracle you know, Cheyenne?"

"What? No." She shook her head. "I told you, I'm done with Oracles."

"Perhaps that one may provide further insight."

"Into a spell? I don't think so. Oracles don't even provide insight into prophecies, and another one of those is the last thing I need right now."

"I am fond of them."

Ember snorted. "Yeah, I bet you are."

The elevator shuddered to a stop, and the lights switched off as Cheyenne grabbed the handle of the Employees Only door in front of them.

They left the elevator for the back of the froyo shop, and Tony looked briefly at them with no other reaction. "That was fast."

"You keep a timer on everybody, or just me?" Cheyenne asked, casting an illusion spell right there so she could stay in drow mode and keep her activator running, just in case.

"Let's put it this way," Tony said as he went back to his magazine, "you couldn't keep up with me."

"Uh-huh." She waited for Ember to cast illusions on herself and Neros before they headed past Tony's checkout counter toward the front of the store. Her phone buzzed in her pocket, and she pulled it out to see Maleshi's name on her screen. *This is either perfect timing or the worst.*

CHAPTER THIRTY-SIX

"Maleshi."

"Hey, kid. Where are you right now?"

Cheyenne paused halfway across the froyo shop, and Neros bumped into her from behind. "Hey, pay attention, huh?"

Maleshi laughed over the phone. "I thought I was."

"Not you. My space-case cousin." Cheyenne gestured at Ember, who raised her eyebrows in curiosity. "We're in Union Hill."

"Froyo shop, right?"

"Yeah. What's up?"

"I'd like your opinion on something. If you have a minute."

"Sure." The line went dead, and Cheyenne stared at her phone before slipping it back into her pocket.

"Who was that?" Ember asked.

"Maleshi wants a second opinion or something."

"Huh."

Neros leaned sideways to peer around Cheyenne and pointed at the space right in front of her. Two seconds later, the general's dark portal bloomed into existence, and Maleshi Hi'et materialized in the center of it.

She spread her arms and smiled. "Come on over."

"Hey, hey!" Tony slapped his magazine down on the counter. "You know how much time and energy I put into keeping this place under wraps from the clueless humans? Come on! Port in and out of someone else's goddamn place of business."

"Later, Tony." Ember tossed him a brief wave before darting through the nightstalker's portal.

Cheyenne nudged Neros forward, and he disappeared a second before she did. The portal closed behind them with a soft pop.

Tony peered through the front windows of his shop, scanning the street for witnesses, then sniffed and picked up his magazine. "Fucking nightstalkers. Think they run both damn worlds."

Maleshi's portal took them into her office in the Computer Science building on the VCU campus. Cheyenne looked around the room she hadn't set foot in for what felt like months and stuck her hands in her pockets. "You're spending your Saturday at work?"

"Don't judge." The general snapped her fingers, and silver light glowed around her before she took on her human illusion, her black fur fading into long black curls and her silver eyes dimming to a glowing green. "We had a hell of a vacation right before Thanksgiving break, and it's not like I can throw a few things together and magic my students' grades into existence."

"So you're playing catch-up," Cheyenne offered.

"Now that we overturned the Spider bitch, healed the blight, and saved both worlds from death and destruction? Yeah, I'm playing catch-up." Maleshi shrugged, and her playful smile faded when she turned to see Neros staring at her. "Oh. No offense about your asshole mom, by the way. At least not aimed toward you."

"Neither Ba'rael's choices nor her mistakes hold any sway over my emotions, nightstalker." Neros blinked, then scanned the cramped, messy office of Professor Maddie Bergman. "Is this your home?"

"Ha! Hardly. Though this weekend, I'd say it's something of a temporary abode." The general tossed her dark human hair out of her eyes. "No matter what I get done—and in the last month, it's been a hell of a lot more than anything I've pulled together over the last few centuries—I always seem to fall irreparably behind."

"I hope you didn't port us all here to ask my opinion on your grading rubric," Cheyenne muttered.

"You're funny." Maleshi pointed at her. "But no. I only waste my own time with useless academic paperwork like that. Speaking of which, have you put any thought into how you're going to pick up the pieces of your missed classes?"

"I'm trying to take one thing at a time."

The general blinked at Cheyenne, the corners of her mouth turned down in consideration. Then she shrugged. "Sure. That's worked for you pretty damn well so far, hasn't it?"

"Why are we here?" Ember asked as she walked past the metal shelves bolted to the walls behind Maleshi's desk. She tilted her head and scanned the titles of the textbooks crammed between more textbooks used as paperweights.

"Not to read those boring-ass books, I'll tell you that much. Come on." Maleshi waved them after her as she jerked open the door to her office and stepped into the hall.

Cheyenne put a hand on Neros' shoulder and practically pushed him out of the office, while Ember jogged a bit to catch up. Maleshi pulled the door shut behind the fae, and her auto-rigged spell turned off the lights and locked up behind her.

"I was hoping you might be able to pick up on something with that activator of yours, kid." The general led them down the hall toward the front entrance of the building. "You know, in case you can see something the rest of us aren't able to see."

"Yeah, that's been happening more than I expected."

"Really? Like what?"

"I'll let you know when I figure it out."

Maleshi shrugged. "Suit yourself. So here's the story. I'm sitting down at my desk, ready to claw my eyeballs out over this farce of an advanced program some little shitstain thought he was clever enough to hide in what most certainly was not his own code design. And I felt something."

Cheyenne snorted. "Whoa. The general's having feelings now, huh?"

"Don't get too excited, kid. I'm talking about the magical kind," Maleshi growled and pointed behind them. "Computer lab's off-limits. Yes, even to a Nor'ieth drow."

Cheyenne turned to see Neros reaching for the doorknob as he peered through the thin vertical window in the computer lab's door. "Neros."

"I got it." Ember approached him and guided the pale-skinned drow, who now looked like a pale-skinned human, away from the door. "Way too much stuff for you to break in there, man. Focus on the general, huh?"

"There is so much energy in that room."

Maleshi chuckled. "Sounds like your cousin picks up on both tech and magic, huh? Of course it's a lot of energy, big guy. How else are we gonna power two dozen computers that can barely run the programs for our curriculum?"

"You were getting to why you ported us here," Cheyenne added as Ember stepped behind Neros and guided him down the hall with her hands on his shoulders.

"Yep. Just outside. Which I'm sure you could've figured out on your own. Magical tingle and everything, right?" They reached the front door, and Maleshi pushed it open before holding it for the others to step out into the brisk, early-afternoon air.

The door clanged shut behind them, and the general folded her arms, nodding at the mound of uprooted earth covered in browning grass. "Same source. Different feeling."

"You felt something at the portal that never officially opened?" Cheyenne took a few steps toward the ruptured mound of earth on the quad about fifty feet from the front of the Computer Sciences building before turning to look at it.

"I felt something. The source of it was a hunch, but at the very least, I figured I'd ask the one drow who can close Border portals before they open."

Cheyenne finally turned to look at the deactivated portal ridge and stopped. Her activator picked up on something, all right, but it wasn't any kind of O'gúl tech, and it didn't warn her of an incoming threat this time.

That's the same damn fire from Peridosh.

She took another step closer and tilted her head, studying the tendrils of opalescent flames seeping out of the almost-sealed crack racing across the quad and filtering up into the air like smoke.

"The way you're checking that out tells me my hunch was right," Maleshi muttered.

"About something happening here? Definitely." The drow studied the flames, which should have disappeared by now if they were anything like what she'd seen in the marketplace. *And when we made the crossing Earthside the last time.*

"But not the part about the activator picking it up, right?" Ember folded her arms, glancing briefly away from Neros to see both Cheyenne and Maleshi staring at her.

"What makes you say that?" the general asked.

"The fact that I don't see anything." Ember tapped behind her ear. "Cheyenne's not the only Earthside magical with a little extra help these days."

"No shit." Maleshi chuckled. "You got Elarit's brainchildren to work over here, huh?"

"On a trial basis," Cheyenne muttered. "Still closed to the general public for now."

"Well, when you open those babies up and the free handouts start, keep your favorite nightstalker in mind."

Cheyenne turned to grin at the general over her shoulder. "Who said you were my favorite?"

"You only know two, kid, as far as I'm aware. Corian's not at the top of anyone's list." Maleshi laughed at herself. "Maybe he should be. Fine. Your favorite professor. How's that?"

"If you want an activator, Maleshi, all you have to do is ask."

"I *am* asking." The general gestured at the ruptured portal ridge. "And now I'm asking what you see right now that no one else can."

Still not a question. It's amazing she and Bianca got along so well.

Cheyenne turned back toward the portal and shrugged, more to relieve herself of the renewed tingle racing across her shoulders than to brush aside the general's half-assed question. "Well, at least it's not the blight spilling through the cracks anymore."

"But there's something else coming through."

"Either that, or it's a bunch of residual magic that doesn't look like it's going anywhere anytime soon." Cheyenne returned to the front of the building and met the general's gaze. "Did you see or hear anything when you got that feeling? Like, a burst of seriously strong magic?"

"Maybe an explosion?" Ember added.

Maleshi chuckled, then stopped when neither of the young magicals questioning her shared the amusement. "Oh. You guys are serious."

Ember nodded at Cheyenne. "It's the same thing from Peridosh, isn't it?"

"Yep. Guess now's as good a time as any to put it all out in the open." Cheyenne shot one final look at the broken portal ridge. "When we brought Bianca back Earthside again and crossed over in Colonial Williamsburg, I saw flames. In the air."

Maleshi frowned. "You said something about it then, didn't you?"

"Apparently, I'm the only one who can see them. At least, as far as I know. That's not including the magical who's been leaving them around like some kind of heavy spell-trail."

"So whoever Maleshi felt on campus was the same magical who blew up over half a dozen shops in the marketplace, and they just happened to be at the new Border portal in Colonial Williamsburg that no one knows about but us." Ember cocked her head. "That sounds more like multiple someones leaving a trail."

"It's not impossible," Cheyenne added. "Whoever they were, I'm pretty sure they were porting themselves in and out of those shops between explosions, and not with nightstalker magic."

Maleshi scoffed. "That's impossible."

"Said pretty much everyone about anything they couldn't see with their own eyes."

The general squinted at Cheyenne and bit the inside of her bottom lip. "Okay, yeah. You have a point. And these exploding portals happened in Peridosh today?"

"Right before you called me."

"What did this mysterious non-nightstalker want?"

Cheyenne shrugged. "Ingredients for a spell, according to the brainiac drow over there."

They all looked at Neros, who had lowered himself to the ground six feet away and now sat cross-legged in the grass, eyes closed, hands resting palms-up on his thighs.

Maleshi leaned toward Cheyenne and muttered, "He looks like L'zar's kid when he pulls shit like that."

"Yeah, I know. It's weird." Cheyenne shrugged. "But he did put together a running list of all the things that were stolen from the shops today, hence the big spell explanation."

"Are you sure it wasn't some kind of personal attack?" Maleshi asked. "Somebody trying to get even with a bunch of shopkeepers hiking prices Earthside because they can?"

Ember shook her head. "Nobody was hurt, which is seriously weird, seeing as there was a lot of flying glass and overturned tables. But it didn't look like it was targeted at anything other than the stolen goods."

"Huh." Frowning, the general turned to look at Neros again, tapping her lips with two fingers.

Stolen goods. Cheyenne grimaced. "The shopkeepers weren't the only victims of successful theft recently, either."

Ember's eyes widened. "Inolu."

"What?" Maleshi chuckled. "Only a complete moron would be stupid enough to steal from a banebreaker."

"A moron would try and probably fail. Maybe even die for their trouble." Cheyenne shook her head. "But a magical who can port in and out of tight spaces without nightstalker magic might be considered a genius. Inolu called me yesterday and accused me of stealing some valuable thing of hers. She was pissed."

"What was it?"

"A calibrax. Ever heard of those?"

Maleshi grimaced and let out a long, hissing breath through her teeth. "Yeah, unfortunately. It's like a superpowered magical generator."

Ember wrinkled her nose. "I'm hoping it's the 'keep your electricity on when the power goes out' kinda generator. But it's not, is it?"

The general shook her head. "No. This is the kind that amplifies the strength behind a large surge of magic. And when I say amplify, I mean like in emergency-broadcast style. Whatever spell or innate ability it's used to pump up would be strong enough to overpower any surrounding magic. Wards. Security. Dampening spells. Attacks. You name it."

"Shit." Cheyenne ran a hand through her hair and studied the portal ridge. "We have an unknown magical darting around Richmond with a calibrax and a bunch of ingredients for a huge spell, according to Neros, that looks like it's gonna be amplified by a bajillion for what? Something to do with the Border portals?"

"That would be an intelligent guess and an extremely unfortunate surprise if it were true," Maleshi said.

Ember scanned the empty quad with a frown. "You think it's all the same magical?"

"Yep."

"Did you at least get a good look at the guy?" Maleshi asked. "Or woman, as it were."

Cheyenne shook her head. "A bunch of colorless flames around the explosions and flying overhead, like I said. Same stuff that's leaking out of this portal right here."

"Flames." The general leaned away from the portal ridge despite it being almost fifty feet away and wrinkled her nose. "I only know of three magicals who use flames with magic that concentrated. As a signature calling card, of course. You, L'zar—"

"And the Sorren Gán?" Cheyenne offered.

"Oh, you can read minds now, can you?"

Cheyenne shot the general a deadpan stare. "No, but the thought occurred to me too. I didn't do all this. L'zar isn't a nightstalker and can't open portals. Plus, I'm sure he wouldn't have attacked me the way he did in Peridosh."

"You were attacked?"

"To get me out of the way. That's it." Cheyenne dug the toe of her black Van into the browning grass and stared at the ground. "Whoever it was moved way too fast for me to see a thing, even in enhanced speed."

"Wow." Maleshi's fingers thoughtfully tapped her lips again. "I'm starting to lean toward a new magical we've never seen before."

"Is that even possible?"

"Beats me, kid. At this point, it's pretty safe to say nothing's impossible, don't you think?"

"It could be the Sorren Gán," Ember added. "Couldn't it?"

Cheyenne and Maleshi both shook their heads. "That thing doesn't leave its cave for anything, Em."

"Well, unless it's a feast of magical discharge exploding out of Hangivol's city limits." Maleshi snorted. "And even that had to be bought and paid for first."

Cheyenne said, "Yeah, don't remind me. And the Sorren Gán wouldn't have any reason to come Earthside to steal a bunch of ingredients from an underground marketplace and a banebreaker. That thing's already way more powerful than any magical has a right to be."

"I'd call it a beast." Maleshi nodded. "But I agree with you. Not the Sorren Gán, but I have no fucking clue what else it could possibly be."

"Great." With a snort, Cheyenne looked at the cloudy November sky and shook her head. "So, someone's storing up stolen goods to get ready for a massive spell powered by the calibrax, and we have absolutely no way to track it down. Not the easiest thing we've ever had to do."

The general stuck a finger in the air and raised an eyebrow. "Not the hardest, either."

"Maybe." *Unless whoever this magical is completes the spell and ends up killing everyone within a hundred-mile radius, I don't think the Olfarim are gonna show up to undo that mess like the last time.*

"The Oracle might be able to offer a suggestion or two," Neros muttered.

Maleshi's raised finger dipped toward Cheyenne's cousin. "Is he talking about Oracles?"

"Yeah. I already told him no."

"It might prove to be a useful conversation, Cheyenne."

"Not happening, Neros." Cheyenne stared at Maleshi as she called to her cousin, who was still sitting cross-legged in the grass. "As cool as Gúrdu is and everything, I'm done with Oracles and prophecies and trying to find answers in a bunch of gibberish."

Maleshi snorted. "Don't let him hear you call it that."

"Right. Because bashing him out of a prophetic state and choking him out to get him to stop was way more respectful."

"Hey, that was one time." Maleshi pointed at Cheyenne. "And it was the wrong damn time for a prophecy."

"It's always the wrong damn time for a prophecy."

The general cocked her head and shrugged. "Very true."

Cheyenne took one last look at the flame-leaking portal. "If you feel anything else like this, let me know, okay?"

"Well, now." The general smoothed the front of her wrinkled mustard-colored cardigan. "I will, kid. And when you finally approve the Black Flame's Earthside Activator Service..."

"Yeah, yeah. I have your number."

Ember helped Neros to his feet, and the three of them turned to Maleshi, waiting.

The general asked, "What?"

"My car's in Union Hill."

"Oh. Right." Chuckling, Maleshi raised her hands, glancing across the empty quad. "Right where I picked you up."

The dark window of light opened up into the froyo shop, immediately followed by Tony's grumble of protest, even though no one was there to see two drow and a fae materialize in his store.

L'zar Verdys stumbled across the open clearing beside the first unregulated Border portal to open in thousands of years, the very one he'd visited with his daughter and his team of loyal followers for their first attempt to make the crossing into Ambar'ogúl together.

That all seemed far away now, like a dream he only thought he'd lived.

No. This is the dream. This isn't real.

A rumbling laugh filled his mind, coming from everywhere and nowhere all at once.

"You've lost touch with reality, little drow. It's finally happened."

L'zar spun, reeling like a drunkard too far in his cups, and shot a blast of bright-white light across the clearing at nothing but dry grass and the few deciduous trees holding onto the last leaves of the season. The laughter in his mind resumed.

"This wasn't the agreement," he muttered, frantically scanning the tree line around him for movement or magic or some sign that he wasn't insane. "This isn't what I wanted."

"That isn't your call to make."

An unseen force spun the drow thief around, making him stagger violently until he faced the glistening pillars of black stone stretching in a jagged ridge for miles to the east and west. L'zar gritted his teeth and blasted two more attacks of white light at the Border portal. A shimmering wall of pink light erupted between the black stone columns where his attack hit, wobbling like a forcefield until the energy of his magic and resistance faded.

"It's all wrong," he muttered, smoothing his white hair away from his face with both hands. "All of it. I was finished."

"Your work has only begun, L'zar," the voice taunted, shoving him forward again.

Like a madman—and maybe he finally was that—the drow thief struggled against the power tugging at him as if his hands had been tied in front of him. The owner of his fate led him forward to the destiny he'd never wanted. He dug his feet into the ground, trying to wrest back control of his body. Dirt and leaves and dry grass puffed up around him as he lurched forward, his shoes digging two-inch trenches in the earth as he was forced toward the portal ridge.

Not my destiny. Not my responsibility.

The portal ridge emitted bursts of colorful light. To L'zar, the magic flaring between those columns seemed to suck all the light out of the air around him instead of lending to it.

"I don't want this!" His golden eyes widened as he slid toward the glistening black stone. "I won't do it!"

The rumbling laughter exploded in his head, drowning out all other sounds. L'zar dropped into a crouch two feet in front of the closest fist of jagged black stone and clapped his hands over his ears. *This can't be happening. I wasn't meant to unravel on this side. Not like this.*

"This is the price you must pay for becoming who you wanted to be, little drow." The roaring chuckle of the voice inside his head softened into a cruel, mocking croon of false sympathy. *"You wished to become the Dark Smiling Weaver. Now your master calls you to fulfill your duty."*

"I am my only master!" L'zar dug his hands into the earth, gritting his teeth and fighting the force threatening to lift him off the ground and bash him against the portal stones.

"You are a master of lies and deceit," the voice rumbled. *"I'll give you that. Stop fighting, L'zar. We're nearly finished."*

With a roar, the drow threw himself away from the portal ridge and staggered across the clearing again, nearly throwing himself face-first to the ground in his struggle to get away. He straightened, spun in a tight circle, and stared at the forest.

How did I get here? What am I doing?

"None of this is the same." He whirled again, his racing heartbeat and heavy breathing rushing together in his ears and drowning out the silent crisp autumn air around him. "I did not see this!"

"*You* will *see, little drow.*" The rumbling laughter overtook him even as he fought to maintain his grip on reality and consciousness. "*Oh, yes. When our work is finished, you will see everything laid out before you the way it was always meant to be. The way I meant it to be.*"

A crushing weight pressed down on L'zar's chest. His breath tightened in his throat, coming in quick, wheezing gasps. "No!"

"*You cannot withstand me.*"

"I won't!" The drow's vision blurred, dancing with black spots as he fought for breath. "Release!"

"*Not yet.*"

The blackness that had been L'zar's existence for the last three days took over again, and his mind was lost to him. It belonged to another now, and even as he struggled against the pressure, he knew he had no choice but to give in yet again.

CHAPTER THIRTY-SEVEN

Back at their apartment, Cheyenne and Ember tossed the sandwiches they'd picked up from Gnarly's in Jackson Ward on the coffee table and sat down for lunch.

Neros stared at the wrapped subs, watching intently as Ember stripped the tape off one end and unrolled the whole thing on the coffee table. "How much of this does one eat?"

"Of the paper?" Ember said, "none of it. Wrappers go in the trash. But feel free to eat as much of the sandwich as you want." She slid it along the coffee table toward him and picked up her sandwich to start the process all over again.

Cheyenne unwrapped hers in her lap in the black leather recliner as Neros struggled to find the best way to hold a sub. "Like this. Two hands. Bite."

He managed to get the sandwich to his mouth, but the whole thing fell apart at the first bite, splattering turkey and cheese, mustard, onions, and lettuce all over his lap and on the paper wrapper on the table. Neros chewed the small bite and stared at the mess in front of him. "It is delicious but difficult."

Ember and Cheyenne looked at each other and snorted. The fae swallowed her mouthful and nodded at Neros' dismembered sandwich. "It takes practice."

"I will not be here long enough to master this skill." He grabbed a tomato slice between two fingers and tilted his head back to stuff the whole thing into his mouth.

"Too bad," Cheyenne said with a smile. "Sandwich-eating skills are highly valued on this side."

Ember fought back a laugh and ended up letting out a squeak before taking another huge bite.

"Are you well?" Neros asked, leaning forward to peer at her face. She nodded vigorously and clenched her eyes shut.

"Eat your lunch." Cheyenne nodded at the rest of the spread on the table. "And that drink's for you, by the way."

He grabbed the paper cup, staring at her, and sniffed the top of the straw before taking a tentative sip. Neros recoiled but smacked his lips. "This is?"

"Lemonade."

"Wonderful."

"There. See?" Cheyenne chuckled as she met Ember's gaze, and her friend fought to keep her food in her mouth as she laughed. "Caffeine's one thing, but give a Nor'ieth drow sugar, and you're in for life."

Ember snatched a napkin from the pile of their takeout bags and clapped it to her mouth as her laughter finally burst out of her and she doubled over her lap.

Two brisk knocks came at the front door, followed by, "It's Matthew."

"Of course it is." Cheyenne leaned forward to grab her paper cup of peach-flavored iced tea and took a long drink. "It's open!"

Matthew cleared his throat, and she heard his feet shuffling on the soft carpet in the hall. "Are you sure?"

"I promise it's not a trick," she called. "Come in."

The front door opened slowly, then Matthew poked his head through and scanned the main room of the apartment. Relief washed over him when he saw all three of them sitting in the living room, and he slipped through the door before closing it behind him. "Hey."

Ember swallowed and wiped her mouth with the napkin. "Hi, Matthew. You hungry?"

"Oh. Uh, you didn't have to get me anything—"

"We didn't." Cheyenne nodded at her cousin, who'd abandoned the scattered half of his sandwich and was wiping globs of mustard and mayo off his light trousers and sucking them off his finger. "But Mr. I Don't Practice With Sandwiches over here isn't gonna eat a whole foot-long."

Matthew gazed at Neros with raised eyebrows. The pale-skinned drow picked up a folded slice of turkey off the splattered wrapper and dangled it in front of him, offering it to their neighbor. "I would be happy to offer you this. What type of flesh did you call it, Cheyenne?"

She choked back a laugh. "Turkey flesh."

"Turnkey? You eat your jailors in this world?"

Ember barked a laugh and quickly covered it.

"It's a bird. We don't eat people, Neros." Cheyenne looked at Matthew and shrugged. "At least most of us don't. And we don't give animals control of our prisoners."

Matthew shook his head. "I stepped into the wrong thing at the wrong time."

"Here. Take the other half of mine." Ember gestured at her sandwich, and Matthew smiled in appreciation.

"Yeah, okay." He sidled between the fae's legs and the coffee table, then sat on the couch between her and Neros. "Thanks, Ember."

"Sure. Plenty to go around."

Matthew leaned forward and set four more star activators on the corner of the coffee table. "These are ready to go."

"Cool." Cheyenne studied the silver four-pointed stars and nodded at him. "Thanks."

"There are more too," he added quickly, looking at Cheyenne and Ember. "I mean, I didn't take all morning to sync up four if that's what you're wondering. I've got a little over half that first trunk ready so far."

"Sounds like good timing to me." Ember smiled at him and took a huge bite of her sandwich.

"You think we can have all two hundred up and running before Monday night?" Cheyenne asked.

"Oh, for sure. I mean, you said you wanted a few more, so I figured I'd stop by and drop these off."

"Hey, Matthew."

He whipped his head toward Cheyenne and blinked. "Yeah."

"You look a little nervous."

"What? I'm not nervous." He shifted on the couch, leaning forward to rest his forearms on his thighs as he clasped his hands together. "I want to make sure I'm doing this right, you know?"

"As long as you're not powering up two hundred activators for the Bull's Head, I'd say you're doing it right."

Matthew nodded at the four stars on the table. "Are they working? The way they're supposed to be?"

"So far, so good." Ember gave him a thumbs-up before picking up her sandwich for another huge bite.

"No glitches? Nothing blocking the use of magic, I guess, or anything else?"

Cheyenne grinned at him. "You do want this to work, don't you?"

Matthew took a deep breath. "Yeah. Look, I know there's not a lot I can do to make up for everything that happened with the last program and my uncle, but I'm trying."

"To redeem yourself." Cheyenne nodded. "I get it. Even if we do find a few bugs in this program and hit a snag here and there, trust me. You're already more than making up for what happened."

He reached for the other half of Ember's sandwich. "Doesn't feel like it." He took a huge, distracted bite and chewed slowly, staring at the table.

Cheyenne studied him with a curious smile. "You hear something about your uncle's trial?"

Crumbs spilled from his mouth, and he tried to catch them before swallowing thickly. "How'd you know?"

"You got this antsy the last time someone updated you on Colonel Thomas' fate." The drow shrugged. "Just a guess."

Ember looked at their neighbor. "What did you hear?"

"I got an email this morning. I guess the FRoE people thought it was a necessary courtesy, or whatever. Verdict came in pretty fast. Guilty on all counts. There were too many to remember." Matthew shook his head. "They're taking him to some prison outside DC. I've never heard of it. Couldn't find it in any federal database, either. Whoever wrote this email tried to reassure me he'd be safe in a non-magical block reserved for humans, I guess."

Cheyenne almost choked on her sandwich and dropped the whole thing in her lap with a wet slap and a crinkle of paper. "They're sending him to Chateau D'rahl?"

"That's not what they called it."

"I'm pretty sure that's just the nickname, right?" Ember asked.

Cheyenne shrugged and wiped her mouth with the back of a hand. "Not like any of us are experts on all the prisons out there for magicals, but there's only one anywhere near DC."

Matthew swallowed again and looked at the women. "Is he gonna be okay in there?"

"Is anyone really okay in prison?"

Ember shot Cheyenne a warning look. "That's not helping."

"It's a fair question, Em." The drow forced herself to hold back the grin that threatened to break through at any minute. *That asshole gets to spend a long-ass time behind bars with the magicals he's been cracking down on for at least the last twenty-one years.* "But hey. Chateau D'rahl has a humans-only block. Who knew?"

"Is that a good thing?" Matthew set the sandwich down on the table and grabbed a napkin. The thin paper was twisted into a rope in two seconds.

"Again, it's prison."

"It's the best of a shitty situation," Ember said slowly, staring at Cheyenne. Then she turned to Matthew and gave him a reassuring smile. "It's a max-security prison that's off the federal map. Nobody knows about it except the FRoE and the magicals locked up in there."

"Right." Cheyenne nodded and took another long drink of her tea. "They probably figured he'd be better off there. Safer, sure. And nobody wants an ex-FRoE officer sitting around with his fellow human inmates and spilling all the beans about magicals and Border portals and the other world they all come from, not to mention FRoE secrets."

"They don't want him in a civilian prison," Matthew muttered.

"Right." Ember nodded slowly. "And Chateau D'rahl's one of the hardest places to get into."

Cheyenne shrugged. "Well, comparatively."

Their neighbor looked at her with a concerned frown. "What does that mean?"

"If you're a drow halfling with a few rogue FRoE agents, a nightstalker, and a troll hacker on your side, it's not impossible to infiltrate—"

"Cheyenne." Ember shook her head.

Matthew wheezed out a breath, his eyes bulging. "You broke into the max-security prison for magicals where they're sending my uncle for military misconduct?"

"Military misconduct." Cheyenne grimaced. "Is that what they're calling it?"

"Oh, my God." Ember rolled her eyes. "Your uncle's doing time for trying to start some serious shit between magicals and humans, Matthew. They're not exactly gonna give him a light sentence."

"Twenty years. Definitely not light."

"Wow." Ember blinked and raised her eyebrows. "That's a long time."

"In a prison that's not impossible to break into." Matthew ran a hand through his hair. "He's not gonna make it through that whole sentence, is he?"

"You don't have anything to worry about," Cheyenne added quickly. "I mean, yeah. It sucks that the uncle you thought you knew was involved with an organization that doesn't even fall under federal juris-diction and tried to singlehandedly carry out mass magical genocide with technology he should never have gotten his hands on. Technology *you* made it possible to operate."

"Jesus, Cheyenne." Ember stared at her.

"But it's not public knowledge." Cheyenne shrugged. "Only the FRoE board and those rogue agents I mentioned know what the colonel did and tried to do, like, the detailed specifics of it. Sure, everyone knows he was stopped and captured and charged, but no one's gonna storm the gates of Chateau D'rahl to get to him."

"Like you did." Matthew gritted his teeth and eyed her.

"Totally different." She sat back in the recliner and dropped her arms on the armrests. "We broke into the place to release a prisoner we needed to take across the Border with us to finish a few things on the other side."

"Saving two worlds and all that," Ember added with another reas-suring smile. "You know how it goes."

Matthew swallowed. "Not really."

"Listen. The point is, your uncle fucked up, and now he's paying for it. If anyone wanted to get at him in there, it would be the Bull's Head."

"So he's not safe in there."

"No, he's safe." Ember set a hand on their neighbor's knee without even thinking about it. "Maleshi killed them all."

He glanced down at her hand on his leg, and she quickly removed it. "I'm in way over my head, aren't I?"

"No. You're doing great." Ember picked up her sandwich and took another huge bite before meeting Cheyenne's gaze.

"You're doing your part, Matthew." Cheyenne nodded at him. "Helping us with these activators is a huge step toward making sure what your uncle tried and almost succeeded in doing never happens again." *Including almost blowing my brains out.* "Colonel Thomas made his bed, and no one's gonna show up to try to drag him out of it."

Matthew swiped a hand across his forehead and nodded. "For as totally insane as this conversation is, I might feel a little better."

"Good. Like I said, you have nothing to worry about."

The living room fell silent. Then the loud slurp of Neros trying to suck down the rest of his empty lemonade cup broke through, and everyone turned to look at him.

The pale-skinned drow popped the straw out of his mouth and pulled away from the to-go cup, staring at the paper and plastic in his hand. "This lemon-helper is better than icy teeth."

Matthew pressed his lips together and jerked a thumb at the drow beside him. "Your cousin's a little off, isn't he?"

"He's not from here." Cheyenne raised an eyebrow at Neros, who smacked his lips loudly as he pried open the cup's plastic lid to peer inside. "Lemonade, Neros. Lemonade and iced tea. Which go pretty damn well together, now that I think about it."

"That is possible?" Neros gazed at her with a growing smile. "What other novelties can be added?"

"I mean, that's kind of up to you," Ember replied.

He looked at her, then frowned and placed a hand on his stomach. "And yet I—" A belch escaped him, startling him out of his intense concentration on lemonade, of all things. "I feel strange."

Cheyenne cocked her head. "First time drinking that much sugar'll do that. Should've got him a smaller size, Em."

"Hey, I thought he could handle it." Ember gestured over Matthew's lap at Neros. "He's a grown-ass magical. Older than all three of us put together times ten."

"Yet as clueless as a three-year-old." With a snort, Cheyenne stood, set her sandwich on the table, and snatched the empty cup out of her cousin's hand.

"What are you doing?" Neros burped again and turned in his seat to watch her as she headed for the kitchen.

"Getting you some water. Then you should probably eat that sandwich."

"I do not eat flesh, Cheyenne."

Ember leaned forward to slide the messy sub wrapper toward him. "Don't eat the turkey then. Everything else is good to go."

The sink turned on in the kitchen, and Neros leaped to his feet. "Wait! I wasn't finished."

"Water." Cheyenne turned off the faucet and lifted the full paper cup toward him. "For the rest of the day. I'm not letting you overload on sugar so you can puke all over the furniture." She paused on her way back to the living room and blinked. *Damn. That was Bianca Summerlin speaking through me, and I didn't even have to try.*

Ember had the same thought and stifled a laugh as she returned to her sandwich.

"Here. You guys have water in Nor'ieth, right?"

Neros sniffed the cup, and for the first time, looked disappointed. "Our water is fresh and sweet. This smells like dirt."

"It's the best tap water you're gonna get. Drink up." Cheyenne returned to the recliner and picked up the four activators Matthew had delivered. She turned them over in her hands, looking at their neighbor as he took another absent bite of Ember's half-sub. "They do work, by the way."

He looked at her with pleading eyes.

This is the part where he's silently wishing for a heartfelt thank you. Cut the guy a break, Cheyenne.

She gave him a small smile. "The first three from this morning went to a troll family I lived next to at my old apartment. You should've seen the looks on their faces."

"Minds blown," Ember added. "This kind of tech doesn't make it across the Border period. Until now."

"But when they put these things on, Matthew," Cheyenne jiggled the four activators in her palm and nodded at him, "there isn't anything to compare it to. These magicals gave up everything they had on the other side to make the crossing into this world, and they've been struggling pretty hard to find that balance, you know? Being a magical Earthside. Living under the radar without being homeless or jobless or hopeless. And they're ridiculously optimistic trolls to begin with. Having an activator, though? Something they recognized from home that made them feel like themselves again? I'd say it canceled out the last few years of them fighting to survive over here."

Ember nodded at Matthew and shot him a winning smile. "Closest thing they have to going home again right now. And who knows? These might even make it easier for Earthside O'gúleesh to go back home if they want to. When it's safe again."

A tiny smile flickered at the corners of their neighbor's mouth. "I thought you guys handled all the…whatever you were doing over there."

"Yeah, we did. But there's an adjustment period." *And O'gúl magic being returned to its original strength after millennia of being abused takes one hell of an adjustment, plus the broken Hangivol system.* "Your program in these activators is gonna change everything, Matthew. That troll family and whoever else ends up getting one of these first activators might not be able to thank you in person, but I can."

Matthew chuckled weakly and hung his head between his shoulders, nodding. "Hell of a compliment, Cheyenne. From you."

She snorted. "Yeah, don't let it go to your head."

"I'll get back to the syncing, then. A hundred and forty-three to go before Monday, right?"

"Or as close to that as you can get."

"Shouldn't be a problem." Matthew stood and pointed at the sandwich half. "Mind if I take that with me?"

"Not at all." Ember scooped her hands under the wrapper and lifted it toward him.

His hands settled briefly under hers, and they stared at each other.

Cheyenne raised an eyebrow. *It's a fucking sandwich. Make goo-goo eyes at each other later.*

Matthew cleared his throat and wrapped the paper around the sub. "Thanks."

"Yeah." Ember jerked her hands into her lap and shrugged, quickly looking away from him. "No problem. Good luck with powering advanced O'gúl tech and everything."

"Let us know if you hit any snags," Cheyenne muttered.

"Sure. Yeah, of course." Matthew stopped halfway to the door, holding the sandwich like it was a fragile relic, and looked from Ember to Cheyenne and finally at Neros. "Later."

Neros cocked his head comically far and blinked at the human standing in the living room. "You are dripping."

"What? Oh. Shit." Matthew wrapped the paper tighter around the sub to keep the mustard and oil and vinegar from spilling on the floor. "Let me get that."

"We got it." Cheyenne flicked her finger at the coffee table and selected her activator's prompt for the simplest, dumbest spell if she thought about it. Two napkins fluttered off the table and landed on the spill at Matthew's feet. She grinned at him. "All good."

"Right." He cleared his throat and turned toward the door. "Talk to you guys soon."

The door opened and shut quickly behind him. Cheyenne heard him muttering to himself as he hurried down the hall.

"What the hell are you doing, man? This is huge. Quit screwing around and do your job."

His apartment door opened and shut, and Cheyenne sat back in the recliner with a grin.

"Stop that," Ember said.

"What?"

"Stop grinning like that." The fae tucked her violet-streaked hair behind her ear and shook her head. "You're creeping me out."

"Are you sure it's me? 'Cause I have a feeling part of our friendly neighbor's motivation for helping us this much is a little more than wanting to redeem himself."

"Don't." Ember looked quickly at her friend and tried to make it a warning glare, but she couldn't hide a tiny smile and the light flush creeping into her already fae-pink cheeks. "He's doing a really good job."

"No argument there." Cheyenne jiggled the star activators in her hand again, then pulled out her phone and scrolled through her contacts. "Biggest test for these things is still ahead of us, though."

"I'm pretty sure his program's gonna hold up, Cheyenne."

"Oh, yeah. Me too. Now we have to see whether or not these things will work for Earthborn magicals, specifically the contracted FRoE-agent variety. More importantly, that they'll be able to handle it."

Ember picked up her sandwich again. "You're calling in more guinea pigs."

"Hey, they were ready and willing to break Venga out of Chateau D'rahl and crash one of the most dangerous human-magical deals with war machines. I'm sure they'll be down for this."

CHAPTER THIRTY-EIGHT

Five minutes after sending the text to Yurik, Cheyenne got her answer.

Are you fucking kidding? You need a favor, C, we're in. Just tell us where and when.

She grinned and sent another text telling them to meet her at Union Hill at 2:00 p.m. *Pretty neutral place. We sure as shit aren't doing this at my place.*

"You look like you hit the jackpot," Ember muttered as she crumpled the sandwich wrappers and stuffed them all into the to-go bags.

"Seems like it. Still have to call a nightstalker about a portal, though. And find a warded place that won't bring the US military down on us while we train." Cheyenne pulled up Corian's number and sent the call.

"You think it's gonna be that intense?"

The drow snorted. "I have no idea what to expect with this one, Em. But now I get why Corian took me to a bunch of places in the middle of nowhere to make me throw everything I had at him." *Never thought I'd be looking back on that fondly.*

The line was picked up, and Corian cleared his throat. "What's up, kid?"

"Hey. I could use some nightstalker-portal help in about half an hour. You busy?"

"Kinda, yeah." A series of loud clinks came over the line. "Why can't Maleshi do it?"

Cheyenne frowned and forced back a wry laugh. "I called you first. Maleshi's playing Maddie Bergman right now and trying to keep her Earthside second life running like normal."

"And you assumed I had nothing better to do, huh?"

"Sounds like someone woke up on the wrong side of the bed this morning." Cheyenne cranked the lever on the recliner and pushed it back all the way. "Which is something I never saw in that unfinished basement you call an apartment. Where do you sleep?"

"Look, Cheyenne," Corian said wearily, "I've been trying to find L'zar since we got back. He's not at the warehouse, not at Bianca's, not anywhere I can think to look for him, and I can't track him. It's like he vanished off the face of the Earth, only that's impossible. He has nowhere else to go."

"I'm sure he's fine."

"Are you, though?"

She leaned back in the chair. "If you wanted to hear me say I'm worried about the disappearing drow whose job for who knows how many centuries has been to disappear, sorry to disappoint."

"Still doesn't sit right with me. And it's my job to make sure he's not playing with something he shouldn't be playing with if you catch my drift."

"Yeah. Corian, forget about L'zar for a second. Can you do that? 'Cause I have some Drow royalty on Earth business to take care of, and I need your help."

"What, did your car break down?"

"Very funny. And no. Meet me in the paid parking lot at Union Hill at two, okay? I only need you for, like, five minutes."

"Yeah, I'll be there." The nightstalker hung up, and Cheyenne snorted at her phone.

"Nightstalker with an attitude today, huh?" Ember asked from the kitchen.

"I guess. He still can't find L'zar, and it's rocking his world, I guess."

"Huh. Maybe L'zar doesn't wanna be found." Ember stepped on the pedal of the trashcan beside the kitchen island and dropped their takeout trash into the open bin. Then she lifted her foot and grinned. "Look at this. I swear. I can step on the trashcan without magic and open it like it was meant to be opened. I love having my legs back!"

Cheyenne chuckled and cranked the recliner's footrest down before standing. "It's the little things, right?"

"All the little things." The fae walked back toward the living room, dusting off her hands in satisfaction. "You have no idea."

"Hey, do you mind hanging out with Neros while I try to get these activators working for a few magicals who didn't even know what an activator was until a week ago?"

Ember stopped beside the end of the couch and looked down at Neros. The pale-skinned drow sat perfectly straight on the couch, the backs of his hands resting on his thighs again and his eyes closed. She waved a hand in front of his face, but his eyelids didn't flicker. "We should be fine."

"You hear that, cuz?" Cheyenne leaned toward him and raised an eyebrow. "I'm heading out. Won't be gone too long. Ember's in charge."

Neros gave no indication that he'd heard her.

Ember snorted. "Having him around is like a crash course in toddlers and teenagers all at the same time."

"Yeah, Em. How many teenagers use meditating as an excuse to ignore whoever's talking to them?"

"Oh, come on. It's the principle of the thing."

Cheyenne grabbed her black trench coat off the armrest of the couch and nodded at her friend. "Should only be a couple of hours."

"Sure. When he snaps out of his drow trance, I'll pop the TV on. Basically the same thing, right?"

At 1:56 p.m., Cheyenne stepped out of her Panamera in the parking lot at Union Hill, just as a shiny black FRoE SUV rolled into the lot. Yurik, Tate, Bhandi, and Jamal shut their doors at the same time before hurrying toward her, all of them wearing their human-illusion masks.

"Yo! Goth drow!" Bhandi threw devil horns at Cheyenne and grinned as she stalked across the parking lot. "What's this mysterious thing you need our help with?"

"Hey, if I told you now, that'd ruin the surprise."

Tate nudged the troll in the side and jerked his chin at Cheyenne. "She's probably gonna start handing out awards. You know, for best rebel agents who almost got canned for insubordination but didn't."

"Well, we sure as shit deserve 'em, don't we?"

Yurik snorted and shook his head, the bullring through his nose flopping against his upper lip even with his illusion mask on. "I'll tell you what, though. Awards or no awards, being out here right now is a hell of a lot better than anything at the base."

Cheyenne nodded at him as he and Jamal caught up to her, Bhandi, and Tate. "Trouble at the home base still?"

They followed her toward the back of the parking lot, where the cars thinned out before the asphalt gave way to a strip of grass.

"Something like that." Yurik shrugged. "It's like Grot's trying to lead a goddamn rebellion or something."

Bhandi scoffed. "Except that he and all the other idiots who hate your guts aren't rebelling against the higher-ups. Just you, Cheyenne."

"I haven't even been there since Sir and Van Lurig made that stupid announcement."

"Yeah, that's probably for the best." Tate rubbed his bald, tattooed head and shrugged. "Not sure how far they'll take it next time you roll up, though. You even know when that is?"

"Monday." Cheyenne searched the parking lot. "The board wants me there for another consultation."

"Shit." Bhandi grimaced. "Any idea what you're gonna tell 'em, or are you planning on pulling something out of your ass at the last minute?"

Tate snorted and shook his head.

The troll lifted both hands in mock surrender. "Hey, don't get me wrong. Cheyenne and last-minute plans tend to work out pretty fucking well."

"Yeah, I have a plan." Cheyenne shot Bhandi a sideways glance, then looked at the parking lot again and saw the small circle of dark light materializing in the air behind a maroon Forerunner. "And if it works, I don't think Grot or whoever else thinks I'm trying to seize control of the FRoE is gonna have anything to complain about anymore."

Jamal grunted. "You gonna take 'em out?"

"What?" Cheyenne and the other agents looked sharply at the huge ogre disguised as an equally huge bald man with a thick brow and jutting lower jaw. "No, Jamal. I'm not taking anyone out."

Bhandi shrugged. "Good guess, though."

"I'm trying to make things easier for everybody, okay? That's why you guys are here to help."

"You said we'd be helping you," Yurik said with a crooked smile, "but you haven't gotten around to that part yet. And we're standing here on the edge of a parking lot."

"I'll tell you when we get there."

Bhandi spun and tossed her arms up. "Get where, halfling?"

Cheyenne nodded at Corian, who stepped away from the shimmering portal of dark light behind the Forerunner and headed toward them, scowling. "Wherever he decides to take us."

The agents turned around to see a pissed-off nightstalker storming toward them. Yurik's hand went to his hip, but where he would have grabbed the butt of his fell pistol strapped there, he only grabbed air. "Dammit. Should we have shown up armed for this little powwow?"

"Hey, yeah." Bhandi folded her arms and squinted. "Isn't that the nightstalker who helped us break into the place none of us are gonna talk about out in the open?"

"The very same." Cheyenne nodded at Corian. "Relax. I asked him to meet us."

The nightstalker slowed when he approached and eyed the agents. "You failed to mention you were throwing a party."

"And you would've been way more excited to show up if I had, right?"

He rolled his eyes in a wide arc. "No. So why am I even here?"

Cheyenne grinned. "To find us a training ground."

Corian stared at her.

"Come on. You know what I'm trying to test here. We need somewhere safe to practice, and you're the only magical I know who can cloak it for us so the rest of the world doesn't start freaking out about a bunch of magic in the middle of wherever."

A slow grin spread across Bhandi's face, and she looked from Corian to the drow. "Did I hear you say 'training ground?'"

"Not the kind you're thinking. Promise."

"That's all you need?" Corian asked with a raised eyebrow.

"Yeah. A portal and a big, safe invisible dome or whatever." Cheyenne shrugged. "Just don't make it a national landmark this time, huh?"

"Uh-huh." Unamused, Corian stepped back and raised both hands to open another portal.

Yurik leaned toward Cheyenne, staring at the growing circle of dark light, and muttered, "Where's he taking us?"

She shrugged. "It's a surprise for me too."

Corian finished the spell, gestured at the portal, and stepped through. "Come on. I'm not keeping this open to wait for a bunch of wide-eyed Earthborns to get with the program."

"Not our first portal," Jamal grumbled before stepping into the dark window.

"You know what?" Bhandi followed him, turning around to look at Tate and Yurik. "We need to get us a nightstalker on the team. How come we've got trolls and goblins and orcs up the ass, but no fucking nightstalkers?"

"You couldn't afford me," Corian muttered from the other side.

"Ha! This guy." The troll pointed at Corian with her thumb as she stepped into a clearing much like Cheyenne's first, back in the days of Corian training her for the drow trials. "He's funny, Cheyenne. A real hoot."

Cheyenne, Yurik, and Tate joined them in the wide field at the top of a hill surrounded by thinned-out trees. The drow looked at Corian as his fingers moved through the air, drawing the symbols in orange light that would form the invisible sparring ring she'd requested. "You should see him on a good day."

The nightstalker drew his hand through the air in a final flourish, and pale orange light burst away from him to form a high, wide dome of shimmering magic over the entire field. Then he said, "Not gonna happen."

He's pissed about L'zar. That's it.

She nodded at him. "Thanks for the portal and the forcefield."

"Yeah." He stalked back toward the portal, shaking his head. "I have to get back to my work. You know, the important kind. Call me when you need to bum a ride back to Richmond."

"Wait." Yurik spun around to call after the nightstalker, "Where are we?"

Corian disappeared through the portal, and it closed behind him with a soft pop.

Bhandi snorted. "Dick."

"Naw, he's pretty okay. He's going through something right now. Come on." Cheyenne waved them forward with her as she headed toward the middle of the field to put plenty of buffer between the trees and whatever else was bound to happen when her agent friends got their hands on O'gúl activators. "Time to get to work."

"Right." Tate rubbed his hands together as he gazed around the field. "Why are we working in the middle of nowhere with nothing to work with?"

"Well, we are starting from scratch. But it's not nothing." Cheyenne withdrew the four activators from her pocket and handed them to the agents.

"Oh, shit." Yurik laughed. "Not awards. Fucking medals."

"Dude, she wouldn't tell a pissed-off nightstalker to port us out to wherever the hell we are to hand out some damn medals that don't mean shit." Bhandi looked at Cheyenne and frowned. "Would you?"

"You said training ground," Tate added.

"Yeah. What the hell are we training for?"

The drow folded her arms and raised her eyebrows. "If you guys wanna shut the hell up and let me explain, we can get started."

"Ha!" Bhandi thumped a fist into Yurik's beefy goblin shoulder. "Yeah, shut up."

Yurik stared at Cheyenne and shook his head. "Don't encourage her, huh?"

"All right, pay attention." Cheyenne removed the activator from behind her ear and held it up to show them.

"Oh, great. We're here to learn magic tricks." Bhandi wiggled the star activator between two fingers. "Always wanted to learn how to pull a coin out of my ear."

Jamal slammed the back of his fist into her shoulder, sending the troll stumbling sideways. Yurik and Tate stepped back to avoid her, sniggering when she straightened and glared at the ogre.

"Hey, what gives, asshole?"

"Shut up and pay attention." Jamal rolled his eyes with a low growl, then nodded at Cheyenne.

They think this is a favor for a friend. Time to ramp up the seriousness level, I guess.

"This is an activator," she said, making sure they all got a good look. "Seriously advanced O'gúl tech that up until two days ago wasn't possible for anyone to use on this side of the Border. Except me."

"And you gave us…" Tate glanced down at the star activator in his hand and chuckled. "ninja throwing stars missing half their points? Hey, kudos for inventing shit, halfling, but I'm good with fell rifles and the occasional RPG lugged around by this guy." The troll stuck his thumb out toward Jamal, who glared at him.

"Okay. Fine." Cheyenne stuck her activator behind her ear again, her eyelids fluttering briefly at the sync-up, and nodded. "You guys remember when I pulled that fell pistol apart by the portal ridge at my mom's house?"

All four agents stared blankly at her.

"Uh, no."

"Why would you pull a pistol apart?"

Yurik's eyes widened. "Oh, shit. Yeah. I mean, we weren't there yet. But I heard about it."

"What, you mean that meathead human's weapon?" Bhandi turned to the goblin and shook her head. "I thought that was a bullshit story to cover how he blew up his own service weapon?"

"Shit," Cheyenne said, "That's right. I had Rhynehart call you guys in after that. Look, the point is that I pulled the dude's gun apart with my activator. Okay? Activators like the ones I handed all of you. That's what you're holding. They're supposed to make things easier. At least, that's the endgame, but we gotta start somewhere, right?"

"How the hell does a dinky metal star pull apart a fell weapon?" Bhandi wrinkled her nose as she studied her activator. "Looks pretty lame to me."

"Fuck, you guys are serious meatheads sometimes." Cheyenne gave a wry laugh and gestured at them. "Put the damn things behind your ears, and we'll take it from there."

"You're not gonna, like, take over our minds or anything with this shit, are you?" Yurik slowly lifted the star toward his head, his hand jerking like he couldn't quite control his own body. "Because you know, you hear all kinds of shit about alien abduction and people getting probed with random shit that doesn't exist on Earth."

"Dude." Bhandi smacked him in the shoulder. "She said behind your ear, not up your ass."

"Just put them on!" Cheyenne spread her arms and stared at them. "Christ, it's like pulling teeth with you guys."

"As long as it's not actually pulling teeth." Tate grinned and pointed at his teeth before the forced smile disappeared. "I just got these babies whitened last week."

Cheyenne blinked at him. "Don't make me blast you across this field, man."

"Idiots," Jamal muttered and slapped the activator behind his ear with a loud smack. His body went rigid, and he let out a choking sound as his eyes rolled back in his head.

"What the fuck?" Bhandi whirled toward Cheyenne. "You said they were supposed to make things easier, halfling!"

"Give it a second. It's syncing up."

"Shit, he's having a fucking seizure." Tate stepped toward the ogre and squeezed Jamal's huge forearm. "Hey, man. Snap out of it."

"He's fine." Cheyenne looked Jamal up and down as spit flew from between the ogre's clenched teeth. *I think.* "This is part of the whole process. Hurts like a bitch at first, but then it's over. Watch."

The agents stared at Jamal. Yurik's mouth fell open, then Jamal let out a low growl and blinked rapidly.

"There he is." Tate whistled. "You okay, big guy?"

Jamal grimaced in pain, still blinking and tilting his head stiffly from side to side to stretch out the bulging muscles of his neck.

"For real, man." Bhandi squinted at him. "If it's still you in there, give us some kinda sign, huh?"

"It didn't take over his mind," Cheyenne muttered.

"You don't know that." Yurik gestured at Jamal, whose heavy breathing was starting to even out, though his eyes twitched independently of each other. "You said we were your damn guinea pigs."

"Hey, you know we got your back, Cheyenne." Bhandi shook her head. "But if that ninja star fucks up Jamal's shit, I'm out."

"Come on, man." Tate leaned sideways and waved a hand in front of the stunned ogre's face. "Say something so we know you're good."

Cheyenne folded her arms and tried not to grimace. *This has to work.*

Jamal grunted again, scrunched his face, and ripped a huge fart. Then he looked down at Tate. "So far, so good."

"Jesus fucking Christ!" Bhandi rolled her eyes and stomped away from the ogre, waving her hand in front of her face. "You couldn't have given us a warning for that one?"

Yurik took a few steps away from the ogre too and chuckled. "Way to draw out the suspense, asshole."

Tate backed toward Cheyenne and flipped Jamal the bird. "You piece of shit. Had us all freaking out, and it's fucking ogre farts."

Jamal rumbled with laughter, his lips peeling back to show the stained yellow teeth behind them. "Put the damn things on, you morons."

"Activators." Cheyenne chuckled and shook her head. "And don't pull shit like that again, okay?"

"What, were you worried too?" Tate asked as he stopped beside her, leaving Jamal plenty of room to air out on his own.

"A little," Cheyenne said, gesturing at the ogre. "That was a reaction I haven't seen before."

Jamal's laughter grew, and his eyes widened as he gazed around the field. "Oh, hell, yeah." He bashed a fist into the opposite palm and grinned. "Let's get this shit started."

"How you feelin'?" Bhandi asked.

"Ready to bash some skulls in." He sneered. "Ninja star behind the ear, troll."

Cheyenne shook her head. "Whatever. Just do what he says."

"So this is how you were fucking juicin', huh, Cheyenne?" Tate snorted and lifted his activator toward his ear. "Magical steroids built into a piece of tech from the other world. This is gonna be awesome."

"Bottoms up." Bhandi raised her activator toward Yurik like a toast. He returned the gesture, and the other three agents attached their activators.

All three of them grew rigid, their eyelids fluttering as the activators synced with organic magic for the first time in a world that wasn't meant to facilitate the link.

Jamal chuckled darkly and grinned at Cheyenne. "Maybe one of them'll shit themselves."

She snorted and rolled her eyes. "I fucking hope not."

CHAPTER THIRTY-NINE

"Aw, goddammit!" Yurik's eyes flew open, and he sucked in a quick, harsh breath.

"Fuck! Fuck, fuck, fuck!" Bhandi slammed the heel of her palm against her temple and wiggled her lower jaw, then blinked rapidly and gazed around the clearing. "Holy shit. What the fuck am I lookin' at right now?"

"Oh-ho, yes!" Tate bounced up and down on his toes, shaking out both hands and blowing out short, quick breaths through loose lips. "What is this shit, Cheyenne? I'm fucking pumped!"

"Good." Cheyenne swept her gaze across the four FRoE agents, who were in various states of surprise and eagerness to get going. "This is O'gúl tech working with your magic. It doesn't give you anything you don't already have, it just makes it better. Easier to control."

"You mean, we can fucking control this?" Yurik burst out laughing. "It's like a goddamn videogame. That virtual reality shit, you know?"

"Yeah, but those stupid nerdy helmets of yours don't feel anything like this." Bhandi rolled her shoulders and clapped her hands together. "Woo!"

"Okay, are you done?" Cheyenne folded her arms. "We still have a lot of ground to cover with these things."

"Whoa, whoa, whoa." Tate lifted his hand in front of his face and slowly wiggled his fingers. "This is like that time I… You know what? Never mind. It's a million fucking times better. You guys seeing a bunch of words floating around your head?"

"Oh yeah."

"Uh-huh."

"Dude, there's a fucking obliterate option!" Yurik stepped back and reached out one hand. "Obliterate what? No goddamn clue!"

"Yurik, hold on," Cheyenne started. "You should probably start slow."

"Why don't I have that?" Bhandi wrinkled her nose and scanned the empty air in front of her as her activator fed her row after row of command prompts. "Man, this is bullshit."

"What does it do?" Jamal asked, smacking his fist into his palm over and over.

Yurik chuckled, his yellow eyes gleaming with excitement. "You asked for it."

"Hold on!" Cheyenne stepped toward him. "Wait!"

An explosion of yellow light in a sunburst shape burst around Yurik's outstretched hand. The magic flared out and sucked back in toward his open palm, then launched in a concentrated stream across the field and blasted into the ground. Dry grass and dirt and small rocks flew twenty feet in the air and peppered the group of magicals.

"Oh, fuck!" Bhandi shielded her face with a forearm, then lowered it quickly to stare at the damage. "Dude. That was insane!"

"What'd you say that was called?" Tate blinked pointedly as he scrolled through the activator prompts in his vision.

"Man, you develop a magical tick or something?" Bhandi laughed.

"I'm looking for that magic."

"You look ridiculous."

Yurik's hand dropped back to his side, and he stared at the last of the dirt and blades of grass fluttering to the ground in front of him.

He dropped to his knees with a grunt. Jamal smacked Tate in the back of his bald head and shoved Bhandi aside with the other hand before stomping toward the hunched-over Yurik.

"Ow. What the hell?" Tate rubbed his head and scowled at the ogre. Then he saw the muscular goblin swaying on his knees. "Shit."

"Cheyenne." Bhandi pointed at Yurik, who accepted Jamal's hand and let the ogre pull him roughly to his feet. "What's wrong with him?"

Cheyenne raised an eyebrow at the troll and shrugged. "He jumped the gun."

Bhandi scoffed. "And you're cool with it? Look at the guy. If he wasn't already green, he'd be turning green."

"You good, man?" Tate muttered as Yurik and Jamal rejoined them.

"I just need a minute." The goblin wiped his forehead with a shaking hand, the bullring through his septum smooshing up against his upper lip when he took a deep breath. "Any suggestions for this fucking headache?"

Cheyenne jerked her chin at him. "Yeah. Don't try to power high-level spells with that thing until you can handle the little ones." *And now I know why Corian was such a dick when he was training me. Pain and failure are pretty much the best teachers for this kinda thing.*

Yurik lifted his head and shot her a crooked smile. "You mean, that wasn't a little one?"

The other agents sniggered.

"No. It wasn't the biggest, though."

"Come on, Cheyenne. They're not all gonna be like this, are they?"

The drow cocked her head. "Not if you pay attention and run through this with me like I tell you to."

"Oh, I get it." Bhandi clapped a hand on Yurik's shoulder, then pointed at Cheyenne. "You're playing drill sergeant."

Tate shook his head, though he couldn't hide a small smile. "You said you needed our help. You wanna train an army of FRoE agents with your special ninja-star gadgets. Is that it?"

Cheyenne looked at each of the agents in turn. "Anyone got a problem with that?"

"As long as you're not training this army to take over the FRoE and rule the world."

Yurik straightened to fix Bhandi with a disbelieving frown. Tate spread his arms and shook his head. Jamal growled.

"What?" Bhandi's eyes widened, and she looked a little scared for a second before she chuckled. "Too soon?"

Rolling his eyes, Yurik straightened fully and gestured at Cheyenne.

"Man, shut up and let Drill Sergeant Drow-Head say what she needs to say."

"Fine." Bhandi turned smartly toward Cheyenne and squared her feet, placing her hands against the center of her lower back. "But we already went through Basic, so skip to the good parts, huh?"

Tate snorted and took up the at-ease posture as well. "Basic doesn't have shit on this."

Jamal eyed Yurik, waiting for the goblin to collect himself enough to stand mostly at-ease beside him until the ogre did the same.

"You gonna tell us how to fire off shit like that without taking ourselves out?" Yurik asked.

"Yeah." Cheyenne looked at them and tried not to laugh. *Soldiers. I have magical FRoE soldiers standing here like I'm a drow Maleshi Hi'et. What the hell is happening?* A grin finally broke through when she said, "Just don't call me 'Sir.'"

The agents sniggered and shouted together, "Sir, yes, sir!"

She rolled her eyes. "Fuck off and listen. Activators. Every single O'gúleesh refugee making the crossing Earthside knows how to use them. They've probably been using them all their lives, or at least most of their lives if they're old."

"So, you're giving them to us because you think we're gonna have to fight them into submission?" Tate asked.

"No." Cheyenne pointed at him. "I'm giving them to you because you guys are all Earthborn. You've never been to the other side."

Bhandi snorted. "Never wanted to either—ow!" Her head jerked forward under the not-quite-slap from Jamal's huge hand. "Dude. First of all, don't touch the hair. And second, didn't anyone ever tell you not to hit a lady?"

The ogre grunted. "If I see one, I'll make sure not to touch her."

Tate and Yurik sniggered.

"Oh, you think that's funny, huh?" Bhandi wagged her finger back and forth between them.

Cheyenne glanced at the gray afternoon sky above the field. *Yep. Corian and Maleshi had every right to toss me around. And that was training one magical.*

"You assholes just wait. As soon as Cheyenne lifts the pin on these things and tells us to go at it with heavy-duty magic, I'm gonna—"

"Hey!" A crackling sphere of black energy burst to life in Cheyenne's palm, and she hurled it at the troll.

Cursing, the other agents lurched away from Bhandi. The troll raised both hands, which flashed dark-purple light, and Cheyenne's attack stopped six inches from her face. "What the fuck, Cheyenne?"

The drow dipped her head in acknowledgment. "That was pretty good."

"Pretty good?" Bhandi's wide scarlet eyes flickered from the crackling black sphere in front of her to Cheyenne's face and back. "You fucking attacked me."

"And you fucking blocked it." Cheyenne tapped behind her ear. "With the activator. Works with your magic better than you knew how to on your own. Now get rid of it."

"What, you mean, like, throw it at one of these dipshits?"

"I mean, pick a command and do it." Cheyenne spread her arms.

Gritting her teeth, Bhandi spread her hands farther apart. Her eyes moved back and forth, staring at activator prompts no one else could see before she drew her hands apart with a shout of effort. Cheyenne's energy sphere launched into the air with a high-pitched whistle before bursting apart like a black and purple firework.

"Damn." Tate folded his arms and watched the magical sparks rain back down toward them before fizzling out. "That works."

"Okay." Cheyenne looked at Bhandi and nodded. "That's one way to do it."

The troll barked a surprised laugh. "How the fuck did I do that?"

"Like I said, it's your magic, but with a concentrated outlet."

"This is gonna be a piece of cake." Tate grinned. "We pick any of the options like it's a damn computer with a mental mouse and do whatever the hell kinda magic we want?"

"I mean, basically." Cheyenne shrugged. "But it's a little more complicated than that when it counts."

"Come on," he said, gesturing at Bhandi, who was still staring at her hands in disbelief. "That looked pretty damn easy."

Cheyenne hurled another energy sphere, this time at the tattooed troll's chest. He had enough time to let out a choked-off shout of surprise before her attack blasted into him and sent him sailing across the field.

He landed on his back and skidded another four feet before stopping. Tate's arms thumped down onto the ground at his sides, and he groaned.

"Ha!" Bhandi grinned at Cheyenne, then whirled and shouted at the downed troll, "Not so easy now, is it, cupcake? Looks like somebody still has a shit-ton of practice to do!"

"That's the idea." Cheyenne hit Bhandi in the back with a smaller energy sphere this time and sent the troll flying forward to crash into the dirt.

"Shit." Yurik stepped back, frantically scanning the options his activator brought up for him.

Jamal roared with laughter.

Bhandi spat out a mouthful of dirt and dry grass and pushed herself up. With one foot on the ground and one knee in the dirt, she turned to glare at Cheyenne. "Dirty fucking shot, Goth drow."

"More complicated." Cheyenne spread her arms. "You get in a fight with magicals who aren't scared of fell weapons, they're not gonna wait for you to turn around before they blast you away. And the in-between monsters you guys saw coming out of that portal ridge at the Summerlin estate? Some of them are even faster."

Tate thumped his fists on the ground and got to his feet. "Are you saying we'll have to fight those gnarly fuckers again?"

"Maybe you will, maybe you won't." Cheyenne jerked her chin at them and spread her arms. "Guess you'll have to get good at using those things. Gotta be ready for whatever comes up, right?"

Yurik closed his eyes and shook his head, then scrolled through his activator prompts again. His fingers twitched at his sides. "Are you opening a sparring ring?"

"If you Earthborn assholes think you can take down a drow halfling, sure." Cheyenne clenched her fists and brought the black flames bursting to life and racing across her skin for half a second, just for fun. Then she snuffed them out and grinned.

"Oh, it's on." Bhandi leaped to her feet and shook out her hands. "Four against one looks like pretty damn good odds to me."

The drow cocked her head and winked at the troll. "I'd say it's almost an even match."

"Ha. Fuck off." Bhandi ran toward her with a shout, a large orb of dark-purple magic growing in one of her open palms.

Jamal slapped his chest with both hands and stomped forward, his fingers igniting with green sparks.

Yurik and Tate stared at each other before taking off after the others, summoning magic they hadn't been trained to use as FRoE agents. Or ever.

Cheyenne brought up a crackling black energy sphere in both hands and stepped back. The agents and their chosen magical attacks lit up in her vision as bright-yellow arrows, and her activator pinpointed each one and fed her real-time data on who was most likely to attack first and with what. She felt the crazed grin grow wider on her face and didn't give a shit how much she might have looked like L'zar. *This is gonna be fun.*

CHAPTER FORTY

T ate let out a blood-curdling scream as he sailed across the field.

Cheyenne had unwrapped her lashing black tendrils from around the troll's legs and let him fly. She raised a shield of dark light in front of her before Yurik's yellow burst of flames and strobing light struck. She shoved forward with one hand, and the telekinetic wave sent the goblin's magic and his body hurtling away from her.

Bhandi picked herself up off the ground, snarled, and raced toward Cheyenne. A spear of dark-purple light blazed to life in her fist, and she drew it back to throw at the drow.

Cheyenne's black tendrils whipped out of her fingertips and coiled around Bhandi's conjured weapon. She jerked up and away, wrenching the spear from the troll's grasp before letting it sail end-over-end behind her. Then she slipped into drow speed and ran toward Bhandi. She stopped behind the troll and slightly to the right, then dropped back into normal speed and shouted right in Bhandi's ear, "Boo!"

"Fuck!"

Cheyenne shoved the troll aside, sending her staggering away and tripping over her own feet. Laughing, she raised another shield to stop Tate's blast of icy blue darts, which shattered against the wall of dark light.

Her activator blared an alarm in her head with a flashing yellow arrow pointing behind her, and she darted aside before Jamal's meaty fists, which crackled with red-brown energy, slammed into the ground where she'd just been standing.

She looked at him and raised her eyebrows. "Close."

Sneering, he launched a spray of copper magic strobing like lit firecrackers with one hand and swung the other fist toward her.

Cheyenne slipped into drow speed to avoid both, then darted behind the ogre and jumped up to latch onto his shoulders with both hands. She tugged the suspended magical down and back. When she entered real-time again, Jamal's head whipped back, and he roared. Copper sparks and big clods of dirt shot into the air when his huge body crashed down beneath the force she'd applied in drow speed. The ground shuddered, and Cheyenne stepped back to take stock of her other opponents.

Her cheeks ached from grinning so much. *I thought Corian was insane for smiling when we fought, but this is the best part.*

Tate ran at her from the left, the column of blue flames in his hands flaring three times larger than he'd managed so far.

He launched the whole handful at her, and Cheyenne ducked. "Hey. You leveled up."

Yurik snarled behind her, sprinting across the dry grass with yellow sunburst magic flaring around his hands and sucking back into his palms again. She turned and dropped to one knee, raising a shield before the column of obliterating yellow light spewed from the goblin's hands and shot toward her. Cheyenne pressed her shoulder against the shield and turned it slightly, redirecting the spray of his attack toward Tate.

"Shit!" The tattooed troll dove away from the ricocheting light, shouting in surprise when Cheyenne reached out with her black lashing tendrils and snagged his ankles. Yurik's attack died out. Cheyenne dropped the shield and stood, putting all the momentum she could into flinging Tate at Yurik. The troll toppled into his fellow agent and sent them both tumbling across the field.

Turning around again, Cheyenne scanned the seemingly empty arena behind her until her activator picked up on Bhandi. The flashing yellow arrow darted back and forth in her vision despite there being no sight whatsoever of the troll. *Clever. I still see you.*

Cheyenne pretended to search the field, and when the flashing arrow came within ten feet, she shoved forward with both hands and sent a rippling shockwave through the ground. Shards of stone and sprays of dirt erupted everywhere, then a startled shout and a furious cry lifted into the air.

Bhandi's cloaking spell sputtered out as she sailed away from the upturned earth. The troll hit the ground with a thud, skidded backward, and didn't bother trying to get back up.

"Jesus Christ," she muttered, her dirt-smeared cheek pressed to the earth. "I thought I had you with that one."

Cheyenne stepped over the ridges of upturned dirt and grass and stopped beside the troll to offer her a hand up. "Well, you get points for pulling off the spell."

Bhandi rolled her eyes but accepted the drow's hand. She climbed to her feet and angrily brushed the clumps of dirt off the front of her shirt. "I was fucking invisible, Cheyenne."

"I know." Cheyenne gave the agent a reassuring thump on the back. "And I have an activator."

"Wait. Hold on." Yurik rolled away from Tate and pushed himself up to sit in the grass. "How come you can see invisible trolls? I didn't see her until she reappeared in the sky."

Tate vigorously rubbed his bald head, sending another small shower of dirt and grass raining down around him. "Lemme guess. Practice, right?"

"I mean, maybe." Cheyenne stuck her hands in her pockets and shrugged. "Might be because my model's slightly better than yours."

The tattooed troll snorted. "I get it. Standard model for the FRoE grunts."

"Shit, Cheyenne." Bhandi gestured toward the drow's activator. "How do I get my hands on one of those?"

"You don't. This one's special."

"Hey, don't be a dick." Yurik's chuckle died in a grimace as he pushed himself to his feet. "They're all special."

Bhandi and Tate shot him mock looks of disgust.

"I'm fucking around, guys. Of course, hers is better."

"Doesn't have anything to do with it," Cheyenne said. *A little white lie never hurt anybody. At least, not as bad as they're hurting right now.*

"Right." Tate accepted Yurik's hand up and dusted off his black t-shirt. "Because you're that much more badass than the rest of us."

With falling dirt clumps and a low growl, Jamal unburied himself from the ogre-sized trench he'd made in the ground and tossed a handful of earth at them. "She is."

"Ooh. The ogre speaks." Tate wiggled his hands beside his face in fake terror.

Cheyenne cocked her head, finally managing to damp her crazed grin down to a playful smile. "Look, the magical who made my activator made yours too. She's one of the best, if not *the* best, and she knew what she was doing. Maybe there'll be upgrades in the future. Who knows? But for now—"

"We gotta learn how to keep our asses from getting kicked with these things." Bhandi rolled one shoulder back in a wide circle, grimacing as she gripped it with the other hand for a brief massage. "But damn. How long's that gonna take?"

"What if we end up going head to head with someone like you, huh?" Yurik gestured toward Cheyenne, then quickly shook his head. "I mean, somebody with a crazy-advanced activator."

"This." Jamal heaved to his feet. "This is what happens."

Tate chuckled. "Yeah, I think we picked up on that."

"As long as you're Earthside," Cheyenne said, "you won't have to worry about fighting magicals with more advanced tech 'cause right now, I'm the only one who can bring it across the Border. As far as I know, there aren't any sparksetters Earthside with whatever materials someone would need to make more of these."

"Sparksetters?" Bhandi snorted and jerked her chin at Jamal. "Sounds like what you were spraying out of your mongo hands, man."

Jamal blinked at her and said nothing.

"It's the name for magicals who make all the tech over there. And trust me, the activators you guys have right now are a hell of an upgrade compared to most on the other side."

Yurik limped forward and hissed, "I think I broke something."

"*You* broke something?" Bhandi rubbed her lower back and bent backward to ease it. "I'll be lucky to get out of bed in the morning."

"Wait." Tate held a bruised wrist and rubbed it as he staggered toward Cheyenne. "If you're the only magical who can get these things across or whatever, why are we testing them? Whatever rez you came through on would've picked these things up and called it the price of guarding the gates."

Cheyenne raised her eyebrows at him. "I didn't come through at a Border rez."

"No shit." Bhandi chuckled. "What, you jumped between worlds, and nobody saw a damn thing?"

"Pretty much."

"Hey, how many of these things do you have, anyway?" Yurik asked.

"Enough. They're not all going to the FRoE, but if you guys can keep from blowing yourself up until Monday when I deliver my master plan to the board, you'll get to train all your friends."

Bhandi grinned. "I like that idea. You know what? You should give one of these things to Grot so I can wipe that fucking drooling smirk off his face when he realizes size isn't everything and I kick his ass across the base."

"Yeah, like Cheyenne kicked yours," Yurik muttered.

"She kicked all our asses." Tate looked the drow up and down, a grimace of pain still twisting his features. "You knew how to fight the first time we were out in the field together, but not like this."

"You been at your secret sparring ring the last couple weeks too, Goth drow?"

Cheyenne looked at them. "Seriously?"

"What?"

"You guys sat down at my mom's dining table and listened to a bunch of O'gúleesh rebels talk about overthrowing the O'gúl Crown before we drew up plans to break a scaleback out of Chateau D'rahl."

"Yeah. You killed your aunt." Tate shot her a dismissive wave and shook his head. "How is that supposed to help us?"

Cheyenne snorted. "I didn't kill her, but trying to stop her from killing me was a hell of a practice round. So yeah."

"Whoa." Yurik stared at her. "Your aunt tried to kill you?"

"Poisoned me too." The drow shrugged. "You know, to cover her bases. But none of that matters now. You guys need to focus on improving your activator skills as much as you can before Monday night."

"When you roll out the FRoE-overhaul plans." Tate nodded. "Yeah, okay. But we're done for now, right? 'Cause I don't think I can handle being thrown across a field, like, even one more time."

She chuckled. "Yeah, neither do I."

"Ha! Goth drow's got some fire today." Bhandi threw her head back and laughed. "She's gonna break you so hard."

"Dude, your ass got thrown out of invisibility by the fucking ground." The tattooed troll spread his arms and shook his head. "The *ground.*"

"You wanna go, Mr. Clean?"

"What?"

"It's because you're bald," Jamal growled. "Not a very good nickname."

As the agents screwed around with each other and tried not to act as sore as Cheyenne knew they were, or at least would be in a few hours, the drow stepped away and pulled out her phone to call Corian for their pickup.

The line rang in her ear. *This'll be a fun one to explain when he gets here and sees the whole place torn apart. No. He won't give a shit.*

She stuck her free hand in her pocket as she waited for him to answer. The line finally clicked, and his answering machine picked up.

"If you called this number, you know who I am. Leave a message. Or not."

The machine beeped, and Cheyenne ended the call. *Sounds like he recorded that in a bad mood too.*

Frowning, she tried again. No answer for that call or the next, so she texted him.

If you're not gonna pick up, don't offer us a ride home.

She sent it, scowling at her phone, and muttered, "Asshole."

"Hey, your furry friend's gonna port us outta here, right?" Tate called. "Never thought I'd miss that rock they call a mattress on the base, but it sounds pretty fucking good right now."

"Give me a minute." Cheyenne nodded briefly at him, then pulled up Maleshi's number instead.

The general picked up almost immediately. "That was fast."

"What?"

"You found the flame guy, right?"

Cheyenne grimaced. "No. Haven't looked anymore today."

"Oh." Maleshi's voice was flat when she asked, "So, what's up?"

"You have a minute to come and port a few magicals out of the middle of nowhere?"

"Cheyenne."

"Maleshi."

The general let out a long, exaggerated sigh. "I told you, I'm up to my eyeballs in grading undergrad papers that make me wanna kill myself."

"Yeah, I know. Corian was supposed to be available for the night-stalker express, but he decided not to answer his phone. I can't exactly carry four friends with certain proprietary tech behind their ears all the way back to Richmond."

Maleshi hissed, followed by the loud rustle of paper and the rumble of her desk chair's wheels rolling across the plastic mat. "Fine. Where are you?"

"I'll send you a map pin. Oh, he made a ward bubble or whatever around this field we're in."

"You know how insulting that is? Of course I can pick through Corian's wards." Maleshi hung up, and Cheyenne raised her eyebrows at her phone's home screen before setting her current GPS location on a map and texting it over.

I hit the jackpot for nightstalkers in shitty moods today.

She shoved her phone into her pocket and headed back toward the agents, who were still rubbing their sore joints and brushing dirt and grass off their standard-issue black fatigues.

Bhandi eyed the drow, and her smile faded. "You look pissed."

"Just hungry."

"Oh, yeah." Yurik rubbed his hands together and grinned. "Man, I could go for half-pounder with cheese and bacon."

"Or we could skip the meal and go straight to the... Hey." Bhandi pointed behind Cheyenne at the window of dark light opening in the air. "Our chariot awaits."

"Man, we should get a nightstalker on the team," Tate said, staring at the growing portal. "You know how much time we'd save in transport between ops if we had portals?" He pointed at Maleshi as she stepped onto the field with them. "That's not the guy who dropped us off."

"Cute, Cheyenne." Maleshi spread her arms and cocked her head. "Your friends have real top-notch observation skills."

"Who are you?" Bhandi asked.

The general stared at the troll, then raised her hands to open a new portal as the old one closed behind her. "I don't have time for this. Where are we going?"

"Union Hill paid parking," Cheyenne muttered, then frowned at Bhandi. "She was there with everyone else when we planned the whole prison break. You seriously don't remember?"

Bhandi shrugged and didn't say anything as she avoided eye contact.

The portal to the parking lot opened, and Maleshi stormed through without bothering to tell anyone it was time.

"Just get through the portal." Shaking her head, Cheyenne stepped through and stood aside for the agents to follow.

Jamal came last, ducking to step through the window of dark light before straightening again on the other side. He took a long sniff of the air and nodded. "I smell burgers."

"Amazing you can smell anything but yourself." Bhandi sniggered at her lame joke and thumped the back of a hand against Cheyenne's shoulder. "Hey, I think this whole 'getting our asses kicked by the Goth drow' thing calls for a celebration."

"Or at least some painkillers." Yurik grimaced and rubbed the back of his neck.

"Froyo shop's right there." Tate gestured down the street at the row of storefronts.

"Not today, guys." Cheyenne caught Maleshi's gaze and nodded. "You mind hanging around for a sec?"

The general folded her arms and said nothing.

"You sure, halfling?" Bhandi turned around to walk backward across the parking lot and spread her arms. "It's been a while. And I have a feeling these things are only gonna get better." She pointed sharply behind her ear. "Might as well throw a party now before we're slammed with all kinds of extra assignments. You know, seeing as we're all capable now and shit."

Tate snorted and headed after her, shaking his head.

"Another time." Cheyenne pointed at them as the agents slipped on their illusion masks and headed for the entrance to Peridosh. "Feel free to have one on me, though. Hey, and nobody talks about what you have on you, got it? That stays under wraps 'til Monday."

"Sir, yes, sir." Yurik shot her a smart salute, then twisted his hand around to flip her the bird. "Relax. We got your back, C."

Jamal slapped the goblin's back with a huge hand and burst out laughing. "Yours too."

"Oh, come on." Yurik stumbled forward and swung his middle finger toward the ogre instead. "I've been hit enough as it is, man. Put that shit away."

Cheyenne watched her FRoE friends step through Tony's front door to head for the underground market.

"You know, I don't see why you'd turn down a chance to drink with those guys," Maleshi muttered. "Real intelligent bunch."

"For as much as they don't know about what's going on, yeah. They're pretty okay." Cheyenne turned toward the general and shrugged.

"So, what was so important to talk about that you had to keep me here and away from my office?"

"Jesus. Are shitty attitudes contagious today, or what?" When Maleshi raised her eyebrows, Cheyenne said, "I'm wondering if you've heard anything from Corian in the last four hours or so."

"Nope. But it's not like we send each other selfies every hour on the dot."

Cheyenne rolled her eyes. "It's weird that he ported us to that field, cloaked it for us, and said to call him when we were done, then suddenly decided not to answer my calls."

"Calls as in plural?"

"Yeah. And I texted him."

Maleshi frowned, then shrugged. "Not your problem, kid. Not mine, either. He's probably still running around the state looking for L'zar. You know, too busy with his immediate tasks to drop everything and come ferry you around."

"I get it, okay? Damn." Cheyenne stepped away from the general and raised both hands. "Figured you wouldn't mind a small favor in return for my consultation this morning."

"Yeesh." Maleshi cocked her head. "Okay, fine. Sorry. You're right. I bit your head off."

"Yeah, thanks."

"Look, kid. I get that you're ready to go all-out with the FRoE overhaul and everything. It's admirable. For real." Maleshi glanced around the empty parking lot and cast another portal with her hands low in front of her, just to be safe. "And you're the kind of magical who needs to have something exciting and meaningful going on at all times to keep your motivation levels up."

Cheyenne snorted. "Who told you that?"

"No one had to tell me anything," Maleshi said. "I've seen enough of you over the last few months to have a pretty good picture of what makes you tick. But you gotta remember the rest of us had been planning an entire O'gúl-regime overhaul for a few hundred years, give or take a decade. I'm sure I speak for Corian too when I say it'd be nice to take a few weeks off to settle into the new normal, you know? Hell, even a few days. It's been over forty-eight hours since we got back."

"Yeah," Cheyenne agreed, wrinkling her nose as she looked around the parking lot. "I get it."

"You should take a break too, huh? Loosen up a little. Give yourself time to unwind and regroup. Nobody's trying to blow up two worlds anymore, okay? You can relax."

"Thanks for the tip."

Maleshi winked at her and stepped through the new portal into her VCU office. The dark window closed behind her.

Cheyenne snorted and ran a hand through her hair. *Yeah. Easy for her to say. She didn't give up the Crown to be a leader for Earthside magicals. She's technically not even a general anymore.*

Pulling her car keys from her pocket and pressing the lock button on the fob, Cheyenne searched for the flashing purple glow of the Panamera's headlights. The little chirp caught her attention, and she smiled as she headed for her car. *At least the Porsche answers when I call.*

CHAPTER FORTY-ONE

When Cheyenne stepped through the front door of her apartment, she froze. "This is weird."

"Hey!" Ember grinned at her and spread her arms. "Check out the new setup."

"Yeah, Em. I'm checking it out, and it's still weird."

Ember had rearranged the living room furniture so the couch faced the front door instead of Cheyenne's bedroom. The recliners had been cleared to one side of the couch, the coffee table to the other, and the fae sat cross-legged on the center cushion. In front of her, Neros lay sprawled out across the black and white rug on his stomach, propping his chin up in his hands and staring at the TV on the entry table beside the door. In front of him was a half-eaten pint of Chunky Monkey ice cream, the spoon sticking halfway out the top.

"We're taking accidental sleepover to a whole new level," Ember added with an extra punch of peppy enthusiasm in her voice. "Right, Neros?"

"Shh." Cheyenne's cousin was fixated on the TV. "If I can't hear what they're saying, I'll have to unwind the movie."

"Uh, 'rewind.'"

"Yes. Rewind." Neros grabbed the edge of the ice cream carton and tipped it toward him to check how much was left inside. "This is a fascinating window into Earthside culture, Cheyenne."

She closed the front door and turned to study the TV. "*Mean Girls.*" With a snort, she looked at Ember and cocked her head. "That's your teaching technique, huh?"

The fae shrugged.

"I'm coming to understand so much more about your world," Neros muttered, dragging the pint toward him and absently pulling out the spoon. His eyes, glued to the flashing screen, widened. "Please be quiet. I wish to hear the entirety of this conversation in the movie box."

"TV. 'Movie box.'" Cheyenne shrugged and walked slowly across her deconstructed living room to join Ember on the couch. She sat and shook her head. "*Mean Girls*? Really?"

"I gave him options, okay? He's the one who picked it." Ember stared at the screen and offered Cheyenne the pint of Rocky Road she'd been working on. "It was either set him in front of a movie or try to keep him from climbing up to the roof so he could 'listen to the world and search for clues' like he'd watched all the superhero movies and thought he'd blend right in."

Cheyenne raised an eyebrow and took the ice cream. "Thanks for keeping an eye on him."

"Oh, don't worry about it. This drow? He's so easy. Such a good listener. Hardly talks back." They hunched over, trying to stifle their laughter.

"Quiet, please," Neros muttered. "Or find somewhere else to hold your conversation where I cannot hear you. Which would most likely be at the bottom of this tall structure you call your compartment."

"Apartment."

"I'm watching this movie, Cheyenne."

She rolled her eyes and jammed a spoonful of Rocky Road into her mouth.

Ember took the pint from her and did the same before whispering, "So, how did it go?"

"Well, they got their asses handed to 'em, but the activators work."

The fae couldn't hold back a dubious smile as she shook her head. "You like being able to throw someone else around for a change and call it training."

"Wow. Everyone's got me totally pinned down today." Cheyenne took the ice cream for one more bite, handed it back, and stood. "I'm gonna go see if there's anything else on that fiery asshole blowing up shops and stealing from the honest, hard-working magicals of Virginia."

Ember chuckled. "Good luck."

Neros thumped a fist on the carpet and pushed himself up enough to turn around and shoot Cheyenne a warning glare.

"Sorry." She lifted both hands in surrender and sidled around the relocated recliners toward the stairs to the mini-loft. "Shutting up now, cuz. Promise."

He stared at her and spooned another heap of Chunky Monkey into his mouth before returning his attention to Cady Heron and the Plastics.

Cheyenne fought back a soft laugh as she climbed the stairs to her loft office. *Maybe Maleshi was right. Everyone else wants to chill and focus on something that isn't overthrowing shitty leaders or saving two worlds or whatever. Somehow, I don't think Ben & Jerry's and high school comedies are gonna hit the spot for me.*

She dropped into her chair and powered up Glenn, then leaned back to wait for her system to fully come online. *If the general has no idea who or what this super-powered portal-casting new magical is, it might be pretty hard to find anything in the Borderlands. Then again, the dark web does tend to be full of surprises.*

Once she'd logged into her desktop and pulled up her VPN, Cheyenne dove into the dark web and found her normal route to Third Quarter Projections and the Borderlands forum behind it. The shrill cat-fighting of movie stars playing entitled teenagers blared louder in the background.

"Whoa." Ember laughed and stood from the couch. "Who said you had remote privileges?"

Neros stared at the TV and absently handed her the device. "You did not say otherwise."

"Okay, well, in this apartment, you have to earn the right to wield the clicker." She took it from him and stepped back to sit on the couch again. "And that's way too loud."

"I thought I heard voices under all the cheerleading."

"Oh, good. You have an overactive imagination too. Good thing we're filling your brain with all the best entertainment Earth has to offer." Ember looked at Cheyenne in the mini-loft and gestured at Neros, rolling her eyes.

Best part about letting your space-case cousin crash on the couch for a few nights is that you get to send him home again. Well, whenever the hell we can figure out how to pop him right back into Nor'ieth.

Cheyenne shook her head and returned her attention to the top of the Borderlands' newest posted topic threads.

The thread had been posted earlier by an avatar she'd seen before, one gu@ardi@n104 admin, and the title was definition eye-catching.

Attack on Peridosh. Seven Storefronts Destroyed, Goods Stolen

Yeah, okay.

She clicked the thread and scrolled through the comments, most of which had been left by magicals who'd either been in the marketplace that morning or who'd heard directly from someone who had. Cheyenne scrolled through the comments. All she had to do was think about running a keyword search for "new magical," "flames," "portal," "ingredients," "spell," and "calibrax," and her activator did the rest of the work for her. It finished scanning the page data before she'd even scrolled to the bottom of the comments and filled her vision with a report in large blinking yellow letters:

Search Results: 0

Figures. Only Neros would keep a running list of everything the mystery guy lifted, and of course, nobody's thinking about making one on the dark web. They're all too freaked out about keeping the market safe.

She scanned the rest of the comments in case something outside the keywords caught her attention. Nothing.

Backing out of the pinned thread, Cheyenne eyed the title again and frowned.

Corian thought it was important enough to stick up here literally right after the place was attacked, but he's too busy chasing L'zar to pick up his damn phone? I call bullshit.

Another scroll of the most recent threads pulled up more of the same

Is Peridosh Still Safe? Have We Missed Something Important?

Open thread for anyone who wants to talk about what they saw this morning. Shit was wack.

Concerned parent looking for anyone skilled in protection wards. Can pay with Earthside money or in trade. Ready to get started NOW.

The list went on and on, taking up a page and a half of the most recent posts until Cheyenne almost gave up looking. Then she reached the end of today's new threads and found herself skimming through yesterday's instead.

Her eyes caught the word "Ironbreak" in a thread opened last night at 10:34 p.m. She blinked and leaned toward the monitor, searching for it again before she found it partially buried in the middle of the posts. "No fucking way."

New Other-World Order. Can the Ironbreak deliver where the Spider fucked it all up?

Looks like someone's trying to improve their magical-journalist skills. If this was posted anywhere else, it'd be a hundred percent clickbait, hands down. And then she clicked on the thread.

RocknTr0ll44: This isn't a drill, assholes. All the rumors you thought you heard about this Persh'al Tenishi, the Ironbreak of Ambar'ogúl, have been confirmed by yours truly. As a T-Class myself, let me be among the first to congratulate the Ironbreak on behalf of T-Class everywhere and the Borderlands in particular. The Spider can suck it! May the Ironbreak reign!

4everHUNG: @RocknTr0ll44 Seriously, dude. You're either a bot, or you've lost your mind. Yeah, we've all heard about the new Cycle. It's all over the place. And *you*, T-Class who posts every two damn hours, need to give it a fucking rest.

Bl00dnHnr: Okay, so I agree with the sentiment behind this post.

Fuck yeah. May the Ironbreak reign, and long live the Black Flame with him, man. Respect. My sister in DC says she heard from a G-Class friend (green, not yellow) that there's something funky happening in Colonial Williamsburg. Like, portal-funky. I mean, yeah, it's all hearsay, but I don't mind the food for thought. The Ironbreak's got his work cut out for him in the homeland, but the Black Flame? Maybe this D-Class felt like paying us a visit. I'd be down, for sure. Beyond that, I'm gonna second @4everHUNG's complaint. @RocknTr0ll44 You really gotta cut it out with this constant posting. You're clogging up the feeds.

RocknTr0ll44: @Bl00dnHnr If you don't like seeing it, don't show up on my thread and agree with me all over the place before telling me to piss off. I'm doing a public service.

DoUBLeev14M: @RocknTr0ll44 And what if the Black Flame told you to piss off, huh? Would that get you to quit smashing keys in front of your computer and hoping something intelligible makes it out on the other side?

PwnPalace420: LOLOLOL! This ^^

OClassHrd0N: If the Black Flame showed up in Virginia and told me to eat my left foot, I'd do it with a fell-damn smile. That D-Class is one badass bitch. And I write that with the utmost respect, for the record.

DoUBLeev14M: @OClassHrd0N IKR? Not like she's gonna waste her time popping into the Borderlands to start reading about herself and what the rest of us displaced refugees think about the whole thing. But damn. How cool would it be to run into her, right? A guy can dream.

OClassHrd0N: @DoUBLeev14M Just make sure to wipe up when you're done. *fistbump*

RocknTr0ll44: @DoUBLeev14M @PwnPalace420 Fuck off. You can't call yourself a true loyalist if you start spouting shit like that. You'll see. MAY THE BLACK FLAME REIGN!!!

Cheyenne shoved herself away from the keyboard and snorted in disgust. *I have no idea which part of that was the most disturbing.*

She clicked out of the Ironbreak thread and scrolled farther down to other posts, searching for mentions of Persh'al, his new Crown moniker, and of course, the Black Flame. *Now I'm never gonna get away from it.*

Her activator pitched in without having to be prompted and pulled up one hundred and seven instances on the rest of this one webpage. She cleared the results and opted for searching on her own, skimming through the post titles without any real idea of what she was looking for. A few more caught her attention:

Anyone know if the Border portals are safe for a homebound crossing?

The Ban on Homeworld Natives Is Lifted! Who wants to take a trip?

Mind-Blowing Shit: A reflection on what the fuck happened on the other side?

Clicking into these didn't pull up anything she didn't already know. *That's a given. I* am *the expert on the subject.*

After a quick refresh on the Borderlands homepage, Cheyenne found one more thread opened four minutes ago by RocknTr0ll44, touting his loyalty to the O'gúl Crown and the Ironbreak's new Cycle and the Black Flame. Other than that, the forum had been overtaken by the news about the attacks on Peridosh and a whole bunch of conjecture from magicals who had or hadn't been there.

But now everyone knows about the new Crown and all the changes in Ambar'ogúl. And this stupid Black Flame won't leave me alone.

Cheyenne blinked at the screen, cocked her head, and wrinkled her nose. *Who posted first?*

Her activator responded instantly to the thought, and Cheyenne lifted her hands away from the mouse and the keyboard as the O'gúl tech navigated the Borderlands forum for her. A new page loaded, and she found herself staring at a single thread title highlighted in bright yellow in her vision.

News From Home! Buckle up, kiddies. You guys won't BELIEVE this shit!

Yeah, super catchy.

She reached for the mouse again, but her activator pulled up the thread before her hand was halfway there.

This thing might be a little too *intuitive.*

Shaking her head, she leaned toward the monitor and read the post.

NotYoMamasMagic: Try to wrap your heads around this, guys. I dare you. News finally came in from the Motherland. A new Cycle turned last week for one Persh'al Tenishi, or as he'll be known for the rest of fucking eternity, the Ironbreak of @mb@ar'ogú! (Come on, I'm not trying to set off any scan alarms. Still gotta be careful around here, right?)

Seriously. This is coming from a direct fucking source. The Spider has been fucking crushed. And not by the Ironbreak. Oh, no. The Black Flame is just one more D-Class hero we get to look up to for the rest of our natural lifetimes, which is a pretty fucking long time. How did this new Cycle (or two Cycles simultaneously) turn so quickly at the thirteenth hour, when it seemed all hope was lost for us Motherland Natives?

Head on over to my blog at NotYoMamasMagic.ogul to read the rest of the story. Don't believe me after that? Go ahead. Check it out on your own. You guys, this shit is FOR REAL. It finally happened. FREEDOM!

Blood and honor, bitches!

Gritting her teeth, Cheyenne reread the post, which sounded like so much sensationalist news with no confirmed facts or supporting and detailed evidence. If she hadn't just read a complete dark-web stranger writing in the occasional all-caps about her own damn life, she would've laughed and kept scrolling.

How the hell did he get all this information?

She studied the URL of the magical nutjob's website, and the activator took her right to it. Only the next webpage pulled up a big fat 'URL Not Found' error, and it turned out the domain name no longer existed.

So he either couldn't handle the heat, or someone else thought he needed to shut things down and did it for him. Probably a waste of time to go diving down that rabbit hole.

And it still didn't explain how news of Ba'rael's fall and the new Cycle turning for Persh'al had gotten all the way over here only a week after the fact. Someone might have made the crossing between the time Cheyenne handed over the O'gúl throne to a troll and almost sixty hours ago when she crossed again and brought an exhausted Bianca Summerlin home.

She went back to the Borderlands homepage and found two new topics already opened. The first was a description of someone's lost dog —and it was hard enough to imagine any magical sitting around in their living room eating O'gúleesh delicacies from Peridosh and patting Fido—but the second made her hiss out a long, slow breath.

Peridosh Thief strikes again? Or just coincidence?

Now the bad news starts rolling in.

She clicked on the thread, which hadn't gotten any comments yet but was sure to explode with everybody's super-important opinion within the next hour or two.

AccNFlames9010: Okay, I know the shit at the market this morning was freaky. Not the weirdest thing that's happened down there, if you ask me, but still pretty weird. Here's the thing, though. My sister's wadeenesh works out on Rez 14. I guess he came home and spilled all the facts to her over dinner or whatever (please don't try to go after the guy. These are weird times. I'm saying this to try to state my sources here). Apparently, the rez had some super weird interaction today. Something funky with the Border tower and a bunch of F-Force tech going haywire for a total of 92 seconds. My sister was adamant about that being the number. Exactly what he told her. I know it doesn't sound like much, especially after all the weird shit any one of us has seen on this side and back home, but pair tech interference and what he thought was concentrated magic for 92 seconds?

Dudes. Something's happening. My gut says it has something to do with the Peridosh attack this morning, but I have no way to put those pieces together. Anybody wanna help a curious O-Class out?

Any and all ideas/suggestions/theories (conspiracy or otherwise)

are welcome. Not trying to argue with anybody on this forum. I want to see if I can pull a few threads and weave them together, as the old saying goes. TIA.

"Shit." Cheyenne sat back in her chair. *Strong magic screwing around with tech on this side too? Sounds a lot like Ambar'ogúl's a lot closer than anyone realizes. And I bet Rez 14 isn't the only place.*

The only thing she had to do now was figure out who was messing with the Border reservations, whether they were connected to the attacks at Peridosh, and how to stop them before a potentially catastrophic combo of malfunctioning reservations and a portal-casting magical wielding a calibrax caused one epic magical mishap.

"Still have to find the bastard first."

CHAPTER FORTY-TWO

After explaining to Ember what she'd found on the Borderlands—in hushed voices, of course, so Neros could finish his first and so far favorite movie in peace—Cheyenne decided to call it a night. She tossed and turned in her bed, unable to wipe the forum's threads out of her mind.

It doesn't make sense. One magical wouldn't be able to spread what sounds like a pretty unbelievable rumor in this short amount of time. Even a dozen couldn't have told enough Earthside magicals to get that much action about the new Cycle on the dark web. Who the hell's spilling O'gúl news bits?

She checked her phone in the darkness of her room, thanks to the perfectly functioning blackout curtains. The screen's backlight was blinding, and she groaned when she saw the time.

Two twenty-five in the morning. What am I doing?

"Go to sleep, Cheyenne." She rolled over, grabbing one of the stray throw pillows and putting it over her face. Eventually, that was what she did.

The next morning, she decided to make the ten-foot trip down the hall outside their apartment to visit Matthew instead of the other way around. Her brisk knock elicited a startled shout of surprise and the clatter of something moving around on the counter before he shouted, "Just a sec!"

She folded her arms and waited for him to open the door. When he did, it was all Cheyenne could do not to laugh in his face. "Looks like I caught you in the middle of breakfast. Literally."

"What?" Matthew followed her gaze down to his shirt. "Oh, jeez. I mean, yeah. Scrambled eggs." He pulled the glob of still-steaming scramble off his cashmere sweater, popped it into his mouth, and swiped at the stain in aggravation, then looked back up at her. "Want some?"

"Only if you haven't worn it all first."

"Ha-ha. Come on in." He stepped aside to let her into his corner loft apartment, then peered into the hall. "What's Ember up to?"

"Trying to instill in my cousin a love for the finer points of folding laundry." Cheyenne shrugged. "I don't think he's buying it."

"Huh." Matthew shut the door and sucked bits of scrambled egg out of his teeth. "How long is he staying with you guys?"

"Hopefully not much longer than it takes us to get the rest of these activators up and running. Then I have to hand them out and hope a bunch of Earthborn FRoE agents can handle their shit long enough for me to escort Neros home." She squinted at the coffee table in his living room and shrugged. "Unless the Underman happens to feel particularly generous in the next couple days and opens a portal for us if we ask nicely."

Matthew looked her up and down. "I have no idea what you said."

"Temporarily, Matthew. That's what that means. Hopefully, my cousin gets home safe and sound in the next couple of days, but you never know."

"Right." He walked around the oddly angled corner toward the kitchen. "I'm guessing you didn't stop by for the eggs."

"I mean, if the offer still stands."

He scooped a pile of eggs scrambled with sausage, bell peppers, and Swiss cheese onto a plate, then pushed it across the island toward her before turning to grab another plate from the cabinet. "I'm almost done with the activators, by the way."

"For real?" She picked up the fork and watched him grab three different hot sauce bottles from the fridge.

"Yeah. Got about twenty left, so the syncing will be over in the next few hours."

"Damn. You stay up all night or something?" It was a poor attempt at a joke, but Matthew looked at her with a self-conscious frown.

"Yeah."

"Oh." *That explains the jumpiness and the eggs all over his sweater. Baggy eyes should've been the first giveaway.* "I don't need them tomorrow. You didn't have to run yourself into the ground or anything."

"Naw, it's fine." Matthew opened a bottle of Cholula and tapped a few drops onto his eggs, then closed it, and grabbed the Red Chili Truffle Sauce for the same treatment. "Been a while since I've had a project keep me up like this. I have a hard time sleeping with unfinished work lying around, you know?"

Cheyenne scooped up a forkful of eggs but couldn't stop staring at her neighbor's attempt to drown his eggs in sauce number three. "I'm familiar with the feeling. You like spicy food, huh?"

"What? Oh." He chuckled and slid the bottles to the side. "On my eggs. My grandma had a secret hot-sauce recipe she took with her to the grave, and this is as close as I can get to the real thing."

Shoveling a forkful of dripping scramble into his mouth, Matthew stared blankly at the counter.

He's gonna fall over any minute. Cheyenne took a tentative bite of eggs, unable to separate the taste of them from the overwhelming scent of all three hot sauces dripping onto Matthew's plate. *I didn't need to eat breakfast with him to check in on the syncing status.*

She slowly lowered her fork to the plate and swallowed. "No problems with those things?"

Matthew started and sucked in a deep breath through his nose as he looked up at her. He shook his head. "No. No problems. I think I nailed the upgrades to the program. I mean, I better have. But everything's working the way it should be, for as much as I have no idea how these things work."

"Good. Thanks for doing all this. And feel free to take a nap or something, huh? You only have twenty left."

"Yeah, okay." He chuckled like she was joking, then his smile disappeared. "I'm fine, Cheyenne. Trying to keep it together while I work through some things."

His eye twitched, and he looked away from her to shovel more eggs into his mouth.

Cheyenne ripped a square of paper towel from the roll on the island and slid it across the granite toward him. Matthew snatched it, quickly wiped his mouth, and nodded. *He's hiding something.*

"Hey, have you heard anything from those mystery maybe-Fed people who wanted to buy your program?"

He froze and swallowed thickly before slowly looking at her. "It's creepy when you do that. You know that, right?"

"Yeah. And I promise I can't read your mind."

Turning quickly toward the sink, Matthew grabbed a glass from the cabinet, filled it at the faucet, and chugged the whole thing in loud, croaking gulps. Then he set the glass down on the counter and turned around again, wiping the sweat from his forehead. "Tastes like grandma's eggs, but hers were never this hot."

"Uh-huh." Cheyenne folded her arms on the island and leaned forward. "What happened?"

"They sent me a message last night. An email." Matthew sniffed and stared at his uneaten eggs. "Reiterating their offer, I guess."

"And it shook you up pretty badly."

"Not the offer." He cleared his throat. "More like the fact that the email address they sent it to is used exclusively for internal company emails, and not even that frequently."

"So, someone's digging into your personal and professional secrets."

"Yeah, maybe. Or maybe I accidentally replied to an external email with that address. I have them all synced up, so it's possible." When he looked up, the easygoing smile he meant to give her didn't look so easygoing. "It's not a big deal, though. When I'm done powering up your metal stars, I'll sit down and try to find that loose end. Nothing to worry about."

"Okay." Cheyenne eyed him. *You're a terrible liar, Matthew Thomas.* "Well, thanks for putting in all the hard hours with the activators. And let me know if you want an extra pair of eyes on anything."

"Yeah, sure. Hey, you're not gonna finish your eggs?"

"Oh. They're good. I'm not that hungry. Thanks."

He nodded and blinked, staring after her as she showed herself out of his apartment.

Somebody's trying hard to get this guy to sell his program. Is that to stop me and the activators or to pick up where Colonel Thomas left off? I guess we'll see.

She spent the rest of that Sunday poring over the constantly updating Borderlands forum, occasionally helping Ember keep Neros out of trouble, and writing a search bot that would ping her with any action she could think of to list that might be related to Matthew Thomas and Combined Reality, Inc.

By the time dinner rolled around, after a brief argument with Neros that no, they couldn't eat sticks of butter for the last meal of the day, or any meal, Cheyenne was tapped.

Ember laid out a spread of sushi rolls from the place two miles away and handed Cheyenne a pair of chopsticks. "You look like you burned down a whole Nimlothar forest and saved a few worlds or something."

"That bad, huh?" Cheyenne snorted and pulled the container holding the Dragon Roll toward her. "I'm trying to put the pieces together, Em. Honestly, this feels a lot like way back in the beginning, you know?"

"Oh, yeah? Way back two months ago when I was in the hospital and you were just another halfling running around under the radar?"

"Yeah. That." Breaking apart her chopsticks, Cheyenne looked at her cousin, who was studying his pair, which were still in the paper wrapper, and snorted. "Here. Trade."

Neros responded willingly enough, taking one of the separated chopsticks in each hand and looking back and forth between them. "I do not understand?"

"Well, in your hands, Neros, I'd say these are a heck of a lot safer than giving you a fork." Ember showed him how to hold the chopsticks, then dug into the food. "I ordered you special veggie rolls, so don't worry about the flesh thing."

"I see." When he quickly discovered he could neither effectively stab the sushi rolls nor hold the chopsticks the way they were meant to be held, he abandoned them and got to work unrolling the rice and seaweed to study what was inside.

Cheyenne ignored her cousin's ridiculous exploration of his food and dug into her portion. "Matthew say anything to you about those suits trying to buy his program?"

"No. But you're bringing it up, so I'm guessing he told you."

"Only after I guessed. Mostly." The drow shrugged and dipped a roll into the plastic cup of soy sauce. "Maybe I'm trying to make the wrong things fit, but I can't help wondering if that's somehow related to the mystery-portal magical and all the weird crap happening on the reservations."

Ember swallowed her mouthful and stared at her friend. "You found more of those today, huh?"

"Five more reservations, yeah. All within a three-hour drive of DC. Not that drive time matters for a magical who isn't a nightstalker but moves faster than one and opens portals at will."

"And no one's seen this guy?"

"No." Cheyenne poked the crunchy flakes of tempura on the top of her roll with the tips of her chopsticks. "No other explosions like the ones in Peridosh, either. I mean, those two things aren't necessarily connected either. I don't have anything other than a gut feeling to link them together."

Ember shrugged. "Well, your gut's got a pretty good track record."

"So far. Until it doesn't." She popped another bite into her mouth and chewed slowly. "Either way, I gotta stick to the plan: rolling up to the FRoE base tomorrow with a case full of working activators to show the board what's up. Hopefully, the human board members take this involuntary-consultant thing as seriously as they want me to take it. I'm out of ideas, otherwise."

"Kinda hard not to take you seriously." The fae shot Neros a sidelong glance and looked quickly away, trying to hide a smile. "Might not be able to say the same thing for any other drow."

"That's not exactly a compliment, Em."

"Take it or leave it." Ember took another bite and watched her friend fiddling around with her food. "And after the board sees what you're doing and gives you the green light to hand out O'gúl tech to as many magical agents as you can?"

"I'm trying to focus on one thing at a time."

"Yeah, that's Cheyenne-speak for you're gonna pour everything you have into finding this portal thief."

"Portal thief." The drow chuckled. "That's a pretty cool name."

"You'll find him. Or her. Or whatever it is. Hey. No." Ember reached out to carefully take the other ramekin of soy sauce out of Neros' hands. "Dude. First, this stuff isn't for drinking. Second, I'm not into cleaning stains out of any of this furniture. Including the rug. Leave this stuff where I put it, huh?"

Neros stared blankly at the ramekin as Ember set it back down beside his veggie rolls. "I smell fish."

"Yeah, it's sushi. You want some?"

He turned slowly to look at the fae and narrowed his eyes. "No."

CHAPTER FORTY-THREE

Cheyenne's Monday morning started with a text from Yurik waiting for her when she got out of the shower.

Ninja stars mastered. Next level unlocked. If you need a demonstration today, we've got your back. FYI.

The text ended with a hand emoji throwing the devil horns, and Cheyenne laughed as she sent him a reply.

Stand by. Might have to take you up on that. Don't obliterate anything.

She spent the rest of the morning searching through more useless conjecture on the Borderlands' newest topic threads, and none of it was any more helpful than what she'd found the night before. Then Matthew showed up with both trunks of program-synced activators in his arms, looking like the weight of the metal trunks would pull him to the floor at any minute.

He staggered when Cheyenne easily lifted them out of his grasp and looked at her with wide eyes. "Okay, I need to up my workout game."

Ember pulled Neros away from the wall, where he'd been trying to reach the smoke detector, presumably to tear it down and study it. "Don't let the super drow strength intimidate you, Matthew. Not sure you're gonna meet the same standards by doubling down at the gym."

He chuckled and ran a hand through his hair. "Is it weird that I'm relieved by that?"

"Not really." Cheyenne set the trunks down on the coffee table and opened them both to check the inventory. Her activator did the counting for her: one hundred and ninety-two, all accounted for. "I wouldn't use it as an excuse to give up, though."

"Yeah, thanks. Hey, let me know how things go with those today, huh?"

She turned to look at him and narrowed her eyes. "You feeling attached to our partner project?"

"More like responsible, Cheyenne. Which I probably should've felt more of the last time. So now I'm trying to turn over a new leaf, I guess."

She nodded and turned away from the cases to face him. "I get the feeling." She stuck out her hand and gave him a small, mostly genuine smile. "You did it."

"Yeah, team effort." Matthew shook her hand and gave her a crooked smile. "Not something I'm used to, but in this situation, I'm pretty sure stepping out of my comfort zone was the only good option I had."

Cheyenne pointed at their neighbor. "You hear this guy, Em?"

"You mean, do I hear him saying all the stuff you're thinking but wouldn't be caught dead saying out loud?" Ember followed Neros across the kitchen and closed the fridge he'd pried open and left that way before moving on. "No! Neros, for the last fucking time, the garbage disposal is off-limits."

Way to throw me under the bus, Em. Eyeing her cousin with a grimace, Cheyenne blinked at Matthew and said, "That wasn't quite what I meant."

"I get it." He couldn't look her fully in the eye either. "We'll call it good at the handshake."

"Deal."

"Yeah." Frowning at Neros, who was now studying Matthew with a tilted head like their neighbor was a specimen, Matthew slowly made his way toward the door. "Your cousin has personal-boundary issues."

"That's a severe understatement."

Matthew opened the front door, shot Neros another uncomfortable look, slipped into the hall, and disappeared.

"Who was that?" Neros asked, staring with the same intensity at the closed front door.

"Our neighbor." Ember blew a few stray violet hairs out of her eyes and folded her arms. "The human you've seen pretty much every day since you've been here."

"He is hiding something."

Cheyenne rolled her eyes. "Who isn't these days, right? Leave him alone. He's a decent guy. I think."

Ember grinned at her friend. "You're being extra complimentary this morning."

"Trying to stay positive, Em. We'll see how I feel after these activators get into a hundred FRoE-agents' hands."

Neros looked down at his own hands and studied his palms. "Hands."

"You feeling okay, Neros?"

"I have forgotten."

Cheyenne frowned at her cousin and shook her head. "We need to get you home."

"That would be preferable, yes."

"Well, after tonight, maybe we can get the Underman to open the door he closed behind you, huh?"

Neros' eyes widened. "Beseeching an *uanáj* is not preferable to being here, Cheyenne."

"Well, we have a saying over here. Beggars can't be choosers."

"I do not understand."

"It means when we find you the first one-way trip home, *uanáj* or no *uanáj*, you're taking it."

At 4:42 p.m., Cheyenne stepped out of her Panamera in the FRoE compound's huge parking lot and smiled when the automatic locks let out their telltale chirp and flash of upgraded purple headlights. *Don't look too happy, Cheyenne. Everyone's gonna think you're hiding something.*

She stuck her hands in the pockets of her trench coat, dropping her keys into one of them and fingering the three extra star activators in the other. *If they want a demonstration, they'll get one.*

The front lobby of the compound was empty, as usual, but the sound of angry voices all talking and shouting at once came from the short hall leading to the common room. The second the front glass doors shut behind the drow, shadows moved along the hallway wall toward the lobby.

"You're so full of shit, Grot," Bhandi shouted. "I swear. Trying to get anything through your thick skull is worse than watching Yurik pick out his clothes at the Goodwill. Which I imagine would be excruciating."

The troll entered the lobby, shaking her head, and froze when she saw Cheyenne.

The drow jerked her chin at the agent. "Hey."

"Shit." Bhandi glanced behind her. "You're early."

"One of those meetings where being early is probably a good thing, right?"

"Yeah." The agent grimaced.

"Well, go on, then, asshole." Grot's rumbling growl grew louder and closer. "Put your money where your goddamn mouth is."

"No problem, dickhead." Yurik emerged from the hall, walking backward with his arms spread wide. "Remember you asked for it. You're gonna eat shit after we—"

"You." Grot stepped out of the hall after Yurik and sneered when he saw Cheyenne. "I knew this had your fucking drow stench all over it. Malfi! Rudy! Get out here. Cleanup at the front of the base."

The ogre stormed forward, shoving Yurik out of his way with a meaty arm and glaring at Cheyenne.

"Don't fucking touch me, you dumb shit." Yurik straightened the standard-issue black t-shirt tucked into his fatigue pants and took off after his pissed-off fellow agent. "You have no idea who you're messing with."

"Shit." Bhandi looked between Cheyenne, Grot, and the group of curiously excited agents spilling out of the hall from the common room. "Yeah, this was why we hoped you wouldn't be early."

Cheyenne held Grot's gaze and slowly shook her head. "It means we have an extra ten minutes to settle whatever needs to be settled, right? Should be plenty of time."

"I'll put you in the ground in less than five, drow." Grot stopped two feet away from her and shoved a sausage-shaped gray finger in her face. "You're one dumb bitch, you know that? Showing your face around here again after what you tried to pull the last time."

She spread her arms and cocked her head. "Last time, I was feeling a little under the weather. Back in top form today, though."

"Okay, wait a fucking minute!" Tate shoved his way through the crowd of magicals who believed Grot's bullshit mixed with the other agents who were curious enough to come see what all the yelling was about. "Cheyenne's got a meeting with the goddamn board, Grot. Back off."

"That's what you're calling it, huh?" The ogre sneered at Cheyenne and leaned forward to loom over her. "I call it a fucking takeover."

"For fuck's sake, man. We've been over this already." Bhandi shoved the ogre's chest with both hands, which only made him sway sideways. He shot her a disgusted look. "Keep looking at me like that, and I'll claw your damn eyes out."

"This isn't helping anyone," Tate added, finally reaching the drow squaring off with the angry ogre. "And I don't know where the hell you got this idea that Cheyenne's trying to tear things apart from the inside out, but it's bullshit."

"She's a drow," Grot snarled.

"Yeah, that's what they do." Malfi stepped up behind the ogre and set a hand on her hip. "This one's no different. Why the fuck else would a drow show up Earthside and weasel her way into this place, huh?"

Cheyenne glanced at the black utility knife strapped to the goblin woman's belt and wrinkled her nose. "Nice try with the scare tactics, guys. Really. I'm not gonna bite, though."

"You don't have a choice," Grot snarled. "Right now. We're gonna settle this."

"Jesus Christ!" Yurik shouted. "You can't pick a fight with her right before she goes upstairs."

"Shut your fat goblin mouth." Growling, the ogre spun away from Cheyenne and swung a massive fist toward Yurik's face.

The goblin ducked and darted aside. Bhandi hissed and reached toward Grot, her fingertips flashing with purple light.

"Whoa, whoa!" Tate darted forward, and a short orc standing behind

Grot stepped in front of the tattooed troll to deliver a nasty right hook to Tate's jaw.

Jamal's bellow preceded him as he stomped out of the hallway, his fists glowing with red and copper light. The floor shook beneath his weight as he barreled toward his brawling fellow agents.

Cheyenne stepped back and raised her hands. *Fuck. Anything I do now is gonna make it worse.*

Tate righted himself with a shout and shot a barrage of roaring blue fireballs at the orc who'd punched him. Bhandi's strobing purple pellets glanced off Grot's bald head and sent him reeling. Jamal's copper-flashing fists crashed into a skaxen agent, trying to stop him before he reached Grot and his misguided followers. The agent flew across the lobby with a shouted curse, and Jamal didn't stop.

Yurik gritted his teeth as the yellow sunburst of his magic burst around his hands before sucking back in again.

Shit. Cheyenne stepped toward him. "Not in here!"

Malfi snarled and charged the muscular goblin. She rammed into him as the spell his activator called Obliteration fired. Instead of reaching Grot, the column of yellow light shot into the ceiling as Malfi tackled Yurik to the ground.

Plaster and thick chunks of the ceiling broke free. Yurik's spell sputtered out as he focused on shoving the goblin off him.

The agents who had gathered to watch the showdown shouted in surprise and anger as the ceiling gave way.

Cheyenne raised a shield with both hands, holding it in place as the huge chunks of plaster that would have cracked Grot's thick skull crumbled around her shield instead and toppled to the lobby floor.

Grot stared at the destroyed ceiling, saw the drow's shield saving him from a bad headache, and snarled.

She lowered the shield as the last wave of plaster dust fell around them, then flipped him the bird. "You're welcome."

A pipe burst in the ruptured ceiling and sprayed a thick stream sideways across the lobby.

"Aw, come on."

"Goddammit. You morons should've taken this outside."

"Fuck you guys."

The FRoE agents who'd come to watch wiped water off their faces and shirts and quickly headed through the hall back to the common room.

Grot clenched his fists, all his knuckles cracking at once as he glared at Cheyenne.

"Damn," Jamal said, shaking his fists out as the copper glow around them flickered out like a dying lightbulb.

Malfi pushed off the floor and shoved Yurik away with a hiss. "What the fuck was that, huh?"

Bhandi tossed her scarlet braids over her shoulder and raised her fists in a fighting stance. "Shit you don't wanna mess with, bitch."

"Cut it out." Tate shook his head at her, and the troll grunted as she lowered her fists.

"I don't know what the fuck you idiots are smoking." Grot stepped away from Cheyenne, his boots crunching on the broken plaster clumps growing soggy under the busted pipe. "But whatever it is, keep it the fuck away from me. You especially." He jabbed a finger at Cheyenne again, glanced at the hole in the ceiling, and stormed across the lobby toward the common room.

Malfi and the other agents who hated Cheyenne's guts glared at her and flipped her off or snarled as they followed the ogre down the hallway. "Better clean this shit up and hope you don't get tossed out on your traitor asses for this."

"Bite me," Bhandi muttered.

"Fuck you."

Then it was Cheyenne and her four FRoE friends standing in the destroyed lobby. She glanced at Yurik and raised an eyebrow. "Mastered, huh? When you said, 'next level unlocked,' I guess I assumed you guys figured out how to keep your shit together with those things."

Yurik cleared his throat and shrugged. "I got carried away."

"Yeah. Which is exactly the kinda thing with a serious potential for sabotaging everything I'm trying to do upstairs."

"We kept it a secret, though," Tate added, wiping water droplets off his bald head and flicking them aside. "Nobody knows shit about the ninja stars."

"No, now everybody thinks we're a team of morons blindly following Cheyenne and fucking shit up with magic we can't control."

Bhandi shoved a clod of plaster aside with her boot. "And we look like idiots."

Cheyenne looked at the broken pipe and studied her activator's command prompt for a quick repair spell. Her twitching finger flashed yellow light and the pipe in the ceiling did the same. With a squeal of metal and a steaming hiss, the pipe sections sealed up again, leaving only a few drops of water to splash into the quickly spreading puddle on the lobby floor.

"Oh, shit." Bhandi frowned at the ceiling and nodded. "Was that all you, or are you tapping into your special headpiece for repair jobs now?"

The drow grinned and headed across the lobby toward the corridor on the opposite side of the common room. "If you guys can figure out how to clean up the rest of this with whatever spells pop up, it might save you some time."

"Right." Yurik's yellow eyes flitted back and forth as he scanned the activator prompts in his vision. "Which one did you use?"

"I didn't mean now." Cheyenne waved them forward. "You guys are coming with me."

"We are?" Tate looked up from the mess on the floor and frowned at the hem of Cheyenne's trench coat disappearing around the corner. "Are we?"

"It's not rocket science," Jamal grumbled as he slapped the back of a huge hand against the troll man's shoulder. "You heard her."

Rubbing his shoulder, Tate glanced at Bhandi. "We're sitting in on a board meeting?"

"Dude, I don't even pretend to know what to expect anymore." She shook her head and stepped around the edge of the puddle to follow Yurik and Jamal toward the other side of the compound.

The tattooed troll grimaced as he surveyed the damage, then rubbed his head and jogged after them to catch up.

CHAPTER FORTY-FOUR

Cheyenne turned the corner on the top floor of the base and stopped. Van Lurig's secretary stood beside the closed door to the conference room, hugging her clipboard to her chest, and looked the drow up and down. She pursed her lips. "You're late. And wet."

"Got a little caught up. You might wanna talk to someone about a building inspection."

"Our adherence to building-code requirements is perfectly fine, thank you. Not that it's any of your business." Helen gestured at the closed conference room door. "This meeting is, though."

"Yeah." Cheyenne ran a hand through her slightly damp hair and headed down the hall. Her four agent friends rounded the corner behind her.

"I'm sorry." Helen raised a hand as she eyed the agents. "These agents haven't been cleared to join you."

"So clear them."

"Miss Summerlin, that's not how things work around here, no matter how much you plan on improving certain tactical processes. On the third floor, the major general calls the shots. And I'm the one who carries them out."

"I told them to come up here with me." Cheyenne looked at the agents, who'd all stopped in the middle of the hall and were staring at

Helen like a bunch of panicked squirrels caught in the middle of a busy highway. She pointed at the chairs lined up along the wall. "Guess you'll have to wait a while."

"There's no need for these operatives to—"

"They're part of my presentation, Helen. Thank you." Cheyenne nodded at the chairs again as she grabbed the doorknob. "Take a seat. I'll bring you in when it's time."

Helen pressed her lips together and stepped aside as Cheyenne opened the door. She looked the agents over one more time as Yurik, Bhandi, and Tate sat in the uncomfortable chairs. Jamal eyed the chair on the end, pressed a hand down on the seat to test it, then opted for sitting on the ground beside it.

Cheyenne stepped into the conference room and found all four remaining board members stepping away from where they'd gathered at the other end of the long table.

"Cheyenne." Major General Van Lurig blinked quickly at the drow and cleared her throat. "We were starting to think you'd lost your nerve for this."

"Lack of nerve isn't the issue, Major General." Cheyenne nodded at Lieutenant Colonel Oppenhaur, Colonel McMillen, and Mr. Weber as they spread out down the table and took their seats. Van Lurig, of course, sat in the chair at the head.

The gray-haired woman folded her hands on the table and nodded at her secretary. "Thank you, Helen. We'll take it from here."

Helen gave her a curt nod and shot Cheyenne a bitter smile before removing herself from the conference room and shutting the door behind her.

The major general lifted her chin and looked Cheyenne over. "There is an issue?"

The other board members took their seats, sniffing and readjusting themselves in the cushy leather executive chairs before rolling toward the table.

"Not yet, but there might be if certain of your agents keep entertaining the idea that I'm here for a takeover."

McMillen snorted and quickly tried to cover it up with a forced cough into his fist.

Van Lurig gave the drow a thin smile and dipped her head. "That's part of leadership. Worrying about pleasing everyone is the best way to gridlock yourself in indecision, and decisions still have to be made."

Cheyenne raised her eyebrows. "Do I look like someone who worries about pleasing everyone?"

"Not in the slightest," Weber muttered.

Van Lurig shot him a quick warning glance and the man shifted in his chair, rising slightly to unbutton his suit jacket before settling back with his arms on the armrests. "No need to bother filing a formal complaint, Cheyenne. If you have specific agents in mind, give us the names, and we'll take care of it."

"No." Cheyenne pulled out the chair at the opposite end of the table and sat. "I didn't come here to tattle on a few agents who have their priorities mixed up. They'll either fall in line, or they won't. I need assurance from the board that if they don't fall in line, it won't blow back on me."

"You're not responsible for any individual member of this organization. And you know that."

"Still."

Van Lurig closed her eyes briefly. "Yes, Cheyenne. You have our assurance. Any outliers among our operatives when it comes to your expertise and willingness to guide us through our systemic overhaul will be dealt with accordingly, independent of your role here. Will that suffice?"

"Yeah, that works. Thanks."

The conference room fell silent, punctured by the monotonous ticking of the clock on the far wall behind the major general. *This feels way too much like a power struggle. Not what I was going for. But they still have to ask.*

Oppenhaur cleared his throat. "So. You've had four days to come up with some initial suggestions. I'm assuming you've prepared something." He looked her over with a small frown. "Or did you leave your proposal in the car?"

"I'm not the three-ring-binder type." *Board meetings aren't my thing either, but here I am.* Cheyenne stood and reached into her jacket pocket to pull out the three activators. She slid them one by one across the table toward Van Lurig, Oppenhaur, and McMillen. Mr. Weber eyed her expectantly, and she shrugged. "Sorry. I only brought three."

Van Lurig stared at the metal four-pointed star in front of her and didn't move to grab it. "What are these?"

"They're called activators. I know you haven't heard the word before because your agents are clueless."

Mr. Weber hummed in poorly concealed frustration. "Insults won't get you anywhere, Miss Summerlin."

"Cheyenne. And anyone who's insulted by the truth isn't ready to hear it."

The man scowled at her. McMillen and Oppenhaur widened their eyes and dipped their heads to hide small smiles.

Van Lurig spread her hands. "So, let's hear the truth about these activators."

Cheyenne leaned back in the rolling executive chair and set her arms on the armrests. "These came straight from Ambar'ogúl."

"I'm sorry." Oppenhaur lifted a finger to stop her and glanced at the major general. "Foreign technology was what got us into this mess in the first place. I'm not a fan."

"The technology isn't the issue, Lieutenant Colonel." Van Lurig raised an eyebrow. "Our oversight and the weakness of character displayed by one former board member are. I'll kindly ask you to keep your comments to yourself until Cheyenne has finished."

The man cocked his head with a bitter grimace, staring at the table as he gestured for Cheyenne to continue.

Someone always comes into a meeting like this with their mind already made up. I'll just have to change it.

The drow nodded at Van Lurig. "These were created by a high-ranking engineer on the other side of the Border. And yes, Ambar'ogúl does have engineers. I'd go so far as to say they're smarter, more skilled, and a lot more capable than anyone on Earth, but that's not the point."

Weber folded his arms and leaned back in his chair with a frown.

I have his attention.

"What are they for?" he asked.

"Oh, good question." Cheyenne shot him a pointed look. "I'm getting to that. The majority of the O'gúleesh population has access to activators like these. The devices range in function and capability, like devices on our market, but they share the same basic purpose. These things sync up with a magical's abilities, whatever they happen to be, and make them more accessible."

Van Lurig narrowed her eyes. "That hardly sounds worth the effort of acquiring one."

"Well, they do a lot more on the other side. You know, where the foundation of O'gúleesh civilization is built on magical technology syncing up across the board through a main database in…" Cheyenne grimaced, noting the increasing confusion in the board members' vapid stares. "Okay, forget all that. These things are the equivalent of cell phones if a cell phone could run our entire lives. Power and steer cars. Open doors. Cook food. Run construction projects and build infrastructure. And help us tap into our innate abilities. Which, in the case of the magicals, is their magic."

The board members blinked at her. McMillen said, "You want to hand our agents these devices."

"Basically, yeah."

"Cheyenne, that would render this board and the entire organization obsolete." He shook his head. "I'm not putting something with this much power and all its various applications into the hands of trained field operatives. They take orders and carry them out, and it works because this organization is structured as a cohesive unit held together by the chain of command. These devices would unravel that chain. Why take orders from a superior when you could rewrite the orders? Or build your own weapons without adhering to inspection regulations? Hell, you might as well have slid three bombs across the table toward us." He tossed his hand in the air and shook his head.

The drow blinked at him. "Are you finished?"

"Yes, he is," Van Lurig answered for him. "You're obviously not, Cheyenne, so please continue."

She nodded. "If we were sitting at this table in the O'gúl capital for the same conversation, then yeah. Your concerns would be pretty damn reasonable, Colonel. But in that world, everybody has an activator. Everybody has access to the core magi-tech system that runs it. It's like the internet, except it powers everything but magic. The O'gúleesh have figured out how to combine the two for commerce, services, trade, and use in their daily lives. But here? On Earth? The activators only work on a small scale."

"Because the numbers are fewer?" Oppenhaur shook his head. "I agree with Colonel McMillen's analogy: one bomb or a thousand, there's still going to be an explosion. And casualties, depending on where it is."

"They're not bombs." Instead of rolling her eyes, Cheyenne closed them and took a deep breath. *You took this on willingly, Cheyenne. Keep it together and channel Bianca if you have to, or they won't take you seriously.* "Okay. Here's a better analogy. I'm assuming at least one of you has a smartphone. Lots of different functions for a phone, right? Sending and receiving calls and text messages. The occasional voicemail. And you have all the apps you could possibly want right there at your fingertips for shopping, social media, car insurance, online banking... You name it, it's probably possible to handle from your phone."

The board members stared at her.

At least they can't disagree with any of that.

"Now, you take a drive up into the mountains for a nice getaway with your dog or whatever. You get all the way up there, and you've got shitty service. Can't make phone calls. Most of the apps slow down when you open them, and it's hard to connect. You're out of range. But you still get the occasional text coming through if you stand on the second-floor balcony and wave your phone around. The camera still works. Your downloaded music is still right there to use if you want a little something for the mood or whatever. The alarm you set will still go off in the morning, and the time and date are still synced with the rest of the world. Emergency calls still go through. And if you need to, you can drive to the closest town to maybe get a few more bars and send an email or make an important call."

"I do believe we understand the basic functions of cell phones." Mr. Weber shifted in his chair. "But if these activators can do what you claim, I don't see why they'd be affected by available internet service or proximity to cell phone towers."

"What?" Cheyenne scrunched her eyes shut and shook her head. "Okay, that went right over your head. In this analogy, activators in Ambar'ogúl are smartphones with full internet access and full cell reception. They're running at full capacity for all functions. The activators on Earth are the same phones but removed from strong signals, so they don't do nearly as much but still perform basic core functions that don't require internet or cell service."

"So, they do or don't also send and receive calls?" Oppenhaur asked slowly.

"Jesus, I don't know how to dumb this down any more for you guys than I already have."

Colonel McMillen spread his arms. "Cheyenne, if you can't accurately explain to this board what these devices will accomplish and why they are not a liability, which seems to be the only real definition for them, you can't expect us to approve of incorporating them into standard operating procedures. It's simple."

"I know it's simple." Cheyenne pointed at the activators on the table. "These are simple. Their core function Earthside isn't to make phone calls, and they're not bombs. Look, I haven't met all your agents or gauged their characters or seen their skills. That doesn't matter. I know a handful fairly well, and I've been in the field with at least four dozen different agents. These are full-blooded magicals, not halflings like me. But they were born Earthside, and they have no idea how to tap into their potential because you put guns and RPGs and fell lasers in their hands."

"Again." Weber pointed at her. "Agent Todd did not have clearance to remove that weapon from our testing facilities."

"Whatever." Cheyenne spread her arms. "The point is that you have magical agents who know nothing about where they come from, what's happening in the other world, or how to help the refugees coming in droves through the Border portals for sanctuary on your reservations. For assimilation. Your magical agents are as unequipped to handle magical situations as you are, and I'm strictly talking about race here. They might as well be humans with weird skin tones and seriously messed-up teeth."

Van Lurig choked back a laugh, then pursed her lips in an attempt to wipe the amused smile off her face. "You have a knack for vivid imagery, Cheyenne. I'll give you that."

"How about you give me a chance to show you what's possible with these things?" The drow nodded at the activators. "There's no risk here beyond the learning curve. Look, this is like setting parental controls on an iPad or something, okay? But the controls are set by your agents being on Earth. They won't have access to the system mainframe on the other side, and even if they did, Earth has a long way to go to build everything out of the kind of energy-and-magic-conducting metal that only exists on the other side. That's how the magic-tech works over there. Here, it's a boost to their magic and a way for them to hone their skills. And make things safer for everyone."

"That is the final objective." Van Lurig dipped her head. "I still struggle to see how."

"Okay." Cheyenne stood and removed her activator from behind her ear, grimacing at the light pinch. She held the silver coil up for them to see. "This is mine."

The board members stared at her device. Oppenhaur tilted his head. "How long have you had that?"

"A few weeks. Trust me, if I'd had this two months ago, I wouldn't have gotten shot in the hip and held hostage here on base for five days. Probably wouldn't have set foot in that building to crash that sting, but that's for different reasons." She set her activator on the table and spread her hands. "Without that, the only things I have in my toolbox are the abilities I was born with. Anyone have a pen?"

Weber scoffed. "What does that have to do with anything?"

Van Lurig cleared her throat and held her hand out toward him. With a surprised scowl, the man reached into the inside pocket of his suit jacket and handed her his pen. "Thank you."

"Okay." Cheyenne nodded. "Throw it at me."

CHAPTER FORTY-FIVE

"This is ridiculous," Oppenhaur muttered.

McMillen sucked on his teeth in aggravation. "Major General, this woman wants to turn our organization into a circus."

Van Lurig chucked the pen across the table. Cheyenne stepped aside and tossed a crackling sphere of black energy at the pen, making sure to aim away from the board members. Her attack hit the writing implement and shattered it into hundreds of metal fragments before the wall of the conference room exploded in a burst of plaster and drywall. Her magic left a dented, charred crater behind and a few trailing wisps of smoke.

Oppenhaur slammed both hands on the table and leaped to his feet. "Now, wait just a minute!"

Van Lurig stared at Cheyenne even as she muttered in a low warning, "Lieutenant Colonel."

"No. This drow shows up claiming advanced magical technology will improve the performance of our operatives and the effectiveness of our organization as a whole, but the only thing she successfully achieves is to blast holes in the walls!"

Weber cleared his throat. "That was a very nice pen."

"Dammit! This isn't a battle you can win through intimidation!"

"Sit down, Oppenhaur," Van Lurig barked.

The lieutenant colonel stiffened, then sank slowly down into his chair again, glaring at Cheyenne.

"I've come to expect that sort of outburst from Major Carson, but not from you." The major general stared at Oppenhaur, then swept her gaze toward Colonel McMillen and finally to Mr. Weber sitting on the other side of her. "I've reached my limit for mediating this discussion. The next person who loses control of himself before the end of this meeting will be dismissed from this room and permanently relieved of any involvement with this proposal. Is that understood?"

"Absolutely," Weber muttered.

McMillen nodded at her.

"Oppenhaur?"

The lieutenant colonel cleared his throat and slowly turned his head to look at her. "Sir."

Folding her hands on the table again, Van Lurig looked at Cheyenne, her nostrils flaring. "Cheyenne, I'm well aware of how tempting it is to leave this room without any willingness to continue the discussion. Thank you for not doing that."

"Yeah, I know I can walk away whenever I want." Cheyenne shrugged. "But I've done enough of that. In more ways than one, I *chose* to be here right now." *It wouldn't mean a damn thing to them if I said I chose this over ruling an entire world as the Crown.* "Just so you know, this whole thing isn't exactly a pet project for me."

"No, you've made your passion for this subject perfectly clear." Van Lurig shot a glance at the charred hole in the wall. "You've been an asset to this organization countless times already. Without compensation, I might add. I hope to do far more in return, but the least we can do is offer you the courtesy of finishing whatever that demonstration was meant to achieve."

"Right." Cheyenne looked at each of the board members in turn, then picked up her activator and showed it to them again. "Before I had this, blowing things up and blasting holes in walls was pretty much the extent of what I could do, with a few exceptions. It's pretty much what your agents are good at too, also with a few exceptions. And yeah, I admit I didn't have nearly as much training for physical engagement, I guess. Or with magic."

"Major Carson told us you were raw and green and pissed off, but you had potential," Van Lurig said. "That was, of course, from his initial report when you were, as you put it, held hostage here on base. His tune has changed a bit over the last few weeks."

The drow let herself return the major general's tiny smile. "If it hadn't, I'd say there's something wrong with both of us."

Van Lurig and Mr. Weber chuckled. McMillen and Oppenhaur exchanged exasperated glances.

"Please continue."

Cheyenne gestured at the hole in the wall. "Obviously, I can aim and fire and destroy, but that's not anywhere close to what's possible. Not for me, not for your agents, not for any magical who makes the crossing Earthside looking for something better over here than what they left behind. Until a few months ago, I didn't know that either. Someone recently tried to teach me how to cast one of the simplest and most important spells for—"

"Spells?" The major general raised her eyebrows. "What do you mean by that?"

Oh, boy. How the hell did these people get this deep into dealing with magicals and not know half the shit they should?

Cheyenne forced herself to smile at the woman. "What it sounds like, Major General. Gestures. Incantations. Specific patterns of magic used in specific ways for a specific outcome. Some need ingredients, some don't. I have full faith in your imagination."

"Try suspension of all disbelief," McMillen muttered. When Van Lurig shot him a warning look, he nodded at Cheyenne and gestured for her to continue. "Which we're willing to provide. Go ahead."

Cheyenne turned the silver coil over in her hand. "I can hold my own in a fight, but I suck at spellwork. That might be an understatement. Most magicals I've met on both sides of the Border have a basic understanding of spells and grasp the concepts around casting them a lot more easily than I do. Except for your agents, of course, because nobody taught them a damn thing about what they're capable of."

"We are not opening a magic school," Oppenhaur muttered.

She snorted without thinking and looked him up and down. "I sure as hell hope not. But that's not what this is about. Training with activators handles both things at once. Tapping into a magical's inherent abilities is one advantage. The other is taking a magical with no skills in spellcasting, even a halfling like me, and giving them at least a basic proficiency."

"This'll be interesting," Weber muttered.

Cheyenne showed them her silver coil again. "Granted, this is one of the more advanced models, so I wouldn't expect anyone with one of those star-shaped activators to be able to cast anything at an advanced level. Or at least not right away. You get the idea."

I'm taking way too long with this. Get to the fucking point.

She stuck the activator behind her ear and waited for it to sync up with her magic. She barely felt the pinch, but her eyelids fluttered all the same. Then she stepped away from the table and studied the scattered pieces of Mr. Weber's exploded pen littering the floor.

A simple thought brought up the activator's command prompt for the repair spell she'd used on the busted pipe downstairs. *This feels way too much like a magic show. Suck it up.*

Cheyenne selected the command, and her hands moved on their own as the activator flooded her synapses with the right magic and the right gestures for casting what she wanted. Yellow light flared on her fingertips, then on every piece of the broken metal pen.

Three seconds later, the shards were floating in the air above the conference table and rearranging themselves into their original state. When it was finished, the pen clattered onto the table in one piece. Cheyenne looked at the board members, all of whom stared at the pen with wide eyes.

Bingo.

She pointed at the pen and sent a small burst of telekinetic energy toward it. It slid down the table toward Weber, spinning around and around, and stopped right in front of him. The man jumped in his chair and clutched the armrests.

"If you'd told me to do that without the activator, I would've told you to piss off." Cheyenne pointed at the pen. "You'll probably have to buy a refill."

The man cleared his throat and reached for the pen, then slowly placed it back in his inside pocket and stared at Van Lurig.

"What about the wall?" Oppenhaur stared at the drow as he pointed at the charred hole in the plaster.

"I mean, I could try. Metal's easier to work with."

"That won't be necessary, Cheyenne," Van Lurig said with a knowing smile. "I think we've heard everything we need to hear about these devices."

"Major General," Oppenhaur muttered, shifting in his chair, "don't you think this is something we should discuss further? In private?"

"Not at all." The woman raised an eyebrow at him. "She knows what she's talking about and can back it up with at least one evidence-based example. Unless you're going to tell me you suddenly don't believe in magic?"

"That's not what I meant."

"Good. Nothing we say here is above Cheyenne's role as our consultant, and that's the point, Lieutenant Colonel. If she is to be consulted, she needs to know what we know. Admittedly, we still know far less than we should. I think that's perfectly obvious."

Weber gestured at Cheyenne. "So we give this woman the green light to distribute her foreign technology to our operatives and hope it all works out?"

Van Lurig shot him a warning glance. "Don't pretend you're not interested in her proposal. We all know you're itching to get your hands on one of those activators."

"Yes, and I'm the only one who wasn't given a sample."

McMillen snorted and flicked the activator in front of him across the table toward Weber. "Be my guest."

The man picked up the metal star and turned toward Cheyenne. "May I?"

"Go for it. Don't try to take it apart or anything, in case you thought that would be a good way to try to figure out how it works."

"Why not?"

She shrugged. "Well, then it might actually be a bomb."

Weber set the activator gingerly down on the table again and sat back in his chair.

"So." Van Lurig stood. "This was a thought-provoking presentation, Cheyenne, and it leaves us with little else to discuss."

"We can't sign off on this without further testing," McMillen said, standing as well.

The major general glanced at the drow. "Which is why—if I may continue uninterrupted, Colonel—we'll need to schedule a more structured demonstration. With one of our operatives, if not several. If what you say is accurate and these devices will benefit the magicals employed by this organization, we need to see it for ourselves. How long do you think you would need to put that together for us?"

Cheyenne stuck her hands in her pockets and grinned. "About as long as it takes to walk outside."

The major general blinked quickly. "I'm sorry?"

"I already tested it." Nodding at the door, Cheyenne turned to let herself out of the conference room. She held the door open as the board members overcame their surprise and moved to follow her.

The agents along the opposite wall of the hallway looked at her expectantly.

"So?" Yurik gave her a hesitant smile. "How did it go?"

"Well, we're about to find out." Cheyenne stepped aside as Van Lurig led the procession out of the conference room.

All four agents stood immediately and came to attention while their superiors filled the hall. Van Lurig studied each of them in turn. "These four were with you and Captain Rhynehart in Westphalia, weren't they?"

"Yep."

"And Agent Todd," Tate added. "Sir."

"That's right. Who is still on suspended leave from active field duty." The major general nodded with a small chuckle. "I'll have to look into his status again."

"And you already tested your devices on these agents?" Oppenhaur wagged a finger back and forth across the line of agents, looking unconvinced.

Cheyenne nodded. "Ask them yourself."

"I asked you."

She rolled her eyes and nodded at the agents. "Show him."

Tate turned his head to show the lieutenant colonel the activator behind his slightly pointed purple ear.

"Are they permanent?"

"No, sir. Just hurts like a bitch to put on and take off."

"Hmm."

Van Lurig turned to the drow. "Then I assume we have everything we need, correct?"

Cheyenne spread her arms. "Wherever you think is best?"

The major general eyed the guinea-pig agents one final time and turned away. She pulled her phone out of her pocket and pressed it to her ear as she headed down the hall. "Helen, if there's anyone in training room B, please clear it. Yes, for the rest of the evening. And close off access to that part of the north wing. I'd like to avoid an audience tonight. Thank you."

Oppenhaur, McMillen, and Weber followed her. Weber turned around again to eye the agents one more time before forcing himself to face forward.

"You heard the woman." Cheyenne headed down the hall and turned around, nodding at her agent friends as she spread her arms. "We have everything we need."

"Wait. Cheyenne. *Cheyenne*," Bhandi hissed, leaning forward and plastering a stern expression on her face when Oppenhaur turned around to look at her. When he disappeared around the corner, the troll leaped after Cheyenne. "What the hell does that mean?"

"You guys said you had my back, right? Time to prove it."

"Holy shit." Tate slapped Jamal's beefy forearm with the back of a hand and hurried after Cheyenne. "Duty calls, big guy. Come on."

"Fuck. Is she for real?" Yurik barked a laugh but choked it down when he caught up to Bhandi. "What the hell did she tell them?"

"Probably threatened to tear 'em apart if they didn't give us a chance." Bhandi punched him in the shoulder and sniggered. "Fucking Goth drow, right?"

CHAPTER FORTY-SIX

Twenty minutes later, Cheyenne, the four FRoE agents with O'gúl activators, and all four members of the board stood in the padded training room in the compound's north wing.

Cheyenne rolled her shoulders back and stared at the walls padded with black dampening foam shaped like the inside of an egg carton. *So fucking weird to be back in here.*

The board members stood along the far wall, waiting patiently. For now. Each of them wore a dampening vest and gloves, and while the officers had refused to add helmets to the ensemble, the civilian Mr. Weber wasn't taking any chances. A light fog thickened and faded against his clear visor with every breath.

"Dude." Bhandi leaned toward Tate and looked at the board members. "What the hell's taking him so long?"

"You think I know him any better than you do?" The tattooed troll sneered at her and shook his head. "He probably thinks this was a fucking joke."

"Yeah, and now he's making us look like a joke. Including Cheyenne."

"Naw, he'll be here." Yurik sniffed and shook out his hands, trying not to stare at the FRoE's top-level officials lined up against the wall.

"Tell you what, though. Feels like lining up a firing squad in here. And we're the ones about to pull out the guns."

Bhandi rolled her eyes. "They already know we can fire our weapons, dumbass."

"Magical guns. You know what I mean."

"Cheyenne," Van Lurig called from across the room. "If we need to reschedule, I suggest you say so now."

"No, we don't." Cheyenne turned around and eyed the narrow vertical windows in the thick metal double doors. "Any minute now."

"Five minutes." The major general glanced at her watch. "And then we—"

The double doors burst open, and Rhynehart stormed into the training room, glaring at Cheyenne. He stopped when he saw his superiors in full dampening gear lined up for their demonstration and came smartly to attention.

"Sorry to keep you waiting, Major General. Lieutenant Colonel. Colonel." The corners of Rhynehart's mouth twitched when he looked at Mr. Weber's helmet. "Mr. Weber. I wasn't sure this was happening today."

"Understandable, Captain. Thank you for joining us." Van Lurig gestured across the padded room. "If you have any final preparations to make, please go right ahead. Make it quick."

"Sir." Rhynehart nodded, then glared at Cheyenne again as he stormed past her toward the far wall beneath the wide two-way mirror. "Why don't you come help me?"

"You need help?"

"Yeah, from you specifically."

"Yep." She nodded at Van Lurig and the others, then fell into line beside Rhynehart as he moved swiftly across the equally padded floors.

"Why the fuck didn't you mention this sooner, Cheyenne?" he snarled loud enough for only her to hear.

"Maybe because you're not a magical or a human board member running your whole organization."

"And yet here I am, pulled into this without knowing what the hell this even is."

"Yeah, thanks for showing up, by the way."

They reached the far wall, and Rhynehart pounded a fist against the black padding. With a soft hiss, a long black drawer emerged from the wall at knee level, and he glared at her before reaching in to pull out a dampening vest, gloves, and helmet for himself. "Twenty minutes' notice. That's the best you could do?"

"You've given me less than that before, Captain." She raised her eyebrows. "Sometimes short notice happens, and we make it work. Right?"

He snorted and pulled the vest over his head. "Don't use my own tactics on me, halfling."

"The receiving end's not so great, huh?"

Gritting his teeth, he jammed a dampening glove on one hand, then the other. "So why am I here?"

"Right. I gave those four agents O'gúl activators I smuggled across the Border and brought online with the better, faster, stronger, updated version of the program that powered the war machines. Your bosses are halfway on board with my plan to hand them out to at least ninety-six other agents, and now they want a demonstration. So here you are, to demonstrate their use of the activators against your training methods."

Slinging the helmet under his arm, Rhynehart kicked the drawer shut with his boot and stared at her.

"That's the condensed version."

"Jesus Christ." He jerked the helmet down over his head and slapped the side of it with a muffled thump. "You need to start thinking things through, you know that?"

Cheyenne snorted. "This *is* me thinking things through."

He rolled his eyes and stomped toward another indiscriminate section of the padded wall. It opened with another thump from his boot, and Rhynehart stooped to pull out a fell rifle. The drawer shut again with a hiss. "Normally, this is the part where I tell you that you owe me one for pulling this kinda shit on me."

"Can't say that now though, huh?"

The agent pointed a gloved finger at her and shook it in warning. "Remember that." He jammed a hand against the side of the rifle, and the weapon powered up with a low whine rising in pitch. The green glow of fell ammunition brightened in the seams between the weapon's segmented pieces. "So, am I trying to make them look good, or am I trying to make them work for it?"

The drow smirked at the four agents staring at them. "Let's go with a happy medium."

"Happy." Rhynehart snorted. "You're a real piece of work."

"Yeah, you too." She clapped him on the shoulder as she raised her voice. "Thanks for doing this, Captain. You're really helping us out here."

He muttered something unintelligible as she passed him, then double-checked the settings on the fell rifle and took his place just past the center of the training room.

Cheyenne returned to the agents and nodded. "You guys ready?"

"Oh, yeah. Sure." Yurik gave her a bitter smile. "Rhynehart's standing there with a gun, and all we have are fucking ninja stars."

Tate grimaced. "He's gonna start shooting at us, isn't he?"

"Think of it this way," Cheyenne said, leaning toward them. "You have about sixty seconds to figure out how you're gonna use those activators. In a real fight, you usually get less than five."

She stepped back, shot them two thumbs-up with a grin, then headed toward the board members.

"She's right." Bhandi clapped her hands together and rubbed them vigorously, jerking her chin at Rhynehart. He slowly shook his head, holding his rifle to his chest at the ready. "We got this. Hey, when was the last time any of you squared off against him?"

"Rhynehart?" Tate rubbed his bald head. "Probably when he kicked my ass in this room."

Jamal grunted. "Which time?"

They all chuckled.

Cheyenne stopped beside the helmeted Mr. Weber and folded her arms. "They're ready when you are, Major General."

Van Lurig shot the drow a sidelong glare. "I have to say, you've already taken this a lot farther than I anticipated."

"Trying to overdeliver." *And get this activator program started so I can focus on the guy blowing up Peridosh and screwing around with portal towers.*

"If this goes the way you think it will, Cheyenne, I'll be the first to tell you you've succeeded in that."

She felt Oppenhaur's gaze on her before he leaned forward to catch her attention. "Shouldn't you be out there with them?"

"What?" Cheyenne couldn't hold back a low chuckle. "No, if I stepped in there, you'd be down a captain, and he just got his job back. But hey, if you don't think you need anyone to stand here and throw up a shield or two in front of any wayward spells or fell rounds, I'm happy to go somewhere else. The view might even be better from the other side of the room."

Oppenhaur ran his tongue along the inside of his cheek and looked away from her. "By all means, Cheyenne. Use your shields."

That sounded so much like Bianca. Cheyenne smirked. *I think I might be coming into my own. About damn time.*

Weber leaned toward her, and Cheyenne stepped aside to avoid the shiny bulb of his helmet looming her way. "You said wayward spells or fell rounds."

"Yep." It was hard not to stare at the fog of his breath growing and shrinking on the visor.

"Does that happen frequently when using these devices?"

"It's a frequent occurrence during training."

"I see." His thick swallow sounded muted and tinny from within the helmet.

He's gotta be their engineering guy. Creates and tests all the weapons, but he's never had the chance to use them. Pressing her lips together, Cheyenne folded her arms and watched the four agents squaring off against Rhynehart, waiting for the final go-ahead.

Major General Van Lurig readjusted one of her dampening gloves and nodded. "You all know why we're here. Let's see it."

The low whine of Rhynehart's fell rifle powering up for its first shot filled the training room. He raised the weapon at the line of magical agents with O'gúl activators and fired.

CHAPTER FORTY-SEVEN

"Shit!"

Tate, Yurik, and Bhandi dove away from the blast. Jamal bashed his fists together and roared. Then he drew his arms away from each other, and the fell blast exploded against a wall of shimmering copper light glowing between his fists. The force knocked the ogre back, but he dug his boots into the mats covering the floor and slid.

"Hmm." Van Lurig tilted her head. "Interesting."

Cheyenne fought back a smile. *Sounds like high praise to me.*

"Dude!" Bhandi stared at Jamal, her mouth open in a surprised grin. "That was fucking insane."

Rhynehart's next shot, set to stun, crashed against the troll woman's ribcage and sent her flying into the padded wall behind her.

"Hey!" Yurik spread his arms and stared at Rhynehart. "Demonstration, not demolition. *Shit!*"

The goblin ducked another blast from Rhynehart's rifle and turned to stare at the fell power crackling over the padded dampening walls.

"He's not fucking around," Tate muttered, raising his hands, which were now flickering with tongues of blue fire.

"Is he ever?"

"Now might be the right time for that Obliterate whatever." Tate nodded at the goblin, then took off running across the room toward Rhynehart.

More fell shots were fired. Tate's blue flames burst toward the man and crashed into Rhynehart's dampening vest. The captain grunted and staggered back, then raised his weapon again. "Don't hold back!"

"Easy for you to say," Tate shouted with a crooked smile. "You're standing in one place with a goddamn rifle. Only one option on your weapon."

"Then why am I not on the ground, agent?"

Tate snorted and stalked in a wide circle around the training room. Rhynehart stepped lightly and slowly, turning with his firearm leveled at the troll's chest. Without warning, he pivoted and fired a shot at Bhandi, who was sneaking up on him from behind.

She dropped to one knee and leaned back, and the fell round sailed two inches above her upturned face and crashed into the wall four feet away from Van Lurig, who didn't even flinch.

"Ha! Did you see that?" Bhandi looked at the wall and jumped to her feet again. "That was some *Matrix* shit right there! I fucking love this ninja star!"

Rhynehart lifted two fingers in the air and aimed his rifle at Yurik. His hand slapped the side for another power-up, and the goblin's eyes widened.

The fell round streaked toward Yurik, who reached out with both hands and grimaced. His activator took care of the rest, illuminating his palms with brilliant white light. The fell shot crashed into the light and ricocheted toward Rhynehart. The mat at the captain's feet crackled with fell energy, making him step back to avoid it before it disappeared.

Jamal stomped toward their sparring partner, his fists and forearms strobing with copper light. Rhynehart leveled his rifle at the ogre's chest and fired. Jamal bashed the stun shot away with one arm, then reached out with the other hand and lit the entire rifle up with copper light.

The rifle jerked toward the ogre, and Rhynehart's eyes widened behind the helmet's visor as he held on tight and was dragged across the mat. Jamal clamped one hand on the rifle's barrel, and he swung his open hand toward Rhynehart's head.

A small compartment Cheyenne recognized only too well opened in the padded wall and unleashed a spray of fell pellets at Jamal, peppering the side of his head. A cloud of green fell energy rose around his face.

Rhynehart ducked the ogre's swinging fist, still hanging on to his weapon, and fired at close range. The fell shot hit Jamal in the hip and sent him staggering sideways with a roar.

Turning in one fluid motion, Rhynehart dropped to one knee with his back to the padded wall and fired three shots in quick succession at Bhandi, Yurik, Tate.

Bhandi's hands moved quickly with her activator's prompted spell. Dark purple light shot in a tall, wide wall away from her hands and crashed into the fell-energy blast. It knocked the green light back toward Rhynehart, then pushed the captain into the padded wall and pinned him there.

Tate wasn't quite fast enough and took a fell round in the shoulder. His next crackling blue attack went wild, arcing across the room and cracking the tempered glass of the two-way mirror.

At the same time, Yurik dove away from the shot meant for him and flicked his wrist toward Rhynehart like he was throwing a frisbee. The spinning disk of yellow light he hurled stuck in the padded wall above Rhynehart's arm, which was pinned to the foam. "Dammit! Gotta work on my aim."

The dampening walls absorbed the goblin's magic, and the disk disappeared.

The force of Bhandi's spell faded, releasing Rhynehart from the wall. He fell to his knees and pounded the padding behind him with a fist. Two-foot segments of the wall opened up every six feet around the room, and thin metal rods six inches long protruded and erupted with crackling fell energy.

"Aw, come on." Tate rubbed his numb shoulder and rolled his eyes. "Don't you think that's a little—"

He yelped when the closest rod shocked him in the back. Spinning around with a snarl, he tossed his hand toward the protruding rod and bent it sideways so it faced the FRoE board members. Oppenhaur and McMillen stepped back. Van Lurig was too busy intently watching the mock battle to notice. Either that, or she didn't care.

The other rods launched fell bursts at the agents darting around the room and trying to figure out their activators. Bhandi barked a laugh and stayed where she was, her eyes wide with realization as she stared at whatever her activator brought up in her vision. Her fingers moved in slow, precise gestures as she stared straight ahead without seeing anything.

Rhynehart leveled his rifle at her, then swung it toward Jamal instead as the ogre lunged toward him. A gust of wind burst from Jamal's fist as he pulled it back for a mighty swing.

Cheyenne gauged the timing of the fell rods' shocks and turned away from the demonstration.

Van Lurig leaned forward, probably thinking the drow was trying to get her attention. "What's she doing? The troll."

"Some kinda spell," Cheyenne muttered and threw a shield up in front of the major general as the bent fell rod hurled a bolt of green energy at her. The blast crackled against Cheyenne's shield, making Van Lurig jump, and the drow whipped her hand toward the metal rod to bend it the other way instead. Then she met the other woman's gaze and lowered the shield with a shrug. "Cutting down her casting time should be part of the basic training."

"Indeed."

Bhandi laughed again as her hands did all the work of casting what had to be a fairly complicated spell if it was taking this long.

Rhynehart fired fell shots and threw hand signals to activate whatever other hidden weapons were stashed around the training room. Yurik dodged more fell rounds and blasts from the electric rods, moving pretty quickly for a goblin with so much muscle. He circled behind Rhynehart as Tate and Jamal closed on him from the front.

"Bhandi, what the fuck?" Tate shouted.

The troll woman grinned as an intricate pattern of pale silver light bloomed and swirled in the air in front of her gesturing hands. "So fucking epic."

The other agents fired magical attacks of their own, for the most part managing to duck Rhynehart's attacks and the fell rods as they closed in.

The rest of it happened all at once. Rhynehart removed a detonating disk from the side of the rifle's barrel, activated it against his thigh, and tossed it into the air. Bhandi's spell finished, looking like a massive, glowing silver spiderweb of geometric patterns. She stepped forward and shoved it with a crazed grin. Yurik had decided to try the obliterating sunburst one more time, and yellow light blazed around his hands.

Bhandi's spell erupted first, sending blazing silver lines across the room and up to the ceiling in a blinding shockwave. The metal rods squealed as they bent in their frames toward the ceiling, then pulled free with fell sparks and whipped into the air. Rhynehart's rifle jerked forward and up, lifting him two feet off the ground before he lost his grip and fell into Yurik. The goblin's obliterating sunburst was already sucking back down into his hands, ready to be unleashed when Rhynehart toppled into him and sent them both to the floor.

The yellow column of destruction burst from Yurik's hands as he bounced across the mat and hit not Rhynehart but the padded wall above Cheyenne's head. She ducked with a hiss and almost launched a black energy sphere at Mr. Weber when the man shouted in surprise and snatched at the watch that ripped away from his wrist and shot up to the ceiling with all the other metal in the room.

Yurik's yellow magic roared as it crashed into the dampening walls in wave after wave and raced over the surface to cover the room. The blazing foam was trying to absorb too much magical energy at once. The mechanisms hidden in the walls sparked and popped open, hissing as metal pieces ripped from their hinges and followed the rest of Bhandi's spell up to the ceiling.

Van Lurig glanced over her shoulder at the crackling yellow walls and took one step toward the center of the room, gesturing for her fellow board members to do the same.

Cheyenne eyed the bits of broken metal and "training implements" hovering in the magnetic field Bhandi had cast toward the ceiling. *Neat trick.*

The walls finally absorbed Yurik's misfired spell, and the yellow light died with a low, menacing hiss. A few more sparks flew from the broken panels in the wall, and everything fell silent.

Rhynehart rolled away from Yurik and pushed off the ground, then whipped his helmet off and stared at the wreckage. "You fucking tore this place apart. And you were trying to hit me with that shit?"

He turned into Yurik's fist.

"Ah, fuck!" Rhynehart doubled over, pressing his hand to his nose and mouth as Yurik shook out his hand.

"Hey, I'm trying to get one hit in."

The human agent chuckled and wiped the blood from under his nose before spitting a bloody glob on the mat. "Good hit, too. Shithead." Rhynehart gazed up at the rifle floating just below the ceiling and spread his arms. "Looks like you win this round, kids."

"Kids. Please." Bhandi folded her arms. "Do you even know—"

The metal pieces clinked together and dropped from the ceiling, released from the spell when she lost her focus. "Oh, shit."

The agents ducked and tried to avoid the falling debris. Cheyenne stepped forward and reached toward the metal pieces. Her activator pinpointed the closest metal shards and broken rods one after the other, and she focused on those first, flinging them into the corner with a mix of telekinetic force and a spell she only realized later was translated as "Redirection."

One by one, the falling pieces flew into the corner of the training room, clattering against the mat-covered floor and each other and embedding into the thick foam covering the walls.

Her activator found the fell rifle for her easily enough. Rhynehart stepped toward the falling rifle, but she beat him to it, wrapping her black tendrils around the stock and the barrel before whipping the weapon toward her. The tendrils retracted before she caught the rifle, spun it around, and slammed her hand against the side of the barrel to power up for another shot.

All the agents turned to her with wide eyes and raised their hands.

CHAPTER FORTY-EIGHT

Rhynehart grimaced and shook his head. "Thought you didn't like guns."

"I don't, but I do like screwing with you." She powered down the rifle and tossed it across the room. *I really, really fucking hate guns.* "I guess that's a wrap."

"Well." Van Lurig took a deep breath through her nose and turned to Cheyenne. "That was illuminating, to say the least."

The drow gestured at the winded agents standing around Rhynehart. "They did all the work."

"In the last ten minutes? Yes. But this is your program." The major general folded her arms and nodded. "I'm impressed, Cheyenne. There's room for improvement, but I *can* say I've never seen any of our agents perform anywhere near this level without weapons or gear."

Bhandi nodded at the board members with a crooked smug smile. "That's right."

Tate shot her a what-the-hell smile and shook his head.

Van Lurig ignored them both. "I'm sure I speak for the board in its entirety when I say your proposal with these activators has the level of potential and merit we need to start implementing it within this organization. Yesterday, preferably."

"I'm glad to hear it." Cheyenne scanned the stunned faces of the other board members. Oppenhaur was glaring at Van Lurig, McMillen was craning his neck to stare at the ceiling despite all the magnetized metal bits now being in a pile in the far corner, and Weber was slapping his dampening helmet as he struggled to rip it off his head. "And I'm grateful for the board's full support."

Oppenhaur scoffed and shook his head.

"And you'll continue to receive our full support," Van Lurig added, "as we roll out the activator training program with you at its head."

Cheyenne snorted. "Good one."

The major general cocked her head. "When I make jokes, Cheyenne, they aren't about the future of this organization."

The smile disappeared from Cheyenne's lips, and she stepped away from the board members to eye Van Lurig. "You're serious?"

"That would be the opposite of joking, so yes. You've proven the benefits of outfitting our magical agents with these devices, and we're accepting your proposal. Feel free to email Helen with a write-up of anything you need to implement your methods and training strategies. Shouldn't take us more than a day or two to fill the order, then you'll come here to start the initial phases of training our operatives."

Cheyenne gritted her teeth and stared at the woman. *That lady has some serious balls. Guess that's why she's at the top.*

"With all due respect, Major General—"

"Don't try to force it, Cheyenne." Van Lurig gave her a reassuring nod, almost winking at the drow but not quite. "At this point, I know the difference between disrespect and anger. You're pissed."

The drow gave a humorless laugh and shook her head. "I didn't say anything about training your agents. All I wanted to do was get these activators up and running so I could show the four of you how stupid it would be not to use them."

"And then what? Let these Earthborn magicals—who, as you put it, have no idea where they came from or what they're capable of—explore the countless nuances of using these devices on their own?" The major general gestured at her fellow board members. "As you also mentioned, none of us are equipped to train these selected operatives. Captain Rhynehart, though remarkably skilled when it comes to combat and weapons training, doesn't have what it takes, and all of his superior officers are human as well."

Cheyenne blinked, her mouth opening and closing in surprise, then she pointed across the training room at the agents standing around Rhynehart and cocked her head. "Them. I gave them activators. Took them out to the middle of nowhere and dragged them through the wringer so they could figure out how to use those things."

"And they're still figuring it out."

"No, you have four magical agents right there who can explain to other magical agents how the hell these things work."

"And give them preferential treatment by promoting them? I don't think so. Especially not after their involvement in our discovery of Colonel Thomas' many transgressions. That's out of the question." Van Lurig clasped her hands behind her back and dipped her head. "You're the perfect magical for the job, Cheyenne. I'm laying the whole thing in your capable hands, and that's the end of it."

The drow shook her head. "I'm not going to be the board's consultant and in charge of running drills."

"I see it more as involved teaching." Van Lurig raised her eyebrows. "You can involve yourself as much or as little as you like, but you will be here."

"I already have a teaching job."

"Then we'll work around your schedule, within reason. And you'll work around ours. Thank you for your time." With a final nod at Rhynehart and the other agents, Van Lurig stripped off her dampening vest and gloves and dropped them right there on the mat. Then she headed for the doors of the training room but paused beside Cheyenne and leaned toward her to whisper, "Add your preferred salary to that prep list when you send it to Helen. Excellent work."

Cheyenne stared at the woman, but Van Lurig raised her chin and strode out. Oppenhaur and McMillen quickly followed her, leaving their dampening gear behind in scattered piles. Neither of them said a thing as they crossed the training room, even when Weber shouted in frustration and struggled with removing his vest.

"These damn things!" He slapped the sides, twisting and squirming within the gear. "If I'd been involved in design protocol from the beginning, we wouldn't have such useless, bulky, infuriating…" The man doubled over with his arms stretched above his head and shimmied out of the vest before he chucked it on the mat. "I'm changing all of it!"

Weber kicked the heavy vest with a well-shined soft-toed loafer and grimaced.

"Upgrades are always appreciated, Mr. Weber," Rhynehart called from across the room.

"I know! And I'll be starting with this mess of a room you destroyed. Good day, Captain." The man stomped across the mat toward the doors and shoved the release bars with a clang. He disappeared down the hallway, the doors clicked shut again, and only the sound of Rhynehart stripping off his gloves and vest broke the silence.

"Well. For a last-minute show-and-tell, I'd say that falls somewhere pretty high on the charts." Rhynehart headed across the room toward the wall beneath the two-way mirror, lugging the gear under one arm and vigorously ran a hand through his hair with his free hand. "Didn't realize you had plans to take over my side gig here, halfling."

"That wasn't my plan." She turned toward him and couldn't seem to focus on any one thing across the room. "Like, at all."

"Well, plans change, don't they?" Rhynehart slapped a hand against the wall and waited for the gear drawer to open. "Gotta roll with the punches." When the drawer didn't open, he kicked the padded wall. "No use in crying over—" The drawer slid open two inches, shuddered with a screech of jamming gears, then tossed a few sparks and hissed.

"Spilled milk?" Bhandi offered, then pressed her lips together to keep her laughter down to a snigger.

"Dammit!" Rhynehart chucked the gear against the semi-open drawer and spun. "You broke my training room."

"Me? Uh-uh. Don't pin that on me." The troll shook her head and pointed at Yurik. "That was all Mr. Exploding Sun Goblin over there."

"How about I blame all four of you?" Rhynehart stalked toward the discarded fell rifle and picked it up. "Or, here's an idea. If you don't get your overconfident asses out of here by the time I count to five"—he slapped a hand against the rifle's barrel and powered it up, making a big show out of switching the setting away from stun to whatever was worse than that—"I'll start firing for real. Anyone who's still standing after that can spend the next week on back-room inventory with Todd."

"Come on, man." Tate sniggered. "That's the worst you can come up with?"

"One. Two."

"Shit, okay."

Rhynehart stepped toward them and raised the fell rifle. "Three."

"We're going. We're going!" Yurik jogged toward the doors, turning back to raise a fist at Cheyenne. "That was fucking epic, Cheyenne."

"Four."

Jamal growled and stormed toward the doors. Yurik spun and shoved them open before the ogre smashed into him.

"Hit us up later, C," Bhandi called as she darted through the doors.

"Five!"

"Move your ass, Bhandi!" Tate shoved the troll the rest of the way into the hall.

The doors clicked shut behind them, and Rhynehart swung the rifle to the right and fired. The fell shot struck the padded wall and crackled violently across ten feet of the dampening foam in either direction before fizzling out. Rhynehart slapped the side of the weapon again to power it down, then tossed it to the floor and grimaced. "At least the foam still works."

Cheyenne watched him walk in a slow circle around the room, kicking scattered pieces of broken metal and ruffling his hair over and over. "I wasn't trying to take over your whole training thing."

"Yeah, I know." He looked at her with a bitter, resigned snarl. "I wasn't trying to fight four of my agents all super-powered with whatever the hell kinda tech you gave them either."

"Activators." *How hard is that to remember?*

"Sure." Rhynehart headed toward her, staring at the mat. When he looked at her again, he seemed embarrassed. "For real, Cheyenne. For a minute there, I had flashbacks about pushing your buttons in this room. Those agents had little control over what they were doing, but there's some serious power behind it."

"It's all theirs. I just gave them something to improve what they can already do."

"Yeah, that's what I figured." He stopped six feet away from her and folded his arms. "That's what you were talking about that night at your mom's estate, right? When you tossed your hand and disassembled a fell pistol in two seconds?"

She had to look away to keep from laughing. "That was the activator helping me out, yeah."

"Brand-new model too. Supposed to be indestructible."

Cheyenne shrugged. "That's what I do. Find the loopholes and make the impossible possible."

"Looks like it's working well for you." Rhynehart nodded at the doors. "I need a shower. And a beer. Let me know if you need anything to get this whole training program set up. Helen's fine for most of it, but she takes fucking bureaucratic paperwork to a whole new level."

"I noticed."

With a disbelieving half-smile, the human agent looked her up and down and headed for the doors. "If she makes you jump through too many hoops, you know how to get ahold of me."

"Thanks for showing up."

"Whatever." Rhynehart turned to shove his back against the doors' release bar, then stepped into the hall and pointed at her. "I don't do sidekick or training assistant or any of that bullshit, so don't even ask."

"Didn't even cross my mind."

"Sure." Chuckling, he slipped through the doors and let them fall shut behind him.

Cheyenne took a deep breath and let it all out in a long, slow exhale. "Fuck."

CHAPTER FORTY-NINE

Fortunately, no one tried to stop Cheyenne for another showdown when she made her way back through the compound and out through the lobby. That might have had something to do with Bhandi and Yurik shouting over each other in the common room as they tried to relay a coherent account of what had happened to their fellow agents.

"You should've seen this shit. I swear, if we'd been anywhere else, you would've seen fucking cars in the sky."

"Man, you don't know how strong it was. Don't take it too far."

"Okay, Mr. Sunshine. You wanna guess how much you could *obliterate* with that fucking solar laser of yours?"

Jamal's rumbling chuckle followed Cheyenne as she pushed the clear glass doors. "Assuming you ever learn how to aim."

The agents burst out laughing, and the sound cut off as the doors closed. Cheyenne headed across the parking lot. *At least somebody's laughing about it. For now. If the rest of them are gonna take this seriously, I guess I better make sure they're too sore and beat up after training to laugh about anything.*

That thought made her stop, and she shook her head with a snort. *Look at me. Already thinking like a FRoE official. Sir would be so proud. Not.*

The Panamera chirped when she pressed the automatic unlock, and when she reached for the driver-side door handle, her phone buzzed in her pocket. It was Bianca, or at least it was the house number. Cheyenne opened the door, slid behind the wheel, and answered the call.

"Hey, Mom."

"I know it's only been the weekend since we saw each other last," Bianca said quickly, breezing straight past the usual pleasantries. "But I didn't want to wait any longer."

Cheyenne frowned and sat back in the seat. "What's wrong?"

"Wrong? Cheyenne, if I'd called to talk about an issue, I would have led the conversation with that."

"Right." *How silly of me.* She punched the Porsche's start button and strapped on her seatbelt, switching the phone from right hand to left. "So, how are you feeling?"

"Much better, thank you."

"Good."

"No, that's an inaccurate assessment. I feel ten years younger. Two weeks ago, if you'd told me I'd be saying that over the phone, I would have asked when you hit your head and how hard."

Cheyenne snorted.

"But I mean it. I'm well aware that this might be a potential peak in my recovery—or return to normalcy—considering the circumstances of the last few weeks and everything we endured. But I intend to ride that peak for as long as it lasts. How are you?"

"Oh." Blinking in surprise, Cheyenne put the phone on speaker and set it in the cupholder before driving out of the base's parking lot toward the large stone gate towers down the road. *She's definitely feeling better if she's asking banal questions like that.* "I'm fine, Mom. Still working through a few things I had to put on hold until we got back, but it's all going well for the most part."

"I assume you're referring to the distribution of those devices that blue woman created for you over there, yes? The trunks you carried over."

"Yeah." Cheyenne smirked. At least Bianca couldn't see or hear it. "That's exactly what I'm talking about."

"I'm glad to hear you didn't waste time and energy planning for something that proved to be useless."

"Thanks, Mom." The line went silent, and Cheyenne glanced at the phone to make sure they hadn't been disconnected. "How's Eleanor?"

"This is exactly why I despise phone calls to check in. There's nothing more to say after the first two minutes."

Yeah, she's feeling like her normal self, all right. "Okay. I'm driving home anyway, so I'll let you go."

"That's fine." Bianca cleared her throat. "There is one more thing I wanted to approach with you, though now that I know you're driving, maybe I should wait."

"You're on speaker. And yes, I'm the only one in the car."

"All right. Cheyenne, something very odd happened this morning at the house. I'm not quite sure what to make of it."

"It wasn't L'zar, was it?"

Bianca chuckled. "No, we've seen no sign of him since Eleanor kicked him out, or so she claims. I expect that has quite a bit to do with her overwhelmingly positive outlook on life over the last few days."

"Okay." Cheyenne turned off the unmarked drive leading to the base and took a left onto the frontage road, trying not to laugh. "So, what happened?"

"I don't know." Her mom paused, then took a sharp breath. "But I felt something."

"What do you mean, you felt something?"

"If I had a better description for it, Cheyenne, I would have used that to clarify. All I can say is that I felt something. Maybe some sort of energy or magic. I don't know. But it was stronger when I went out onto the veranda."

"But you didn't see anything?"

"Nothing beyond what has become the new normal. The portal in the yard. That was destroyed, correct?"

Cheyenne grimaced. "Absolutely."

"Good. It did make me wonder. I understand quite a bit more about how difficult it is to trust something you think you know after having had so many foundations of reality ripped out from under you."

"You're not going crazy, Mom. Don't worry about that."

"I would never. I know I'm perfectly sane. It's the rest of the world that can't seem to make up its damn mind."

"Huh." Cheyenne frowned at the road. "Well said."

"Anyway, if you're certain there's no reason for concern…"

"Yes. I'm certain. But if you feel something like that again or see anything that doesn't look right, it's probably best if you don't wait twelve hours to tell me about it."

The clink of ice in a glass came over the line, followed by Eleanor's heavy whisper. "Tell her I said hello."

"Eleanor says hello. And I'll tell her you said the same." Bianca paused again, this time to drink.

Cheyenne bit her lip when she heard two loud gulps. *She's drinking like normal again. Things are looking up.*

"And yes, Cheyenne. I realize I could have called you sooner, but I honestly don't enjoy the idea of calling you every time a feeling hits me. I prefer to think of it as residual whatever-it-was from our recent travels, but in case it was something else, it seemed appropriate to inform you."

"I appreciate it. That portal's been destroyed from the inside out, and it's not coming back. I do know that much."

"Well, that settles it then. Thank you."

"Sure. Anything else?"

"No, Cheyenne. I believe that's all. Enjoy your night."

"You too, Mom."

The call ended with a sharp click. "Nice talking to you too. Call again soon. Love you. Never gonna happen."

She tightened her grip on the steering wheel and turned on her brights. The tree branches curving overhead were almost bare already, and the moon strobed through them as she headed back toward the highway and Richmond.

She felt something, just like Maleshi. Both of them were right next to a portal ridge that's closed. I bet I'd see a bunch of clear flames around the one in Mom's back yard too. Who would want to fuck around with the deactivated portals? And why?

The thought turned over and over in her mind as she drove, and she kept coming back to the growing accounts of issues with the Border towers on the FRoE reservations.

Maybe it doesn't have anything to do with the portals but what they're made of. All that black stone. All that magic. It has to be the same magical who attacked Peridosh.

Cheyenne said dryly, "The portal thief. That asshole's throwing a wrench in my 'drow royalty on Earth' plans."

She reached for the dashboard to turn on the radio, but her phone buzzed again in the cupholder. She answered and put it on speaker. "Hey, Em."

"Okay, please don't kill me."

"What happened?"

"I just went to the bathroom. That's it. Maybe, like, two minutes? I mean, it's not like I was gonna take him in there with me so I could keep an eye on him. It's been four days, Cheyenne. I thought he could handle himself by now."

"Whoa, slow down. You are talking about Neros, right?"

Ember groaned. "Yeah."

"What did he do?"

"That's the problem! I have no fucking clue. He could be anywhere! It's blowing my mind right now how somebody who can't even figure out how to close a damn drawer or stab food with a fork suddenly walks right out of the apartment and uses the fucking elevator. Did you know he knew how to use an elevator?"

"He left?"

"I can't find him. So yeah, I can only assume he's gone. I went all the way down to the lobby. Nothing."

Cheyenne slammed her palm on the steering wheel. "Shit."

"I'm so sorry."

"Stop. It's not your fault. Don't be sorry. Do you have any idea where he might've gone?"

Ember clicked her tongue and said, "He wouldn't shut up about the Oracles."

"And I wouldn't take him, so he figured he'd go by himself."

"Cheyenne, how does he even know where to find an Oracle? You didn't tell him, did you?"

"No, but I dropped Gúrdu's name in casual conversation. Shit. You stay at the apartment in case he comes back, okay?"

"Are you sure?"

"Yeah. And if he does come back before I do, hit him with that crazy magic-chain spell you used on me at Bianca's."

"The one that pinned you down so I could force a healing potion down your throat?"

Cheyenne grimaced but forced the frustration out of her voice. "That's the one, Em."

"Yeah, I'll try. If he comes back without you. Might not be very effective if he's using his magic to track down a raug Oracle by name and nothing else."

"I'll find him. Hang tight."

"Yeah, okay. Sorry." Ember hung up before Cheyenne had a chance to tell her to quit apologizing.

"Dammit, Neros." She glanced in her rearview mirror, finding the road dark and empty, and stepped on the gas. *So now I get to go visit an Oracle I have absolutely no desire to see, and if he's not there? Finding a lost puppy in Richmond would be a hell of a lot easier than this.*

CHAPTER FIFTY

Cheyenne pulled up in front of Gúrdu's apartment building beneath the old railroad tracks and forced herself not to slam the car door when she got out.

If he's not in there, I'm gonna lose my shit. If he is? I'll probably lose my shit anyway. What does he think he's doing?

The murky glass front door to the apartment building was closed against the autumn chill, and she jerked it open before storming down the leaf-littered hallway toward Gúrdu's apartment. The door was open a few inches when she reached it, and she slipped into drow mode without bothering to hide beneath an illusion spell.

They're all magicals living here anyway.

Summoning a black energy sphere in one hand, she opened the door enough to slip inside and made her way silently through the raug's dark, dusty, smokey apartment. "Gúrdu? It's Cheyenne. Had any drow visitors lately?"

"Ah." The raug's low, rumbling voice came from the main room on the left at the end of the hall. "That was very well-timed."

"Off by about thirty seconds," Neros muttered.

Goddammit. Cheyenne brushed aside the curtain of beads separating the hall from the back room and stormed in. "Hey! I told you no Oracles for a reason."

Sitting cross-legged on a pile of old, frayed, soiled pillows, Neros turned slowly to look over his shoulder at her. "That was your reason, Cheyenne. I have my own for coming here, though it seems I waited too long."

"Look, I don't care what your reasons are for wanting to see an Oracle. I do care that you up and left the apartment without telling anyone. By yourself. I'm amazed you made it here, but what if you hadn't, huh? The last thing Richmond needs right now is a drow from Nor'ieth who doesn't know how to order a burger or that the little white person on the traffic light means it's safe to cross the street. Not okay."

"No." Neros turned back around again to face the large platform where Gúrdu the raug preferred to deliver his prophecies. "What we need is an Oracle. And unfortunately—"

Gúrdu's chuckle quickly escalated into a harsh, wheezing cough. "Unfortunately, this one is out of commission."

Cheyenne finally took the time to look at the raug sitting cross-legged on his platform. Gúrdu's gray skin had taken on an ashy, mottled whiteness in patches. Dark circles had formed beneath his glowing red eyes, and he was hunched over his crossed legs as if straightening his back either took too much energy or caused too much pain, or both.

"Gúrdu." Cheyenne snuffed out the energy sphere in her hand and stepped forward, squinting through the musty light from the magical lanterns hanging around the room. "What happened?"

The Oracle scratched the side of his face with a long black claw and shrugged. "Someone has blocked me from reading the Weave."

"What?"

He coughed into his fist again, wheezing for breath, then turned and spat a thick glob of phlegm into the corner. "No prophecies today, Cheyenne. Not for you. Not for your strange-looking kin. And no magic for me."

"I don't get it." When she stopped beside Neros on his pillows, he looked at her with his usual blank expression.

"I told you we needed to see an Oracle, and now it's too late."

"Why? Because he's sick?"

"Ha!" Gúrdu slapped his knee and ran his thick gray tongue along the edge of his teeth. "Not sick, *hinya*. Disconnected. Do you understand?"

She shook her head. "I didn't even know that was possible."

"Neither did I, but here we are, eh?" The raug spread his arms and chuckled again, this time without coughing. "It has been almost fourteen hours since I first felt the effects. Whoever it is knows far more about cutting an Oracle off from their magic than I could have anticipated. More, perhaps, than even I was aware of." He coughed again, then cleared his throat.

Cheyenne tilted her head and studied him. "So you're blind, then. I mean magically, not literally."

Gúrdu rumbled—she couldn't tell if it was more laughter or more coughing—and nodded. "I could not draw a prophecy for myself from the Weave if you threatened me with all the might of the Black Flame."

"That's not good."

"No, Cheyenne, but it is a temporary nuisance." The raug batted a huge hand through the air, then reached toward the tray beside him and picked up something that looked suspiciously like a skinned, cooked rat on a skewer. He bit off almost half the unfortunate creature and chewed noisily. Flecks of crispy skin and crunched bone flew between his lips. "In the larger scheme of things, that is. How long specifically? It could be years. It could be days."

"Shit." Cheyenne ran a hand through her hair and spun to check out the room. *Not like I'm gonna find my answers in dusty corners and all the cobwebs.* "Someone did this to you on purpose. Blinded you to the future and from seeing anything in the Weave."

"If you know what this someone did not want me to see, *hinya*, I would enjoy hearing it."

"I don't know for sure." She turned back to the huge raug and grimaced. "But I have a hunch. Someone's out there messing with Border portals, the ones that work at the reservations and the ones that have been deactivated in the last few weeks. Those are the ones I know about."

"Tampering." Gúrdu's red eyes narrowed. "To what end?"

Cheyenne shrugged. "Know of any magicals who can port themselves all over the place like a nightstalker and leave behind a bunch of flames in the air?"

He stared at her. "That cannot be a serious question."

"Yeah, I didn't think so. Look, it might not be the same magical dipping into the portals, but I think it is. Those flames are pretty hard to miss. For me, at least. There is someone out there stealing a bunch of ingredients for some kind of huge spell." She gestured at her cousin. "Neros figured that one out."

"Your cousin's sight is less affected than mine." Gúrdu let out a low growl of consideration. "Can you see, pale drow?"

Neros lifted his chin toward the raug, though he remained expressionless. "I see nothing, Oracle."

So, either he's blind too, or he doesn't wanna tap into that big ol' magical database in the sky. Or wherever it is.

"Then we only have your hunch to move us forward, Cheyenne."

Cheyenne nodded. "Which now includes whoever it was that cut you off from the Weave. Temporarily or otherwise."

"A shared endeavor." Gúrdu nodded slowly and scratched the side of his face again with one thick claw. "Shut out one of only a few Oracles in this world so no one sees when or where or how. Or who."

"For a giant spell powered by all the stolen ingredients and a calibrax. Yeah."

"Hmm. I would like to help you more than this. For now, I only seem to take up more space than I inhabit." Gúrdu chuckled again and stuck the other half of the crispy critter in his mouth.

"I'm trying to figure this out," Cheyenne mused. "I think whoever's behind this paid my mom a visit this morning, and I'm not into that. I'll let you know if I find anything that'll help, or at least tell you more about what you're dealing with."

"I will be fine." He nodded and fell into another coughing fit that sounded like he was choking on his snack. "Reversing the effects of what was done to me will take time, but we all have more of that now than any of us expected. Thanks to you."

Cheyenne wrinkled her nose. "I can't take all the credit. Hey, but I can give you something."

"Oh?"

"Yeah. I'll be right back." She pointed at her cousin and hoped the look she gave him was warning enough. "You stay right here. I'm serious. If you try to leave, the raug has my permission to pin you down and tie you up."

"Permission or no, I would not do that," Gúrdu muttered as he chewed.

"Fine, then I'm telling you as the Black Flame. If Neros tries to sneak out of here before I come back, pin him down and tie him up." She plastered a thin smile onto her lips, then spun and tossed aside the curtain of beads. "Two minutes."

It took more like a minute and a half, but when she darted back into the musty back room, she found Neros and Gúrdu exactly where she'd left them.

"Okay. Magicals are finally starting to listen around here." She stepped over piles of fraying cushions, some of them wafting up the stench of mildew when she kicked them with the side of her shoe. Cheyenne paid more attention to keeping her balance than anything else, but when she reached the Oracle's platform, she slapped a hand on the edge of the wooden raug throne and thrust the other under Gúrdu's face. "For you."

Rumbling, he slowly opened his palm below hers, and she dropped a metal four-pointed star into it. "I don't accept advanced payment for prophecy, I'll have you know."

"And I don't hand out presents just to turn around and call it leverage when I need a favor."

Gúrdu picked the activator up between two black claws and squinted at it in the low light. "So, what is this gift?"

Cheyenne tapped behind her ear and nodded. "Straight from the Motherland."

His red eyes widened, and he looked at the star activator, then the drow who'd handed it over. A sharp bark of laughter escaped him. "You brought an activator all this way to give it to me?"

"Trust me, it's not the only one."

The raug threw his head back and roared with laughter, rocking backward until it looked like he'd fall over and never get up.

Cheyenne headed through the maze of nasty cushions toward her cousin and extended a hand to help him up. "Come on. Let's let him laugh it off in peace."

"Where are we going?" Neros asked, ignoring her hand and standing in one fluid, seamless movement.

She stuck her hands in her pockets instead and nodded at the hallway. "Home. My home for now. Yours very, very soon, hopefully."

Her cousin followed her obediently out of the Oracle's main room, turning back every few steps to look over his shoulder at the huge raug cracking up over an Earthside activator.

"I knew from the very beginning, *hinya!*" Gúrdu shouted after her between fits of thunderous laughter. "I knew! May your story never end!"

As Cheyenne opened the front door and held it for Neros, the Oracle's laughter sputtered into another fit of coughing between growling chuckles.

"May the Black Flame reign on this side too!"

She rolled her eyes, shut the door, and grabbed Neros' flowing sleeve to tug him down the hall. *At least the guy got the Earthside part right. The Black Flame of Earth. Eh, maybe not as catchy, but it feels a hell of a lot better.*

CHAPTER FIFTY-ONE

The next morning, after a painstaking twenty minutes of trying to explain to Neros how waffle-makers worked and why he couldn't touch the thing to "feel its power," Ember and Cheyenne guided the pale-skinned drow back to their regular setup in the living room to eat at the coffee table.

Ember tried to clear enough space for her coffee mug amidst three large plates, the butter, syrup, powdered sugar, silverware, and a plate of extra bacon. "Huh. You know, I never thought about it until our third wheel showed up, but I'm thinking we should get a table for actual meals."

"Like, a kitchen table?" Cheyenne asked and crunched down on a slice of bacon.

"No. That would be right in front of my bedroom." Ember gestured at the space between the coffee table and the wall of windows. "Right there. Like, a bistro table, right? The tall kind."

"Yeah, that's a bistro table." The drow eyed her cousin, who seemed way more interested in poking his finger into every waffle hole than in eating. "But our third wheel's not gonna be around forever, Em. Seems kinda silly to buy a dining set for the next couple days."

"You seriously think Neros is the only person who's ever gonna come over for a meal?"

Cheyenne slowly sipped her coffee and stared at her friend over the rim of her mug. "You're talking about Matthew, aren't you?"

"Not exclusively." Ember shrugged. "I mean, yeah. Sure. He's the most likely person to come over on any given day. He does live right across the hall. We also have nightstalkers popping in and out of here like it's their day job. And what if Bianca and Eleanor decided they wanted to drive down for the day and stay for dinner, huh?"

"You think those two would make a forty-five-minute drive here and back again to sit at a bistro table?"

"Cheyenne. Listen to yourself." Ember leaned over her lap and nodded slowly, enunciating her next words like the drow had just started learning English. "Bianca made the crossing and got her drink on with a bunch of rebels who now rule an entire world. Forty-five minutes still sound unlikely to you?"

Cheyenne cut another bite of waffle and jammed it in her mouth, trying not to laugh.

"Yeah, that's what I thought." Ember straightened on the couch and looked at the space in front of the huge windows again. "Bistro table. You wanna pick it out?"

"Sounds like it's already decided. Get whatever you want."

"Huh. That was weirdly easy."

"I do not understand this food." Neros poked at the waffle holes again, buttery syrup dripping from his finger. "What is the point?"

"It's fun, for starters." Ember laughed and slapped a napkin down in front of him. "And you're supposed to eat it all together, man. Fill all the little holes with syrup, and if you cut it right, you have the perfect bite every time."

"Syrup."

"Yeah, the drippy stuff. Jeez, do I need to cut it up for you too?"

"No." Neros stuck his syrupy finger in his mouth and smiled around it. "I like this very much." He reached for the syrup bottle, and Ember slapped his hand away.

"Dude, I filled all the waffle holes. You don't need any more than that."

Cheyenne snorted and shook her head. "Too much, and you're dipping your syrup in a little bit of waffle."

"See?" Ember gestured at her friend, then set the syrup on the opposite end of the coffee table. "We know what we're talking about. Just eat your waffle."

The women exchanged amused looks and went back to diligently eating their breakfast at almost 11:00 a.m.

"I want to watch the movie box." Neros turned to stare at Ember. "Please."

"Really?" Ember shot him a playful frown. "We're eating."

"Your food here tastes better when I can focus on the movie box at the same time."

Cheyenne choked on a laugh and almost sprayed waffle chunks all over herself. "Hell of a compliment."

"Hey, if you don't like the waffles, blame the mix, not the cook. When I make things from scratch, no one thinks about anything else."

"Yeah, but how often do you cook from scratch?" Cheyenne muttered.

"Not often enough, apparently. Fine." Ember snatched the remote from where she'd wedged it between her side of the couch and the armrest. "But we're watching something everybody likes, okay?"

Neros stared at her with a tiny smile. "You are a gracious and conceding host, Ember Gaderow."

"Wow. Thank you. That's…wait. Who told you my last name?"

"I saw it." He frowned. "Why? Is it a secret?"

"No, but the way you said it is creepy."

Neros raised his eyebrows and looked at the remote in her hand instead. "You will forget all about it once the movie box is working."

"TV." She clenched her eyes shut and shook her head. "It's a TV. That's it. And now I'm turning it on."

After a click, a low hum rose from the entry table as the flatscreen rose slowly into place. Then the screen turned on, and the local news station flickered across it.

Ember spun to glare at Neros. "Did you mess with the remote last night?"

"That is a good movie." Neros nodded at the TV. "Though it never seems to end like the others."

"It's not a movie. It's the news. My God." Ember slumped back on the couch and lifted the remote toward the TV again. "I know you've already had, like, a few thousand birthdays or whatever, but if I wasn't sure about the whole no-kids thing before you showed up in this world, I am now."

"Wait, Em. Hold on." Cheyenne leaned forward and pointed at the TV. "Look at that."

"What, the burning building. Happens a lot."

"Oh, yeah? You see a lot of magical safehouses blowing up and making state news in the middle of the day?"

"Oh, shit. Is that Persh'al's warehouse?"

"Turn it up."

Ember did as she was told, and the newscaster's voice filled their living room.

"…explosion at this abandoned warehouse outside downtown DC this morning. Firefighters were called in at nine-thirty this morning by the owner of an apartment complex who saw the flames from the next block down. So far, authorities tell us the warehouse was abandoned and empty, though evidence suggests there might have been up to three individuals squatting on the property. Though it's still unconfirmed, that may also be the cause of the explosion and ensuing fire that took firefighters over an hour to get under control. So far, the owner of the property remains unknown. Now we head over to Bradley for your mid-morning weather report."

Ember muted the TV and dropped the remote on the couch when the image switched from Persh'al's burning warehouse to a man with a fake tan and likely fake hair waving his hands in front of the green screen. "What the fuck?"

"Yeah." Cheyenne stared at the TV, but the weatherman was taking up his full allotted time. "Squatters. That's such bullshit."

"I mean, no one had been there for a while." Ember stared at her friend as Cheyenne stood from the chair and headed to her bedroom. "The goblins and Persh'al are in Hangivol. Maleshi and Corian are in Richmond. And L'zar never went back, right?"

Cheyenne emerged from her room with her cell phone and pulled up Corian's number. "Yeah, but no way in hell did a couple of squatters walk right through the wards around that place. Whoever blew it either knew exactly how to get in, or they were powerful enough to wipe out the wards. Either option is pretty shitty if you ask me."

"Who would even do that?"

Pressing the phone to her ear, Cheyenne felt her stomach drop a little lower each time it rang and Corian didn't pick up.

"If you called this number, you already know who I am."

"Shit." Cheyenne hung up and tried again.

"He's still not answering?"

"No, and that better stop real soon." Cheyenne gritted her teeth and hissed when his answering machine picked up again. After the beep, she had to force herself not to crush her phone as she snarled a voicemail. "Pick up your phone, asshole. I'm not calling about a free ride this time, so whatever you're doing, it better be a hell of a lot more important than a burning warehouse."

She hung up and selected Maleshi's number.

"It doesn't make sense." Ember pulled her legs onto the couch and stared at the coffee table. "It's been four days since you've talked to him? Why would he stop picking up?"

"Why do any magicals do anything, Em?" Cheyenne paced in front of the bathroom. "I gave up trying to figure that out a long time ago."

Maleshi answered, "Hey, kid."

"You watch the news this morning?"

"Well, seeing as I just got out of my last class, I'd have to go with Hell No for four hundred."

"Great. I'm gonna send you something. If it feels important, you can find me at home." Cheyenne hung up and did a quick internet search for the burning warehouse outside DC. She sent the most recent article with updates and the news clip to Maleshi's number and shoved her phone into her back pocket. "Something's seriously off about this."

"Yeah, no kidding. You think someone was trying to—"

"Oh, what is that?" Neros pointed at the TV. "And why is it falling apart?"

Ember glanced at the TV and instantly turned it off.

His shoulders sagged in disappointment. "That was unnecessary."

"Commercials rot your brain cells, Neros. That's why we have Netflix."

Cheyenne picked up her pacing again, clenching and unclenching her fists. She stopped when a circle of dark light materialized in front of her. Maleshi stepped swiftly through the portal and snarled at her.

"Do you have any idea how infuriating it is to be hung up on like that and sent this bullshit?"

She thrust her phone into Cheyenne's face, and the drow slapped her hand away. "Yeah, but at least I'm paying attention to what's going on right now, and it's way bigger than you teaching your stupid computer classes. Where the hell is Corian?"

Maleshi blinked quickly, then looked at Ember. "How the hell should I know?"

"He's not picking up. Still. And he's usually the first magical who calls when something goes wrong." Cheyenne spread her arms. "Something's very wrong."

"Fuck." Hissing, the general spun away and raised her hands to open another portal. "Maybe he's there already."

"Sure. And he assumed we'd go there without him."

"I get that you're pissed, kid, but the attitude isn't helping."

"It sure got your attention."

"Cheyenne." Ember stood slowly from the couch and looked questioningly at Neros.

"Yeah, of course you're coming. Both of you."

"How nice. The whole happy family." Maleshi's portal opened all the way and she stepped back, waving the cloud of thick smoke out of her face. "Jesus."

"Is it still burning?"

"No." Maleshi coughed, then poked her head through. "Maybe some leftovers. Come on."

Ember nudged Neros forward, keeping an eye on him as they followed the general into the warehouse. The portal closed behind them with a pop and another puff of smoke that quickly dissipated in the middle of their living room.

"Oh, man." Cheyenne stepped slowly across the huge empty space in the middle of the warehouse, which was now covered in ash, soot, and piles of charred fallen shingles. Steel beams hung at precarious angles above them, and the chill breeze blew in through the open ceiling and the nonexistent top four feet of the walls. "How the hell did this happen?"

Maleshi spun in tight circles, her silver eyes flashing as she scanned the wreckage. "No."

"Yeah, it sucks."

"No, no, no. Fuck." The general darted toward a particularly large pile of charred wreckage in a burst of silver light. A huge cloud of ash burst away from her when she slipped out of enhanced speed, and the half-burned timber cracked and toppled to the floor. Snarling, the general grabbed huge chunks of debris and tossed them over her shoulders. "Dammit!"

"Whoa." Ember staggered back when Maleshi burst across the warehouse again toward another pile, the shockwave pushing her hair away from her face and kicking up a small tornado of ash. "What's going on?"

"It was all here. The safest goddamn place any of us could think of, and it still wasn't enough." Maleshi tossed more rubble across the warehouse and hissed, "We were so stupid!"

"Maleshi." Cheyenne stepped toward her, but the general darted toward the toppled computer tables and the burnt, melted husks of Persh'al's computer setup, then to the couch on the opposite wall that was nothing more than a few metal springs and charred fabric, then all the way across to the small square office in the back that had served as L'zar's room for weeks.

That room seemed fairly stable, at least, but when Maleshi grabbed the doorknob and pulled, the door flew off its hinges and sailed across the warehouse, crumbling in charred pieces as it went. "All of it! No!"

"Hey!" Cheyenne darted into enhanced speed to get a head start and grabbed the general by the shoulders before slipping back into real-time again. "Take a breath and—"

Maleshi roared and spun, swinging a fist toward Cheyenne's head. The halfling moved quicker than either of them expected and caught the general's wrist. Four-inch silver claws glinted in the pale light spilling through the burned ceiling, winking at Cheyenne from a mere two inches away. The drow snarled and glared at the nightstalker. "Pull your shit together, Hi'et. Now."

The general's eyes twitched, then she realized what she'd almost done and jerked her wrist out of Cheyenne's grasp. Her deadly claws retracted with a metallic slice, and she stormed past the drow toward the side door leading into the parking lot behind the warehouse.

"This is the part where you start talking," Cheyenne muttered. "Then we can forget you almost shish-kebabbed my eyeballs."

"I brought them all here, Cheyenne." Maleshi took a shuddering breath and stared at the side door. "Every war machine from that event center. Every crate of old-world tech. Every stack of ammo. Every control box."

"Shit."

"Yeah." The general whirled and spread her arms. "A nice fucking cache inside our secret warehouse surrounded in the most complicated wards I've seen Earthside, and I've been here a while."

"Oh, my God." Ember rubbed her mouth and stared at the night-stalker. "You think someone broke in and stole it all?"

"I don't see a goddamn spec of O'gúl metal in here, fae. Do you?"

"Hey, watch it." Cheyenne shot Maleshi a warning glare. "It wasn't us, so don't start acting like it."

"I know it wasn't you," the general growled at her and paced in front of the side door, muttering under her breath.

"So who else?"

"That's what I'm trying to figure out. Shut up." Maleshi's hands worked in quick, jerky movements as she paced and muttered whatever intense spell took all her concentration. Then she jerked both hands toward the side door, and a flash of silver light hit the metal. Her spell illuminated the ghostly outline of what had once been active wards before the magical light faded to nothing.

Maleshi roared and slashed across the door. Her claws shrieked on the thick metal and peeled back thin, curling strips as sparks flew.

Ember stuck her fingers in her ears and winced at the sound. It hurt Cheyenne's teeth, but she grimaced through it and waited for the general's fit to come to an end.

The nightstalker pounded her fist on the door, breathing heavily, and hung her head.

"What happened to the wards?" Cheyenne muttered.

"Removed." Straightening slowly, Maleshi smoothed her hair away from her face and took a long, slow breath through her nose. "By someone who knew they were here. Someone who knew which wards to take down in which order and how."

"That's a pretty narrow range of options."

"No shit." Storming toward Cheyenne, Maleshi reached out with both hands like she meant to wrap them around the drow's neck and stopped. "I'm only gonna ask this once in a way that doesn't hurt either of us."

"Don't you dare threaten me."

"Cheyenne."

"Take it down a goddamn notch and just say it."

Maleshi growled. "Any of your Earthborn pets in black combat gear know a single fucking thing about wards?"

The drow barked a dry laugh. "I gave four of them their very first activator a few days ago, and they're the only FRoE agents in existence who've ever seen one up close and personal. No, they don't know shit about wards."

Maleshi nodded, unable to look Cheyenne in the eye as she spun and took up pacing on another path. "The goblins are with Persh'al. Corian's MIA."

"Corian wouldn't take all the war machines you stashed here, then blow this place sky-high to cover it up."

"No. But the Weaver would."

"Bullshit." Ember folded her arms and shook her head. "He's crazy, yeah, but L'zar wouldn't do this to us. To you guys. What's in it for him?"

"Only L'zar knows what L'zar's getting out of his plans."

"I'm not buying it." Cheyenne turned to look at Neros, who stood in the center of the warehouse and stared at the cold gray sky. Fluttering bits of ash rained down around him when the wind kicked up, and he blinked when a large flake landed on his eyelash.

Raining ash in both worlds now. Not a good sign no matter how you spin it.

"You getting any Nor'ieth hints about what happened here?" she asked.

"Fire." Neros searched the sky through the open roof. "And more fire."

"It's like you're only useful in my dreams, and even that's stretching it." Cheyenne shook her head and pulled out her phone. "I'm gonna try him again."

"Who?" Maleshi stalked toward her.

"Corian."

"Put your phone away, Cheyenne. Those things are a waste of time."

The general raised both hands for another quickly cast portal, then marched through it with a snarl.

Cheyenne and Ember exchanged wary looks, interrupted by Neros walking between them and stepping through the portal without being prompted.

Guess he's learned something.

Ember lowered her head and hurried through the dark window of light. Cheyenne took one final look around the destroyed warehouse, secret hideout of L'zar Verdys and his rebels for at least the last two hundred years, and left it behind.

CHAPTER FIFTY-TWO

"Are we supposed to know what this place is?" Ember stepped across the concrete floor in the dark, narrow room but quickly lifted her foot when she felt and heard glass crunching beneath it.

"Cheyenne knows." Maleshi's silver eyes glowed in the darkness as she crossed the single room, her boots sending unknown items skittering across the floor.

Cheyenne squinted, catching only the glint of the general's eyes, but she felt the strength of the concentrated magic that had been here some number of hours ago. It was strong and raced across her shoulders and her upper back. *No flames. Plenty of time for them to disappear but leave a pretty clear magical footprint behind.*

"This is Corian's apartment," she muttered.

The jingle and click of Maleshi pulling the string of the uncovered lightbulb overhead filled the room, followed by a brief burst of light and a pop before everything went black again.

"Shit." Glass rained down around the general, then an orb of silver light crackled to life in her hand. She tossed it toward the ceiling, where it disbursed over the water stains in the thin panels and bathed the room in a pale silver glow. The general swiped pieces of the shattered light bulb off her sleeves and out of her hair, then straightened and looked around.

"Jesus." Cheyenne rubbed the side of her face as she took in the state of Corian's basement apartment. The long row of metal shelves had been kicked away from the wall and slanted sideways, and their contents were strewn across the concrete floor. The folding card table and the single chair had been flipped over and hurled across the room. Corian's laptop lay broken in three pieces in the corner. All the small boxes and crates where he'd stored magical artifacts for centuries were overturned, delicate items crunched underfoot and scattered throughout the indecipherable mess.

Then she looked at the door that opened to the slippery, moss-covered cement staircase and swallowed. "This was a break-in."

"What?" Maleshi stomped across the glass and debris and raised her eyebrows when she saw the door. The thing had been ripped halfway off its hinges, and a massive indent buckled it in at the center, like a fist the size of a steel beam had rammed into it to get inside. "What did you do this time, *vae shra'ni?*" the general whispered.

"Not like anyone would be able to tell," Ember said as she stepped tentatively across the wreckage, "but you guys see anything missing? Other than Corian, obviously."

Cheyenne stepped back and scanned the ruined apartment that had never looked like a home. "I should've paid way more attention when I was here. He has so much stuff."

Her foot came down on something small and hard that sent an electric buzz of magical energy up her leg and into her hip. The drow stepped quickly back again and lifted her foot. "Holy shit."

Maleshi turned toward her. "Tell me that's the good kind this time."

"Probably not." Cheyenne stooped to pick up the small metal four-pointed star that had zapped her, sucking in a breath when a buzzing tingle raced up her arm and into the side of her neck. "Well, we know this isn't his."

The general squinted at the magic condensed into physical form, her upper lip twitching in a sneer, then drew away in confusion. "That makes no sense."

"Add it to the list. Neros." When her cousin turned toward her, Cheyenne flicked the four-pointed star his way. He caught it deftly and stared at her. "Look familiar?"

The pale-skinned drow slowly opened his hand and tilted his head. "Our magical signature. Forged into this state quite recently."

"Yep. My guess is a few hours. Maybe even before the warehouse blew up."

"An educated guess, kid?"

Cheyenne grimaced at the general. "More like I can feel it. That's not an activator, either."

"So, what?" Ember spread her arms. "A drow of the Verdys bloodline was here in Corian's apartment?"

"Well, two of them are right now." Cheyenne nodded at her cousin. "No lies or riddles, Neros. Did you—"

"I did not set foot in this room until two minutes ago, Cheyenne." Neros closed his fist around the four-pointed star and sniffed, his nostrils flaring. "I would have remembered the stench."

"Fair enough."

"Then who?" Maleshi closed her eyes and shook her head. "That only leaves L'zar and Ba'rael. I don't know any other Verdys drow."

"You seemed pretty convinced L'zar wouldn't have a problem taking down the wards around the warehouse and stealing all the war machines. Not to mention the explosion."

"I know what I said, Cheyenne. But this?" The general gestured at the wreckage and the bashed-in metal door. "Corian is his *Nós Aní*. L'zar's capable of doing something like this to any other magical in two worlds, but not Corian."

True. I don't think he'd hesitate to break into my place if he convinced himself he had a good reason.

"So then it's Ba'rael." Ember stared at them with wide eyes. "It has to be, right? She's the only other magical who'd attack Corian and leave a piece of her magic shaped like that behind."

"Easy enough to find out." Cheyenne pulled out her phone again and called Inolu.

The line picked up halfway through the first ring. "You must have hit your head in Ambar'ogúl and cracked it wide open. That's the only reasonable explanation I can come up with for why you're still fucking calling me."

Cheyenne rolled her eyes. "Good to hear your voice too, Inolu."

"Is there a reason we're having this conversation?"

"Yeah. You still have the Spider in that cage?"

The banebreaker sniggered. "You're cute."

"I'm serious."

"Yes, she's still in the cage. Harboring at least six *uanáj* in my physical flesh doesn't make me an idiot. Okay, fine. Ten *uanáj*. But still."

"Any way you can prove it?" Cheyenne asked. "Seeing as I've been banned from your house and everything."

"Ugh. You're so boring." Footsteps carried over the line, then Inolu's voice was slightly fainter as she held the phone away from her. "Someone wants to know if you're taking phone calls today, darling."

Cheyenne recognized the ensuing snarl even before fists pounded on metal bars and Ba'rael hissed, "Rot in the abyss, *uanáj* whore."

"Ooh, what a mouth on this one, huh?" Inolu chuckled, but it cut it off abruptly when she pressed the phone to her ear again. "Satisfied, drow?"

"Yeah. Thanks."

"Now go bother someone else. I'm busy." The banebreaker hung up, and Cheyenne slipped her phone back into her pocket.

"Ba'rael's still locked up tight. Still pissed. I don't think Inolu would let her out for thirty seconds, even if she thought she could get away with it. I'm paying her way too much not to."

Maleshi bared her teeth in a snarl, her silver eyes darting around as she raced through one possibility after another. "It doesn't add up. No way was this L'zar, but that has to be his magic."

"So, someone else showed up when they were both here and tore the place apart." Cheyenne shrugged. "Maybe took them both?"

"What fucking *dae'bruj* in his right mind would take on L'zar Verdys and Corian Vedi'im at the same time?"

"Someone who's not in their right mind?" Ember suggested.

"No, that's too obvious." Maleshi spun again, hissing when she slipped on some broken object before kicking it across the room.

"Maybe we should go with the obvious answer."

"Cheyenne, I know it seems simple, but trust me. It's the exact opposite. An idiot with a death wish would take them both on, but an idiot wouldn't be able to sniff out the wards around this apartment. Or the warehouse. And an idiot certainly wouldn't have the means to remove a whole goddamn army's worth of war machines and ammo from that warehouse without setting off any alarms. Whoever this fucker is, we need to find him."

Cheyenne spread her arms and stepped back. "Couldn't agree more."

The general pulled out her phone to call Corian, glanced sideways at Cheyenne, and pressed the phone to her ear. "I know what I said about phones, but I'm out of ideas."

Pressing her lips together, Cheyenne exchanged wary looks with Ember. Then she frowned at Neros as he sniffed the metal four-pointed star and touched his tongue against it. "Hey, come on."

"I want to be sure." He nodded. "It *is* what we think it is."

"Great. No, I don't want it back. You can keep it or ditch it or whatever."

Maleshi growled and shook her phone in frustration before pocketing it again. "What is going on?"

"Who else do we know over here who might've heard from him?"

"You're asking the wrong damn magical, kid. I've been Earthside for almost four hundred years and only found out Corian was here a few weeks ago. I don't know anyone." The general opened a portal into Cheyenne and Ember's apartment and stepped back to allow them through. "You go handle your own business, whatever that is. I'll keep trying to find them."

"We can help," Ember offered. "Tell us what you need."

"I need to be alone, Ember. In case I can't help but take out my frustration on the closest thing to me. Moving targets are a lot more attractive like that."

Ember raised her hands and stepped toward the portal. "Fine."

Neros tossed the metal star, caught it, and followed the fae without a word.

"Let me know when you find something, okay?" Cheyenne paused, studying the general's scowl. "I'll do the same."

"Deal. Go on." Maleshi stared at the crooked bookshelf and didn't meet the drow's gaze. Cheyenne finally gave up.

"We'll find them."

"I know. Now it's a matter of timing. And not fucking it up." Maleshi nodded at the portal, and Cheyenne bit her lip as she stepped through it into her living room.

"Hey, what if I—" The portal closed behind her and she grimaced. "Guess that's a no."

Ember slumped on the couch and leaned forward to pick at her cold, syrup-soggy waffle with her fork. "That was rough."

"Yep. Something's still not adding up." Cheyenne headed for the stairs to the mini-loft. Her black Vans clomped on the metal steps as she took them two at a time. "When in doubt, go search through the one place everyone puts the crap they don't want traced back to them."

"Not every Earthside magical is part of the dark web pool, Cheyenne."

"You'd be surprised how many are, though, and even if they don't know about Corian, everyone knows who the Weaver is. There's gotta be something."

CHAPTER FIFTY-THREE

For the next three hours, Cheyenne and her activator pored through every new topic thread on the Borderlands forum, searching for mentions of L'zar, Corian, a break-in, a blown-up warehouse, more randomly stolen ingredients, and anything else.

She found absolutely nothing.

There's nothing on this stupid forum because nobody has any clue what's happening around here. She thumped her fist on the desk and sent a pen clattering off it. It dropped through the banisters around the mini-loft and hit the hardwood below. *Things would be a hell of a lot different if Earthside magicals had fucking activators and a way to deal with bullshit.*

"Nothing, huh?" Ember looked at her friend and grimaced.

"No. Nothing, Em." Cheyenne pushed away from the desk. "Everyone was talking about Peridosh and the weird shit with magical blackouts at the reservations, and that's it. Nothing else. It's like the last twenty-four hours never happened."

Or everyone's been too distracted by Peridosh and the reservations to pay attention to anything else.

"I still don't get why whoever took them, if we're assuming two of the most powerful magicals in this world were taken, would want to take the war machines too. Again, assuming it's the same magical."

"We're missing a crucial part of this, and it's driving me insane."

Cheyenne squinted at her monitor, but she had already run everything she could think of through her activator's search protocols. "The why doesn't matter as much as the who, though. The war machines are down for now, yeah, but the thief didn't just take those. They took all the ammo. All the controls. Everything anyone would need to have a working artillery battery."

"Except for Matthew's program."

"Right, but someone else could easily replicate it. Sure, not exactly, but close enough to get things going."

Ember stood up and wrinkled her nose. "And take Corian and L'zar with them on some crackpot crusade to blaze a trail across Earth with old-world tech? That's kind of a stretch."

"Again, only assuming the same asshole who bashed down Corian's door also broke into the warehouse." Cheyenne stood from her chair, forcing herself to breathe and take a break as she gripped the iron rail around the loft. "Those crates, Em. They had the same stuff Colonel Thomas and the Bull's Head used to take me down with my own special DNA poison."

"Right, but you destroyed that machine."

"That one was for me. When we found those crates smuggled in at the portal ridge the first time, some asshole fired this blood-seeker canister thing. It was like a magical heat-seeking missile but by race."

"Oh, yeah. That orc did the same thing to give the colonel a demonstration."

"Yeah. I'm not worried about another machine coming after me so much as I am about the wrong asshole getting their hands on all that tech." Cheyenne ran a hand through her hair and stared out the wall of windows at the northern part of Richmond and the first bit of DC in the distance. "Those machines could be used for anything. Genocide by magical race if that's what someone was going for. Human genocide too, probably."

"It wouldn't take old-world tech to wipe out humans on Earth if someone put their mind to it."

"No, but it would be a hell of a lot easier with an army of machines that don't need food or supplies or medics. Maleshi took out the rest of the Bull's Head. I have no idea who else would want to do this."

Ember nodded and patted the back of the couch in contemplation.

"You'd think anyone who could handle L'zar and Corian at the same time wouldn't care about something like magical race wars and Earthside destruction. Like the Sorren Gán, right? That thing didn't give a shit about Hangivol almost blowing itself off the map beyond how much magic it could eat and how long it would take to get there."

"Right. This looks like a simple master plan to start a whole bunch of shit over here, but Maleshi was right. Maybe it's *too* simple."

Neros let out a startlingly loud groan as he stretched out on the couch, raising his hands high above his head and kicking out his bare feet. "Simplicity is a form of mastery, cousin."

"Oh, good. You're back to the riddles."

"What else remains when all the complications are cast aside?" He looked at her and raised his eyebrows. "The truth."

"The truth is we're in deep shit if Corian and L'zar don't show up real soon." Cheyenne stretched her stiff legs and clomped down the stairs. "I need a shower. Maybe that'll simplify the brainstorming process for me."

Neros shrugged. "Water is a conduit."

"It's just a shower. Go ahead and turn on some cartoons or something." Cheyenne disappeared into the bathroom, and the showerhead turned on two seconds after she'd locked the door.

Neros pushed up against the armrest and tilted his head at Ember. "You did not mention cartons."

"Cartoons." She frowned at him. "You're only listening to what people say around you, like, half the time, aren't you?"

"Roughly. Sometimes less. Are cartoons as enlightening as your superhero movies?"

"Probably not. Here." Ember handed him the remote and patted his shoulder. "I'm gonna stare at pictures of food and pretend I'm hungry enough to cook something."

Neros aimed the remote at the TV.

Cheyenne checked her phone at least a dozen times while she toweled off, got dressed, and dried her hair. Nothing from Maleshi and nothing from Corian, but as soon as she gave up on hearing from either of them, her phone buzzed on top of her dresser.

She leaped over the bed toward it, scraping her thigh on one of the skull-shaped drawer knobs and ignoring the sting as she snatched it up. It was Rhynehart.

Come on. I have at least a few more days before everyone in the FRoE and their mother needs to call the drow trainer.

Still, she had to answer.

"What's up?"

"Cheyenne." He cleared his throat. "You busy?"

Naw, just trying to track down my crazy dad and his nightstalker best friend and a few hundred tons of O'gúl weaponry on tracks. "Depends on why you're calling, honestly."

"Fair enough. Listen, I'm not in the position to call you up and order you out into the field anymore. None of us are. I'm hoping you might come out anyway as a personal favor."

Cheyenne raised an eyebrow and sat on her purple crushed-velvet bedspread. "Out where?"

"Res 9. It's about an hour south of Five Forks. I know it's kind of a stretch on short notice, but you've made two hours in forty-five minutes before. Figured it wouldn't be that hard."

"Maybe. If you tell me what's got you so freaked out that you're calling in a personal favor."

"Yeah, I'm probably the least freaked-out person here." The sound of a door shutting came over the line, then Rhynehart lowered his voice. "Something's wrong with the tower. The giant black—"

"I know what a Border tower is. What's it doing?"

"Fuck if I know, Cheyenne. I'm not an expert on the reservations' inner workings, but I haven't seen anything like this since I signed up for the job. Not sure how long the people and magicals around here are gonna be able to keep it together before someone starts screaming about the end of the world and shit hits the fan."

"Anyone show up at the rez who's not supposed to be there?"

Rhynehart swallowed thickly. "Like who?"

"Anyone."

"No. Sorry. I could seriously use an extra pair of eyes out here, and maybe your fancy earpiece skills."

"Activator, Rhynehart. Activator." Cheyenne glanced around the room and tapped her feet on the floor. *Border towers acting up. Rez guards and refugees freaking out. Wanna bet this is related?* "Okay, fine. Pin it on a map or something and send it over."

"Done. Thanks."

"Don't thank me until I've done something. I'll probably be there sometime in the next hour."

"Yeah, sooner would be better than later, but I get it. I'll keep an eye out." He hung up and sent her a GPS location for Rez 9 less than thirty seconds later.

In the middle of the woods with no one around to see all the freaky shit happening. Perfect place to hide magicals from the human world. Perfect place to hide an attack too.

CHAPTER FIFTY-FOUR

Half an hour later, Maleshi's portal opened in the middle of the woods south of Five Forks, and Cheyenne and the general stepped through together.

"You sure this is the place, kid?"

"Rhynehart gave me the GPS location, and that's what I gave you." Cheyenne scanned the quiet, seemingly empty forest, then looked at the nightstalker. "As long as you brought us to the same coordinates."

"Don't start that with me. My aim is perfect."

They walked through the thinly spaced trees, searching for signs of Rez 9.

Not like the other reservations. No gate. No road. They built a rez around a portal in the middle of the woods?

"You think we'll find something about that fiery-portal magical out here at a reservation?" Maleshi asked.

"It sounds exactly like everything else I've heard about weird shit going down at other portals." Cheyenne shrugged. "Sure, it's all hearsay, but that was why I asked you to come with me. So we can both see it for ourselves."

The general asked, "You mean, you didn't just wanna use me for quick, free transportation?"

"Well, there's that, too. You know, if you wanted to leave the higher-education realm, I bet you could make a killing ferrying magicals through space even just four hours a day. Nightstalker Uber, right?"

Maleshi cocked her head. "Less physical contact than driving, too."

A shimmering light blinked through the trees a quarter-mile ahead of them. They stopped and stared.

"That look like an illusion shimmer to you?" Cheyenne whispered.

"Look at you, kid, identifying different kinds of magical light. You've come a long way since you stepped into my office trying to pretend you weren't what you are."

"Yeah, thanks."

The light shimmered again for half a second longer this time, accompanied by a brief burst of sound, loud voices, metal banging, and a surprised shout. It all cut off again when the light disappeared.

"I think we found Rez 9." Maleshi gestured through the trees. "Whenever you're ready."

Cheyenne stalked ahead of the general, fixing her gaze on where the illusion had flickered off and back on again. When they reached that spot, a slight tingle raced across her skin, and without any resistance, they were standing on the reservation.

The trees had been cleared to leave room for the FRoE operations buildings, the barracks, and the guard towers.

"What the hell?" Cheyenne stared at the huge pillar of the black stone Border tower, which rose forty feet above the tops of the tallest trees surrounding the reservation. Bursts of that same wavering illusory light sputtered up and down the tower in waves, echoed by lights flashing randomly around what should have been Q1.

"Shit with the Border tower." Maleshi snorted. "I think your FRoE friend sold himself short with that explanation."

"Yeah, no kidding."

Magicals flashed in and out of Q1, FRoE rez guards and personnel and O'gúleesh refugees who should have been contained in either Q3's marketplace or Q4's rows of cookie-cutter houses. The agents looked pissed whenever they blinked into Q1. The refugees looked terrified, staring around and leaping away from transport vehicles and agents in full dampening gear patrolling the area.

"We gotta find Rhynehart." Cheyenne headed into the unpredictably shifting layers of multiple dimensions held together by the Border towers.

"Hey!" An orc guard wearing the dark blue rez uniform with Rez 9 across his baseball cap in bright yellow letters headed toward her. "Who the fuck are you?"

"Rhynehart called me."

"Throwing names around now, huh?"

"Yeah, and I need to find him."

The orc eyed her and readjusted his grip on the fell rifle. "You're that consultant, huh?"

Great. That's what I've become to these guys. Cheyenne shrugged. "You heard it straight from the major general's announcement last week. So yeah. I'm the consultant."

"And I'm her assistant," Maleshi added as she stepped up behind the drow.

"What the fuck!" The orc staggered back and leveled his rifle at the general.

"She's with me." Cheyenne gestured for him to lower his weapon. "Stand down, man. Come on."

"What the fuck are you?"

"Aw." Maleshi tilted her head. "That's cute."

"No." The orc shook his head and pointed at Cheyenne. "You stay right here. Security's tight, and this whatever ain't on the list."

"Nightstalker. And she's with me." Cheyenne tried to brush past him.

"I said, stay there!" The orc's yellow eyes narrowed as he looked at Maleshi, and he grabbed the radio on his shoulder. "Cameron. It's Torg." He stepped back, still aiming his rifle at the general's chest. "We've got a—"

He disappeared in a wavering flash of light like he'd stepped into another illusion, and he didn't come back.

"Well, that was convenient," Cheyenne said to Maleshi. "Try not to rile any more of them up, okay? You're a novelty."

"Oh, sure. Like a drow and a nightstalker showing up on a malfunctioning reservation together."

"Yeah. Magicals are probably gonna freak out." Cheyenne took off toward a collection of single-story metal buildings arranged almost exactly like the ones she'd seen in Rez 38's Q1.

Before they got halfway to the main building where she figured she'd find Rhynehart, a family of skaxen, two terrified adults and three small orange children, materialized in front of them. The skaxen woman saw Cheyenne and dropped a woven basket of brightly colored cloth. Then she saw Maleshi and let out a shriek.

The man tried to calm her down as the little rat-like kids clutched at their mother's skirts. FRoE agents shouted at each other and headed toward the family.

"Got a whole family popping into Q1," a troll guard muttered in his radio. "Goddamn refugees need to stay—" He disappeared, and the two guards jogging behind him toward the terrified skaxen woman stopped in their tracks.

They saw Cheyenne and Maleshi and raised their weapons. "Hands up!"

"How the hell'd you get in here?"

Cheyenne spread her arms. "Are your radios going out too? Come on. I'm looking for Rhynehart."

"Skaxen! Back away from those two!"

The mother jerked her children away, and the father stood frozen in fear, glancing between Cheyenne and the rez guards with raised weapons.

"I'm not gonna hurt you," Cheyenne reassured him. "And neither are they."

"I said, hands up!"

"Come on, guys. Call Rhynehart and tell him I'm—"

"Look out!"

The roar of a diesel engine started out of nowhere behind the wary guards, transported from Q2 without warning. The ogre guard behind the wheel laid on the horn and the skaxen family scattered, the mother shrieking and dragging her children after her.

The guards shouting at Cheyenne dove out of the way as the driver of the transport vehicle slammed on the brakes, but he couldn't quite stop fast enough.

"That's our cue." Cheyenne darted into drow speed and ran around the slow-moving truck with a spray of dirt thrown up by its wheels suspended in the air.

Maleshi joined her in enhanced speed a second later. "Why'd you stop, kid?"

Cheyenne gazed at the chaotic stasis of Q1. "You don't see this?"

"I see what I always see when I'm moving faster than the rest of the world."

"The flames, Maleshi." She gestured at the streaks of opalescent fire she'd seen in every other place where things had gone wrong over the last few days. Lines of shimmering flames crossed in every direction, diagonally up and down, shooting into the sky, racing across the reservation, and flickering as if she stood in regular time instead of enhanced speed. "They're everywhere."

"Shit." The general scanned the air and shook her head. "Still don't see it, kid, but I'd bet whoever's leaving this trail—"

"Has a hand in the Border tower freaking out. I knew they were connected." The drow pulled herself out of her surprise and headed swiftly for the main FRoE building. She slipped out of enhanced speed in front of the door, and the rest of Q1 burst into chaos again. The transport vehicle's horn blared, the skaxen family shrieked and darted away, and guards shouted and aimed their rifles all over the place.

Cheyenne jerked open the door and stepped into the main ops building, with Maleshi close on her heels.

Rhynehart stood at the high counter on the left, leaning forward to talk in low tones to two human guards behind the desk who were typing furiously on two bulky computer's keyboards. When the noise burst through the open door, he quickly looked up and stepped away from the desk. "Cheyenne."

The door swung shut with a metallic bang.

"You guys have a serious problem out here."

"What—" Three agents at the back of the building raised their weapons. "Q1 is restricted, no civilians. What the fuck are you doing here?"

"What the fuck are *you*?" Another human guard's hands shook as he tried to aim his pistol at Maleshi.

"Friends," Rhynehart said and raised a hand toward the startled guards. "Both of them. Stand down."

"Captain, they just—"

"I said to stand the fuck down." Rhynehart glared at the three agents in the back, and they warily lowered their weapons. He turned back toward Cheyenne. "Didn't ask you to bring any friends."

"But I did." Cheyenne shot Maleshi a sidelong look. "We're gonna add nightstalker study to the list of things your guys need to learn before they take up their posts."

"Whatever." Rhynehart tapped the counter and nodded at the guards behind it. "Keep working on it, huh? It'll settle out eventually."

"Having system problems too?" Cheyenne stepped toward the counter, and both guards pulled their hands away from the keyboards to step back.

"The whole damn thing's on the fritz." Rhynehart ran a hand over his mouth. "Can't look up shit. All the orders coming in, lists of residents, boxes to check off any given day at a given hour. Whatever's happening out there with the tower is leaving us blind with our tech too. Wouldn't surprise me if the radios go out next."

"I think they already have." Cheyenne studied the backs of the computer monitors, which normally would have offered information, with her activator feeding the data to her line by line. Now all the code lines scrolling across her vision flashed error messages. "Mind if I take a look?"

Rhynehart shot Maleshi a wary look, then shrugged. "Go ahead."

The human agents behind the counter backed up even farther until they were pressed against the wall, eyes darting from the first drow they'd seen in person to the first nightstalker they'd seen in person. Cheyenne ignored them and stepped around the counter to stand at the monitors.

Both screens had new command boxes flashing in and out, the lists of supplies, orders, protocols, O'gúleesh names, and employee rosters blinking on top of each other. Her fingers flew over the keyboard as she tried to force a manual restart. Instead, the monitors flashed even faster.

She grimaced and tried to read what was coming up on each screen, but it came too fast.

"What are you—"

Cheyenne slipped into drow speed to slow down the flashing

programs on the computers. Leaning closer, she frowned and studied the information frozen on the screen. *It's all scrambled. Not even legible.*

The monitors flashed again in slowed time, and the same thing popped up on both.

Magic is shorting out the system here and rearranging all the data.

She reached for the keyboard again to try something else, but a bright flash illuminated the air around her.

A streak of opalescent flames had burst through the far wall of the main building, and it shot across the room toward the door. It flickered in front of Maleshi's face and crackled softly into existence, then continued into Q1.

Shit.

Cheyenne slipped out of drow speed.

"—looking for?" Rhynehart finished.

The screens flashed faster, then went white.

"What?" She stared at them, and her activator displayed a warning message.

System Nonexistent

"I have no idea," she muttered and looked at the line of fire racing across the room, which slowly faded from her view. "But I think something's about to—"

A loud bang and a blood-curdling scream came from outside.

"Shit." Rhynehart pointed at the human guards in the back. "Go. Make sure nobody loses their shit out there. And no one touches the magicals, understand? We're here to help them, not gun them down."

"Sir." The guards jogged across the room and bolted through the door, weapons drawn.

The chaos outside was deafening. Crashes everywhere, O'gúleesh screaming, rez guards and FRoE agents shouting at each other. Magical light of every color burst like a fireworks display outside, then the door banged shut again.

Rhynehart stormed toward the right side of the building and grabbed a dampening vest and gloves from a pile of them on a bench. "Any idea what we'll find out there?"

"Not really." Cheyenne walked around the desk to rejoin Maleshi, who studied the walls and cocked her head as she listened to the noises outside. "But your system's totally fried."

Shrugging quickly into the heavy vest, Rhynehart spun toward her. "What?"

"It's gone."

The guards behind the counter approached the computers. "What the hell did you do?"

"I didn't do anything. It was already happening."

"Screens don't just go white." The other guard typed furiously, scowling at a monitor that didn't change. "Fuck. We're down."

Cheyenne looked at the spot where the stream of flames had been. It was gone now. "Someone's messing with the whole thing."

"The whole thing what, Cheyenne?" Rhynehart tugged on his gloves and headed for the door.

"All of it. Your tech systems. The Border tower. The illusions for all your Qs." Cheyenne followed him through the door.

Maleshi grinned at the dumbfounded guards behind the computer counter. "Hang tight, boys."

She slipped through the door behind Cheyenne.

CHAPTER FIFTY-FIVE

"What do you mean, someone's messing with it?" Rhynehart snarled, swerving around a line of armed guards jogging toward a burst of green light racing from behind the next building over. The last two guards disappeared without the other two noticing. "Like, some kind of spell? An issue with the Borders from the other side like that sludge shit?"

"The blight's gone," Maleshi told him, catching up on the other side of Cheyenne. "Not coming back. We made sure of that."

"Then what is it?"

"I don't know." Cheyenne shook her head. "But whatever it is, I think it's just getting started."

An orc materialized in front of them, her eyes wide in panic as she raced into Q1 from whichever other quarter she'd been in. A burst of green light arced over her head from behind, and the woman stumbled to a stop to avoid running into Rhynehart. "Help him! Help him!" She turned around again, noticed she wasn't where she thought she was, and gasped. "Maldu? *Maldu!* Where are you?"

"Head back that way." Rhynehart pointed. "You'll have to walk back across."

The orc blinked at him and gazed at all the flashing light blazing through the air. Rhynehart, Cheyenne, and Maleshi kept walking.

"Hey, watch it!" A human guard ducked beneath a red shower of sparks bursting from a displaced gremlin's hands and spun to level his fell rifle on the terrified magical. "You can't do that out here! Hands up!"

The gremlin raised both hands, and another burst of red sparks shot into the air. He started, backed away from his uncontrolled magic, and spun to dart between the buildings.

"Dammit! Get back here!" The guard fired a warning shot and started to race after the gremlin.

"Hey!" Rhynehart stepped in front of him and shoved him back. "Open fire on a magical again, and you'll be sitting behind a desk stamping classified reports for the next fifteen years. Understand?"

"Sir, he attacked—"

A huge explosion wracked the closest building to the Border tower. Half the debris flying into the air vanished along with the growing fire-ball as guards and agents and O'gúleesh scattered away from the blast.

"Go check into that." Rhynehart shoved the guard toward the explosion, then whirled at the sound of screams behind them.

Two trolls raced across the busy lane of Q1, one of them engulfed in strobing purple light, the other blasting small blue orbs of energy in every direction from his hands. He darted away from his magic, terrified and shaking out his hands as more attacks escaped without conscious control. He looked at the purple-engulfed troll and opened his mouth to shout something, then disappeared.

"This is fucked." Rhynehart spun again, surveying civilians and FRoE personnel popping in and out of Q1. A burst of fire materialized in the air from some other quarter, then winked out. "How the hell?"

Cheyenne stepped back when an emaciated gremlin appeared at her feet, groaning and blinking through the blood spilling from a cut in his forehead. "Hey. You okay?"

He looked at her, stuttering incomprehensibly despite accepting her help up. After one quick look at Maleshi, the gremlin leaped away in a burst of green-yellow light and raced around the closest building.

Cheyenne turned toward Rhynehart. "We need to get everyone off the reservation. Rhynehart!"

He stared at the Border tower, his mouth open and eyes wide. "Bigger problem, Cheyenne."

She looked at the tower and froze.

The whole pillar of glistening black stone flashed in and out of existence, throwing off multicolored sparks as blazing lines of magical energy crackled up and down its surface. The ground trembled, and a sound like thunder and whipping wind and a long, low moan came from the tower.

"Rhynehart. How many of those things have come crashing down onto a rez before?"

"None."

Maleshi put a hand on Cheyenne's shoulder. "You're right. We need to get everyone out."

Rhynehart turned toward the main building. "I'll send a—"

An even larger explosion rose from the far end of Q1, followed by more screams and shouts of fear and anger.

They all turned that way, and Cheyenne's breath caught in her throat. "That's him."

"Who?" Maleshi and Rhynehart asked together.

"The fucking portal thief." She shook her head. "The flaming magical, Maleshi. He's here."

A balloon of opalescent flames rose from the explosion, filling the air with a thick, crackling tingle like ozone mixed with too much magic in one place.

"That's him." Cheyenne sprinted toward the flames, darting around another transport vehicle blaring its horn at her as it materialized from nowhere. It disappeared again, and she slid sideways across the ground to avoid barreling into some guards running to safety.

"Cheyenne!" Maleshi darted after her with a snarl.

Rhynehart growled and followed, drawing his fell pistol from the holster at his waist.

"You think running toward it is the best idea?" the general shouted.

"We stop this asshole, then we can get the rest of this shit under control." Cheyenne ducked a wayward spell of strobing orange light bursting from a troll's hands as she ran away from the blast. "So help me do that!"

"Cheyenne, I have no idea—"

The next explosion came from their right between two of the squat Q1 buildings. A sheet of metal hurtled toward them and Cheyenne reached out to grab it with her telekinesis, shouting at the effort as she propelled it toward the trees. Opalescent flames roared to life in front of her, stinging her nose with the bitter and sour scent of concentrated magic.

Another column of flames blasted into existence behind her against the side of a transport truck. O'gúleesh and guards scattered as the truck toppled onto its side, covered in the fire only Cheyenne could see.

More lines of the flames darted through the air, zigzagging toward the Border tower.

"Wait." She grabbed Maleshi's arm and jerked the general back around to face the same way. "He's heading for the tower."

"Jesus Christ, Cheyenne. How do you even—"

"I can fucking see it!" She darted into drow speed again, not caring if Maleshi followed. *This has to stop. If that asshole makes it to the tower...*

Maleshi joined her in enhanced speed, running through the suspended chaos around them to catch up with the drow. "Cheyenne! This isn't something we know how to handle!"

"So we figure it out!" Snarling, Cheyenne followed the racing lines of shimmering fire through a maze of metal buildings and skidded to a stop. Maleshi nearly barreled right into her when she rounded the corner, and they both stared at the crackling, growling Border tower. "That thing needs to stay where it is because whoever this is wants to—"

Maleshi grabbed her arm and hurled the drow sideways as a blazing portal of white light and shimmering fire burst into existence right where Cheyenne had stood. A slate-gray hand emerged from the white light. Long, slender fingers reached toward the closest line of flames, then a silver flash burst within the portal, and the arm retracted.

The portal disappeared.

"Cheyenne." Maleshi's voice was barely above a whisper. "Was that..."

"A drow hand? I think so." Breathing heavily, Cheyenne scanned the suspended Q1 as more flaming lines crossed the air. *It looked like L'zar's hand, and neither of us wants to say it out loud.*

"There!" Maleshi pointed at another white blaze twenty feet closer to the Border tower. Flames erupted from the blinding circle of white light as another portal reappeared. Someone snarled, and they caught the glint of four-inch silver claws swiped at something they couldn't see. Nightstalker claws.

"What?" Maleshi darted forward, but the portal disappeared again.

Two seconds later, another opened on the surface of the Border tower fifty feet in the air. And whether it was the angle or the battle within that portal dimming the light, Cheyenne and Maleshi both saw a lot more than a dismembered hand and blinding whiteness.

Two voices shouted in unison as Corian and L'zar appeared within the portal on the tower wall. Corian's silver eyes burned as he swiped toward L'zar's face with his claws extended. L'zar caught the nightstalker's wrist, snarled, and sent a fist toward Corian's gut. Before he made contact, the portal disappeared in a mushrooming burst of opalescent flames and they were gone.

Cheyenne searched the Border tower and the trampled dirt of Q1 beneath it. All the racing lines of shimmering fire disappeared. Snarling, she kept searching, running behind the next building to be sure.

The energy slowly crackling over the tower's black stone surface vanished, leaving the faint smell of vinegar behind. The thick presence of concentrated magic was sucked out of Rez 9, making Cheyenne stumble and gasp as if someone had suddenly removed a two-hundred-pound weight from her shoulders. Everything was silent.

"No." She straightened and whirled toward Maleshi as the general turned the corner around the building.

"Cheyenne."

"They're gone. And the fire. All of it's gone."

"Hold on—"

"Maleshi, they were right here!" Cheyenne stared at the Border tower.

"Fighting each other." The general frowned in confusion as she slowly approached the baffled drow.

"Were they? I don't know how that even makes sense."

"That was what it looked like." Maleshi grimaced and set a hand on Cheyenne's shoulder. "But we might not get the whole picture from a few quick glimpses through a kind of portal I don't know how to explain."

They both slipped back into real-time, and the roaring explosions around them died out as magicals and humans shouted and ran away.

The ground had stopped trembling, and the tower's howling roar was gone.

"Maybe they were fighting something else." Cheyenne turned to look at the general. "Whoever's been attacking all these places and stealing shit for who knows what. Right?"

"We don't know." Maleshi saw a troll guard flash into existence from a different Quarter and realize where he was. He ran toward the others, shouting for help and searching for casualties. "We don't know anything for sure."

"It doesn't make sense. It has to be someone else."

"But if it's not, kid…"

"Don't. Don't say it. We don't know." Cheyenne stared into the general's silver eyes and could hardly even think it.

Then L'zar's the one blowing up stores and stealing ingredients for some massive spell, and no one would know how to stop him.

CHAPTER FIFTY-SIX

In a dark, windowless room beneath the streets of Washington DC, Corian lifted his head and blinked in the semi-darkness. His temples throbbed, and the silhouette standing between him and the single source of muted yellow light wavered in and out of his swimming vision. The cords of opalescent flames wrapped around his wrists burned his flesh, filling the room with the scent of singed hair and the deeper, almost sweet scent of cooking meat.

Already, the pain had started to fade into a warm, tingling numbness.

Corian struggled weakly against the bonds and groaned, his chest heaving. "Why are you doing this?"

It came out as a rasping croak after the crushing blow he'd taken to his windpipe, and it hurt like hell.

The dark silhouette turned from the small wooden table and stepped aside to allow soft yellow light to spill onto Corian's face.

The nightstalker squinted against the sudden brightness and turned his head away. "I asked you a question."

Trying to speak made him fall into a fit of rasping coughs, and he sucked in a wheezing breath as he leaned back against the concrete wall behind him.

"No. No, it's not time yet."

"Hey." Corian fought to catch his breath. "Look at me."

"You want to take the whole fucking world down with you, don't you? That'll never work." The dark silhouette jerked sideways, flashing with multicolored lights that seemed to come from within. "I will not! Yes. It's always been the way we… We never agreed to anything." A loud hiss filled the room. "The calibrax can't possibly stretch that far, and you know it. But I don't. I don't know. I don't."

Corian grimaced at the growing pain in his pounding head. *I have to get through. He's finally lost it.*

"That doesn't go there! The whole thing. Ruined. We'll take as much as we need and—"

"L'zar!" Corian shouted. "Look at me!"

The figure blazing with multicolored light spun away from the wall. There was a sharp crack, then a burst of air knocked Corian's head against the wall as L'zar reappeared in front of him.

"Stop talking," L'zar growled.

Corian blinked against the dark spots dancing in his vision and focused on his friend's face. "You're lost, brother."

The Weaver tilted his head. "I know. And if you don't shut up, I'll send you to the final deathflame."

"What are you doing?"

L'zar turned away as if he might back away from his *Nós Aní*, who was constrained by flaming bonds too powerful for him to break. "Don't answer that. No. It's not—" He whipped his head back toward Corian, his golden eyes blazing. "I have no choice, *vae shra'ni*. It must be done."

Corian gritted his teeth and stared into those glowing golden eyes. "You? The Dark Smiling Weaver who broke through countless prophecies by choice? Whoever's feeding you these lies, L'zar—"

"This is what I was made for!" L'zar snarled. "What I was created to do, but you can't possibly understand how strong that bond is." His mouth opened and closed soundlessly as he studied the beat-up nightstalker breathing heavily in front of him. "I still don't, but I'm the only one who can do this."

A wickedly sharp knife materialized in L'zar's hand, glinting in the soft light. He shoved it under Corian's chin until the point pressed delicately against the nightstalker's fur and the flesh beneath.

Corian didn't flinch. "Don't."

"I must." The glow behind L'zar's eyes pulsed, then purple flames burst from within them, and a voice that was his and not his at the same time emerged from his curled lips. "And you're the only one who can help me."

"L'zar. I'm here with you. Let me help—"

"Too late." The drow grabbed the front of Corian's shirt and jerked down, ripping the fabric away until the collar dangled in shreds over the nightstalker's stomach. Then he pressed the tip of the blade against Corian's fur-covered chest and slashed across in one swift movement.

Corian hissed and pressed his back against the wall. "This isn't you."

"This is all I am, *vae shra'ni.*" Pressing the edge of the blade against the nightstalker's chest, L'zar stared at the blood dripping from the gash and pooling on the blade of the dagger. "And I'm taking all you are. You've done everything I've asked of you. Don't make me slit your throat."

He removed the blade and stood to carry it carefully back to the table in front of the bright light. Then he took up the unintelligible muttering again, and the clink of metal on stone drifted through the room.

Corian dropped his head against the wall and closed his eyes. *That's all I am now, huh? Just a nightstalker blood bag he won't think twice about draining dry if that's what it takes. What are you planning, L'zar?*

Six feet away from him, his cell phone buzzed noisily on the cement floor, turning slowly with each new pulse. The backlight felt harsh and blinding, and no matter how hard he focused, he couldn't read the name on the screen.

CHAPTER FIFTY-SEVEN

Cheyenne Summerlin stared at the Border tower on Rez 9. She felt Rhynehart approaching behind her but was unable to look at him.

We're in deep shit now.

"Please tell me you pulled some drow trick out of your sleeve and put everything back together," Rhynehart muttered, whipping off his dampening gloves as he stopped beside her to study the Border tower. "Otherwise, I have no fucking idea what to think."

She shook her head and glanced at Maleshi. The general stood with her hands behind her back, intently studying the Border portal they'd all thought was on the brink of toppling over on Rez 9.

Who knows what kind of awful mess that would've stirred up?

"Whoever this was," Maleshi said cautiously, "I'd say they got what they came for."

"Oh, yeah?" Rhynehart narrowed his eyes at the first nightstalker to set foot on this particular reservation. Then he turned back to Cheyenne and cocked his head. "You gonna tell me you don't know who this asshole was? 'Cause you looked eager to take off after him."

Cheyenne bit the inside of her bottom lip and took one final look at the restabilized Border tower. *I'm done with secrets, and I'm gonna need his help as much as he needs mine.*

"I know exactly who it was," she muttered.

"Cheyenne." Maleshi stepped toward them, raising an eyebrow half in warning and half in a plea.

The drow ignored her and met Rhynehart's gaze. "I have no idea why."

"All right." He looked at them. "Look. These agents and guards out here are scrambling to pick up the pieces of whatever the hell happened, and while I'm here, it's my job to make sure everything's running the way it should be."

"Then perhaps you should go tend to those duties of yours," Maleshi hissed, taking a warning step toward him.

Rhynehart ignored her and stared intently at Cheyenne. "But I'm willing to stand here and ignore all of it until you tell me exactly what I need to know."

"The only thing you need to know, Captain, is that this is more of a personal matter than we realized." The general grimaced. "And it doesn't concern you in the least."

He whirled on the general, his hand falling to the fell pistol on his hip. "I wasn't talking to you."

"Well, I'm talking to you."

"Okay, stop." Cheyenne stepped between them and grabbed Maleshi's upper arm to give it a warning squeeze. She eyed Rhynehart's hand on the grip of his pistol, then looked back at him and shook her head. "I need both of you because whatever's coming next is gonna take a lot more resources and manpower than any of us have on our own. Got it?"

Rhynehart's upper lip twitched in frustration, but he removed his hand from his service weapon and folded his arms instead. "So tell me what the fuck I saw."

"Cheyenne, we need to discuss this."

"We are discussing this."

"These humans have been scrambling to get their hands on him since they realized he was gone."

"They have access to a lot more than we do right now!" Cheyenne glared at the general and pointed at the black stone monolith of the Border tower. "Whatever's going on with those two, it isn't over, or we would've heard from Corian by now. And you know it."

"Cheyenne."

"If you don't want to hear me tell him, Hi'et, feel free to step aside." Cheyenne ignored the quick flash of surprise that darted across Maleshi's features before it was covered by a scowl. Then she turned back to Rhynehart. "You remember Corian."

"The other nightstalker. This was him?"

"No. This was L'zar."

Maleshi hissed in frustration and shook her head.

"L'zar Verdys." Rhynehart's eyes widened. "Your drow dad decided he'd pop into a Border Reservation and start blowing shit up for fun?"

"That's an oversimplification." Cheyenne ran a hand through her hair. "I don't know what's wrong with him. Corian's been looking for him since we made the crossing Earthside on Friday. Then we couldn't find Corian, and we think that's because they've been fighting each other over whatever L'zar's trying to do."

"He's trying to bring down a fucking Border tower, Cheyenne."

"I don't think he even knows what he's trying to do. But if Corian found him and tried to stop him?"

"The door was busted down in his apartment, Cheyenne." Maleshi gestured at the black stone tower. "L'zar found him."

"I know. And now we need to find them both."

"Why am I hearing about this now?" Rhynehart smacked his dampening gloves together and glared at her. "I called you here to help me out with the system and the Quarters going haywire. And you knew?"

"I didn't know anything until twenty minutes ago." Cheyenne took a deep breath and forced her anger back under control. *It shouldn't be this hard to get everyone on the same damn page.* "Look, this wasn't the first attack."

"Oh, so L'zar's been on a rampage for the last five days, and you're just now telling me about it?"

"I didn't know it was him!" She turned quickly and studied the rez guards and FRoE agents running back and forth across Q1, which had settled down into its regular state without FRoE employees or O'gúleesh refugees popping in and out through the different Quarter illusions. "And I still don't really think it *is* him. None of us have seen anything like this, okay? Maleshi didn't recognize the signs. Corian didn't either, or he wouldn't have been caught up in this mess like he was. The only clue I had was this fire in the air wherever L'zar's been showing up lately. This isn't a part of him any of us have seen before, okay? I'm still not convinced it's him anyway."

"What, like someone brainwashed him?" Rhynehart scoffed. "You've been protecting him way too long, Cheyenne. You told me he wasn't a threat."

"He wasn't. Not before this. Something's wrong with him."

"Yeah. He's the drow piece of shit who had another twenty-five years on his sentence and decided to parole his own damn self." Rhynehart shook his head and turned away from her. "I shouldn't have given you the benefit of the doubt on that one. Jesus Christ, I helped him break into Chateau D'rahl for one of the most dangerous fucking inmates!"

"This isn't about Venga. He's not Earthside anymore anyway. This is about something else."

The captain took a deep breath and let it out as almost a growl. "Then tell me what the hell it's about so I can give the right orders to be carried out."

Cheyenne stared at him. "I don't know yet. But I'll figure it out."

"Yeah, you better." Rhynehart sneered at Maleshi. "Both of you."

"I came here to help," the general snarled.

"Yeah, some fucking help you were. The entire reservation went up in flames, we endangered who knows how many lives, and yeah, I'm counting my agents here and the guards and the magicals, and neither of you did a goddamn thing to stop it."

"Hey, if either of us had known how to stop it, we would have." Cheyenne stepped back as Rhynehart whisked his phone out of his pocket and grimaced at the screen. "Am I boring you all of a sudden?"

"Shit." His eyes widened, and he scrolled through whatever had popped up on his phone.

"Rhynehart."

"This is way bigger than two asshole magicals fighting over Rez 9." Rhynehart looked up at her. "Whatever he did here, it's happening at ten other reservations."

"Eleven." Her activator had picked up the data streaming to his phone through an external system independent of everything she'd seen go haywire in Q1's main building. "Twelve now."

"What?" He looked back down at his phone. "Shit."

"He can't be at twelve different reservations all at once," Maleshi muttered. "That's too much even for L'zar, especially if Corian's fighting him along the way."

"No, these have been sending out signals for a while." Rhynehart whipped the dampening vest over his head and shoulders and slung it under his arm. "I'm just getting the alerts now."

"Twelve different Border towers in Virginia and the surrounding areas." Cheyenne scanned the data lines her activator pulled up, even after Rhynehart jammed his phone back into his pocket. "Looks like he hit them all before he came here."

"So, you think this was the last stop?" Rhynehart asked.

"No. Maybe the last reservation stop, but he's planning something." Cheyenne nodded at Maleshi. "We need to get moving."

The general spread her arms and offered a bitter smile. "I'm waiting for the plan."

Rhynehart grunted. "Yeah, me too."

"Same plan." Cheyenne nodded at the general. "Just a faster timeline. I should've done this yesterday. We need to stop by my car first."

Maleshi stepped back and raised her arms to cast another portal.

"Feel like letting me in on the secret?"

Cheyenne turned to the FRoE captain. "I have almost two hundred activators turned on and ready to go. If we're gonna be prepared to face L'zar and whatever he thinks he's doing, your agents need to have them, and they need to learn how the fuck they work."

"Kinda your agents now too, wouldn't you say?"

She gave him a deadpan stare. "Don't be cute."

"Did you already move on those materials for Van Lurig's assistant?" He sniffed and readjusted the dampening vest under his arm. "I thought I heard something about putting in an order for supplies and writing up a structured training program."

"Yeah, that's the last item on the prep list." Cheyenne turned to the dark circle of light opening in front of Maleshi. "We don't have time for any of that."

"So you're gonna hand out a bunch of those devices no one knows how to use? Cheyenne, the board gave you an okay for training, not active field use."

"The board can suck it. I'm not waiting around for Van Lurig to take her sweet time weighing the pros and cons." She shrugged. "You're welcome to tag along."

"No. I'm here. I need to stay and make sure these guys have what they need to clean up and get things running as close to normal as they can." Rhynehart grimaced and shook his head. "You sure you know what you're doing?"

"No." Cheyenne sighed. "But I'm sure that if we don't do something right now, L'zar and whoever else has a hand in this is gonna catch us all with our pants down. This isn't about the Border anymore. This is something way bigger."

"Fine. I'll see you back on the base, then."

"Sure." With a final nod at the FRoE agent, Cheyenne stepped through the portal into the parking lot of her apartment complex.

Maleshi raised her eyebrows at Rhynehart. "Don't try going after him yourself and screw this up. I hope it's obvious how badly your people failed at that already."

She disappeared, and the portal closed behind her.

Rhynehart glared at the space where they'd been standing, then chucked the dampening vest on the ground and flipped his middle finger at nothing but air.

An orc guard stepped up behind him and grunted. "Sir?"

"Fuck." Rhynehart spun. "What?"

"Got a headcount after the explosion. Minor injuries, including one native. Everyone else is accounted for."

"Great."

The guard stared at him, his lips puckering around his jutting tusks. "So, what now?"

"Yeah, when I figure that out, I'll let you know."

CHAPTER FIFTY-EIGHT

Cheyenne forced herself not to slam the trunk of her Panamera, which would have been hard with both metal boxes of activators stacked in her arms anyway. She turned toward Maleshi and dropped them into the general's arms.

"I can't port us with an armful of tech," Maleshi muttered.

"I need a minute." Cheyenne pulled out her phone and found Ember's number, glancing briefly at the top floor of their apartment building. Her friend answered almost immediately.

"Hey. Everything okay?"

"Not really." Cheyenne turned away from the buildings. "Rez 9 was attacked, so I'm moving up the activator training. I'll be gone for the rest of the day, at least. Probably most of the night."

"Shit. Want me to come with you?"

"No. Right now, Em, keep watching Neros for me. If you're cool with that."

"Yeah. He hasn't looked away from the TV in the last hour." Ember snorted. "I'd probably feel a lot worse about using *Dexter* as a babysitter if the guy wasn't, you know, a few thousand years old or whatever."

"Well, whatever works. I'm with Maleshi, so if you need me—"

"Yeah, I'll call you."

"Thanks, Em."

"Sure. Cheyenne, did you catch the guy?"

The drow grimaced and shook her head. "No. It's L'zar."

The fae paused on the other end of the line, then whispered, "Fuck. Keep me updated."

"Yep." After hanging up, Cheyenne stuck her phone back in her pocket and took the activator trunks out of Maleshi's arms. "Think you can port us right onto the base?"

"I'm pretty sure I can manage." The general's grin wasn't nearly as playful as usual as she raised her hands to open another portal in the parking lot. "Do *you* think you can get a bunch of Earthborn magicals ready to face whatever he's doing?"

"I'm pretty sure I can manage."

"Touché." The general's lips moved soundlessly as she opened another window of dark shimmering light in front of them.

Cheyenne readjusted the trunks in her arms, gritted her teeth, and stepped through the portal into the huge parking lot of the FRoE compound halfway between Richmond and Washington, DC.

Maleshi stepped through without hesitation and snorted at the long line of shiny black FRoE vehicles parked beside them. "These guys take their all-black look to a whole new level, don't they?"

"I guess they're going for some kind of federal vibe. Not like it's all that successful."

A blaring siren sounded within the main compound building. Red and white lights flashed every twelve feet along the roof, and the siren grew louder. The garbled sound of shouting and agents jumping into action inside was muted through the thick walls and glass front doors.

Maleshi raised her eyebrows. "So, this is how they welcome their guests."

"I think that's for you." Cheyenne said, "You're breaking a few night-stalker records today. Come on."

The general chuckled wryly and followed Cheyenne toward the front doors of the compound. As soon as they reached the last vehicle in the line, a low hum rose from the asphalt beneath their feet, followed by a series of short echoing clicks. Then two panels separated in the asphalt, splitting open to launch a wall of crackling bright green fell energy in front of them.

In two seconds, the energy wall whipped around them and enclosed them in a ten-foot-square fell box. Cheyenne rolled her eyes and stared through the shimmering wall at the front doors of the compound. "What the hell are they doing?"

"Looks like they don't discriminate."

"Very funny."

The front doors burst open and a dozen FRoE agents barreled outside, all of them in full field gear with their fell rifles powering up, adding their high-pitched whine to the buzz and crackle of the fell cage around the drow and the nightstalker. Another side door burst open and clanged against the exterior wall on the east side of the building, letting out another flood of agents. They all ran toward the cage and their captured intruders, aiming weapons at the fuzzy forms of the two magicals inside.

"I'm pretty sure I could cut through this if I had to." Maleshi's claws extended from one hand as she stepped toward the energy wall. She brought two of them slowly down across the green fell surface, and sparks flew.

"Yeah, and you could cut through all these agents too." Cheyenne snorted. "It's not gonna come to that, okay? Let me handle it."

"Uh-huh." The general stepped back but didn't retract her claws as she scanned the squad of geared-up agents running toward them.

"Hands up!" The first agent slowed to a stop six feet from the front of the fell cage and raised his rifle. "Right now!"

The other agents fanned out around the fairly useless trap, their dampening helmets glinting in the late-afternoon light. The fell energy threw an eerie green glow across their shiny surfaces.

Cheyenne cocked her head. "You don't recognize me?"

"I said, hands up!"

She shrugged, glancing at the activator trunks in her arms. "Little hard to do right now. These are pretty valuable."

"What the hell is that?" a troll shouted, swinging the barrel of his fell rifle toward Maleshi.

"Cheyenne, I'm particularly unimpressed by your friends," the general muttered.

"You and me both." The drow scanned the faces behind the helmet visors and called out to the agents surrounding them as another wave came out of the compound. "This is General Maleshi Hi'et, and she's a friend."

"Bullshit. That was an unauthorized entrance."

Maleshi grinned at the agent. "I think 'portal' is the word you're looking for."

Cheyenne glared at her. "I said, let me handle it."

"And it's going so well."

"You're fucking kidding me," Grot growled, his voice cracking across the parking lot as the huge, boil-covered ogre stomped through the rows of agents surrounding the fell trap. "I knew it!"

"Jesus." Cheyenne rolled her eyes. "You have no clue what's going on, do you?"

He lowered his weapon to remove his helmet, chucked it on the ground, and swung his rifle up again to level it at her head. "I know exactly what's going on here. You thought you'd seize the moment and bring in backup for an attack."

Maleshi folded her arms. "Well, you've caught us. Foiled all our plans."

"Maleshi!"

"Hey, it talks." Grot sneered at the general and swung his weapon toward her. "Back away from the wall. Whatever you are."

"If you're going to threaten me, you warty cretin, at least have the wherewithal to call me what I am."

"We don't give a shit what you are," Malfi shouted, sidestepping around the side of the fell cage and training her weapon on the general. "Fact is, you're trespassing. And you're in a cage."

"What the hell?" Yurik stopped behind the rows of agents surrounding the crackling fell box and whipped off his helmet. "Cheyenne."

"Hey." She jerked her chin at him. "What gives?"

"How did you end up in there?" Bhandi shouted. The troll slapped the visor of her helmet to lift it and get a better look. "Damn, Goth drow. These the kinda friends you run around with on the outside?"

"The outside?" Maleshi raised an eyebrow at Cheyenne and snorted. "You got yourself in deep with these idiots."

Cheyenne ignored her and stepped closer to the cage wall. "Okay, everybody shut up and listen."

"Not this time, bitch." Grot approached the cage and raised his rifle higher, steadying the stock against his shoulder. "You're not coming in to tear us up from the inside out. You couldn't do it alone, and you sure as shit won't do it with that furry friend of yours."

Maleshi rolled her eyes. "I'm so offended."

"Somebody needs to turn off this fucking box," Cheyenne snarled.

"Nobody move," Grot roared, leering at her. "This drow's been lying through her fucking teeth the whole time. She just stepped in the wrong pile of shit."

A goblin leaned toward the ogre and muttered, "Want me to call it in to—"

"Fuck that, Belra. Let the drow rot in her cage like her goddamn daddy was supposed to." Grot snarled and adjusted his grip on his rifle. "Anyone else wanna see this traitor let out so she can slit all our throats?"

A good third of the agents closed in tighter around the fell box, weapons at the ready.

"What the hell is wrong with you guys?" Tate shouted. He holstered his fell pistol and pushed his way through the agents toward Grot. "If you keep this up, man, you're gonna be thrown in the brig."

"Don't fucking touch me." The huge ogre whirled and cracked the side of his fist against the tattooed troll's helmet. Tate staggered back, and the agents around them erupted in shouting, half in protest, the other half in encouragement.

Jamal stomped toward them and drew Tate away by clamping a huge hand on the troll's shoulder. "Time to give it up, Grot."

"No. She's brainwashed you morons into thinking she's here to help us. You can all go to hell."

"The board gave her access!" another agent shouted.

Grot swung his rifle toward Cheyenne again and snarled. "The board's been compromised too, you fucking idiots. Anybody else tries to change my mind, I'll blast a hole through this bitch's head right now."

Cheyenne cocked her head and glared at him. *Who the fuck thought it was a good idea to let them all out here to fight for command over this?*

Maleshi leaned toward her. "Would now be the right time?"

"No." Cheyenne bent to set the metal activator trunks at her feet and spread her arms. "I don't know how many times I have to repeat myself, but you guys need to listen!"

"Fuck you and your drow lies." Grot took another step toward the fell wall. "You're the one in the cage."

"We don't have time for this shit." She stepped back and scanned the asphalt around her.

"You'll have all the time you need when you're rotting in a Chateau D'rahl cell," Grot snarled, reaching toward the back of his belt for a pair of dampening cuffs. "That's exactly where you're headed now."

Cheyenne's activator pinpointed six different mechanisms beneath the asphalt, lighting them up in her vision with flashing orange arrows. She drowned out the sound of Grot's power trip and focused on the energy running beneath her feet, all six points of the security system she and Maleshi had tripped.

"You're done fucking around with this organization," Grot snarled. "I'm gonna make sure of it."

She selected the command prompt to deactivate the fell cage, then she reached out with her magic to find the thin threads of resistance in the ground beneath her and clenched both hands into fists. A series of loud snaps rose as the parking lot trembled. The deactivated security panels crunched beneath the weight of the earth closing around them all at once.

The green wall of fell light dropped with a few wayward sparks, and Cheyenne opened her eyes to stare at the furious, misguided ogre agent. "You done yet?"

CHAPTER FIFTY-NINE

"What the fuck?" Grot staggered back, his head bobbing wildly as he looked from Cheyenne to the broken fell cage and back. "How did you—"

"It doesn't matter how. I need you to quit running your mouth so I can say what I came here to say."

The ogre roared and raised his rifle again, launching a fell round at her head.

Cheyenne tossed up a shield and the fell attack ricocheted with a metallic ping. It sailed over the heads of the gathered agents, who ducked and backed away, shouting. "Any other day, asshole, I wouldn't be willing to ignore that. Don't try it again."

"Get her!" Before the ogre could squeeze the trigger again, Cheyenne reached out with her black tendrils, coiled them around his rifle, and jerked the thing out of his grip. Grot staggered forward, his yellow eyes wide as his weapon went sailing through the air to crash into one of the last FRoE vehicles in the line, denting the hood.

"Shut up and listen to me!"

Two other agents as stupid as Grot fired at her. Cheyenne snarled and raised another shield to deflect the shots before darting around the shimmering walls of black drow light toward the agents who'd stepped out of line. She reached toward the first one, jerked the goblin agent's rifle out of his hands with a telekinetic wave, and sent a second wave barreling toward his chest. He flew into the operatives gathered behind him, sending two of them to the ground beneath his weight.

The rest of the agents backed up, many of them lowering their weapons to stare at the drow literally fighting to be heard.

Grot roared and charged toward her. Cheyenne launched a spray of purple sparks at his mottled face to get him to back off, but he just roared, shook his head, and charged again.

Malfi fired a shot that went wide as she ran toward Cheyenne, and the fell round whizzed past Maleshi's head. The general spun to see it smash the windshield of a black SUV and snarled.

"Get her on the ground!" Grot shouted.

"You fucking moron!" Bhandi darted through the surrounding agents and trained her weapon on the ogre. "Cut it out, man!"

Malfi swung her weapon toward the troll and hissed, "Back the fuck up, bitch."

Three more agents, convinced this was a drow takeover, moved toward Cheyenne and fired. Before she had the chance to raise a shield or blast the agents out of the way, her black drow fire took over for her. Flames burst to life and flickered across every inch of her skin. The six fell shots hit the black fire with a crackle of green light and nothing more.

Strength she hadn't felt before flooded Cheyenne's veins. The heat of her drow magic flared with double the usual intensity up her spine, pulsing as the black fire around her swelled and expanded. Black flames appeared behind her eyes, and she drew in a shuddering breath of surprise and something else—dark, vengeful pleasure. *Holy shit.*

The agents stared at her and staggered away. "What the fuck is that?"

"I said, put her down!" Grot roared and reached toward Cheyenne with one huge, wart-covered hand. The dampening cuffs dangling from his other hand whipped toward her.

Cheyenne shot a thin stream of black flames toward the huge ogre. He stopped instantly in his tracks, frozen within her magic as a halo of dark fire blazed around him.

She sneered. "You're pathetic."

"Hey!" The other agents stared at the ogre, rigid within the circle of black fire. "Hey, what the fuck are you doing?"

"I said you need to listen." Cheyenne turned toward the four agents shouting at her. Without thinking about it or having to reach toward them, she shot more streams of black flames at Grot's followers and engulfed them too. Fell weapons clattered to the ground. An orc clutched at her throat as Cheyenne's power flooded through her body.

The drow raised both hands at her sides, and all five operatives captured within bubbles of black fire rose off the ground. Grot let out guttural sputters. The other agents struggled, kicking their legs feebly against nothing but air.

Malfi bellowed and ran toward the drow, squeezing the trigger of her fell rifle.

With a mere glance, Cheyenne sent the fell rounds whizzing away from her across the parking lot. Then black flames leaped from her body and engulfed the orc agent, stopping Malfi in her tracks. The orc's surprised scream cut out as the drow fire squeezed her throat and her lungs, pressing powerfully around her body and lifting her into the air with the others. Her rifle fell, cracking against the asphalt, and the six misinformed FRoE agents dangled six feet in the air, choking and bucking helplessly.

"Is this enough to get you to shut up?" Cheyenne called to them, raising her arms even higher. Part of her recognized the voice coming from her mouth, hers and yet not. The strength of her power flooded through her, overwhelming nearly every conscious thought. She could feel the magicals struggling in her grasp, their lifeforces waiting to be taken and used however she saw fit.

What the fuck am I doing?

"Cheyenne?" Yurik stepped forward, flinging his removed helmet to the ground. His eyes darted from one hovering black-fire-engulfed operative to the next. "I think you made your point."

She drew in another shuddering breath, feeling like her whole body was on fire with the power coursing through her.

"Yeah, you got their attention," Bhandi added, dropping her weapon to the asphalt and heading slowly toward the drow. "Maybe it's time to—"

Cheyenne's burning eyes darted toward the troll, who raised her hands in surrender and stopped.

"Okay, kid." Maleshi stepped toward her. "I think they get it."

"Not yet." Cheyenne reached toward Grot, who was hanging above the other startled agents. "I haven't finished."

Maleshi darted around her and grabbed the drow by both shoulders, then gave her a brisk shake. "Snap the fuck out of it, Cheyenne."

"You want to stand in my way too?" Cheyenne heard herself snarl at the general. She couldn't quite see Maleshi's face through the blazing flames consuming everything.

Maleshi snarled and stepped back. Her arm moved faster than anyone could see, but the echoing smack of her palm on Cheyenne's cheek was unmistakable.

The drow's head whipped back, and she blinked.

"Get it together!" the general growled.

"What?" The drow magic rippled up her spine and sputtered out, interrupted by the sting on her cheek she knew she should have felt a lot more. She lowered all six of the dangling agents to the asphalt again. They crumpled in heaps around her, and she wrested the black fire under her control again and snuffed it all out.

"Yeah. Like that." Maleshi turned to scan the operatives, who were groaning and coughing and gasping for air. She slapped the back of her hand against Cheyenne's arm and snorted. "Maybe rein that one in next time, huh?"

"Shit." Cheyenne dropped her arms to her sides, then stuffed her hands into the pockets of her trench coat.

"If you get a welt or something, sorry."

She looked at the general and shook her head. "I hardly felt it."

"Huh."

Grot snarled, pushed himself off the asphalt to support himself with his hands, and glared at her.

The parking lot grew eerily silent as the other agents she'd almost killed in midair caught their breath and rolled out of whatever positions they'd landed in.

I almost blew this whole thing before I even started.

Cheyenne scanned the shocked, disbelieving faces of the crowd of geared-up FRoE agents. "Anyone else wanna come at me before I can tell you what's going on?"

Bhandi barked a laugh. "That was fucking epic!"

Jamal grunted and offered Grot a hand up. The other ogre slapped his hand away and stood on his own, swaying when he got to his feet.

Tate folded his arms, scanned the agents around him, and nodded. "Go ahead. What's up?"

At least someone's willing to listen.

A small shudder of interrupted magic like an overwhelming itch that never fully turned into a sneeze skittered down Cheyenne's spine. She took another deep breath and studied the agents staring at her. "Listen up. I didn't come here to rip apart the FRoE. General Hi'et's with me as a friend. I'm here because we all need to be ready for what's coming."

"You mean, something worse than whatever the hell that was," a goblin shouted.

"No, that was badass." Bhandi pointed at the goblin. "And that wasn't even Cheyenne at full throttle. So shut the fuck up and listen, Krolig."

"This is bullshit," Grot snarled.

Cheyenne glared at him, and he quickly looked away. "Anyone who still thinks I'm here to take over the board or overthrow whatever you've got going on in this organization needs to open their eyes. That's a small-picture issue a few of you are hung up on, but it doesn't mean anything. If you're not ready to listen to me, you need to get lost or get fucked. We don't have time to screw around like this."

Another slow scan of the operatives' faces showed her confusion, excitement, and admiration, but no one said a word.

Good.

"I came here to help you guys because I need help. So do a lot of people who have no clue what's coming and even fewer means to stop it." Cheyenne approached the metal trunks on the asphalt, bent to flip up the latches on the top one, and opened the lid, then drew out one of the star activators. "You guys are getting geared up in a new way."

"Oh shit!" Bhandi laughed and pointed at the trunks. "Looks like ninja stars for all you bitches."

"Bhandi." Tate snorted and shook his head.

"What's she talking about?" a goblin asked, holstering her pistol.

Cheyenne stepped away from the open trunk and gestured at it. "Everybody gets one. That's all you need, and you're not the only agents getting a delivery today. Just take one. Then I'll run you through how they work."

Bhandi rubbed her hands together vigorously. "You assholes are in for it now."

Jamal turned toward the troll and growled. "You're getting annoying."

"What? A troll can't be excited about this?" She scoffed. "Come on, big guy. You know this is gonna be good."

As the agents slowly moved toward the open activator trunk in something resembling a line, Maleshi stepped up beside Cheyenne and leaned toward her. "You think they're gonna deal with this? Especially that big ugly bastard over there."

Cheyenne studied Grot, who stood back with his arms folded, presumably to wait until everyone else took an activator before subjecting himself to the same. "I think they're more afraid of me than of what they don't know. I'm not worried about the ogre. Maybe keep an eye on Malfi, though. If you want."

"The orc with the bad hair?" Maleshi dipped her head. "Yeah, it's always the ones in the background you gotta worry about the most."

"I'm not worried."

The general winked at Malfi when the orc turned her glare on the drow and the nightstalker who were speaking in hushed tones. "Yeah, but she should be."

CHAPTER SIXTY

"You guys are gonna lose your shit when you see what these things do." Bhandi folded her arms and sniggered. "You have no idea."

Yurik stepped up beside her, shaking his head. "Maybe let them figure it out for themselves, huh?"

She gestured at Cheyenne. "What does it look like I'm doing?"

Tate joined them, rubbing his hand vigorously over his bald head. "Looks like you're trying to take credit for this."

"Man, you're as stoked as I am. Shut up."

When every agent had taken a star activator and returned to stand in a line across the parking lot, Cheyenne stepped toward the trunk and peered inside. The remaining activators lit up in her vision, and the silver coil behind her ear brought up a remaining count of forty-two.

Seems like a lot less than fifty out here. Guess it's as good a start as I'm gonna get.

"What are these things?" a gremlin asked, grimacing at the activator before closing his hand around it and letting it fall to his side. "Doesn't have any kinda button."

"It's not a toy, Lug," Bhandi muttered.

"Looks more like the shit my mom sticks up on her mantle," another agent offered, receiving a round of hushed chuckles and sniggers.

"Earthborn." Maleshi clicked her tongue. "They have way too much to learn."

"Yeah, well, a crash course is gonna have to cut it." Cheyenne stepped away from the trunks. "These are activators. Advanced O'gúl tech I brought back with me from the other side."

"They're what?"

"Man, those backwoods natives don't have tech."

"Great. We got sloppy seconds from across the Border."

Cheyenne stared at the operatives and fought down her growing frustration. *Rein it in, Cheyenne. Patience. Not your strong suit, but the only thing that's gonna get this done.*

"What the hell are they for?" someone else shouted.

Jamal whirled and snarled at the agent. Those behind him stepped back, chuckling nervously.

"Hey, calm down, big guy."

"Shut up and let her explain, shitstain." The ogre cracked his knuckles while glaring at his fellow operatives.

"They go behind your ear," Cheyenne continued, raising her voice. "Hurts a little the first time, but after they sync with your magic, you shouldn't have any reason to take them off in the short-term. Every single one of you with an activator needs to figure out how to use these. We need to be ready. The next couple of days are gonna be rough."

"You still haven't told us what we're supposed to be ready for," a goblin shouted. "You know somebody who is trying to take over the FRoE?"

"Jesus, for the last fucking time, this isn't about the FRoE." Cheyenne shook her head. "So quit trying to guess and pay attention. Any other stupid questions?"

Nobody said a thing. Half the agents were staring at the star activators in their hands, trying to figure them out.

Cheyenne said, "We're taking this one step at a time." When no one moved, she stepped forward and spread her arms. "Put the damn things on, huh?"

"Behind your ear." Bhandi turned to the closest agents and showed them her activator.

Amidst doubtful grumbles and whispered objections no one was willing to offer any louder, the agents lifted the activators to their ears one by one and did as they were told.

A round of shouts, grunts, and pained grimaces rose from the operatives as the devices synced with their magic for the first time. An orc growled and stumbled to one knee. Bhandi threw her head back and cackled. "Look at you, Herman! Hurts like a bitch, huh?"

The orc blinked furiously, snarled, and pushed back up.

Maleshi chuckled. "Little cruder than I expected if I'm honest."

Cheyenne answered, "They're running on an Earthside program, okay? This is the best we have."

"If they can handle that pinch, kid, I guess they can handle what comes next."

Cheyenne waited until all the agents were back on their feet, blinking away the pain of the first piece of O'gúl tech any of them had ever had access to. "This is how things work on the other side. Most O'gúleesh have access to an activator at any given time. They're made to sync with your magic and whatever inherent abilities you have. They help you use your abilities like you were meant to, whether you've been Earthside your whole lives or not."

"When do we get that creepy black fire shit?" someone shouted.

Laughter and cheers rose across the parking lot.

Cheyenne looked at the gray sky and shook her head. "You don't. That one's mine. I have no idea what the rest of you are capable of. Bhandi did some freaky shit with a magnetic spell yesterday."

"Spells? We didn't sign up for this shit so we could go to magic class."

"Shut the hell up, Orden." Bhandi pointed at the agent. "Or I'll magnetize your ass."

Cheyenne dipped her head and pinched the bridge of her nose. *This is gonna take forever.*

"Bhandi."

"Yeah?"

"Get up here."

The troll grinned at Cheyenne, then realized she was serious and jumped to attention. "Shit. Yeah, okay."

"Tate, Yurik, Jamal. Come on." The drow waved them forward, and the three agents followed Bhandi toward the cracks in the asphalt and the drow beckoning to them.

Jamal growled over Grot's shoulder, waiting for the other ogre to step aside. For a minute, Cheyenne thought she'd have to break up another standoff, but Grot finally moved out of the way, flipping Jamal the bird as he stepped through the crowd of agents.

Yurik sniffed and swiped under his nose with the back of a hand. "We doing another demonstration?"

"Yeah. Go ahead and narrate it if you can. The best way to get through to the rest of these guys is if they hear it straight from you, right? Someone they trust."

"Don't worry about it." Bhandi clapped her hands. "We'll whip their asses into shape."

"Right. Maybe start with aiming away from your eager new students, huh?" Cheyenne clapped a hand on the troll woman's back and nodded. "Just to start."

Bhandi scoffed. "Tell that to the greenskin over here. He's the one with the aiming problem."

Yurik glared at her. "You try aiming a blast like that when everyone's always falling on top of you."

"Shut up." Tate whacked them both on their shoulders. Jamal grunted and folded his arms.

"All right, listen up, noobs." Bhandi stepped forward, clearly loving the limelight, and reached out with both hands, wiggling her fingers. "I know none of you dipshits had any idea that we can cast spells and shit, but now you're running with the big dogs."

Tate and Yurik rolled their eyes.

Cheyenne stepped away from her willing assistants to join Maleshi a few yards behind the open activator trunks. "I have no idea if this is gonna work, but it has to."

The general cocked her head with a knowing smile. "Good choice to let them teach themselves. Now they'll all be trying to one-up each other instead of hanging back, knowing they can't possibly do what the Black Flame's capable of."

Cheyenne stared at her. "They've never heard that name."

"They will after this. When everything's said and done." Maleshi's smile faded as she eyed the drow. "You okay, kid?"

"I'm fine."

"Good. 'Cause it looked like you were riding some kinda power trip back there for a minute."

"With the activators?"

Maleshi looked at the scowling Malfi, who was whispering to one of the doubting agents beside her. "With the small band of dedicated and highly deluded go-getters."

"Oh." Cheyenne shot a quick look at Grot, who was easy to find since he stood a good two feet above the tallest orc among the gathered agents. "That asshole's had it in for me since he saw my drow face."

"You sure put a stop to that, didn't you?"

"It won't happen again." Cheyenne watched the four agents she'd called up to teach the others. Everything Bhandi was shouting at her fellow operatives blended into a drone, including the punchline to the troll woman's joke that brought a wave of raucous laughter from others. "Not now that I know what it feels like."

"Stronger magic, huh?"

She turned to the general and nodded. "Yeah. The kind I didn't know I could tap into."

Maleshi nodded slowly. "I feel it too, kid. From the second we stepped onto that reservation today."

"I think it's the towers."

"That would be my guess, yeah."

"Can he do that?" Cheyenne grimaced at the memory of L'zar and Corian fighting within a blazing white portal halfway up Rez 9's tower. "Turn up the dial on magic flooding into Earth?"

The general shrugged. "None of us knew he could port all over the place like he did. It'd be pretty stupid of us to start doubting him now."

"It's not him, Maleshi. At least, not just L'zar. There's something else going on."

"I have to agree with you there." Maleshi sniggered. "And once you get your little squad up and running with those activators, we'll figure out what that is."

Cheyenne said, "Sooner's better than later. I have a feeling we're running way too low on time."

"That never stopped you before."

"Well, before, I didn't have to train a bunch of Earthborn magicals with overblown egos on how to use O'gúl tech to stop whatever L'zar's trying to do." *I still have no idea what that is.*

A cheer rose from the gathered agents as Jamal's spellcasting demonstration threw a glistening red-brown glow across the parking lot.

"Damn, big guy," a troll shouted. "You gonna pull out more than a few fireworks, or what?"

"Hey, don't get him started." Bhandi pointed at the jesting troll. "Jamal's got this shit on lock, man. What you wanna be careful about is Yurik with his goddamn exploding sun—whoa!"

She leaped away from a thick stream of black-green light bursting in swirling orbs from Grot's outstretched hands. The bulk of whatever spell he'd cast flashed past Bhandi and smashed into the last two SUVs in the long line of black vehicles. A wayward trail of bubbling magic struck Jamal's shoulder, making him grunt and lose concentration on his spell. The copper light in front of his hands exploded and rocketed into the air with a whistle before exploding.

"Shit." Cheyenne stalked away from Maleshi as shards of glass from the last of the blasted-out SUV windows tinkled onto the asphalt.

"Grot, you dumb fucking shit," Bhandi snarled at the huge ogre. "You almost hit me in the face! You know that?"

The ogre stared at his hands and let out a dark, disbelieving chuckle. "I wasn't even trying."

Jamal stared at the last bit of his interrupted spell fading in the sky and snorted. "Motherfucker."

"All right. Who threw the green blobs?" Cheyenne stopped on the other side of Jamal and folded her arms.

Bhandi leaned forward to peer around the big guy's body and stared at the drow in disbelief. "You saw who did it," she hissed.

"Now I'm asking." Cheyenne studied the gathered agents, most of whom studied all the information their new activators delivered across their vision. *Any second now, someone's gonna start drooling.*

The agents closest to Grot stepped away from the boil-and-wart-covered ogre and either nodded at him or flat-out pointed.

"Grot." Cheyenne raised her eyebrows as the ogre chuckled and looked away from his hands to meet her gaze.

"Yeah, it was me." He sneered at her. "What're you gonna do about it?"

"I'm gonna teach you how to control that shit so you hit an actual target and not your team members. 'Cause I guarantee you won't be the laughing ogre out in the field if you take another agent's head off with a powerful spell like that. If you screw this up when it's time to use these things, I won't be able to help you."

Grot's yellow eyes narrowed as he looked her up and down. "Fucking teach me, then."

"Damn." Bhandi looked at them and barked a laugh. "You mean, all it took for you two to play nice was for this mountain of an asshole to almost blast my face off?"

"Too bad it didn't get you to shut up, troll." Grot summoned the beginning of some other spell on his fingertips, his magic darting around his hands as they moved on their own to cast the spell. Tate and Yurik chuckled and clapped Bhandi on the back in macabre support.

"Kill it." Cheyenne snapped her fingers and pointed at the ogre.

"What?" The black-green light flared around the ogre's hand.

"I said, kill the spell. Should be a command prompt for that, like the one you picked to cast the damn thing."

Grot's eyes flitted back and forth as he searched through what his activator fed him. "What fucking prompt?"

"Holy shit, man." Yurik raised a hand to shield his eyes from the bright flashes of Grot's growing spell, and he stepped back. "Fucking turn it off."

"Easy for you to say, greenskin. You've had yours for how long?" Grot stepped back, both hands outstretched as his spell grew out of control. "Fuck. How do I—"

The spinning orbs of dark light burst from his hands and headed toward Cheyenne and her demonstrating friends. The newly equipped agents darted away from the grotesque ogre, shouting for the others to take cover.

Cheyenne raised a shield to block the first of the black-green orbs streaking toward her, then pivoted and aimed it at the sky. Grot's spell bounced off the wall of shimmering black light and careened into the air, but he couldn't get the rest of it under control. He roared and stomped forward, staring in horror at his hands as they blasted out an explosive spell he had no idea how to use.

Slipping into enhanced speed, Cheyenne darted around her shield and came up behind the ogre. She hopped up onto his back, wrapped one arm around his thick throat, and ripped the activator from behind his ear. Then she fell out of drow speed and released him.

Grot groaned, his eyelids fluttering violently, and staggered forward. The spell died instantly, throwing the two final black-green orbs to the asphalt at his feet. He opened his eyes, grunted, and searched his vision for the activator's feed that wasn't there. "What the fuck?"

She smacked his meaty arm and opened her hand to offer him his activator again. "That would be the manual off switch. I seriously hope you don't have to use it again."

The ogre snarled at the activator and snatched it. "Cheap trick."

"Not a trick, just advanced tech." She grinned at him, then returned to the agents who'd had four more days' practice with activators than the rest of them. *They're not up to par, either.*

"You all trained with firearms," she shouted to the gathered agents. "Explosives, and whatever fell gear this organization is handed by Mr. Weber's testing facilities, right?"

"Looks like he's done a shit job of it," someone shouted, and a round of laughter and jeering agreement rose from the operatives.

"Or maybe he's doing the best he can with what he has, like the rest of you. Fell weapons and ammunition have worked fine so far, right? Why bother figuring out how to use anything else?"

"Good fucking question."

Tate snapped his fingers and pointed at the agent who'd said it. "Shut it, Ollerson."

Cheyenne ignored them. "I'll tell you why. The weapons you know how to use wouldn't have done shit against what Colonel Thomas had planned for all of you. And don't play dumb; I know everybody's heard by now about the war machines."

A murmur of assent passed through the agents. Some of them turned and spat.

"If the FRoE wants to be the last line of defense along the Borders and on Earth, you guys need to seriously up your game." Cheyenne pointed at Grot as he stuck his activator behind his ear again and grew rigid as it synced back up with his magic. "That's what the activators are for, and the only magicals Earthside who have one got it from me. No one else is bringing them across. No one else can. If you can't figure out how to work with the most advanced tech on this side of the Border, you shouldn't be here."

She paced beside the line of her agent friends who'd tried and failed to demonstrate the activators. "None of you have been to the other side. You don't know how things work over there because this organization's been keeping you in the dark. I mean, it's owned by humans, after all."

Cheyenne spread her arms with a smile, and the operatives replied with another round of laughter, this time in agreement.

"The activators don't give you magic," she continued. "You already have it. They help you tap into it, and trust me when I say you all need serious help. If you can't learn how to use the command prompts to cast the spells you want and to cut them off when it's the wrong fucking time, like Agent What-Command-Prompt over there, feel free to hand the devices back. Or you can choose for me to take them from you. I'm not dishing out the most powerful tech on this side of the Border to a bunch of Earthborn magicals who'd rather stick with their big guns. Any questions?"

The agents were silent, staring at her with their full attention now.

"Good." Cheyenne scanned their faces as she paced back to the line of vehicles. "So, we're gonna start with the simple but apparently very confusing concept of cutting off spells halfway through. You're working *with* your activator, not *for* it. Anyone who can't keep their magic under control and lets off so much as a spark without me giving the go-ahead is gonna run laps around the base, and I mean the whole property, not just that tiny building back there."

A few agents chuckled at that, but most of them groaned or grimaced at the thought.

"You think you're some kinda drill sergeant at Basic?" Malfi shouted. "This is bullshit."

"This is your training." Cheyenne glared at the orc. "Like I said, if you have a problem with it, hand over that metal star behind your ear and get the fuck back inside."

Malfi snarled but didn't remove her activator.

"Great. Time's up for all the smart-ass remarks. Does everyone get the picture?"

"Sir, yes, sir!"

The dedicated shout from fifty FRoE agents was deafening as it echoed across the huge parking lot. Cheyenne blinked and scanned the agents' faces, looking for a smirk or a poorly hidden snigger and finding none. *They train them like soldiers, huh? I guess it's better than "Hail the Black Flame."*

She nodded. "Then get to work."

The agents spread out into a long line between their drow trainer and the front of the main building, ready to practice casting spells they wouldn't get to finish.

Maleshi folded her arms and watched Cheyenne walk down the line of Earthborn magicals with no clue how to use their new O'gúl tech. "Not a bad start, kid. Give 'em hell."

CHAPTER SIXTY-ONE

Four hours later, beneath the yellow-orange light of the huge streetlamps dotting the FRoE parking lot, they were still at it.

"Wait, wait." Cheyenne reached toward a goblin casting an overly complicated spell and grimaced. "What are you doing? Don't fight it."

"I'm not fighting," she growled. "It's too fucking big."

"Yeah, say that to the next threat you're up against in the field." Cheyenne summoned a black energy sphere in one hand and waved it in front of the agent's face. "You're not gonna let me blast you across the parking lot with this, are you?"

Silver light flashed at the goblin's fingertips, her eyes widening when she saw the drow's attack. "I thought you wanted me to hit those trees."

"I do. Better hurry up, though."

"Don't. I can't!"

"You say that to your targets when you're out there gunning them down with a rifle?" The crackling black sphere doubled in size. "I don't think so."

"I just got this damn thing, okay?"

"You've had it for four hours. Everyone else hit the trees." Cheyenne wracked her brain for the goblin's name. "You gotta be faster than that, Tani."

"I'm trying."

"Not hard enough." Cheyenne stalked toward the agent, turning up the power behind her energy sphere to make it as menacing as she could. *I have a whole new appreciation for everyone who tried to train me by being a dick.*

"Wait. I'll get it."

"I'm not waiting, Tani."

"Give me a goddamn minute!" The goblin snarled and turned to the trees surrounding the parking lot. The silver attack spell she'd tried to cast burst from her outstretched hands and cracked into three of the closest trees as Cheyenne launched her energy sphere. Tani spun back to the drow and threw her hand up in front of her face. Another burst of silver light hit the crackling black sphere and sent it into the sky.

They both stopped and stared at the magic that flew into the night sky before disappearing. Cheyenne cocked her head. "Well, that worked."

"Holy shit, Tani!" A gremlin agent turned to her and gestured at the trees. "You trying to take down the whole damn forest or what?"

"What?"

The three trees her spell had finally hit cracked even farther, splitting halfway up their trunks like she'd taken a chainsaw to them. Then the bare branches dropped toward the asphalt as the trees groaned and toppled over.

"Timber!" another agent shouted, laughing as he stepped away from the falling trees. They smashed into the edge of the parking lot, bouncing and cracking and sending splinters and smaller branches shooting in all directions.

Half the other agents stopped their activator-enhanced sparring to watch the wreckage and cheer. The other half didn't give a shit and kept fighting with spells.

"That's how to take down a few trees." Cheyenne brought a hand down on Tani's shoulder as she passed the goblin. "Time to practice on something that can move."

Tani stared at the felled trees, her mouth hanging open, then stalked off to find a sparring partner.

"Look at you." Maleshi approached the FRoE's new activator trainer and grinned. "Give you a team of willing subjects and a few hours, and you're building your own army."

Cheyenne said, "Yeah, the army that's gonna have to take a stand against L'zar. And I'll be the one to give the order."

"See? That sounds natural coming out of your mouth."

"It's not funny." Cheyenne stuck her hands in her pockets and gazed around the parking lot at the magical FRoE agents launching brilliant flashes of light at each other. Some of the attacks went wild, but most of them crashed against other agents' dampening vests with little more effect than knocking the targets backward. "They need to know how to do this anyway."

"I know, kid. We'll make sure they're ready, and then we'll do our damnedest to make sure they don't have to stand against him." Maleshi tossed her black hair over her shoulders. "I'm not convinced they'd last very long anyway."

"Well, at the very least, they'll be able to handle themselves in the field and with the refugees crossing over. It's a good start." *As long as we find L'zar first. All the activators in two worlds aren't gonna mean shit if he finishes whatever massive spell he's been gearing up for.* "Have you tried calling Corian again?"

Maleshi's smile faded. "More than once. Still no answer."

"Yeah, we need to—"

A car horn blared urgently on the far side of the parking lot as a black Jeep barreled toward them from the access road.

"Oh, look. Only took him four hours to get back."

Rhynehart's Jeep squealed to a stop fifty feet from the end of the vehicle line and he leaped out, slamming the door behind him.

"He looks pissed." Maleshi cocked her head. "Didn't know he was gonna miss all this action, did he?"

"Cheyenne." Tate jogged over to her, shooting a wary look at Rhynehart as the man stalked toward them with his fists clenched. "You want us to stop?"

"No, keep going. I'm just doing my job. So are you." She nodded at his sparring partner.

"Okay." With a final glance at Rhynehart, the tattooed troll headed back to the other agents, ducking a flying spear of blue magic. "Jesus, Kinol! You trying to take my head off with that thing?"

"Maybe."

Tate slapped his bald head. "No helmet, idiot. Come on."

Rhynehart stared after him and flinched away from a wayward spell hurtling across the parking lot on his right. He grimaced when the blazing red light glanced off the back of a black SUV, rocking the vehicle on its tires and leaving a massive dent in the back fender. "I didn't think you were coming here to train our agents to destroy FRoE property."

"Part of the deal." Cheyenne turned to look at him and shrugged. "Not enough space in the training wing, and honestly, I'd say replacing a few cars won't cost nearly as much as replacing all the tech in the training-room walls."

He bit down on his bottom lip and grunted. "Maybe."

"How'd it go at Rez 9?"

"How'd it go?" Rhynehart let out a bitter laugh. "The place is fucked. That's how it went. The system still hasn't come back online, so they're blind out there. We have radios and cell phones, but the rez-to-rez comms are down, and nobody has time to make a personal call for every little thing."

"Right. The other reservations going through the same thing?"

"Yeah. I did make a few calls before I headed out. It's the same shit everywhere. I have no idea how to fix one reservation, let alone a dozen."

Cheyenne looked at Maleshi. "We might be out later than I thought tonight."

"I'm following your lead, kid."

A vortex of purple energy burst across the parking lot, spinning and swirling like a cyclone before it crashed into the thick concrete base of one of the streetlights. The light buzzed and rained a shower of sparks on the asphalt, then the bulb shattered. A group of agents cheered.

"Looks like your plan went over well," Rhynehart muttered.

"It could be worse."

The glass front doors to the compound burst open, and out stormed a blustering red-faced Major Carson. "What in the torturous hell that's become my life is going on out here?"

"Did you know he was here?" Maleshi asked.

Cheyenne shook her head, watching Sir stomp across the parking lot, ducking wayward spells. "But I'm wondering why it took him so long to join us."

Then she saw Malfi stalking after the major, a leering grin curving around her orcish tusks.

"I thought you said you'd keep an eye on her."

Maleshi shrugged. "Whoops. Honestly, kid, I was focused on watching you rock this new position of yours."

"Great. Thanks so much."

"Halfling!" Sir stopped in the center of the parking lot and waved her forward. Behind him, Malfi stopped and folded her arms, looking way too full of herself.

Cheyenne asked, "Anyone wanna join me?"

"I think you're equipped to handle this one on your own," Rhynehart muttered.

Maleshi chuckled. "I'd be happy to. Lead the way, kid."

The drow headed toward Sir and Malfi, occasionally glancing at a particularly bright spell flying through the darkness. When she reached them, Sir's mustache was twitching. *Not a good sign. He knew this was gonna happen.*

"Major." She nodded at him and shot Malfi a warning glare.

"Don't 'Major' me, Cheyenne." Sir stepped back and gestured at the orc agent beside him. "I'm up in my goddamn office trying to figure out who shit the bed on a dozen of the closest reservations, and you know why I'm out here?"

Maleshi grinned at him. "To watch the show, I assume."

Sir looked the general up and down with a snort. He stepped away from her, vigorously rubbed his mustache beneath his nose, then cleared his throat. "I wasn't talking to you, lady."

"I'm flattered."

"What happened?" Cheyenne asked.

"That's what I'm asking you, Cheyenne." Sir jabbed a finger at Malfi again. "Because I'm hearing some real bullshit. I thought you said you were gonna train these agents with your fancy magic tech?"

"Yep."

"So why the hell haven't you gotten this one to fall in line?"

Malfi blinked in surprise and looked at the red-faced major beside her. "Sir?"

"You heard me." Grunting, he folded his arms and turned to the orc. "Go ahead. Tell her what you were so fucking excited to tell me. If it was important enough to interrupt my real goddamn work, it's important enough to repeat to your fucking superior."

Malfi glared at Cheyenne. "Permission to speak freely, Sir?"

"I should goddamn hope so."

The orc turned to him. "She's out here turning everyone against each other. Look at this!"

"Looks like a bunch of dumb twats blasting magic at each other, yeah."

"Sir, this isn't what we do. This drow appeared on base with this *thing*." Malfi gestured flippantly at Maleshi. "And then she hands out a bunch of metal stars she says are supposed to help us. It's some kinda brainwashing or something. No drow would show up here just to help us be better at our jobs. She's hiding something, and I don't trust her. That was why I came to you."

"Hiding something, huh?" Sir looked Cheyenne up and down. One of his eyes twitched. "Let me see your hands, drow."

Cheyenne spread her arms, stretching her empty hands out wide.

"Yeah, look at that." Sir pointed at her and turned to Malfi again. "She's hiding something, all right. Her fist in your goddamn face if you don't get this bullshit story out of your head and take orders like you were trained to do. That's your fucking job, agent!"

"Sir, I don't—"

"You don't understand? Let me make it simple for you." He stepped over to Malfi and leaned in. "I got in front of a fucking camera and told every agent, guard, and official in this organization that this drow is now one of us. As much as she can be, anyway. You trying to tell me I made an asshole of myself for no reason?"

"No, Sir."

"You accept one of those damn devices?"

The orc looked sharply at Cheyenne. "Yeah."

"Then get your head out of your ass and do what she tells you to do with it! Not that hard to understand. And if you try to undermine this objective again, I swear to whatever goddamn gods your native ancestors pray to, I will strip you of everything you have and toss you out on your dumb green ass. Understand?"

Malfi stared straight ahead, breathing slowly as her lower lip curled around her jutting tusks. "Sir."

"You're goddamn right. Now go make yourself useful and learn how to blow shit up the right way with the rest of your team!" Sir pointed behind him and glared at the agent.

Malfi grimaced and spun sharply away before heading toward the agents sparring with magic instead of fell weapons.

"Jesus H. Christmas." Sir ran a hand over his receding hairline and met Cheyenne's gaze.

She grinned at him. "That was unexpected."

"Don't get all mushy about it, halfling. I already apologized to you once. You're not getting another one."

"Why would I want an apology for that?"

"You goddamn shouldn't, that's why! You should be thanking me."

Cheyenne fought back a laugh. "Thanks, Major."

"Shut up."

Rhynehart approached them, glancing over his shoulder at the crackling wall of yellow and green light that raced across the parking lot, then darted into the sky and detonated for seemingly no reason.

"What took you so goddamn long?" Sir muttered.

"Wasn't sure what I'd be stepping into." Rhynehart tried to wipe a smile off his lips as he nodded at Major Carson. "Sir."

"Well, you stepped in it now, Captain. Why the hell wasn't I told training starts today?"

"We had to move up the timeline," Cheyenne explained.

"I'm dealing with thirteen reservations that up and disappeared from the system, Cheyenne. What fucking timeline?"

Cheyenne looked at Rhynehart. "You wanna tell him or should I?"

The captain grimaced. "Might be something to—"

"Fire in the hole!" an agent shouted, followed immediately by a deep-purple blast of magic crashing into the closest black SUV.

The spell consumed the vehicle in an instant, lifting it off its tires as the whole thing erupted in a mushroom cloud of purple magic and real flames exploding from the engine and the gas line. Glass and metal shreds flew in all directions, and the SUV slammed back down to the asphalt with a hiss as two of its tires burst.

"Oh shit!"

"Randy, what the fuck?"

"I did it!" Randy jumped up and down and pointed at the flaming wreckage. "I fucking did it!"

Sir grunted, his mustache glowing purple and yellow in the reflection of the explosion. "Some training."

"Yeah." Cheyenne stormed away from him and launched a spray of purple sparks into the air. "Everybody listen up!"

The laughter and excited jeers from the agents died. Fortunately, most of the spells started by a handful of agents winked out. One troll noticed the flickering chains of green light in his fingers hadn't disappeared, and he shook out his hand, trying to get rid of it. His other hand pounded the activator behind his ear, then he grimaced and the spell snuffed out.

At least they're figuring out how to shut it down.

Cheyenne pointed at the main building. "We're calling it a night. Good work for your first few hours, but you still have a long way to go. Get back to whatever you were doing, keep the activators on, and try not to blow up your rooms before you can figure out how to fully control those things, huh?"

The agents stared at her, waiting intently for the part of the speech she'd left out.

Sir growled and stomped toward her. "You heard her. You're fucking dismissed."

Trying to hide their amusement at Sir's embellished order, the agents nodded at Cheyenne and turned swiftly away, jostling each other as they headed back to the door to the main building.

"Cheyenne." Yurik jogged up to her, looking over his shoulder once at the retreating agents. "Hey, real quick—"

"Did you not fucking hear me?" Sir growled.

"Thanks, Major Carson," Cheyenne said, "I can handle it."

Sir grumbled something under his breath and folded his arms.

"I'm just checking." Yurik hesitantly reached up to touch the activator behind his ear and frowned at her. "Not like I'm trying to argue with you or anything."

Cheyenne snorted. "Just say it, man. I'm not gonna bite your head off."

The muscular goblin muttered, "Yeah, but *he* might."

"I think Sir's here more for backup than anything else. What's going on?"

Yurik rubbed the back of his neck. "You want us to keep these things on all the time?"

She shot him a playful frown. "That's a problem all of a sudden?"

"No. Hell, no. These things are awesome. I just was wondering, 'cause that's a whole lot of agents with magic and the ability to blast each other into pieces if someone gets pissed off."

"That's the point." Cheyenne nodded. "Not to get pissed off. Look, if we had more time, I'd tell everyone to only use these things for training. That's technically twenty-four-seven right now."

He studied her gaze and wrinkled his nose. "Something happen?"

"Kinda." Cheyenne wasn't quite sure what to do with her hands, so she stuck them in her pockets again. "Until I have more information, I don't wanna distract everybody. Just a bunch of conjecture at this point, you know?"

"Uh-huh." Yurik's eyes darted to Sir again. "He knows?"

"Not yet. We'll take care of it, all right? Go take a break. Do whatever you do at the end of a day here."

He snorted. "Nothing to write home about."

"Yeah, I figured. And maybe don't try that Obliterate thing of yours until we're back out here working on better control, huh?"

Yurik rolled his eyes and turned away. "Never gonna live that down."

"Because you haven't done it right yet!" Bhandi shouted from in front of the glass front doors.

"How the fuck did you hear that?"

The troll grinned and pointed at her ear. "Turns up the volume too, asshole."

"Shit."

"Hey, Cheyenne! You let us know if you need anything else."

"Yep." Cheyenne raised a hand at the cackling Bhandi as the troll slapped a hand on Yurik's shoulder and shoved him through the front doors.

"Those two?" Sir shook his head, staring after the agents Cheyenne pretty much considered her friends at this point. "You picked those two for that demonstration I heard about?"

She turned to the major and plastered on a fake grin. "Tate and Jamal too."

"They any better than the goblin who could bounce a quarter off his ass cheeks?"

Cheyenne and Rhynehart exchanged amused looks. "They do okay, yeah."

Maleshi leaned toward Sir and muttered, "That was an illuminating visual, Major."

Sir started and ducked away from her. "Don't fucking sneak up on me like that. Jesus."

The general chuckled and clasped her hands behind her back.

"I'd say we should go somewhere to hash all this out," Cheyenne added, "but Maleshi and I are gonna leave again, and I'm not a fan of tripping another alarm system when we head out."

"That was you, huh?" Sir raised an eyebrow and glared at the buckled asphalt where she'd destroyed the fell cage hours before. "Something tells me that alarm won't be doing shit for a few days."

"Repairs will have to wait longer than a few days, probably."

"Why the hell is that?" Sir barked out the question, but his eyes had widened in interest.

Cheyenne ran a hand through her hair. "Here's what I know about what's happening at the reservations."

CHAPTER SIXTY-TWO

After she explained to Sir what they'd seen at Rez 9 and shared her plans to distribute at least another fifty activators to magical FRoE agents and rez guards at the twelve reservations that had gone dark around Virginia, Sir looked like he was going to have an aneurism.

"I knew it!" He shoved a pudgy finger in her face and shook it. "I knew that fucking drow was up to something."

"Really?" Cheyenne stared at his finger until he lowered it. "Because then I'd have to ask why you didn't let any of us in on it."

Sir scoffed. "I'm not your personal secretary, Cheyenne. You can't run around like you own the place and expect everyone else to—"

Rhynehart cleared his throat.

"What?"

"We'll take care of it, Major."

Sir's upper lip twitched, then he backed away from Cheyenne and patted down his jacket pockets. "You sure as shit better. I'm up to my neck in phone calls trying to get those goddamn rez systems back online, and now I get to explain why five vehicles and half the fucking parking lot look like they got hit by a goddamn RPG party." He pulled a rattling bottle of pills from one of his pockets and growled when it dropped to the asphalt. "Dammit."

In the blink of an eye, Maleshi bent and picked it up to offer it to him.

Sir scowled at her, then snatched the bottle from her hands.

"You're welcome, Major."

"What, you want a fucking cookie?" He shook out two pills and popped them into his mouth, then looked her up and down as he swallowed. "Or maybe it's catnip for you, huh?"

"Very cute."

"I'll keep you guys updated." Cheyenne nodded and caught Maleshi's gaze. *She's gonna drive him up the wall.* "We have to get more activators out to magicals at the reservations and hope they can figure out enough on their own."

Sir grimaced and thumped a fist on his chest. "You mean you can't turn back time like fucking Santa Claus and drop down every chimney before sunrise?"

Everyone stared at him.

"Fine." The major headed toward the building. "You do what you gotta do. All this shit falls on your head if it hits the fan, halfling,"

"You know, there is a way to keep that from happening," she called after him. "Or at least to hold it off."

"Yeah, yeah. Fuck. I'll cover for you. Leave a goddamn glowing review of your fucked-up training methods with the board." Sir spun and pointed at her. "But if you need anything else after this, you go tell them yourself."

"Deal."

Grunting, Sir turned and jerked open the door. They watched him stomp across the lobby to the west wing and disappear down the hall.

"That went better than I expected." Rhynehart folded his arms. "I think you're starting to grow on him."

"I'm glad I can't say the same thing for him."

Maleshi chuckled. "I don't know, kid. You nailed that officer impression pretty well."

"What?"

"'Get lost or get fucked,' right?"

Rhynehart snorted. "You said that?"

Cheyenne rolled her eyes. "I was making it up as I went."

He slapped her arm with the back of his hand and nodded. "Yeah, you're doing fine. I'm sending you that list of the reservations on black-out, and I'm keeping my phone on."

"You'll hear from me."

Rhynehart turned to shoot her a crooked half-smile, then shoved his hands into his pockets as he headed for the front doors.

Maleshi snorted. "Time to blow this FRoE stand or what?"

"Yep." They returned to the metal activator trunks stacked behind the cracked asphalt and Cheyenne snorted. "You're gonna give him a heart attack if you keep that up. You know that, right?"

"You mean the soft-spoken man whose mustache has a life of its own?"

They chuckled softly as Cheyenne bent to close the lid of the top trunk and latch it. "I'm fairly sure that was his blood pressure medica-tion. Heard it straight from his wife." She lifted the trunks in both arms and stood. "Can't handle a lot of physical labor."

"How unfortunate for him." Maleshi studied the compound's lobby through the glass doors. "I enjoy making him jump."

"Well, maybe put the cat-and-mouse game on the back burner for now, huh?" Cheyenne's phone buzzed in her pocket, and she grimaced.

"Right pocket?"

"In my jacket. Yeah."

Maleshi pulled out Cheyenne's phone and skimmed the first line of the text. "We've got our first reservation right here. I hope they're expecting us."

"If they aren't, we'll have to deal with it."

"True." After pocketing Cheyenne's phone, the general raised both hands and opened another portal in the parking lot to take them to Rez 38.

As soon as the window of dark light opened, a weak alarm blazed from a speaker mounted on the building and another spinning light flashed. Maleshi pointed at it, and a silver streak of lightning hit the roof. The light and the speaker exploded in a shower of sparks and squealing metal. "They should fine-tune their security out here."

Shaking her head, Cheyenne stepped through the portal.

It took them five hours to hit all twelve reservations whose Border towers and FRoE systems had been affected by whatever L'zar had done. The first three took the longest because the agents and guards there hadn't been expecting them, but once the guards overseeing each reservation took the time to listen to Cheyenne explain the situation and to call Rhynehart for confirmation, they got on board with the plan, however doubtfully.

The fourth and fifth reservations were still cleaning up from unexplained explosions they'd incurred early that morning, and Cheyenne offered to help with a few quick spells to stack up the piles of rubble before she got the guards' full attention. By the time Maleshi ported them to the sixth stop, the agents and guards on duty had already been contacted through radio and a few scattered phone calls and were expecting a visit from the drow and the nightstalker and their trunks of metal four-pointed stars.

The only thing she could tell them before heading to the next place was, "Hand these out to your best ten agents and tell them to put them behind their ears. We'll contact you with more instructions."

Maleshi followed every time with a wink and added, "Maybe tell them to sit down before connecting."

The last three reservations had apparently been alerted to the process and already had ten agents and guards gathered to take the activators. Some of them even stuck them behind their ears before Cheyenne and Maleshi ported out again, but no one bombarded her with the questions she'd expected.

At least they can take orders and shut up about it. Hopefully, that lasts when I tell them what those next steps are.

When they finished, Maleshi ported them back into Cheyenne's living room. The drow gently lowered one empty trunk and then the other, which had twenty-two activators left inside, then looked at Neros, who was sprawled out and seemingly asleep on the couch. She straightened and smoothed her hair away from her face. "What time is it?"

Maleshi pulled out Cheyenne's phone and checked the home screen. "Five-oh-two. That's a.m."

With a snort, the drow held her hand out for her phone, and Maleshi passed it to her. "Seriously, thanks for your help with this."

"Well, I'd say it's the least I can do, but it's the only thing I can do right now, given the circumstances."

"Not for long." Cheyenne pocketed her phone and nodded. "We'll find them."

"Yes, we will." Maleshi turned and raised her hands to open another portal, then paused. "You did well today, kid. All things considered."

"I had help." Giving the general a tired smile, Cheyenne nodded at Maleshi's outstretched arms. "You going home?"

"Why? Is there another errand you needed me to run?" The general chuckled when Cheyenne rolled her eyes. "I'm not giving up on trying to find either of them, but I'm useless if I keep running on empty. I need some sleep. We both do."

"Yeah, I'm gonna go look through a few dark-web forums first. You know, just in case anybody's seen anything we can fit into this screwed-up puzzle. I don't think I'll be able to get to sleep for a while anyway."

"Whatever works. I'll let you know what I find."

"Same."

The general paused, cocking her head in thought, then flicked her silver gaze up to meet Cheyenne's. "There is a spell."

"For real?"

"Cheyenne, it's a long shot, and I mean longer than any of the other shots we've taken in the last few months."

Glancing at Neros, then at Ember's closed bedroom door, Cheyenne stepped over to Maleshi and lowered her voice. "Not like that's ever stopped us."

"Well, what's stopping us now is the shortage of supplies Earthside for this one. That and its complexity."

"Doesn't matter. Send me a list, and I'll start looking."

A small frown flashed across Maleshi's brow. "I'm not sure it's worth trying to find all the ingredients on our own. That by itself could take days."

"Well, then tell me the spell and send me a list. I'll look into it." Cheyenne cracked a smile, trying to make it look reassuring. "We won't be looking on our own. You know Corian was running the Borderlands forum, right?"

Maleshi chuckled weakly and rolled her eyes. "He tries so hard to be clever. *Borderlands*. No, Cheyenne. I had no idea."

"I think he might even have started it. Or Persh'al did, and Corian took over. I can access more O'gúleesh and Earthborn magicals through that than pretty much any other avenue, so send me the list and the name of the spell, okay? If anyone has the ingredients, I'll find them."

"Sure. I'll send it all to you before I turn in." Maleshi's hands worked quickly to cast one final portal in the living room, then she nodded and stepped through into her house without another word.

Once the portal closed, Cheyenne turned to Neros on the couch. Her cousin's chest rose and fell in a steady rhythm, his hands folded on top of his chest. *He doesn't need sleep, my ass.*

Smirking, she headed as quietly as she could up the steps to the loft.

CHAPTER SIXTY-THREE

Once she had Glenn powered up, Cheyenne switched to her VPN and dove into the dark web. Before she could get to Third Quarter Projections and the Borderlands forum, her phone buzzed in her pocket with the text from Maleshi.

She pulled it out and opened the text with the name of this spell and a list of seven ingredients she'd never heard of.

Of course, I haven't heard of them. I don't know shit about this stuff.

The name of the spell was promising: Soulstring.

Not like that can be confused for anything else.

She paused and stared at her phone, then almost slammed it down on her desk before stopping herself.

Cell phone. How could I be so stupid?

With the help of her activator, she input Corian's number and scoured through the cell phone company databases and cell tower ping-back records, trying to track his phone. It took her three minutes to find the list of his number's most recent incoming and outgoing calls. There were seven from that afternoon alone, all incoming, two from her number, and the other five from Maleshi. But nothing outgoing.

Cheyenne gritted her teeth and looked through the tower ping-backs. Corian's phone had stopped sending out signals at 3:02 p.m., and the last cell tower it had broadcast to was on the outskirts of DC. Technically that was yesterday. Right after she and Maleshi had seen L'zar and Corian battling each other in a blazing-white portal in the sky. After that, there was nothing.

No, no, no. Come on.

She widened her search, looking through records from the surrounding areas and even a fifty-mile radius beyond the rough half-circle of the thirteen Border towers that had gone haywire along the east coast. Nothing. Even when she expanded the search even farther to check the cell towers across the entire Continental US, Corian's phone had gone dark. No signal. No power.

So either it died, or L'zar got smart and decided to smash it.

Cheyenne scanned the data her activator pulled up for her in real-time, then selected the command prompt in her vision for an activity alert. If Corian's phone was off, not destroyed, and turned back on again, she'd know about it. Then she'd be able to find them both.

She sat back in her chair, rolled the thing closer to the desk, and got ready to switch gears.

Time to tap into the collective magical database on Earth.

When she clicked into the Borderlands forum, it took her a moment to fully understand what was happening.

The forum had descended into chaos, or at least as much chaos as a constantly monitored forum on the dark web could become.

The new topic threads, which were usually double-checked and approved by Corian as gu@rdi@n104 as the admin, had no longer been funneled through the process. The first page with the most recently opened topics updated every ten seconds with at least five newly opened threads every time, and the thread titles were just as chaotic.

What the hell is going on at the Border rezes?
> **New Magic Surges – I know you know what I'm talking about.**
> **Our Friendly Forum Admin left us here to rot.**
> **The Motherland is coming Earthside. Not a pretty picture.**

Even the pinned post, which had been stuck up there by someone who obviously wanted to make a splash, was against what Cheyenne had come to recognize as the purpose of the Borderlands forum:

It's the end of the fucking world. Get out while you can.

With an exasperated snort, Cheyenne clicked on it and read the initial post.

MacOn43: It's been three days. No gu@rdi@n104. He's abandoned us. You know who else has abandoned us? Pretty much anyone who ever had a chance to do anything useful for any of us natives on this side. We're fucked, plain and simple.

Border reservations are blowing up all over the place. And no, I don't mean virtually. Shit's getting weird. I've been trying to cast my own customized work, and for the last three days, nothing works. I almost took my cat's head off, and Mr. Pickles won't come out from under the bed.

We need to do something. For Mr. Pickles. For all of us.

Seriously, if anybody has a shred of hope left, share it here. Probably won't do much, but I'm running on empty.

We heard the Motherland was healed. I say it's shit. The Motherland is dying. So this is the end of both worlds. All you motherfuckers will be meeting the final deathflame any minute now. I'm serious.

I shouldn't even be here posting this. I should be getting my shit together. I should be running far, far away, only the farthest place I can get from here is over the fucking Border, and that's a deathtrap.

Save yourselves! I need to find Mr. Pickles. Maybe I'll build us both a funeral pyre and—

The post cut off at the end like the poster had up and vanished.

Except that the asshole pressed Enter to make the fucking post.

Cheyenne scrolled through the comments on the thread, which fell into two categories: half of the users telling the OP to go fuck himself for sowing panic like this, and the other half begging the OP to share some insight on what the hell was going on.

Screw this.

Her activator pulled up the access channel into the Borderlands forum, and after five minutes of darting down one security rabbit hole after another, she managed to hack into the forum and grant herself admin access. Then she tore down the pinned topic thread and put up her own to replace it.

Admin approval by ShyHand71. OP ShyHand71. Topic pinned on Nov 13th, 2021 at 5:23 a.m. Topic Title: gu@rdi@n104 Needs Your Help. So Do I.

ShyHand71: I know people are starting to freak out, but I want to remind everyone that losing our heads over this isn't going to get us anywhere. I've been a lurker for a while, but I can't do that anymore. So listen up.

gu@rdi@n104 is in serious trouble. I know him personally, and I know he's gone missing. It's related to the spike in magical energy everyone's been feeling the last few days and to the apparent attacks on the Border Reservations. I saw one of them with my own eyes on Rez 9 yesterday. Something big is coming, and I need your help. We need to find gu@rdi@n104.

A close friend of his told me about the Soulstring. If anyone has any information on this one or any of the ingredients needed to cast it, please reach out.

I know this sounds like another nutjob posting on the forum, but this is serious. You guys have questions. I have answers. Not all of them, but enough to put together a plan. Check the pinned topic stats. I have admin access, and there's a lot more I can do to help you guys if we help each other.

If anybody's interested in making a difference right now when it counts, reply here. I'm also sending this out as a forum-wide message. Anyone who gets back to me and is willing to pitch in will be added to a private chat.

Don't listen to some crackpot asshole saying all hope is lost. The Motherland isn't dying. I was just there. But we have to move quickly because whatever's coming is coming soon.

I'll be checking my DMs constantly. Don't hold back. gu@rdi@n104 needs us right now, and we all need each other.

Once that was posted, she copied the whole thing and did what the post said she'd do. A forum-wide message went out to every registered user Corian had approved as gu@rdi@n104. Cheyenne didn't have to wait long before the responses came rolling in.

Avis500: @ShyHand71 Go fuck yourself. This is obviously just trolling for sympathy. Go get some real friends and leave the rest of us to handle the end of the world in peace.

NativeBornBi@tch07: Fake! No way is this real. Who the fuck are you? Some admin, posting shit like this to get us all riled up. I'm with @Avis500. Get a life.

Masks4Dayz: Has anyone vetted @ShyHand71 beyond approval into the forum? I can only find two other posts by this dumbshit, and they all center around us "getting together." If this asshole isn't F-Force, I'll eat my eyeballs. Careful.

Jesus.

Cheyenne sat back in her chair and watched one comment after another pop up on her pinned post. They were all from delusional magicals who didn't want to open their eyes to the truth. She gave herself another ten minutes to watch the comments and wait for any replies that had value.

Eight more frightened, pissed-off, juvenile comments calling bullshit rolled in, then she got her first reply through the forum-wide messaging.

GCatLady44: @ShyHand71 You don't sound like a nutjob. I'm interested in more. Add me to that private chat.

She pulled up a new private chatroom before sending GCatLady44 an invite. It was accepted immediately.

Then she had to ignore the comments on her post as the responses on the open chat rolled in.

LongHaulMaster1132: This is why the Borderlands was started in the first place, right? So we can help each other. Add me too.

MessinwiththeMaster000: @ShyHand71 Takes a lot of balls to send out something like that. Yeah, it might look like some kind of

takeover, but it's a lot harder to try to give out hope when people are panicking than to cater to the panic. I believe you. Sign me up.

DarkWing8008: Best post I've seen in the last 72 hours. I'm in.

DoubleorN0thin: @ShyHand71 Thanks for the open invite. Add me to the private chat when you get a chance, please.

@Thing1OnP0int You might wanna look at this more closely. Kinda hard to sift through all the bullshit floating around in here the last few days.

Thing1OnP0int: @DoubleorN0thin Thanks. @Shyhand I'm down.

T0pH@t314: Endaru's balls, man. I'm so fucking tired of all these idiots posting like they have no idea how to interact with other sentient beings. You'd think if someone has the wherewithal to get this far on the dark web and navigate their way to the Borderlands, they'd have enough common sense to recognize a fellow native wanting to help the rest of us in troubled times. Maybe I'm old-school like that. @ShyHand71 I would love to be a part of whatever you're creating here. Please add me to the private chat, and I'm all ears. Virtually, of course.

Cheyenne let out a small, muffled laugh of disbelief and sent out invitations to the six new users who'd shown interest. They all accepted the private-chat invite immediately, but no one posted.

Everyone's waiting for me to make the next move. Who knew this many magicals were up and on the dark web at five-thirty in the morning?

She gathered her thoughts and sent out the first message in the private chat, which had a total of seven users plus her. Eight was a good start, and it would have to be good enough.

ShyHand71: Thanks for showing interest. I'll be focusing on this chat and any incoming messages from the forum-wide chat. The comments on the pinned post seem to be a little less open-minded. If anyone here catches interest from someone else, feel free to tag me so I can check them out.

Like I said in the pinned topic, gu@rdi@n104's missing. Honestly, I think someone took him against his will, and we need to find him. Anyone ever heard the name Corian Vedi'im?

The wait for responses felt like it lasted an eternity. *I put Corian's identity out on the dark web. Here's to leaning on good old-fashioned magical comradery and hoping nobody tries to use it against him.*

The private chat was filled with incoming messages.

DarkWing8008: Good idea to ignore the idiots commenting on your post directly. Some magicals never learn. Never heard that name, but I'm guessing that's gu@rdi@n104?

MessinwiththeMaster000: Don't recognize the name, but I have heard of the Soulstring. Might be able to help you with that.

GCatLady44: New name to me too. I'd love to get to the Q&A, though. @ShyHand71 Sounds like you know a hell of a lot more than most of these other dae'bruj on here.

T0pH@t314: I recognize the name. @private_chat_all I also believe it's in our best interest and his not to repeat that name here. Anyone who's looking would find it easy enough to trace, even in a private chat. I recommend we get together in person, if at all possible. @ShyHand71 I'm familiar with the Soulstring as well, though I think I may have something a bit easier for you to use. That spell's rather complicated, in my experience. How do we feel about a meetup?

DarkWing8008: If that's something we're going to consider, we should make sure this is all for real, right? @ShyHand71 I hate to be "one of those," but how do we know you are who you say you are? Or at least that you know what you claim to know. Meeting up with strangers and all that, right?

DoubleorN0thin: I second this. You caught our interest with your post, but still. Better safe than sorry.

GCatLady44: Or dead.

The chat fell virtually silent as everyone waited for Cheyenne to prove to them that she wasn't full of shit. *Guess now's as good a time as any. If they need more after a meet, I'll give them more.*

It took her five seconds to pull up a video clip from her activator as she had with the proof needed to convince Matthew Thomas that his program wasn't being used for benign technology. She cut it to a ten-second segment of what she'd seen at Rez 9, explosions with opalescent flames and the Border tower flickering in and out of solidity, though she cut it off right before Corian and L'zar appeared in their mid-air portal near the tower. She uploaded it to the private chat and sat back to wait.

Thing1OnP0int: Holy shit. Is this for real?

LongHaulMaster1132: It has to be. Can't doctor footage from a Border rez unless you've been there to grab the footage in the first place.

DarkWing8008: Looks clean to me. And fucking scary.

T0pH@t314: I appreciate this more than I can say. And I agree with @DarkWing8008. This is disturbing to say the least and it doesn't look tampered with. I stand by my original assertion that an in-person meeting would benefit all parties involved.

Cheyenne let out a sigh of relief and nodded. *Okay. One obstacle out of the way. As long as I can keep proving I'm not making all this shit up.*

ShyHand71: @T0pH@t314 I think that's probably the next best step. Any suggestions?

LongHaulMaster1132: Tbh, I didn't think this was gonna turn into a meetup irl. But I'm down.

Thing1OnP0int: Same.

DoubleorN0thin: Count me in.

DarkWing8008: Ditto.

T0pH@t314: Since time is of the essence, as @ShyHand71 said (and I also believe to be true), I'd like to propose we meet up this afternoon. I'm in Roanoke. Not sure how many of you are in the area. If anyone needs assistance getting here, I'm more than willing to purchase last-minute plane tickets. No strings attached. For anyone else in the area or who can make the drive, I'd say 3:00 p.m. EST would be the best time. After the lunch rush dies down and before rush-hour picks up. I also don't stay up much later than 8:00 p.m. Medical condition, you understand. But I do have a facility we can use to host this meetup. Completely neutral and private. Feel free to vet on your own time.

T0pH@t314 followed that up with a pinned GPS location and an address in Roanoke. Cheyenne's activator pulled up a satellite view of the area, and she zoomed in to see the address was an old book-binding factory that had been out of commission for the last twenty years at least.

ShyHand71: @T0pH@t314: You own this place?

T0pH@t314: I do.

DarkWing8008: Looks good to me.

LongHaulMaster1132: Perfect. I'm right by you in Penhook.

MessinwiththeMaster000: Doable. Good thing I'm off today.

Thing1OnP0int: I'll be there.

DoubleorN0thin: @T0pH@t314: I appreciate you putting yourself out there to host this thing. I'm in MI. Not sure I can make the drive in ten hours. I can buy my ticket, but it sounds like you have a few extra resources for getting those last-minute, so check your DMs. Thanks for everything. You too @ShyHand71 for putting this together.

GCatLady44: It'll be tight for me. If I leave now, I can make it at 3 or a little later. We all set on this, then? Just need confirmation, and I'll be out the door.

Cheyenne stared at the messages rolling through the private chat. *We're really doing this. Dark-web magicals meeting face to face in Roanoke. Good thing I've been brushing up on my people skills.*

She snorted, then hunched over and typed her reply.

ShyHand71: It's a yes from me too. Thanks @T0pH@t314 for the offer. And thanks to everyone else too. Not sure what I expected out of that post, but I'm glad to see magicals out there who can still think for themselves and want to help. gu@rdi@n104 will appreciate it too.

T0pH@t314: Then it's settled. Feel free to message me if you have any other questions. And come in on the north side if you would. The back parking lot. The front is a little outdated and not particularly suited for receiving visitors.

Cheyenne looked at the time and stifled a groan.

I've been up for twenty-one hours straight. Guess I'm making up for all the time I spent unconscious in the last week.

She clicked out of the Borderlands, logged off the dark web, and shut down her VPN, then let Glenn cycle through a shutdown before rolling her chair away from the desk. Looking away from her monitor made her dizzy, and her eyelids drooped when she passed a hand in front of her face and saw tracers floating behind it.

The second she stood and clamped her hand on the metal banister of the loft, Ember's bedroom door opened. The fae shuffled out of her room with a yawn as Cheyenne tried to step quietly down the staircase. "Morning. You're up early."

Cheyenne reached the bottom of the stairs and lifted her hand in a tired, unenthusiastic wave. "Never went to sleep."

"Seriously?"

"Yeah, Em. Got home about an hour ago."

"Wow. Then I guess it's 'good night' instead."

"Yeah. I'm gonna set an alarm, but if I'm not up by noon, you mind banging on my door?"

Ember yawned again and headed toward the coffee maker. "One wake-up call at twelve. You got it."

"Thanks."

Neros took a deep breath, blinked open his pale eyes, then shot up on the couch and looked around. "Cheyenne."

"I need to sleep, Neros."

"Did you not?"

"Nope. Looks like you finally figured out how nice it is, though. Please don't run off anywhere again, okay?"

"The Oracle is no longer a viable option, Cheyenne. I have no reason to."

Cheyenne's bedroom door closed behind her, and her cousin stared at it in confusion.

"She'll be fine." Ember waved dismissively in the direction of her friend's room and returned to brewing a fresh pot of coffee. "Hang tight for like twenty minutes, okay? Coffee first, then we'll figure out what we're doing today."

"Coffee." Neros smacked his lips and brushed his long white hair out of his face. "I would like to have coffee."

"No, this is high-octane stuff, Neros. But we have orange juice."

"Then I will have that." Neros stared at Cheyenne's bedroom door, then grabbed the remote off the coffee table. "And while I wait—"

The remote zipped out of his hand with a flash of violet light and sailed across the apartment. Ember caught it without looking and set it down on the counter beside the coffee maker. "I need twenty minutes and coffee. Thanks."

CHAPTER SIXTY-FOUR

Cheyenne woke with a start, covered in cold sweat, and tossed the covers off. The last image from her dream took at least thirty seconds to fade from her mind. *All my friends, all the Hangivol drow, Bianca, everyone sprawled across the scorched Earth after their battle with the blight and the Vessel's unleashed power. All of them dead while ash from the burned Nimlothar forest rained down around them.*

"Fuck."

She smoothed her sweat-dampened hair away from her face and let out a heavy breath. *Why can't I leave this shit behind me where it belongs?*

Her hand slapped the phone on the nightstand, and she blinked at the bright backlight when she checked the time. *Great. I wanted two more hours.*

Gazing around the darkness of her room, she dropped her phone on the mattress beside her and sank slowly back down on the pillow. *Just two more hours. No more dreams. I just want to sleep.*

"Neros, what the fuck?" Ember shouted in the living room. "You can't… Oh, my God, what are you doing?"

Cheyenne jumped out of bed, almost tripped over her trench coat lying on the floor, and jerked open the bedroom door.

Neros sat on the floor between the couch and the wall of windows, a knife in one hand and a pair of Ember's jeans in the other. All around him were scattered articles of clothing—pants, shirts, sweaters, socks, underwear, bras—and half of them had seen the sharp end of the kitchen knife.

"Dude. What the hell?" Cheyenne stalked over to him, glancing at the shreds of silk underwear draped over the back of one of the black leather recliners.

"Fuck." Ember spread her arms and stared around their apartment at her scattered clothes. "This is, like, everything I own. What were you thinking? I can't right now. I just can't."

Cheyenne stopped in front of her cousin and scowled at him as she extended her open hand. "Knife."

Neros blinked up at her and handed over the knife. "I don't understand."

"You don't understand what's wrong with this picture?" Ember barked a crazed laugh. "You know who cuts up people's clothes like this? Psychopaths, that's who."

"Em!"

"No, seriously. What the hell are you trying to do?"

"I wanted to see how they were put together." Neros shrugged. "The craftsmanship isn't particularly impressive."

"Yeah, well, you didn't do shit to improve that, did you? How many things did you need to cut up to understand how they're put together?"

The drow lifted the pair of jeans out of his lap and shrugged. "All of them."

"Come on!"

Cheyenne headed quickly back to the kitchen and dropped the knife into the open drawer below the counter, then slammed it shut with a bang. Her activator pulled up a command prompt for a locking spell, which she almost accepted but didn't. *A spell won't keep him out. We need physical locks.*

"What is wrong with you?" Ember shouted.

"I merely wanted to understand."

"Sure. Okay. Great. But you can't cut things open to understand them. Jesus, next it's gonna be small animals gutted and scattered all over the place because you wanna know more about Earthside creatures!"

"Knives are off-limits," Cheyenne muttered as she headed back into the living room.

"That's it? Just off-limits?" Ember grabbed the back of the couch and leaned over it. "Cheyenne, I'm sorry. I woke you up, didn't I?"

"No, I was already awake." Cheyenne folded her arms and stared at her cousin. "But this isn't what anyone wants to wake up to."

Neros searched her gaze and lifted his chin. "Dreams again?"

"What?"

"You are plagued by dreams, Cheyenne. I can see it." He raised a hand and stretched long, slender fingers toward her. "All over your face. I told you to release it."

"Yeah, we're not talking about my dreams. Ever." She turned to look at Ember. "How long was he—"

"I jumped in the shower." Ember closed her eyes. "He was watching TV, so I took a shower and blow-dried my hair. I come out, and all my drawers are open, and all my clothes are out here with this crazy asshole, already in pieces." She grabbed a button-up shirt off the back of the couch, holding it by the collar, and slid her hand through the huge slash down the middle. "What's the point of this, huh? If you wanted to cut open the seams, I'd get that, but down the middle?"

Neros blinked at her. "The buttons fell off when I did that. They were not sewn on well."

"Oh, my God." Ember's gaze flicked to Cheyenne. "I can't do this. I'm sorry. I know it's just stuff, but I can't—"

Neros took a deep breath and pushed to his feet. "I apologize for upsetting you, Ember. That was not my intention."

"You didn't think that one through very well, did you?"

He stared at the fae and slowly raised a hand before snapping his fingers. A sound like scissors cutting through paper filled the living room, and the shredded articles of Ember's clothing sewed themselves back together in two seconds.

Ember jerked her hand through the rip in her button-down shirt before a fae hand was added to the garment, then held the shirt out in both hands and blinked. "Okay. You could've started with that."

Cheyenne eyed her cousin. "As easy as that, huh? Snapping your fingers?"

"You sound frustrated, Cheyenne."

"Out of all the things you could've done to help us, you choose cutting up Ember's clothes and putting them back together again. That's it?"

Neros stared blankly at her. "I wanted to help."

"How about helping us find Corian, huh? Or L'zar? Maybe you can snap your fingers and summon them into the living room with us. That'd be great. You know, just reach up into the air, pluck a few threads, and bring everybody back to life. The useful stuff."

"That was already done and is no longer necessary."

"What?" Ember slapped her shirt on the back of the couch again and looked at Cheyenne. "Who died?"

"Nobody." Everybody. Cheyenne dropped into the closest recliner, ignoring the pairs of Ember's reassembled underwear hanging over the back. She closed her eyes and dropped her head against the cushion.

Her cousin stood where he was and looked her over. "You did not tell your friend."

"Neros, shut up."

"Cheyenne." Ember looked at them, then walked around the side of the couch and sat. "What's he talking about?"

"It doesn't matter. It's all over."

"You need to release it," Neros added. "Which you have not done."

"I can't!" Cheyenne's eyes flew open, and she stared at the ceiling.

"Seriously." Ember cleared her throat. "We're talking about somebody coming back to life, and I didn't even know somebody died. I'm ready for an explanation whenever you are."

"Jesus." Rubbing her hands over her face, Cheyenne sat up in her chair and glared at her cousin. "You have a real talent for bringing everything out in the open where no one wants it. You know that?"

"Thank you."

She blinked at him, then looked at Ember. "I didn't tell you 'cause I didn't wanna freak you out."

Ember let out a nervous chuckle. "It's a little too late for that now, don't you think?"

"Neros."

"Cheyenne."

"Be honest with me right now. Can you find Corian or L'zar? Or both?"

"I cannot see beyond my own eyes, cousin." Neros gestured at the scattered piles of Ember's clothes. "This, I can see. And I mended it. But something has hidden the Weave from me in your world."

"That's a no, then?"

"Correct."

Cheyenne buried her face in her hands and took a deep breath. When she looked at Ember, her friend was still staring at her. "Okay, look. I didn't tell you before because it didn't matter. We got rid of the blight. We healed the Nimlothar. I'm the only one who remembers anything because I'm the only one who—"

"Who what?"

"I'm the only one who survived, Em." A long, shuddering sigh escaped the drow, and she couldn't quite bring herself to look Ember in the eye. "When we went out to burn the trees. I was the only one left."

Ember shot her a disbelieving smile. "I don't get it."

"Everyone else died. I think it was Bianca as the Vessel or whatever, but that's what happened. She blasted the poison right out of me, and when I woke up, everyone was dead."

"No." Ember's smile widened, then faded when she realized her friend wasn't joking. "You're serious?"

"Well, I know this sounds like something I'd be into. Death and destruction and drow darkness or whatever." Cheyenne ran a hand through her hair and finally met the fae's gaze again. "Turns out it's not as awesome as it sounds."

"Wait. You're telling me I died?"

"All of you. Corian. Maleshi. The goblins." Cheyenne swallowed thickly. "Bianca. Everyone who was there. All the drow. It was just me."

"She completed her pattern in the Weave," Neros added.

Both women gave him scathing looks, and he clasped his hands behind his back, seemingly unaffected by their irritation.

"That doesn't make any sense," Ember whispered. "I don't feel like I died."

"Probably a side effect of being brought back to life by an Olfarím who popped in for a little fun playing god. No big deal."

"Cheyenne."

"See? There's no point in telling anyone because for everyone else, it's like it never happened. So forget it."

"That's not gonna be as easy as you make it sound."

Cheyenne grimaced. "Yeah, I know."

"You haven't told anybody?"

"Just you. And I'm sure that if we don't find L'zar and Corian before my mad-drow father finishes whatever he's planning, I'll be living that day all over again, except this time, it'll be a lot bigger. And without an Olfarím to save the day after giving me a pat on the back and an 'attagirl.'"

"Shit." Ember slowly straightened, then leaned back against the couch. "Why wouldn't you tell me something like that?"

"Because it's highly disturbing and is still giving me nightmares. I guess I figured I'd spare you and everyone else from the gory details."

"That's a lot to carry."

"I'm fine, Em."

"Obviously not if you're still having nightmares."

Cheyenne closed her eyes. "They'll go away eventually."

"Not until you release it," Neros added.

"You've been saying the same thing over and over like I didn't hear you the first time."

"Cheyenne, if you do not let yourself move past what is no longer serving you, you will not be prepared for what you must still do."

"How do you know what I must do?" She sat up quickly and glared at her cousin. "You said you can't read the Weave here, so are you giving me some kind of Nor'ieth prophecy, or are you trying your hand as a therapist?"

Neros spread his arms and dipped his head. "I am reminding you of your strength, Cheyenne. Which you will need if L'zar is as involved in the changing tides as you believe he is."

"Changing tides?" Ember gave a small, confused smile. "You mean, the problems at the Border Reservations?"

"Okay." Cheyenne pinched the bridge of her nose and forced herself to calm down. "I have a lot to catch you up on."

CHAPTER SIXTY-FIVE

By the time Cheyenne had finished telling Ember what she and Maleshi had seen at Rez 9, that they'd spent all night handing out activators to FRoE agents at the base and on the malfunctioning Border reservations, and about the plans she'd made with a bunch of strangers from the Borderlands forum, she was ready to go lie back down and try to sleep off the knot her gut was in.

Neros had laid down on the hardwood floor beside the wall of windows and stretched out, arms and legs nearly touching the furniture and the windows on the other side. Thankfully, he didn't offer any more useless suggestions for Cheyenne's mental health, and Ember listened intently from the couch.

"And I'm supposed to be in Roanoke at three." Cheyenne's alarm went off in her bedroom, and she stood from the recliner. "That's my wake-up call."

"You're leaving right now?"

"After I eat something." Cheyenne headed into her room to grab her phone and found her cousin and her friend right where she'd left them in the living room. "You hungry?"

Ember choked out a wry laugh. "Not anymore."

"I'm sorry, Em. I should've told you everything sooner."

"The rez stuff, I understand. You didn't have a chance. It's the dying part I can't quite get over."

"I know. That's why I didn't tell you."

"I'm glad you did." Ember drummed her fingers on her thighs and gazed around their clothing-strewn living room. "I think."

Cheyenne headed for the kitchen, took a quick peek into the cabinets and the fridge, then opted for a peanut butter and jelly sandwich. Ember listened to her friend opening jars and taking down a plate, then stood and stepped over Neros to join the other drow at the kitchen island.

"I'm happy to make you one." Cheyenne pointed at the fae with a jelly-covered knife. "While I'm here."

"No, thanks." Ember grabbed the edge of the island's countertop. "But I wanna come with you to this meeting. You know, with your dark-web friends."

Cheyenne snorted. "I wouldn't call them that. And honestly, I think I should go alone for this one. Otherwise, I'd call Maleshi again and have her port me to Roanoke in a few hours."

"What, like you need a secret password to get in?"

"Very funny." Cheyenne pressed the slices of jellied and peanut-buttered bread together and licked the end of the knife, then tossed it into the sink. "There's enough highly valued privacy to go around when you're on a forum like the Borderlands. I didn't expect anyone to want to meet up in person, but I guess I made a convincing enough case."

"How'd you do that?"

"Dropped Corian's name and uploaded a video clip of what I saw at Rez 9 yesterday."

"Not the part with Corian and L'zar fighting each other, though, right?"

"No, Em. If they're still down to hear me out when we see each other, that fun little reveal will come later. But this is one of those things where there isn't a lot of trust to start with, and if you come, Neros has to tag along, and I didn't tell anyone I was bringing friends. Sorry."

"No, I get it." Ember looked over her shoulder at Neros, who was still sprawled on the floor. "I can't wait 'til we get to send him home."

"First thing on my list, Em. You know, after all this other shit."

Cheyenne took a huge bite of her sandwich and stared at her prone cousin as she chewed. *Hopefully, nothing else life- or world-threatening pops up before that.*

The pale-skinned drow on the floor slowly tilted his head back and forth. "Can you feel it?"

Ember and Cheyenne looked at each other, and the drow shook her head. "Feel what?"

"Like a dam has been opened. It grows stronger, cousin."

Tapping her fingers on the countertop, Ember widened her eyes. "You have any idea what he's talking about?"

"Magic. Right?"

Neros said, "All of it."

"Yeah, I can feel it." Cheyenne took another bite and gave up hoping Ember wouldn't ask any more questions when her friend peered expectantly at her. "On the FRoE base yesterday. I was trying to make a point with a wart-faced ogre and his posse."

Ember snorted. "Posse. Paints a perfect image."

"I might've gotten a little carried away with it. If you feel your magic turning up to a thousand percent, you're not the only one."

"You said the magicals on Rez 9 were freaking out about their magic too."

"Yeah. And there were a few posts about it on the Borderlands forum."

Ember stared at Cheyenne's sandwich. "So it's affecting everybody."

"That's what I mean, Em. Whatever L'zar's trying to do, it's big." Cheyenne stuck the rest of her sandwich in her mouth and nodded at her cousin. "Maybe it'll keep him from conducting any more experiments."

"I hope so." Ember pointed at the silverware drawer, which opened with a flash of violet light. Another butter knife sailed past Cheyenne's head and into the fae's hand, and she grinned. "Sandwich looked good."

"Yeah, it was."

"Neros, you want a PB&J?"

"Is that like the juice that was orange this morning?"

"No, it's food. Forget it. I'll make you one."

Cheyenne gave her friend a sympathetic smile before sticking her plate in the sink. "I know you didn't sign up for babysitting duty."

"But you're paying the bills and letting me live here for free." Ember shrugged as she pulled out bread for two sandwiches. "And I'm your *Nós Aní*. I guess it's part of the job."

"Still. Thanks." Cheyenne eyed her cousin as she headed for her room. When she came back out with her trench coat in hand, Neros was still lying there, eyes closed, one hand lifted in the air as his fingers twisted slowly above him. "Seriously, Neros. No more experiments, okay?"

"As you wish."

"Oh, hey." Ember turned to point at her friend with the butter knife. "Maybe he can help me pick out that bistro table. And put it together if we have to. Better to create than destroy, right?"

Cheyenne squatted in front of the metal trunk with the remaining twenty-two activators and unloaded them into her jacket pockets. "Isn't it 'Easier to destroy than to create?'"

"Not for the point I'm trying to make, thanks."

Closing the second empty trunk, Cheyenne rose with her pockets full of activators and nodded. "Call me if you need anything."

"Yeah, that's kind of a given at this point. Go meet your internet friends."

"Right." Cheyenne stepped out of the apartment, ready to make the drive to Roanoke to meet a bunch of strangers she hoped were interested in helping her. *And that they can. Out of all the weird meetings I've had in the last few months, this one'll probably take the cake.*

At 2:51 p.m., Cheyenne parked her Panamera across the street from the address T0pH@t314 had given and stepped into the brisk afternoon air. The gray sky and quiet street made the whole neighborhood seem as empty as she imagined the old book-binding factory would be. Even the chirp of her car's automatic locks seemed strangely loud as she crossed the street and headed for the building.

She'd parked on the south side to give herself a viable excuse to walk around the property and give it a quick once over. Her activator pulled up a simple data stream coming from one security camera on the south side of the building and another on the north.

Regular security for what's pretty much another abandoned warehouse? Probably not. Persh'al should've had cameras on his.

As she walked down the cement path along the west wall, she

studied the brick exterior and found her vision clearing away the building materials to show her the figures inside the room. Four of them sat in the middle of the main room, two goblins and an orc, based on the colors of their glowing outlines, and a magical with a bright pink outline, which she hadn't seen before.

At least I'm not early and not the last one.

Cheyenne scanned the rest of the building but didn't see any other magicals' outlines. Her activator didn't pick up on any other tech lying in wait beyond the two security cameras either. Then she walked down the wall of the building, turned to the north-facing wall, and found the metal door facing the back parking lot. She knocked three times and waited.

The glowing pink outline inside stood and grew larger and brighter as the magical approached the door. She was surprised to find an old man on the other side when it opened. He was in his late seventies, wrinkled face, silver-framed glasses, and a bald head covered in age spots, and his blue eyes glistened as he studied her without the expression of shock and distaste she usually got from humans of all ages.

"Can I help you?"

"Hi." Cheyenne tried to smile. *We should've settled on a password.* "I had a meeting scheduled here to go over Third Quarter Projections."

The old man smiled back, though it was tinged with a little extra suspicion. "When did you schedule this meeting?"

"This morning."

"Excellent." He grinned and opened the door for her to come in. "Please. Join us."

Cheyenne stepped into the old book-binding factory and looked around as the man shut the door behind her. The place had been cleared out except for the eight chairs arranged in a semi-circle in the center of the main room. Steel beams crossed below the ceiling, giving it an open, dusty feel. Despite how long the place had been out of commission, she could still smell the warm, earthy scent of paper and a lingering trace of glue and ink.

"Are you T0pH@t314?"

The man chuckled and waved her off, his shoulders slightly stooped as he headed back to the chairs. "If that's what you want to call me for now, that's fine. I'm sure we'll make the proper introductions in time.

Though I will ask you, as I've asked the others, to keep your aliases to yourself until we're all here. That way, we're all coming into this at the same time without any preconceived notions of each other."

Cheyenne stuck her hands in her pockets and followed him to the chair. "Except you, right?"

"Ha. Indeed. It's a little difficult to maintain anonymity when you're here at one of my facilities, isn't it?" He lowered himself into the chair on one end of the circle with a groan. "And illusions stay on for now if you don't mind."

"It's your factory." Cheyenne took the chair on the other end of the half-circle and nodded at the three other magicals, who were all wearing human illusions as well. "Hey."

"'Sup." A guy in his last twenties who looked like every pizza delivery driver she'd ever met at her front door jerked his chin at her.

The woman sitting two chairs away from him looked like she'd never been in on a secret meeting in her life. Her blonde hair was pulled back in a tight, neat bun above a tasteful maroon blazer and matching pencil skirt. She crossed her ankles demurely in front of her, functional brown pumps kissing the dusty cement floor, and she clutched her matching brown handbag close to her chest as she looked at Cheyenne.

The magical sitting close to the old man could have hopped right out of an eighteen-wheeler before joining them here. Tufts of black hair poked out between his ears and the bottom of his camo trucker hat, and the left breast pocket of his bomber jacket had Terry embroidered over it in bright red thread.

Cheyenne nodded at him and glanced at his unintended nametag. "Kinda defeats the purpose of anonymity, right?"

The trucker looked down at his jacket and grunted. "Got this from the Goodwill. Just don't call me Terry, and we'll be fine."

"Right."

The pizza guy leaned forward and propped his forearms on his thighs, squinting as he looked Cheyenne up and down. "You chose that illusion? I mean, with all the piercings and the makeup."

She raised her eyebrows and cocked her head. "Something like that."

"Otherwise, that'd be a hell of a lot to keep up, right? And I heard that shit through the middle of your nose hurts like a bitch."

"Huh. I didn't feel a thing, honestly."

"Oh, shit. That's all real?"

Cheyenne sat back in the folding metal chair and crossed one black Van over the other, her hands still in her pockets. "Yep."

"Damn. That's serious commitment. I mean, I can't remember the last time I cut my hair, but who gives a shit when everybody else in this world sees—"

A brisk knock came at the door, and the purse lady jumped in her chair.

"Everyone always comes at the last minute, don't they?" The old man grunted as he pushed to his feet again and headed across the room. "Should've set a chair by the door."

"I gotcha." Not-Terry stood and grabbed the old man's chair before following him.

Two other magicals stood outside and answered the same series of questions before being let in.

"Have a seat, please." The old man gestured at the center of the warehouse and sat again. "All aliases off the table for now. We're waiting for one more, then we can start putting names to faces. Real or virtual, I suppose."

Trucker stepped back and eyed the newcomers warily as they headed for the circle of chairs. "Y'all come together?"

The man in his mid-thirties wearing a newsboy cap dipped his head. "Yep."

"Y'all know each other personally?"

The woman who took her seat behind Newsboy looked at Trucker and folded her hands in her lap. "Is that a problem?"

"No. Kinda defeats the old guy's talk 'bout keepin' it anonymous, but I'd reckon y'all were hidin' somethin' if you'd said no."

"True that." Pizza Boy folded his arms and stared at the two newest members. "You two related or what?"

"If you don't mind," the old guy called from his chair beside the back door, "I'd rather we wait with the personal questions until everyone has arrived and we're all sitting down."

There was another knock, and he sighed before rising again to answer. "May I help you?"

"Hi. I have a reservation for nine, but only eight of us are showing up."

Cheyenne turned in her chair to face the door, but the old man was still blocking whoever stood outside. *Why do I recognize her voice?*

The old man chuckled. "Clever. You're number eight, my dear. So please, come on in, and we can begin."

When the woman stepped into the warehouse, Cheyenne sat straighter in her chair. "What?"

It was one of her students, Tori something. The chick with half her head shaved who almost rivaled Cheyenne when it came to writing programs and digging up the right kind of information.

Tori's eyes widened when she saw Cheyenne. "Hey."

"Hey." She couldn't help but give a surprised laugh. "I had no idea."

"I figured." Tori shrugged and readjusted the strap of her red-and-black flannel tote over her shoulder. "Didn't know you were in on this, or I would've reached out to ask about a carpool."

Cheyenne snorted.

"Y'all know each other too?" Trucker asked.

"Now, wait a moment." The old man waved at them as he bent to lift the folding metal chair that seemed way too heavy for him. "Let's all get settled first. I don't want to miss anything."

Tori turned to look at him, then stepped forward when she saw him struggling with the chair. "Can I help you with that?"

"The chair?" The old man straightened suddenly, whipped the chair up with one hand, and grinned. "You're sweet, my dear. But I'm perfectly capable."

Pizza Boy scoffed and rolled his eyes. "You're not really an old dude."

"Oh, I'm much older than I look, son. You can bet on that. But the strength hasn't left this body nearly as much as it seems." The man chuckled and walked briskly back to the half-circle of chairs before settling his firmly back into place with a metallic clang. "How else am I supposed to convince the rest of this world I'm coming up on the end of my human days here?"

The purse lady frowned at him. "Why would you choose an illusion like that?"

He sat, folded his arms, and nodded at her. "Excellent question, my dear. The answer to that, as much as it seems appropriate to give, is that I've made something of a reputation for myself in this world, buying and selling properties like this one. The illusion changes with the decades, of course. Ha. Give me another ten years, and I'll put this illusion and the name that goes with it to rest."

"What's that supposed to mean?" Pizza Boy asked.

The old guy smiled at him. "I'll die. Or at least, the name I've been keeping and everything with it will die. I'll start again as someone new."

"Huh."

Everyone in the circle of chairs fell into an awkward silence.

Cheyenne studied the old man, who wasn't nearly as old as he wanted to seem. *I wonder if he's had as many new names and new lives as Maleshi? If he recognized Corian's name, he might know her.*

"So, then. Let's begin." The old man clapped his illusion-wrinkled hands and grinned. "Let's go around in order, shall we?"

CHAPTER SIXTY-SIX

"You all know me already as T0pH@t314," the old man continued. "And for the last fifty years, my name has been Kenneth. I like to think of myself as something of an original old-school member of the Borderlands forum. Found it when it was created forty years ago. This is the first time I've ever met up with other users in person, so I must say I'm particularly excited to meet all of you like this. Thank you for coming."

Purse Lady shook her head. "The internet wasn't open to the public until the '90s."

"Ah, but I'm not talking about what's open to the public, my dear. I don't believe any of us are."

"Wait," Pizza Boy cut in, "why do you look eighty if you've only been this guy for fifty years?"

The woman related to Newsboy shot Pizza Boy a dirty look. "He can't start a new alias as an infant."

"Somebody hasn't been here long enough to need a new life," Newsboy muttered beside her.

"Oh, yeah. Shit. I didn't think about that."

"Clearly."

"All right. How about you, then?" Kenneth nodded at Trucker, sitting beside him.

The man ran his tongue over the inside of his cheek and grunted. "Jeff. Or MessinwiththeMaster000. I ain't fixin' to say more'n that 'til we get to the reason why we're here."

"Yes, I would very much like to move this along if we can," Purse Lady added. "To talk about the Border reservations and that video we were sent by… Now that I think about it, I don't know which one of you is ShyHand."

Newsboy nodded. "That's why we're here."

"No one else wishes to introduce themselves first?" Kenneth looked genuinely crestfallen as he scanned the seven faces of the other magicals. "Very well. You all did me the courtesy of joining me here, so I suppose I'll return it in kind. So ShyHand71, the floor is yours."

The warehouse fell silent again as everyone looked at each other. Cheyenne briefly raised her hand. "That's me."

"No shit." Pizza Boy sniggered. "How the hell did someone like you get onto a Border rez to take that video?"

"Not sure what that question's supposed to mean." She raised an eyebrow at him. "But the answer has at least four different variations."

"Hey, man." Newsboy shook his head and shot Pizza Boy a warning glare. "Maybe we should hold off on the questions 'til she's done talking."

"Jeeze. It was just a question."

The others ignored him and gave Cheyenne their full attention. She looked at Tori on the other side of Pizza Boy, who sat back in her chair with her arms folded and her legs stretched out in front of her. *So weird to see someone I know in here. No way to keep work life and personal life separate, I guess.*

Tori met her gaze and gave her the same smirk she'd given in every one of Cheyenne's classes.

"Well?" Purse Lady prompted.

Cheyenne cleared her throat and ran a hand through her hair. "Yeah, okay. As a precursor, guys, I'm well aware of how crazy this is gonna sound, so bear with me."

The seven strangers watched her intently.

"That video I sent you guys was taken yesterday morning at Rez 9 outside Five Forks. I was called in as a consultant to take a look at what the agents there thought were a few bugs in their system."

"A consultant for the FRoE?" Kenneth asked.

"Yeah."

"Yo, this chick is F-Force?" Pizza Boy stood quickly from his chair and shook his head. "I'm out, man. Should've seen that coming from a mile away."

"Sit down and shut the fuck up," Purse Lady barked, releasing her handbag long enough to summon a warning crackle of yellow and black light in her palm that made the warehouse smell like hot metal. "She said consultant, not agent."

"Yeah, but she could still—"

"Better listen to her, boy." Jeff folded his arms and nodded. "I ain't seen a broad that pent up in a long time, but what I have seen, I never forgot."

Pizza Boy's eyes widened, and he lowered himself hesitantly back into his chair, leaning away from Cheyenne with a grimace. "F-Force comes crashing in to break up our little powwow, I know exactly who to blame."

Cheyenne leaned forward, rested her forearms on her thighs, and clasped her hands. "Nobody gives a shit about whatever petty crime you think you're gonna get popped for. Especially the FRoE."

"You don't know that."

"Yes, I do." She looked at him and raised an eyebrow. "Wanna let me finish?"

"Man." He sniffed, crossed one leg over the other, and folded his arms. "Knew I should've stayed home."

Cheyenne closed her eyes and took a deep breath. *You'd think Earth-side magicals would be a hell of a lot easier to convince about this shit than the humans running the FRoE. Keep it simple.*

"Okay, to sum it up, there are thirteen Border towers in Virginia and surrounding states that are experiencing some interference. The kind that's been turning up the dial on the strength of magic flooding across the Border from Ambar'ogúl. I honestly didn't know that was a thing until a few days ago. It's messing with the Border portals way more than anything should be able to mess with them, and I need your help to stop whatever's coming next."

"What *is* coming next?" The woman beside Newsboy raised an eyebrow. "This sounds like conjecture to me, honestly."

"I wish I knew for sure what it was." Cheyenne shrugged. "But I do know the magical behind it is setting up for some kind of huge spell, most likely powered by the Border towers and a calibrax."

"What the fuck is that?" Pizza Boy asked, wrinkling his nose.

"Magical generator, son," Kenneth muttered. "Now, if you don't mind, please keep your mouth shut until the floor's open for questions."

Cheyenne stared at the dusty concrete floor in the center of the half-circle. *If I have to tell them it is L'zar, I'm gonna have to tell them who I am first. This is gonna be weird.*

Fortunately, Kenneth saved her from having to figure out how to do that without confusing everybody. "You mentioned Corian Vedi'im."

She nodded at him. "Yeah."

"Is he the one behind this?"

"No. No, but he probably stands to lose the most if we're talking about the very short term. It sounds stupid, but he was kidnapped by the magical who's setting up for this spell, which can't be anything but big and bad if he's hit thirteen Border towers in the last four days. Plus Peridosh in Richmond for supplies."

"Sounds like you know who he is," Jeff muttered. "Do ya?"

"I don't know for sure. But I know he has Corian, and Corian is probably the only magical in both worlds these days who can stop him."

"Which is why you called us together, right?" Tori asked. "Because you want to find this Corian guy?"

"Right. Using the Soulstring. Or whatever Kenneth mentioned that might do the same thing."

"Okay." Purse Lady clutched her purse and narrowed her eyes at Cheyenne. "It's a fairly believable story so far, but it's not enough to convince me that this is something we need to take action on right now."

Pizza Boy snorted. "What have you got to lose, huh? She's not trying to take your purse."

The woman's nostrils flared above a scowl aimed at him. "Judging by the complete lack of intelligence spewing from your mouth, I'm going to assume you have no idea what horisband is. Or an ethronian squall."

He rolled his eyes. "Can't be that important."

"They're ingredients for the Soulstring," Cheyenne said.

"And incredibly hard to find this side of the Border. Not to mention the price tag." Purse Lady lifted her chin and looked Pizza Boy up and down. "Which I imagine is more than your entire yearly salary. As a rough estimate."

"Bitch."

"Whoa. Okay." Tori leaned forward and looked at each of them before gesturing at Cheyenne. "Can we let the woman finish or what?"

Purse Lady blinked furiously and shifted in her seat. Pizza Boy sat back to focus on picking the dirt out from under his fingernails.

Cheyenne looked around the half-circle. *Maybe I should break out the L'zar part first.*

"Please continue," Kenneth prompted.

"Yeah." She stood quickly from the chair and paced in front of the seven strangers. *You knew you'd have to put it all out there. Just do it.* "Okay. I need help with this, which isn't usually something I ask for. Or accept. But this is bigger than me, bigger than all of us, so I'm just gonna lay it all out there."

Newsboy chuckled. "You're that kinda magical, huh?"

"What?"

The woman sitting beside him, probably his sister, elbowed him in the ribs and shook her head. It made him laugh again. "You know, more comfortable sitting behind a keyboard than walking down the street in broad daylight. Got some kinda tech job where you don't have to talk to people. Nobody knows who you are until some F-Force admin gets wind of you and decides you might be useful. Bet that was the first time you set foot on a rez since crossing over, huh?"

A small smile flickered at the corner of Cheyenne's mouth, and she pointed at him. "You got me all figured out. Do you know how I know? 'Cause you're the kinda magical who likes to pick everyone else apart but doesn't know shit about strangers and only guesses correctly about five percent of the time."

Tori snorted and pressed a fist against her mouth to cover a laugh.

Pizza Boy didn't bother. He threw his head back with a cackle, then leaned forward and shook a finger at Newsboy. "Oh, shit! You got your ass handed to you by this…this… Huh." He turned in his chair to look at Cheyenne. "I have no fucking clue what you are."

"Yeah, that seems to be a theme right now." She paced some more, feeling a little more confident about the whole thing when she caught Purse Lady's small, amused smile from the corner of her eye. "I do know who's behind the Border tower interference. I haven't figured out why magic's growing stronger and what spell's being cooked up, or what it will do. He's the same magical who kidnapped Corian Vedi'im. Who, if you haven't figured it out by now, is Guardian104."

"You said you knew Guardian personally," Purse Lady added. "So that doesn't come as much of a surprise. I'm interested in this other magical you still haven't named."

Yeah, get in line, lady.

Cheyenne stopped pacing and spread her arms. "It's L'zar Verdys."

"Whoa, whoa, whoa. What?" Pizza Boy sliced his hands through the air and shook his head. "This is going into complete bullshit territory. L'zar Verdys is—"

"An escaped inmate from Chateau D'rahl? A thief? An asshole?" Cheyenne nodded. "Yeah, I know."

"He's a drow, man. You want us to help you track down a drow so we can stop him from doing what? You don't even know."

"I know it's not gonna be good if he succeeds." She shook her head and scanned the others' expressions, looking for a sign that any of them believed her. "I wish I had more proof. All I'm asking for right now is help to track him down. You guys are gonna have to figure out on your own whether you want to be part of all the rest. Though I hope you'll choose standing up and doing something about it over staying quiet and watching to see what everyone else does. I picked that second option not too long ago and figured out pretty quickly it was the wrong decision."

A few of the others shifted in their seats. Jeff popped a stick of gum in his mouth and chewed noisily. "Who're you? That's what I wanna know."

"Yep. Also a good question." Cheyenne stopped pacing and scanned their faces again, though this time, she let her activator pry for her until she had seven cell phone signals from the seven phones in front of her. "If I were you, I'd be wondering the same thing, so I'm glad I prepared for this."

"For what?" Newsboy's sister asked.

Cheyenne pulled up the file she'd put together with all her details, full name, address, phone number, IP address, and even her connection to Bianca.

Not like I expect any of these magicals to know who she is, but any little bit helps at this point.

"Hey." Pizza Boy spread his arms. "She asked you a question."

"And I'll answer it in two seconds." When her activator had locked onto each phone number around the half-circle, she sent the document to all of them and folded her arms to watch their reactions.

Seven phones buzzed or dinged one right after the other. *Bad to the Bone* by George Thorogood & The Destroyers blared from Pizza Boy's cell phone, and he scrambled wildly to pull it out of his pocket and shut off the music. Everyone else stared at their incoming texts with varying degrees of skepticism before the reality of what they were looking at sank in.

"Whoa." Newsboy looked up at her. "Are you serious right now?"

Cheyenne shrugged. "Kind of a messed-up thing to joke about, right?"

"Man." Jeff sniffed and shifted his weight from left to right in the chair as he scrolled through the information. "Takes balls to send this out to a bunch of strangers."

"Cheyenne Summerlin." Kenneth chuckled and looked up at her. "ShyHand71. Not the kind of inspiration I expected for an avatar, but I can't say it doesn't fit."

"Hold on." Purse Lady held her phone out to the side and looked around the circle. "I didn't give her my number."

"Neither did we." Newsboy's sister folded her arms and stared at Cheyenne. "I'll admit you caught my interest with this one but with the wrong thing."

"Shit, that's right!" Pizza Boy spun toward her in his chair, looking quickly between his phone and Cheyenne. "How the fuck did you get my number, man? I *know* my VPN is solid, and I don't put this shit out on the internet for anyone to find it."

"Good choice. But it wasn't the internet."

"Whatever it was," Newsboy said, narrowing his eyes at her with a small shake of his head, "you better have a damn good explanation for it. Right now. Or I'm out."

Cheyenne nodded at him and reached behind her ear to remove the silver coil. Her eyelids fluttered as the activator released its connection with her magic, then she held it up for everyone to see. "I hope this counts as a good explanation 'cause it's all I've got."

"*Majiya iya*," Purse Lady whispered. Then her mouth fell open, and she shut it promptly.

"No fucking way." Pizza Boy's mouth fell open too, but he didn't bother to close it.

"Cheyenne." Kenneth cleared his throat. "Is that what I think it is?"

"That's an activator," Newsboy muttered. "Isn't it? It has to be. How did you get that across the Border?"

"Just something I figured out I could do. I've made the crossing more times than I can count in the last few months. Discovered it by accident." Cheyenne replaced the coil behind her ear and managed to keep one eye open while the other twitched with the sync-up.

"Aw, don't." Pizza Boy let out an exaggerated sigh. "Come on, man. You know what? I don't even care about all that metal shit in your face. You do you. Whatever style you've got goin' on. But for the love of everything I fucking left behind to come Earthside, please let me use that thing for like twenty minutes."

"Can't." Cheyenne shrugged. "Sorry. I already tested it out on a few friends, and it doesn't work for anyone but me."

"That's fucking bullshit."

"Man, I'm tired of your fuckin' mouth," Jeff snarled. "You ain't said one useful thing since you showed your ugly human-lookin' face in here, and I'm this close to shuttin' it for you. Permanently."

"You need to start using your head," Newsboy's sister muttered. "She didn't post on the Borderlands and bring us together so she could give us her activator."

Cheyenne smirked. "Well…"

The bickering stopped immediately.

Kenneth ran his hands down the legs of his jeans and straightened. "Well what, my dear?"

She fingered the star activators inside her jacket pockets, three in the left hand, four in the right, and stepped toward Kenneth first. "I kinda did. Granted, they're not mine."

"What?" He cupped his palms together and stared at the metal star she dropped into them.

"You're joking," Purse Lady whispered. "This has to be a joke."

Cheyenne moved around the half-circle and handed out activators in order. Jeff swallowed his gum when she dropped one into his hand, then coughed and grunted and couldn't stop blinking. "Go ahead and try it. Then tell me if you think I'm joking."

Purse Lady didn't shy away from her like Cheyenne had expected when she received her activator. She didn't even look at Cheyenne but stared at the activator, flipping it over and over in her hands. The safety of her handbag was forgotten.

Newsboy and his sister were speechless. Tori shot Cheyenne a coy smile and stared at the drow until Cheyenne moved on to offer the last activator to Pizza Boy.

He didn't seem to find it as amusing as Cheyenne's surprise-magical student. "What the fuck is this?"

"An opportunity you seriously don't wanna pass up." She shook the last activator at him, and the guy leaned away from her.

"Is it?"

"Totally real. Fully functional. No catch."

Pizza Boy's brown human eyes flickered between the activator and Cheyenne's human eyes. "Nobody gives something like this away for free."

"Yeah, I do a lot of things nobody else does. You don't have to say thank you or anything. Just take the damn activator."

He snatched it from her grasp, then turned it over in his hands, grimacing. "Not a fan of handouts, honestly."

"You'll be a fan of this one." Cheyenne stopped on the other side of her chair, folding her arms. "If you shut up and put it on."

One by one, her tentative new friends slowly placed the activators behind their ears. The energy of so many devices syncing up to individual magic all at once brought the faint odor of vinegar to Cheyenne's nose. Each one of them grew rigid, eyelids fluttering, hands clenching at pantlegs or purses or each other.

"Wowee!" Jeff shouted, jerking his head from side to side. "Shit packs a punch, I tell you what."

Purse Lady blinked rapidly, taking in short, shallow breaths before letting herself gaze around the warehouse. "Oh, my."

"You good?" Newsboy turned to his sister and gently touched her shoulder. She nodded, cleared her throat, and gave him a hesitant smile.

"It works." The woman looked at Cheyenne and whispered, "How did you get them to work?"

Cheyenne shrugged. "I have a guy."

Kenneth drew a long breath and ran a slightly trembling hand over his bald head. "In all my time spent Earthside, Cheyenne," he said as he looked at her, his eyes shimmering with tears that faded almost instantly, "I never imagined this was possible."

"Now it is." She stuck her hands in her pockets and felt the remaining activators clinking against each other. "These are all brand-new, straight from Hangivol's best sparksetter. They've never been used before, so if you hang onto them, I'm sure they'll end up pairing only with you. At least, mine did."

Tori leaned back in her chair and swept her gaze across the warehouse, grinning. "How many more of these do you have?"

"Fifteen. I'm sure I can get more eventually, but right now, the most important thing is finding L'zar Verdys and Corian Vedi'im. Which I'm hoping you guys are still willing to help me with."

Purse Lady's mouth opened and closed in amazement before she found her voice. "Ms. Summerlin."

"Cheyenne. Please."

"Yes, of course." The woman cleared her throat. "Cheyenne, I must admit that after this, I'm far more inclined to say I'll stand with you for whatever you need. As much as I can, that is."

"Anything helps. Thank you."

"See, that's what's rubbing me the wrong way." Pizza Boy shook his head. "You said no catch. This sounds like a fucking catch to me, lady."

"I'm not gonna take away your activator if you decide you don't want anything to do with this." Cheyenne stepped away from her chair to get a better look at him. "This isn't a tit-for-tat kinda thing."

He snorted. "Tit."

Newsboy's sister hissed, "You're as juvenile as the idiots who tried to derail her call for help on the forum. Did you even mean it when you said you were interested, or are you another troll in the flesh this time?"

"Oh, screw me for being cautious, huh?"

"Please. Please." Kenneth raised his hands for everyone to calm down while Pizza Boy and Newsboy's sister glared at each other. "This isn't why we're here, and quite frankly, I'm tired of listening to useless banter between strangers. That won't get us anywhere, and I'm quite sure you both know that. We all do. What we've been given," he said, shaking his head, his wrinkled lips curving in and out of a smile, "I don't entirely understand, but I can say it's one of the most genuine gifts I've received since I made the crossing into this world. Whatever Cheyenne's reasons are, I appreciate where they've led her more than I can say. So thank you, Cheyenne."

She nodded. "You're welcome."

"What *are* your reasons?" Jeff asked, finally loosening up his tight grip on his kneecaps. "I ain't sayin' I don't appreciate this as much as the next magical with a working activator, but I reckon there's somethin' else behind the givin' away of somethin' so valuable. Care to share what that is?"

Cheyenne slowly sat in her chair again and took a moment to put her words together. *Opening up isn't my strong suit, is it?* "The reason I'm handing out activators is that I can. Earthside magicals deserve that much, O'gúleesh and Earthborn. If one magical can bring O'gúl tech across the Border and it works on the other side, that kinda carries a responsibility to do it for more than just myself."

"That's very altruistic of you," Purse Lady muttered.

"Well, I'm trying something new."

"How about you try one more thing, huh?" Newsboy folded his arms. "Show us who you really are."

Cheyenne laughed and spread her arms. "I am who I really am."

"No illusions." He looked from stranger to stranger and nodded. "You gave us personal info and want us to think that's enough. I'm not buying it."

"I'll second that," Jeff muttered, folding his arms and kicking his legs out in front of him. "You want our trust? Show us why we should give it."

"She gave us an activator," Purse Lady whispered in disbelief.

"I ain't talkin' 'bout activators."

"She won't do it." Pizza Boy leaned away from her with a sneer. "Told you there was a catch."

Cheyenne raised an eyebrow at Kenneth, who put both hands in the air in surrender. "I'm not the one to call the shots on this, Cheyenne. We're in my building, but you arranged this meeting."

"Yeah, I did." She stood again and shrugged out of her trench coat.

CHAPTER SIXTY-SEVEN

"Ooh!" Pizza Boy sniggered. "You getting ready to fight somebody?"

"Hey, you need to shut up," Tori said. "For real."

"Yeah? Just watch." He pointed at Cheyenne, who rolled up her sleeves and blinked at her activator's command prompt to take down her human illusion. "She's either gonna tear this place down or bolt."

Cheyenne spread her arms and shot him a deadpan stare. "Maybe you should leave."

"Why? 'Cause I'm—"

Her fingers flickered at her sides as her activator took over dissolving the human illusion, and she stood there in drow form among a group of magicals who'd been passing as human just as well as she had.

"Holy fuck!" Pizza Boy practically threw himself on Tori in surprise. The woman shoved him off with a growl, and he grabbed at the sides of his chair to steady himself.

"You're an idiot," Purse Lady hissed at him.

"I'll be damned." Jeff nodded. "I asked, you delivered."

Newsboy and his sister stared at her with matching grins. Kenneth leaned forward in his chair and studied Cheyenne with a thoughtful frown. Tori laughed. "I knew it wasn't a costume."

Cheyenne pointed at her. "That stays between us."

"Hey, who am I gonna tell?"

"When did you join the Borderlands?" Kenneth asked.

"Almost two months ago."

Newsboy's sister widened her eyes and just kept grinning. "Right around the time all those threads about a new D-Class friend showed up. Right?"

"No fucking way." Pizza Boy's mouth fell open. "That was you?"

Cheyenne dropped her hands to her sides and shot him a brief dismissive look. "I'm not sure you're gonna believe anything I say."

"Who gives a shit what that numbskull thinks?" Jeff said. "I sure as hell don't. Naw, I think you're showin' us exactly who you are now."

Newsboy's sister stood abruptly and walked across the half-circle toward the drow, her hand extended. "I'm Melody. DoubleorN0thin online."

Cheyenne couldn't help but smile. "Nice to meet you. Officially."

Newsboy grimaced. "Mel, come on."

"And my brother Henry. Thing1onP0int."

Cheyenne nodded at him, and he returned it brusquely before looking away and shifting uncomfortably in his chair. "He's never seen a drow, has he?"

"Not like this." Melody stepped back and eyed her. "I'm in. Whatever you need help with, I'm ready to do whatever I can."

With a small frown of surprise—and a little less discomfort now that she'd put almost everything on the table—Cheyenne studied the other woman's gaze. "Thanks."

"Thank *you*."

"My name is Cassandra." Purse Lady stood and took one small step forward. "And I'll tell you the same thing."

Cheyenne couldn't think of a reply quickly enough, so she gave the other magical a crooked smile instead. *At least they're not banging on the chairs and their chests. This is way better.*

"All right." Jeff pulled his legs in and cleared his throat. "You already know my name, but now I'm convinced. Whatever you need, Cheyenne. I reckon we'll be a lot more helpful to you with activators anyway."

"That's not—"

"I know that ain't why you did it. I'm just sayin'."

"Okay. Cool."

"They *will* make us more helpful," Cassandra added. "And useful."

"I guess I should put something along the same lines in there too, huh?" Tori chuckled and didn't even try to stand.

"That would be an excellent show of support, yes," Kenneth replied, still studying Cheyenne with a curious frown.

"She already knows I'm in."

Cheyenne tried not to laugh. "I better not get a bunch of undergrad emails after this."

"What?" Tori snorted. "Like I talk to anybody in that class."

The other gathered magicals eventually turned their attention to Pizza Boy, who still hadn't offered his name or an agreement that he'd help Cheyenne with her issues. He was staring at the factory ceiling, his mouth hanging open as he searched through his activator's data.

Melody cleared her throat. Tori had to lean over to the guy and smack him on the arm. "Hey. Get with the program, man."

"What?" Pizza Boy blinked quickly and scanned their faces. "What?"

"You're the only one of us ain't said shit after knowin' what we now know," Jeff said.

"What do you want me to say?"

"Whether or not you're going to join us in helping her," Cassandra growled.

He stared at Cheyenne and shrugged. "I don't know. Something's still itchy about this whole thing."

Henry rolled his eyes. "This guy."

"Something's not quite right. I'm just being honest."

The others groaned and rolled their eyes. Melody gestured at the door. "Then maybe you should leave."

"Well, give him a moment," Kenneth added. "He can think about it, and in the meantime, I have a few more questions for Cheyenne."

She looked at the old man who wasn't an old man and raised her eyebrows. "Like I said, I have answers. Maybe not all of them, but enough."

"I believe you do." Kenneth studied her and stroked his chin. "Though whether or not you have these answers is a bit more important to me than what they may happen to be."

Cheyenne narrowed her eyes. "Okay."

"Just for my own curiosity, you understand. And perhaps in an effort to alleviate any confusion on our fellow natives' behalf." He gestured at Pizza Boy, who snorted and shook his head.

"Just ask." The drow dipped her head to meet the old man's gaze directly. "Trying to hide anything stopped serving me a while ago."

"An excellent lesson to learn." Kenneth sat back in his chair and tilted his head. Cassandra and Melody glanced at each other and headed back to their chairs. "First, I'm particularly interested in knowing why you're so interested in finding L'zar Verdys. Yes, you're a drow. Most drow, in my experience, would rather see him fall into the Abyss with the Spider."

"You can say that again," Pizza Boy muttered.

Kenneth shot him a warning look before continuing, "The last time I set foot in Hangivol, the inner circle had not yet come to a decision one way or the other regarding their feelings about Ba'rael Verdys. I suspect that has changed."

Cheyenne couldn't help herself. "You said you had questions."

"Indeed. Why do you care so much about what happens to the Weaver? And how is it that a drow who's only recently appeared on our radar, at least on the Borderlands forum, knows as much as she does about him and Corian Vedi'im?"

"His *Nós Aní*." She nodded when Kenneth's eyes widened in recognition. "As much as I wish it weren't true most of the time, I've pretty much accepted that I can't get away from him. I'm his daughter."

Cassandra let out a squeak of surprise. "You're *what*?"

Henry leaned forward in his seat. "That's a big claim."

"I know. I try to make a habit of only making big claims I know are true."

"Prove it." Jeff tilted his head to the other side, as if a different angle would show him the truth.

"Prove it." Cheyenne snorted and scanned the beams stretching across the old factory's ceiling. "Guess I should've expected that. No one knows what to believe on this side anymore, do they?"

"What's that supposed to mean, huh?" Pizza Boy jeered. "You think you're better than the rest of us or something just because you're a fucking drow?"

"It means with me, what you see is what you get." She stepped back and spread her arms, part of her hating that she had to put herself on display as black flames burst to life all over her skin. The other magicals leaned back in their chairs and stared at the drow fire racing up and down her arms, flickering over her fingers, and burning in her hair and behind her eyes without harming her.

"What's that?" Henry whispered. Melody slapped his arm with the back of a hand and scowled at him.

"You know what the fuck that is," Pizza Boy said breathlessly, all traces of doubt wiped away by his amazement. "I don't believe it."

"Then you're still the same moron who didn't believe it before." Cassandra blinked when the others looked at her in surprise and shrugged. "I merely said what we're all thinking. Whoever he is, he doesn't care about seeing the truth."

Pizza Boy's chair screeched across the dusty concrete floor when he leaped to his feet. Cheyenne cut off the black fire, shook out her hands, and stared at him.

"The truth, huh?" He took a step toward her. "Yeah. This is the fell-damn truth right here."

"Now, son," Kenneth warned.

The skeptical nameless magical gritted his teeth and dropped to one knee, then thumped a hand on his chest. At the same time, his human illusion fell away to reveal a wide-eyed orc. His huge brown-stained tusks turned inward at the end, making Cheyenne think of a warthog before she pushed the thought out of her mind and cocked her head. "Don't."

"My life for the Black Flame of Ambar'ogúl." He said it in a low growl, yellow eyes blazing as he stared unblinkingly at her. "And I know you motherfuckers just heard me say that."

Tori burst out laughing. The others were still too surprised to care. "Right here in Roanoke." She kept laughing. "Using the Borderlands forum to get us all out here in the same place. Are you kidding me?"

The orc whirled on one knee and snarled at her. "Now who's being stupid?"

"Hey, man. I get it." She raised both hands and grinned at Cheyenne. "Right there with you. I'm just putting way more pieces together than I expected right now."

Cheyenne shot her a warning look. "Pieces you weren't supposed to see."

"Uh-huh. Everything makes so much more sense now."

Henry slid slowly toward the edge of his seat to lower himself onto one knee. Cheyenne pointed at him. "Don't do that."

He froze.

"No kneeling. No bowing. I don't need anyone to pledge their life for whatever. This is Earth."

Cassandra grabbed her brother's arm and hauled him back into his seat.

"Come on. Get up." Cheyenne extended a hand to Pizza Boy, and he took it without hesitation. She helped him to his feet. "You don't have to do that here."

He chuckled around his tusks. "Who the fuck told you that?"

"No one. *I'm* telling *you*." She released his hand. "I had enough of that on the other side, and it got old really fast."

"Was that a command?"

"What? No. Look, orc, I'm not here to give anyone commands either."

"Brúj." He thumped his chest again. "My given name. Ended up bastardizing it for Earthside living to Bruce."

"Huh." Tori crossed one leg over the other and cocked her head. "Your illusion doesn't look like a Bruce. I would've thought something more like Chad. Or Benny."

"You know what?" Brúj flipped her the bird without turning around. "You can use whatever name you want. The Black Flame put it all out there."

"Come on. Just call me Cheyenne."

"So I'll do the same fell-damn thing." He nodded curtly, then slowly stepped back and almost sat on thin air until he realized his chair was three more feet behind him.

"If that's who you are," Jeff said slowly, "then what about all them rumors? Everythin' that's been floatin' around on the Borderlands. They true?"

"Not if you're talking about the trash everyone's been plastering all over the front page since Corian went missing."

"Naw. I mean about the Spider. The new Cycle turning for a drow first and ending on a troll."

"Persh'al. Yeah." Cheyenne folded her arms. "The Ironbreak. That part's all true."

"*Hishmál,*" Henry whispered.

Melody let out a low whistle. "You can say that again."

"Good thing we were all on board with her from the very beginning." Tori looked over her shoulder at the orc as he grabbed his chair. "Right, Bruce?"

"Just keep talking." He whipped the chair forward and sat gruffly. "I'm allowed to change my mind just like the next guy when I have all the facts."

"Uh-huh."

"Cheyenne." Kenneth gestured at her empty chair, and she headed toward it. "For the Black Flame—"

She grimaced and opened her mouth to stop him.

"No, hear me out. Please. For the Black Flame, I have a few more questions."

Frowning, she slowly sat in her chair again and leaned forward. "You don't believe me."

"Everything you've said and shown us so far has been airtight." Kenneth spread his arms in supplication. "You'll have to forgive me for being a cautious old magical. It's rather hard to make it this long Earthside without a healthy level of skepticism."

Jesus Christ. What else do I have to do to make this convincing? Take them all across the Border?

She took a deep breath. "Ask away, then."

The wrinkles around his human-looking eyes deepened when he squinted at her. "How fares the Vessel these days?"

"What?"

Kenneth nodded slowly. "You heard me."

"She's fine. Better, thanks."

"Who the fuck is the Vessel?" Brúj asked.

The old magical raised a hand to shut him up and kept staring at Cheyenne. "And what of the necromancer?"

Cheyenne straightened in her chair. "I'm pretty sure he's pissed that

I brought the Vessel back home with me after burning an entire forest and everyone in it."

"Whoa." Henry shook his head. "What?"

"This just jumped to a whole new level of what the fuck," Jeff muttered.

"A forest of what?" Kenneth asked.

"Nimlothars."

He leaned even farther toward her. "The Black Flame has another name, which was given after that morning. What is it?"

Cheyenne pressed her lips together and turned slightly away from him. "You're interrogating me now."

"I am asking questions I imagine you haven't yet heard."

"*Lainarí.*"

"And the drow who escorted you through the city afterward?"

She barked a laugh. "What is this?"

"Answer the question."

"Glís. Ban'oru. Haslin. Now tell me how the hell you know all that."

A small smile bloomed on Kenneth's lips. "I'll show you, my dear. As soon as everyone else in this building drops the illusions like you and Brnew. Allow me to start."

A flash of light-pink light raced down Kenneth's body from head to toe, and the old-man illusion disappeared.

Cheyenne blinked. "You're a fae."

"Would I be anything else?"

"I didn't think there were very many around. Well, I guess that explains the pink." She looked at the others and shrugged. "Might as well, right?"

CHAPTER SIXTY-EIGHT

One by one, they removed their illusions and revealed themselves. She knew Jeff and Cassandra were goblins before their green-blue skin and yellow hair and eyes emerged. She didn't expect to find a pair of skaxen siblings sitting in Henry's and Melody's seats or that skaxens could smile with such sharp teeth and not look like lunatics.

Tori took a few seconds longer than the others to remove her illusion. Her hair and eyebrows disappeared, her ears grew twice the size of Cheyenne's with even more prominent points, and her skin shimmered like it had been painted with mercury. Two eyes split into four, the second pair just below the first, and two silver batlike wings stretched away from her back when she leaned forward in her chair.

"Whoa," Jeff muttered. "That's, uh…"

"Wonderful," Kenneth finished for him.

Tori looked from face to face, the two sets of eyes blinking independently. "Pretty much the reaction I always get."

"How long have you been Earthside?" Cassandra asked.

"I was born here. Or hatched if we're technical. But my parents still follow the old laws as much as they can. Haven't made the crossing yet, but who gives a fuck, right?"

Cheyenne grinned at her. "Took the words right out my mouth." *And the attention off this Black Flame shit. Thank you, Tori.*

"Well." Kenneth clapped his hands and stood in one fluid movement.

Cheyenne stepped back to take in what must have been seven and a half feet of violet-haired fae and chuckled.

"I believe our next steps are simple." He gazed around the half-circle of magicals, who couldn't decide whether to stare at him or Tori. "Everyone in this building is expected to keep what they've seen and heard here today private. I assume that's understood."

"Quite." Cassandra nodded.

"Not like anyone would believe us anyway," Henry added, his whiskers twitching at the end of his rat-like orange nose.

"Belief is not the issue." Kenneth clasped his hands behind his back. "The anonymity we all valued on the Borderlands no longer exists. Anyone talks, the rest of us will have little trouble finding them, if any. Am I understood?"

They nodded, and Cheyenne bowed her head to hide the smile she couldn't wipe off her face. *Played the polite old man card to perfection and got everyone to show up without any secrets. He's been in this world for a long time.*

"Good." Kenneth smiled sweetly, though the effect was more disturbing coming from a seven-foot fae than from a wrinkled old human. "Excuse me for a moment."

He turned swiftly and headed across the dusty floor of the old factory to a crooked wooden table with thick legs on the far side of the room.

"Fae." Tori shook her head as she watched him walk away. "Wouldn't have guessed that one."

"Compared to seeing you?" Brúj snorted. "I might as well see fae out in the open every damn day."

"Yeah, okay."

"All right." Jeff sniffed. "I know I ain't the brightest fella on the block, but what the hell are you?"

"Huh. I figured native O'gúleesh wouldn't have a problem putting the pieces together."

He stared at her with narrowed eyes and muttered, "I wanna hear you say it."

"I'm Verati."

Brúj clapped his hands, then pumped a fist. "I fucking knew it."

"No, you did not," Cassandra hissed.

"You calling me a liar, lady?"

"You're so full of lies, it's amazing that new activator is of any use to you."

Jeff nodded and rubbed his mouth, staring at Tori without a word.

"Okay, we got that out in the open, so everyone can say they saw a real-live Verati and leave it at that." Tori gave Cheyenne a confused smile. "Why are you looking at me like that?"

"I'm impressed. You figured out how to hide that a lot better than I did."

"Yeah, well, I had help. And I can't walk around in a bubble of black fire or anything, so it's not the same." The Verati cocked her head. "I know L'zar broke out of prison a few weeks ago."

"Man, everybody knows that," Brúj added with a snort.

Tori ignored him. "I'm guessing he wasn't around much before you showed up on campus, right?"

Cheyenne let out a wry, humorless laugh and glanced at the ceiling. "That's one way to put it."

"Isn't Bianca Summerlin human?"

The others stared at Cheyenne again, and she sighed. *And all the shock and surprise is back on the drow. Nice move.* "As far as I know, Bianca's human."

"Bianca Summerlin," Kenneth interrupted as he moved swiftly toward them with a large wooden crate in his arms, "is the Vessel."

"No." Cheyenne pointed at him. "She *was* the Vessel."

He chuckled and slowly lowered himself into his chair once more before setting the crate on the ground between his old-man loafers. "Vessel. 'A hollow container, especially one used to hold liquid, such as a bowl or cask.' Does a bowl stop being a bowl once all the soup inside has been eaten?"

"There was no soup in the forest, Kenneth." Cheyenne fixed him with her usually intimidating blank stare, but it had no effect on the fae. "And my mom isn't a bowl, so that analogy is crap."

"The analogy is perfect, Cheyenne." He shot her a quick smile before opening the lid of the crate. "She is still the Vessel."

"But is she human?" Melody asked. "Because that would mean—"

"That would mean everything we thought we knew about the way both worlds work isn't true, wouldn't it? Which I do believe we've already discovered." Kenneth cleared his throat and withdrew a much smaller, six-inch square box from the crate. "Looking to the future matters more than trying to solve the riddles of the past, and those are hardly riddles if one knows how to draw the threads together. Do sit down, everyone. Unless anyone wishes to argue that we've learned enough and are already finished."

The magicals who hadn't stayed in their chairs returned to them, eyeing the small box in the fae's hands.

Cheyenne leaned back in her chair. "What's that?"

"This, my dear drow, is an ardorium. While I'm sure the eight of us could pool our resources to find you the ingredients needed to perform the Soulstring, like you, I'd rather not waste what precious time we have looking for pieces of the solution when something whole and fully functional is right here in front of us." Kenneth stretched his long arm out to her with the box in hand. "Take it."

She stood and walked across the circle to take it from him, then opened the lid to take a look inside. "It's a mirror."

"Only made to look like one. The ardorium is a rather ancient form of communication. Magical, not technological, of course, or it wouldn't be here. It's almost as old as I am, believe it or not. Most O'gúleesh would call the ardorium hopelessly outdated, but I prefer to place my bets on what worked without fail for countless millennia before the Spider decided to overrun the Motherland with her far more advanced technology."

"And it's for tracking down magicals?" Cheyenne slowly returned to her chair, staring at the small hand mirror inside that looked way too tarnished and dented to be of much use.

"It connects the user to whoever they most urgently desire to see. And yes, my dear, it does function beyond the confines of the Border portals and between worlds. Plus, it's a great deal faster than casting a complicated spell like the Soulstring, even if we had all the ingredients with us at this moment."

She leaned away from Brúj, who was trying to peek over her shoulder, but tipped the box toward him to give him a better look. The orc's lips curled around his tusks as he wrinkled his nose. "You sure you didn't pull this outta your grandma's purse or something?"

"I don't feel the need to dignify that question with a response." Kenneth folded his hands in his lap and smiled at the small box in Cheyenne's hands. "You may use it."

"Thanks. I'll bring it back as soon as I find—"

"Oh, no, Cheyenne. I said you could use it, not take it with you. The ardorium remains here. Please and thank you."

"You don't trust her enough to borrow a mirror?" Henry scratched the side of his long orange face, his beady black eyes flicking between the fae and the drow. "Still?"

"That is mine." Kenneth pointed at the box. "And I won't let it out of my sight. Making the crossing with an ardorium was no small feat, believe me."

Cassandra licked her lips in interest and leaned forward. She tried to peer into the box, but it was too far away. "How so?"

The fae cleared his throat. "The polite way to say it is that I hid that highly valuable device in places that still give me phantom pains on occasion to make the crossing with it on my person."

"Aw, dude." Brúj leaned away from Cheyenne, cringing as he lifted a fist to his mouth. "Not an image any of us needed."

"Whatever image you have is entirely the product of your own mind. And Cheyenne, you may stay long enough to use the ardorium here. I'll show you how it works."

She grimaced at the box and slowly closed the lid. "As long as you've cleaned it."

"Several times. Yes." Kenneth lifted his chin and smiled at the rest of them. "Let's move on, shall we?"

"Not much to move on to when we're waitin' for her to use that thing you stashed in your—" Jeff snorted. "Damn, Ken."

"Kenneth, if you don't mind. Then I suppose now would be the time for the rest of you to take your leave."

Cheyenne looked at the circle of magicals. "I know how to contact all of you. Once I find L'zar and Corian and can track them down, I'll need help stopping whatever L'zar is trying to do before he does it. Or at the very least, to get to him in time to shut down his final spell."

"You have no idea what that is?" Melody asked.

"Not yet, but I will. We have to be ready to go as soon as I do. If he's already managed to make thirteen Border towers freak out in a way they're not supposed to, it's gonna take a lot more than one drow casting one spell."

Cassandra nodded. "I absolutely agree."

"Well." Jeff slapped his thighs and stood. "I reckon you can reach out on the Borderlands when you get your next clue, or whatever."

Cheyenne shook her head. "That takes way too much time. And it's not the best route for getting information across quickly. Texting's a little slow, too. And I'm hoping we can get more than eight magicals to show up when the time comes."

"Well, it's not like we have a fucking emergency alert system for Earthside magicals," Brúj added. "Especially since most of us don't have activators. Everyone else is shit outta luck."

"I made an app." Tori glanced at Cheyenne and shrugged.

"An app?" Jeff gave a wry laugh. "As fun as all this sounds, it ain't a game."

"It's not a *game*." The Verati glared at him. "It's a self-contained VPN that can run on a large number of different devices all at once. It's cloaked but not connected to the dark web, a strong closed channel that needs a one-time randomized password to access."

Henry's whiskers twitched. "You mean, like Slack or something?"

"I mean like something with air-tight security and high accessibility that didn't exist, so I created it," Tori replied curtly.

"Good." Cheyenne nodded and looked at the Verati's two pairs of eyes, which didn't seem to have one true color. "That's really good."

"Thanks."

"We'll use that. Send us all the information we need to get in and to get anyone else on board who wants to be a part of this. Not to stop L'zar if we have to, but to keep the Border working like it should. I have a feeling he's gonna try to change that."

"Yeah, no problem." Tori studied the concrete floor, and her wings twitched away from her back before folding in again. "I'll send everyone an invite with passwords and instructions on how to spread it to any other magical with a phone or computer or tablet. Whatever."

"Good. We'll need as many magicals as we can get on this thing." Cheyenne looked at her trench coat hanging over the back of her chair and frowned. "And I still have fifteen activators. Any of you know other magicals who'd wanna show up and make a stand when the time comes? Who'd also want a working activator Earthside?"

Cassandra burst out laughing, shaking her head vigorously as she stood and clutched her purse against her chest. It looked a lot more ridiculous on a goblin in a blazer and pencil skirt than when she'd appeared to be human. "I'm sorry. So sorry. Forgive me." She cleared her throat and nodded. "I'm sure we all know a few magicals who would fit that description."

"Damn straight, we do." Brúj chuckled. "Pretty much every fucking non-human on this world. Are you kidding?"

"Yeah, that's what I thought." Cheyenne emptied her pockets of the remaining activators and handed two out to each of them. She gave Henry three. "So get these out there. Depending on how you're running that app, Tori, I might be able to put a few extra things together."

The Verati gave her a crooked smile, flashing one dangerous shark-like incisor. "Cool."

"Excellent." Kenneth gestured at the door. "Now, if you don't mind, Cheyenne has an ardorium to use, and I need to be getting home to my cats."

"Oh, how many?" Cassandra's face lit up. "How many cats do you have?"

"Five. For now. Thank you all for coming. This undoubtedly will not be the last time we see each other. And everyone, keep an eye out for the application."

"It's just called an app." Tori stared at the fae, then shook her head. "You know what? Never mind. I'll get it out to you guys."

Jeff headed for the door first, his fingers flickering briefly at his sides before his goblin form disappeared within the cross-country-trucker illusion again. "Damn. These things work like I ain't standin' in a world full of humans."

"That's the point." Cheyenne gave him a small, grateful smile as he passed her, but it disappeared when he thumped his chest and chuckled.

"Whatever we gotta do." Brnew thumped his chest too, and his illusion reappeared. "May the Black Flame reign."

"Get outta here." Cheyenne waved him off, unable to hide her amusement as the orc headed across the factory. He now looked like any other skinny dude with baggy pants and a delivery job.

Henry and Melody stopped to shake Cheyenne's hand but didn't say a word. Cassandra slung her purse over her shoulder and stopped in front of the drow next, her eyes shifting as she struggled to find the words she wanted. "Remind me not to judge a magical by their illusion again."

"I think you already figured that out."

"Yes. Good. Thank you, Cheyenne."

"You too."

With a final amazed look at Tori, Cassandra skirted past them and joined the others filtering out of the back door of the warehouse.

"So." Grinning, Tori recast her illusion into the student Cheyenne recognized. "If this whole 'stop L'zar from breaking the Border' thing happens to fall on a Wednesday or a Friday, does that mean I still have to show up for class?"

Cheyenne snorted. "I'm not gonna make that decision for you. I can't even figure it out myself. First get us those invites, okay?"

"Yep." The Verati winked at Kenneth before turning to the door. "Later, fae."

"Good afternoon." Kenneth's lips twitched in a smile, and he waited until he and Cheyenne stood alone in the center of his defunct bookbinding factory. "Well. That was an illuminating gathering, wouldn't you say?"

"I would, yeah." She craned her neck to look up at him. "Surprises all around. I'd love for the surprises to be over once you show me how to use that ardorium."

"Of course."

Grabbing the box from her chair, Cheyenne opened the lid again and handed it to the fae when he extended his hand. Then she pulled out the small mirror and tried to keep a straight face. *Don't think about how he got it here. You'll be fine.*

"It's simple. Your reflection in the mirror will only greet you for a second or two before the ardorium handles the rest for you. Be sure you're clear about the intention to find the magical with whom you most fervently desire to communicate."

"He'll be able to see me too?"

"Oh, yes." Kenneth chuckled. "Think of it as the magical Facetime that predates the invention of the wheel in this world. I'll be across the building to give you some privacy."

"Thanks."

The magical took off toward the front of the factory, working a short spell with one hand as his long legs carried him swiftly away. His chair rattled and flashed violet light, then rose into the air and trailed after him. "Ha. Activators. Who would have thought?"

CHAPTER SIXTY-NINE

With a deep exhale, Cheyenne sat in the metal chair and leaned forward, gazing into the stained, foggy glass of the ardorium's mirror in its tarnished metal frame.

Okay, let's get to work. You and me, ardorium. Show me the magical I most want to see.

Her reflection hardly looked like her, marred as it was by the imperfections in the glassy surface. A tingling buzz of very strong magic shot through her fingers where her skin met the metal, then raced up her arms into her shoulders, growing so intense she almost dropped the ardorium. Cheyenne sucked a sharp breath through her teeth and held on, staring into the glass.

Then the sensation stopped, and the surface of the mirror rippled, not only visually but physically as if the glass had melted into liquid form. She saw the glowing golden eyes first, followed by the long bone-white hair she shared with L'zar and the entire drow race.

Yes! Holy shit, it's working.

Cheyenne leaned toward the ardorium, ready to give L'zar her special version of hell once the mirror's rippling faded and he became aware of who was reaching out to him, if not why. But when the mirror finally settled into place, along with the features of a face that was like

L'zar's but not quite, she almost dropped the ardorium. "What the fuck?"

R'leer's kohl-smeared eyes widened in the mirror, and his lips pressed together in a thin line without any trace of a smile. "I could ask you the same thing, Cheyenne."

"No." She shut her eyes and shook her head before opening them again. "Come on. I wasn't trying to talk to you."

"Are you sure?" R'leer looked around the inside of his darkseller shop, then chuckled. "I thought you'd returned Earthside."

"Well, I'm not sitting in some O'gúl Goldsmile den, in case you were wondering."

"I was not. There isn't nearly enough smoke around you for that."

There's no smoke. Cheyenne glanced across the factory to see Kenneth sitting in the long chair at the far end, facing her with his eyes closed and his hands resting calmly on his thighs. *Everyone's fucking meditating, huh?*

"Seriously, R'leer. I wasn't trying to contact you."

He flashed her a wide, feral grin and leaned close to whatever version of her he saw in front of him. For a moment, she half-expected him to cross through and climb out of the ardorium's surface to join her. "You have an ardorium."

"Yeah, it's a loaner."

"And it brought you to me." His golden eyes widened, then narrowed again as he withdrew slightly to bring his entire face back into view. "How illuminating."

"It's old. Must be malfunctioning or something."

Kenneth cleared his throat. "Old magic like that doesn't malfunction, Cheyenne."

"Hey, I thought you were offering privacy."

The fae opened one violet eye and fixed it on her. "My apologies. Carry on."

"Who's that with you?" R'leer asked.

"The owner of this stupid thing." Cheyenne returned her attention to the mirror and shook her head. "Don't worry. I trust him." Mostly.

"Oh, I'm not worried about a thing." The darkseller smoothed his white hair away from his face, his grin fading a little as he cocked his head. "You shouldn't be either. Obviously, your deepest desire at this moment is to dive head-first into the darker side of your drow heritage. I'm flattered that you believe I can offer you what you seek."

She snorted. "That's not what happened."

"The device sent you to me."

"I was trying to reach L'zar, okay?" *And I will be trying that again after this little stunt is over.*

"L'zar." R'leer frowned and looked around his shop again. He nodded at the back, most likely directing Gyla to leave him for this impromptu conversation. Heavy footsteps faded into nothing, then his golden eyes focused on Cheyenne again. "You've lost the Weaver?"

"I didn't lose him. I'm not his keeper."

"All signs point to the contrary, Cheyenne, but if you insist."

"Yeah, I insist. Look, I'm not responsible for L'zar's insane decisions. I'm not taking that on. I have no idea why this ardorium pulled you up instead of him, but it obviously means you have something I can use to find him."

The darkseller blinked slowly. "What is he up to?"

She gritted her teeth. "I don't know yet."

"Then perhaps you should take this surprisingly pleasant opportunity to share with me what you do know." The corners of his mouth twitched. "Or not."

"Fine. He was already gone when we made the Earthside crossing five days ago. Corian tried to find him, then Corian went missing too."

"Interesting."

"I'm pretty sure L'zar took him. By force."

R'leer tilted his head to the other side, looking like an actual bird now with his golden eyes and the feathers of his mantled cloak rising around his shoulders and neck, fluttering with the movement. "His *Nós Aní?*"

"Yeah. We found proof of that and had no idea what had happened or where they were until we saw them yesterday morning. At a Border reservation."

He hissed and shoved his face so close to whatever he saw of her that the ardorium's mirror filled with one blazing golden eye. "A pathetic attempt to snatch our freedoms from us, Cheyenne."

"They're falling apart, R'leer." Cheyenne took a deep breath. *Might as well put everything out there again. I'd be an idiot not to trust whatever this stupid mirror's trying to show me.* "Whatever insane plan he's cooked up, it has something to do with the Border towers. Thirteen of them, at least. Maybe more. I don't know."

"You saw him tampering with the towers?"

"No. I saw lines of clear fire in the air and explosions. Apparently, I'm the only one who can. And I saw one tower fading in and out, looking like it was gonna crack and fall over at any minute." They stared at each other, and she let out another slow breath to steel herself. "Then a portal opened in the air, a white one ringed with the same fire. L'zar and Corian were fighting each other."

R'leer narrowed his eyes again. "Are you certain?"

"Not of that last part, no. But everything else? Yes."

"Hmm."

"You think I'm making it up? That I think this is a fun prank?"

"Don't direct your anger at me, Cheyenne," he said casually, though the warning in his voice was unmistakable. "It is sorely misplaced."

"I know." She swallowed. "Sorry. Any idea what the flames are about?"

"Not in the slightest. But it hardly seems concerning enough to warrant the use of an ardorium to find him. I realize it was before your time, but L'zar and his *Nós Aní* aren't particularly known for their peaceful relationship."

"Yeah, that doesn't surprise me at all."

"Then what's the issue?"

Cheyenne blinked. *The more I have to tell this stupid story, the more I forget everyone else doesn't know.* "He's planning some kind of spell. Stole a bunch of ingredients from Peridosh by porting in and out of shops and blowing things up. I saw that too, but I didn't know it was him at the time. Neros recognized the ingredients."

"Neros." R'leer stepped away, growing smaller in the mirror's surface. "The Spider's hidden offspring is with you too?"

"Accidentally, yeah. I'll figure that part out once I handle L'zar."

"What was stolen?"

Cheyenne paused, fighting down her irritation at being interrupted so many times. "Snaregut, Idlewór, and a camphrus bone. And a jar of prism something."

"Prismus pellet." R'leer's gaze darted around his shop, his lips curling in a pondering sneer. "Was that it?"

"No. I can't remember the rest of the list."

"Do vendicat and bloodcrow sound familiar?"

"Yeah. Yeah, that's it. Plus whatever he was doing at the Border towers. I don't know if he was trying to cut the stone apart or if there was something else."

"It doesn't matter. If that's the list so far, it still isn't complete."

Cheyenne sat back in the chair and raised the ardorium in both hands to keep his gaze. "What does he need next? If I know that, I can find it over here and cut him off." *If he hasn't found it already.*

"The spell requiring those particular supplies is unfathomably powerful, Cheyenne." When the darkseller shook his head, the faint echo of all the beads and bones strung through his hair joined her in the abandoned factory. "More power than L'zar could possibly possess. Unless some Earthside *dae'bruj* as insane as he is has the ability to amplify his magic, it would be impossible for him to use."

"Shit." A lump caught in Cheyenne's throat, and she forced herself not to chuck the ardorium across the room.

"Not entirely where I was headed, but—"

"R'leer, he has a calibrax too." She stared at him in the mirror, and for a moment, she thought he hadn't heard her. "You there?"

His lips curled away from his teeth, which she could hear grinding through the mirror as he growled, "How in two worlds did he get his hands on one?"

"It's Inolu's."

R'leer roared and spun away from whatever allowed them to see each other on his side. Cheyenne had to look away from the ardorium as the view spun wildly, showing her a blurred rush of shelves and dangling artifacts and darkseller wares. R'leer's fists crashed down on one of the display counters, scattering items with crashes and the quickly dying clink of something light and metal bouncing away from him. When his short-lived outburst was over, he was breathing heavily, staring not at Cheyenne but at something above where her face was in his shop.

She cleared her throat. "If you know what this spell does, now would be the time to tell me."

He growled and met her gaze again. "I will not give its name,

Cheyenne, but that spell is meant to create permanent changes in magical boundaries such as those running through Ambar'ogúl along the lifeforce veins. Do you understand?"

"Like the Border portals."

Another hiss escaped him, and he straightened from where he'd loomed over his counter. "Yes. The Border itself, even."

"And magicals use this spell?" She scoffed. "Doesn't sound like something anyone else would have the guts or the strength to pull off."

"It's not. The last magical to attempt the casting of it changed the course of O'gúl history. Of drow history."

"What? Please don't tell me Ba'rael and L'zar are drawing from the same spell."

"The Spider couldn't use her own magic to save her life, Cheyenne. Everything she did was manufactured for her. I was referring to Sylra."

Cheyenne blinked. "Nightflame? You mean, the first ruler of Hangivol?"

"The very same." R'leer whirled again, bringing another wave of dizziness. She had to look away from the ardorium again. He started pulling item after item off the shelves around him and setting them firmly down in a quickly growing collection on the newly cleared counter. "Sylra Nightflame cast this spell around Hangivol to bring it to power. To shift the balance of energy within the lifeforce vein to redirect to a city of his own making. For the drow."

"Shit."

"Yes."

"Why the hell would L'zar want to do something like that?" Cheyenne shook her head at Kenneth again, who hadn't moved an inch and seemed to be far away in his own world. *Not fucking likely. He's listening in on all of this.* "It sounds like he's trying to open the portals for himself again, back to Ambar'ogúl. But he can't do that with Ba'rael's curse. It'll kill him unless there's some part of this spell that breaks curses too."

"Not that I am aware of." The darkseller drew in a sharp breath of realization. "And therein may lie the downfall of his plan." He rummaged urgently through the items on his shelves. "L'zar would need direct access to the lifeforce veins and the magic in this world, to draw from it and use it as the source of change as Sylra Nightflame did for

Hangivol. If Ba'rael's curse prevents him from crossing over, that might be exactly what he plans to do."

"You lost me."

R'leer nodded slowly, his gaze darting around the shop and occasionally flicking back to Cheyenne as he worked on gathering more of his inventory she couldn't see. "Has he shown any interest in returning to Ambar'ogúl?"

"No. He says he hates it there. Didn't even care about the curse when the Spider cast it."

"He's lying." The darkseller's shop filled with the thump and rustle of R'leer collecting his armful of items, then he carried them to the main counter on the other side of the room. "It seems like an impossibility. One would have to be insane to attempt something like this."

"L'zar *is* insane," Cheyenne growled.

"Perhaps. Or perhaps he's merely fueled by the call to return home. Out of all of us, Cheyenne, the Weaver is the most likely to be strongly affected by the balance you restored with the Nimlothars. He did not receive that name on a whim."

"So, he felt Ambar'ogúl heal itself and drow magic grow stronger, and he lost what was left of his sanity because he knows he can't cross the Border without his sister's curse killing him?"

"Quite possibly, yes. I imagine he's attempting to permanently open the portals. Perhaps even eliminate the in-between, which is the plane where that curse would come into effect and carry out its intention."

"Is that even possible?"

R'leer stopped his busywork and fixed her with his blazing golden gaze. "With that spell and the calibrax, Cheyenne, there is no conceivable way of knowing what's possible. And L'zar's the type of magical who would try to use that to his advantage."

"He's an idiot."

"In many ways, yes. If he plans to rip open those holes within the fabric of the Border, there will be no barrier between worlds. And with no barrier comes the inability to rebuild them without repeating the process in reverse."

"Jesus Christ." Cheyenne closed her eyes. *L'zar's taking it way too far this time. There's no way he can manipulate himself out of this one.*

"The part that concerns me now is what L'zar still requires to affect the portals specifically."

"Like, more magic?" A humorless laugh escaped her. "If he's coming after me, I'm way beyond ready. I have no problem standing against him."

R'leer frowned. "Do you possess the ability to open portals?"

"What?"

"L'zar requires magical energy on both sides of the Border to affect the portals. Magic specifically suited to portals."

"No. I can't open portals."

"Then he's not coming for you."

"So who is he going after?" she shouted. "Spit it out, R'leer. I'm not in the mood for this riddle bullshit."

"He already has it!" R'leer hissed. "Sylra Nightflame required a life-force vein, redirecting the flow of the magic from everyone else in this world to affect Hangivol specifically. That was why he built the city around the Nimlothar and above one such vein. L'zar means to change the portals or the Border, but the specifics don't matter. He may already have a force in Ambar'ogúl willing and ready to aid him from this side, but if you saw him with his *Nós Aní*, L'zar most certainly has portal magic at his command on that side. Do you understand?"

"No. Wait." Cheyenne's fingers went numb when the realization hit her. "Corian. He's the source of the magic L'zar needs to aim this spell at portals."

"You understand perfectly." R'leer returned to his quick, methodical organization of whatever items he'd pulled from his shelves.

"Fuck. Nightstalker blood opens portals for any other magical to wherever they want."

"As long as the supply is readily available."

"That makes sense." She shut her eyes. *That was why he broke into Corian's apartment and why he dragged Corian with him to the reservations. He already has everything he needs.* "He's definitely trying to open portals. Maybe to change them. And it's not just the working portals. L'zar's hit every deactivated portal ridge in Virginia too."

"Where?"

"Here, R'leer. Right here! Right where I live. Where everything is centered." Her mind raced to put the rest of the pieces together. "And his power source in Ambar'ogúl is the Sorren Gán."

The darkseller's golden eyes flashed with dark, foreboding light when he looked sharply at her. "What?"

"Yeah. Has to be. The Sorren Gán created a brand-new portal in the fellfire pits that also leads to Virginia."

"That is an astounding conclusion you've arrived at," he muttered. "I'm sure you have your reasons to suspect as much, Cheyenne, but a Sorren Gán does not take orders from a drow. They eat us."

"Oh, I know." *And that one made L'zar its bitch.* "But L'zar might not be the one giving orders."

"That would be unfortunate."

"To say the least." She smoothed her hair out of her face and quickly returned the hand to the ardorium. "So, assuming I can't get to L'zar before he casts that fucked-up spell, seeing as this thing won't lead me to him, how do I stop the spell?"

"The source of the magic fueling it must be removed by any means necessary. Another spell, though I suspect that would take the same amount of power to get through. Or physically."

"So, get rid of the power source. Simple enough."

"In theory." He looked away from her and continued rearranging his items, looking a lot more distracted now despite a crooked smile curving along one side of his mouth. "Inolu will not be pleased to hear the Weaver has taken possession of her calibrax."

"She accused me of taking it. If L'zar survives this, if any of us survive, she'll probably kill him."

"She can try. I assume you had no cause to use the displacer, then."

"The what?"

R'leer chuckled. "The item I gave you when you told me you were after a banebreaker."

"Oh. No. Showing it to her was enough to get what we wanted. Mostly."

"Should Inolu present a threat, which she very well might when she finds L'zar with her stolen calibrax, you would do well to use the displacer. It separates non-physical beings from physical bodies, such as each of the banebreaker's intimately incorporated *uanáj.*"

"Wow. That's why she was so terrified of it."

He grinned at her. "Was she?"

"Yeah. The *uanáj* didn't seem to care much. Thanks for explaining it after the fact, though." That sounded way more sarcastic than she intended, but R'leer either didn't notice or didn't care how much his lack of detailed instructions frustrated her. "How do I use it?"

R'leer blinked in surprise, then threw his head back and filled both his shop and Kenneth's factory with dark laughter. She stared at him through the ardorium. "It only requires you to power it. Intention is all that matters with that one."

"Wonderful advice. Very specific."

"As long as you're aware of your intentions when you do so." His grin faded into a small smile as he studied her face and slowly licked his lips. "You may want to work on honing yours more succinctly. A wise lesson to take from the ardorium contacting the drow you didn't even realize you wished to see."

"Don't let it go to your head."

"I wouldn't dream of it." R'leer leaned closer, his face filling the mirror's surface again. "Did L'zar never reveal the Don'adurr Thread to you?"

Cheyenne's mouth fell open. *Well, that was a stupid oversight.* "L'zar only reveals what L'zar wants to reveal."

"You didn't answer the question."

"I don't have to. Thanks for helping me put this together."

He chuckled and returned his gaze to his work. "I'm happy to aid the Black Flame in maintaining the integrity of our worlds' separation."

"Uh-huh. How's everything over there? With the system shortage and the high possibility of a Hangivol revolt."

R'leer shrugged. "It could be worse. It has been worse."

"Right. So far, so good, then." Cheyenne paused, waiting for him to look at her again, but he didn't. "I'm leaving now."

"Blood and honor, Cheyenne." His lips turned up in a tiny smile, but his gaze remained focused on whatever work was suddenly so important.

Cocky asshole. She scoffed and turned the ardorium face-down on her lap, finally freeing it from both hands. The buzz of the mirror's magic faded from her shoulders, arms, and fingertips, and she looked at Kenneth. *Okay. Get my intentions in check. Let's try this one more time.*

Turning the ardorium over again, she clenched her teeth and breathed slowly, closing her eyes to focus one more time on the magical she wanted to find. *Show me L'zar. Just the Dark Smiling Bastard trying to rip a hole in two worlds. L'zar, L'zar, L'zar.*

The ardorium's magic flared up her arms again, and she opened her eyes to see the mirror's surface ripple and settle into clarity much faster than before. "Come on. Seriously?"

R'leer looked up at her and grinned. "You are dedicated, I'll give you that."

"Fuck off."

His careless chuckle made her smile, and she turned the ardorium over again to cut off the connection.

Useless for finding L'zar, but if I ever need a darkseller, I know exactly where to go in either world.

Rolling her eyes, she stood and grabbed the ardorium's box and lid from the chair where Kenneth had set them. After packing the thing up again, she headed across the factory floor. The fae didn't open his eyes until she stopped six feet in front of him. "A successful chat, I hope?"

"More or less." Cheyenne handed him the box, and he stood to take it. "Thank you."

"It's the least I could do at the moment. I assume there will be more opportunity for mc to be of use in the future."

"Definitely. You could start by telling the others what you overheard so they know more about what we're facing if you don't mind. It'll free up some time for me to get a few other things done."

Kenneth pressed his lips together to hold back a smile. "Of course."

"Cool. I'll be in touch."

"I look forward to it."

Cheyenne headed swiftly back to her chair, snatched up her trench coat and shrugged into it. Kenneth silently watched her leave, and the metal door shut briskly behind her when she stepped into the cool air of early evening.

The sun had already set, casting Roanoke in a wash of pale gray-blue light while the stars glimmered faintly in the growing darkness.

She headed around the building to the south side and crossed the street to her car. The purple glow flashing on the headlights when she unlocked the Panamera was a lot brighter in the twilight. *The fucking Don'adurr Thread. I can't believe I didn't think of that. Showing up in L'zar's head is the last thing I wanna do, but apparently, it's my only option.*

CHAPTER SEVENTY

She ended up back in Jackson Ward just past 7:00 without knowing why that was the area of Richmond she'd picked. Driving past Gnarly's Pub on East Clay Street brought that night two months ago racing through her mind again. Ember watching her drow form slip through without any control. Ember talking about the myth of halflings and saying that magicals like them had to stick together. Take care of each other. Ember racing off to the skatepark a few blocks north without a word because Cheyenne was busy freaking out in the alley.

Feels like forever ago. I was so full of myself.

Cheyenne pulled her Panamera into the parking lot at the end of the row of shops and restaurants, locked the doors, and crossed the street to head for the park.

The streetlamps cast yellow pools of muted light on the asphalt as she crossed Brook Road, then lit up the browning grass along the edge of the park, which would most likely be covered with frost in the morning. Somewhere on the east side of the park, car doors opened and shut quickly and voices rose in greeting.

Regular people getting out of their regular cars to go about their regular lives. That's how I'd want it to be if some magical I didn't even know existed was planning to rip holes through two worlds and do what? Guess I'm about to find out.

She reached the end of the grass and the border of the skatepark. The pavilion in front was empty, of course. The chain-link fence around the concrete playground for kids on wheels looked the same as the last time she'd been here, after the fence and the blasted chunks of cement had been repaired.

Cheyenne slipped through the gate, the fence rattling when she opened it, and stepped across the concrete pavement along the dipping edge of the halfpipe. The dark stain on the ground could have been what was left of Ember's blood, impossible to wash out. It could have been an oil stain or the mostly dried splash of someone's spilled water bottle too.

Kind of a macabre place to return to for a little privacy. I guess that's the way I like it.

With a final glance at that dark stain, she turned to face the fence and the empty park on the other side, then sat on the cement and crossed her legs.

L'zar and his fucking meditations. If this doesn't work, I'm out of ideas.

The drow closed her eyes and exhaled a long, slow breath. Her hands rested palms-up on her thighs. A thin breeze rippled across the skatepark, rattling the fence again and brushing her High-Voltage Raven Black hair away from her face and back over her shoulders. It was a lot colder now than the night Ember had tried to break up a magical fight and was shot in the spine for her trouble. Cheyenne didn't feel the cold.

She focused on L'zar.

Wherever you are, I'm gonna find you. Bet you never thought getting into my head would come back to bite you in the ass like this. Even the Weaver can't see everything.

Her breathing slowed into a long, easy rhythm, and she tried to imagine L'zar's face without letting her anger get the better of her. A dog barked somewhere in the neighborhood behind her. Two cars rolled slowly past the park, the whir and occasional crunch of tires on asphalt fading toward Jackson Ward's East Clay Street.

Then something shifted, and at the same time, Cheyenne felt her body and the rest of her float away into deep meditation, reaching for L'zar's mind.

All the sounds around her in the park faded away, replaced by

L'zar's low muttering. Everything around him was white and perfectly blank, but she saw him as clearly as if he were standing right in front of her. He was hunched over a table, working quickly with tools she couldn't see.

"No, no, no," he muttered. "If that's connected on the wrong end, you'll make a mess. I'll make a mess? Who do you think has more experience? I don't care what they say. This isn't...hmm. Yes. This one's much more responsive—"

"What the *fuck* are you doing?"

L'zar's head whipped up from his work, and he hissed madly at her. "You."

"Yeah, me." Cheyenne's eyes widened at the strobing lights in every color flashing behind his eyes. "I've been trying to find you."

"What is that? A fence?" L'zar scanned the area around her, obviously seeing at least part of the skatepark. "If you think you can stop this with a cage, you're stupider than I thought—Stop!" He snarled and smacked himself on the cheek.

"L'zar."

"Don't. Don't even look. Eyes on the task. The endgame. The rip, rip, rip... What the hell is this!" He snatched something off the invisible table and turned to hurl it across whatever room he was in. "If you even think about—"

"Where are you?" Cheyenne asked. "I'll come to you. Just tell me."

"Say nothing. See nothing. Do nothing!" The flashing lights behind his golden eyes spread to his entire body, flickering from within him and lighting every inch of his slate-gray skin. "This is the rest of it. The rest, and the last, and the beginning, over and over and over."

L'zar's arms and hands moved sporadically, like a puppet being handled by someone who didn't quite understand how bodies were supposed to move.

This is it. He's officially lost his mind. If he's even still in there.

"L'zar. It's Cheyenne."

The Weaver muttered unintelligibly and shook his head in sharp, jerky movements as he focused on his work.

"I know you can see me. I found you. Tell me where you are."

L'zar flung another unseen item away from him and whirled to snarl, "If you don't shut your fell-damn mouth, I will. You're too dry to do a thing about it!"

"Is that Corian?" Cheyenne wanted to step over to her father but couldn't move. "He's with you, isn't he?"

Her father snarled again and returned to his work, the colored lights beneath his skin pulsing as they changed.

At least Corian's still alive. I hope.

"L'zar, listen to me!"

"Enough! Your pattern is ended, *mór úcare*. Leave the Weaver to his." He raised his hand as if to strike her, then lunged forward and slapped both hands on the table in front of him. For a split second, the golden glow of his drow eyes broke through the flashing colored lights, and L'zar Verdys was lucid. And terrified. "Cheyenne, pay attention. It's all right there. Everything you need to— Get out!"

The voice at the end wasn't entirely his. It was fueled by a brilliant burst of multicolored lights that came from his eyes and his mouth and his nostrils.

"Pay attention to what?" Cheyenne's heartbeat raced furiously. "L'zar, what are you—"

The intensity of the vision blasting into her mind took everything over. She saw the front gates of Chateau D'rahl in broad daylight, the bodies of four guards strewn across the ground. The air around the prison rippled with multicolored lights and opalescent flames, then the screams reached her.

She saw magicals and humans fleeing in panic but unable to get away. The lines of fire streaked toward body after body, striking them down and pulsing even brighter as they shrieked and howled at the magic being torn from them. Humans convulsed on the asphalt of the prison's parking lot, in the grass surrounding the property, and among the trees blocking Chateau D'rahl from the rest of DC.

Then the Sorren Gán's face was in her mind, its gaping black maw spilling black smoke as opalescent flames flickered around its lips and dripped to the ground like water.

Or blood.

The creature's laugh rumbled through her head as it drew one line of opalescent flames after another toward itself and crammed them into its mouth. A thunderous crack like breaking and tumbling stone joined its laughter, then its fiery eyes settled on Cheyenne as the world around her burned.

"You cannot stop this. I made you what you are!"

The creature thrust one deathly-sharp claw at her chest and struck her.

Cheyenne fell back and heard the crack of her head hitting the concrete of the skatepark before she felt it. "Fuck."

She lay there for a moment, breathing heavily and gritting her teeth against the growing throb of pain shooting down the back of her head into her neck. When she opened her eyes, she saw only the dark sky studded with stars.

Was that from L'zar? Is that what he's trying to do?

With a grunt of effort, she pushed herself up to sit on the cement again, blinking through the pain, and recrossed her legs. "We're not done."

She closed her eyes and tried to steady her breathing. *One more time. He's still in there. He recognized me.*

The feeling of rising through her body and simultaneously sitting there returned as she called on the *Don'adurr* Thread again, but it took her nowhere. She should have been able to feel L'zar and find him again, but the magic reaching out to her father was weak and ineffective—not hers, but his.

"Shit." Cheyenne's eyelids fluttered open, and she scanned the fence in front of her. *I was right. L'zar's not calling the shots. He can't. And the Sorren Gán wants to, what, rip open a bunch of portals to feed on everyone in this world?*

The sound of at least four different pairs of footsteps briefly caught her attention, but she ignored them. They were out in the grass.

Doesn't make sense. That thing doesn't go through any trouble just to feed on magic. It's still full from Hangivol, so it wants what? Fuck. What does it want?

A growl of frustration escaped her, and she slapped her thighs. "Why can't I fucking figure this out?"

"Whoa!"

"Benny, hold up."

"Where the heck did she come from?"

Cheyenne leaped to her feet and snarled, almost summoning a black energy sphere in her hand before she saw four boys who couldn't have been older than fourteen standing rigidly on the other side of the fence. They stared at her, and one of them opened and closed his mouth before muttering, "You okay?"

"You guys shouldn't be out this late by yourselves."

"But it's only—"

"Beat it." She stepped forward and the kids jumped into action, pulling each other away from the skatepark and scrambling toward the other side of the park. One of them looked over his shoulder and saw her staring after them. He tripped into his friend, then kept running.

Cheyenne took a deep breath and stared at the edge of the park even after the boys had disappeared across the street into the neighborhood. *Be glad they're freaked out by a Goth girl in the skatepark and not a drow on a rampage.*

Something rustled in the trashcan beneath the pavilion, and she spun toward it. This time, the dark light of her crackling black energy sphere flared in her palm. "If you don't step out and show yourself, I'll blow the whole thing to pieces."

A low, grunting chuckle rose in reply, followed by more rustling. Then a small yellow head with a shock of red hair burst from the top of the trashcan, sending empty candy bar wrappers fluttering to the ground. "You seem a little jumpy."

Cheyenne snuffed out the energy sphere and grimaced. "Says the gremlin eating out of a public trashcan."

"What, you expect me to go through private trash?" He scoffed and lifted a half-eaten pack of mini doughnuts to the pale light. "Please. You only find the good stuff out where people think they've finally gotten rid of it. Hey, how's your head?"

"What?"

"Heard you hit it." The gremlin ripped open the package and shoved a chocolate mini doughnut into his mouth. "I wouldn't go to sleep right away if I were you. One time, I cracked my head open on the bottom of a dumpster lid. Thought I'd left the thing open. Those damn raccoons!"

"Have a good night." Cheyenne slipped through the gate in the fence.

"You found him, right? The Weaver?"

She cocked her head and watched him cram two more doughnuts

into his mouth. "If you wanna know, go check out the Borderlands. Enjoy your snack."

"Hey, thanks. Blood and honor for the—"

"Don't say it."

Chuckling, the gremlin lifted the last doughnut toward her in a toast, crumbs spilling from his overfull mouth, then ducked back into the trashcan.

Feels like I'm being watched from every angle all the time. That's gonna stop as soon as I figure out where the hell L'zar's holing up. No way am I gonna let him get to that prison.

CHAPTER SEVENTY-ONE

Whether the vision had come from L'zar or had spilled over from the Sorren Gán's connection to him, it turned over and over in Cheyenne's mind as she left Jackson Ward and drove north to her apartment. Ember's and Neros' voices rose from the other side of the door as soon as she stepped off the elevator, but she didn't expect to find Matthew Thomas sitting in the living room with them when she opened the door and practically slammed it behind her.

"Hey." Ember's surprised smile disappeared when she noticed her friend's distracted scowl. "What happened?"

"A lot and nothing, all at the same time, Em." Cheyenne looked at Matthew and nodded curtly. "You look like you're feeling better."

"Thanks." His smile looked like someone had put a gun to his head and told him to enjoy stepping across broken glass. "Helps when I'm not sitting alone in my apartment. I can leave if you—"

"No, you're fine." The drow dropped into the recliner closest to the door and frowned at Neros. "What are you doing?"

"Trying to make out these symbols." Her cousin crouched over a book in his lap, scowling at the open pages. "Whoever was responsible for creating such a pointless alphabet needs to start over."

Matthew glanced at Ember and muttered, "He can't read?"

"Not English." The fae leaned toward Neros and spun the book on his lap. "Might help if you're not trying to read sideways."

Neros closed the book and shook his head. "I don't think it matters which way I read it."

"What happens when you're alone?" Cheyenne asked.

"What?"

She gestured at Matthew. "You said it's better when you're not alone at your place."

"Oh." He ran a hand through his hair. "It's hard to get out of my head."

"I feel you."

Matthew leaned back on the couch and rubbed his hands down his pant legs. "I got another call today. From those people who wanna buy my program."

"And?"

"And I told them I was still undecided. They're getting pushy, though. Showing more of their hand to squeeze me into it." Their neighbor gazed nervously around the apartment until he decided to spit out the rest. "They said Les had made them certain promises he obviously couldn't keep anymore, so now it's my job to follow through."

"Sounds like a threat."

"Kinda, yeah."

"Did they mention anything about magicals?" Cheyenne dropped her arms on the armrests. "Or say anything that sounded like they know?"

Matthew shook his head. "Les knew, obviously. These guys know about the program, and that's all they ever talk about."

"I don't get why humans would want it," Ember said, "if they don't know about the machines."

"We don't know who knows about the war machines." Cheyenne closed her eyes and grimaced at the dull throb in her head when she rested it against the back of the recliner. "Maleshi stashed them in the warehouse, remember? Now they're gone."

"L'zar was the one who broke into the warehouse, though, wasn't he?"

"That's a pretty firm 'I think so,' Em."

"What do you want me to do about it?" Matthew asked.

"Hang tight. I'll look into who those jerks are and find out why they're bothering you."

"Thanks, Cheyenne."

"Yeah." She stood and pointed at him as she turned to head for the stairs to the loft. "First thing on my list after I send a giant alert message to as many magicals as Tori got on her app in the last three hours."

"What?" Ember and Matthew watched the drow climb the staircase.

"I found L'zar. Kind of. He's not doing this on his own. Honestly, I think he used the last of what little control he had left over his mind to tell me where they're gonna strike."

"Oh, jeez." Ember started to get up off the couch but decided against it and asked, "Who's 'they?'"

"As far as I know? Just L'zar and the Sorren Gán." Cheyenne sat in her desk chair and powered Glenn up.

Ember stared wordlessly up at the loft. Beside her, Neros straightened and cocked his head. "Is that so?"

Cheyenne shivered when she saw him with the same expression and in the same position as R'leer. *How do all the drow dudes I know manage to be the exact same level of creepy in the exact same way?*

"Well, Neros." She pulled up her VPN and waited for it to cycle before logging onto the dark web. "I'm aware that I might be wrong, but I don't think I am. Drow mind-meld showed me L'zar, all right. Nothing else. I couldn't even see what he was holding in his hands. But I'm pretty sure he was talking to Corian at one point, and the rest of it was probably the Sorren Gán."

"Holy shit," Ember whispered.

"Yep." She navigated her way to Third Quarter Projections and entered the Borderlands forum one more time. "As far as I could tell, L'zar's still working on the last bit of whatever he's trying to do, so we have a little more time. How much? I have no clue. R'leer and I pretty much agree L'zar's trying to rip open a bunch of Border portals and keep them open. Or get rid of them altogether."

"Wait, R'leer? He's still on the other side."

"Talked to him through a magic mirror a fae loaned me."

"Okay, you guys lost me at Sorren whatever." Matthew shook his head. "But judging by Ember's face right now, I get a feeling it's bad."

"Well, it's not good, that's for sure."

Ember stared at her hands, then shot Matthew a confused look before gesturing at the loft. "And all that new information makes you wanna play around on your computer for a while?"

Cheyenne leaned sideways to shoot her friend a warning look through the metal bars of the rail.

"Sorry."

"One of the magicals at the Borderlands meeting wrote an app for anyone who wants to help us to communicate with each other all at once." She clicked into the new private message from DarkWing8008 that had a single line of text: Special Invitation. Below that was a link and a password. Cheyenne clicked the link. "And I'm gonna make it better."

"So, you're improving the technology to stop L'zar."

"Hopefully." The drow looked down through the bars and raised an eyebrow. "Would you believe it was Tori who built this app?"

"Tori?"

"Yeah, my student, remember? Oh, hey. She's the one who dug up all that conflicting info about your Uncle Matthew. You know what? If you're ever looking for an intern or someone to fill an entry-level position at Thomas Safe…"

He leaned against the couch's armrest, looking pale. "I don't know if that's a good idea."

"You're probably right. She'd be way too bored at entry-level. I can write a great letter of recommendation for her, though. Keep it in the back of your mind." Cheyenne dove back into her Borderlands messaging and opened the link to download Tori's new app. It gave her the option to download to her phone as well, which of course she did.

Matthew looked at Ember and whispered, "It can't be that bad if she's talking about helping someone else get a job, right?"

"Oh, no. It's still bad. She's gotten a lot better at multitasking."

Pulling out her phone, Cheyenne downloaded the new app through the private link texted to her, then she was in. The main message board was full of speculation, magicals talking about how cool it was to have an activator, others asking how the hell anyone could have a working activator Earthside. Altogether, there were twenty-one members on the app, including everyone who'd met at Kenneth's warehouse a few hours before.

Cheyenne paused with her fingers over the keyboard on her phone and wrinkled her nose. *Well, they believed everything else I told them. Guess I don't need to worry about how insane this is gonna sound.*

ShyHand71: Hey, guys. Good to see you here. Here's what's happening. Whatever's going down will happen at Chateau D'rahl. Can't say when exactly, but it'll be soon, so we all need to be ready. I'm hooking up something extra to help us stay connected. Not sure we'll always have the time to text on an app, even one that works as well as this one seems to. I want anybody who has an activator to let me know when they get it. Stand by.

Nobody else said a thing in the chat, so she focused on the next step. *At least they're not using this thing like the forum.*

Her activator simultaneously pulled up the code within Tori's app and her phone's operating system, and with a series of short command prompts, she rearranged the access lines to include bits of the activator's programming. It wasn't the same as Matthew's program, but his program had been created here on Earth to meld human innovation with O'gúl tech.

Pretty basic transfer. If it works.

She studied her phone, waiting for someone to send a response.

It'll work.

The next message came from Brúj, which she wouldn't have known if it had just pulled up his username on the app and nothing else. The message also came through her activator and lit up in the top right corner of her vision.

Brúj: Holy shit. This is for real.

She snorted and didn't have to bother typing. All she needed was to think her message and the activator took care of the rest, posting for her in the app and simultaneously across the new activator network she'd just created with Matthew's program.

Cheyenne: It's real. Everyone else can see this too, right?

Cassandra: I don't know how it's possible, but yes.

Kenneth: This is outstanding. Well done.

Henry: Great. Just what I needed, a whole gang of magical techies in my head.

Melody: Don't pretend this isn't a dream come true for you.

Jeff: Well, fuck me sideways. Y'all know how hard it is to surprise me these days?

Bucky: Cheyenne. You're the drow?

She frowned and looked at her computer screen, though she didn't even see the monitor because she was focused on the active chat in the corner of her vision. *Word will get out so much faster this way.*

Cheyenne: That's me. Thanks for joining us.

Jeff: I brought him.

Brúj: Great. She'll probably hand out gold stars later. You know, after the whole "stop the Border from being ripped apart" thing.

Lit&Loaded4Real: You guys all have activators?

Henry: Yup.

Lit&Loaded4Real: Shit. How do I get in on that?

UptownGClass10: Yeah, me too.

A whole slew of other magicals who'd installed the app posted their own questions about the activators and their next move. Cheyenne could hardly read each one before it was replaced by the next.

Cheyenne: Okay, we need to keep this channel clear. The bottom line right now is that all the available activators have been handed out. Anyone who was at the factory today and who still has one or both their extras should hand them out to magicals they trust. Everyone else, keep your notifications on for the main chat. PM somebody if you're not trying to get in touch with everyone. And reach out to everyone you know who has a phone. Tell them to download this thing. Get them on board. Anyone who's willing to stand up against some serious magic needs to be ready.

Tori: Any idea when that might be?

Cheyenne: Soon. That's all I have right now. When I know more, this is the first place that information's going.

She sat back in her chair and watched a string of thumbs-up and fist-bump emojis roll in from the app's users. "It's a start, I guess."

"Uh-oh." The voice blasted into her mind, a little tinny as if it had come through a phone but all around her.

Cheyenne spun in her chair. "What?"

Kenneth's chuckle filled her mind. "I believe you've also discovered audio communication through these things. We can hear you, Cheyenne."

As he spoke, his activator transcribed everything into the main chat, which she saw also contained her brief line.

Anderson Weber would piss himself if he heard these activators now work like phones. I don't have to tell him anything.

Cheyenne rolled her eyes. "Anyone else online with audio?"

A chorus of yeses and affirmative grunts filled her head and scrolled across the active chat.

"Wow. Okay." She gripped the armrests of her chair against the blare of voices and quickly selected her activator's prompt to cut the volume by half. "You guys know how to use those things. Cut off audio until we need it. And Tori?"

"Yeah."

"Good work with this app."

"Does that mean I get an A for the semester?"

Cheyenne snorted. "Remind me to tell you about a job opportunity when all this is over. Now seriously. Everybody off."

She disabled the audio on her end and spun back around in her chair. *Turned out better than I expected. Now I need these guys to go out and collect an army on this app.*

After quickly logging out of the dark web and shutting down the VPN, Cheyenne rolled her chair away from the desk and looked down at Ember and Matthew through the bars. "That went well."

"You look way too happy right now," Ember muttered and folded her arms.

"Appreciating the little things, Em." The drow stood and headed for the top of the stairs.

"That's normal for you?" Matthew asked.

"Trying to make it that way, yeah."

Ember slowly shook her head. "Cheyenne, you were talking to yourself."

"And I wouldn't call that a little thing."

Cheyenne spun at the bottom of the stairs and stopped. "Oh. You guys think I've lost my mind too, huh?"

"I mean…"

A laugh burst out of the drow, and she pointed at the silver coil behind her ear. "Activator, Em. Turns out Matthew's program also turns these things into Bluetooth headsets. Who knew?"

"Wow." Matthew cocked his head. "I didn't write anything into it that should be able to do that."

"Of course you didn't. Collaboration at its finest, Matthew. Tori built an app, I have an activator that doesn't need your program, and *bam.* Just stick 'em all together." She winked at him and walked swiftly across the living room to the kitchen. "You guys eat yet?"

"No." Ember slung an arm over the back of the couch. "Are you feeling okay?"

"I'm fine." Cheyenne opened the fridge, then shut it and grabbed a frozen mushroom risotto out of the freezer instead. "You cool if I eat this?"

"Yeah."

"Seriously, I'm fine. It's not like this is the worst thing we've faced, right?"

Ember squinted as her friend nonchalantly punctured the container's plastic wrapper and tossed the thing in the microwave. "Depends on how you look at it, I guess. But you seem really peppy. For you."

"'Peppy?'" Cheyenne leaned against the counter and folded her arms as the microwave hummed for two minutes. "That's the word you're going with."

"Compared to your baseline, yeah. And it's weird that you're not more worried about this."

"Maybe I'm grateful that something's working out the way it's supposed to, Em. We've got two hundred activators floating around with magical citizens and FRoE agents. This app helped. I figured out how to turn on a giant magical comm unit linking all of them. Oh! Hold on." Cheyenne pulled up the app and sent Tori a quick message.

Invite to this number. Thanks.

The Verati didn't reply, but only because she hadn't wasted any time in doing what Cheyenne asked.

Ember's phone dinged, and she pulled it out of her pocket to frown at the text banner.

"What's that?" Matthew asked.

"I have no clue."

"That's for you, Em. Download it, then you'll understand what I'm talking about. Make sure the audio's off."

Ember took a minute to click through the prompts on her phone, then her eyelids fluttered, and she spun on the couch to sink back against the cushion, staring at the ceiling. "Oh!"

"Yep."

"This is awesome." The fae laughed in disbelief and scanned the messages in the app's main chat that now showed up in her vision. "Okay, I take it back. You're not insane."

"Thank you so much for that glowing bill of health, Healer." Cheyenne almost bowed, but the image of L'zar doing the same thing flashed through her head. She gripped the edge of the countertop and scowled instead.

"She's right." Ember nudged Matthew's arm and nodded. "You need to give this Tori chick a job."

He let out a tired, unsure chuckle. "I'll think about it."

CHAPTER SEVENTY-TWO

Cheyenne ate her formerly frozen dinner standing over the kitchen island and wondered if her activator could draw from Matthew's program for other hands-free functions. It gave her three different prompts for interacting with her cell phone, and she snorted before selecting the outgoing call option. The second she thought about pulling up Maleshi's number, the ring filled her mind.

We made this way too easy.

The general answered on the third ring. "Please tell me you've found something useful, kid. I sure as shit haven't."

"Okay."

"Okay, what?"

"I found something. Lots of things. You have some time to listen to it all?"

Maleshi sighed. "I just opened a bag of chips, so as long as you don't mind talking over the crunching, fill me in."

Cheyenne relayed everything she'd learned from her ardorium call with R'leer and the creepy connection with L'zar when she'd used the *Don'adurr* Thread. When she got to the part about Tori's app syncing with the activators, Maleshi groaned in disappointment. "You gave them all out, huh?"

"Shit. Sorry."

"It's fine, kid. You've been on a mission, and I'm not exactly the most helpless magical without one anyway. I'll wait for the next shipment to come in."

The drow snorted. "Yeah, I'll make sure that happens sooner rather than later."

"Excellent."

"You know anything about this spell R'leer mentioned? If he knew the name, he didn't seem too happy about saying it out loud."

"Honestly, it sounds like a drow spell, kid. Or something only a complete idiot would cook up in his own spare time. Wish I could be more helpful."

"It's fine."

"So, what's the plan?"

Cheyenne dropped her fork in the empty risotto container and cocked her head. "You're asking me?"

"You're running this show, Cheyenne. As much as it sucks that we have to deal with this right now, with L'zar, I'd say it's about damn time you took the lead a hundred percent."

"Huh." *You chose Drow royalty on Earth, Cheyenne. Time to step into the shoes.* "Okay. You keep looking for L'zar and Corian any way you can. I don't think he's ready to move yet, but he will be in one, maybe two days. If we can find them first, we can keep everybody out of it."

"And if we can't?"

The drow said, "Then I need to get as many magicals as I can to Chateau D'rahl. Every rez L'zar hit in the last few days has about ten with activators. As soon they know the Border towers aren't the main issue anymore, I'll get them re-stationed at the prison. And get everyone else geared up for the same, I guess."

"Sounds good to me."

"Hey, I'll get an invite to that app out to you. Just for fun."

Maleshi chuckled dryly. "I'm overjoyed."

"Yeah, sounds like it. Keep your phone on, huh?"

"As long as I'm not the next nightstalker on L'zar's ingredients list, then yeah. I'll keep it on." The general ended the call, and Cheyenne looked up to see Neros and Ember on the couch with the TV on. Her cousin stared with rapt attention at the screen while the fae browsed through something on her phone.

"Where's Matthew?"

"He went home." Ember nodded at the door. "Said he wanted to find out what you did to change his program."

"I didn't change it." Cheyenne tossed the empty container in the trash and stuck the fork in the dishwasher. "Just rerouted a few things."

"Either way, I think he wanted a distraction, and I was probably ignoring him by accident. These magicals you got together on this app, Cheyenne? They're ready to go."

"What?" Cheyenne stepped out of the kitchen and glanced at Neros, who didn't seem to hear a word of their conversation. *Probably for the best. At least he's occupied.*

"Yeah. Forty-six on there now. Granted, most of them don't have activators, but they don't seem to care."

Cheyenne pulled up the app's main chat, but there hadn't been any new messages there since she'd signed off with the others. "You're messaging them all personally."

"Well, yeah." Ember finally looked up from her phone and grinned. "Somebody has to update the new ones, right?"

"Sounds like you've got virtual hospitality handled." Cheyenne blinked heavily and fought back a yawn. "I'm gonna go lie down and make a few more calls."

"Yeah." Ember had gone back to her phone.

"You know you can just think messages, right?" Cheyenne pointed at her own activator.

"I am. And while those send, I'm typing other ones." Ember shook her head. "I'm pretty sure I mastered multitasking way before you did."

"Right. Thanks for keeping everybody in the loop." When the fae didn't offer a response, Cheyenne headed into her room and closed the door behind her. The blackout curtains blocked even the city lights below their apartment, but she didn't need to see to make a beeline for her bed. After flopping on the mattress, she pulled up Rhynehart's number with her activator and made the call.

"What do we need to do?" he answered gruffly.

"Yeah, hi."

"Come on, Cheyenne. I've been waiting for this call all day. What's the plan?"

She told him as much as she could without adding too many confusing magical details, but the main points got across fine.

"This is fucking insane," Rhynehart muttered.

"I know. We need to be ready for it anyway."

"What do you want me to do?"

"Ten agents at every rez that was hit have activators. We need to pull them and send them to Chateau D'rahl to cover our bases."

"Shit," he said, frustrated. "I can't."

She sat up quickly and stared into the darkness of her room. "What do you mean, you can't?"

"Don't have the clearance. Otherwise, I hope you know I'd make the calls myself."

"Yeah. Okay."

"Even if I made the calls right now, they won't mean anything without approval from the top."

"I get it." Cheyenne ran a hand through her hair, then turned on the mattress to kick her black Vans onto the floor. "I'll talk to Van Lurig."

"Perks of being a consultant, I guess."

"You know, there haven't been nearly as many as I expected. Kinda surprising."

Rhynehart snorted. "Let me know how it goes."

He hung up, and Cheyenne's activator pulled up the number for Helen Holder. That was all she had.

The phone rang six times, then the click of the answering machine came through. Cheyenne ended the call and tried one more time with the same results. *So, the agents are on call, Sir and Rhynehart don't have regular hours, but Helen the assistant calls it a night before eight o'clock. Figures.*

The yawn she'd managed to hold back in the living room returned with full force. She didn't stop it this time and let herself fall back on the mattress with a heavy sigh. *I can't sleep now. Can't stay up waiting for L'zar to make his move, either. Van Lurig can wait.*

She thought she'd be up for hours staring at the ceiling, but it only took her two minutes to pass out in her clothes on top of the bedspread.

The smell of coffee wafting under her door woke her up. Cheyenne groaned and rolled over, reaching for the covers to pull them over her head before she realized she'd slept the whole night on top of them. She blinked against her phone's backlight and stared at the time.

Twelve hours. Uninterrupted. No nightmares. Fucking finally.

Neros and Ember were already up and sitting at a tall black bistro table between the couch and the wall of windows. Cheyenne paused when she saw them, Ember with both hands around a mug of coffee and Neros sipping orange juice through a straw. "When did this happen?"

"About an hour ago." Ember grinned and patted the table's surface. "Nice, right?"

"Since when did the two of you figure out how to build a table like that without making a sound?"

"Perks of having a weirdo cousin from a different dimension couch-surfing in your apartment." Ember sipped her coffee, then nodded at Neros. "He made himself useful and decided to magic the table together instead of cutting up more of my clothes."

"Huh. Good choice."

"I still do not understand why this seemed to be such a complicated process." Neros gulped down more orange juice and pulled away from the straw with a contented sigh. "It took me five seconds."

"Well, 'cuz, most people in this world don't have Nor'ieth magic to do everything for them. And I'm guessing it takes most O'gúleesh a lot longer than five seconds to figure out how to assemble anything over here without an activator or a system mainframe to do it all for them."

"I am surprised, Cheyenne. I did not think Earth would be so primitive."

Ember scoffed, "Ambar'ogúl has advanced tech, sure, but we don't throw each other into fighting pits and burn ourselves with healing fire to boost the economy."

Neros' eyes widened. "Neither do I."

Cheyenne poured herself a cup of coffee and took a minute to enjoy not feeling like a zombie after more than a full night's sleep. Then she pulled up Helen's number one more time and tried again.

"Helen Holder."

"Cheyenne Summerlin."

"Oh." The woman paused. "What can I do for you?"

"I need to talk to Catherine, but I don't have her number. Is she there?"

Helen cleared her throat, and the sound of papers shuffling on a desk came over the line. "Major General Van Lurig is currently unavailable, Cheyenne. Would you like to leave a message?"

"No. When will she be available?"

"Oh, I'm so sorry. It looks like she's in back-to-back meetings all day. Maybe I can squeeze you in sometime at the end of the week?"

"We don't have 'til the end of the week, Helen. Tell her I need to speak to her."

"As I said, the major general is in meetings all day. I'll hardly see her myself. How about Friday at ten-thirty?"

Cheyenne ended the call, took a huge sip of coffee, and stormed to her room to grab her jacket.

"Everything okay?" Ember asked.

"That lady likes to fuck with me." Shrugging into her jacket, Cheyenne crossed the living room again and headed for the door. "I'm heading out to the FRoE base. Shouldn't take very long."

"Good luck."

"I hope so." *Otherwise, I'm gonna have to step out of my consultant pants and go all drow dictator on the board. Last resort. Can't say I'm not looking forward to it.*

CHAPTER SEVENTY-THREE

When she rolled up on the base, Cheyenne parked the Panamera at the far end of the huge parking lot, which was filled with activator-wielding agents practicing spells on their own time. She got out, locked the doors, and stalked across the lot to the front doors of the main building.

Spells flew in all directions, followed by laughter and loud, jeering calls as the agents egged each other on. Most of the agents paused when they saw her, lifting hands or nodding in greeting. She returned the nods of a few of them but was a lot more focused on getting inside to find Van Lurig.

"Hey! Cheyenne!" Yurik whipped off his dampening helmet and jogged over to her. "Back for more training?"

"What? No. I told you guys to stick with it on your own." She scanned the agents, who'd returned to their sparring. One agent sent a blast of four-foot-diameter multicolored orbs across the parking lot. They bounced and spun, chasing the other agents. A skinny troll shouted and crashed to the asphalt when one of the orbs hit his back and threw him forward, eliciting a round of roaring laughter and crude jokes from the other operatives. "Doesn't seem like anybody's taking it too seriously, though."

"We take it seriously, sure. These things are awesome."

"Then why am I seeing magic tricks instead of sparring?"

Yurik frowned at her and straightened. "There's only so much pummeling each other to go around. The next step would be to take these out in the field."

"So take them into the field. We seriously need you guys to be ready for what's coming." Cheyenne shook her head. "Which I never told you about. Look, I'm here to see Van Lurig. There's gonna be an attack on Chateau D'rahl."

"Another one?" Yurik folded his arms and gazed around the parking lot, but no one was paying attention. "Cheyenne, that was fun and all, but Rhynehart's got his job back, and I don't think any of us are down to break in again."

"I said attack, not break in."

The muscular goblin scrunched his nose. "Okay."

"We need a huge number of agents at the prison to be ready. That's why I'm here."

"Can you prove it?"

"Do I need to?"

He shrugged. "Probably. But I doubt you'll get the green light to send out a bunch of agents who just had their first taste of using real magic in the last seventy-two hours."

"Tell everyone to stop screwing around and use those things the way they were meant to be used. I'll worry about the green light."

Yurik nodded at her curtly and turned to watch her stalk toward the front doors.

"Hey. Drow." Grot thumped his gloved fists together, then nodded across the parking lot. "That your Porsche?"

Cheyenne pointed at him and kept walking. "Touch my car, and I'll end you."

He chuckled and folded his arms, staring after her until she disappeared across the lobby and down the hall on the west wing.

Fortunately, Helen was patrolling the halls of the third floor when Cheyenne stepped out of the elevator. *Meetings all day, huh? Fine. Should make her easy to find.*

She threw open every door she passed, checking it for Van Lurig and whatever meeting she might or might not be conducting. The conference room where she'd met with the board every time was also empty, but it wasn't the last door.

Then Helen rounded the corner, saw Cheyenne, and stopped. "Excuse me."

"Sure." Cheyenne kept moving down the hall, opening doors left and right.

"Ms. Summerlin, what do you think you're doing?"

"Saving two worlds from death and destruction. Again. Where is she?"

"I told you, the major general's in meetings all day. You can't come storming in here to interrupt." The woman stopped and scowled when the next door Cheyenne opened revealed what she was looking for.

She turned back to look at Helen and shot her a winning smile. "I'll take it from here, Helen. Thank you." Then she slipped inside the room and closed the door behind her.

There were only four people in this particular meeting: Van Lurig and three other humans in plain black suits sitting across the table from her, two men and a woman. The conversation paused as they all turned to look at her.

"Cheyenne." Van Lurig folded her hands on the table and frowned. "We're in a meeting."

"So I heard. Normally, I'd schedule an appointment with your secretary, but this can't wait."

"But it can. We're in the middle of something I've moved my schedule around to accommodate."

"It won't take very long." Cheyenne stepped over to Van Lurig's side of the table and nodded at the three suits staring at her with blank expressions. "Excuse us for a second. Two things, Major General. First, those agents need to be out in the field using their new gear in real-time. Or at least approved for it."

"Cheyenne, this isn't—"

The drow looked at the three stoic humans. "And I need ten agents from each of the thirteen reservations that were affected two days ago to be moved from their current posts and stationed on the prison grounds."

"We can discuss your requests later," Van Lurig replied through clenched teeth. "Now please let me return to—"

"Look, later's not gonna cut it. Something's coming, and it's coming for the prison. I can give you details later, but right now, I need the all-clear to get those agents off the reservations."

"That is quite enough, Cheyenne." Van Lurig scooted violently away from the table and stood, gesturing at the door. "You need to step outside and wait until I'm finished."

"You need to listen to me."

"Excuse me, Major General." The suit on the far right with the adolescent sideburns lifted a finger. Van Lurig and Cheyenne turned to stare at him. "Is this woman the Cheyenne Summerlin you mentioned?"

"Oh, great. You mentioned me." The drow glared at Van Lurig. "Who are these guys?"

"This is—"

"Ms. Summerlin," the woman suit added, "we've heard about your work in preparing this organization's operatives with certain new technology, and we're very interested."

"Yeah, it's a work in progress. And it would work a lot better if the major general would hear me out and get these operatives moved to where they need to be."

Van Lurig shot the drow a warning glare.

"You wouldn't happen to have any extra devices on you, would you?" Sideburns asked. "Those…what did you call them?"

The second man in the suit with a massive zit on his chin grunted. "Activators."

"Right. Cheyenne?"

"You want an activator?" Cheyenne frowned at them and folded her arms. "Take off your mask first."

"I'm sorry?" The woman blinked and shot Cheyenne a confused smile that would have looked more natural on a corpse.

Van Lurig shook her head. "Cheyenne, they're not…"

"That's what I thought." *Three humans sitting in a meeting with the head FRoE official and wanting to get their hands on an activator. Matthew did say they looked like feds.* "What's going on?"

"Ms. Summerlin, we have been down every avenue we could think of for this endeavor," the anonymous woman continued. "Except we haven't yet had the opportunity to speak with you, so it's lucky for us that you barged into this meeting uninvited."

"Every avenue." Cheyenne looked at Van Lurig. "Does that include trying to strongarm Matthew Thomas?"

The major general rubbed her eyebrow in frustration.

Sideburns cocked his head. "You know him?"

"A little. Sure. He said you've been showing up at his apartment. Calling him. Raising the stakes. Seems kinda weird that you'd come here looking for the same thing."

"Mr. Thomas' uncle was a member of this organization's board."

"The colonel. I know."

"Of course you do." The woman leaned forward and folded her hands on the table. "And before he was incarcerated, Colonel Thomas engaged in a number of business deals with us and our organization. His mistakes were unfortunate, but they've also left us with our hands empty and our clients waiting for us to fulfill our end of the deal with merchandise and services the colonel can no longer provide."

"So we reached out to Major General Van Lurig to see how our two organizations can help each other," Sideburns added. "Which is where those activators might be very useful."

Business deals with the colonel? How does Van Lurig not see what a shit-show this could turn into? Bet they know something about the stolen war machines.

Cheyenne looked from one expressionless face to the next and shrugged. "Sorry. Van Lurig can't make a deal for the activators. Neither can the board or anyone in the FRoE because they don't own the things. Not even a patent. Can't give it away. Can't sell it. That's part of the agreement."

"Cheyenne," Van Lurig muttered.

"That *was* part of the agreement." Cheyenne stared at the major general until she looked away.

"We only want one of those devices." Sideburns spread his arms. "Wouldn't hurt to throw us a bone, would it?"

"I'm guessing it would." Cheyenne wrinkled her nose in mock sympathy. "And the activators don't run on the program you're looking for. Just so you know."

"We don't mind a few updates," the woman said. "As long as the core is—"

"It's not the same. Completely rewritten. Totally different. And it only works with activators. Sorry."

Sideburns leaned over the table to exchange knowing looks with his partners, then stood and nodded at Van Lurig. "This obviously isn't the right time, Major General."

"It was. I apologize for the interruption."

"No need." The woman stood next, followed by Zit, who'd still only said one word. "We'll let you handle your internal affairs, and when you're ready to pick this discussion back up, you know how to contact us."

Van Lurig nodded as the suits left the room without another word. As soon as the door closed, she whirled on Cheyenne. "I don't know what you think you're doing barging in on a private meeting, but it's unacceptable."

"Necessary, though." The drow shrugged. "And those people don't want to see how they can help the FRoE. They're only interested in helping themselves."

"You have no idea who those people are, Cheyenne!" Van Lurig gestured sharply at the door. "They've already made an offer."

"Well, good fucking thing you didn't get the chance to accept it."

"Watch yourself."

"Listen, those guys have been after Matthew Thomas for days now. Threatening him. Practically stalking him because they want the program he wrote. You know, the one that powered the war machines Colonel Thomas paid for with FRoE money? This isn't about technology. This is seriously dangerous stuff in the wrong hands. Their hands, specifically."

Van Lurig stared at her and then lowered herself into her chair again. "I'm sorry to hear that."

"Don't be sorry. Just don't make a deal with whoever the hell those people are. You're not gonna be able to give them an activator anyway. No one's gonna give theirs up."

"They will if I order it."

"Come on."

The general major pressed the side of her fist into the table and grimaced. "Cheyenne, Colonel Thomas was, among other things, this organization's top investor. That was what got him a seat on the board, and that was why we didn't do as much as we could have to question his initiative and look into what we now know he did. I regret that, but it doesn't change the reality."

"Of what? That you have an empty seat on the board? I can think of a dozen people off the top of my head who'd be a way better choice than getting into bed with those assholes."

"If they're willing to contribute the same level of funding as Colonel Thomas did for the last twenty-one years, I'd be willing to consider it. But it can't wait."

"You're out of money already?" Cheyenne leaned against the table and folded her arms. "He's only been behind bars for a week."

"Yes. If it had been anyone else, we would have been in the black for at least the next six months, but the colonel's accounts have all been frozen, with good reason. Including the ones he was responsible for handling on the FRoE's behalf. Even if that weren't the case, I'd be acting against my conscience by continuing to use that man's funds after what he tried to do to this organization and who knows how many others. So yes, we're out of money already." Van Lurig glared at the table, her nostrils flaring.

At least she's got some *ethical backbone.*

"How long can you keep things running?"

"Before we fall apart at the seams?" Van Lurig shook her head. "Another week, and that's stretching it. Without the colonel's contributions and the accounts I wish we'd never handed over to him, not to mention the various networking groups he was a member of that were interested enough to support various projects of ours, we won't have the resources to keep doing what this organization was founded to do. And I'm certain there's no one else even remotely prepared enough to take over for us."

"I get it." Cheyenne pulled out a chair beside the woman and rolled it down the table a bit to give them both more space. Then she sat and nodded. "You're stuck between a rock and a hard place. Trust me, I know that sucks, but you can't go into business with those people. It'll be a Colonel Thomas repeat. I promise."

"Then by all means, send me a list of contacts you have enough faith in to recommend. You said twelve, didn't you?"

Cheyenne bit her bottom lip. *Maybe I exaggerated a little.* "I'll work on it. And I'll help you figure this out if you want. I'm sure that falls under a consultant's job description, right?"

Van Lurig let out a dry laugh and looked at the ceiling. "If you say so."

"And if you want me to keep being a consultant, I actually need to be consulted. Especially about who's being brought into this whole thing when we're in the middle of restructuring everything."

The major general glared at her. "I can't help but feel like I'm getting a lecture from my mother right now."

"Nobody wants that." Cheyenne raised both hands in concession. "My bad. Look, what we need to focus on right now is what I came here to talk to you about pulling a hundred and thirty agents from thirteen reservations and sending them to Chateau D'rahl."

"That's a large order, Cheyenne."

"Yeah, I know. It's a large customer. Something's going to happen there in the next few days. An attack. Magical. We need to double up on security, and I want the agents with working activators to be out there so they at least have a chance of handling it before it gets any worse. They're the people most likely to be able to deal with what's coming."

"Which is?"

"An attack. I just said that."

Van Lurig studied the drow's gaze. "Where did you get this information?"

"Jesus. I have to explain it to you, too?"

"Excuse me?"

"I saw it, okay? Plans for the attack. Not all of them, but we have to—"

"Who is it? Where did you find the plans? Anyone who leaves them out in the open doesn't sound smart enough to pull this off. I'm sure the operatives we have at the prison already can handle it."

"No, they can't!" Cheyenne pounded a fist on the table. The major general didn't even flinch. "I'm talking about L'zar, okay? He's gone off the deep end into some seriously crazy stuff, and I can't find him to stop him, but I know he's going to show up at the prison with a fuck-load of magical power behind him and no one to get in his way unless we move those agents right now."

"So he told you about his plan."

Cheyenne grimaced. "Not exactly."

"Then where's your proof?"

Fuck. She's not gonna budge, and I'm gonna sound as crazy as he *is.* "It's in my head, okay? Drow thing. I told you that when you tried to interrogate me about him, and it's true. I saw what he's doing."

"Cheyenne, I understand you might feel responsible for L'zar's poor choices."

"What? No. This doesn't have anything to do with—"

"He was captured and detained once already. Before the FRoE had its hands on that prison. We're much better than those who came before us, I promise."

Cheyenne growled in frustration, "He walked out of that place like the walls were made of paper. And he wasn't there because he got caught. L'zar only stayed behind bars for seventy-five years because that was exactly where he wanted to be. Now he's coming back, and it's not to turn himself in again."

"I'm sorry, Cheyenne." Van Lurig shook her head. "If you don't have concrete evidence of a viable threat, forget it."

"Major General!"

"I'm not going to reassign our operatives on a hunch. That's the end of it."

"Catherine, you're being an idiot."

Van Lurig stood abruptly from her chair and stepped toward the drow, her eyes burning with anger. "Major General, Cheyenne. You may not be on the payroll, but I am *not* your friend. Don't do that again. And stay out of my meetings."

With that, the leader of the FRoE stormed past Cheyenne and jerked open the conference room door. It hit the wall with a bang before slowly swinging shut again.

Cheyenne slammed her fist on the table again, this time hitting it hard enough to crack the wooden surface and leave an imprint of her anger.

"Shit." She stuck her hands in her pockets and waited long enough that she wouldn't have to share an elevator with the woman on the way down.

It's more than a hunch. The last time no one in this place would listen to me, a bunch of kids got kidnapped and tortured because I didn't have proof. It's magic!

Her footsteps thumped down the hall. Helen emerged from a doorway on her left, holding her tablet against her chest. "Looks like that didn't go nearly as well as you expected."

Cheyenne flipped her the bird and kept moving. *Screw protocol and chain of command. The FRoE's gonna go through an overhaul, all right. I'm not fucking around anymore.*

CHAPTER SEVENTY-FOUR

When she entered the lobby, the agents had come inside from their playtime with activators and were milling around the lobby on their way to the hall that led to the common room.

"Goth drow! Hey!" Bhandi clapped her hands to get Cheyenne's attention. When she saw the drow's scowl, she cursed and headed after her. "Hey! What's going on?"

"Tell everyone who's willing to do whatever it takes to be ready for anything, including rolling out of here fully geared-up. Got it?"

"Yeah, yeah. Sure. You talk to Van Lurig?"

"Yeah. Waste of time." Cheyenne shoved the glass front doors open and headed toward the parking lot.

"Wait." Bhandi darted after her, looking briefly over her shoulder at the other agents, who didn't seem to notice anything was wrong. "Yurik said you went up for the go-ahead. You didn't get it?"

"I don't need it." Cheyenne stopped and faced the troll woman. "Neither do you. Tell anyone who cares more about the chain of command than holding off one of the biggest threats to both worlds that they're free to stay home, but we need everyone else. I'll let you know when that is."

"Sure." Bhandi eyed her, smile gone now. "Anything else?"

Cheyenne headed for her car. "Tell Yurik to check his phone."

As she said it, she pulled up the private app with her activator and sent Tori a message with the goblin's number. *The rules won't matter anyway if L'zar goes through with this.*

Halfway home, she got a call and almost reached into her pocket for her phone before remembering she didn't have to anymore. "Hello?"

"That's a rather odd way to answer my call, Cheyenne."

"Hey, Mom. Sorry. Hands-free headset, and I'm driving."

"I see. I received a strange phone call from a gentleman asking if he and his associates could meet with me to discuss your involvement with that secret organization you've been running."

"The FRoE?"

"If that's what they're called, then yes."

Cheyenne's grip tightened on the steering wheel. "Did they give any names?"

"Unfortunately, no. But he sounded lobotomized."

Jesus Christ. Those suits just won't stop. "What did you tell them?"

"I told them absolutely not. They could speak to you themselves if they wanted to know your business. I am curious, though. What's going on?"

Cheyenne took a deep breath and slowly exhaled. "In a nutshell, the FRoE's lost its funding. Or it was pretty much ripped out from under them, and the board's desperate to make some new connections."

"What happened?"

"They lost a member. The creeps who called you made an offer, but they're the wrong kind of people."

Bianca hummed in acknowledgment. "I understand."

"If they call again, Mom, don't answer."

"I'm not concerned about a little pressure from someone who wouldn't even give me the courtesy of his name, Cheyenne. They seemed well aware of my capabilities and my connections. I believe the call was meant as a courtesy on their part, but I think maybe they were trying to get to you."

"Yeah, I know. Sorry they bothered you with that. I'll take care of it."

"I have no doubt."

"Hey, nothing else has happened at the house, right? With the stone rubble out back or otherwise?"

"If it had, I would have called you about it."

"Okay. Thanks for calling me about this."

"Enjoy the rest of your morning." Bianca hung up, and Cheyenne snorted.

The lack of pleasantries only means she cares.

Once she'd reached the highway to head back to North Richmond, she pulled up Maleshi's number with her activator and called.

"You found him?"

"No. Sorry." Cheyenne cleared her throat. "Little side favor. Some seriously weird people called Bianca wanting to talk about me. It's a bunch of bullshit aftermath from Colonel Thomas, but do you mind paying her a quick visit and putting up some wards around the estate to keep them away from her?"

"You think they'll try something?"

"Not really, but I can't just brush it off and do nothing."

"Sure, kid. Should only take me about twenty minutes."

"Thanks. I'll try not to call you again unless I have news."

Maleshi chuckled. "I'm happy to help, and I enjoy the woman's company. It'll be a fun twenty minutes at the very least."

"Yeah, just don't start drinking with her."

With a laugh, Maleshi hung up.

Cheyenne stared at the road, stretching her hands out on the steering wheel to flex her fingers. *At least I'm trying to stay ahead of the game instead of barely managing to catch up. I thought it'd be more satisfying.*

When she returned to her apartment, she found Ember sitting at the new bistro table with Maleshi's unbound spellbook spread out in front of her. The shower was running in the bathroom beneath the loft. Cheyenne shut the front door and pointed at the bathroom. "You left him alone in there?"

Ember lowered the page she'd been reading and raised an eyebrow at her friend. "I have no problem being the adult-drow babysitter, but I draw the line at supervision in the bathroom."

Cheyenne shrugged and headed over to the table. "Not a lot he can do in there, right?"

"I mean, he could try to take apart the showerhead, or the curtain, or the drain. Maybe he's trying to flood the bathroom. Or going through your makeup."

"Very funny."

Ember returned her attention to the spellbook. "I was serious. Those are all very real possibilities."

"I think he learned his lesson with your clothes."

"I fucking hope so."

Cheyenne climbed into one of the tall bistro chairs and shifted around to test it. "At least you bought a sturdy set."

"You don't like it, do you?"

"I don't have an opinion about a table."

"Good. 'Cause if you did, we'd still be keeping it."

Cheyenne shrugged out of her trench coat and hung it over the back of the chair. "What are you looking for?"

"Anything that could help us track down L'zar. Or Corian. Or the calibrax. Disruption spells. Insanely powerful battle magic." Ember shrugged. "Take your pick."

"And?"

"I haven't found anything yet."

"Shit." Cheyenne ran both hands through her hair, then drummed her fingers on the tabletop. "There has to be something else we can do. Nobody sees a fire heading toward them from two miles away and sits around waiting for it to burn everything down."

"No." Ember looked at her. "In that scenario, most people evacuate."

"Firefighters, Em. That's the analogy I'm trying to make."

"Well, then, good analogy."

The drow folded her arms on the table and peered at Maleshi's upside-down writing on the spellbook pages. "Except we can't see the fire."

"Maybe not. I can tell you're feeling the heat, though."

"We should all be able to feel it. The stronger magic. The shift. Something awful about to happen."

Ember finally gave her friend her full attention. "We'll stop him, Cheyenne."

"I want to find him, Em, not stop him at the last minute with two worlds on the line and have to pick up a mess we could've avoided by being more on top of it."

"What else can we do until he makes a move?"

"Cast our own spell." Cheyenne stared at the table and pulled up the private app in her vision. She opened a new chat with the seven magicals who were at the factory the day before. *I should've asked for these ingredients anyway. Bad idea to rely on one quick fix when the ardorium didn't take me anywhere near L'zar.*

Before she had any words down in the message, the shower turned off, followed by the squeak of wet feet on the floor before the bathroom door opened. "Or you could call the fire to you."

"What?" Cheyenne spun in her chair and immediately turned away again. "Dude!"

"Oh, my God." Ember thumped her elbow on the table and cupped her hand over her eyes to stave off the image. "Neros, I put the towel right there on the counter for you."

"Yes. It was not very efficient for bathing."

"For real?" Cheyenne and Ember stared at each other, then burst out laughing. "I mean, it *is* called a bath towel."

"He took a shower, Cheyenne."

"In a bathtub."

"Okay, forget the towel, Neros. At least put some clothes on."

Neros leaned back through the doorway and looked at the counter. "When they finish soaking."

Cheyenne closed her eyes as her laughter settled back down. "You magicked Ember's entire shredded wardrobe back together. Go ahead and spell-dry your clothes, okay?"

"I prefer the natural way."

Ember shook her head vigorously and stared at her friend, her eyes wide and still hidden behind her hand. "I can't sit here and focus on spells while he's standing there like that."

"Yeah." Cheyenne slid off the chair and pointed in the general direction of her cousin. "Get back in the bathroom and close the door."

"Why?"

"Because I'm getting you a towel, and if I get one more unwanted image forced into my head, I'm pretty sure it'll explode."

"I do not see the—"

"In. Door. Closed."

Neros slowly backed into the bathroom, the door creaking as he pulled it shut.

Cheyenne went quickly to the closet with the washer and dryer and pulled a clean towel down from the shelf. Then she knocked on the bathroom door and turned away. "Here."

Neros threw the door open again.

"Ah!" Ember whipped her head to the wall of windows beside her and stared outside.

"I already used one, Cheyenne."

"Wrap this one around your waist at the very least. Or stay in the bathroom until your clothes are ready."

He eyed her, then snatched the towel from her hand and quickly covered himself. "Ah. I see."

Ember barked a laugh. "Yeah, and I've seen too much."

"It is meant for drying oneself."

"There you go." Cheyenne turned back around and almost clapped a hand on his shoulder before realizing he was still covered in water, his hair sticking in streaming white clumps to his neck and shoulders. "Now, what were you saying about calling the fire?"

"You know it is coming. You can feel it." Neros shrugged. "If you do not wish to wait, leave it no other choice. Call it to you."

"I tried the *Don'adurr* Thread already. The Sorren Gán threw me out."

"That was a communion, Cheyenne." He raised a surprisingly condescending eyebrow at her. "Not a summons."

She lifted her chin and eyed him warily. "You want me to summon L'zar."

"I am being perfectly clear, and still you twist my words into different meanings." Neros looked down to readjust the towel around his waist, then stepped toward her. "I find it both fascinating and infuriating."

"Wow. Okay." She stepped away from him. "Why don't you spell it out for me? Pretend I'm an idiot."

"Hmm."

"Yeah, I get it. You think I *am* one because I haven't figured this out yet. Just tell me, man."

Neros stepped into the bathroom again and fished through the sopping clothes he'd stuffed into the sink and covered with water. When he returned, he extended his open palm to her. On it was the four-pointed star of L'zar's magic they'd found in Corian's apartment. "Summon him."

Cheyenne took the metal piece and turned it over in her hand. Then she looked at her cousin and grinned. "Except for stopping Ba'rael from striking the mortal blow in the Heart, this is the most helpful thing you've done."

"What is it?" Ember asked.

"L'zar's magic." Cheyenne pulled up Maleshi's number for one more call.

The line picked up, and the general cleared her throat. "Yes?"

"No, it's not time yet, and I didn't find them, but I'm pretty sure I figured out how to do that. Depending on how long it takes."

There was a long pause. "Well, do go on."

"Okay, the first time we stormed Hangivol so I could drop my coin on the altar. That pin L'zar gave me. You remember that thing, right?"

"The *Nalís*. Yeah, kid. I remember you pinned against the Nimlothar about to eat shit, then porting L'zar right into the Heart with you."

"Right." Cheyenne tossed the four-pointed star, caught it, and grinned. "You know how to make one of these?"

"Sure, but we're missing the two main ingredients: a magical tie to the one you want to open the portal to and nightstalker blood."

"Well, I'm holding L'zar's four-pointed star in my hand right now."

The general snorted. "And that's why you called me."

"You think it'll work?"

"Unfortunately, I know it will, and there's a reason I haven't done it since I left Ambar'ogúl. You home?"

"Yep."

"Hang tight." Maleshi hung up, and ten seconds later, the window of dark light opened beside the front door. The general stepped through in nightstalker form, wearing gray joggers and a rainbow tie-dye hoodie. "Hey, I like that table."

Ember laughed. "Thank you."

"All right, kid." Maleshi headed swiftly over to the table, glancing at the half-naked Neros. "I hate bleeding, so let's get this over with."

<h1 style="text-align:center">CHAPTER SEVENTY-FIVE</h1>

It took them an hour to find the right carrier for the new nightstalker-powered summoning portal. Maleshi refused every metal trinket and piece of jewelry Ember and Cheyenne offered as a possible ingredient until Cheyenne finally found a thick silver skull pin she'd stuck on her jackets in high school and asked if it would work.

"I guess it's okay," the general muttered, wrinkling her nose in distaste when she peered at it.

"That's better than the flat-out no you gave everything else."

"Are you sure you can't find something better?"

From the kitchen, Ember called over her shoulder, "Sounds like you're stalling."

Maleshi scowled at Cheyenne and sat back against the couch. "Fine. It's fine, kid. I need a few minutes to get into the right headspace."

"Okay. I'm gonna make a call." Cheyenne stepped into her bedroom for privacy and pulled up Inolu's number.

The banebreaker answered immediately. "What the fuck do you want, drow?"

"More like what do *you* want." Cheyenne stopped beside her closed bedroom door and leaned against it. "I know who has your calibrax."

"Tell me!"

"I figured maybe you'd like to come get it yourself when it's time.

The magical who has it right now is planning something that needs to be stopped. You know where Chateau D'rahl is?"

"Don't insult my intelligence, Cheyenne."

The drow folded her arms. "I'll take that as a yes."

"You can't play these games with me. If you don't tell me where my artifact is right now, I'll—"

"I still have the displacer, Inolu." The banebreaker's angry hiss brought a small smile to Cheyenne's lips. "I'll use it if I have to, but I'd rather do this another way."

"What do you want?" Inolu's voice was low and angry, but she obviously didn't want anything to do with R'leer's fancy jeweler's loupe that could rip all her *uanáj* right out of her body.

"Show up when your artifact is being used. Could be any day now, but it'll be soon. At the prison. I'll be there. The calibrax will be there. If you happen to pop in and join us, you might have to fight a little to get it back." *Hopefully with some help from a few powerful uanáj.*

"You want me to join your pathetic militia. I'm not concerned with whatever useless spats you've gotten yourself into."

"You'll probably care about this one." Cheyenne shrugged. "But even if you don't, I know you care about getting back what's yours, so when it's time, I'll text you."

There was a long pause on the other end. "Fine. Don't call me again unless you have something useful to tell me."

The banebreaker hung up, and Cheyenne headed back into the living room with a tight smile. *She saved my number. And we can use all the help we can get.*

"You find your headspace?"

Maleshi pressed her lips together and stared at the drow. "The full scope of it eludes me at the moment. I don't think I'll be any more ready than this."

"Okay. What do we do now?"

"Now we drain me dry."

The cabinet door slammed shut beneath Ember's hand. "You're not serious."

"Nope." Folding her arms, the general glared at the floor. "But that's what it feels like when you're drawing blood for one of these things."

Cheyenne eyed the general and lowered the skull pin to her side.

"It's not just about the blood, is it? It's about you being willing to give it too. The magic of it."

"Trust me, Cheyenne. I'm willing. Doesn't mean I have to be happy about it."

"Story of my life over the last two months," Cheyenne said, and the Nightstalker rolled her eyes.

"Do we need a specific kind of bowl for this?" Ember asked, opening the cabinets again.

"If you have a quarter-cup measuring cup, that'll do just fine." Maleshi closed her eyes. "Two ounces is pretty much the sweet spot."

Ember grimaced and bent beneath the counter to open the spinning shelf in the corner. "That sounds like a lot."

"The average adult human body holds around one and a quarter gallons. Not sure how nightstalkers compare to that, but I can't imagine it's any less. That would make this, what? One percent?" Maleshi looked up to see Cheyenne frowning at her and shrugged. "I Googled it, okay? Trying to give myself some peace of mind."

"Did you find it?"

"Not really."

"Okay. Quarter-cup." Ember closed the cabinet and joined them by the couch. "Now what?"

"Hmm." Maleshi nodded at the coffee table, grimacing, and Ember set the measuring cup in front of her. "You're the healer, Ember. Stand by with the healing."

The fae looked at Cheyenne with wide eyes. "Yeah, okay."

Cheyenne sat on the couch beside the general and stared at her. "What do you want me to do?"

"Just sit here. It's not a pleasant experience."

Neros emerged from the bathroom again, fully dressed. He'd agreed to let Ember stick his sink-washed clothes in the dryer. He sat beside the coffee table on the floor and crossed his legs beneath him. "I find this rather intriguing."

"Of course you do." Maleshi shot him a scathing look, then slid the measuring cup toward her until it sat at the edge of the coffee table. "Don't let me stop until this is full. Got it?"

"As long as I don't have to fight you." Cheyenne had meant it as a joke, but it did nothing to lighten the general's mood.

"No. I'll be doing the fighting." Maleshi took a deep breath and turned over her right wrist, resting the back of her forearm on her lap. Then she raised her left hand and extended a four-inch claw from her index finger. The blade-like tip sang as it shot out. Grimacing, the general began her incantation in a soft murmur and cut a thin slice three inches long from the bottom of her palm down her wrist. A hiss escaped her through the muttered words of her spell.

"Whoa. Wait a minute." Ember moved toward the couch, meaning to step in with the healing.

"Hold on, Em." Cheyenne lifted a hand for her friend to wait. "She knows what she's doing."

"This is how people die," the fae whispered.

"It's okay." Cheyenne stared at the blood pooling around Maleshi's claw and trickling over the sides of her wrist. *This is exactly how someone bleeds out.*

Except that Maleshi seemed to bleed in slow motion.

The general kept up her incantation, scowling at the blood leaving her body. Before the thick streams of blood made it down her arm to stain her gray pants, a faint silver light flashed within it and within the slice on her wrist. Bit by bit, the general's blood rose into the air like giant strands of spider silk, then it floated with agonizing slowness toward the measuring cup. The first few wavering lines dropped into the container, and the rest followed.

Neros stared at the floating streams of crimson, one corner of his mouth turning up either in awe or amusement. Cheyenne frowned at her cousin. *He's still a drow, all right. Drawn to dark magic and anything that has to do with someone else's blood. Nor'ieth couldn't wash that out of him.*

Ember winced and pressed her fingers against her mouth. "Is it supposed to take this long?" she whispered.

"No idea, Em." *Probably. A cut like that should've made that thing overflow by now, but it's not about the blood.*

Maleshi groaned through her muttered incantation, her eyelids fluttering briefly.

"Whoa. Hey." Cheyenne leaned forward to peer at the general's face. "You're okay."

The general's silver eyes flashed with light, then rolled back into her head. Still, she kept muttering the incantation and sat rigidly on the couch without moving.

Ember let out a high-pitched whine. "Is that supposed to happen?"

"She said to make sure she keeps going." Cheyenne shook her head. "I'm guessing this is why."

The words of Maleshi's spell caught in her throat and her head tipped backward, eyes still rolling. The threads of her blood moving within the silver light paused in the air on their way to the measuring cup.

"Shit." Cheyenne set a gentle hand on the general's shoulder. "Keep going."

"It's only half-full," Ember whispered.

"I know. Maleshi." Giving the general's shoulder a firm squeeze, Cheyenne leaned in. "Keep going."

Maleshi's lips barely moved, but somehow she managed to continue muttering the spell.

Yeah, she's fighting, all right. Fighting herself.

She whispered in the general's ear, "Don't stop. This is how we find them. Got it? You have to keep going."

The general made no reply, and her lips barely moved. The floating threads of blood had slowed to less than a snail's pace and were rippling in thin waves toward the table.

Cheyenne closed her eyes and thought of the Nimlothar—not only the seed she'd taken to start her trials but the single tree in the Heart of Hangivol and the entire forest they'd restored in the mountains. Her fingers tingled with heat where she squeezed Maleshi's shoulder. *A little boost. That's all.*

Magic flared up her spine and through her chest, then raced through her arm and hand into Maleshi.

The general drew a gasping breath and her eyes flew open, blazing with silver light. Her head whipped back down so she could stare at her blood moving toward the cup, and her nearly soundless muttering burst from her mouth in a desperate shout. The incantation in O'gúleesh sped up, as did the lines of blood drawing themselves from her arm. Maleshi's voice grew louder, rising in pitch, and the rest of the measuring cup filled to the brim and overflowed.

"That's it! Stop!" Ember rushed to the general's side.

Cheyenne let go of Maleshi's shoulder and leaned away.

"Holy fuck!" Maleshi shouted, drawing huge, heaving breaths as Ember clamped both hands around the general's wrist to start the healing.

"Sorry." Cheyenne raised both hands. "You said—"

"I know what I said, kid." Grimacing, Maleshi closed her eyes and calmed her breathing. Gold light bloomed beneath Ember's hands and healed the gash in the general's flesh. When the nightstalker finally opened her eyes, she slowly turned her head to meet Cheyenne's gaze. "That certainly helped."

"Okay. Good."

The general chuckled. "Hell of a power boost too."

Cheyenne sighed with relief. "You're welcome?"

Ember withdrew her hands, straightened, and took a deep breath. "Okay. I'm pretty sure that did it."

Maleshi rubbed her wrist, the black fur matted with blood, and nodded at her. "Yes, it did. You know, if I'd had both of you with me the last time I attempted this, I don't think I would've been as hesitant about it this time."

"Well, that's good. I think." Ember stared at her bloody hands.

The living room fell into a tense silence, punctured by the steady patter of Maleshi's overflowing blood dripping off the edge of the coffee table onto the rug.

"Oh, shit." Maleshi started to stand. "Sorry."

"Nope. You sit down." Cheyenne put her hand back on the general's shoulder and stood instead. "I got it."

Neros leaned toward the table and gazed at the blood dripping thickly from it. "Beautiful."

Cheyenne grabbed a handful of rags from the laundry closet and tossed two of them at her cousin's face as she returned. "That's creepy. How about you help with the cleanup, huh?"

"What?" He blinked and stared at her as he pulled the rags off his shoulder and chest.

"I'll do it." Ember grabbed the cloths from him and knelt beside the coffee table to press them into the rug and catch the last drips.

Cheyenne carefully lifted the measuring cup, somehow managing not to spill it, and set the cup on another rag so she could wipe up the puddle.

Maleshi laughed softly. "It's not generally this messy."

"We have no problem getting our hands dirty." She looked at the general. "You taught me a little bit about that."

"Ha. Flattery during one of my worst moments, huh?" Maleshi leaned back against the couch, rested her head on the cushion, and closed her eyes. "I could get used to that."

"We shouldn't get used to any of this." Ember came back with a spray bottle of cleaner and handed it to Cheyenne. "Please."

"You have a problem with a little blood, healer?" Maleshi asked with a grin, her eyes still closed.

"Maybe when it's being used to power spells." Ember met Cheyenne's eyes, and the drow knew they were thinking the same thing.

Like L'zar's planning with Corian, only on a way bigger scale and without backup in case something goes wrong.

Once they'd cleaned up and Maleshi had downed two large glasses of water, the general asked for another bowl to dump her blood into, and they gathered around the coffee table again.

"Last part. This is on you, kid."

"Okay." Cheyenne fingered L'zar's four-pointed star in one hand and the skull pin in the other.

"The skull pin first."

It dropped into the glass mixing bowl with a thick plop.

Maleshi nodded. "Now the other bit."

Cheyenne eyed the four-pointed star and delicately dropped it into the crimson mess. The metal manifestation of L'zar's magic quickly disappeared beneath the surface. *This has to work. That's all we have left.*

"All right." Maleshi tossed her black hair over her shoulder and stared at the drow. "Repeat after me."

Cheyenne nodded, listening intently to the pronunciation of the O'gúleesh words she still didn't understand. Once she got the first three out, her activator blazed to life in her vision, scrolling through lines of coded spells. Everything flashed with dark-purple light and Cheyenne's eyelids fluttered, then words she didn't recognize and had never uttered in her life flew from her lips.

Maleshi leaned away from her and stared.

"What's happening?" Ember asked.

"Looks like she knows this one."

The rest of the incantation came out quickly and succinctly, and the purple filter across Cheyenne's vision disappeared. She caught her breath and blinked. "Whoa."

"I'll second that, kid." The general chuckled. "You giving credit to your activator for that one too?"

The drow asked sarcastically, "You mean, you don't think I've been brushing up on my ancient-blood-magic skills?"

"Either way, it's impressive."

"But did it work?"

Maleshi turned to the mixing bowl again.

As soon as they returned their attention to their odd concoction, the pool of Maleshi's blood in the bottom of the bowl began to shrink. Ten seconds later, all of it was gone, no streaks on the glass, no leftover drops in the bottom. The skull pin looked exactly the same.

Cheyenne frowned. "That's it?"

"Ha. I hope you weren't expecting some kind of explosion. Go ahead, kid. Pick it up."

Reaching slowly into the bowl, Cheyenne picked up the skull pin, which would now open a direct portal to L'zar when she was ready to use it. She turned it over in her hand, her eyes widening at the lack of blood. "We did it."

"It would seem so."

Ember cleared her throat. "Where's that metal star thing?"

Cheyenne shrugged. "Looks like this thing sucked it right up with everything else."

"It's his magic." The general pushed herself higher on the couch cushion. "He made the last one himself, in person. That was the next best thing."

"And it'll work?"

"It has to, Em."

"We're gonna try it. Right?"

Cheyenne glanced at Maleshi, whose eyes were closed again above a small, knowing smile. "General?"

"That took a little out of me. Give it another twenty minutes, and I'll be fine."

Ember and Cheyenne exchanged looks, then the fae sat on the other side of the general and studied how weak she looked. "We might not have twenty minutes."

"I'll hardly be of any use to anyone if Cheyenne opens that portal now and I stumble through it like this."

"We have another option." Ember pressed both hands against Maleshi's chest.

The general opened her eyes. "What?"

A much brighter strobe of gold light burst beneath Ember's hands. The general jerked back against the couch, staring in shock at nothing. She gasped, then Ember removed her hands, and the nightstalker burst out laughing.

"How about now?"

Maleshi's fists clenched at her sides. Then she bolted upright on the couch and clapped her hands together. "You two!" Another harsh laugh escaped her. "Wow. If I didn't know better, I'd say you guys have been doing this forever."

Cheyenne tightened her grip on the skull pin. "So, no twenty-minute wait?"

Maleshi leaped to her feet, shaking out her hands and hopping on her toes. "Let's do this. I'm fucking pumped."

Ember stood from the couch and stared at the bouncing general buzzing with energy. "I'll turn it down a notch next time."

"There won't be a next time, Ember." Maleshi flashed her a feral grin. "We're stopping this right now."

"Okay." Cheyenne nodded.

Staring at the skull pin, she pulled up the private app in her vision and thought out a message on the main chat.

Cheyenne: Found L'zar. On the way now. Stand by.

Her activator showed her a hundred and four nearly instant views of her message. Only one magical sent her a reply.

Yurik: We're in. Got your back.

Cheyenne looked at the nightstalker, the fae, and the paled-skinned drow standing in her living room. "Here we go."

Maleshi's head bobbed as she stared at the skull pin. "Ready when you are, kid. Ready for this shot of fae energy to die down a little too."

"Sorry," Ember muttered.

"I'll be fine. Good for a fight anyway, right?"

Cheyenne held the skull pin in one open palm and took a deep breath. "Here we go." She slapped her other hand on top of the new *Nalís* they'd made. "L'zar."

A flare of heat raced up both arms, then a dark window of light opened three feet to her left.

Cheyenne summoned a black energy sphere in each hand and ran toward the portal to L'zar.

CHAPTER SEVENTY-SIX

They barreled through the portal in quick succession. Only Neros stepped through as casually as everything else he did.

"L'zar!" Cheyenne shouted, raising her hand with her attack at the ready and scouring the dark, musky room. Then she saw the portal of blazing-white light at the other end, flickering within a ring of opalescent flames.

Everything seemed to happen all at once. L'zar threw something through the portal, and his other hand clenched around Corian's arm. The nightstalker's wrists were bound behind his back with the same flames, his shirt torn open at the front. He whirled toward them with wide eyes, struggling to stay on his feet. "Cheyenne!"

L'zar's golden eyes burst with multi-colored lights, and he grinned at his daughter.

"Don't!" She darted into drow speed and hurled a black sphere at the Weaver, who had been overrun by the Sorren Gán.

He was too fast.

L'zar stepped into the white portal and dragged Corian behind him, disappearing before her attack even got halfway. Maleshi joined her in enhanced speed and ran toward them, claws outstretched. The white portal vanished as Cheyenne's spell struck the far wall and blew off huge shards of concrete. They hung suspended in the air, falling slowly.

600

"No. No!" Maleshi roared and spun, searching the dark room. "Corian!"

"They're gone." Cheyenne dropped back to normal speed and stared at the shimmering outline of opalescent flames in the air where the portal had been. The chunks of wall fell to the floor. "Fuck."

Maleshi darted around the room in a silver streak, then stopped in front of the wall beside the fading outline of the portal and slashed the concrete wall with her claws. More chunks crumbled amidst a spray of sparks, and the general roared again.

Ember swallowed. "What happened?"

"They're gone, Em." Cheyenne whirled and studied the room. "We were too late."

"How?" Maleshi shouted. "How did he know we were coming?"

"I don't think he did." Gritting her teeth, Cheyenne studied the room. A knot tightened in her stomach. "We had really bad timing."

"Can't you follow him?" Ember asked. "Portals leave signatures, right?"

"Nightstalker portals, yeah." Maleshi took a breath and snarled. "That was something else."

Cheyenne turned and saw the ring of opalescent flames had already disappeared. "Shit. Twenty seconds sooner, and we would've had him."

"Oh, my God." Ember pressed her hands against her eyes, then removed them to study the room. "That means he just left for the prison, right?"

Nodding at the wall behind where they'd entered, Cheyenne grimaced. "Looks like he got everything he needed."

The wall was splattered with blood, and thick, mostly dry streaks ran across the concrete floor, occasionally broken up by a handprint. Two other pools of it had collected farther from the wall too. In the corner were the shattered remains of what had to be Corian's cell phone.

She walked to the wooden table in the center of the room and studied the contents, vials, and jars streaked with different-colored fluids, all of them empty. It was covered with mixing bowls, a mortar and pestle, cut bits of string that had been tied around bundles of stolen ingredients, and rubber tubes covered in blood, some of which still oozed crimson at the ends. "He didn't bother to clean up."

"Why would he? He doesn't need to hide this anymore. He's already there." Maleshi turned to her and raised her hands. "We need to go. Now."

"Yeah." Cheyenne stepped away from the table, trying to ignore the splatters of blood she hadn't noticed on the bare walls before. "Right in front of the—"

A massive explosion came from above them, making the walls and floors of the doorless, windowless room shudder. Everyone ducked, then looked up at the trembling ceiling. Dust sifted down, and two glass vials rattled against each other before rolling off the table and shattering on the floor.

"He couldn't work that fast, could he?" Ember asked.

"I have no idea what he can and can't do right now." Cheyenne nodded at Maleshi. "Open it."

A siren blared overhead, honking over and over. Cheyenne frowned at the ceiling. "Motherfucker."

"What?"

"That's the prison siren."

Maleshi's portal opened in front of her, and she lowered her hands. "Are you sure?"

"Yeah, I'm sure! I set it off on purpose the first time I met L'zar, and I heard the same thing when we broke Venga out."

"He's been here the whole time," Ember muttered.

"Under the prison." Cheyenne hissed and nodded at the portal. "Let's go."

"Cheyenne." Neros' voice was weak, but it carried well enough in the small, bare room. They all turned to him to see the pale-skinned drow flickering in and out of existence. He slowly tilted his head. "I feel strange."

"You look like the Border towers." Cheyenne headed over to him. "Strange like how, Neros? Can you walk?"

"I can walk, but I do not..." His eyes widened as he faded into a ghostly outline of himself, then settled into normal solidity again and stayed that way. "The balance is tipping again. This time, I do not understand."

"Well, we'll figure it out, but we need to move. Come on." Cheyenne set a hand on his back to guide him to Maleshi's portal, from which emerged the sounds of shouting and a loud security alarm.

Neros stumbled and finally got his feet under him as she urged him forward.

"This is it." Maleshi nodded at the portal. "We need to find Corian before there's nothing left of him."

"Yeah." Cheyenne sent another message through her activator to the private chat as she hurried her cousin through the portal.

Cheyenne: It's happening now. Chateau D'rahl. Get here however you can.

She received replies, but she couldn't focus on reading them in the corner of her vision because she stood outside the front gates of Chateau D'rahl with her hand on Neros' back and watched the place erupt into chaos.

"Oh, my God," Ember muttered.

A huge plume of smoke rose from the center of the prison building, where flames burst from the hole in the ceiling and roared in the open air. The siren blared, and beneath it, Cheyenne could hear snippets of radio conversation and the guards shouting at one another inside and outside the prison.

"Explosion in Alpha Block. We need more guards down here! Shit!"

"Charlie Block's been breached. I repeat. Charlie Block breached."

There was another explosion burst on the west end of the building, followed by screams, the rumble of crumbling stone, and gunfire.

"Get down on the ground! I said, get down!"

"Where the fuck do you think you're going, inmate?"

"Guard Tower, they're heading for the front. Do you copy?"

Cheyenne shook her head and studied the outside of the building. "Where the hell is he?"

"Inside, right?" Ember gestured at the prison but flinched and stepped back when another explosion blasted sideways out of the eastern wall and flung huge chunks of stone into the chain-link fence around the prison. They knocked a section of fence down and thumped into the surrounding trees.

"No. This is a distraction."

"Are you sure?" Maleshi asked.

"Yeah. Nobody's talking about L'zar, just a bunch of escaped prisoners."

"Oh, lovely."

Ember stepped forward but stopped, and for a moment, she couldn't find her voice. "Shouldn't we help?"

"Well, if we had agents with activators out here like I fucking told Van Lurig we needed…" Snarling, Cheyenne finally checked the corner of her vision to scroll through the app messages with her activator. "Okay. Shit. Five vehicles coming from the base. More after that, and, like, sixty more groups from at least five different cities. Nobody's gonna be able to get here in time."

"I'll do it." Maleshi nodded. "I need a list of locations. If they're all ready to go, it'll be fast."

"Yeah. Oh, shit. You don't have an activator."

"Take mine."

"You sure, Em?"

"I'm already with you." Ember ripped hers off, grimacing at the pinch as her eyelids fluttered. She puffed out a breath and handed the star activator to Maleshi. "I made a map this morning of where everybody is. It's under files."

Cheyenne pulled the map up in her vision as Maleshi took the activator and stuck it behind her ear. "Wow, Em. Good work."

"Felt like a good idea. You know, stay organized."

Maleshi grunted and shook her head as the activator synced with her magic. Then she blinked quickly, her eyes scanning her version of Ember's map. "Okay. Got it. Reservations first, right?"

"That's where most of them are, yeah." Cheyenne nodded at her. "Thanks."

"Gotta make use of my portals before L'zar has a chance to change who knows how much of what works and what doesn't." The general raised her hands to open another portal and stepped quickly through. Shouts of alarm came through the portal to join the chaos in front of the prison, but they quickly faded. "Everyone who's ready to go, get the fuck over here!"

Maleshi reappeared and shot Cheyenne an urgent smile. "First wave through." Then she stepped aside to open another portal to the next reservation.

Ten agents in full gear stormed through the open window of dark light and fanned out. "Holy shit."

"That asshole's gone too far this time."

Some of them noticed Cheyenne as they jammed on their helmets and nodded at her.

An orc agent stopped beside her. "He in there?"

"No!"

The doors burst open, and a thirty-foot-long black snake slid through them and stopped in front of the prison.

"Stop!" A guard in the left tower aimed his gun at the magical who'd decided slithering was the best way to make its escape. "Did you hear me?"

The snake spat a wad of shimmering yellow goo at the tower and lit the whole thing up with an electrical charge, laughing.

Two other inmates in Chateau D'rahl's standard-issue gray sweatpants and white t-shirts burst through the doors and flung spells at the other guard tower. "Can't hold us down, motherfuckers!"

The tower guard who hadn't been fried fired round after round of fell shots at them, then another wave of inmates surged through the open doors.

"Yeah, we got this." The orc agent beside Cheyenne nodded at her and slapped down the visor of his helmet. "Move!"

The ten agents surged forward to meet the rush of escaped inmates, weapons up and firing fell shots into the fray.

Maleshi stepped through her second portal with another group of rez agents. "Get after them! Go!"

Cheyenne ducked a spray of electric yellow goo from the huge black snake, which was racing toward her. She snarled and threw a crackling black energy sphere at the shapeshifting magical. It hit the snake in the belly, and the magical curled into a ball with a shriek before reemerging as a massive creature that looked like a panther but was five times the normal size with a barbed tail and horns on its head.

The second wave of FRoE agents converged on it, firing fellfire rounds and magical blasts of their own.

"You should be looking for him," Maleshi shouted as her third portal opened.

"I am!" Cheyenne tried to ignore the fighting in front of the prison as she scanned the lot, the road leading off the property, and the trees surrounding Chateau D'rahl. "I don't know where he is!"

The ground trembled, but not from another explosion. Staggering backward, Cheyenne stared at the blazing column of opalescent light that was now shooting into the sky from within the trees at least two miles behind the prison complex. The air filled with a static buzz, making the top of her back and her shoulders burn with the strength of the magic suddenly released in the sky.

Ember pointed at the column of light. "I'd say that's a pretty good start."

"Yeah. Come on."

Maleshi stepped halfway through her open portal. "Everybody through. Now!" She waved agents onto the pavement beyond the front gates, then turned to Cheyenne. "If he's not there, tell me. Otherwise, I'll find you."

"Yeah." Cheyenne grabbed Neros' arm and tugged him along behind her. "Come on."

Her cousin stared at the rising column of smoke with unblinking eyes. "It smells like home."

"Well, it sure as hell isn't. Neros, we have to go." She paused when his body flickered in and out of existence again, growing intermittently cold and hot beneath her grasp. "And if you can fight, I seriously recommend reconsidering whatever you have against it. Ember!"

"Let's go." Ember nodded and raced toward them, blasting a wall of purple light at two inmates who'd cleared a path through the FRoE agents. The prisoners shrieked as they were hurled back into the fighting. "So we're running off into the forest?"

"Pretty much." Cheyenne summoned a black energy sphere and released Neros' arm. "Can you keep up on your own?"

"I want to see this." He stared at the column of light clawing into the sky and jogged to catch up with her. "Yes."

"Good. Be ready for whatever we find." *And it better be L'zar and Corian. Alive.*

CHAPTER SEVENTY-SEVEN

As they moved around the west side of the building between the trees and the tall chain-link fence topped with rows of concertina wire, Cheyenne could hear shouts of warning and a few fell-fire shots from the other side of the thick stone wall.

"Wait. Hold on." She scanned the wall ahead of them and extended her arm to stop Neros and Ember beside her. "Something's happening."

"You think?" Ember pushed her friend's arm down.

"Stop!" Cheyenne grabbed the fae's wrist and hauled her back a second before another massive explosion rocked the side of the building in front of them. Huge chunks of stone struck the chain-link fence, followed by fireworks of orange and green light streaking into the forest. The two closest trees splintered when the magical blasts hit them, but they stayed upright.

Ember turned to stare at Cheyenne and whispered, "Thanks."

"Come on, you fucking Earthborn piece of shit!" An orc in prison garb roared with laughter and dragged out a human guard by the collar of his uniform shirt. "We're gonna have us some fun, ain't we, Muz?"

A crooked, hobbling skaxen thumped down one clawed foot with each step and dragged the other one uselessly behind him. His black eyes darted in all directions but constantly returned to the struggling guard as he slavered and cackled. "Lotsa fun. Hey, Relaude. You're gonna let me get one in too, right?"

"You want in?" The orc bashed aside a section of the partially destroyed wall and dragged the guard through it. "What's the magic word?" He stopped when he saw Ember, Neros, and Cheyenne staring at them from the other side of the fence. "Would ya look at them, Muz?"

"At what, huh? I wanna see the light, man. Hey, ain't that a drow?"

"It's two." Relaude chuckled. "Though that one with the whitewash doesn't look too good."

Neros tilted his head, then turned to stare at the massive column of magical light.

Cheyenne summoned another black energy sphere in one hand and pointed at the guard with the other. "Let him go."

"Who? This flabby piece?" The orc jiggled the guard's collar, jerking the man back and forth. The guard flopped around like a useless sack, grunting at the abuse until he finally looked up at Cheyenne through swollen eyes beneath a massive cut bleeding on his forehead. "Looks like we got some new friends wanna play too."

The skaxen hissed in delight and wrung his hands, tittering. "Let's play, then. By the Mother's oozing tit, man, it's been way too long."

"I said, put him down," Cheyenne repeated.

"Yeah, let's play." With a grunt, Relaude stooped and lifted the guard in both hands. With a roar, he tossed the man high into the air and straight at the coils of barbed wire that ran along the top of the fence.

Cheyenne shot her energy sphere at the orc, ignoring the fact that he bashed it aside with a huge forearm like she'd thrown a rock instead. She was a lot more focused on reaching the beaten guard and lifting him high above the barbed wire. The hem of his uniform pants snagged and ripped as her telekinesis drew him safely away. He settled to the ground in front of them, and Ember rushed to his side.

"Fucking hero, huh?" Relaude bashed a fist against his other palm. "Bad day for you."

"Not any worse than most of them." She lunged at the fence and sent her lashing tendrils from both hands through the gaps in the chain-link. They coiled around Muz's wrists. Cheyenne stepped back and jerked hard. The skaxen flew across the prison's side yard and bashed into the fence, spit flying from his snarling mouth as his orange flesh squeezed through the gaps in the metal wire.

"You fucking bitch!"

She released her tendrils and kicked him in the face, sending him crashing to the ground.

The orc laughed at his groaning fellow inmate, then lunged at the fence and drew his hands apart like he was trying to rip apart the air in front of him. Orange and green light burst from his hands and crackled along the chain-link fence. His spell rippled along the metal wires in two waves spreading away from each other, leaving nothing behind but an open gap between the rolled barbed wire and the bottom rail of the fence against the ground.

Cheyenne stared at the hole and cocked her head. "That's useful."

Relaude stormed through the fence, glaring at the human guard on the ground as Ember finished healing the guy. "We're not done, human."

"Yeah, you are." Cheyenne summoned another energy sphere as a warning. "Back off."

"Fuck you. I blasted a hole in Chateau D'rahl. If I wanna get back at this prick for any number of things, I'm gonna do that." He snarled at Cheyenne, then stepped past her toward Ember and the guard.

Cheyenne grabbed him by the back of his t-shirt and hauled him away. He stumbled back through the fence as another explosion wracked the prison. Raising both hands, she felt for the magical resistance within the crumbled chunks of the prison's stone wall and lifted them all. The rubble swarmed around Relaude, buffeting him from side to side as the stone hunks returned to the hole in the wall. He tried to punch through them and duck, but more rose and pushed him back.

The escaped prisoner bellowed when he was shoved back inside the prison, and Cheyenne fitted all the chunks back together in a heaping pile, shoving them into place to block the escape route.

"You're gonna die, drow!" The orc's furious roar was muffled from the other side of the wall.

Cheyenne glanced at Muz the skaxen, lying unconscious beside the nonexistent fence. *He's fine where he is.*

"Okay, come on." She turned to Ember, who was helping the human guard to his feet. "We need to get outta here. Neros."

Her cousin stared blankly at the column of light in the sky. "I am ready."

"Yeah, I hope so." She nodded at the guard. "You need to get outta here too."

The man stared at the blazing magical light too. "What is that?"

"Above your paygrade."

The hole she'd filled with chunks of stone wall exploded open again, huge boulders and smaller shards tumbling to the ground. This time, it wasn't just one orc and one skaxen blowing through the prison wall. It looked like an entire cell block.

"Go!" Cheyenne shoved the guard toward the front of the prison, then grabbed Neros' wrist and dragged him toward the tree line, still heading for the back of the prison and the forest behind it. "Ember!"

Her friend took one look at the dozens of escaped prisoners stepping through the hole, laughing, shoving each other, lifting their faces to the sky, and taking deep breaths. Before anyone could notice her staring, she ran after Cheyenne and Neros.

Cheyenne stared at the huge column of light, and when they reached the back of the prison's main building, she paused. *That's a lot farther away than I thought.*

"What's wrong?" Ember fought to catch her breath, bending over with her hands on her thighs.

"Nothing. I hope that's where he is."

"Who else would cast some crazy shit like that?" Ember looked over her shoulder, and her eyes widened. "Shit. Escaped prisoners heading this way."

"What?" Cheyenne turned to see a wave of inmates moving swiftly toward the back of the prison, though no one ran or seemed to be in a particular hurry. "Why?"

"You sure this isn't L'zar breaking his prison buddies out to try to take them all home?"

"Yeah, I'm sure. Come on." She pulled Neros with her again and headed into the thick forest behind the farthest wall. A few spells from prisoners flew overhead, crashing into trees and sending branches raining down around them.

"That kinda feels like they're after us, doesn't it?" Ember shouted, stepping quickly away from a falling branch.

"I have no idea. Keep moving." The closer they got to the column of light, the harder it was for Cheyenne to think about much more than the buzz of strong magic that had become a constant burn along the back of her neck and shoulders and the fact that she now smelled and tasted nothing but vinegar. But she couldn't pause to try to figure anything out. *We need to stop L'zar before he rips open these portals and before he kills Corian trying to power them all.*

Instead, as she ran and ducked flying spells and occasionally turned with Ember to fling an attack at the laughing prisoners, she composed a message to Maleshi through their activators. Her fingers flickered at her sides while she tried to focus on sending a pinpoint of their location while not getting blown to pieces.

More explosions came from behind them. The air rang with fellfire shots, the crackle and hiss of magic, tumbling stone, screaming magicals, and mad laughter.

Then another tremor shook the ground, making all three of them stumble. "What was that?"

Frowning, Neros turned slowly to the west and pointed. "The next one."

As soon as he said it, another blazing column of light shot into the sky. It looked small compared to the one over a mile away in the forest, but it couldn't be mistaken for anything else. *That's either a rez portal opening, or L'zar set one giant power circle.*

"Neros, let's go." She grabbed his arm and tugged him along. Six feet in front of them, a portal opened, and Maleshi barreled through to join them in the forest. Behind her came another two dozen FRoE agents with activators, geared up. "Hold them off," she told them, pointing at the prisoners racing toward them through the trees.

The agents covered the ground quickly, firing as they passed Cheyenne and Ember.

"Maleshi." Cheyenne had to shout over the noise of the battle so close behind them now. "How many more do you have left?

"About fifty. O'gúleesh, not Earthborn."

"Okay. They'll probably be able to think quicker on their feet for this anyway. That's where we're going." The drow pointed at the vertical light, and the general's eyes widened when she saw it for the first time. "I'm guessing that's where he is."

"Ya think?"

"Port everyone else to that light. Then maybe we can draw some more guards out here if they can get the prison under control."

"Yeah, kid. I got it." Maleshi darted into enhanced speed and leaped away from a sizzling strand of purple light whizzing through the forest. She dropped back out again and snarled at the inmate who'd flung the spell. "You wanna do this, asshole? Right now!"

"Maleshi!" Cheyenne pointed at the light. "You can fight when everyone's here."

The general scowled but opened another portal and disappeared.

"Neros, come on." Cheyenne reached out for her cousin's arm, but he flickered in and out of his physical form, and her fingers closed on air. "Shit. What's happening?"

"I will remain, Cheyenne. But I can't…now. You have to…without me…"

His voice disappeared every time his body flickered, and Cheyenne gritted her teeth. "We gotta go. I'm not gonna leave you here to disappear."

"I won't if you go now." He looked perfectly calm as he nodded at her and looked at the vertical light reaching to the sky.

"I'll stay with him," Ember said. "Go. You'll get there faster anyway."

"I won't be able to reach you!"

"Go, Cheyenne!" Ember turned to search the fighting between FRoE agents and Chateau D'rahl's escaped prisoners. A goblin prisoner who'd either ripped his shirt open or gotten it snagged on something else raced toward her, sneering and moving his hands to summon an attack. Ember blasted him back. "We got this."

"Okay. See you there." Cheyenne fired a black energy sphere at two ogres who looked like twins who were hauling agents aside left and right. Then she slipped into drow speed to head for the column of light.

Tree branches tugged her hair and trench coat as she ran, scratching her cheeks and hands. Moving this quickly, with the explosions and the sounds of battling magicals slowed to a soft, low rumble, she could hear the vertical light pulsing with energy less than a mile ahead of her. It buzzed and hummed rhythmically, rising and dropping in pitch as pulses of different strengths raced up its length.

She felt the next surge of intensely strong magic rippling beneath her feet at the speed of a car rolling casually through a residential neighborhood. It was heading southwest. Turning in that direction, she thought she saw flames moving beneath the earth but couldn't be sure. She hardly noticed the tremble of the ground beneath her as a third magical column rose miles away. It soared above the top of the forest and stretched who knew how far, a thin stream of light ballooning at the top before disappearing through the clouds.

"Shit." Cheyenne forced herself to turn back to the closest column and book it.

Two portals already. That has to be what they are.

With thirteen border reservations and the three deactivated portal ridges she knew of—where the Bull's Head smuggled in the war machines, on the VCU campus, and in Bianca's back yard—that left sixteen for L'zar to finish what he started.

Assuming he needs all of them. I can't assume anything at this point, can I? Just have to fucking stop him.

She pushed herself as hard as she could, racing through the trees toward the column of blinding light and the thickening waves of intense magical energy pulsing away from it. The closer she got, the harder it was to run in a straight line, even when she had a clear path between the trees.

Not now.

Cheyenne's shoulder bumped into the rough bark of a pine, its trunk bare of branches for the first ten feet. At drow speed, the impact splintered the tree and rocked it sideways. As soon as the wood separated, the tree hung suspended in air, needles jolted from their branches and waiting to drop with the rest of the foliage. She pushed away from the tree with a grunt and kept moving.

That's part of this spell of his, isn't it? No drow speed to get the drop on him. Fuck that.

Tears blurred her vision as the sharp stink of vinegar overtook every other scent. She spat as she stumbled forward, tasting it as well. Her skin buzzed with intense cold and heat, and she could hardly keep her balance.

Her activator blared an alarm in her head, lighting up the closest tree with a flashing yellow arrow. Despite seeing the damn thing and trying to turn away from it, the drow stumbled head-first into another pine and split that one too.

Cheyenne pushed away with a grunt, her head spinning. *I'll never get there like this.*

Taking a deep breath, she tried to steady herself so she wouldn't crash into anything else when she dropped out of drow speed.

The wave of dizziness lifted instantly, and the splintering crash of the first tree she'd hit filled the forest. She looked up and saw a thick cloud of pine needles dropping toward her, then the second trunk splintered and threw shards in all directions.

She raised a shield, breathing heavily, and blinked back tears as the tree groaned and crashed away from her. Then she saw the light.

Thirty yards in front of her, the dense growth of trees thinned. All she could see from here was the blinding haze of the pulsing column, but she knew who she'd find when she reached the clearing. Cheyenne stalked through the trees and headed for the light.

"I'm coming, asshole. And I'm hoping for you to do something stupid this time."

CHAPTER SEVENTY-EIGHT

Cheyenne's ears rang with the pulsing hum of the vertical light, less from the sound and more from the thickness of the magic racing through it. Then she made it through the trees and entered the clearing.

The blinding light rose from the center of a pile of black stones that had crumbled decades ago and were covered in moss. Long grass had grown between the fallen shards of black rock, and though it only stretched about twenty feet across the clearing, she knew exactly what it was.

Border portal a few miles away from the prison. How did anyone miss that?

Clenching her teeth, Cheyenne scanned the deactivated portal ridge and the column of light, searching for L'zar. Instead, she found a thick pool of blood at the base of the ridge, running in rivers down the crumbled stone and stretching across the dry grass. Dark crimson drops fell rhythmically from above, and she looked up to see Corian strapped to a bare tree branch.

"Shit." She darted toward him, her stomach clenching.

He'd been strung up by endless yards of the same opalescent flames that bound his hands behind his back. They crossed each other as they wound around his body, pinning his arms to his sides and holding him fast to the thick branch. He'd been secured at a slight angle, with his head lower than his feet, and his blood spilled from several cuts on his chest and shoulders.

"Corian. Can you hear me? Hey."

The nightstalker's eyes fluttered open, and he groaned.

"Jesus, I can't believe he did this to you. I'm gonna get you down. Hold on."

"N-no."

Cheyenne summoned an energy sphere and hurled it at the branch behind his feet. A shimmer of opalescent flames erupted around the branch and sent her attack right back at her. She leaped aside as her magic blasted into the earth and sent up a spray of dirt and dry grass and small stones. "Are you fucking kidding me?"

She hurled two more attacks and dodged them each time they were deflected by the spell around the tree. *I'm never gonna get through like this.*

"Corian, I'm gonna stop this. Don't bleed out on me, okay?"

"Not until…h-he's…finished." His silver eyes fluttered again as he tried to focus on her face. "Remove the…r-remove…"

"I know."

Another tremor raced across the ground, and it almost threw Cheyenne on the blood-covered ridge. As she righted herself, another column of light shot into the sky miles to the south. *That's four. Dammit.*

She ran into the center of the clearing, hating herself for leaving Corian. *We'll get him down. As soon as the others show up and we stop this.*

"L'zar!" she roared, spinning furiously. "You have to stop this!"

Staggering and turning in tight circles, she moved across the clearing and found him on the other side of the portal ridge behind the column of light stretching into the sky. L'zar stood within a smaller, murkier dome of pulsing light. His hands were lifted slightly at his sides, fingers curling and flicking and darting in whatever insane gestures this spell required. With his head thrown back and his white hair fluttering behind him, he looked like he was staring in ecstasy at the magic he'd unleashed instead of controlling it.

If it's even him anymore. I'm not so sure.

"Hey!" She ran toward him. "L'zar. Do you hear me? You're gonna tear both worlds apart!"

The Weaver made no response as he muttered his incantation over and over, staring blankly at the vertical column of light. Flashes of it pulsed across his body, illuminating him from the inside and rippling across his limbs.

Cheyenne searched the ground within his dome of weak light and saw the circle of stolen ingredients laid out around him. Every item was smeared with blood like he'd rolled each object in a huge pool of it before placing it there. *Because he had.*

Inside the circle, a yard in front of L'zar's feet was a two-foot pyramid of glass glowing with inner gold light. *And there's the calibrax.*

The second she thought it, her activator confirmed it with a description. She waved the data aside and studied the dome around her father. "L'zar! You can't keep this up!"

Still no response. Another shockwave tore across the ground, spreading away from the vertical light to race to the next Border tower on his list. Cheyenne staggered forward but didn't try to find the next spear of light miles away bursting into the air like the others. Instead, she ran full throttle at her father, summoning energy spheres in both hands.

When she came within two feet of the dome, a pulse of dim light exploded from the magical wall and struck her in the chest. Her energy spheres went wild as she was thrown back across the clearing; one of them sailed over the treetops, and the other shot into the vertical light and disappeared without any effect.

Cheyenne crashed into the ground and skidded backward in the dry grass, shuddering as the attack from L'zar's protective field jolted through her body. When it finally stopped, she collapsed on her back and blinked fiercely at the sky and the blazing pulse of magic.

I should've expected that.

Shouts came from the prison side of the clearing, interspersed with fellfire shots and the crash of spells hitting trees, earth, flesh, and dampening vests.

Groaning, Cheyenne rolled onto her side. The first wave of battling inmates and FRoE agents emerged from the trees, bringing even more chaos with it. She pushed off the ground and headed back toward L'zar and the protective dome around him. More inmates emerged from the trees behind her, having gone wide around the prison to avoid the agents trying to capture them. The first huge magical with horns like a bull and two whipping tails stepped into the clearing first, grinning in dumb awe at the vertical light.

Cheyenne turned to him and summoned two more energy spheres. The horned magical noticed her and sneered. "Now it's our time."

A portal opened between them, and a crackling blast of silver lightning burst from the dark window. The inmates on the far side of the clearing tried to dodge the attack, though some of them were more concerned with the trees bursting into flames beside them. Others were caught in the silver lightning and bucked furiously before dropping to the ground.

Maleshi emerged from the portal, followed by almost two dozen O'gúleesh with activators. The magicals shrieked and screamed their battle cries as they charged the inmates streaming into the clearing. The crackle and buzz of spells and magic of every color and form made Cheyenne stagger. Her ears rang from the noise, which drowned out everything else until she noticed her activator had given her a prompt to turn down the volume.

Then she backed away from the battle toward L'zar's dome, scanning all the magicals Maleshi had brought in to join the fight. *They weren't supposed to fight a bunch of prison escapees. We need them for L'zar.*

The general shot another flaring bolt of silver lightning at the inmates, then spun and saw Cheyenne standing six feet away from the muted dome of light and L'zar within it. "What are you waiting for, kid? Shut it down!"

"I can't. Not like this."

Maleshi launched more lightning at L'zar's dome. The protective magic crackled when the silver light met it, covering L'zar in streaking patterns until the general's attack faded. "Shit. Get the calibrax, then."

"Yeah, I'll figure it out."

Stepping away from the battles, Maleshi opened another portal. She didn't step through it this time but waved urgently for the magicals on the other side to join them. Another two dozen poured through.

Whatever the general shouted to them, Cheyenne didn't hear. She didn't recognize any of the faces appearing from the other side of the portal, and she barely avoided a magical net of blue ooze flying through the air. The only thing she could focus on now was the burst of intensified magic burning across her skin and the growing brightness of the column of rippling light.

She turned to stare at L'zar, who slowly lifted his arms as his voice rose in an incomprehensible growl, repeating his spell. The vertical light flashed once and spread down the broken portal ridge's length.

No. No, we can't be too late. What did we miss?

The Border tower at Rez 9 let out a groan like a falling tree. The agents and guards stationed there stepped out of their buildings in Q1 and stared at the black stone monolith, which crackled with opalescent light and flickered in and out of existence. The ground trembled, and one agent found his wits enough to shout, "Everyone out! Get out now!"

On Rez 74 on the southern edge of Pennsylvania, O'gúleesh refugees screamed and scrambled away from the Border tower standing tall in Q4. Burning white light rose from the black stone, filling the reservation with magic so thick that many of the magicals found themselves unable to move. Parents scooped children into their arms and forced themselves to run across four different quarters to get off the reservation. Some tried to take their few belongings with them until their neighbors grabbed them by the hand or the arm or the tunic and dragged them away. The light shooting up the tower's walls into the sky began to expand, spreading outward from the pillar of stone.

Five other Border towers on five other reservations along the eastern coast of the United States erupted with shimmering multicolored light.

A portal ridge that had been hidden, buried in vines and palm fronds, in the Yucatán forest along the Mexican coast for centuries, shuddered and split, the buried black stone blinking in and out. Towers in China, Malaysia, Istanbul, Germany, France, and Sweden split up the sides, groaning and giving off wave after wave of powerful magic the

Earth wasn't built to withstand. Earthquakes rippled across the continents.

A tidal wave built and hurtled toward the coast of Morocco, picking up speed as it was propelled forward by a quivering portal ridge in the Atlantic Ocean.

The Border between worlds was splitting.

CHAPTER SEVENTY-NINE

Cheyenne backed away from the expanding column of blazing light on the crumbled portal ridge. The battles raging around her died down as a thunderous crack split the air, followed by the roars of a thousand voices laughing as one. Smoking claws as long as a car emerged from the wide vertical light and ripped through the magical wall, tearing it open to reveal a blinding collection of multi-colored flames flickering in and out. Then the Sorren Gán's burning, fiery eyes appeared thirty feet in the air.

No fucking way.

L'zar didn't notice the creature's half-emergence between worlds. He was caught in the casting of his spell, unaware of anything around him.

The magicals in the clearing—agents, inmates, and O'gúleesh refugees—backed away from the shimmering form of the fiery creature that was struggling to break free.

"A new age dawns," the Sorren Gán roared. "And I will come for all of it."

"What the fuck is that thing?" the horned inmate snarled.

Cheyenne saw the prisoner from the corner of her eye, unable to look away from the muted veil between their world and Ambar'ogúl.

The spell isn't finished. That thing can talk to us, but it can't get through. Not yet.

"It's the only fucking thing any of us needs to fight right now," she muttered.

It didn't matter if the inmate heard her. The Sorren Gán's claws pressed against the muted film of reality holding it on the other side, chuckled again in its thousands of otherworldly voices, and pointed at L'zar. The Weaver's hands jerked high above his head and he bent over backward, suspended by magic alone as he kept muttering the incantation and fueling the rest of the spell. "We will have this world, little drow. But first, a taste…"

The creature withdrew from within the massive rip between one world and the other. Its deafening laughter receded with it, then the column of light darkened with shadows.

"Cheyenne." Maleshi appeared beside her, staring at the shadows cast by purple flames converging on the tear in reality. "Any ideas?"

The first figure composed of purple flame emerged, floating over the top of the crumbled portal ridge and coalescing into a humanoid shape. Its face was contorted into a permanent scream, sockets spewing black smoke where eyes should have been. Others followed, shrieking, wailing, and reaching out to the magicals scattered around the clearing.

"Right from the lake of fire," Cheyenne muttered.

The general scowled at her. "What?"

Someone in the clearing flung a bolt of searing blue light at the souls from the Sorren Gán's lair. The attack did nothing to stop the emerging army.

Cheyenne flickered through the spells her activator prompted, not knowing what she was looking for until she found it. Then she cast the spell, her hands working on their own as if she'd been doing this her whole life.

A black dart burst from between her hands, growing as it hurtled toward the closest soul trapped in purple flames. By the time it reached the undead creature, it had ballooned to twice the thing's size, and it wrapped around the fiery body. The figure's shriek died, and it disappeared. The other beings of purple flames filled the gap and floated slowly across the clearing, unaffected by the one who had vanished.

"This banishing spell." Cheyenne sent the name of it to Maleshi's activator and walked away from the screeching horde toward L'zar, who was frozen in his protective dome. "Make sure everyone knows those things are here to siphon magic. Can't kill them, but we can send them right back."

Maleshi cast a banishing spell and grinned fiercely when it took out two of the fiery souls. She shouted to the others, and Cheyenne barely registered the message appearing in the corner of her vision with the name of the banishing spell. She focused on L'zar again; his feet were still planted firmly on the ground, arms stretched over his head as his back curved in an inverted U.

That thing's just fucking with him now. Making L'zar its puppet for real.

As the magicals who'd been fighting each other now fought off the Sorren Gán's fiery army, Cheyenne sifted through every spell her activator could pull up. Each flashed red with an error message.

Projected failure.

Yeah, no shit.

"L'zar!" She stepped cautiously over to the dome and reached toward him. "I know you can hear me."

A gnarled, stooped figure of purple flames, its arms dangling at the wrong angles, passed through L'zar's protective wall and emerged unaffected on the other side, reaching toward Cheyenne. She stumbled back and hurled the banishing spell at it. The black orb struck the howling creature, stopping the thing for only a second. The purple-flamed prisoner of the Sorren Gán continued toward her.

Knowing drow speed was a bad idea, Cheyenne turned and ran toward the opposite side of the clearing, ducking flying banishing spells and trying to get far enough away to cast her own. She'd almost reached the forest when a burst of startling cold and a shimmering wave of air appeared in front of the trees. It wasn't a portal, but out stepped a small figure in a dark cloak and hood. In the darkness of that hood were two eerily glowing green eyes and a glowing sickly grin.

Inolu raised both hands, the veins glowing green through her gray skin, and blasted a wave of dark light at the oncoming horde. Cheyenne dropped to her knees to avoid the banebreaker's attack. Her head felt like it would split as the powerful spell seared through the air.

The undead creatures of purple fire screamed and wailed, their shrieks adding to the din until the banebreaker's wall shattered them into fragments that disappeared a moment later.

Inolu lowered her arms, and the glowing eyes looked at Cheyenne. "Where is the calibrax?"

Shit. That's the Underman.

Cheyenne staggered to her feet and stepped around the banebreaker's small figure to point at L'zar. On the other side of the clearing, the magicals focused on the much smaller number of fiery souls to banish, spell orbs flying through the air and growing to consume them. One unfortunate inmate got too close, and the Sorren Gán's enslaved soul struck him in the chest. The inmate fell to his knees, screaming over and over as shimmering light was pulled from his body and hurled through the veil.

The Underman turned toward the scream and laughed. "Well, isn't this exciting?"

"It's next to L'zar," Cheyenne shouted.

"We want it, drow." The green grin turned to her, and the Underman tilted his borrowed head. "Now."

"So go get it!" Cheyenne shot another banishing spell at the closest undead thing. "I can't get to him. Maybe you can."

"The only way to stop this spell is to remove the source of the magic fueling it." The Underman chuckled. "Hadn't you heard?"

"Yeah, I heard. If I can't get to the calibrax—"

"Not the calibrax, you adorably blind creature." The Underman flicked a glowing hand at another wave of purple-flaming souls and shattered them. He threw his head back and roared with laughter in half a dozen tones, then a glowing green finger indicated the dome around the drow. "That's the source on this side."

"L'zar." Cheyenne stared at her father, caught helplessly in his power fueled by the Sorren Gán. "Remove him? No. I'm not gonna kill him." The sounds of the raging battle between the Earthside magicals and the undead souls melted into an incomprehensible warble. A knot formed in Cheyenne's stomach. *If I don't do something, that fucking drow-eater is gonna come tearing through that veil and destroy everything it touches.*

"You do you, Cheyenne." The Underman cackled again. "I'm here for the fun."

Inolu's body pranced across the clearing, the cloak fluttering behind her as the Underman ignored some of the purple souls and blasted others to bits at random.

Cheyenne spun when the earth shuddered again, and she saw two more pillars of light bursting into the air from hundreds of miles away. *I can't kill him. He's not the one doing this.*

"Cheyenne!" Ember burst through the trees, dragging Neros behind her by the hand. The pale-skinned drow stared with wide eyes at the open veil spilling purple figures into the clearing. Ember jerked him forward until they stood beside Cheyenne. "Why are you standing here? What the hell are those? Where's L'zar?"

The drow pointed at her father in the dome. "I can't break through. The Underman said I have to kill him. Remove the source of the magic, but I don't…"

Neros' hand flickered as he reached out to his cousin and put it on her shoulder. He leaned slowly toward her ear and muttered, "You do not need to kill him, cousin. Merely remove him. As I removed Ba'rael."

Cheyenne blinked. "What?"

He nodded. "Only one of us can get to him."

"Shit. Okay."

Ember jumped away from a stray floating soul heading their way, and Cheyenne blasted it to nothingness with a banishing spell as she ran toward L'zar. Halfway there, she burst into black flames and pushed herself to top speed. *This better fucking work.*

The dome unleashed another attack as she approached, but her drow fire deflected it like armor. Then she was through the wall, halted by the thickness of the magic protecting the Weaver. Her eyes watered, and she pushed the thick force that was trying to toss her back out.

"L'zar!" Cheyenne gritted her teeth and managed to step forward and lean into the center of the dome. "Stop!"

He didn't react to her presence, so she reached out with one black flaming hand. A stream of drow fire shot from her fingertip and glanced off L'zar's skin like she'd tossed water at him. It caught his attention.

Slowly, he straightened, his arms lowering back down to his sides, and he turned his head to her. His eyes blazed with the same flashing, colorful lights as his body, and the grin splitting his face didn't belong to him.

"You're too late." The Sorren Gán's voice poured from L'zar's barely moving mouth. "L'zar is gone. Powerless. I may let you join him if you behave."

Fuck. Cheyenne shot another stream of black flames at her father, but it wasn't any use.

Remove the source of the magic fueling it. I don't have to remove L'zar.

It was easier to reach into the pocket of her trench coat than it was to reach out to the Weaver. With a shout of effort and still rippling with black fire, Cheyenne forced her legs forward one step at a time, leaning at a steep angle to keep her feet planted on the ground.

"L'zar! I know you're still there."

He threw his head back and laughed with the Sorren Gán's thousand voices. "You know nothing."

She was only three feet away now. Through the dim light of the dome's outer wall, she saw the magicals battling an army that couldn't die. Maleshi darted around the clearing in silver streaks. A purple light bloomed around the seven-foot Kenneth, protecting him as he hurled banishing spells through his shield. Tori swooped down in full Verati form, shooting black orbs out of the sky. Tate and Bhandi screamed together and sent fiery souls back through the veil.

Don't stop now, Cheyenne, or all this will be gone.

Two feet. One.

L'zar's flashing eyes widened, as did his grin, which should have been impossible. "You are remarkable, Cheyenne. I'll give you that much."

"Fuck you." She threw herself at her father, crashed into his rigid body, and wrapped him in her arms. Searing heat flowed through her as black fire roared around them in the dome, engulfing them both. With R'leer's displacer pressed to the Weaver's back, Cheyenne willed the thing to do what it was meant to do and whispered in L'zar's ear, "It's over."

L'zar's mouth slowly opened, his terrified shout growing louder and louder in one long, unending breath. Black flames whipped around them. The dome exploded, sending a shockwave of ruptured concentrated magic in every direction. It blew the fighting magicals off their feet and across the ground. The souls howled and wailed, writhing where they stood until they burst and shot back through the veil in streams of purple flames.

Cheyenne's head pounded with L'zar's screaming so close to her face. Then he dropped like an empty sack, slithering out of her arms and writhing on the ground. The flashing lights within him condensed into a thick stream, and she had to clench the displacer in both hands to keep from dropping it as it absorbed the pieces the Sorren Gán had inserted into L'zar Verdys, biding its time. The displacer rattled and shook, jerking her arms back and forth before the last of the Sorren Gán's magic disappeared inside it.

The column of light shooting into the sky cracked, sending a buckling ripple through the earth before it shriveled into itself and sank beneath the rubble of the destroyed portal ridge. The crumbled black stones exploded, and huge chunks flew into the air and sailed over the forest.

Every other visible column of light did the same, cracking and shrinking before one explosion after another wracked the sites affected by the Sorren Gán's spell.

The rear wall of the prison crumbled into a pile of rubble beneath the shuddering blast. For a few heart-stopping seconds, everything was silent.

Unless I just went deaf.

CHAPTER EIGHTY

The only beings left standing in the clearing behind the prison were Cheyenne and the Underman in Inolu's petite body. The drow stepped away from her father, still holding the flickering displacer in both hands, and stared at the fallen magicals. *Not again. Please, not again.*

An inmate groaned and coughed out a mouthful of dirt. Two geared-up FRoE agents slapped their hands on their helmets to take them off before dropping their heads back onto the browning grass. Then everyone else started stirring, taking time to recover.

"What happened?"

"I think I broke my back."

"You look like you broke your fucking face."

"Holy shit. The light's gone."

Cheyenne heaved a relieved breath and blinked back the tears stinging her eyes.

"Oh, wonderful," the Underman droned. "We're right back to the boring stuff." He stalked toward Cheyenne and lifted a finger. "I don't want to deal with this anymore, so consider this the end of our arrangement, however amusing your part in it was. And I hate that thing."

The Underman whipped his hand away from Cheyenne, pulling the displacer with it. She stumbled after it and watched the thing hurtle end over end through the air. A white portal burst open in time to let the displacer through.

"Wait!" Neros shouted, leaping to his feet. He raced past Cheyenne and slipped into drow speed.

She followed a second later. "What are you doing?"

"Returning home, Cheyenne." He turned and grinned at her. "I am ready. Do not worry about me, cousin. I will return when I am more prepared."

"Okay." That was all she could say as her cousin spun again and ran toward the shrinking portal that led to Nor'ieth. He stepped through before the circle disappeared, and Cheyenne dropped back into regular time.

The portal was gone.

That was easy.

The Underman stalked over to her as magicals all over the clearing picked themselves up and shook off their injuries. "There. That's the end of it. Don't make me clean up after you again. If I wanted to do that, I would have found my own body." He stooped to scoop up the calibrax with both hands, and the grin glowed even brighter as he straightened and stared at Cheyenne. "But feel free to come say hello. You're so unpredictable."

A flash of green light burst around Inolu's cloaked figure, then she and the Underman and whatever other *uanáj* she hosted were gone.

Yeah, nobody ever wants to stay for the cleanup.

Cheyenne knelt beside L'zar's crumpled body and pressed her fingers to the side of his neck. Relieved, she tried to shake him awake, but he wouldn't budge. *I've passed out enough times to recognize this for what it is.*

"Oh, shit. Corian."

She darted through the grumbling magicals as the inmates regained their wits enough to pick fights with the agents. Weapons were drawn again, spells and attacks conjured in warning. "Maleshi!"

When she skirted the destroyed portal ridge, the tree branch was empty.

With a hiss, the general raced forward with a burst of light and dropped into regular speed, sliding across the ground on her knees. *"Vae shra'ni."*

Corian lay in a heap in the rock-strewn, blood-soaked grass. His eyelids fluttered, the pale silver glow behind them dangerously weakened.

"Oh, no. Ember!"

"Stop yelling. I'm right here." Ember raised a purple-glowing hand in front of her to ward off two inmates as she headed toward the fallen nightstalker.

They blinked in surprise, and one of them thumped the other in the chest. "Fae's not worth it, man."

"She could be."

Ember ignored them and knelt beside Maleshi. "Let me look."

The general didn't hear her as she bent over Corian's face and ran her fingers through his hair. "I'm so sorry, *ma gairin*. I should have been here sooner."

"Maleshi." The fae leaned forward to catch her attention. "Let me help."

With a shuddering breath, Maleshi kissed Corian's furry blood-covered cheek and growled.

"General Hi'et," Cheyenne barked. "You need to back up and let the healer do her job."

That snapped the nightstalker out of her grief. She whipped her head up to blink at Cheyenne, then scrambled to her feet and stepped back. "It's not too late. Right?"

Ember ran her hands over Corian's cut, bloody, bruised flesh and closed her eyes. "Not for him. I'm gonna need a minute."

The gold light of her healing magic bloomed beneath her palms as she worked Corian over from head to toe.

"Back the fuck up, Earthborn *nilsch úcat*!" A battered orc inmate summoned attack spells in his hands and hissed at the FRoE agents closing on him. "I came out here for a reason, and now it's fucking gone. I ain't goin' back to that."

"Hands up!" Gloved hands slammed against the sides of fell rifles as multiple agents powered up their weapons to employ simpler tactics. "You didn't make parole. This is over."

"Eat shit."

Fights broke out across the clearing as inmates tried to flee and agents worked together to round them up. The horned magical with two barbed tails backed away from the crowd and tried to disappear into the forest. A dark form swooped down from the treetops and barreled into him, knocking him back on his ass.

"What the—"

Tori landed in front of him, her silver bat-like wings fully outstretched as she spread her arms. "I don't think any of your prison buddies would be too happy to hear you got up and ran off without them, would they?"

"Get the fuck outta my way." The inmate scrambled to his feet and launched an oily black spray at her.

Tori stepped aside, deflecting his attack with a swipe of her hand and a burst of silver light, then stormed toward him and threw a web of glittering strands in his face. The spell whipped his head back, and a mesh net unfolded around the horned guy's head, then spilled down his shoulders, chest, and back until he stood there like a mummy wrapped in glistening magic. She stepped over to him and poked his chest with a silver finger. The inmate snarled at her, then fell on his back with a thump.

The prisoners watching her cursed and scattered. Agents shouted and took off after them, firing shots across the clearing and tossing mechanical devices powered by fellfire.

The highest whine of all rose from the prison side of the clearing, and there stood Agent Michael Todd in full field gear with the fell laser secured to his hip. "If any of you assholes try to run for it, I'll blast you all back to—"

The laser fired, spraying a stream of devastating fell energy across the clearing. Agents darted toward him as he lost control and the weapon sprayed the ground, throwing up dust and grass and chunks of portal stone.

"Goddammit, Todd!" Bhandi raced over to him and dropped to the ground to avoid the beam he swung her way. Inmates and operatives both leaped aside.

"Cut it off!" Cheyenne shouted.

Yurik stormed toward his fellow agent and clapped. The roiling flash of his Obliterate spell's yellow light flared around his hands, then was sucked back in. The blast erupted from his palms and hit Todd's fell cannon halfway up the massive fellfire-spewing barrel. It erupted in a spray of green energy and shrapnel. Todd reeled away, staring at his empty hands, and Tate ran up behind him to shove him in the back.

"What?"

"Yeah, what the fuck, Todd?"

"Who told you to bring that shit out here?"

"Hey." Yurik stared at his hands in disbelief. "I fucking did it this time."

The human agent stared at everyone picking themselves up off the ground and glaring at him. "You're letting them get away." He pointed at the inmates who were using his exploded weapon as a distraction, and the other agents hurried after the escapees to tackle them to the ground and slap dampening cuffs on their wrists.

Cheyenne folded her arms and watched the magical agents working with their activators as well as their weapons. *At least they're using them in the field now.*

"You guys good?" she shouted over the thumps of prisoners hitting the ground and a few more shots.

"Yeah, you stick to training and consulting," an agent shouted, and most of them burst out laughing as they hauled detained prisoners to their feet.

Tate headed over to her, glancing around the impromptu battlefield and shaking his head. "You were right."

"Thanks. It's good to hear and everything, but if I had to choose between—"

"Between saving two worlds and being right? Yeah, I get it." He rubbed his bald head and nodded at the agents roughly escorting the recaptured prisoners back to the blown-up prison. "We'll figure something out to keep them contained, I guess, until we can put the cell blocks back together." The tattooed troll clapped a hand on her shoulder and nodded. "But you don't have to worry about that part."

"That's appreciated."

"Hey, hey! Watch that asshole's tail, will ya?" Tate pointed at two agents dragging an inmate into the trees and jogged after them.

Ember sat back on her heels and took a deep breath. "Okay."

Maleshi studied Corian intently and groaned when the nightstalker stirred and rolled onto his side. "By the—"

She couldn't finish her sentence but dropped to the ground next to him to help him sit up, brushing loose grass off his shoulders, touching his cheeks, and checking him like she thought he'd fall into a hundred pieces at any minute.

Corian blinked at her and suffered the unusual attention. Finally, he grabbed her wrists in both hands and leaned toward her. "General Hi'et."

"What?" She studied his silver eyes, which were now glowing with their usual strength.

"I do believe you're fussing."

Maleshi hissed and jerked her wrists out of his grasp. "Don't be an idiot."

Corian chuckled and rose unsteadily to his feet. "No, I think I've reached my quota for that already."

"Can you walk?"

Ember snorted. "What kind of a healer would I be if he couldn't?"

Corian smiled weakly at Maleshi as she stepped smartly aside and clasped her hands behind her back. Then he approached Ember and stopped mere inches from her.

"What?" Her luminous violet eyes widened. "Did I miss something?"

Corian wrapped her in his arms, making her squeak in surprise, and muttered, "I heard the deathflame call my name, healer. Then I heard you call me back. Thank you."

Ember swallowed thickly, but before she could return the embrace, he released her and stepped away. "L'zar?"

Cheyenne nodded at the other side of the clearing. "He's sleeping it off. Pretty sure nobody's gonna bother him at this point."

She was right. Another group of agents entered the clearing to help with the cleanup, while Maleshi opened portals for the remaining magical civilians who'd come to join in the fight. Most of them stopped to thank Cheyenne for the activators and for calling on them to take a stand however they could. It was a little awkward to be thanked by the magicals who'd fought off the Sorren Gán's horde while Cheyenne focused on L'zar, but she let it slide.

This is what I signed up for anyway. Drow royalty on Earth, right?

The Earthside magicals and FRoE agents had all left the clearing one way or another. Only Cheyenne, Ember, Maleshi, L'zar, and Corian remained.

The general folded her arms and studied the border portal, then gazed into the sky as if the column of light were still there. "What happened?"

"A lot of things all at once." Shrugging, the drow turned to her father and waved the others forward with her. "If anyone wants to port us back to my place, we can get him away from this prison. Then I'll fill you in on everything you missed while you were bleeding out and fighting off an undead army. How's that sound?" She looked at Corian and Maleshi over her shoulder and smiled crookedly.

"Sounds like we might be returning to a semblance of normalcy," Corian muttered. "But I think I'll hold off on portals for now."

The general elbowed him gently. "No one asked you to do a thing."

"I know. For the first time, I think I might take advantage of it."

They returned to Cheyenne's and Ember's apartment, where they laid L'zar on the couch to let him sleep and recover for as long as he needed. Cheyenne told the others about having seen the undead souls in the Sorren Gán's lake of fire, drawing the creature's magic from L'zar, the Underman tossing R'leer's displacer filled with that magic back through dimensions and into Nor'ieth, and Neros' joyful return home.

Standing behind the recliner where Corian sat, Maleshi drummed her fingers on the leather cushion. "Honestly, kid, it sounds like all the pieces of the fucked-up puzzle fell into place at the right time."

"Lucky, I think."

Corian turned to look up at the general, and they both burst out laughing. "If that's what you wanna call it."

"So, what about the Border?" Ember asked from her seat at the bistro table. "Is it broken, or did we stop that part?"

"I don't know, Em." From the other leather recliner, Cheyenne studied her sleeping father. "But I think no news is good news as far as that goes. If there are any issues, I'm sure I'll be hearing about it soon."

"And in the meantime?" Corian added.

"In the meantime, what?"

He nodded at L'zar. "What will the—"

L'zar stirred on the couch and let out a massive groan. Then he started and bolted upright, his gold eyes darting everywhere at once. "Corian! *Vae shra'ni*, I never—"

"I'm right here." Corian stayed where he was in the chair, gripping the leather armrests as he nodded calmly at the Weaver. "And it's finished."

L'zar stared at him. "I didn't…did it…" His mouth worked soundlessly as he tried to recall anything from the last five days. "I can't see."

"What?" Cheyenne stood abruptly, not even thinking about how odd the others probably thought it was to see her race over to the couch and kneel in front of her father.

L'zar's head whipped back and forth as he stared blankly around. With a grimace, he slowly lowered himself onto the couch again, waving one hand and then the other in front of his face. "Cheyenne?"

"Yeah, I'm here."

"Cheyenne, I can't see."

"Yeah, I heard you." She grabbed one of his flailing hands and lowered it to his side, holding it there firmly. "Look at me."

L'zar turned his head toward her, and his gold eyes found hers. "What happened?"

Frowning, Cheyenne waved a hand in front of his face, and he blinked. "I think you can see fine. You sure you're awake?"

He let out a soft, exhausted chuckle and sank deeper into the couch cushions. "Being awake and being able to see are not always the same."

"Uh-huh."

"I'm talking about the Weave, Cheyenne." L'zar scanned the room one more time, then returned his gaze to his daughter's face. "My eyes are perfectly fine, but the Threads are gone."

Corian sat up straighter in the armchair and cleared his throat.

Cheyenne dipped her head toward her father, frowning. "Are you sure?"

He laughed. "I know what the world looks like without reading it in every molecule." His voice was soft, and his eyes lost their clarity as his physical weakness caught up with him. He pushed through it enough to raise his hand toward Cheyenne's cheek, pausing there without touching her. "I can no longer see the Weave. I can only see you."

She swallowed thickly. *He's delirious. No way would any of this make him happy enough for that dopey smile.*

Grabbing his hand again, she lowered it back down to his side and nodded. "If that's true, I think I know why?"

"It doesn't matter."

"It might. I pulled the Sorren Gán out of you with a displacer. Probably all of it if you can't read the Weave anymore."

Her father stared at her, his ridiculous blank smile still on his face.

"I'd do it again in a heartbeat, L'zar, but I'm sorry that got taken from you."

The drow's slow, steady breathing was the only sound in the living room for a moment. Then he blinked and said, "Honestly, Cheyenne, I don't give a fuck."

His smile widened briefly, then his eyes rolled back in his head, and he passed out again.

She sat back on her heels and looked him over. *Nobody changes that much, do they? Nobody gives up everything they wanted for nothing.*

"Well." Maleshi clapped her hands together and stepped out from behind Corian's chair. "That was a little more intimate than I think any of us were ready for. If you don't mind, kid, I feel like calling it a day."

"Yeah." Cheyenne stood and backed away from the couch. "I think we all are."

"Excellent."

Corian pushed out of the chair with a grimace and raised his eyebrows. "I should thank you for the timely rescue."

She snorted. "Probably."

"Thank you, Cheyenne. You've done more than you might understand right now."

Maleshi nudged him into silence. "Don't insult her, *ma gairín*. She knows exactly what she did."

"What we all did." Cheyenne nodded at them. "Don't wait too long to get a new phone, huh?"

Corian blinked at her. "Point taken."

Chuckling wryly, Maleshi opened another portal in the living room, then turned to wink at the drow. "Here's to many more close calls."

"Hopefully not with my blood," Corian added. He reached out to take Maleshi's hand, and they stepped quickly through the portal. After it closed behind them, Cheyenne ran her hands through her hair and closed her eyes.

"You okay?"

"I think so." The drow turned to look at Ember, who was sitting at the bistro table. "Are you?"

"I don't know yet. I was looking forward to not having an insane drow crashing on our couch for a while."

Cheyenne gave a dry, tired laugh and climbed into the chair across from her friend. They both stared at L'zar for a moment. "I don't think he'll be here long. That's the way he is."

CHAPTER EIGHTY-ONE

Four days later

Cheyenne was in another conference at the FRoE base, waiting for the meeting to begin. Also waiting were Major General Van Lurig and the three remaining members of the board. The clock on the wall at the far end of the room ticked obnoxiously, and Cheyenne spun back and forth in her chair, reading her latest emails.

The one that had caught her attention first was short, simple, and to the point.

Dear Miss Summerlin,

We have reviewed and discussed your previous email, and we understand your decision to withdraw from the graduate program. On behalf of VCU's entire Computer Sciences Department, I would like to extend to you an invitation to re-enroll in the graduate program at any time, if you should see fit to do so. Your current credits will remain applicable indefinitely.

We wish you the best of luck in your endeavors.

Sincerely,

Dr. Maddie Bergmann, Ph. D.

Computer Sciences Department

Virginia Commonwealth University

Cheyenne held back a laugh as she read the email one more time. *I bet she's the one who got them to agree to those non-expiring credits.*

Her phone buzzed once with an incoming text, and she opened it to find a picture from Inolu and a short text beneath.

Just another Monday. Subdued and manageable, and we're getting along fine.

The picture was a selfie the banebreaker had taken, grinning with her arm around a blank-faced, complacent Ba'rael. Despite her vapid stare, the Spider held up a middle finger to the camera.

Looks like the banebreaker's been teaching her Earthside manners.

Cheyenne snorted.

"I don't find this funny in the least," Van Lurig muttered, turning around in her chair to look at the clock on the wall. "We should have started this meeting ten minutes ago."

"I'm sure they'll show up." The drow looked up at her briefly and shook her head. "I don't like waiting either."

"You seem to be entertaining yourself just fine."

"Going through some emails. That's all."

None of the board members had a response to that, and Cheyenne returned her attention to her phone, typing her message to Inolu instead of using her activator to make herself look busy. *You'd think whoever called this meeting would show up on time. This is a total power play.*

Looks like you're having fun. We should talk about getting her involved in community service when she's ready.

Inolu immediately responded with a devil-face emoji and a thumbs-up. Cheyenne fought back another smile.

Then her activator pinged her with an incoming message through the system, and she opened it to find another update from Persh'al.

Ironbreak: Just had a visit from the Golra. I thought Nu'ek was the exception, but it seems good manners are built into them. They

wanted to talk about opening up territory rule again. I have no problem with it. I wanted to check with you.

Cheyenne: You don't have to check with me about anything. But I appreciate it. You know how I feel.

Ironbreak: Yep. Then I'll start dishing it out to whatever tribes want it back.

Cheyenne: Any more issues with the mainframe?

Ironbreak: Nope. I still don't get how the Sorren Gán managed to put up that wall, but now that the bastard's gone, everything's working like it's supposed to. Looks like magicals over here learned a few things about gratitude over the last week. So far, no attempted takeovers.

Cheyenne: So far, so good, right? How's the next shipment coming?

Ironbreak: She's almost finished. We might have to charge for the next one, though.

Cheyenne: I don't think anyone's gonna complain. Thanks for the update.

Ironbreak: See you soon, kid. Blood and honor.

Cheyenne swiped the message out of her vision and stopped spinning in the executive office chair. *A few things about gratitude. Right. Like that the Border still exists, even after it was ripped open enough to let Earthside activators access Hangivol's system. Who knew there could be a silver lining to that one?*

She looked at the clock, which was now showing 2:15, and drummed her fingers on the chair's armrests. "You guys did say two o'clock when you talked to whoever, right?"

Mr. Weber shot her an exasperated look. "Helen would be the last person to have a typo in her email."

"Yeah, I bet."

"Either they got caught up in something else, or they're trying to make us squirm," Lieutenant Colonel Oppenhaur added.

"Or they've decided to pull out and leave us sitting here like a conference room full of desperate idiots." Van Lurig closed her eyes and took a deep breath. "It's impossible to tell."

"Do you guys even know who this new investor is?" Cheyenne asked. "Any previous connections?"

"No." The major general eyed the door. "The only correspondence we've had was with an unaffiliated third party working on the investor's behalf. They were quite adamant about sitting down with us to discuss our next steps. Two o'clock was the investor's idea."

"Cheyenne." Colonel McMillen folded his hands on the table and raised his eyebrows. "You wouldn't happen to have a hunch about who this mystery person is, would you?"

"Nope. I'm as clueless as the rest of you." The board members scowled, and Cheyenne dropped her gaze to her phone again. "Whether or not this meeting happens, we still need to move forward with changes. A lot of them."

"That isn't why—"

"I'm sorry, Colonel, but that *is* why we're here." Cheyenne looked up again and met each of the board member's gazes. "The Border isn't closed, and the standard operations on the reservations need massive improvements, not to mention everything we can now offer the Earth-side magicals. And should."

"You brought them activators!" Weber exclaimed incredulously.

"That's a tiny sliver of it, and you know that. There's a hell of a lot more to be done."

Van Lurig nodded. "We understand your concerns, Cheyenne, and we'll address them after this meeting with our new investor. With as much as they'll be pouring into this organization, they're entitled to hear your proposals before we put any of them into action."

Cheyenne shook her head and stared at her phone again. *More bureaucratic bullshit. And I bet this new investor's gonna be a real shithead about the whole thing.*

There was a brisk knock on the door.

"Finally," Van Lurig whispered. She cleared her throat and called, "Please come in."

The door opened swiftly. "My apologies for making the board wait so long. It's been some time since I made the drive into the city."

Cheyenne whipped her head up to see her mother step into the conference room with a leather portfolio under one arm. *What the actual fuck?*

The woman closed the door softly behind her, then approached the chair at the head of the table opposite Van Lurig. Everyone stared at her as she took the seat Cheyenne usually sat in. Bianca set the portfolio on the table before rolling the chair forward and gazing at all of them. "I assumed formal introductions wouldn't be necessary, but if I'm mistaken, please let me know."

Van Lurig blinked at her. "No, Ms. Summerlin. We know who you are."

"Wonderful. I must say it's lovely to finally meet all of you, Major General. Lieutenant Colonel. Colonel. Mr. Weber." Bianca gave each of them a nod, saving her daughter for last. "Cheyenne."

The drow's eyes widened, and she couldn't think of anything to say. *What is she doing?*

"Now, I'd like to start this meeting with a proposal of my own," Bianca added, unzipping the leather portfolio and opening it. She removed three sheets of paper and briefly scanned them. "Seeing as I've recently purchased a controlling interest in this organization with my contribution and pledge, I'd like to be more involved than what's usually afforded private investors."

Van Lurig stared at the papers in Bianca's hand. "Such as?"

"Such as Board Director, Major General." Bianca nodded at the woman. "Now, please don't mistake me. You've run this organization efficiently and effectively according to its previous standard protocols and functions, and you handled the highly problematic situation with Colonel Thomas far better than most, but I'm not interested in funding this organization's operations, only to be stonewalled at every turn. Or having to drive down from Henry County on a whim to make my case should I see fit to implement any changes. Neither is Cheyenne."

"I'm sorry?" Van Lurig asked.

"What?" Cheyenne whispered.

Bianca ignored them both. "She has agreed to hold Power of Attorney for my responsibilities here as Board Director and the allocation of funds provided to this organization by my estate."

The major general looked between the Summerlin women. "Cheyenne didn't mention any of this beforehand."

"We decided it was best to go over everything at once and in person with the other members of the board. I'm sure you understand the delicate nature of what's at stake for this organization. I'm much more effective when I can ensure no one will be running their mouths about my involvement in any business transactions. And despite what you may have heard, Major General, I still conduct many of them."

"And this is already settled?" McMillen asked.

"Of course." Bianca handed the paperwork to Cheyenne. "Would you mind passing those around, Cheyenne?"

"Sure." She took the papers and briefly skimmed them. There it was, a legal statement from Bianca Summerlin, pledging her continued financial investments to the "independent organization" on the condition that she retain controlling interest and her seat as Board Director. Beneath that was a Power of Attorney laying out the terms Bianca had mentioned, with a Notary Public seal stamped on the bottom beside two signatures. Bianca's and Cheyenne's.

She forged my signature.

Oppenhaur cleared his throat, and she slid the papers across the table toward him. The man had to stand to grab the documents, and he skimmed them before passing them to McMillen. The documents made their way around the table for the other board members to inspect, and Bianca shot her daughter a sidelong look.

A tiny smile flickered at the corner of the woman's mouth, and Cheyenne stifled a laugh.

Jesus. I told her there was an opening on the board. Practically gave her the okay for all this.

"As you can see, everything's already been signed and filed with the state. That's merely for tax purposes. This organization's anonymity has been maintained in its entirety."

"Yes, that's certainly clear." Van Lurig frowned at Cheyenne, then quickly removed the expression to address Bianca. "I'm curious, Ms. Summerlin, as to why you called this meeting. It seems you already have everything perfectly handled."

"I prefer not to enter new partnerships without at least one face-to-face discussion, though, admittedly, very few of them make it necessary for me to leave my estate." Bianca lifted her chin and scanned the board members' faces. "I also wanted to offer the board the opportunity to refuse my terms and my investment, should it deem this proposal an unfit arrangement. In person."

The question hung thickly in the air without anyone having to say it. Did Van Lurig value her seat as Board Director over the staggering amount of Bianca's initial contribution and her commitment to continue making the same indefinitely?

Weber glanced at Van Lurig. "I don't see any reason why we should reject this proposal."

"Mr. Weber."

"The engineering department only needs a fraction of what she's offering!"

"That's enough." Van Lurig stared him down and the man sank back in his chair, clasping his hands together in his lap, but he kept staring at the major general with pleading eyes. She turned to McMillen and Oppenhaur to gauge their reactions. All she received from either of them was a dip of the head as they deferred to her final decision. "Ms. Summerlin, this organization, this board, could not be more grateful for your contributions and your swift attention to detail. We gladly accept your proposal."

"Excellent. That final document on the bottom includes each board member's name. Your signatures are required to complete this agreement, then we can move forward. You'll see Cheyenne and I have already signed."

Cheyenne bowed her head and tried to hide the smile threatening to overwhelm her. *Should've told her about all this sooner.*

Van Lurig smiled politely at Bianca. "Does anyone have a pen?"

Cheyenne almost burst out laughing when Weber removed the pen she'd obliterated and restored from the inside pocket of his blazer.

"Thank you." The major general signed first. The other board members added their signatures, then the documents were passed around the table to Bianca.

The woman took them from Cheyenne with a curt nod before setting them neatly back in the leather portfolio and zipping it closed. When she stood, every member of the board stood with her. Cheyenne rose to her feet as well.

"Thank you all for your cooperation and understanding. I trust that moving forward, the operation of this entire organization will reach its fullest potential. I look forward to seeing the first report."

"Thank you, Ms. Summerlin." Van Lurig looked like she'd bitten into a lemon. "I'll have Helen show you out."

"That's kind, Major General, but I'll see myself out. However efficient your assistant may be, and I'm certain she is, she's a bit coarse. Good afternoon."

With that, Bianca stuck her portfolio under her arm and turned to head for the door. It shut behind her with a soft click, and the conference room fell silent.

Cheyenne gazed at the board members—her board members—and sat in her chair again with a smile. "So, let's talk about what needs to happen next."

The others sat stiffly, still in shock seconds after Bianca's unexpected takeover. Oppenhaur scowled at the drow, but that was apparently the resting state of his face. Van Lurig licked her lips, clearly holding back another outburst, and folded her hands on the table. "Whenever you're ready. Director."

Cheyenne sat back in her chair. Her phone buzzed in her pocket, and a command prompt appeared on her activator to read the message privately and hands-free. She selected the prompt and pulled the text from Bianca into the top right corner of her vision.

Consider it an early Christmas present.

L'zar stood on a rolling hillside in the mountains of Virginia, looking out over Henry County. From here, he could see the swath of perfectly manicured lawn behind the small glint of sunlight reflecting off the back windows of Bianca Summerlin's estate house. With his hands clasped behind his back, he closed his eyes and inhaled deeply. "Mountain air, *vae shra'ni*. That's what I enjoy most about this place. I imagine it's very much the same for her."

Corian turned to look at the drow standing beside him. "Which one?"

"Bianca."

"Of course." Corian studied the empty lawn behind Bianca's house. From here, the destroyed portal ridge would have been visible as a line of black stone rubble, but that was before the Border had almost been ripped to shreds beneath the Sorren Gán's magic. Those glistening black hunks of rock were gone. "What about Cheyenne?"

"What about her?"

"She pulled together Threads even we couldn't see."

L'zar nodded. "Indeed. She is my daughter, after all."

The nightstalker chuckled. "There was never any doubt."

"Only her own." The drow tilted his head and gazed past the valley of the Summerlin Estate at the still-green mountains beyond, brown and bare in patches where deciduous groves had lost their leaves for the coming winter. "I imagine I'll have more doubts in the times to come. That's rather a prerequisite of no longer reading the Weave, wouldn't you say?"

"I have nothing to compare it to."

"No. Of course, you don't."

"But doubts about her, L'zar? No. I wouldn't call those a prerequisite."

The drow thief shot his *Nós Aní* an annoyed look. "I wasn't talking about my daughter."

They stood silently for a few minutes longer, the cool mountain breeze tossing L'zar's white hair behind his head and ruffling Corian's tawny fur.

"What are you planning now?" Corian asked, eyeing his friend.

"It's not so much a plan as a long-time dream of mine." The drow chuckled. "Would it surprise you to hear I'm thinking about opening a school?"

"A school." The nightstalker pressed his lips together and forced himself to look away from his friend and out over the valley. "The Academy of How Not to Unravel the Weave, you mean?"

L'zar shrugged, a small smile dancing across his lips. "Just a school. For magicals, of course. And no, Corian, I don't mean I want to run a daycare for pups learning to cast on their own."

"You and children? I wouldn't dream of it."

"There's so much knowledge to be shared, brother. So much knowledge I gathered and sat on for far too long. I can no longer read the Weave, but that doesn't mean I've forgotten what I've seen."

"Hmm. I suppose not." Corian stuck his hands in his pockets and frowned. "But somehow, I can't imagine you sitting behind a desk all day and writing on a chalkboard."

"You're living way too far in the past, *vae shra'ni*. They're all smartboards and projectors now. I think."

"Removing the Sorren Gán didn't leave you with a sudden propensity for technology, did it?"

L'zar snorted. "Don't be an ass. Everything will be virtual. I hear Elarit's ready to send another thousand activators across the Border."

"Ah, yes." Corian nodded sagely. "The Earthside Crown returns with her bounty of activators so L'zar can finally fulfill his dream."

The drow turned slowly to his friend and cocked his head. "You think that's all I feel for her?"

"No. I know you're proud of her. As you should be. I know I am." Corian clapped a hand on the drow's shoulder and nodded. "The Black Flame isn't finished yet. Neither are you, I think. Come on. I'm hungry."

The nightstalker headed back into the trees for his descent down the mountainside. L'zar took one more sweeping look at the valley and the Summerlin Estate before dipping his head to look at his own hands.

"Yes," he muttered. "On Earth, may the Black Flame reign."

He snapped his fingers, and a burst of black fire flickered around his fingertips before snuffing out again.

"Don't make me haul you down this mountain, L'zar," Corian called from the forest.

L'zar grinned. "Never."

The End

Get sneak peeks, exclusive giveaways, behind the scenes content, and more.
PLUS you'll be notified of special **one day only fan pricing** on new releases.

Sign up today to get free stories.

or visit: https://marthacarr.com/read-free-stories/

AUTHOR NOTES - MARTHA CARR
DECEMBER 8, 2020

It's almost the end of the year. It's the time when I generally update or clean out things. For once, something in 2020 is no different. That includes author notes and the leftover bits and pieces of news.

The neighborhood around the dream house continues to expand. I hear there are going to be a CVS Pharmacy and a McDonald's near the entrance. And on the far side, there are going to be apartments and maybe even a hotel. I'm happy to say I'm a distance from all of it back in my quiet corner at least a mile away from all of it. Across the street from me is a greenbelt. My little piece of suburban heaven.

I have told the Offspring (who likes to point out that some day all of this will be his) that I'm creating my idea of assisted living here. It's a new idea for me to put down real roots instead of wondering where I will go next.

During this phase of staying apart, I can either lament what I can't do or do what I can and get ready for what I can do next. I can take advantage of this enforced extra time in the house and make this place welcoming for when the doors can open. And enjoy it myself in the meantime. With that in mind, I've been sprucing up the place.

The garage got cleaned out once at the beginning of quarantining and somehow stuff crept back in there. This week things started getting cleaned out again, along with my closet. It's time to let go of the 'maybe

I'll use that someday' items and let them go on to where they actually will get used. Leave spaces for new ideas, new adventures.

Light switches that have never really worked right are getting fixed and curtains are getting hung. I've found some cool photographs of Austin concerts and places around Chicago that have been framed and are getting hung on my walls. Handles are finally going on the drawers in the two bathrooms. There are even new board games waiting in the closet.

This weekend I'll be doing my annual cookie baking and leaving them on neighbors' doorsteps. This year I'm going for a good sugar cookie with sprinkles. Something simple (and gluten free). I'll get the last presents out that need to be mailed and relax – or at least my version of it.

Sunday, I'll be taking my first kayaking lesson. I know this probably made every reader in the mid-west shiver, but here it'll be in the low seventies. I've also gotten something called the Quiet Punch that lets you set up a mini punching bag in a doorframe. I'm getting kind of close to having my own home gym here, but when I can I'll go back to the Y. I like being seeing the familiar faces and secretly competing with everyone near me. You do that too, right?

Okay, back to writing for me. A lot of new stories to tell as the year winds down. Hope you've enjoyed this series and as my father used to love saying, I'll see you in the funny papers. (No, I don't know what it means either.) More adventures to follow.

AUTHOR NOTES - MICHAEL ANDERLE

DECEMBER 8, 2020

Thank you for reading to the very end of not only the books but the WHOLE SERIES. At least, for now.

What you have just finished is the sixth of the trilogies containing the eighteen books total that make up the series.

Normally, Martha and I would have put out the eighteen books and put up the boxed sets of trilogies sometime either during the releases or at the very end. This time, the stories were put out in their trilogies and the audio released as the large books, and the individual stories will be released next.

It was different. We tried it with this and many other of our stories, and we learned.

We learned a lot. For example: When you release such large books, it takes a LONG time, and you had either be able to write and publish fast or hold them back to publish quicker. Our answer was a little of both.

Further, when you do multiple series this way, pay attention to about a year from when you start, and remember you have to finish this set of stories before you start new ones. Should you NOT pay attention, you might end up with a month of nothing but books 4, 5, and 6 and no new storylines for fans to read who don't wish to read the ongoing (long) books.

In short, you might screw yourself.

Ok, so enough of "What did LMBPN learn today." Let's talk a bit about the character.

I've never been a Goth person (or a drow, but I assumed you knew that.) Given all the characters Martha and I have created, it is occasionally a challenge to think of something new we want to play around with.

Fortunately for me, she was on board for a Goth Drow. I mean, how cool would it be that our main character didn't actually have to wear makeup to look Goth? Okay, okay, so she did...but then she also didn't.

Kinda, sorta. It's all confusing. She's a walking, talking Halloween cos-player.

I really liked her mom's situation in this story. The lady is super-connected, yet is doing whatever she needs to protect her daughter. So connected that those in power come to her house to talk.

That's power, in my book.

But she isn't perfect. She is dealing with her past and the decisions she has had to make. We see her grow...well, a tiny bit, through the book. However, she's a rock, and people crash against her, cracking under the weight of her attitude.

She might not be magical, but she *is* powerful.

I am so happy you enjoyed this set of stories. The eighteen breakout books will not be new per se, but they will have new covers. Do take a peek sometime and see if you like the new art direction!

Ad Aeternitatem,

Michael Anderle

P.S. – Have you read *Dwarf Bounty Hunter* yet? If not, grab your copy at Amazon!

CONNECT WITH THE AUTHORS

Martha Carr Social

Website:
http://www.marthacarr.com

Facebook:
https://www.facebook.com/groups/MarthaCarrFans/

Michael Anderle Social

Website:
http://www.lmbpn.com

Email List:
http://lmbpn.com/email/

Facebook
https://twitter.com/lmbpn

Instagram
https://www.instagram.com/lmbpn_publishing/

BookBub
https://www.bookbub.com/authors/michael-anderle

OTHER BOOKS BY MARTHA CARR

Series in the Oriceran Universe:

THE LEIRA CHRONICLES
THE FAIRHAVEN CHRONICLES
MIDWEST MAGIC CHRONICLES
SOUL STONE MAGE
THE KACY CHRONICLES
THE DANIEL CODEX SERIES
I FEAR NO EVIL
SCHOOL OF NECESSARY MAGIC
THE UNBELIEVABLE MR. BROWNSTONE
SCHOOL OF NECESSARY MAGIC: RAINE CAMPBELL
ALISON BROWNSTONE
FEDERAL AGENTS OF MAGIC
SCIONS OF MAGIC

Series in The Terranavis Universe:

The Adventures of Maggie Parker Series
The Witches of Pressler Street
The Adventures of Finnegan Dragonbender

9 781649 713674